Kala

Also in Arrow by Nicholas Luard

GONDAR

KALA

Nicholas Luard

ARROW BOOKS

Arrow Books Limited
20 Vauxhall Bridge Road, London SW1V 2SA

An imprint of Random Century Group

London Melbourne Sydney Auckland
Johannesburg and agencies throughout
the world

First published in Great Britain by Century 1990
Arrow edition 1991

Filmset by Deltatype Ltd, Ellesmere Port
Printed and bound in Great Britain by
Cox & Wyman Ltd, Reading

ISBN 0 09 9682 80X

For Poppy Luard

Kala

— 1 —

She held the huge diamond whenever she was frightened.

She was frightened now.

Fire frightened her. So did the storms that swept the desert in front of the rains. So too did the great black-maned hunting lions which had once challenged her for prey. There was no firc or storms or lions here. They were all far away. Like so much else, they belonged to what had happened before. Here there was only the icy, misty chill – November 1882 was the start of the coldest London winter in years. The chill, and the tall man shouting in fury far below her.

The man terrified her more than anything had ever done.

'Kala! Kala! Where the hell is the little bitch? Find her, for Christ's sake!'

The enraged cries rang on.

High above him she gripped the diamond until her knuckles whitened. She threaded her fingers together as tightly as if they were woven reeds in a delta fish-trap. She had to. The stone was so brilliant, so charged with radiance, that like the river's waters its light threatened to seep out through the tiniest chink.

The diamond was her lodestar. It was almost her life. If she was going to protect herself against him, she had to guard every fragment of the stone's incandescence.

'Kala!'

Kala-Xkung-na-Kjota. 'The little she-hare that fell from the sky with the rains'. The San people of the African desert had given her the name. Later the white men who trapped her had shortened it to Kala. She recognized the sound of the word. The word itself meant nothing. She had been given so many names over the years. Except when she used them in her own private and silent language, words had no meaning to her.

She was mute.

The idea of a 'theatre' was meaningless too. To her the towering Victorian building was simply a structure like one of the giant African termite mounds. She had been locked away somewhere inside it. She'd found a gap between the roof beams over her dank little room, and had crawled out. Then she'd climbed a ladder to the catwalks above.

Now she was lying on a narrow, swaying metal bridge. Below her there was nothing except the vertical plunging fall to the stage floor a hundred feet below. It would be a dizzying perch for eagles or high-climbing leopards. She had swung herself up on to it as easily as if it had been the branch of a low tree.

Apart from her short leather skirt, she was naked. The rusting slats pressed uncomfortably against her breasts, patterning her pale olive-coloured skin with freezing bars of whiteness.

'Where's that goddamn cripple-carpenter? Ben! Where the hell are you?'

'Here, Mr Farini!'

'You've got the key to the little savage's room. Where is she? For Christ's sake, she's my goddamn star. What have you done with her?'

'Her room's still locked, sir. She won't have gone far. We'll find her, Mr Farini –'

The second voice started to shout. 'Kala! Kala!'

The call was picked up by the other men as they searched the theatre. She could see plumes of steam rising from their mouths. They began to climb from the stalls to the dress circle. They would continue upwards until they shone their lanterns on the catwalks and found her.

She gripped the diamond even more tightly.

Trapped between her palms it was no longer a stone irradiated by fire. It was a bright-eyed living creature of the lagoons. She could almost feel its heart beating. She gazed down at it. Her own eyes were opaque and unblinking. The stone's eyes – the glittering points of light that shone back at her – belonged to a rapacious fish eagle or a hunting falcon. The diamond's eyes changed all the time, but they always carried reflections.

They carried reflections now.

She could see a young man wielding a mallet. She knew him well. He was one of the carpenters who worked on the stage. He was the person the other man, the man who frightened her so much, had bellowed at. For some reason the young carpenter had been made her keeper. His body was humped and misshapen, but he used his tools with care and skill. The tapping of his hammer was familiar. It echoed sounds she knew from long ago.

She frowned, searching in her mind for where she had first heard the tapping. The memory refused to come back. She shook her head and concentrated on the stone again.

This time she saw a young woman. The woman was perhaps twenty, four years older than Kala was herself. Kala sensed she knew the young woman, that their spoor – the imprint of their tracks on the earth – had crossed. But the young woman's face was sheeted with blood in the stone's reflections, and she could not make out her features.

The blood troubled her.

She drew in her breath. The image was so vivid, Kala knew the young woman was somewhere close. Kala lifted her head and scanned the darkness.

Although her sight was as keen as any night-hunting animal's, she could see nothing. A tangle of smells coiled over her face. She inhaled, sifting through them. Something registered on her skin. It was the emanation of heat from a living body. She tensed. She tried to focus on the heat's source. Before she could trace it, the field of warmth had gone.

Kala wrinkled her face.

She was right. The young woman had been there. Now

she had vanished. Not yet, not yet, something told her. For the moment she was trapped in this musty tower. But both the carpenter and the young woman were vitally important to her. Somehow they represented her freedom.

'Kala! Kala!'

The shouts were much closer now.

Kala glanced round. There was nowhere she could hide. She tucked the diamond back into the pouch at her waist. Hidden beneath the apron of her skirt it was safe.

Soon the lanterns would find her. She would be taken down and dragged in front of the man. She would snarl and spit at him, but it would make no difference. He was used to that now. She could already see his eyes. Brutal and greedy, they would pierce savagely through her. She knew what he would do. He would whip her first. He had done that before. Then he would make her dance.

Trembling, she rested her head on her arms. She had no defence against him. Sleep was her only escape. Sleep, and what in dreams it brought to her.

Sometimes in dreams she saw other worlds. She seemed to have inhabited so many different worlds in the brief seventeen years of her life. Fragments of one in particular sometimes came back when she slept. It was the first she had known. It was a strange and secret world. A world filled not with animals – they had come later – but with people.

A world that was immensely ancient, older than anything her lost and tormented mind now had the power to understand.

Somehow she knew that in its far-off beginnings were her own beginnings too.

— 2 —

'I want him now!'

The queen's voice was still husky and quiet, but the edges of the words were fretted with tension.

Semirotis closed her eyes in despair. The old servant woman knew the signs all too well. Under the calm imperiousness, the queen's volcanic anger was beginning to simmer and rise. At any instant it might erupt in blind, wilful rage.

'Let him sleep for another hour, my lady,' Semirotis pleaded. 'He has been up all night with the ships. He must rest.'

'I want him now. Bring him to me.'

The words came out flat and dull but the ferocity behind them was chilling.

'Listen to me, little *chatla* –'

In ancient Egyptian *chatla* meant duckling. It had been Semirotis' term of endearment for the queen when she had nursed her as a child. Semirotis seldom dared use it now except when the situation was desperate.

'There is no other girl with him. He is alone. I have looked into his chamber myself, I promise you. But he has to sleep, he needs his strength for the morning. All his captains say so. They have begged me to see he is not disturbed. Please, *chatla*.'

The queen was standing with her back towards the old woman. For a moment she said nothing. Hardly daring to breathe, Semirotis thought her plea had been successful. Then she saw the pulse behind the queen's ear begin to throb and her shoulders tremble.

'Never again call me *chatla* –'

Her voice was icy. Suddenly it rose to a scream.

'Get him here – now!'

Semirotis recoiled. She had experienced the fury before. Each time its violence was so swift and brutal it was like a blow in the face. She bowed and mumbled and backed out of the room.

Her wrists shaking, Cleopatra watched her go.

As the Persian damask curtain swung down behind the old woman's departing back, the queen's rage vanished as quickly as it had boiled up. Cleopatra rubbed her eyes. It was almost dawn. She too had been up all night and she was tired. She ran her fingers through her hair and walked over to the open window.

She stood looking down from the palace over the harbour.

The year was 30 BC. For Cleopatra, Queen of Egypt, it was to prove the last and most disastrous year of her life. At thirty-eight the queen bore no resemblance to the pictograms the court scribes drew on the temple walls throughout the city. There, to Cleopatra's irritation, she was shown as a small thin woman with bulging eyes and severely cut black hair. The scribes were doing no more than obeying tradition. Egypt's first recorded queen had been painted like that. They knew no other way of portraying its present one.

The reality was very different.

For generations since that first queen, Cleopatra's ancestry had been almost wholly Greek. Occasionally a Sudanese princess from the south had been brought into the dynasty, bearing with her the golden genes of the desert people. Across the years, as the swarthy Egyptian stock was bred out, the Greek and the gold had blended.

The result was Cleopatra.

She was short – but there the resemblance to the pictograms ended. The queen's skin was a dusky bronze. Her mane of hair, almost lion-like in its texture and the despair of Semirotis when Cleopatra was a child, was thick and copper-coloured. Her brown eyes were flecked with chips of silvery-grey. Her figure was strong and voluptuous, with heavy breasts set above wide hips, and strong legs that narrowed down to finely set ankles.

The common people of Alexandria called her the she-beisa – the elegant and unpredictable Arabian oryx. They had named her with the shrewd, observant eyes of peasants. In its duns and golds and umbers, in its scything horns and glittering chestnut-coloured eyes, the oryx antelope was a true creature of the desert. It was beautiful and dangerous. So was Egypt's queen.

Cleopatra stared thoughtfully at the water.

He might be bleached with tiredness, but he would come. He always came when she called for him. In the shimmering reflection from the surface she seemed to see his face. Ravaged and lined, the hair grey and tousled, the gentian-blue eyes shadowed from the night's drinking and the skin blotched with what he laughingly dismissed as 'the blossoms of Egypt's grape'.

In spite of Semirotis' claim, he probably had a girl in his bed. He hated sleeping alone. Any pair of plump breasts, any firm buttocks, drew him like a magnet. Mostly Cleopatra tolerated his infidelities. When she saw him licking his lips at one of her servant girls, she would chuckle and throw him the young woman as though she were tossing a hubara bustard to one of the palace leopards.

Occasionally she rebelled. Then, in jealousy, her vengeance could be fearsome. Two weeks earlier she discovered that a dark-haired Assyrian had become his regular night-time companion.

Cleopatra had the girl garrotted and butchered in the palace kitchens. She personally selected four of the girl's ribs and dropped them into the stew for that night's banquet. She told him what she had done as he was gnawing at one of them. He dropped the rib and vomited. Then he hit her across the mouth. Afterwards he stumbled from the dining hall bellowing incoherently.

He stayed away for five days. Then he came back to her. He always came back. He would come now.

'Why? Why in the name of sun and wind and fortune can you not let me be just for a few hours?'

He had come.

He entered the chamber yawning and rubbing the sleep from his eyes. As the curtain swung back, Cleopatra saw the eight members of his personal bodyguard standing grim-faced and hostile outside. They wanted him to rest. She didn't care. There were more important matters than sleep.

'Somewhere to sea out there,' he gestured towards the window, 'that jackal Octavian is waiting with his ships. We sail today to find them. But we will go when the wind is fair and I am sharp. The wind, the captains say, will change at noon. But will I be sharp then? No! I will be a drowned, destroyed, decayed cane rat. And why? Because of you, you bitch! Because you will not let me sleep –'

His eyes blearily searched the room. He saw the turquoise-glazed pitcher of wine and advanced on it.

'Let me be, Egypt,' he finished. 'Let me rest and dream. If you do, I promise you this. I will dream only of you.'

The pitcher was in his hand. Before he raised it to his mouth he tilted his head to one side, half closed his eyelids, and gave her one of his most vulnerable and winsome smiles.

Cleopatra's face remained impassive.

She knew his smiles better than anyone alive. Seductive and beguiling, they had captivated and manipulated the Roman world since his boyhood. They had seduced and enchanted her. They would do so again – and she would not care if they were contrived, just as she had not minded in the past. But not now. Now she wanted something else.

She waited until he had drunk and the warmth of the wine began to flow through him. Then she crossed the floor.

'Antony!'

She held him to her. She let him nuzzle her neck, kiss her on the lips, slip his hands into the gold tapestry sheath of her gown and hold her breasts. Then, as his breathing began to quicken, she pushed him abruptly away.

'What are you doing?' he protested.

'I wish to talk,' Cleopatra answered.

'Of course, we will talk,' he agreed. 'We will lie down together and talk. Then I will rest. And then it will be as it should have been before – except it will be better. Because between talking and sleeping, we will have done other things.'

Chuckling, Antony reached for her again.

'No.' She struck away his hand as he began to unbuckle the serpent's-head clasp of the belt at her waist. 'Semirotis!'

The old woman was waiting outside the entrance that led to the queen's private quarters. She came in instantly.

'Bring me Osiris.'

Semirotis bowed and withdrew.

'Osiris? What do you want with that old witch?' Antony asked frowning.

'Octavian's fleet is gathered at Actium,' Cleopatra replied. 'We will confront him there. Today we go to war.'

'*We* will fight Octavian, not that wizened, foul-smelling little monkey, Osiris. What has she got to do with it?'

'*We* will fight Octavian. But *we* also have a daughter.' Cleopatra paused. 'What happens to us happens to her. I wish to know what that will be, so I can determine now what shall be done with her.'

Antony stared at her.

He came from the Roman world. It was a rational, masculine world which honoured its gods but knew that men decided their own affairs and their own fate. Egypt was different. It was much older. Its cast of mind was feminine. It was dark and devious and riddled with superstition. He despised and hated its dependence on the priests, soothsayers and sibyls who thronged Alexandria like a plague of parasites.

They held the people in thrall and sucked their blood. Most of all Antony hated the old woman known as Osiris. He hated her not least because Cleopatra trusted her and her spells more than anyone – more even than her childhood nurse, Semirotis.

Anger flushed Antony's face.

The child was his daughter too. He was not about to let her fate be decided by an illiterate and wizened old hag from some backwater in the Nile's delta. He opened his mouth to roar in protest.

Antony was too late. The curtain parted again and Osiris appeared.

— 3 —

The sibyl, Osiris, was carried into the chamber on a tall high-backed stool.

The stool was borne on poles by four young women in sea-green cotton tunics fastened at the neck by golden clasps. They put her down in the centre of the floor. They withdrew the poles from the iron hoops below the stool's curved arms. Then they backed away.

As they vanished behind the curtain, Cleopatra glimpsed another throng of watchers on the far side. Antony's bodyguards on the left, the sibyl's retinue on the right. Behind both groups were ranks of her own soldiers. Beyond them there would be more people. Functionaries, scribes, officials, servants, and slaves, spreading out in rippling waves north to the sea, east and west into the desert, southwards down through the Nile's delta.

Cleopatra shivered. She was Egypt, and Egypt was never alone. Cleopatra glanced back.

The woman hunched on the stool was small and immensely old. Her bones were as thin as a Ghaza sparrow's, and her skin had the dull crumpled darkness of oasis mud at the summer's end. But her eyes, darting, staring, flickering backwards and forwards, were as keen and penetrating as a viper's.

'What does Egypt wish to know?' she demanded suddenly, fixing her gaze on Cleopatra.

The queen came forward. 'I have questions –'

'Then kneel, child, kneel, before you ask them,' the old woman's voice rasped as she cut Cleopatra off. 'You may be Egypt. I am Osiris. You are human. I am divine. Show your respect.'

Cleopatra flushed with anger. She *was* Egypt and this puckered little harridan, old as she might be, was no more than the daughter of a peasant farmer from the delta.

Beside her Antony seethed too.

'Pull her off her arse,' he muttered. 'Make the old baggage kiss the tiles in front of you. If you don't dare, I will.'

His face reddening, Antony lurched forward. Cleopatra pulled him back. She dropped to her knees. Gripping Antony's wrist with all her strength, she dragged him down beside her.

'I kneel, Osiris,' she said.

Cleopatra lowered her head. Furious and muttering, Antony dipped his head too.

The old woman grunted.

'Now give it to me so that I may see.'

Cleopatra looked up. She lifted her hands to her hair and lifted the diadem from her head.

The diadem was a circle of gold vine leaves. It had been wrought, it was said, by the master-goldsmiths of Crete. They had made it at the king's instructions to crown the head of Theseus, after he had sailed to the island and slain the beast of the Labyrinth.

Theseus was the son of Poseidon, the god of the ocean. He wore the diadem only once. Then he threw it into the sea to thank his father for safeguarding him on his voyages. Although it was carved from the purest and heaviest gold, the diadem didn't sink. It was carried east on the waves towards Egypt.

The diadem came ashore in the Nile delta. The night the sea washed it up, a star shook itself free from the jewelled ropes of the constellations and fell to earth. It landed on the golden vine leaves. The star's heat melted the gold and fused its heart, a huge diamond, into the diadem's arching prow.

Next morning a fisherman casting his nets from the shore found the diadem. He carried it inland a short distance and laid it on the ground. The place where he put it down became the site of Alexandria. The diamond was the Star of Egypt.

No one was allowed to touch the circle of vine leaves and the glory at their centre except for the queen herself and the anointed priests. The stone was Egypt even more than Cleopatra was. Osiris was neither a priest nor, least of all, the queen. She was a seer, a sibyl. At this moment she was more important than any priest.

Osiris knew the future.

Cleopatra gave the diadem to the old woman. She waited while Osiris peered into the constantly shifting bowl of glittering light that radiated out from the diamond.

'The dark ships are gathered,' Osiris said. 'The wind blows cold from Egypt's shore. The fleets meet, but yours and your Roman ram's are scattered and lost. It is over.'

Cleopatra shuddered. The pronouncement was short and brutal. She knew exactly what it meant.

At her shoulder Antony, not understanding the old woman's dialect, heaved and grumbled fretfully.

'What of the child?' Cleopatra asked.

'There is no safety for her here,' Osiris said. 'After you, if you so will it, she will be Egypt. But there will never be safety for Egypt while the waves ride to her doors.'

'Where can she and Egypt be safe?' Cleopatra demanded desperately.

The old woman stared into the diamond again. For a while she mumbled to herself. Then she looked up. Her eyes were vacant and remote.

'For Egypt danger comes from the deep waters of the ocean,' she answered. 'It always has, it always will. For the child and Egypt to be safe, they must go where the waters run shallow. Where rivers run inland and spill themselves on sand. Where no ships can raise their sails.'

Bewildered, Cleopatra shook her head. 'Rivers run to the sea. No river runs inland.'

'There is a river which runs to land. I can see it here in the stone.'

'But where is it?'

'I do not know. It is far towards the south. The stone will lead me to it –'

The old woman gazed at Cleopatra with a terrible searching intensity.

'You are finished, Egypt. So is your man. Egypt dies with you both.' The old woman paused. 'If you wish Egypt to live, give me the child and the stone. Give me guards and engineers. I will take them south into Africa. When the stone has led us to the place, Egypt will be rebuilt. There the child and all who follow her in line will be safe. Safe until the sails of the ships appear again on the water. That will be never. For where we go, there will be only land beyond –'

Osiris paused. 'The great stone I cannot do without. But if you are wise, Egypt, you will give me all your other treasure too.'

'All?'

Cleopatra gasped. The store of diamonds that had come to her with the Ptolemaic inheritance was the largest in the world. It was beyond price.

'What do you wish should happen to the jewelled harvest of your ancestors?' the old woman rasped. 'That it should be plundered and lost to the scum of Rome when Rome has broken you? Or that it too should travel to safety and remain Egypt's for ever? The choice is yours.'

Cleopatra was silent. Then she bowed her head, weeping. Antony tugged at her elbow.

'What is it?' he demanded. 'What does the old jackal say?'

'That Octavian defeats us,' the queen replied between her sobs. 'That we are both lost and Egypt with us. That the child and the stone must flee with her –'

'I will kill her!' Antony interrupted shouting. 'With traitors like this among us, Octavian does not need ships!'

Fumbling at his waist for his sword, Antony struggled to stand up.

'No –!'

Cleopatra pulled him down again. The old woman watched them impassively.

'Listen to me, Antony,' Cleopatra implored. 'Maybe we are not lost. Maybe the outcome still lies with the gods. But that is for you and me to prove. I will not hazard my daughter in the endeavour. If she goes with the old woman she will be safe however the day turns.'

'She is my daughter too!' Antony bellowed.

Cleopatra cut him off. 'You are not Egypt. I am. If I die, you will still not be Egypt. Our child will.'

Antony was silent.

Cleopatra stood up. Her tears had dried and she was Egypt again, resolute and implacable. Antony stared at her, partly in awe and partly in despair. She had bewitched Caesar and she had bewitched him, the two most powerful men in the world. But that was as a woman, as any forked and female human with a honey pot between her legs.

Now, Antony realized bitterly, she was just as much an uncontrollable force of nature as a queen.

'You shall have what you ask,' she said to the old woman. 'I will place my daughter, the great stone, and Egypt's treasure in your hands. I will give you all you need and Herontas to lead the column. Guard my child well, Osiris. The gods may forgive you if anything happens to her. Wherever I am, believe me, I will not.'

The old woman said nothing. Her attendants came into the chamber and carried her out. Cleopatra called for Semirotis again.

'Bring me Herontas,' she commanded.

Herontas was the commander of her personal bodyguard. Still a young man, strong, intelligent and loyal, he was the best and bravest soldier who had ever served her. Today he should have sailed for Greece at her shoulder on the deck of her flagship.

Not now. Now he was needed for a more important task still.

Herontas was shown into the chamber. He stood stiffly in front of her. Cleopatra poured him a mug of wine and told him to be seated. She spoke to him for almost an hour. Herontas listened attentively, nodding from time to time. Finally she gestured for him to leave.

Cleopatra glanced round. There were only two more things to be done. She summoned Semirotis again.

'Bring me my daughter,' she said.

Semirotis reappeared with the child. Cleopatra held her in her arms.

The child was asleep. Twice Cleopatra tried to wake her, stroking her under her chin and touching the child's lips with her finger. The baby refused to respond. She turned her head away and nuzzled deeper into the pale cotton wraps that enfolded her.

Suddenly tears filled Cleopatra's eyes. She raised the child to her face and pressed her lips against her cheek. Under her breath, Cleopatra prayed. Then quickly and resolutely she handed her back to Semirotis.

'Take her away,' she instructed curtly.

Almost blinded with tears, Cleopatra made her way to the window. She blinked until the tears dried and she could look out.

It was dawn. The Nile estuary was starting to glow with ribbons of lemon and rose as the early morning light cut down through the night's mist. On either side she could see the gleaming white walls and towers of Alexandria. Fishermen were casting their nets in the lagoons. Water-birds were calling and skeins of flamingoes clamoured across the sky.

Cleopatra sniffed the air. It was cool and soft and clean. She raised her eyes beyond the estuary and gazed into the distance. Out there beyond the sand dunes and the gentle flow of the river was the sea.

Unlike the delta the sea looked dark and ominous. As she watched, a harbouring dhow came into view. The wind was blowing from the north. Running before the wind, the boat's sail filled until it resembled a swollen venomous blossom.

Cleopatra shivered and turned away.

Antony was sprawled on a couch at the back of the

room. He had finished the pitcher of wine, and fallen asleep. She walked over and gazed down at him. He looked peaceful and untroubled, his greying hair rumpled untidily over his forehead and his square hands resting lightly on his growing paunch.

Cleopatra smiled. She bent down and kissed him on his lips. He muttered and stirred.

'If you must sleep,' she said, 'I can offer you softer cushions on which to lie.'

She caught his hand. Grumbling and bleary-eyed, Antony stood up.

Cleopatra paused. There had been two things which needed to be done. Two farewells, she realized, she needed to make. One had been done. This was the other.

Still smiling, Egypt's queen led what the old woman had called, in the blunt terms of the delta peasantry, her 'Roman ram' towards her bedchamber. It was the last time, Cleopatra knew with a bleak and absolute certainty, they would lie together there.

By the time they woke and sailed for their fateful encounter with Octavian, all that was left of her life – the child, the great diamond that had fallen from the sky, and Egypt's treasure – would be hurrying south. To the south lay Africa.

If Osiris was right, somewhere in the dark and unknown heart of Africa was a river that spent itself on land. On the river's waters Egypt would at last find sanctuary from the ships that had always destroyed her.

Cleopatra put her arms round Antony and bound him tightly to her.

— 4 —

Vasco Dao stared at the diamond in disbelief.

'Where does it come from, Inchelele?' he asked.

Across the table the Matabele warlord shrugged, but didn't reply.

Dao pushed his sweat-stained leather hat back on his head. He rubbed his beard. Then he examined the stone again.

It was the summer of 1868. Dao was sitting at his camp on the plain in modern Zimbabwe just to the south of 'the smoke that thunders' – the waterfalls that the great explorer, Dr Livingstone, had named after the mighty Queen-Empress, Victoria.

The diamond was one of the finest Dao had ever seen. Dao was a trader and hunter, not a diamond merchant, but he'd once worked a claim at Kimberley. He'd learnt enough to guess the stone weighed about thirty carats. If he was right, it would fetch ten thousand escudos in Lourenco Marques. That was the equivalent of five prime years of ivory.

He looked at Inchelele.

The African chieftain's face was slack and bloated, but he was watching Dao through cold shrewd eyes. Not for nothing did Inchelele's name mean 'Slippery Sides' in the Matabele dialect. Behind Inchelele a dozen of his warriors were leaning on their spears.

'How did you get it, Inchelele?'

Inchelele twitched his shoulders again. He went on gazing impassively at the Portuguese. Dao glanced up at the morning sky.

'The heat is heavy,' he said. 'We will talk later.'

Dao put the diamond back on the table between them. He walked back to his waggon. His servants had stretched out a canvas awning from the bow-shaped hoop at the rear. Dao threw himself down on a chair in the shade beneath it.

The air was hot and humid, but then it always was before the rains. It wasn't the heat that had made him cut short the meeting.

Dao wanted to think.

Portuguese by birth, Vasco Dao was fifty. Thirty-two years earlier as a young sailor out of Lisbon, Dao jumped ship at Beira in the Portuguese colony of Mozambique. From there he set out into the African forest to make his fortune as an elephant hunter.

In the second half of the nineteenth century the southern tip of the African continent was in turmoil. The immigrant white Boers were surging up from the Cape. The psychopathic Zulu chieftain, Shaka, had carved out his murderous empire to the north and east. The land beyond was virgin territory where bold and resourceful men, armed with European rifles, could win vast kingdoms for themselves – and become legends as they did so.

Dao was bold and resourceful. By the time of his meeting with Inchelele, Dao was one of the best-known white hunters between Zanzibar and Durban. His only rival in that vast stretch of the African landscape was another hunter and trader, a British adventurer named Wilson. Both were known by the names of the tribes with whom they had the closest links. Wilson was 'Matabele Wilson'. Dao was 'Mashona Dao'.

Ironically, as the bearded Dao sprawled back in his chair that morning, it was not his own Mashona he was among. His trek had taken him into Wilson's tribal territory.

Dao was among the Matabele.

When Shaka's empire began to crumble, a number of the leaders of the Zulu impis took their regiments out into the plains and forests to claim land and kingdoms of their own. Inchelele was one of them. Inchelele headed north and then west. Finally he established his kraal – his village, power-base, and fortress – near the Victoria Falls.

Dao could hear the roar of the cascading water from where he sat. If he stood up he could even see the spray that rose hundreds of feet into the air above the forest. Dao didn't stand. He pulled his hat down over his face and closed his eyes.

Dao needed to think. Tactically he also needed to wait.

Dao didn't return to Inchelele's kraal that afternoon. Nor the following day. Nor the day after. The Portuguese built up the already thick boma of acacia thorn that walled his waggons, and stayed in his camp. Dao had only thirty men with him, while Inchelele's kraal housed several thousand. Inchelele's men too were Matabele, they were warriors. Dao's were Mashona – and the Mashona were not known as fighters.

Yet Dao's Mashona had been with him for many years. They were tried and faithful. Most important of all, he had armed them with rifles. If Inchelele attacked him, Dao would have backed his thirty Mashona against a hundred times as many Matabele.

That, in Africa, was the difference the rifle made.

Inchelele would not attack him. Not only because of Dao's rifles but because the Portuguese had nothing Inchelele wanted. Nothing except knowledge. Knowledge of the white man's world of trade. To acquire that, the Matabele spears were useless. Inchelele would have to come and treat.

Inchelele came on the third day.

He came sullenly and reluctantly, accompanied by one hundred of his morans, his young warriors. Inchelele pretended he hadn't even come to see Dao at all. He was merely passing by Dao's waggons on his way to hunt. But when Dao invited him into the boma to take coffee, he accepted. He even told his morans to wait for him outside the thorn fence.

As Dao led the chieftain towards his fire, a satisfied smile crossed the face of the Portuguese. No Matabele leader would have sat down alone in a white bwana's camp unless he wanted to do business.

'So,' Dao said after the coffee had been brewed and drunk, and they had exchanged the elaborate courtesies of the bush, 'I will hide nothing from you, Inchelele. Three sunrises ago you showed me a stone. The stone interests me.'

Without comment Inchelele reached inside his cloak and pulled out the diamond again. He put it down on the table.

'It is said for such a stone, men will trade one hundred guns.'

Inchelele's eyes slid away as he spoke. Dao laughed as if he were sharing a joke.

The Matabele had no idea of the diamond's worth. All Inchelele had heard was that the white men treasured the desert rocks, and he was hazarding a wild guess at its value.

'A hundred guns?' Dao went on chuckling. 'Inchelele, you are my friend. I will answer you in truth. This stone is worth five guns, maybe ten. No more. But –'

Dao raised his hand as Inchelele began to scowl in anger.

'Such stones are not found singly. Where this stone came from, there will be others too. Take me there. If I am right and we can secure them, I will make you a promise. You will have not one hundred guns, but a thousand.'

'How do I know you will do as you say?' Inchelele demanded.

'Because you know of me well,' Dao answered. 'You have treated with Matabele Wilson. You know he keeps his word. You have heard of Mashona Dao. You know he does the same. But there is more than that –'

Dao paused. 'Where there are stones like this, there will be men to dig and guard them. I will need more warriors than I have. I will need your help. We need each other.'

Inchelele considered the matter in silence. Grudgingly he nodded. He gestured vaguely over his shoulder towards the west.

'The stone comes from where the sun lays itself down,' he said. 'From the waters.'

'The waters?'

'The waters beyond the Great Thirst.'

The Great Thirst was the Kalahari desert. At its end there was supposed to be a region of lakes and lagoons. Dao had never been there. The desert was too brutal and daunting a barrier. Nor, as far as he knew, had any European – apart from the English missionary, Livingstone, who claimed to have seen the outer rim of the lakes.

Livingstone was famously crazed and Dao had always taken the story of the waters as another African legend.

'Have you been to the place?' Dao asked.

Inchelele shook his head. 'It is many days' march.'

'Then how do you know the stone comes from there?'

'An impi of Okatai's people passed by here at the last harvesting,' Inchelele answered. 'They said they had been working for white men who had built a kraal on the waters. They were given the stone in payment for their labour. They were taking it to the coast to trade, but their hunting was bad and they had no food. They offered it to me for corn.'

Dao stared at him. 'White men?'

'Not white as you are, but as the Felindi. Except they were not Felindi.'

Dao was astonished.

Felindi was the Matabele name for the olive-skinned Arab traders who for centuries had raided coastal Africa for slaves. A kraal could mean anything in size from a hunting camp upwards. If this kraal provided employment for three hundred men, it was nothing less than a town.

If that was so, somewhere in the waters beyond the Great Thirst was a permanent settlement of fair-skinned people who were not Arabs. And a people who had diamonds.

'I think we should make safari to this kraal,' Dao said.

Inchelele frowned. 'The men of Okatai's impi say the

kraal has been there for many, many years. It is strongly guarded with great walls of ironwood. Unless the walls can be breached there is no way in –'

The chieftain paused thoughtfully.

'Okatai's people say one thing more,' Inchelele went on. 'The men of the kraal had heard stories of a white man travelling the Great Thirst. They were curious about him. Often they asked Okatai's impi to tell them what they knew of white men.'

Dao thought.

The white man was almost certainly Livingstone. However crazed the missionary might have been, no one now doubted that twenty years before he had managed to cross the Kalahari from south to north. A few Europeans had crossed the desert since, but it was Livingstone who was known and remembered.

Perhaps, Dao thought suddenly, Livingstone's stories of the waters were true after all.

'What do you mean by this, Inchelele?'

'The people of the kraal are interested in the white man,' Inchelele replied. 'You are a white man. Maybe if you come to the kraal gates, they will open them and let you in.'

Dao rubbed his face.

'Whereas if you come with your morans and their spears, they would arm their walls against you,' Dao said. 'But if I get in with my Mashona, I can open the gates for your Matabele. Then the kraal is ours. Is that what you are suggesting?'

Inchelele shrugged. 'You have rifles. The people of the kraal in the waters do not.'

Dao stared at him. The Portuguese burst into laughter.

'You are a scoundrel, Inchelele,' he said. 'A devious, treacherous, thieving scoundrel. But, by *Cristos*, you would make a good general.'

For the first time the Matabele chieftain laughed.

'Do we march together, Mashona Dao?' he asked.

Dao nodded. 'We march together, Inchelele. And when we return, you and your morans will have rifles too.'

Inchelele turned.

Still chuckling, he called through the gap in the boma fence to the young warriors waiting outside. As he finished speaking they hammered their spears on the hard dry earth. An excited roar went up and a wall of red dust lifted into the air. Then they began to chant.

Inchelele went out. Dao listened to the deep rhythmic song. The Matabele had abandoned the idea of hunting. Instead they were readying themselves for war.

For a long time after Inchelele left and the chant faded, Dao sat in thought at the table. Then he called for Mashuana.

'Yes, bwana?'

Mashuana was his headman. Still in his early twenties, he was the second son of a legendary chieftain named Sechele.

Sechele had been captured as a child by Arab slavers. Sold as a cabin boy to the owner of a coastal-trading dhow, he had risen through his skill and courage to become the captain of his own ship somewhere in the seas far to the north.

Sechele returned to his homeland speaking Arabic, Spanish and Portuguese. For years he was invaluable to the European traders and hunters who ventured inland from the coast. Dao had always recruited his bearers from Sechele's people. The chieftain's second son, Mashuana, had been his father's favourite child.

Sechele was dead now. But on the chieftain's deathbed, Dao had promised he would always give employment to Mashuana.

'We go into the Great Thirst,' Dao said.

He told Mashuana what he planned to do.

'What do you think?' Dao finished.

Young as Mashuana was, Dao had learned to trust his judgement. Mashuana had inherited many of the qualities of his father. Dao never set out on an expedition now without consulting him.

Mashuana considered the matter.

'The rains are far off,' he replied. 'The Great Thirst will

be bad. This kraal and the waters where it lies are unknown. I think this will be a hard journey.'

'Would Sechele have embarked on it?' Dao asked, chuckling.

It was an old joke between them. The test of any dangerous enterprise was whether Mashuana's father would have attempted it.

Mashuana grinned back.

'For diamonds he would have made it.' Mashuana paused. 'But to get into the kraal, bwana, I think Sechele would make a plan.'

'What do you mean?'

'You come there as a white man,' Mashuana said. 'They have interest in the white man, but surely they will be cautious. They will treat with you, I think, outside their kraal. That is no use. You must be within their boma walls. Now, Inchelele says they are also white, even if in the manner of the Felindi. I know of only one time when a white man will take another into his kraal without question – when the second is sick.'

Dao frowned.

'If I arrive with the fever, they will let me enter?'

Mashuana nodded. 'With the fever and a few men, you can be no threat to them, bwana.'

Dao laughed. He stood up and clapped Mashuana round the shoulder.

'You are as cunning as Inchelele,' Dao said.

Mashuana beamed proudly. Among the Africans, cunning was the most prized of all qualities.

'More so than that dog,' Mashuana replied. 'As much as my father. And for such an enterprise we will need all of his cunning –'

He paused. The young African's face became grave.

'Bwana, I have a young brother by my father's last wife,' Mashuana went on. 'I promised my father I would support them both. I have kept my promise. But they are not favoured in the tribe. My elder brother is jealous of them. I do not fear for myself. But if anything should happen to me, I fear for them.'

Dao nodded.

The Portuguese knew well the rivalries and jealousies that tormented the lives of the African tribal groupings. They stemmed from the complex laws and traditions of inheritance. The disputes they caused were bad enough in the case of an ordinary family. In the case of a chieftain, with several wives and as many lines of descent, they were worse.

They could lead to death or – worst of all in the catalogue of Mashona vengeance and humiliation – to exile. Exile from the tribe and its homelands was a punishment not even death could match.

'What are you saying, Mashuana?' Dao asked.

'That this endeavour is filled with hazard,' the African replied. 'Should we fail, my little brother and his mother are in peril.'

Dao looked at him. Mashuana's eyes were troubled.

'How shall we not fail?' Dao asked.

Mashuana hesitated before answering.

'I do not think these people lack cunning either, bwana,' he answered. 'You will need to be truly sick if they are to take you inside their walls.'

Dao laughed.

'Then make the waggons ready,' he said. 'We outspan tomorrow. We will cross the Thirst. And I promise you, Sechele's son, when we come to the waters I will be as sick as even your father could wish for.'

— 5 —

The mosquitoes came as the light started to fade.

They rose from the earth and hung in a dark pulsing barrier that drifted backwards and forwards across the water like a curtain blown in the wind. They thronged the delta all the time, but it was at the start and end of the day that they were most visible and tormenting. There were so many millions that they dimmed the light of the lowering sun from the ground to high above the treetops.

Dao rolled up his sleeves and got to his feet.

He walked deliberately away from the camp's smoking fire to the water's edge. From fifty yards the mosquitoes seemed to be silent. As soon as the curtain swung round him, the air throbbed with an incessant whine. Within seconds every millimetre of his exposed skin was blackened with insects.

'Bwana! What are you doing? Come back!'

The shout came from Dao's second boy, Hlue. Hlue leapt up and raced shouting towards the lagoon.

'Leave me alone!' Dao waved him angrily away. 'This must be done. Mashuana will explain.'

Hlue stood frozen. He could not ask Mashuana. The headman had left the camp to check the game traps. As the mosquitoes attacked him too, Hlue retreated. Back at the fire he watched appalled as Dao stood unmoving on the shore of the lagoon. The Portuguese was covered so thickly with insects he seemed to have grown a rippling black fur.

Hlue shuddered.

The bwana must have gone mad. The white man's vulnerability to the yellow sickness was known all over

Africa. And when the white man fell sick, there was no hunting, no food, no wages.

Hlue closed his eyes in despair.

By the time Dao walked back to the camp five minutes later, Mashuana had returned. The Mashona headman had told the other boys what the bwana was doing. Unconvinced by the explanation, they squatted on their haunches staring at Dao, frightened and bewildered.

'Listen to me, all of you,' Dao said. 'What Mashuana says is true. I have exposed myself to sickness and the fever will come. When it does, this is what you must do –'

As he spoke the corrugated red lumps on Dao's exposed skin were beginning to swell. His eyelids, where the tissue was more sensitive than the rest of his body, were already so puffy he could barely see through them. Soon he would be sightless for at least several hours. But Dao knew he had done what he intended.

He had infected himself with malaria.

'Tomorrow, or maybe the day after, I will become delirious,' Dao went on. 'It does not matter. We are travelling upstream. We will continue whatever happens to me. You must put me in the makoro and keep paddling towards where the sun rises. Understand?'

The boys nodded fearfully.

'Good,' Dao said. 'You will do as Mashuana tells you. You must keep travelling towards the sun. Sometime soon men will come down to the river and tell you to stop. They will be like the Felindi, white men with Felindi skins. You will say your bwana has the yellowing fever. You will ask for their help –'

Dao breathed in. His mouth was so enlarged it was difficult to suck air between his lips. Even his tongue was engorged with the insect bites.

'Do as the bwana says,' Mashuana instructed.

As the terrified Hlue scurried away, Dao lay back on the sand beside the fire.

Two months had passed since his agreement with Inchelele. Since then Dao, with his thirty Mashona, and Inchelele, marching behind with an impi of two thousand morans, had trekked west along the banks of the Chobe river.

They had not altogether been able to avoid the Great Thirst of the Kalahari, but wherever possible they had held to the river's bank. They crossed the Moremi plain, and travelled through the drylands of Savuti. Two weeks ago they entered the Okovango delta. Now they were a hundred miles into its waterways.

Twenty-four hours later, when the fever invaded Dao, his last thought before he lost consciousness was the same as when he first set eyes on the network of lagoons. The crazed explorer, Livingstone, was right.

There was water at the desert's end. Water and diamonds.

Like every European traveller in Africa, Dao had suffered attacks of malaria before. Dao's system was well used to producing antibodies to combat the fever. This time the response of his natural defences was weak and sluggish. Instead of fighting back, for five days he remained in a torpor. His skin turned a gangrenous yellow and his breath slowed by the hour. All the while, following his orders, Dao's makoros, the hollowed-out canoes of the delta's waterways, pressed deeper into the lagoons.

The Mashona bearers grew more and more uneasy and distressed. Eventually even Mashuana became frightened.

'Bwana, we must go back,' Mashuana pleaded in one of Dao's few moments of consciousness.

'No! Do as I say, continue upwards against the stream.'

'But, bwana, the sickness comes from the waters. The insects feed on you every hour.'

'Listen to me –'

Dao tried to shout. It was impossible. His voice shrivelled in his throat. Sweating and trembling, he forced himself upright in the stern of the boat.

'Would Sechele have gone on?' he managed to whisper.

Mashuana was silent. Then he smiled.

'Sechele would go on,' he replied.

Dao nodded. He tried to smile back, but the muscles of his face were too weak. He relapsed into unconsciousness again.

The makoros pressed on through the swamps.

Two days later, as the party beached for the night beside an oxbow lake, they were surrounded by a group of men carrying spears and swords. Most of the men were black Africans. As far as Mashuana could tell from their tribal markings, they came from Tswana tribes.

A few were different. They were unlike any race Mashuana had ever seen. Their skins were pale, but they were neither Felindi nor European. From their bearing they were clearly in command of the Tswana.

Mashuana tossed his own spear into the water. Then, with his arms spread wide and his open palms held upwards, he approached the man who appeared to be their leader.

'My master is sick with the fever,' Mashuana said. 'I am his headman. I ask for your help.'

The pale-skinned man glanced down into the makoro.

Dao was lying limp and unconscious on a thin bed of dry reeds between the paddlers' seats. His face was almost skeletally thin and the fever sweat was running down his emaciated cheeks. A trickle of saliva dripped down from his mouth and he moaned.

'Pick him up,' the man said curtly in the Tswana tongue to the Africans with him. 'You –'

He gestured at Mashuana and Dao's other bearers.

'You may come with him.'

An hour later Dao and the thirty Mashona found themselves inside what seemed to be a city floating on the waters of the Okovango river. Dao was still unconscious, but Mashuana's eyes swung alertly from side to side as he followed the pale-skinned men and their Tswana servants.

'How do you name your kraal?' he asked the party's leader, using the same Tswana tongue that the man had used.

'Ophir,' the man replied.

The man glanced back.

The expression on Mashuana's face indicated he was dazed by the height of the buildings and the width of the streets. The man smiled. Another primitive black, the man thought, who had never seen anything other than a kraal of baked earth and mud huts.

'Ophir has been here for two thousand years,' the man added. 'It will be here for two thousand years more.'

'Yes, bwana,' Mashuana said humbly.

Exactly two weeks afterwards, Dao rose to his feet in the darkness.

The Portuguese was weaker and thinner than he had ever been. When he walked he had bouts of shivering. Occasionally his head swam dizzily. Dao knew it would happen for another month at least. It did not matter.

He was inside the city's walls and the fever had burnt itself out.

'Are they all ready, Mashuana?' he asked softly.

'They have their rifles,' Mashuana replied. 'They are ready, bwana.'

'And my rifle?'

'Here, bwana. I have loaded it for you.'

Dao took the gun. As he checked the breech in the starlight from the window, he felt a wave of giddiness sweep over him. He staggered and clutched at the sill.

For a moment Dao leant against it, trembling.

He shook his head and forced himself to think of the diamonds. He had not seen them yet, but the conviction that they were somewhere close to him in the extraordinary wooden-walled city he had still only glimpsed through the windows was overwhelming.

It was too late, much too late, to let the legacy of the fever weaken his resolve now. He had dared everything for this. Inchelele and two thousand of his morans were waiting outside the walls. Dao and the Mashona were within. They had learnt the site of every gate and the position of every guard – Mashuana had seen to that.

And they had the rifles. The rifles. In Africa, Dao

repeated it to himself again and again as he struggled to throw off the giddiness, rifles were everything.

'Are you sick again, bwana?'

Dao heard Mashuana's worried voice at his shoulder. Dao heaved himself to his feet. Cursing, he pushed himself away from the windowsill.

'Of course I'm not sick,' Dao answered furiously. 'I am as ready as you are. Would not Sechele attack now?'

In the darkness Mashuana's teeth flashed white in a grin.

'Sechele would attack,' he replied.

'Then let us go.'

Dao led the armed column of the Mashona out of the buildings where they had been quartered into the silent early-morning city.

Fifteen minutes later, for the first time in their two-thousand-year history, the streets of Ophir rang with the sound of gunfire.

— 6 —

The old woman ran at a steady trot for seventy-two hours.

For the first hour she could hear the occasional crackle of gunfire. She didn't know the sound came from rifles. She had no idea what a rifle was. All she knew was that something terrible had happened in the great kraal behind her, the floating city on the river's waters, and the night had been rent with explosions like the thunder that came with the rains.

Gradually the sounds faded.

What didn't fade was the pressure against her wizened breasts of the infant who had been thrust into her arms before she fled from the city.

The old woman's name was Go-Ki. Go-Ki was tiny. Well under five feet in height, she came from a clan of Kalahari Bushmen – the 'San' people, as the apricot-skinned hunter-gatherers of the desert called themselves. As a young woman, Go-Ki had been captured by the people of the kraal. For the past thirty years the kraal had been her home.

When Go-Ki was taken there, she was set to work in what she came to recognize was the city's royal household. She had been in turn a menial servant, a wet nurse, and finally, as the years passed, a trusted playmate and companion to the royal children. When the rifle-fire began to detonate, she was asleep in the arched byres below the palace.

Fifteen minutes later she was standing in front of the woman she knew as Serapis.

'I bond her to you, Go-Ki –!'

Serapis held the child out to her.

Serapis, a tall, intelligent and commanding woman, was the senior lady of the household and one of the few people in the kraal who spoke the language of the San. In recent years a plague of tsetse fever had swept the kraal. Most of the royal children had died. The infant Serapis gave her, the little bundled girl, was the only one who had survived.

'Men have entered the kraal, evil men,' Serapis went on. 'They are bent on destroying it. You understand?'

Go-Ki nodded. It was impossible not to understand. The deadly tumult was raging all round her. She gripped the child to her breast.

'They will not succeed,' Serapis said 'The waters will stop them. But whatever happens here tonight, the child must live. She must go away until she can return. You know the waterways. You are the only one amongst us who does. With you she can travel to safety. With you she lives and Egypt lives. Guard her, Go-Ki, guard her with your own life! Now, go!'

Serapis began to push the old woman away.

Fires were blazing round them, and the air was thick with smoke and cascading sparks. As Go-Ki headed in the direction Serapis was urging her, she heard a cry.

'Wait –!'

Serapis' hands fell from Go-Ki's shoulders. Serapis glanced back. The old woman stopped and turned too. Someone else, another younger woman, was racing towards them, dodging the falling debris from the burning buildings. Go-Ki peered at her through the haze. She knew the younger woman. Her name was Flavia. She was one of Serapis' maids.

'The child must take this!' Flavia screamed.

She halted panting beside them. In her hand was a belt of oiled buffalo-skin with a bulging pouch at its centre. Serapis looked down at it. She frowned. Then she nodded in understanding. Serapis seized the belt and threaded it round the child's waist.

'Run, old woman, run!' Serapis shouted. 'Remember

what I have said. Egypt and now her star are in your care!'

Go-Ki turned and ran.

Serapis' words, fluently as they had been uttered in the clicking and whistling intonations of the San language, meant little to the old woman.

All Go-Ki had registered was the meaning behind them. Like an incantation it had entered her spirit. She had been given charge of life. The child's life and her own were one. Together they were all of life.

All of life was in her keeping.

At the beginning of her journey, darkness lay like a great cloak over the delta. The night made no difference to Go-Ki. The old woman knew, or she sensed, the course of every path that threaded the network of waterways.

Unerringly in the starlight she headed south.

Often, in the first night, she was aware of a flare against the sky behind her. A terrible fire was raging somewhere at her back. Go-Ki took no notice. She trotted steadily on. As dawn came the glow of the flames faded against the brilliance of the morning sky. All that day plumes of smoke stood like dark towers on the horizon at her back. When evening came again they were lost among the Kalahari stars.

Go-Ki trotted on throughout that second night.

Occasionally she paused and rested. She squatted in a thorn bush's narrow cone of shadow. She leant against a low dune's wall, her back to the sun. She sheltered under the trunk of a mopani tree uprooted by browsing elephants. Always within minutes she was on her way again.

And always, held tight to her breast, was the child Serapis had pressed into her arms.

Go-Ki ran on.

And then in the early afternoon of the third day, she stopped. She had been stumbling more and more all morning. Now she dropped panting to her haunches. She was old. She had been travelling for three days and nights. She had covered over one hundred and fifty miles, weighed down not only by the child but by the leather pitcher of milk and wheat gruel she had been given to feed her.

Go-Ki had come to the end of her powers.

She gave the child the last of the gruel and tossed the pitcher away. For an hour the old woman rested. Then she rose wearily to her feet.

Go-Ki had stopped beneath a tall camel-thorn acacia tree. She climbed the branches until she was ten feet above the ground. There she tied the child with leather thongs to the trunk. At least the infant would be safe for a while from anything except leopard and lion.

Go-Ki scrambled back to the earth.

The bush stretched out on every side, threaded with meandering game-paths between the scrub and thorn trees. For a long time Go-Ki studied the tracks imprinted on the sand. Finally she set off.

An hour later Go-Ki found what she was looking for.

Ahead of her the ground rose in a series of curving ripples like earthbound waves. The ripples sheered up into a bank that enclosed a smooth flat circle of sand. Formed by the action of rain and swirling winds, the circle was one of the Kalahari's many 'pans' – perfectly rounded depressions in the desert's surface that looked from the air like the pockmarks of craters on the moon.

Set into the bank that surrounded this particular pan were a number of large burrows. At the approach to each burrow the sand had been compacted and fretted with animal tracks.

Go-Ki squatted again.

She waited for another two hours. By the time evening came again her eyes were crusted and the bush was wavering dizzily in and out of focus. Her skin was so dehydrated it felt as brittle as the bronze mopani leaves at the dry season's end. If she touched it, Go-Ki sensed, it would break and flutter away from her flesh. Her head reeled and her mouth was so dry she couldn't part her lips.

Suddenly, as the light began to fade, her head jerked up. The tiredness dropped away from her.

An animal was emerging from one of the burrows. Massively built at its forequarters with a broad lowered head and a hide covered in thick smoke- and oatmeal-coloured fur, it was a female spotted hyena. Go-Ki glanced at its belly. The hanging dugs were swollen and damp. The animal had a litter hidden in the earth below.

Go-Ki had been sure from the pattern of the tracks on the earth that it was the case. Even so, she blinked momentarily in relief.

The hyena stared over the trenched clearing that surrounded the burrow. Go-Ki was hidden in a clump of dried grass at its edge and the evening breeze was behind her. The hyena didn't notice the old woman. The animal grunted and barked. Seconds later it was joined by eight other hyenas. All of them had been resting in adjoining burrows or lying up unseen among the ridges round the pan.

For a while the pack greeted and nuzzled each other. Then, without an apparent instruction, they trotted up on to the top of the ridge and vanished towards the west.

They had left, Go-Ki knew, to hunt.

Silently the old woman backed away through the grass. She returned to the tree. She climbed up and untied the still sleeping child. Then she went back to the burrows. There she knelt down and crawled into the entrance from which the female hyena had emerged.

It was impenetrably dark inside. The stench of animal odour, decayed meat, and hyena faeces was almost overpowering. Unperturbed, Go-Ki headed on, squirming forward on her belly. The tunnel opened into a chamber. Go-Ki raised her head and stretched out her hand. Her fingers touched a small warm bundle. Teeth tugged tentatively at her thumb and a tongue licked at her wrist.

It was a hyena cub.

Go-Ki shook the cub away and her hand explored further. There were four cubs in the litter. She grabbed the nearest by its head and pulled it squealing behind her as she slid back to the burrow's entrance. Outside, she broke the cub's neck with a single chop of her flattened hand. Then she reached for the child.

From the moment the child had been placed in her arms, it had been swaddled in a tiny kaross, a blanket of genet hides. Go-Ki unwound the kaross and rubbed the hyena cub's limp body all over the child's now naked skin. When she finished the child reeked of the same feral odour as the den. Pushing the child before her, Go-Ki crawled back into the tunnel and nudged the infant into the foul-smelling nest where the other three cubs were whimpering.

Go-Ki retreated again.

On the sand outside she climbed to her feet and glanced up. Night had dropped over the Kalahari and the sky was brilliant with multitudes of stars. To a stranger to the desert they would have been dizzying and incomprehensible in their numbers and brightness. Not to Go-Ki. For the old woman they made a pattern that was as clear and familiar as the simplest map.

Without conscious thought she orientated herself. Then she set off into the darkness, a tiny figure in the immensity of the bush. As she walked she spoke softly to herself in a series of rhythmic clicks and snaps.

She was talking to the spirits of the San people.

Go-Ki's journey, she knew, would take her days, through some of the most inhospitable terrain on earth. Its end, even if she reached the end, was doubtful. There was no guarantee she would find what she was looking for. And afterwards?

The 'afterwards' was far beyond the scope of Go-Ki's thought processes. Her mind, an extraordinarily flexible and sensitive instrument in terms of what her body asked of it, encompassed only one goal at a time. For now, all she had to do was reach another pan, a pan known to the San as *Iquat-Nmaka*, the pan of the lone thorn.

Lone Thorn Pan was a gathering place of her people, the San hunter-gatherers. When she arrived there, *if* she arrived there, her brain would change direction and set another target before her. Meanwhile she needed all the nurture and support the spirits of the San could give her.

As the Kalahari lions roared out their night hunting calls, she strode on through the darkness.

Go-Ki never reached Lone Thorn Pan.

As dawn approached, the old woman encountered the hyena pack returning from their night's hunt. The hunt had been unsuccessful. The moon was full. As always at full moon the pack's intended prey, the antelope of the plains, had scattered to take advantage of the security the moonlight gave them while they fed. The hyenas had made three separate attacks on wildebeest cows and one on a young gemsbok. All the attacks had failed.

Now, heading back to their den, the hyenas were hungry and fretful. The leading hyena, the lactating female who was the pack's matriarch, scented Go-Ki first. The early breeze was behind the hyenas and their pungent smell came to the old woman at almost the same instant.

Go-Ki knew exactly what the smell meant. Danger. Desperate imminent danger.

Adrenaline surged through the old woman's body.

She glanced quickly round. She was exhausted, but if there had been a tree close, the pumping energy of primal fear would have carried her at a run to it and up into the branches. There were no trees in sight. She was isolated in a patch of low thorn scrub.

The other hyenas had scented her now. The pack galloped forward. As their nostrils picked up the old woman's body odour, they called to each other in high-pitched screams. Go-Ki heard the light drum of their paws on the sand and the brush of their flanks against the thorn.

Go-Ki gave one final glance at the Kalahari stars as if still, at this last moment, the spirits of the San people would reach down and save her. Then, realizing the spirits wanted to take her to themselves, she squatted on the ground.

The old woman came from the sun. Like the racing hyenas, she was part of the life with which the sun's energy had canopied the earth. They were all bound together in the intricate pyramids of living. Now Go-Ki's force, the still vital protein stored in her body, would be handed on to the pack and she would return to the sun. Sooner or later she and the hyenas would come back to feed another cycle of life on the Kalahari sand.

Fatalistic and quite calm, she wrapped her arms round her knees and waited.

The hyenas killed Go-Ki very quickly.

The pack's matriarch tore away Go-Ki's throat with a swift pluck of her massive jaws. Then the hyena settled down to feed. The rest of the pack gathered round her and began edging forward hungrily. Each time they came too close, the big female bristled and snarled and chased them away.

She had four cubs to feed. The other members of the pack could wait.

Eventually the female hyena was satisfied. She raised her head. She yawned and belched. The rest of the pack, recognizing the signal, fell upon what was left of Go-Ki. Within minutes the old woman had vanished. Even the smallest of her bones had been cracked and eaten. Ten minutes later nothing remained of Go-Ki's presence on earth except a scuffed and empty space of bloodstained Kalahari sand.

By then the female hyena was trotting back towards her den.

Inside her stomach the protein was already beginning to be digested and converted into milk to fill her dugs. She needed to lactate. She had a litter to feed. The ancient imperative of sustenance came before even the demands of sex and territory.

Ahead of her in the lair lay her cubs. Not four now, but three. Three infant desert predators from the prehistory of animal evolution – and, tucked away beside them in the fetid darkness, a human child. Round the child's waist, tied tightly and buttressed awkwardly on her tiny hips, was a thick leather belt.

Inside the child's belt was the Star of Egypt.

The female hyena was unaware of the child and the diamond. She registered only the mewling, plucking, demanding mouths. She crawled into the burrow and settled down to let them suckle from her.

— 7 —

The child, Kala, opened her eyes.

As she did so she was assaulted by four sensations.

Weight was the first. Something warm and heavy was bearing down on her. Next she registered dark. It was darker than she had ever known. The faintest, thinnest trace of light had been blotted out. Not even the edge of a distant star's reflection penetrated the blackness.

After that the child's nostrils caught the smell. Raw and warm and rancid, the stench saturated the air. An instant later, mingled with the darkness and the smell, she picked up sounds – small snuffling and yelping sounds.

Drowsy with dehydration and heat exhaustion the child moaned and concentrated on the weight. She tried to push it away. Her hands touched something soft and damp. Fumbling, her fingers explored it. There was a new smell now, milky and moist. The new smell triggered a fifth sensation.

Hunger. Uncontrollable ravening hunger.

Instantly all the other impressions vanished. The child seized her discovery and pulled it to her lips. She began to suck greedily, drawing spurts of sweet thick fluid into her mouth.

From above her a massive heavy-jawed head came down and nudged the child into a more comfortable position among the other cubs. Then the animal rolled away and waited, panting, as the four little creatures suckled at its teats. It made no difference to the hyena that one of them was a two-year-old human child.

The child, smeared with the dead cub's urine and gland

scents, had become a member of the litter on equal terms with the rest.

Later the child dropped back into sleep.

Kala had no will of her own.

Once, although she was never to know it, she had been a strong-minded truculent infant – a pugnacious puppy of a child, tumbling and nosing and enquiring and demanding everywhere. No longer. That was in a different world. It had all gone, snuffed out like a candle in the wind. Now, submerged in a sea of darkness, she was just a tiny ripple of energy moulded and shaped and rocked by the vast ocean tide of the rhythms of animal life.

All she had left was her resilience, the unconscious spark of being that relentlessly kept her alive. For the rest there was only the sightless burrow and the flux of the unseen hyenas' movements round her.

Tides. They ebbed and flowed with the moon, rocking the young creatures in the den between food and sleep.

Mostly the child slept. At intervals the hollow of hunger in her belly woke her. Drowsily she would reach up for the teat that had fed her on the night she was thrust into the lair. For the first week the teat was often absent. She would lie mewling for an hour or more while the other cubs slumbered round her. Then the plump wet nipple would slap against her face. The cubs would waken, and they would all feed.

Soon her pattern of sleeping and feeding adjusted to the litter's. The four woke together, they suckled together, they dropped back into sleep together. The cubs adapted to the child just as much as the child adapted to the litter.

With the adjustment came a hierarchy. The lactating hyena had two rows of nipples. The nipples closest to her hind legs gave the biggest supply of milk. Inevitably they were the ones most fought over by the litter. In the struggle to win them, the child was at an advantage. She was bigger and stronger than any of the cubs.

By the end of the second week her position was secure. At the expense of many scratches on her arms and wrists, she established the right to draw from the teat that swung against the inside of the hyena's rear thigh. Across from the urinary duct that separated them, the litter's largest cub, the only male, fed hungrily.

Kala fed hungrily too.

Light.

It was only a tiny glow, a wavering halo against the darkness. But to the child it was as vivid and strange as if it were the first light she had ever seen. She blinked and the light had gone. Rubbing her eyes – the gleam had been as painful to her pupils as a scraping claw – she felt something shouldering its way past her. It was one of the cubs.

She reached out her hand and explored the thick-haired grunting shape.

Akula.

In her two weeks in the underground lair she had 'named' every member of the litter. Names, in terms of ordinary human speech, meant nothing to her. She had no idea what she was doing. What she felt was a need to identify the separateness of each of the cubs. She found she could label them with different sounds.

Akula was the male cub. She had labelled him after the grunting noise he made when he struggled for the teat. 'Akula! Akula!' was the sound that came to her ears. The sound became the name and the name became the cub.

Akula wriggled past her.

His shoulders filled up the tunnel's mouth. Then he was gone and the disc of light came back. The child wriggled after him. She worked her way round a bend in the tunnel. Suddenly the full force of the glow hit her.

The child squirmed and moaned and pressed the backs of her hands to her eyes. After a while warmth began to trickle through her fingers. The sharpness of the light's assault faded. She cautiously lowered her hands. For several moments, blinking under a tightly wrinkled forehead, she peered out at a dazzling pattern of sunshine and shadow.

Her eyes focused and she began to see.

Akula was a few yards in front of her, his head hunched awkwardly on his paws as he peered intently forward. Close to him was Ochla – the elder of the two female cubs in the litter. Like Akula, the child had named Ochla after the throaty sounds she made as she demanded the teat. To their right was Kwic-kwa, a tiny aggressive ball of fur, the second female and the runt of the litter.

Beyond them all, stretched out in a scoop of sand, was the sleeping body of the cubs' mother.

To the child until then the female had no name. She had simply been the vast warm presence which had periodically filled the lair and swung her nipples above the cubs. Without a voice – unlike her young she had never called or yapped or mewed – the hyena had given the child no means of identifying her.

Now she did.

Little Kwic-kwa bounded over and tried to nuzzle in under her mother's stomach. The female hyena tolerated her for a moment. Then she lost patience. She reached out with her forepaw and knocked her away, sending the cub tumbling head over heels in the sand. As she did so the hyena grunted.

To the child the grunt sounded like 'Herut'.

From that moment on Herut was how she mentally referred to the litter's mother. The litter's mother – and now her own.

She was no longer the child of humans. She had been absorbed into the world of animals. She had a new family. Her nurture and guidance, her comfort and safety, came from one of the desert's boldest and most efficient predators.

The child's role model – the model on which she would begin to create the patterns of her own life and behaviour – was a hyena.

— 8 —

Kala shuddered and cried out at the sudden sharp pain.

Something was gripping her round her neck. She struggled and flailed out wildly with her small plump fists, trying to fight free. It was useless. The grip tightened and she felt herself begin to move. At the same instant she recognized the smell of Herut.

The big female hyena had picked her up in her jaws, and was dragging her towards the den's entrance.

It was two weeks after the old woman, Go-Ki, left her with the hyenas – although the child had no concept of time, let alone any way of measuring its passing. All she knew was that she had been asleep in the darkness, and she had woken to an agonizing pressure on either side of her throat.

A moment later they came out into the light. As the child howled from pain, fear, and the blinding glare of the morning sun, Herut carried her fifty yards round the rim of the pan until she reached another tunnel in the bank of sand. Herut crawled inside and deposited the child in a new sleeping chamber. Then she backed out and trotted away to fetch her other cubs.

The child stretched out her hand and rubbed her neck. The pain was fading quickly. In spite of the discomfort that lingered for several minutes, Herut had carried her so gently that the hyena's teeth hadn't even punctured her skin.

Half an hour later all the cubs were installed beside her in their new home.

Burrowing among them, Kala slept again.

There were half a dozen different underground dens

within a few hundred yards of the first one. Over the weeks and then the months that followed, the child came to know them all. The movements of the litter between the dens in the jaws of Herut were one of the regular features in the life of the Merula Pan hyena clan.

As Kala unconsciously began to register with the unquestioning acceptance of a child's mind, it was a life almost as intricate and complex as the world of humans she had been plucked from.

Go-Ki had seen nine hyenas setting out to hunt on the evening she squatted above the pan's rim.

The nine were less than one-quarter of the Merula Pan clan's full strength – the clan, as the San people referred to hyena packs, took their name from the tall merula tree that grew beside the pan. In all, the clan consisted of almost forty individuals.

Their home territory was an oval of the northern Kalahari that spread out a mile in width and two miles in length from the pan. On every side the land marched with the territories of other hyena clans. On the ground the boundaries between the neighbouring territories were invisible, but to the nose – the hyena's nose – they were as clear and precise as if they were enclosed by posts and fences. They were marked daily by scent smeared on the grass from glands inside the animals' rear legs.

The land was the clan's private kingdom. Within its borders, like an ancient warrior tribe, the Merula Pan hyenas had won by battle and conquest jealously guarded rights to roam, breed, and above all to hunt. Only at its peril did an animal from another hyena clan cross the scent boundary into their preserve.

The forty Merula Pan hyenas varied widely in age. There were cubs like Herut's litter. There were young males and females. Breeding mothers like Herut herself. Older males and females. But the biggest and most important difference between them all was neither age nor sex.

It was seniority and rank.

Like every hyena clan, the Merula Pan hyenas were a matriarchal society. The clan was dominated and led by its breeding females. They in turn had their own hierarchy. The females at the top weren't necessarily the oldest. They were simply the most powerful and intelligent, the best equipped – in the collective judgement of the rest – to guide the destinies of everyone.

Herut was not only a breeding female. She ranked first of the four breeding females which made up the clan's ruling 'council'. Although Kala was never to appreciate it, Herut's status – effectively the leader of the entire Merula Pan clan – was to have a profound effect on the child's life. Indeed, through the complicated rhythms of hyena cub rearing, it almost certainly saved Kala's life.

Adopted by the great hyena as one of her own, from then on Kala was constantly under Herut's protection. If she had been placed in the litter of a lower-ranking female, Kala would probably have died within a few weeks as many other cubs did.

To have Herut as a mother was like becoming the favoured child of an autocratic and all-powerful queen.

Weighing one hundred and seventy-five pounds and standing just over three feet tall at her massive shoulders, Herut had a broad head, yellow eyes, alert pricked ears, and a steeply sloping back. Her mane was short and her smooth sand-coloured hide was patterned with a scattering of the round black spots that give the spotted hyena its name.

Everything about Herut's muscle-corded body radiated strength, boldness and aggression. She weighed as much as a large leopard yet, particularly in the company of her fellow hunters, was infinitely more dangerous than any leopard. She could run in short bursts at forty miles an hour, faster than almost any other animal of the desert. She was armed with the terrifying weapon of her jaws.

The same jaws which had carried Kala so gently could crack open the tree-like thighbone of an elephant to extract its marrow. Not satisfied even then, Herut would use the crushing vice of her teeth to grind and pulverize the remaining fragments of bone for her stomach to digest.

More than anything Herut was utterly fearless.

For a long time the furtive scuttling movements of hyenas and their chilling 'laughing' screams gave them a reputation for timidity and cowardice. They were animals, it was believed, which lurked in darkness, fed on carrion and stole from others. The muddled observations which created the reputation were made by white men newly come to Africa. Fettered by their preconceptions, blind and fearful about the true nature of the dark continent's wildlife, the white men invented a myth.

Had they consulted the dwellers and observers of Africa, above all its most ancient people, the San hunter-gatherers, they would have formed a very different opinion.

They would have learned that hyenas such as Herut are the bravest and most ruthless of all Africa's predators. They will feed off carrion if it becomes available. Far more often they hunt for themselves. They will not hesitate to attack animals as large as young rhino and elephant, even when the young are protected by parents armed with tusks and horns and weighing a hundred times as much as a hyena.

They will tackle a pride of lions feeding on a kill, challenging the lions and driving them from the carcass. They will hound leopards and rob them of their prey. They will drive wildebeest into rivers, dive into the water, and battle – and feed – swimming below the surface. They will brave fires and raid human settlements, defying guard dogs and guns.

Like all hyena matriarchs, Herut was cunning, resourceful and patient. She was superbly equipped as a single hunting machine in her own right, but she was always supported by the network of the clan.

The other clan members were only marginally less well endowed with courage and intelligence, but Herut held the edge over them all.

Yellow eyes gleaming as bright and translucent as the sun-dried stalks of the Kalahari's wavering trimedra grass, belts of muscle coiling tight and hard beneath her scarred and pitted hide, saliva dripping from her great jaws – saliva that her cubs, and soon Kala too, delighted in licking up for the salts and minerals it contained – Herut was the undisputed monarch of the clan.

Her leadership directed the lives of the others. Her intuition determined how they hunted and fed. Her dictatorship decided how they chose their mates, how they bred, and where and in what manner their cubs were raised.

She settled disputes with a flash of her fangs. She gave her approval with a grunt, a lick of her tongue, or a quiet roll on her back. She was more than a monarch. To the hyenas she was God, and her 'word' – her grunted or screamed instructions of warning, advice or encouragement – was Holy Law.

Over the weeks, months and then the years that followed, it was by Herut that Kala was imprinted with the lore of survival under the canopy of the Kalahari's oxygen, water and sunlight.

Kala's beginnings were very distant now. They survived only as a wavering memory in the darkest and most remote caverns of her child's recollections. Sometimes, dreaming between sleep and waking in the ever-changing dens where the litter was dragged, she heard the tap of carpenters' mallets, the sound of singing voices. Occasionally she even registered the features of a human face.

The occasions were rare and the images vanished quickly.

Deep and dark in the Merula Pan's burrow, the child, Kala, like a desert cobra, unconsciously began to slough off one skin and put on another. The skin she discarded was the wrapping of humanity. What she put on in its place was not so much a skin as a hide.

Kala became a hyena.

Only the glittering stone in the belt at her waist remained as a silent witness of her past.

— 9 —

'Make sure you look at Lkabe's foot,' Mrs Ramsay called after Mary-Ellen. 'I pulled the thorn out yesterday and put on some mercury-chrome, but it was still very swollen.'

'Yes, Mama.'

'And on your way back, check that Harimi really did feed the chickens this morning. You won't forget?'

'No, Mama.'

'And put your head into old Nkosi's hut to see if there's any news about that young wife of his.'

Twenty yards away by now, Mary-Ellen turned on the soft deep sand of the compound. Her mother was standing on the steps of the mission dwelling-house. Mary-Ellen pushed the broad-brimmed sunhat back from her forehead.

'Shall I pin the leaves back on to the baobab too?'

Mary-Ellen's face was a mask of innocent enquiry. Mrs Ramsay peered at her through the already fierce glare of the Kalahari morning.

'What, dear?'

'Never mind, Mama.'

Mary-Ellen waved affectionately. Then she set off again for the compound fence.

Mrs Ramsay watched her go.

The tiny village of Kuruman stood in what the Church Missionary Society colourfully but effectively described to its members as: 'The desolate and arid wastes of the extremity of the African continent, a place where even the savages must battle nature to survive'. More specifically, the village was set on the southern edge of the immense plateau of upland stone and sand known as the Kalahari desert.

To the south and west of Kuruman lay the prosperous but troubled British and Dutch settlements of South Africa. Stretching out on either side were the parched lands of the native Tswana tribes. To the north there was nothing but the great desert.

Dusty and sun-seared, swarming with flies and shadowed by vultures, the little settlement lay like a lonely bird's nest blown down by the wind on to the emptiness of the pale Kalahari sand.

The Kuruman mission post had been founded half a century earlier by a Scottish missionary, the Revd Robert Moffat. Moffat was at heart a gardener, not a missionary. He grew good cabbages at Kuruman, but in all his time there Moffat reckoned he saved only one African soul. Moffat's fame came at one remove. Another missionary was brought to Kuruman after being mauled close to death by a lion.

Much younger than Moffat, the missionary was nursed back to health by Moffat's daughter. Inevitably the two young people fell in love. Not long afterwards they married. The missionary's name was David Livingstone. The legendary journeyings of the great explorer – Dr Livingstone opened up more of the planet than anyone before or since – began in Moffat's home and with the encouragement of Moffat's daughter.

To Mrs Ramsay the story of the mission's founding and Livingstone's epic adventures belonged to history.

Although Livingstone himself had died only a few years earlier, his connection with Kuruman had been severed long ago. Yet his presence – dark, brooding, almost demonic in its intensity – still seemed to haunt the remote little village. Livingstone was just one of the many shadows over Mrs Ramsay's life.

Mrs Ramsay hated Africa. She hated being a missionary's wife. Most of all she hated the bleak wilderness of the Kalahari which imprisoned her. It was the last place in all the world she would have chosen to live – not that she'd been given any choice in the matter. Her mother had arranged it, but then she'd arranged everything. She'd even arranged her marriage.

Mrs Ramsay shuddered as she remembered.

When her mother discovered what had happened, she had written to the secretary of the Church Missionary Society. The Society published a newsletter in which bachelor missionaries in the far-flung territories overseas advertised for wives. It was the only way, in their isolated outposts of Christianity among the heathens, that they could reach respectable, white young women with the same beliefs and values.

The secretary sent back a list of names to her mother. The third name on the list – the first two, it transpired, had died of fever – was the Revd George Ramsay.

Mr Ramsay had been entrusted by the CMS with the small but celebrated mission at Kuruman – celebrated, of course, for its links with Dr Livingstone. Mr Ramsay was, in the report of the examining commissioners who had given him the appointment:

'A taciturn and, to the appearance, a somewhat cold man and a strict, it has been alleged over-strict, disciplinarian. Earnest for truth, he is impatient of error. By temperament he is said to be choleric. Physical chastisement, he said to us, he regards as essential for the correction of transgressions.

'He would not be suited, we feel, for an appointment in a temperate clime where manners and morals are modest. However, his forthright approach and his undoubted convictions may well find their appropriate expression amid the rigours of the Kalahari.'

Fifty years later the Church Missionary Society would almost certainly have rejected Ramsay for what he undoubtedly was – a violent and psychopathic bully with an uncontrollable temper. At the time, desperate to engage staff for the hazardous and unpopular African missions, they accepted him in spite of their evident misgivings.

Ramsay was posted to Kuruman. After nine years in

the isolation of the desert village, he advertised in the CMS newsletter for a wife. Eighteen months later the young woman who the following day became Mrs Ramsay – Ramsay conducted the marriage service himself –arrived at the mission.

The events of her past were of no interest to him. Ramsay wanted a wife and housekeeper. Now he had one. He would provide for her and he would be a good father, a *strict* father, to any child that might arrive. Ramsay believed that the boot, the fist and the whip – particularly the knotted rhino-skin sjambok – were chief among the Almighty's chosen instruments of correction and instruction for black and white, adult and child alike.

What Mrs Ramsay believed didn't matter, it had never mattered. Once she had had her dreams – she had even dreamed of Paris. The dreams had ended with a brutal finality that morning twenty-one years ago when she stepped down from the waggon, and walked through the mission gates. All she'd known ever since was the Kalahari desert and a cold, bigoted and sadistic husband.

The one saving grace had been her daughter. Through watering eyes Mrs Ramsay followed Mary-Ellen down to the stockade fence.

Even at this early hour the African light was brutal. The huts that rimmed the compound were small and stark and coarse – dark bundles of twigs against the pitiless white sky. The fence posts of the compound's perimeter, adze-chipped stakes of hardwood, lifted like bars against the horizon. One of the Tswana staff had killed a springbok antelope two days before. The stench of the drying flesh hung pungent and rancid in the morning air.

Yet even in that unlikely setting there was something unmistakably elegant in the way Mary-Ellen walked – a grace in the swirl of the sun-bleached cotton dress, a poise in the angle of her neck, a delicate balance in the stride of her long legs.

Mary-Ellen moved like a dancer across a ballroom floor.

Something caught at Mrs Ramsay's throat. Then Mary-Ellen disappeared through the gates that led to the secondary compound which housed the blacks. Behind her she left only a billowing cloud of dust raised by her footsteps, and the vanishing shadow of her parasol.

'Mama Ram'y! Mama Ram'y!'

Saduka, one of the mission girls, came padding towards Mrs Ramsay, vacant-eyed and swollen-bellied with pregnancy. Mrs Ramsay answered her question and scolded her back to work.

A dancer.

Mrs Ramsay stepped inside. The windows of the large living room were shaded from the sun by a steeply sloping straw awning outside. Inside it was dusky and almost cool. Mrs Ramsay stood in the well of shadow, her hands resting on one of the windowsills as she gazed back into the glare beyond.

A dancer.

Her nails dug into the wood. Like the compound stakes, the sill was made of African hardwood. Her nails should have broken as she pressed them against it. They didn't. Hard as the wood was, termites had burrowed into it and reduced the timber to a soft honeycomb of yielding fibres. In Africa nothing, not even iroko, was what it seemed.

A dancer.

Dancers came from dancing-masters. That was something Mary-Ellen would never know.

— 10 —

Mary-Ellen walked steadily in the little pool of shadow cast by her parasol.

At twenty-two Mary-Ellen was unmistakably Mrs Ramsay's daughter. She had her mother's tall poised figure, her firm breasts and her long well-made legs. She had her mother's flawlessly even features, and the long tawny-blonde hair – although her mother's was dry and greying now.

But there were differences between them. The most striking ones were in their mouths and eyes.

Mrs Ramsay's mouth had always been narrow. The long years of frustration and unhappiness had made it more so. Mary-Ellen's mouth was broad, generous and laughing. Where her mother's eyes were a washed-out grey, Mary-Ellen's were a deep chestnut brown flecked with gold and green. Bold, sparkling, and often remote as if they looked on horizons Mrs Ramsay had not even dreamed of, Mary-Ellen's eyes could never have belonged to her mother.

Mary-Ellen's eyes drew their depth and strength from somewhere else.

The heat inside the stockade round the mission house was stifling. At least the compound was shaded by a group of baobab trees. Beyond the gates there was nothing except bare sand and a pulsing white sky. At ground level on the plain the air was like a furnace. A few vultures floated lazily on the invisible pillars of the thermals, the currents of hot rising air which supported their huge wings, and a yellow-billed kite coasted hungrily overhead.

Otherwise the desert beyond was silent and still.

It was high summer. Unlike her mother, Mary-Ellen was hardly troubled by even the worst of the dry season's heat. Mrs Ramsay seldom ventured beyond the compound gates. She had never adjusted to the temperatures of the Kalahari, and she clung to the baobabs' shade like an insecure child to its security blanket.

Mary-Ellen was a true child of the ancient stone plateau. She had been born there. She had grown up there. The Kalahari's moods, the unrelenting ferocity of its sun, the swirling sandstorms that blew out of the north, the occasional brief days of softness and damp shining green, were all she had ever known.

To Mary-Ellen the desert was her home.

In fact the Kalahari wasn't really a desert at all. Certainly not in the sense the Sahara was a desert – boulders and shifting sand dunes and constant unremitting drought. The Kalahari had been named a desert by Africa's early European explorers like Livingstone. The reason was its lack of any permanent water. Certainly the rains often failed. When they did, the Kalahari could be among the most desolate landscapes on earth.

But when the rains came, the Kalahari could flower as rich and green as any part of Africa. Even in its cycles of dryness, the Kalahari's hardy vegetation, rooting deep in the sand on the desert's stone floor, still supported one of the largest populations of birds and animals in the entire continent.

'*Pula*, Mama Mary!' Moffat greeted her.

Moffat must have seen her coming. As she turned into the sprawling cluster of native huts that lay to the west of the compound, he stepped out into the sun to meet her.

'*Pula*, Moffat!' Mary-Ellen replied.

In Batswana, the main language of the settlement, *pula* meant rain. The Tswana tribes used it as their traditional greeting. To the people of the desert, *pula* was the most potent and magical of all incantations. *Pula*, rain, was life.

'What do you do today?' Moffat went on.

The same age as Mary-Ellen, Moffat was black. Unlike most of the other Africans at Kuruman, he wasn't a native Tswana but a member of one of the warlike Mashona tribes from somewhere far to the east. Moffat's origins had always been a mystery.

He had arrived as a child at the mission one night with his mother. According to the woman, her husband, Moffat's father, had been a chieftain who died soon after Moffat's birth. Later there had been a quarrel over inheritance. She and the child had been expelled from the tribal lands. They had been travelling ever since.

At least that was what the Ramsays, who were unfamiliar with the Mashona dialect, understood. The outline of the story was certainly common enough. In different shapes and forms, it featured in almost every account of African misfortune. What was clear was that both mother and child were on the point of starvation.

As good Christians, the Ramsays gave them food and shelter. The woman's condition was even worse than it seemed. Her body never got over her ordeal, and within a few weeks she was dead. The child, on the other hand, recovered quickly. In contrast to the somnolent Tswana children, he returned to health as an energetic and alert little boy.

Mrs Ramsay decided he would make an excellent playmate for Mary-Ellen. Mrs Ramsay had never managed to grasp the boy's native heathen name. It wasn't important. The child was christened Robert Moffat after the mission's founder, and moved into the mission house. Since then he and Mary-Ellen had grown up together. When he reached puberty, Moffat – only his second name was ever used – was sent back to the African compound, and told to address Mary-Ellen as Mama Mary.

In public he always did. When they were alone together, at Mary-Ellen's insistence Moffat used her own name. To Mary-Ellen he was far more than her childhood companion. To all intents and purposes Moffat was her brother.

'As usual Mama's given me a whole list of things to do.' Mary-Ellen ran through her mother's instructions. 'When I've finished, I'll go to the river.'

'I will come with you round the huts,' Moffat said.

They set off together through the village.

The errands took them half an hour to complete. There was no need for Moffat to escort her. Mary-Ellen had known the villagers as long as he had, and spoke their various dialects just as fluently. But she was always happy to be with him, and she knew it gave Moffat pleasure too.

'Thank you,' she said as they finished.

They were standing at the far end of the village with the mission compound almost half a mile behind them.

Moffat looked at her, frowning.

He had grown up into a tall and well-made young man, with the spare graceful frame of the Mashona and their keen fierce eyes. He could read and write English without hesitation – he had learnt alongside Mary-Ellen in the mission schoolroom. He helped Mr Ramsay with the mission's business. He was well fed and well paid. Young as he was, by African standards Moffat had an extraordinarily rewarding life.

Yet as she looked back at him, Mary-Ellen knew he wasn't content. It wasn't just the banishment to the compound after his years in the mission house. Moffat had never been content. She had sensed it when they were both children. Moffat was haunted by the missing spaces, the blind windows, in his past. He was a Mashona among Tswana. It was like being, as he told her once, a warrior without a spear among goats.

His name and his past were his spear. They had been taken from him and lost. Now they were beyond finding.

'You be careful at the river, Mary-Ellen,' he said. 'Very careful. There are many crocodiles this year.'

'Moffat, I've been going to the river almost every day for three years now. There are always many crocodiles –'

Mary-Ellen laughed. She gave him a quick kiss on the cheek and patted his arm reassuringly.

'But, yes, I'll be careful. I promise!'

Moffat smiled back. He turned away.

Mary-Ellen set off again. She didn't head directly for the river. In Africa every step of life was controlled by ritual. Her walk through the village with Moffat was just one of many.

Before she approached the waters there was another unchanging ritual she had to go through.

— 11 —

Beyond the village was another, smaller, encampment of grass-roofed huts, most of them little more than hovels.

Mary-Ellen headed towards them.

'Chi-mona!' Mary-Ellen called.

'Mama Mary!'

It was not so much a hut as a tiny hovel. There was a stir in the dusk at the back. Jagged tobacco-stained teeth gleamed in a welcoming smile and an old woman shuffled forward.

'Where have you been, child? It is five days since you came. That has not been so since the rains.'

The old woman embraced her. She barely reached Mary Ellen's chest. Mary-Ellen stooped and held her round her shoulders.

'I have been busy helping Mama Ram'y,' Mary-Ellen replied. 'I am happy to be back.'

The two squatted on the beaten earth floor and began to talk.

They spoke not in Tswana, the language Mary-Ellen had used in the village proper, but in a mishmash of dialects. Some of the phrases they exchanged were in Herero, some in Xhosa, some in Hottentot. But the majority were in the guttural click language of the San people – the ancient desert Bushmen.

The satellite village housed the servants of the black Tswana who in turn provided the servants for the mission. By 1876 slavery had technically not existed in Africa for almost half a century, and certainly not in the continent's mission posts. To the Revd Ramsay, who found the whole business too taxing to sort out clearly, the hovel dwellers were his congregation's paid help.

The hovel dwellers were San.

They acted as herders for the Tswana. They gathered the Tswana's wood, drew their water, and built their huts. They did everything the Tswana ordered them to. In return they were given a little maize and allowed space to erect their primitive dwellings. To Ramsay it appeared a reasonable exchange of services for goods.

Mary-Ellen had a different view.

To her the mixed interbred community of Herero, Xhosa, San, and half a dozen other dispossessed races – speaking out of necessity the mongrel tongue she used with old Chi-mona – were as much slaves as any column of black Africans trudging west in chains to be laden into the West Indian sugar ships.

One word of defiance to their effective owners, the Tswana, and they would forfeit both shelter and food. They would be turned loose into the desert to die. Worse, if they attempted to escape even without a dispute, the Tswana would saddle their horses, ride out to round them up, and whip them back to the village.

Mary-Ellen had a deep affection for the Tswana. She had a deeper affection still for the community of outcasts who were their slaves. Of all the outcast races the one she loved best was the little people, the San. Mama Chi-mona was a purebred San – however much in her long years of enslavement she had lost of her native tongue.

'So, my child,' Mama Chi-mona said as they finished discussing the affairs of the village, 'you wish to go to the river?'

'I am thirsty for its waters,' Mary-Ellen answered.

'I know your thirst for the waters. If I let you, you would drink the river dry!' The old woman rocked with laughter. 'Your clothes are here where they will always be. I will call my grandchildren.'

Mama Chi-mona handed Mary-Ellen a jackal-hide sack. The old woman got to her feet and called for her grandchildren.

Mary-Ellen moved through into a larger hut beyond, and began to undress.

It was a laborious process. Her mother had always insisted she wear the full range of clothing of a New England young lady, from the complicated undergarments to the buttoned and hooked skirt and long-sleeved blouse. Mary-Ellen had learnt not to argue with her. There were more important battles to be won than over stays, laced boots and ribboned hats.

She stepped out of her knee-length drawers. For a moment she stood naked.

As always, she felt a sense of exhilaration and freedom. Her body shining white in the hovel's darkness, she swung round on her feet. Her hair flared out round her head and her eyes shone with pleasure. She paused. The year before she had given Mama Chi-mona a mirror as a present. She stopped to inspect herself in its dim reflection, as shadowed and silvery as the water under the river's bending trees.

She saw her neck and lifted her chin to bring out its length. She passed her hands over her breasts. She tilted them up slightly and felt her nipples. She slid her fingers down across her flat stomach to the triangle of golden hair at her groin. She touched the hair, feeling its crispness. She moved her hands further down along her thighs.

Then she swung her head up again and laughed.

She dressed herself in the clothes that for three years now she had kept in Mama Chi-mona's hut. It took her only moments. The clothes were very simple. A length of cotton folded round her waist. Another shorter length to drape her chest and shoulders. A pair of woven grass sandals on her feet. It was what the native women wore. Dressed in them, Mary-Ellen felt cool and comfortable. Most of all she felt free in a way that the tight and claustrophobic clothes her mother demanded never allowed her to be.

'They are ready, Mama Mary,' the old woman called from the hut's entrance.

Mary-Ellen went outside. Waiting for her were the old woman's three grandchildren, two little girls and a ten-year-old boy.

They twisted their hands together shyly as Mary-Ellen greeted them. With a wave to the old woman, she and the children set off for the river.

Without food a human can live for at least a month and sometimes longer. Without water, and above all in the ferocious moisture-sapping dryness of wastes like the Kalahari, life expectancy dwindles to a day or two, or even hours. Every mission in Africa, like every African village, was sited close to water.

The mission at Kuruman took its name from the river that ran by it.

For the half mile that bordered the village and the mission compound, the Kuruman flowed between low banks through a stretch of open plain. Half a mile upstream its waters narrowed. The bush closed in and the river began to twist and turn. On either side trees and scrub plunged down their roots to reach for its life-giving moisture.

It was there that Mary-Ellen and her three small companions headed.

As they approached a little oxbow lagoon, the boy broke away from them and took up his position under the shade of a young merula tree. Mary-Ellen went on with the little girls until they were standing on the sandy bank by the water's edge.

'Men or crocodiles,' she said. 'Which is worse?'

The girls covered their mouths and giggled.

'Until you discover, watch out for them both,' Mary-Ellen added.

She slipped out of her clothes. She handed the cotton wraps to the children. They stood gazing up and down the stream.

Mary-Ellen stepped naked into the river.

She waded forward until it was lapping at her body just below her breasts. The river was golden-brown. The gold was the colour of the Kalahari sand at dawn, the dusky brown the hue of the thorn bush that swept down across its banks. Below the surface tendrils of green weed coiled in the pull of the flow.

Gold and brown and green.

The colour of her eyes. She stared down into the opaque brilliance. The tapestry of light flared back at her. Mary-Ellen laughed. She plunged her head into the current and set out for the far bank. Five minutes later, glistening and fresh and cool, she swam back and clambered out.

'Right,' she said as she wrapped the cotton skirt round her hips and slung the bodice over her shoulders, 'call your brother. We have work to do.'

As one of the girls ran back into the bush, Mary-Ellen took the little hide bag from the other child. She rummaged inside and pulled out a leather-bound note-book. She had just reminded herself of the last entry when the boy came springing down the bank.

'I hope you know where those baboons have got to,' she said. 'If you've lost them, both Dr Darwin and I are going to be very cross.'

She scowled theatrically.

The boy threw back his head with delight. He had no idea who Dr Darwin was, nor what Mama Mary was doing in the endless expeditions she made in pursuit of the Boteti's baboon packs. It didn't matter. Mama Mary was second in his pantheon of idols only to the great sun-god Xa.

'Come with me, Mama Mary,' he said. 'I've been watching them ever since you were here last. They are feeding two bends up the river. I shall show you now.'

He seized her hand and tugged Mary-Ellen forward.

As she followed him Mary-Ellen was remembering the sight of her body in the mirror of Mama Chi-mona's hut.

She had reacted happily to the images thrown back at her from the chipped glass. She had touched and stroked herself, on her breasts and across her groin and along her legs. The sensation had been warm and pleasurable. But then, of course, it should have been. It would have been very strange if it hadn't.

She had been grooming herself.

Animals responded to visual images. As the images reached them, they often instinctively groomed themselves. There were many reasons for the grooming. As often as not, Mary-Ellen had noticed, it was to arouse them for the most vital function of all in an animal's life – for sex.

It was months after she recorded it before she could bring herself to put the observation to Dr Darwin. When she wrote the letter, her face had been flushed and her hand shaking as the pen covered the paper. Darwin's reply had been characteristically crisp and to the point.

'Of course, my dear,' he replied. 'Look in a mirror and, if I may with delicacy suggest an experiment, test the matter with yourself. I venture you will find the same – for you are an animal too.'

Mary-Ellen shook her head as she thought of his words.

Darwin was right. The great doctor, of course, was always right. He had been from the time when, even at the vast distance which still separated them, he entered her life. That had been the most momentous event in her entire existence.

In time, Mary-Ellen sometimes thought, she might forget the horror of what else happened then. Her parents never would – and, mercifully, they only knew half of the truth. If her father discovered what had really taken place, he would certainly have killed her. But her father would never know. He didn't even know about Darwin.

Only Mary-Ellen knew the full story. It had changed her life for ever. Dr Darwin was the one saving grace to have emerged from the nightmare. She would never meet him. He remained her salvation – and yet in a way her curse, the albatross tied round her neck.

The Revd Ramsay might somehow find it in himself to forgive James Cotton Oswell as a common lecher and fornicator. Darwin he would never forgive even if the gates of hell were closing round him.

Mary-Ellen shivered.

She caught the boy's hand and walked on. She tried to listen as he spoke to her about the baboons. She could not. Her concentration wavered and drifted away.

Mary-Ellen was thinking of the day almost five years before when the young man who announced himself as James Cotton Oswell walked into the lonely little world of the Kuruman mission.

— 12 —

'Good evening, ma'am –'

The man took off his wide-brimmed leather hat. He lowered his head in a swift graceful bow.

'James Cotton Oswell at your service. I was wondering if I might trespass on your hospitality and make my camp inside the compound tonight.'

Mrs Ramsay started.

To her astonishment the visitor was a gentleman. His accent was the most refined she had ever heard in Africa. So were his manners. The bow was almost courtly. Her hand went to her throat and she flushed in confusion.

Then she managed a flustered smile.

'Of course,' Mrs Ramsay replied. 'I – we – would be delighted.'

'I am infinitely obliged.' The man returned her smile. 'I will set my servants about their business. Then, if I may, I will return to pay my respects to your husband.'

He bowed again and turned.

'Who is he, Mama?' Mary-Ellen whispered as she stood behind her.

'His name is Mr Oswell,' Mrs Ramsay replied. 'Much more important, he is evidently a gentleman.'

Mrs Ramsay stared rapturously into the darkness where the traveller was walking away.

Mary-Ellen gazed after him. The man was tall and narrow-hipped with long arms and a wrist that flashed white as he removed his hat. His hair was short and curling. His face was fine-drawn, and his eyes in the lamplight had shone a deep gentian blue. Across his shoulders he wore a tweed cloak. As he disappeared it swung out like a bell.

Mrs Ramsay drew in her breath. She closed her eyes. For an instant the sounds of the Kalahari evening faded. She heard instead the distant strains of a waltz rising and falling like the sea, and she saw a silhouette watching her across the floor.

A lion roared and the moment passed. She shook her head and went inside. Mary-Ellen followed her. Mr Oswell reminded her of nothing at all.

He was simply the most beautiful man Mary-Ellen had ever seen.

'I'll take it, Mama,' Mary-Ellen said eagerly.

The family were at breakfast the following morning.

Oswell had camped at the edge of the compound, just out of sight of the dining room window. Mary-Ellen had already been up for two hours watching from her own window. She saw Oswell appear from his tent. She stared fascinated as he stripped to his waist to wash and shave in a tiny canvas washing-bowl mounted on a tripod of sticks. When he finished he sat down by his fire and lit a pipe.

When Oswell had returned the night before to introduce himself to Mr Ramsay, Mrs Ramsay had promised him a freshly baked loaf. Now she was about to take it out to him. Mrs Ramsay hesitated.

'Don't be so stupid, Mary-Ellen,' her father snapped before his wife could answer. 'He doesn't want to be bothered with a child.'

Mary-Ellen held her breath. Mrs Ramsay very seldom contradicted her husband. She did now.

'I think Mr Oswell might enjoy Mary-Ellen's company,' she said. 'Furthermore, it would do the girl nothing but good to listen to an educated voice. Mr Oswell's cadences are truly charming.'

Without giving her husband the chance to disagree, she turned to her daughter and added, 'Make sure you don't trespass on Mr Oswell's time, dear. But if he does wish to converse, listen very carefully to his modulations.'

'Yes, Mama.'

Before her father could object, Mary-Ellen seized the loaf and ran outside.

Oswell had finished breakfast by the time she reached his fire. His Tswana servants were scouring the dishes with sand, and Oswell was cleaning a rifle. Mary-Ellen approached him shyly. She held out the loaf.

'Mama asked me to give you this,' she said. 'It was baked this morning.'

'Why, thank you, young lady.' Oswell jumped to his feet. 'And please give my warmest thanks to your dear mother for her kindness.'

He took the loaf and smiled. Mary-Ellen smiled back. There was silence.

'Well, thank you again,' Oswell said.

In growing despair Mary-Ellen watched him swing round and head for the provision box mounted on the back of his waggon.

'Excuse me.' Her voice was tremulous as she hurried after him. 'I saw you were cleaning your rifle. Have you come here to hunt?'

'Indeed I have,' Oswell answered with his back to her.

'I might be able to help you. I know quite a deal about hunting and the game of the neighbourhood.'

Oswell paused and glanced back. 'How very interesting. You hunt lion and elephant yourself, do you?'

'No, I don't hunt myself –'

Oswell's eyes were twinkling. For a moment in her eagerness to talk to him, Mary-Ellen only registered his words.

'But I have many friends among the Bushmen who live here. They call themselves the San and they're the best hunters in all Africa –'

She stopped. Oswell, she realized suddenly, was struggling not to laugh. Mary-Ellen's cheeks flushed scarlet.

'You're laughing at me.' A surge of anger succeeded her embarrassment. 'You think I'm a silly young girl who doesn't know what she's talking about. Well, you're wrong. I really could have helped you. Now –'

She didn't finish. She gazed at him furiously, her face hot and smarting. Then she swung round on her heel.

'Please don't go –'

There was a hand on her elbow and a voice speaking close to her but from somewhere, it seemed, high above her head. The voice was Oswell's.

'I owe you my deep apologies. Please accept them.'

Mary-Ellen's eyes were damp with tears. She blinked them away and glanced up. Oswell was no longer smiling. Against the Kalahari sky his face was filled with remorse.

'It is a wretched excuse,' he went on, 'but when I looked at you in your delightful frock with that enchanting parasol and imagined you hunting those terrifying beasts, my frivolous sense of humour got the better of my judgement. Let me think how I can atone –'

Oswell paused.

To Mary-Ellen's astonishment, he suddenly let go of her elbow. He dropped to his knees before her, and spread out his arms in a theatrical gesture of entreaty.

'Take pity on a penitent, I implore you! Allow me to make my peace. Agree to sit by my hearth and accept as a small token of my repentance a cup of my fragrant Lapsang Suchong.'

His eyes rolled upwards in anguish and he struck his brow with his wrist. Mary-Ellen stared at him in confusion. Then she burst into laughter.

'I don't know what that is but, yes, I'd like to very much.'

Oswell jumped up.

He clapped his hands and shouted for his servants. 'Tea for the lady instantly! We are all guilty. We all have restitution to make. Hurry! Hurry!'

A few minutes later Mary-Ellen was perched opposite him across the embers of the fire with a tin mug of steaming hot tea in her hands.

'Peace?' Oswell asked as she raised the mug to her lips.

His auburn hair was tumbling forward over his forehead. His eyes sparkled, and his smile was irresistible. She laughed and nodded.

'Peace,' she replied.

'Now to business.' Oswell rubbed his face thoughtfully. 'First, I suppose, who am I?'

'I beg your pardon?' Mary-Ellen said, startled.

'Although I was too obtuse to notice it,' he said, 'you clearly wish to talk to me. *Ergo* you'll need the basic information. To save you the trouble, young lady, I thought I'd put the questions and answer them myself. Sensible?'

Mary-Ellen nodded. 'Except I'm not really a young lady. I'm just Mary-Ellen.'

'You're young and you're a lady, *ça se voit*. But Mary-Ellen –?'

Oswell's voice was doubtful. He put his head on one side and examined her carefully.

'I think not. Somehow the name is too domestic, too antiseptic and earnest. You need something wilder, more passionate.' He snapped his fingers. 'Of course, I have it. Clarissa to the very last straying curl! How do you like that?'

Mary-Ellen's hand went to her hair. 'But I'm still only Mary-Ellen –'

'But me no buts,' he interrupted her. 'Clarissa you are and Clarissa you shall be. And now you shall have your answers. Name: James Cotton Oswell. Title: Gentleman – or at least an overseas member of that club. Occupation: Bad hat.'

Mary-Ellen glanced instinctively at the battered leather hat on Oswell's head. 'You make bad hats?'

Oswell shook with laughter.

'The world, Clarissa, is divided into good eggs and bad hats. Most people, like my parents and no doubt yours, come into the first category. A few come into the second. I'm one of them.'

Mary-Ellen frowned. 'I still don't see.'

'Good eggs are virtuous. Prudent, honest, loyal, hardworking. Bad hats are just the reverse. They're idle, they're spendthrift, they gamble, they haunt low taverns and visit houses of – well, they do a number of other unmentionable things too.'

Mary-Ellen's eyes widened in understanding. 'You're a sinner.'

'How admirably put! In my case an utterly, incurably, and happily congenital sinner.'

If Mary-Ellen was capable of regarding the stranger with greater interest and respect than before, she did so then. She knew all about sinners from her father's thunderous denunciations of them in his sermons. Like any child they had become invested for her with the glamour and mystery of the unknown. Now, for the very first time, here was one of them sitting face to face before her. Instead of the sunken-eyed despair she'd imagined, this one was brimming with exuberant vitality and laughter.

She smiled at him.

'Papa says one finds the worst sinners in cities. Why have you come to the desert?'

Oswell slapped his thigh in pleasure. 'Clarissa, you are pure gold. Why indeed, as you so quaintly imply, did I abandon my home pastures of Sodom and Gomorrah for the Great Thirst –?'

He paused. His tone changed.

'Even the worst hats are allowed to know a few good eggs,' Oswell said quietly. 'I came here because of my best egg. He was my father.'

'Your father?'

He nodded. 'He died last year. While he lived I have to confess we did not get on well. To be frank, I thought him a sanctimonious prig. What he felt about me I dread to think. But he left me the estate which my grandfather had passed on to him, and I finally decided I owed them this pilgrimage, if you like. They both loved the Kalahari better than anywhere else on earth. I came to see why.'

The name Oswell had been plucking insistently at the back of Mary-Ellen's mind ever since he first introduced himself. She suddenly realized why. The name was so famous she was astonished neither of her parents had made the connection.

'Was your father the Mr Oswell who crossed the desert with Dr Livingstone?'

Oswell chuckled. 'You are destined to be the grave of all my vanities, Clarissa. I am assuredly old but not yet, I protest, that ancient. No, it was not my father who accompanied the great doctor but my grandfather.'

'But your father came here too?'

Oswell nodded. 'We have both trodden in Grandfather's footsteps in more ways than one. He was a Coldstreamer, so was my father, so was I.'

'Coldstreamer?' Mary-Ellen's face was puzzled again.

'A soldier,' Oswell replied. 'An officer in Her Majesty's Coldstream Guards. The most exalted and, to my mind, the most ineffably boring role life has to offer. I took it on because of "tradition" and because I knew no better. Mercifully a misunderstanding over cards resulted in a request for me to resign. It was the happiest day in my life – and the one that solidified my father's growing *froideur* into ice.'

'What did you do then?' Mary-Ellen demanded.

Some of Oswell's words and phrases were beyond her comprehension. But even when she didn't understand them Mary-Ellen knew beyond any doubt that she was listening to the most fearsome and exciting catalogue of sins she had ever heard.

'I went to Paris,' Oswell said. 'I studied how to paint. If you really want to know, I painted naked ladies.'

Mary-Ellen gasped. 'You mean without their clothes on?'

'Without *any* of their clothes on.' Oswell wagged his finger at her.

Mary-Ellen stared at him. Oswell gazed back at her. Then his shoulders began to heave with laughter.

'You're teasing me again,' she protested. 'You promised you wouldn't.'

'No, Clarissa, I'm not teasing you,' he said as the tears ran down his face. 'That is truly the way you learn how to paint people. Think about it. How can you paint them if you don't know the way their bodies are shaped under their cloaks and coats and dresses? I'll tell you what, I'll paint you.'

'Me –?'

In an agony of confusion and embarrassment Mary-Ellen gathered her dress protectively round her legs.

She had absorbed what Oswell said. With her quick perceptive mind, she knew after only an instant that it made sense. How could any artist paint someone without knowing the lines of the figure beneath the clothes? Yet that was one thing. For her to strip naked before a stranger, even the most beautiful stranger in the world, was totally different.

Even her mother knocked on her door now and waited outside until Mary-Ellen was dressed before coming into her room. The blush on her cheeks deepened to crimson.

'Don't worry, Clarissa.' Oswell cut the agony short. 'Yes, I want to paint you. Goodness knows, I'm a dolt for not thinking of it sooner. But, no, not as a naked lady. I'll draw on Paris, on the past, for the way your skin and bones and muscles run –'

He was reaching for his sketchpad as he spoke.

'I'll paint you just as you are right now in front of me. And when it's done, we'll give the painting to your parents as a souvenir of the bad hat's visit. Agreed?'

The colour began to ebb from Mary-Ellen's cheeks. She smiled shyly and nodded.

'Only, let's keep everything we talk about here a secret,' he added. 'Paris and cards and naked ladies, good eggs and bad hats, they're just for us. A compact, right?'

It was another word whose meaning Mary-Ellen didn't know, but she nodded again.

'Shake on it, Clarissa,' Oswell instructed.

She reached out and they gravely shook hands. Then she settled back and composed herself.

Immediately Oswell's hand began to move over the white paper.

— 13 —

Oswell stayed at the mission for ten days.

He dined once in the mission house. Apart from that, to Mrs Ramsay's chagrin, he kept to his camp. His rejections of her invitations were made with such elegance and gallantry she was unable to be offended.

'You must forgive me, dear lady,' he would say with a disarming smile. 'But for someone condemned to live his life amid a city's dark and noisy clutter, every moment away from God's clear skies is a moment begrudged.'

He lifted his head and gazed soulfully at the desert's horizon.

'How disappointing,' Mrs Ramsay remarked afterwards. 'But what sentiment, what sensitivity! You're most fortunate he's taken such a liking to you, Mary-Ellen. At least you have the benefit of his company. Don't waste a moment of it.'

'Yes, Mama.'

Mrs Ramsay watched proudly as her daughter set off on one of what had now become Mary-Ellen's twice-daily visits to Oswell's camp.

'A fondness for children is an invariable sign of a true gentleman,' she observed to her husband.

The Revd Ramsay grunted noncommittally. Although there was something about the visitor he didn't altogether trust, the name Oswell was too potent in Kuruman for him to object.

Oswell's rejection of Mrs Ramsay's invitations had nothing to do with the Kalahari skies. He had tried the missionary and his wife once. He found them excruciatingly boring. Mary-Ellen was very different.

The girl was a little solemn on the surface. With those parents, who wouldn't have been? But only a little prompting produced a ready laugh. She was bright and bold and spirited. And with her clear gold-flecked eyes, her long shining hair and her supple figure, she was already a delight to look at. Before long she would be a head-turning beauty.

In fact, Oswell reflected, studying the lift of her breasts and the alluring spread of her long legs beneath her skirt, she was already old enough to provide some excellent sport.

To his immense pleasure, Mary-Ellen was also wholly and wonderfully innocent. All she had ever known was the tiny hermetic world of the mission post, the life of the native settlement at its gates, and the fundamentalist values of her father. Oswell had attended the Sunday service and heard the Revd Ramsay preach.

The sermon made him shudder.

Mary-Ellen's innocence was like a curtain keeping a strong enquiring intelligence in the dark. Once the curtain was drawn and light poured in, God alone knew what direction her mind would take and what havoc would follow.

Indeed God himself, Oswell thought, might well be one of the first casualties.

Oswell decided to take it in stages. Mary-Ellen visited his camp every day after breakfast and again before the family supper. When she arrived one evening she found him hunched over a book. Apparently absorbed in what he was reading, he waved her to sit down. Mary-Ellen sat on the leather stool on the other side of the fire. As she waited she studied him.

By now Mary-Ellen had memorized almost every plane and contour of his body. The angle of his high cheek-bones. The set of his neck into his sloping shoulders. The way his eyes narrowed at the firelight, the toss of his hair when he threw his head back in laughter, the graceful patterns of his wrists when he gestured.

From the first moment she saw him, Mary-Ellen knew

Oswell was the most wonderful man she would ever meet. She knew she could not keep him. He was a migrant, a passer-by, a traveller who came and would go in the night. All she could do was print him so deeply on her memory that in a sense he would never be lost.

That night Mary-Ellen was storing up in her mind even the smallest of the pale hairs that curled over the backs of his hands.

'Monkeys,' Oswell said abruptly, lifting his eyes at last from the book.

Mary-Ellen wrinkled her face.

They'd talked several times about the Kalahari's animals. Mr Oswell, she sensed, wasn't quite as keen a hunter as she assumed, but he always seemed interested in what she had to tell him about the wildlife of the desert.

Monkeys were a different matter. Not even the most dedicated sportsman attached any importance to them.

'Monkeys?' she echoed, puzzled.

'Little creatures which climb trees and look rather like us,' Oswell said. 'Never seen them?'

'Of course I have,' Mary-Ellen protested. 'There are some up in the baobabs here right now. People call them green monkeys. But no one hunts them unless they're terribly hungry.'

'I wasn't thinking of hunting them. I was thinking of observing them.'

'Then all you have to do is raise your head.'

Oswell laughed. 'How delightfully practical you are, Clarissa. I shall do just that.'

They both looked up.

In the gathering dusk a group of little vervet monkeys were chattering and quarrelling as they jostled for their night-time perches in the branches. At the flash of white from the two upturned faces they momentarily fell silent. Then, losing interest, they started to bicker among themselves again.

Oswell glanced back at the fire. He closed the book and leant forward.

'Where do we humans come from, Clarissa?'

Mary-Ellen started. 'From God, of course,' she answered.

'Who made us in his own image out of the mould he created in Adam and Eve?'

She nodded.

'Yes, that's what I was taught too,' Oswell went on. 'It's a very convenient way of explaining everything, isn't it? I mean, if one accepts that, everything else falls into place.'

Mary-Ellen shrugged. She had never considered anything else. 'Of course God made us. Everyone knows that,' she said.

'Not Dr Darwin.'

'Who's Dr Darwin?'

'A very wise and distinguished scientist. He believes we came from monkeys.'

Mary-Ellen looked at him, shocked. 'But that's not in the Bible. That's blasphemy.'

She had been brought up on the word. It was her father's strongest term of condemnation for anything he disapproved of. To commit blasphemy was to commit the worst sin of all. The consequence was to be thrown into outer darkness.

'Maybe not –'

Oswell approached the subject cautiously.

'Dr Darwin certainly believes in the Bible,' he continued. 'But he sees it more as a symbol of God's word rather than the literal truth. A poem, if you like, rather than a history book. When Darwin tried to discover how we actually came to exist, his studies led him back to the animals. I'll try to explain –'

Oswell leant forward and began to talk. An hour later he sat back.

'That's it in what might be called a nutshell,' Oswell ended. 'I've simplified a great deal of what he found out and I've skipped over even more. But broadly that's how Dr Darwin thinks it all happened. He's convinced a great many people – and I may say I'm one of them.'

Mary-Ellen was sitting gazing at the flames as if in a trance.

For several moments she didn't seem to realize Oswell had finished. Then she shook her head and jumped to her feet, flustered. Dusk was settling down swiftly over the mission compound and the lamps were glowing in the house.

'I must be getting back,' she said. 'Papa is always cross if I'm late for supper.'

'Then you must run along, Clarissa.' Oswell stood up too. 'I trust I didn't fatigue you with Darwin's theories?'

'No, certainly not. It was the –'

She shook her head, searching for the right words. 'The most extraordinary, the most interesting idea I've ever heard.'

Oswell smiled. 'I'm glad. Remember our compact.'

'Compact?'

Mary-Ellen's mind and concentration were still remote from the camp fire and the tall languid man who towered above her.

'That anything we discuss here is a secret between us,' he reminded her. 'Dr Darwin's conclusions are still, to say the least, controversial. I doubt they would find favour with your admirable father.'

Mary-Ellen smiled back. 'I won't mention anything.'

She set off for the house.

Oswell watched her cross the dusty compound and climb the flight of steps that led inside. For several minutes after she disappeared, he remained gazing at the door and stroking his moustache. He felt very satisfied. The evening, he sensed, had been a capital success.

Oswell chuckled. He turned and called for his servants to bring his supper.

— 14 —

'You're very quiet tonight, child.'

Mrs Ramsay glanced at her daughter across the table as the houseboy shuffled round behind the chairs with the platter of roasted mealies and springbok venison.

Mary-Ellen was staring through the window. She didn't answer.

'Your mother addressed you, young woman,' Mr Ramsay said sharply. 'Kindly have the ordinary good manners to reply.'

Mary-Ellen's head swung round.

'I'm so sorry, Mama. I was talking to Mr Oswell and I think I forgot to put my bonnet on. Perhaps I was overlong in the sun.'

'What were you discussing with Mr Oswell?' Ramsay put down his fork and glowered across the table.

'Only animals, Papa. He leaves to hunt in a few days. I was telling what Xugu-San had told me about the eland herds.'

'That old villain Xugu is a Bushman, a heathen. Call him by his rightful name,' her father snapped. 'I cannot abide this affectation of referring to him and his kind as San.'

'Yes, Papa. I'm sorry, Papa.'

'George, I beg you not to chide the child,' Mrs Ramsay interjected. 'She's the only one of us who can communicate with the creatures. And I'm sure she's been giving Mr Oswell most useful advice –'

She turned to her daughter.

'Why don't you run along to bed, Mary? You may leave your supper. Take a glass of water and a pinch of laudanum from the jar in my cabinet. You will feel better in the morning.'

'Thank you, Mama.'

Mary-Ellen stood up. She embraced her mother, who clucked fussily at her and repeated the instructions about the laudanum. Then she kissed her father on the forehead. His skin felt cold and he gave the merest grunt of acknowledgement in response.

'You really should be more charitable towards your daughter,' Mrs Ramsay said as the door closed. 'She's being so helpful to that excellent young man. I truly believe she's been the making of his visit.'

'I don't know what he finds to talk to the child about, but I don't like it,' Mr Ramsay replied. 'Too much long hair and too many fancy gestures. The sooner he outspans from here, the better in my view.'

'George!' Mrs Ramsay stared at him, shocked. 'Remember his name.'

'Handsome is as handsome does.' Ramsay speared a last chunk of meat. 'That, in the vulgar proverb, is what I was encouraged to reflect on as a child. It is an admonition hard to better. I doubt his grandfather would have given Mr Oswell the time of day.'

He munched angrily.

Mary-Ellen didn't go to bed. She walked down the passage and went into her room.

The single floor-to-ceiling window gave on to a narrow balcony. She stepped through it, swung herself over the low balcony railing, and walked towards the compound's stockade wall. The wall was set with a number of lookout platforms. In the case of an attack by natives, they were designed to be manned by defenders with rifles. Mary-Ellen climbed the steps to one of them, and gazed out over the desert.

The platform faced due north.

From where she was standing the Kalahari ran flat and uninterrupted for almost five hundred miles. In the darkness all Mary-Ellen could see were faint ripples of thorn bush and the immense bowl of the night sky.

A thin dry wind came to her from out of the night. The wind smelt faintly of sand and sun-bleached wood. Apart from its tentative movement against her skin, all she was aware of were stars. Ice bright and dazzling, they seemed to cascade in hundreds of thousands down the heavens across infinities of distance and space.

God spoke through the wind and lived among the stars.

So Mary-Ellen had known and believed all her life. Until now. Now everything had changed. She had been told a story and gazed at a photograph – Oswell had shown her the frontispiece to the new edition of *On the Origin of Species*. She had seen a solemn, haunted man with mournful eyes and a long slanting jaw. With a spearing intensity of perception, Mary-Ellen knew he had found the truth.

Nothing would ever be the same again.

'You're early today,' Oswell said a few evenings later when Mary-Ellen arrived at his fire.

'Yes,' she replied as she sat down, 'Papa's ridden out to give communion to old Mrs Ryecroft at her son's ranch at Kukung. She's very ill, poor old lady. For once Mama went with him in case it's the last time she'll see her. They won't be back until late. I thought I'd make the most of it.'

Mary-Ellen smiled happily.

For a moment Oswell stiffened. Then he smiled too.

It was almost too good to be true. Everything had come together at precisely the right moment. Fresh oxen had arrived that morning from Mafeking for his waggons, and he'd been deliberating when to move on. He was already bored with Kuruman. Only Mary-Ellen still kept him there.

There was one final thing that remained to be done with her. Now he'd been given the perfect opportunity to do it.

'Well, well,' Oswell said. 'How admirably Providence arranges these matters. Because I was about to ask a favour of you – a favour best given, I think, in privacy.'

'A favour –?' Mary-Ellen began, puzzled.

'Wait!' Oswell raised his hand and cut her off. 'Favours are a reward for other favours. We have business to transact before we come to that.'

He reached down beside him and picked up his portrait of Mary-Ellen.

The portrait was finished now. Oswell had painted her from the waist up. Mary-Ellen was sitting by the fire, wearing a high-buttoned blouse and a straw hat. It was an excellent, even an outstanding, likeness of her, and Oswell smiled in satisfaction as he examined it.

He had caught the boldness of her face. The coils of hair straying youthfully and untidily down from the hat's brim. The wide intense eyes, thoughtful but edged with the vulnerability of her seventeen years. Most of all he had captured her innocence, the confident, untroubled innocence of the child of the isolated mission post in the benighted wilderness of the Kalahari.

That would be his true present to the Revd and Mrs Ramsay. An eternal chilling reminder of their daughter as they wished her to be – as she was when she believed in God, and God believed in her. That was before Oswell's arrival. Oswell didn't know if either God or the young woman believed in the other any longer.

He had done everything in his power to destroy the faith of both. With any luck he had succeeded.

Oswell had no interest in Mrs Ramsay. She was a vain, empty-headed woman. The Revd Ramsay was very different. Little as Oswell had seen of him, he felt through Mary-Ellen he knew Ramsay well. Ramsay reminded him vividly of his father. There was no vengeance Oswell could take on his own father. He was dead. Ramsay, on the other hand, was alive and no doubt fiercely proud of his only child.

Oswell hoped his paintings of Mary-Ellen – for there was a second to come – would haunt Ramsay to the grave.

'May I see?'

Mary-Ellen took the portrait from him. She studied it for a moment. Then she glanced up, frowning.

'Well?' Oswell demanded.

She hesitated. 'It's me, I suppose, but not the me I see when I look in the mirror. I think I see someone older, someone who knows more.'

Oswell burst into delighted laughter.

'Clarissa,' he said, 'you've just paid me the greatest compliment I've ever had. Of course you're absolutely right. I've painted you as you were when I arrived. Since then you've changed. Modestly, if I may say so, the change is due to me. So now I have two Clarissas. One that I've captured and one I've created. This one –' Oswell took the painting back from her '– goes to your parents. The other I want for myself.'

Mary-Ellen frowned. 'But there isn't another one.'

'Be patient and all will be explained!'

Oswell reached beneath his chair again. He pulled out a neatly wrapped parcel.

'It will not, I fear, be a surprise,' he said. 'But as a token of respect and admiration, I beg you to accept it nonetheless. Inside are my own copies of all Dr Darwin's works. I have taken the liberty of inscribing them to you from your devoted and humble servant –'

Oswell smiled.

'I hope they will not only be a worthy souvenir of my visit to Kuruman, but a lifelong source of interest and enlightenment.'

Mary-Ellen took the books. For a moment, stunned with pleasure and surprise, she stood silent. Then she threw her arms round Oswell's neck and kissed him on the mouth.

'Thank you,' she said.

Mary-Ellen had never kissed anyone on the mouth before. As she realized what she had done, she stepped back in confusion. Then something else struck her.

'You are giving presents,' Mary-Ellen said. 'Does this mean you're leaving?'

His face grave, Oswell nodded. 'I've already stayed far longer than I intended. That, needless to say, was due to you. But very soon now I must go.'

'You can't go!' Mary-Ellen exclaimed. 'Not yet. I mean –'

Her voice trailed away. Then she added wildly and forlornly, 'What about the other painting you mentioned?'

'We are going to do that now.'

Oswell slung over his shoulder the leather hunting bag that contained his sketching materials, and reached out his hand. In a daze Mary-Ellen took it. She followed him out through the compound gates and down towards the river.

'Here!' Oswell said. 'Sit down.'

Mary-Ellen stopped. She sat where he indicated on the trunk of a fallen tree.

Oswell had chosen the place on one of his morning walks beyond the compound. It was a small sandy bay carved out from the river's banks. Tall golden trimedra grass ran down almost to the water's edge, and thick shrubs and trees overshadowed the stream. None of the Kuruman villagers, Oswell had observed, came there.

Apart from the occasional plunge of a pied kingfisher, the bay was silent and deserted.

'Listen to me.' Oswell knelt in front of her. He held Mary-Ellen's hands. 'Do you remember the first day you came to my camp? When I talked about Paris and how I'd learnt to paint people naked?'

Mary-Ellen nodded. Of course she remembered. Like everything else Oswell had said to her, it had been unforgettable.

'I told you the reason,' Oswell went on, 'but only half the reason. Yes, every artist must learn how human bodies look. Yet there's more to it than that. It's only when people are naked, undecorated, exposed in the way they were when they were born, that they truly reveal themselves. It's only then that an artist can fully capture their spirit –'

Oswell paused.

He gazed at Mary-Ellen. In the dappled shade of the bank, his eyes were clearer and more commanding than they had ever been.

'I want you as you are,' Oswell said. 'I want to paint your spirit for myself alone. I want to keep you and hold you in my heart for ever. Take off your clothes and lie down for me here on the bank between the grass and the water.'

Mary-Ellen stared back at him.

Even if she had wanted to deny him, she knew it would have been impossible. He had painted her once. He had opened worlds to her. He had given her presents and changed her life. He was also, as he would always be, the most beautiful man she had ever seen. Now he wanted something from her. He had no need even to ask.

She stood up and undressed.

'Here?' she said as the last of her clothes dropped to the ground and she stepped naked on to the sand.

Oswell nodded. 'Lie on your back with one knee raised,' he instructed.

She lay down in a trance. The sand was warm beneath her. The afternoon sunlight cascaded over her face. On one side she could hear the bending rustling grasses. On the other the ripples of the stream plucked by the darting Kalahari dragonflies.

'Capital!'

Mary-Ellen shook her head. She sat up and glanced round dizzily. From the angle of the sun more than an hour had passed. She looked down and suddenly remembered she was naked. Scarlet with embarrassment, she huddled her legs together and folded her arms across her breasts.

'Have you finished?' she asked timidly.

Oswell nodded.

Mary-Ellen got to her feet. Standing with her back to him she began to scramble back into her clothes as quickly as she could.

'May I see it?' she asked when she was dressed again.

Oswell shook his head. 'Much as I hate to deny you anything, Clarissa, for once I am going to say no. This is for me alone. To remind me of you and Kuruman. To warm me and make me smile when winter comes –'

He paused. 'You will have to take my word that it is exactly what I want. It is perfection.'

Oswell smiled at her.

He'd often smiled at her before – it was one of the things Mary-Ellen liked best about him. There was something different about his smile now. On the surface it was as warm and delightful as ever. Somehow Mary-Ellen sensed something darker lay beneath it. A feeling of triumph, of malevolence, almost of savagery.

She looked at him uncertainly. The moment passed and she smiled too.

'I'm glad,' she said.

Oswell took her hand. They walked together back through the trees until the mission came into view. There Oswell stopped. He let go of Mary-Ellen's hand and swung round to look down at her.

'This is where our paths divide,' he said. 'You must go back to prepare the house for your parents' return. I am going to take one last walk alone to imprint the landscape of Kuruman even more indelibly on my memory than it is now. Between friends and lovers there should be neither sentiment nor ceremony in parting. Let there be none between us.'

Oswell bent down and kissed Mary-Ellen quickly on the forehead. Without a further word he turned and strode away.

Mary-Ellen looked after him, appalled. She felt cold and numb. For ten days he had filled the drab, empty world of the lonely mission with the flare and brilliance of a meteor that had fallen from the sky. Now as abruptly as he'd appeared, Oswell was vanishing.

'Surely I can come and see you off in the morning?' she called after him desperately.

'No!' Oswell called back. 'Remember what I said. Neither sentiment nor ceremony.'

Mary-Ellen's eyes filled with tears.

'I'll never forget you!' she shouted again.

Oswell paused then. He glanced back and smiled. The light was starting to fade, but Mary-Ellen could see it was the same disturbing smile that had unsettled her by the river fifteen minutes earlier.

'I'm quite sure you won't!'

Oswell touched his hat to her. Then he was gone. Sobbing, Mary-Ellen ran back to the mission.

Exhausted by the turmoil of the day, Mary-Ellen went to bed early and fell asleep quickly. She woke twice during the night. The first time was close to midnight when her father and mother returned from their visit to Kukung. She listened to their horses being led away, and their muttered conversation on their way to bed.

The second time Mary-Ellen woke was close to dawn. Waggon-wheels were rumbling somewhere outside. She got out of bed and went to the window. Craning her head, she could just see the space in the compound where Oswell had made his camp. The tents had been folded away, and the fire extinguished. Oswell was leaving.

His waggons creaked out first. Then she saw his mounted servants depart. Finally she saw Oswell himself. He rode up to the door of the house, and swung himself off his horse. He was carrying something under his arm. Oswell placed it against the steps.

Oswell seemed to be studying what he had left there. He lifted his head. The moon was low and the Kalahari stars were dull, but even in the darkness Mary-Ellen could see Oswell was smiling. He turned away and climbed back on his horse. A moment later he vanished through the gates behind his waggons.

Unaccountably, Mary-Ellen shivered.

She returned to bed. This time she slept only fitfully. She tossed and dozed and then turned restlessly beneath the sheet again. When she finally dropped into a deep slumber, it seemed only moments before she was woken once more. She opened her eyes and stiffened.

Someone in the mission was screaming. The screams were endless and despairing. It took Mary-Ellen only an instant to realize they came from her mother.

— 15 —

Mary-Ellen ran frantically along the passage.

The screams were coming from her father's study. Mary-Ellen paused outside the door. She had never heard her mother scream like this before. It could only be something terrible. In a frenzy of guilt, she wondered if it was anything to do with her. Her mind went instantly to Oswell.

For a moment Mary-Ellen shivered. Then she shook her head. Oswell had been gone that morning before her parents woke. It had to be something else. Trembling but not quite as frightened as before, Mary-Ellen raised her hand to knock on the door. As she did so the door swung open in front of her. Her father threw himself out.

The two of them almost collided. For an instant they stood face to face. Her father, Mary-Ellen knew, had been coming to find her.

'You –!'

Ramsay broke off incoherently.

He was a strong, broad-shouldered man with thinning hair, a fleshy nose and a scarlet-veined face. Mary-Ellen had often seen him angry. She had never seen him so convulsed with rage as he was now. His entire body was shaking. Saliva was trickling down his chin and his eyes were maddened with fury.

Ramsay found his voice again. 'You filthy whore!' he bellowed.

He drew back his hand and hit her violently across the face. Mary-Ellen was thrown against the wall. She slipped to the floorboards and lay there half stunned. The blow had cut her mouth and blood was flowing down her chin.

'What have I done?' she managed to whisper.

'You have the vain impertinence to ask *me* what *you* have done? I will not foul my lips with what you must know too well. Instead, let your own eyes be your witness!'

Ramsay reached down. He caught Mary-Ellen by the wrist. He heaved her up and hurled her into the room.

As she stumbled across the floor, Mary-Ellen heard her mother scream again. Mary-Ellen was vaguely aware of Mrs Ramsay clutching a chair for support. Her mother's face was white and streaked with tears, and her chest was heaving. Then she felt Ramsay's hand grip her neck.

Her father drove her forward. They came to his desk. Brutally, as if he were making an untrained dog inspect its mess, he forced her head down.

'Look!' Ramsay shouted. 'Look, you little harlot, at what you have done!'

Mary-Ellen looked. Her knees buckled and she felt sick. Dizzily she managed to recover herself. As the pressure of Ramsay's fingers tightened round her neck, she looked again.

Propped against the desk were the contents of the package she had seen Oswell leave at the mission house steps a few hours earlier – the brown paper wrapping was tossed to the side. The package should have contained one painting, the demure and youthful portrait Oswell had done of her. The portrait was there. So was the other painting.

Mary-Ellen choked as she stared at it.

It was the sketch Oswell had done as she lay naked on her back. Unlike the hours he'd spent on the first painting, this one had been executed quickly. Somehow the speed made it all the more vivid.

She was no longer an eager vulnerable girl. She was a woman. Her eyes were closed languorously. One arm was crossed over her chest as if she were fondling her breasts. Her legs were splayed out limply as if the muscles had been exhausted with passion. And the insides of her thighs were streaked with bright ribbons of blood.

Mary-Ellen looked at the blood in disbelief. There had been no blood on her skin – and then she suddenly realized. Oswell had portrayed her as if she had just lost her virginity.

The painting blurred and dissolved. She dropped to her knees. Her head fell away from Ramsay's hand and rested on the floor. Behind her Mary-Ellen heard a rustling sound. She realized Ramsay was removing the heavy buffalo-hide belt with its metal studs from his waist.

'Whore!' he bellowed. 'Whore of Babylon!'

The belt slashed down. It went on rising and falling until Mary-Ellen lost consciousness.

As Mary-Ellen's screams faded, Moffat rose to his feet outside the mission house.

He stood for a moment in the pool of shadow where he'd been crouching. His face was an impenetrable black mask and his eyes unblinking. Then he slipped out through the gates and vanished into the village behind. Five minutes later he reappeared and set off towards the south.

For an hour he loped steadily through the bush in the gathering dawn. The tracks of the white man's waggon and horses stretched out in front of him. Spooring them at that hour was an easy task. Later, when the sun bore down, the prints would blur and crumble in the heat. Now, in the half-light, they stood out crisp and clear in the frost and dew.

Moffat came to a junction in the paths which criss-crossed the scrub. He paused briefly. The horse and waggon tracks led to the right. He knew where the group was heading, the nearby ford where they could cross the Kuruman river. There was a shorter, narrower route to it on the left.

Striding more quickly now, Moffat set off along the left-hand path.

For once Moffat wasn't dressed in his mission house-boy's clothing of cheap grey cotton slacks and shirt, and straw-soled sandals – Mrs Ramsay could not abide the houseboys walking around without shoes. Moffat was barefoot and wearing nothing but a short leather apron. In his hand was a long sharp-bladed throwing spear.

The leather apron and the spear were all that had been left to him by the mother he barely remembered. They had been kept for him by the enigmatic old San woman, Mama Chi-mona, who had looked after his mother until she died. When Moffat came to puberty, Mama Chi-mona gave them to him. All she had said was that he was a Mashona and these were the mark of a Mashona warrior. Not even Mary-Ellen knew he had them.

Since then Moffat had sometimes put on the apron in secret, and often – in secret too – practised throwing the spear. He had become so adept at hurling the weapon that once he had even killed an impala antelope from a distance of thirty yards. Apart from that he had no use for them. Like so much else, they were no more than relics from Moffat's unknown and unknowable past.

Until now. Now they had a deadly and vengeful purpose.

Moffat came to the ford. He waded across and positioned himself in the shadow of a merula tree on the other side. A few minutes afterwards Moffat heard what he expected to hear – the sound of a horseman advancing through the bush. The white man was riding ahead of his waggon and servants as the white men always did.

Moffat balanced the spear on his outspread palm. His fingers tightened round the shaft.

A moment later Oswell came into sight. His rifle was in his hand. He paused at the edge of the water and scanned the banks on either side, in case any game had come to drink. There was nothing. Oswell slung the rifle over his back. Using both hands on the reins he urged the horse into the river.

Moffat waited until Oswell was in mid-stream. Then he stepped out from the tree's shadow and walked forward into the shallows.

The rising sun was behind Moffat's head. Oswell didn't see him until barely twelve feet separated them. As he did, Oswell reached instinctively for his gun.

'Stop!' Moffat called.

The spear's tip gleamed as Moffat raised it. Oswell froze. He gazed down at the man below him in the water.

Oswell blinked at the flare of light from the ripples. Then he recognized Moffat. The African was one of the Ramsays' houseboys. Oswell had seen him often during his stay at the mission.

Often – but never like this. Moffat's body was naked to the waist. His face was drawn tight with hatred.

'What the hell is this?' Oswell shouted angrily. 'Get out of my horse's way, boy! There are crocs here –'

'Listen to me –!' Moffat interrupted him. His dark eyes held Oswell's and stared them down with disgust and contempt.

'Mama Mary-Ellen is my sister,' Moffat went on. 'You dishonoured and betrayed her. For that I hold you to account!'

Oswell understood then.

The bizarre young coon must have followed him and the missionary's daughter to the Kuruman. He had seen Oswell make her undress. Now, in the absurd jargon the black boy must have learnt at the mission, he was presenting himself as the girl's defender.

Oswell rocked with laughter.

'Get back to the mission, you little savage!' he shouted. 'Don't ever again interfere in the business of your superiors!'

Still laughing, Oswell dug his spurs into the horse's flanks and drove the animal forward.

Moffat pulled back his arm. Trembling not with fear but with rage, he hurled the spear upwards with a strength and ferocity he had never known before. The razor-sharp point caught Oswell just below his ribcage. The blade buried itself deep in his body. Oswell's mouth opened in astonishment. He clutched his stomach. Then he toppled sideways off his horse. The terrified and riderless animal surged past Moffat, and vanished up the bank.

Relentlessly, Moffat waded forward.

Jerking and twitching convulsively, Oswell was floating on his face on the river's surface. Moffat rolled him over. Putting his foot on Oswell's chest, Moffat forced him to the bottom. He wrenched out the spear and waited for several moments. Then he stood back.

The water was darkening with plumes of blood. Oswell's body bobbed up again and began to drift away on the current. Already Moffat could hear the splash of crocodiles dropping into the river. He waded back to the far bank and washed the spear clean.

Oswell was right. Moffat had disliked and distrusted the white man from the day Oswell arrived at Kuruman. With growing unease, Moffat watched Mary-Ellen's visits to his camp. When Oswell led her down to the river the day before, Moffat was behind them in the trees.

He saw what took place there, and the expression of triumph on Oswell's face when he'd looked at the painting. Moffat hadn't understood the reason, but he'd seen Oswell leave the package by the door and had heard Mary-Ellen's agonized screams of pain. Everything had become clear then. Moffat knew too why he had been given the spear and leather apron of a Mashona warrior.

Mary-Ellen had been violated by deceit as surely as if she'd been violated by force. For a man to violate another's sister was one of the most unpardonable crimes in the code of every African nation. Moffat had been given the spear for vengeance.

Moffat set off back for Kuruman.

Mary-Ellen walked slowly through the breast-high grass.

Six months had passed. It was early May and the start of the Kalahari winter. In the desert it was the season she loved best. The days were hot and dry. The nights chill and canopied with the most brilliant stars of the whole year. Six months ago the grass had been green and succulent after the rains. Slowly the colour of the stems had changed to a rich red-bronze as they fed their seeds.

Now they were a pale delicate gold. Their seeds were scattered. In the morning wind they seemed to chime like bells in celebration of a task well discharged.

Mary-Ellen came to one of the pans that ringed Kuruman, as they patterned the entire desert. On the surface below her there was spoor of the scimitar-horned gemsbok, spiral-antlered hartebeest, jackal, lion, hyena, and many more. She could read all the tracks as easily as if they had been labelled with written words.

Mary-Ellen lay down on the bank round the pan. She rested her chin on her arms and gazed out across the sand.

Six months. It was exactly six months since Oswell's waggons had rumbled out of the mission and left her with the legacy of his visit. They had been the worst, the unhappiest and most troubled months of her life.

For the first month she had been confined to her room. Then there had been the daily beatings with the studded belt or, more painful still, with his sjambok, the rhino-hide whip Ramsay used on the Tswana. The beatings had lasted for much longer than a month.

Her father had administered the punishment in the name of the Lord. The Revd Ramsay was an obsessive student of the scriptures and the numbers they revealed to him. He had whipped her first for forty days to remind her of Christ's torment in the wilderness. Then for a further forty days because while the Lord had been tempted and cast aside the temptation, she had been tempted and embraced it.

The torment – numb and hardened to it as she had become – would still be continuing had it not been for her mother.

Mrs Ramsay, weak and helpless as she was in the face of her husband's implacable certainty, had inherited something from her own mother who had dispatched her to Africa. Mrs Ramsay was also a pragmatist.

'You cannot continue with this, my dear,' she implored as once again she sent Mary-Ellen's bloodstained clothes out to be laundered by the Tswana women at the river. 'Her back is becoming disfigured. No man will take a wife as permanently scarred as she will be.'

'I do not punish her,' Ramsay snapped. 'Her correction comes from the Lord. He will decide its term and its measure.'

He beat Mary-Ellen even more savagely the next morning. It was the last time he did.

Ramsay had taken his wife's words to heart. He had no idea where Mary-Ellen would find a husband in the Kalahari. He simply wanted the young whore away from his household as quickly and decently as possible. Furthermore, he sensed with satisfaction, by now he had given her a taste she would never forget of the retribution she could expect if she lusted and sinned again.

Mary-Ellen knew nothing of the exchange between her parents.

She had accepted the daily beatings almost without question. Her father was her father. Her mother, her mother. She belonged to them. From her earliest childhood, Mary-Ellen had often felt she hated Ramsay. Whenever she did she was always overcome by guilt. Cold, brutal and intemperate as her father might be, he was still the dominant figure of authority she had been brought up to respect and obey.

This time his punishment of her was even just. She might have betrayed her parents. Far worse, Mary-Ellen had betrayed herself. She felt disgusted and humiliated. She had been a naïve fool, a wide-eyed, mindless child. Each time she thought about it, her cheeks flushed scarlet and her hatred for Oswell, for his smile and his cunning and the cynical game he had played with her, rose in her throat like sour, choking bile.

In time the still raw and jagged edges of the memory might blunt and fade. The memory itself wouldn't vanish until she died. With the complete and utter certainty of a distraught and passionate seventeen-year-old, she knew she would never trust a man again.

Mary-Ellen stared across the pan.

She had been lying on the bank for an hour or more, long enough for any animals of the bush to have registered and disregarded her presence. No antelope or any of their predators, lion, hyena or leopard, had come down on to the surface of the pan. As Mary-Ellen watched, a pack of baboons appeared.

They came warily and skittishly. The leaders leapt on to the sand. They examined and tested the pan's surface. They barked, and bounded back into the bush. Then they reappeared. This time they had with them the entire pack – the grizzled grandmothers, the lactating mothers, the confident young males, the scampering and inquisitive children.

As the baboon pack spread out below her and began to lick the pan's salts, something happened to Mary-Ellen.

Mary-Ellen was lying on her stomach because the wounds on her shoulders from her father's beatings were still too raw to let her lie on her back. She was seventeen and her life was over. She was an eternal prisoner of Kuruman and her past just as her mother was. The blood that kept staining her blouse proved that.

Except it did not. The blood was as much a challenge as a padlock on her life.

Mary-Ellen knew about baboons. She suddenly realized she knew more about them, about their ways and behaviour, than perhaps anyone alive. Dr Darwin had referred often to baboons in his books – but even he, the greatest scientist of modern times, had only a fragment of her knowledge of the Kalahari's major primates.

Mary-Ellen knew something else too. She was a friend and companion of the San, the Bushmen. The San, as they had often told her, were the baboon's companions.

She stood up. The baboons below her scattered as they registered her presence. They screamed and bared their teeth at her. Then, accepting she was not a threat, they composed themselves. They continued with their life's business of hunting, gathering, and licking the pan's sandy grains for minerals.

Mary-Ellen smiled. It was exactly what the San did.

Oswell, she had thought for the past six months, had left her life in ruins. Perhaps he had not. Perhaps after all he had given her salvation. Out of the wreckage, out of the degradation and betrayal, she had been left with the books he had given her. The books were intended, she knew, to be as deceitful and destructive a present as the painting he had left for her parents.

The books carried the photograph of a bearded and thoughtful old man.

— 16 —

'Dear Dr Darwin,' Mary-Ellen wrote. 'Please have the kindness to accept my apologies that I, a stranger, address you without introduction –'

The candlelight wavered over the neat flowing script she had been taught by her mother.

Mary-Ellen paused and chewed thoughtfully on the end of the porcupine-quill pen.

Oswell had left her with three of the great scientist's books: *The Voyage of the 'Beagle'*, *On the Origin of Species by Means of Natural Selection*, and *The Descent of Man*. Over the six months since Oswell left Kuruman, Mary-Ellen had read the three books not once but several times.

Like many children of isolated missions Mary-Ellen was formidably well educated. The Revd Ramsay was a Scot. As was the case with many expatriate Scots, he had a passionate love of reading. Ramsay's famous predecessor, Robert Moffat, had been content with the mission garden. Ramsay instead had his library. It was the one pride and delight of his embittered life.

Mary-Ellen had been taught to read at an early age. From then on she was not merely encouraged to read on her own. Ramsay demanded it of her – often for hours at a time. The works she was made to study were austere. The Bible came first. After that there were endless stern volumes of theology, classical history and moral philosophy.

Daunting as the books were, reading them was never any hardship to the child. Beyond the compound fence and the village huts, there was nothing but the forbidding

– and forbidden – Kalahari. Books were the only alternative to the desert. The grim tracts on Ramsay's shelves became half of Mary-Ellen's life and world.

Mary-Ellen dipped the pen in the horn inkwell and continued with her letter.

'I live here at the Kuruman mission post on the southern edge of the Kalahari. Few Europeans pass this way. One who by chance did had with him certain of your learned works. He, for the traveller was a gentleman although his name escapes me now, urged me to read them.

'I yielded to his entreaties. I was deeply affected by your arguments and your conclusions. Words cannot convey their impress upon me. Suffice it to say, one life has been changed for ever by what you wrote –'

Mary-Ellen paused again. She wanted to be very careful how she expressed herself next.

Apart from the omission of Oswell's name – she couldn't yet bring herself to write it – everything so far was true. What followed would have to be equally true, even if it also had to be tailored to the position she found herself in.

'And so, if I may be so bold, to business,' Mary-Ellen went on. 'You have a noble vision. You say many more studies are needed before the vision can be made manifest as demonstrable truth.

'May I volunteer my services in the quest?

'I referred before to my circumstances. Kuruman is remote from civilization. I live here surrounded by animals and birds of every size and nature. They are before me day and by night. Among them, might there be a candidate for observation, the results of which I could communicate to you for contemplation –?'

In Mary-Ellen Oswell had thought he was dealing with an innocent whom he could turn against her father.

Mary-Ellen was indeed an innocent. Oswell fell into the ancient trap of believing innocence and weakness were the same. He was badly mistaken. He half-realized his mistake on the morning he left Kuruman. As his waggons rumbled away, a puzzling – and disturbing – thought had occurred to him. He had intended to corrupt the young woman. Was it possible he had done something entirely different? That he had in fact released her – not as a venomous cancer on the Revd Ramsay's life, but as a liberating wave on the flood of life itself?

Oswell frowned. Dismissing the idea from his mind, he had spurred his horse on towards the ford in the Kuruman river.

'I wish neither to mislead you, nor to waste your valuable time,' Mary-Ellen wrote on.

'I am young. I shall be aged eighteen this forthcoming March. I have scant knowledge of the scientific disciplines, although I have long had the mathematical tables by heart. I have a strong constitution. I breathe well. My eye, I venture, is keen. My friends among the San people, whom many erroneously call Bushmen, say that I am really a San hunter in an over-large white skin.

'More than anything, Dr Darwin, I am ardent to my heart's depths. Each life, I have been taught, requires a cause for its fulfilment. In you I have found mine. For me, the world – together with its past, present and future – now has a different hue. I have become a soldier in your bold army. I want nothing more –'

Mary-Ellen raised her head.

She had gnawed so hard on the quill that its end was worn down to a frayed stub. Mary-Ellen wrinkled her forehead and pondered again.

Dr Darwin would, of course, write back to her. There was no question of his reply being sent to the mission. Her parents – which more specifically meant her father – would demand to know who the letter came from and what it contained. Dr Darwin's reply would have to go somewhere else. The question was where.

It took Mary-Ellen several minutes before she solved the problem.

The European community round Kuruman was very small. There were perhaps a dozen settlers within a hundred miles of the mission. All of them were cattle ranchers and most were of Afrikaner stock. However a few were British. One such family was named Appleby.

The Applebys had three daughters. The eldest, Beth, was Mary-Ellen's exact contemporary.

Mary-Ellen and Beth had shared a governess for a year. The mission post and the Appleby ranch were a long day's ride apart. The two girls had spent alternate weeks in each other's homes. Sharing a bedroom as well as the governess, they had become close friends.

Beth Appleby had cousins in Britain. Letters from them to her were common and caused no comment in the Appleby household. If Darwin wrote to Mary-Ellen through Beth, Beth could simply pass the letter on to her and neither the Applebys nor the Ramsays would ever know.

'If you will be so obliging as to reply, I would ask you to do so through the care of my friend, Miss Beth Appleby, whose address I append below. Miss Appleby will deliver your communication to me.

'My father, for whom my respect knows no bounds, is a minister employed by the Church Missionary Society. I feel sure I need say no more.'

It was enough.

Mary-Ellen signed the letter boldly. She folded the pages into an envelope, and wrote out the address – the name of Dr Darwin's house and his county of residence were given at the end of the preface to *The Descent of Man*. She sealed the envelope with wax.

Afterwards Mary-Ellen sat in thought.

Her parents had gone to bed hours ago. Around her the wooden house creaked and heaved like a ship moving with the tide. White ants were gnawing into its timbers from beneath.

Sooner or later the ants would cause the mission to crumble and fall. Mary-Ellen had known about the termites since she was a child. Often the stir of the joists had made her fearful. Sometimes it had given her nightmares. Not now. The mission was no longer the castle it had been in her childish imagination. It was a temporary shelter, a tent of eland hide, even one of the thorn-bush canopies the San threw up at sunset.

Mary-Ellen had no need of a castle any more. She had grown up. Like the little people of the desert in their eternal questings, she was about to embark on a journey.

'Mama,' Mary-Ellen said to Mrs Ramsay after breakfast next morning, 'it's been almost two months since I visited the Applebys. I would so much like to see Beth again. May I ride over there at the week's end?'

'If your father has no objection, my dear, I certainly have none.'

Ramsay was in his study.

The events of six months ago still hung like a dark shadow over them all. Today Ramsay's mind was concentrated on the forthcoming Sunday's sermon. For once he agreed to Mary-Ellen's request without his usual suspicious interrogation.

'I will give you a text of mine Mr Appleby has been pestering me for,' he said. 'Be sure you're back early on Monday. That old blackguard, Tope, is bringing his headmen in for a judgement. I may need your services to translate the arguments.'

'Of course I'll be back, Papa.'

Ramsay waved her irritably away and returned to his sermon. By chance its inspiration was the very Mr Appleby whose daughter Mary-Ellen was going to visit.

Appleby was a leading member of the local mission council. He had been over to Kuruman last month with the latest directives from the Society's headquarters in London. The pernicious ideas of the new so-called Humanist movement were gaining ground everywhere. Led by self-styled 'scientists', who trumpeted their heresies under the banner of the infamous Charles Darwin, they were questioning the very origins of faith itself.

The Church Missionary Society had instructed its members to refute the unholy new dogma at every opportunity. It was a cause dear to Ramsay's heart. His pen gouged deep into the paper.

'I shall take as my text Genesis chapter one, verse one: *In the beginning God created the heaven and the earth. And the earth was without form and void; and darkness was upon the face of the deep.* I tell you, brethren, the armies of evil are marching once more out of that darkness –'

Ramsay came to the foot of the page. He blotted the ink quickly in the tray of sand, and started on a new sheet.

'Their emblem is the serpent. Now the serpent, as the Good Book reminds us, is more subtle than any beast of the field. The wretched Eve learned to her eternal shame and damnation where the path of the serpent leads –'

In full flow Ramsay wrote on.

As he wrote, Mary-Ellen was riding out of Kuruman on her way to the Applebys.

In the pocket of her tunic was a letter to the man who had challenged the foundations of Ramsay's text, his universe, and his very existence.

— 17 —

'No! No! Stop him! He'll die!'

The noise of the falls was so loud Farini could barely hear the woman's screams, although she was standing only a few feet away, out of his sight on the other side of the canvas.

Barston withdrew his head from the chink in the canvas.

'She's scaring the shit out of their pants,' he said. 'If you're sure you're ready, let's go.'

Momentarily there was an anxious expression on his face as he looked at Farini.

'I'm as ready as a racoon in heat,' Farini answered. 'The kid's doing a good job. Give her another couple of minutes just to make sure they're all wetting themselves.'

He smiled confidently and sprawled back in his chair, stretching his legs out in front of him.

Barston watched him. It was 1876, the same year in which Mary-Ellen wrote to Darwin from the little mission at Kuruman. Farini and his agent, Barston, were waiting in the tent that Barston had arranged to be erected on the edge of the Niagara Falls on the border between Canada and the USA.

At thirty-six Farini was a tall, imposing man with dark hair, heavily pomaded and parted in the middle, and a great luxuriant moustache that swept down on either side of his full mouth. His face was long, craggy and saturnine, and his eyes stared out from beneath a pair of bushy eyebrows. Pale and flint-coloured, there was something at once menacing and seductive in their piercing gaze.

More than anything, as Barston had often noticed, Farini's eyes were hungry.

Farini's appetite was gargantuan. For food, for drink, for women, for success – above all for money. Barston knew little about Farini or where he came from, but somewhere in the past he must have been starved. The experience had left him insatiable. He had to be almost insanely hungry, Barston thought, to attempt what he was about to do now.

It was early spring and the Niagara was in full spate.

Spray was dripping through the tent's roof, and the noise of the cascading water was an unending roar. Barston wouldn't have tried to cross the falls for all the gold, fanny and territory in North America. But there was no blood in Farini's veins, Barston had long since realized, only Alaskan ice threaded with nerves of beaten steel.

Barston shrugged and drummed his fingers nervously on the tent pole. Outside, the woman's terrified screams went on. She was screaming well, Farini thought, but so she should be. She was being paid enough.

Farini yawned and scratched himself.

'Sorry, gents, my throat's gone –'

The tent flap swung open and a young woman stumbled in. Her dress and shawl were soaked and her hair glistened with water. She shook her head, sending a shower of drops across the floor. Then she grinned.

'Like a bleeding rainstorm it is out there,' she went on. 'It's sent me hoarse. But I reckon the job's done. They're all going now like a load of banshees. Listen!'

Farini lifted his head. The girl was right. A chorus of entreaties and shouts of 'No!' was ringing through the air.

'You did well, young lady,' Farini said. 'Give her what she was promised, Barston.'

As Barston reached into his pocket, Farini inspected the girl. She had a good strong figure, a bold impudent face, and she was looking at him provocatively.

'Wait for me afterwards down by the bridge,' he said. 'There could be a little bonus to celebrate with.'

Farini stood up. As he passed the girl on the way to the flap, he pinched her thigh and winked. She grinned back at him. Farini reached for his hat.

Farini's top hat, a majestic creation from Paris in heavy blue velvet with a golden buckle on its band, was his trademark. He put it on, tilting it rakishly forward over one eye, and glanced back at Barston.

'Ready?' Farini asked.

'I'm ready but –'

Barston paused.

As the wind swung the tent flap back he glimpsed the cascading torrent and the whirlpool where it met the river beneath. The drop in between was sickeningly, almost unimaginably vast. The spectators gathered on the rocks below looked like ants. One slip of Farini's foot on the spray-drenched rope and the spectacle would turn into tragedy.

Barston creased his face unhappily. He was both Farini's oldest friend and his agent. As his agent Barston stood to make a great deal of money out of the performance. But there were moments even in an agent's life when friendship was more important than money.

'Are you really sure you want to go ahead? We could still cancel it. We could say you twisted your ankle on the climb up –'

'Cancel it?' Farini cut him off. 'For Christ's sake, Barston, your tiles are slipping off! This is the big one, the breakthrough. Look at the crowds. Listen –'

He leant forward and gripped Barston by the lapel of his jacket, thrusting his face close to the little man's.

'Blondin did it. Look what it did for him. And what that little French shyster can do, I can do in spades. Did he have the newspapers here? Nuts he did! We've got them all. In a couple of days we'll be front-page news across the country. You know what they'll be calling me – ?'

Farini grinned. 'Not just Farini, but the *Great* Farini!'

Barston smiled weakly back. It was still madness, but as always Farini's energy and confidence had trampled over his doubts.

'I'll be right behind you.'

'Keep your feet on the ground and that's an excellent place to be.' Farini chuckled and tapped Barston's cheek. 'Just make sure you don't miss any late wagers. One gets five if I don't make it to the other side.'

With Barston scurrying behind him he stepped outside.

As he appeared, a roar of applause greeted him that was audible even over the thunder of the water. Farini swept off his hat and bowed low, his cloak streaming out behind him in the wind. With his head level with his knees he glanced quickly round. The crowd was in four parts. One clustered round the tent he'd just left, the second on the far side of the falls, and the other two on either side of the river below.

In all there must have been five thousand people there. It was twice as many as Blondin had attracted. Most of them had paid fifty cents to enter the roped-off spectators' enclosures. With the betting money and the sale of the souvenir posters and programmes, the total take should be close to four thousand dollars.

Farini smiled.

Slowly he stood up. He handed his hat and cloak to Barston. The young woman, her voice recovered, ran from the tent and flung her arms round his legs. She knelt at his feet and sobbed hysterically.

'Stop! Stop! You'll be killed!'

Farini gently disengaged her. He raised his arm in a final solemn salute to the audience. Then, with his face grave and his eyes fixed unwaveringly on the far side, he set foot on the rope that spanned the falls.

The roar of the churning water battered his ears. Within seconds all his clothes were sodden with spray. All he could see was tumbling and whirling clouds of grey moisture.

Surely and unhesitatingly, not even rocking in the sudden gusts of wind, Farini walked on.

He could not see them but all he was aware of was the audience. Behind and beneath the spray, people, thousands of people, were gasping and holding their breath as they watched him. Watching him, Farini knew, as if he were the most important man in the world – the representative of all their hopes, dreams and fears.

He had become their god on earth. In spirit they were on the tightrope at his side but it was he, Farini, who was making the crossing for them. At that moment it delivered them all into his power.

Farini reached the far side of the falls. He jumped down from the rope and bowed again. Dimly above the ceaseless tumult of the swollen river, he heard another roar. People broke through the rope of the enclosure and enveloped him. Many were weeping. They touched him, embraced him, tried to fold themselves round him.

Farini pushed them away.

Suddenly he climbed back on to the platform. He pulled a black silk handkerchief from his pocket and tied it round his eyes, blindfolding himself like a condemned man. Then he stepped out on to the rope again. Farini spread out his arms. He stumbled. For an instant he seemed about to fall. Somehow he regained his balance, and set off once more.

On the far side of the falls Barston watched him, appalled.

This was not part of the performance. The audience had been promised one crossing only. Farini must have gone mad. What he was doing now was suicidal – and doubly so because there was no reason for it.

'Get back!' Barston screamed.

If Farini heard Barston, he ignored him. Farini went on. Rocking perilously from side to side, he reached the middle of the rope. There he stopped. Very slowly he knelt on one knee. Still blindfolded he lowered his head. Like a lover courting a mistress he blew kisses to the four parts of the crowd in turn. Then he stood up and completed the crossing.

'You're insane – !' Barston shouted at him as Farini tore the handkerchief from his face and jumped down to the ground again. 'Find yourself another agent! I'm never going to act for a maniac again!'

Farini shook with laughter. The acclaim from the crowd was so loud now it had almost drowned out the tumult of the water.

'If I'm a maniac, you should get me to bite your other clients,' he said. 'Listen to the punters, Barston. We won't just be front-page news. We'll be headlines. And, believe me, old friend, this is just the start. Tomorrow we're moving on.'

Farini turned to acknowledge the continuing shouts from the audience.

A week later in New York Farini sat hunched forward reading the pile of newspapers that was waiting for him.

Barston waited. The newspapers carried the reports of his Niagara crossing. Farini wasn't in fact so much reading them, it seemed to Barston, as devouring them. When he had sucked each one dry, he tossed it on to the floor and started greedily on another.

Barston watched Farini as the pile grew.

Farini wasn't his real name. According to the Bronx Hospital of Our Lady of Lourdes he was William Leonard Hunt. Farini himself sometimes wondered if Hunt was his real name either. It was what was written on the label tied round his neck thirty-six years earlier, when the hospital sent him to the adoption agency after his birth. For all Farini knew, Hunt might have been a name the hospital made up for convenience.

It no longer mattered though. He had chosen his own name, a truly *real* name, long ago.

He was Farini.

He'd seen it written on the side of a conjurer's tent in a travelling circus which passed through the Bronx when he was six. The visit to the circus was the only treat his foster parents, a grim and cold pair of fundamentalist Christians, had ever given him. It provided Hunt not only with a new name, but with a vision of what his life would be.

When he ran away from home ten bitter years later, Farini had known for a long time that one day he would be the greatest showman in the world.

Farini threw the last of the papers away. He sprawled back and crossed his legs. For a moment he closed his eyes, smiling to himself. Then he laughed out loud.

'Didn't I tell you, you doubting Thomas!' he shouted. 'Look at these and weep in penance!'

He gestured at the floor.

Barston smiled. He'd already read the newspapers. Farini was right. The Niagara crossing had made the front page of every one. The reporters who'd written the stories must have been infected with the drama of the occasion as much as the watching crowds had been. The praise for Farini's boldness and courage was close to adulation.

'You did fine,' Barston said.

'Fine? For Christ's sake, man! Inside a week I've become a national figure, and that's the best you can do? It's not fine! It's extraordinary, a miracle! Who remembers that frog Blondin now?'

'Exactly. Who indeed – ?'

Barston's smile vanished. His voice took on the quiet, calculating tone of the professional agent.

'The Frenchman never capitalized on what he did,' Barston went on. 'He didn't make any real money and he's been forgotten. Sure, you made a lot out of Niagara. But it wasn't the Comstock Lode and it won't last for ever. You don't need to repeat Blondin's mistake. For you Niagara's just a platform.'

Farini stared at him.

His eyes narrowed in anger. Barston was everything that he was not. Small and plump and timid with shifty eyes, a wispy beard, and a manner that even the paid women found repellent. Barston was not merely second rate, he was third rate. Now he was jealous – jealous of what Farini had done, of how it had shown up his own fear and inadequacy.

Farini swore. He swept the papers aside with his foot and started to rise. Suddenly he stopped. Scowling he sank back into the chair again.

Barston was right. Niagara had been a triumph but it

was still only a platform, a stepping stone. He was going the whole way and he needed the little agent to show him the next step.

'So where the hell does Niagara lead to?' Farini demanded.

'Upstate a little north from here,' Barston replied. 'Right now the place is just beginning. But, believe me, when you look at it, you'll be looking at the future.'

'What's it called?'

'Coney Island.'

— 18 —

'How much?' Farini asked.

Unsettled by the abruptness of the question, the young man tugged at his cravat.

'I beg your pardon?'

'I'm asking what's the gelt?'

'Gelt?'

'Jesus, man, what do you want for it?'

'Ah, the consideration –'

The young man coughed to cover his confusion.

The three of them, Farini, Barston and the young man, were standing on the steps of the London theatre known as the Westminster Aquarium. The theatre's lease was up for sale and the landlords, an old-established Victorian savings bank, had appointed the young man their agent.

'The consideration –' the young man repeated, still struggling.

The young man was used to a world where one showed a client a property and retired to a high-class tavern to discuss its merits over a leisurely pint of ale. Farini's approach was unlike anything he'd ever encountered. But then almost everything about the tall flamboyant American had been disconcerting since they'd met an hour earlier.

'The rental is seven hundred guineas per annum,' he ventured. 'The lease is for seven years, renewable on negotiation. In addition there is a repairing covenant –'

His confidence returning, he swept out his hands towards the pillars. Farini cut him off.

'Hold it, son, hold it! I only arrived in Britain yesterday. I'm going to need a little help.' Farini turned to

Barston. 'This seven hundred guineas. Translate it for me.'

The plump little man calculated and ticked off the figures on his fingers.

'Thirty-five hundred dollars,' he said.

'Thirty-five hundred – !'

Farini stared at Barston. At the same moment both of them began to heave with laughter. The agent watched them bemused.

'You're wasted, kid, wasted.' Farini seemed to be struggling to contain himself as he looked at the agent again. 'With a sense of humour like that, you should be on the boards. In my business you'd make a fortune. Listen –'

He gripped the young man by the arm.

'Today I'm not here to audition comics. I'm here to deal. I'll level with you. I like you and I like the place. Maybe it's got possibilities. So let's forget the jokes about thirty-five hundred dollars and go somewhere we can talk – and I mean talk goddamn sense.'

Across the cobbled street was a tavern. Pulling the agent behind him, Farini set off down the theatre steps towards it.

The young man was still bewildered. He had no idea what had provoked the laughter. Somehow in the company of the two Americans he sensed he was out of his depth. They were sharper, blunter and bolder than any clients he had ever dealt with. He wasn't sure it really mattered.

He had been told to sell the lease. The Americans were clearly interested. At least sitting down in the tavern with a drink in front of him he'd have a chance to gather his wits.

Unprotestingly he hurried after Farini.

It was the late summer of 1880, four years after Farini's crossing of the Niagara Falls.

Farini had spent the years between at the new amusement park on Coney Island to the north of New York. At

Barston's instigation he imported from Paris the first cannon seen in America capable of firing a man. Farini opened his site on Coney Island by setting what he claimed was a world record for a human cannonball.

The adulation of the press and the public was even greater than for his feats at Niagara. Within weeks he was drawing larger crowds than any other entrepreneur in the park. Four years later the crowds were as big as ever, but Farini was restless. The Niagara crossing had given him national notoriety. Coney Island had brought him money and further fame. In the entertainment business, he was known throughout the country.

His success was heady and potent. To Farini it was not enough. He dominated Coney Island, but the sandy sprawl of the island's dunes still only amounted to no more than a little fairground satellite of New York. New York, in turn, was no more than a fledgling town. Compared with the great and ancient capitals of Europe, New York was a village.

On Manhattan Island, the last foul-smelling clusters of Indian teepees were still being pulled down by sullen immigrants whipping at ox-drawn waggons. Europe, in contrast, dazzled and glittered.

On a sudden impulse Farini sold his Coney Island site. He turned his ambitious gaze east towards the monuments and displays of a more ancient, more sophisticated, and still much richer world. It was a world he was obsessed with conquering. Farini hungered for Europe.

As so often Barston gave him the key.

The little agent with the wispy beard and the damp eyes had become one of the first trans-Atlantic commuters. Every spring and autumn he crossed the ocean, looking for new acts he could sell in America or placing American performers in Europe. On one of his trips he learnt about the London theatre called the Westminster Aquarium.

'It's in the centre of the city, close to the river,' Barston said. 'The last tenant went bankrupt, but that was only because he didn't know entertainment from a snake's ass. The site's perfect and it's up for grabs. Handled right, it could become the finest theatre in the world. Put in an offer and its yours.'

A week later Farini was on a boat heading for Britain. Forty-eight hours after landing at the port of Southampton, he and Barston were standing on the steps of the Aquarium.

At his first calculating glance, Farini knew the theatre was everything he had ever dreamed of. The Coney Island pavilions were small tawdry structures of plaster and cheap wood. The Aquarium was vast. Built of granite and marble and seating over two thousand people, it towered above the surrounding streets like an imperial palace.

The exterior had fluted pillars and pediments and statues. Inside, there were great domed corridors painted with frescos. Yard upon yard of old mahogany panelling. Immense cascading crystal chandeliers. Deep Wilton carpets, rows of plush seats upholstered in velvet, and glowing brocade on the walls.

The whole building was stamped with splendour and power. Farini, the Great Farini as he had insisted on being known since Niagara, had found a setting that destiny might have designed for him. He had come home.

'Okay. Let's go over it once again,' Farini said to the owner's agent. I'll figure it in dollars. You can translate back into pounds. With that keen brain of yours, it shouldn't be any hardship. Right?'

Farini grinned at the young man. The agent smiled weakly back.

They had been in the tavern for two hours. The young man didn't know how much he had drunk, although it was certainly far more than his usual single cautious glass of ale. The glasses of all three of them seemed to have been emptied and refilled with the same bewildering speed with which the American had done his calculations.

Farini ran through the sums even more quickly than he had ordered the drinks. Then he leant back in his chair. He shook his head ruefully and chuckled.

'Know what, kid?' Farini said. 'You and your

principals are going to come out of this covered in gold leaf. While me? I take all the risk and do the earning for you. I get the feeling you've just danced rings round me. But what the hell? Farini makes a deal. He sticks with the deal –'

The young man tried to interrupt. Some of the figures didn't sound quite like the ones he thought they'd agreed. Before he could speak Farini turned to Barston.

'You got it all noted down?' Farini asked.

Barston nodded. He'd been writing away furiously for the past twenty minutes.

'Then let's sign it.' Farini took the paper from him. He scrawled his signature at the foot of the page. 'Like my mother used to say back in Boston, there's no better time to infuse than when the kettle's boiled.'

He pushed the paper in front of the young man. Almost hypnotized, the young man took out his pen.

'And while we're waiting for the ink to dry,' Farini added, 'let's make it a real celebration.'

Farini snapped his fingers. The bar-boy hurried over. Farini ordered a bottle of champagne. As the champagne foamed up in their glasses, the young man signed the paper.

Six months later Farini's first production opened at the Aquarium. The following year he wrote urgently to Barston who by then was back in New York. The letter started jovially. Then its tone changed. Much more urgently it continued:

'Max Barston, I need you.'

'Max! Max!' Farini gripped Barston by the shoulders and embraced him. 'My oldest friend! Jesus, am I glad to see you!'

It was several moments before the little man could disentangle himself from Farini's bear-like grasp.

Barston plucked at his beard and panted. Farini's presence, the sheer physical vigour of the man, always unsettled him. As a showman he was unquestionably a genius, but to be with him was exhausting.

Farini hurried him inside the theatre and swept out his arms.

'So what do you think?'

They were standing in the stalls of the Aquarium.

It was the first time Barston had seen the theatre since Farini bought the lease. Barston's ship from New York had docked the day before. He hadn't even been to his hotel yet. Farini's own carriage, painted black with Farini's name in gold on the doors, had been waiting for him at the station. The carriage had taken him direct to the Aquarium, where Farini was restlessly pacing the steps.

Barston drew on the cigar Farini had just pressed upon him, and glanced round.

'I think it's sensational,' Barston answered. 'But then I always did. Isn't it just what I told you?'

'Wait until you see the show tonight,' Farini said. 'We start with jugglers, an act from Moscow, the best I've ever seen. Then a singer, a kid I found in a beerhouse near the docks. I don't understand a goddamn word she says, but she's got a voice like a bluebird. They *love* her. After the kid, something of my very own. Watch this – !'

He shouted instructions at one of the stagehands who was crossing the footlights.

The man scuttled away. A few moments later there was the sound of machinery grinding, and two huge glass tanks rolled on to the stage from either side of the wings. Both the tanks were filled with water dyed a vivid aquamarine.

'In the one on the left, a mermaid,' Farini explained. 'On the right, a seal. And not just any seal, he's the brightest animal you ever met. The mermaid throws him a sardine. He catches it in his mouth. He tosses it over to a boy with a skillet, waits for the kid to fry it. Then he catches it again straight off the fire and throws it back to her. The girl eats it and pitches one back to the seal. They feed each other –'

Farini chuckled. 'Some nights I can run it for fifteen minutes. Wait until you see the mermaid's boobs. I've got her putting oil inside her bodice. When she leans over the tank after the fifth sardine, you can damn near see down to her pussy!'

Farini shook with laughter. He shouted at the stagehand again and the tanks were trundled away.

'So,' Barston said in the silence which followed, 'you've got a fine place, and what sounds like a terrific show. What's the problem?'

Farini hadn't spelt it out in his letter, but there had to be a problem – a serious problem. Only that could have explained Farini's urgency in writing, and his promise to pay for Barston's passage.

'I'm playing eighty, Max, and it's sliding. Not fast, but it's on the way down.'

'Eighty – ?'

Barston raised his eyebrows. In the shorthand of the entertainment business, eighty meant that the show was running at eighty per cent of the theatre's seating capacity.

'Eighty should be great,' Barston went on. 'You're clearing at what? Fifty?'

'Forty-five.'

'Then you're running in straight profit. You can let the show roll until you're down to forty-five. Then cut it and put on a new production –' Barston frowned. 'I don't see any problem.'

Farini took Barston's arm and led him back through the stalls towards the entrance.

'Sure, I'm in front, Max,' Farini said as they walked. 'But I didn't come here for that. I've always been in front. I was way out front on Coney Island, for Christ's sake. It's not enough. I gave up all that. I came here to win. That's different. And eighty's not a winning call, least of all when it's sliding –'

They reached the foyer. Farini gestured round the walls.

They were hung with posters, prints and lithographs. They depicted acts in a dozen earlier shows at the theatre, some going back twenty years or more.

'Look at them,' Farini went on. 'Jugglers, singers, dancers, novelty acts. That's what I've got, Max. The same goddamn show as these artists were drawing way back before even you or I ever heard of this place –'

Farini shook his head.

'Okay, so my show's better. It's got a shine, it's faster, it's more exciting. The trouble is the public's seen it before. I can put it on again when we drop to forty-five with different names and different faces. It'll still be the same. Next time I'll open not at eighty but at sixty, and I'll drop even quicker –'

He clenched his hands in frustration.

'I've got everything, Max,' Farini finished. 'Everything except what I really want. The city, the site, the platform. It's all round us and it's perfect. Add me to that, add what I can do, and it should be unbeatable. But there's something missing. I can't find it and it's sending me insane.'

Barston looked at him.

For once Farini wasn't using hyperbole. The skin on his face was stretched as tight and pale as a drum, and his wrists were shaking. His stone-coloured eyes had always been unsettling. Now, in their ferocious, unblinking intensity, they looked almost mad.

For anyone else, acquiring the most famous theatre in London and mounting a production that had filled it for weeks would have been a triumph to satisfy them for the rest of their lives. Not Farini. To him it was still not enough. He wanted the Aquarium to play at capacity for ever.

At least that was what he claimed.

Even that, Barston knew, wasn't true. If he achieved it, Farini would still ask for more. Something was gnawing at the deepest roots of his being. Farini kept feeding it, but the demon that had fastened on to him was insatiable. It would go on demanding until it killed him.

Barston could do nothing about that. But there was something that might assuage the creature's hunger for a while. Its appetite was also the public's appetite. To feed his demon, Farini needed to tempt the public again. He needed a breathtaking act that would be a complete break with the past.

Barston knew where Farini could find it.

'Africa,' Barston said.

'Africa?' Farini looked at him, astonished.

Barston nodded.

'What the Christ has Africa got to do with entertainment? Only coons come from Africa.'

'I'm not talking about coons,' Barston said. 'There's more in Africa than coons. There's something called pygmies. Herman Wagnell discovered them. Wagnell opened them at Coney early this fall. Over here you'll have missed out on it, but they've been the most spectacular success the island's ever seen.'

'What the hell are pygmies?'

Barston explained.

Wagnell was another of Coney Island's impresarios. Until Farini's departure he had been Farini's only serious rival. Now he was unchallenged as the island's leading entrepreneur. Wagnell's position of triumph had come with what he had billed as, 'The dances of the pygmies from the unknown centre of the earth'.

'Christ knows how he heard of them first,' Barston said. 'They live way out in the jungle in somewhere called the Kalahari. Like I say, they're not coons. They've got yellow skins. They walk round butt-naked. They're no bigger than tiny kids – they'd fit inside a doll's house. And they dance like a dream. Wagnell got news of them. He sent off to Africa and bought himself a bunch. They're a sensation.'

'Africa!' Farini was shaking his head in disbelief. 'You mean on Coney, punters are paying to see midget African coons dancing?'

'They're paying Wagnell by the thousand,' Barston said. 'The world's changing fast. Changing, opening up, discovering things it never knew before. Take this guy Darwin. He said we grew from monkeys. Darwin was a Brit. Other Brits have been checking out Africa ever since. Africa's full of monkeys, they're there in waggonloads –'

Barston paused. 'You ever heard of the missing link?'

Farini shook his head again.

'It's what comes between the monkeys and us,' Barston said. 'Monkeys first, then the missing link, then you and me. So what if these pygmies are the famous link that's got lost? That's how Wagnell's playing it. I tell you, he's hit the public in the belly –'

Barston wasn't naturally eloquent. For a few moments he became so.

'Africa's the new dream.' He gripped Farini by the arm. 'It's strange, it's dark, it's magic. Africa's the past, the present and the future. It's nursery and school, cradle and death. That's why they're paying Wagnell on Coney. Africa is us –'

He breathed in deeply and tugged at his beard.

'What you need is Africa. Africa's your salvation –'

Barston paused. 'There's one more thing. The pygmies look like people, but they're animals. It means you can show the women pygmies' titties in public on stage.'

Farini looked down at the little man.

Most of what Barston had said was beyond him. To Farini, Africa was somewhere large and undefined to the remote south. He had heard vaguely of Darwin. He knew equally vaguely of the explorers who had been trying to penetrate the dark continent. He had read of the New York reporter named Stanley who had followed a man called Dr Livingstone into the jungles.

Stanley had made his own name and the name of his newspaper famous throughout the world.

What had silenced Farini was Barston's final comment about pygmies. No one had ever put a bare-breasted woman on a public London stage.

'Where can I find me my own bunch of pygmies?' he demanded. Farini leant down and gripped Barston by the elbows.

In the intensity of his conviction, a conviction that Barston had found the answer to all his problems, Farini lifted the little man up until their eyes were level. Convulsed with eagerness, Farini shook him like a dog shaking a rat.

'There's a man named Frouw, Gert Frouw,' Barston spluttered. 'He's a South African. He travelled over on the boat with me. He's here in London. He got Wagnell his group. I guess he can do the same for you.'

Farini lowered Barston back to the ground.

'I want to do business with him,' Farini shouted. 'I want to do business right now!'

Scarlet-faced, Barston smoothed down his jacket.

'If you'll give me a chance to breathe,' Barston said, 'we'll go and find him.'

— 19 —

Seven thousand miles from London on the southern edge of the Kalahari, Mary-Ellen stood in the shade beneath a tall acacia tree.

Mary-Ellen had been there for two hours.

The tree had rooted on a mound. From the mound's top she could see out over the surrounding bush. Every few minutes she peered towards the west. Mary-Ellen looked across the tawny winter-grey scrub again. Still there was nothing to disturb the stillness of the desert air.

She lowered her head and plucked impatiently at her hair. Somewhere close a robin was singing. She tried to listen to it. The Kalahari robin could mimic almost perfectly the song of at least a dozen other desert birds. The little San hunters had taught her to recognize both the robin's song, and the calls it imitated.

Mary-Ellen counted seven melodies soaring from the robin's throat. Then fretfully she gave up. She brushed the sweat from her face. She pushed her hat back on her head and stared out once more.

This time she tensed.

There was a tiny cloud of dust on the horizon. As the cloud came closer, it grew larger. Mary-Ellen saw the shape of the horse beneath the wind-blown sand, and finally the silhouette of Moffat. The slim young African rode up to the tree, and swung himself down from the saddle.

'You've got it, Moffat?' Mary-Ellen said breathlessly before he could speak.

Moffat nodded. 'Mama Beth was waiting by the Tbisi waterhole. She gave me this.'

Moffat handed her an envelope. Mary-Ellen seized it.

'Shall I wait for you?' Moffat added, 'You can ride back behind me.'

For a moment Mary-Ellen didn't answer.

She was staring at the envelope, her eyes transfixed by the bold angular writing that ran across it. Then she took in what Moffat had said. She glanced up and shook her head.

'Thank you, Moffat,' she replied. 'Thank you for everything. But, no, I want to read this alone. I'll walk back when I've finished.'

As Moffat trotted away, she stepped back into the tree's shadow.

Mary-Ellen held the envelope for a long time before opening it. She knew what it contained. She had known from the moment Beth Appleby had sent a message that a letter had arrived for her at the Appleby ranch. Mary-Ellen had contrived for Moffat to ride over and collect it.

The letter could only be her reply from Dr Darwin. She closed her eyes. She heard the robin singing again and felt the sun, filtered through the acacia's leaves, on her face. Then she slit the envelope open.

The letter from the great scientist was brief.

'Dear Miss Ramsay, I am indebted for your communication and gratified by your interest in my studies. However, I fear I am unable to assist you. The field of my research is complex and, indeed, contentious. It is not one appropriate either to your years or your sex. Nor, as a Christian, would I countenance a deception in regard to parental authority.

'With my sincere regards nonetheless, Yours etc Charles Darwin.'

The signature was neat and underlined with a crisp firm flourish.

Mary-Ellen read the few lines over and over again.

Her initial reaction was shocked disbelief.

Darwin's books had moved and enthralled her more than anything she had ever read. They had changed not just her world, but the entire world – the desert and the remote stars and the myriad forms of life that thronged the air between them. She had not even been fearful of writing to their author. Mary-Ellen believed that her passionate enthusiasm for what he had done, for the great windows he had thrown open, needed no explanation.

She was wrong. Dr Darwin had dismissed her like a frivolous child.

Afterwards, pouring in over the shock, came waves of humiliation. She had written offering her entire life to advancing Darwin's work. She had been contemptuously put in her place. She was an infant, an ignoramus. Worst of all, she was a woman.

Anger came to Mary-Ellen then.

At first the anger was mixed with tears. Tears of shame and frustration. Then, like steel repelling the acids of her other emotions, Mary-Ellen was left with anger alone. A fierce, hot anger that was also thoughtful and determined.

The destructive Oswell, who believed his assessments of people, of the common herd, were flawless, had misjudged Mary-Ellen on almost every level. His worst mistake was in regarding her as 'just a woman'.

Mary-Ellen did not see herself as a woman. She saw herself as a person.

A week later Mary-Ellen picked up her pen again. The great scientist was about to learn his profound error.

'Dear Dr Darwin,' she wrote. 'Your letter was received. I answer as follows. I am young but I have a mind, a mind, I may say, as good as anyone's. My sex you rightly deduce from my name. In your book you say the burdens and travails of child-bearing may well have formed the female stronger than the male. Furthermore –'

Mary-Ellen remembered the flourish beneath Darwin's signature. She smiled and underlined the word with the same firm authority.

'*Furthermore*, have you observed prides of lion at the hunt? I venture not. I can be so bold as to assert that I have. On many occasions. Each time, in my observation, it is the females who encircle and pull down the prey. The males – the *men*, if I may be permitted an anthropomorphic comment – then slink in to feed off the carcass –'

Mary-Ellen smiled again.

It was very late. Her parents were asleep. Apart from the creaking of the joists, the house was as dark and silent as it had been when she first wrote.

Then, in spite of her conviction about what she and Darwin shared, Mary-Ellen had been apprehensive. She had written as a supplicant, as a child to an old and venerable man. Not now. Now, in anger and conviction, she was addressing an equal – and she was furious.

She had, Mary-Ellen believed, good reasons to be furious. Not disappointment or childish petulance at his rejection of her. She had strong and hard scientific reasons – and she spelled them out with a cold controlled fury.

'You argue our descent from the apes. Might there not then be links between us and the apes? Let me tell you this. My friend Xtau is one of the little people, the San or the "Bushmen" as they are wrongly and ignorantly named, as I have mentioned previously. The San were here before we or even the black man came to Africa. They say they are the oldest people in the world.

'I go often with Xtau to his camp – I cannot call it a village. His people sleep under shelters of brushwood supported by a sapling shaped to a bow-frame. The mouths of the shelters face always to the east. I asked Xtau why this was so. He could not tell me. "They have always been set thus," he said. "It is right and natural. Besides, look at our companions, the baboons. Do they not also set their nests towards the rising sun?"

'I observed the tree roosts of a baboon pack near the mission the next day. Xtau spoke the truth. The branches are piled so the entrance is to the east.

'Before I read your books this puzzled me. No longer. We trace our past to the apes. We have advanced but the apes have stood still in time. Yet they are still with us, they walk beside us. Would it not be passing strange if they did not show us the manners and furnishings of our beginnings?

'For where else did Xtau and his people learn to set their shelters – ?'

The nib of the pen snapped. Mary-Ellen sharpened another quill. She dipped the point in the ink. She hesitated. Then she hunched herself resolutely forward over the page again.

She had come to the point, to the meat of the letter. She frowned intently as she tried to get the words right.

'Dr Darwin, I have many more experiences to put at your disposal. I truly believe that, although I am painfully conscious of my shortcomings and my lack of formal scientific education, I can supply you with ample and detailed observations which cannot be obtained under any other circumstances but those in which I find myself.

'You have deduced the source of human life. Here in the Kalahari desert, I suggest, I can provide the evidence which will turn your deduction into proven fact. To you, Xtau and his people are for the moment the San or the Bushmen, the little people or the Baswara – it matters not what you choose to name them. To me they are my brothers and sisters, my family. To the world they may turn out to be the fount of all our beginnings.

'As a scientist you ignore them and their companions, the monkeys, at the peril of your research. I am the companion and observer of both the San and the Kalahari's baboon packs. You have spurned my offer. My communications go unanswered. Your silence, sir, is ignoble. Worse, I venture, in spurning me you put yourself at peril – the peril to your own reputation for honesty, justice and sound judgement.

'I remain your humble and devoted disciple . . .'

Mary-Ellen signed her name in her careful script.

Next morning she gave the letter to Moffat and told him to deliver it to Beth Appleby at the Appleby farm. From there, stamped by Beth, it would travel by waggon to Johannesburg, by waggon again from Johannesburg to the Cape, and then by packet boat to Britain. Unloaded with the rest of the colony's mail at the Tilbury docks, it would be sorted and put on a train to Kent.

The letter completed its journey.

Nine weeks after leaving Kuruman it arrived in the south-eastern county of Kent.

— 20 —

Leaning on his stick, Charles Darwin walked slowly out into the clear June sunshine.

The white roof of the dovecote at the end of the garden dazzled in the early-morning light. The pigeons, *his* pigeons, the carefully selected and meticulously bred fantails and Cape buffs, swooped in and out of the shadowed entrances that led to the nesting boxes.

Darwin watched them for a moment. The air was heavy with the scent of roses. A fox that had been hungrily circling the dovecote's central pillar raced away into the woods beyond.

Darwin smiled. Limping painfully, his eyes watering at the brightness, he set off for the lichen-covered bench at the end of the lawn.

He was eighty-one and his health had been bad for years. Every day now even the smallest of journeys was increasingly not so much a trial as a torment. Yet his morning walk in the garden among his beloved pigeons was something he would never give up – not, at least, until he was carried out of the door in a pine box.

Darwin reached the bench and lowered himself on to the seat in the well of shadow beneath the towering elm. As he leant back a shaft of sunlight falling through the leaves flared off something in his hand. Darwin glanced down.

The letter.

'Dear Dr Darwin,' The writing was youthful but bold. 'Your letter was received. I answer as follows. I am young but I have a mind, a mind, I may say, as good as anyone's –'

He read it again slowly and carefully. Then he raised his head and frowned. Bees circled round him and a swallow hawking insects dipped past his feet.

'I am young but I have a mind.'

The phrase reverberated in Darwin's brain.

He received more than fifty letters a day. He'd done so for the past forty years, ever since the publication of *On the Origin of Species*. When, fifteen years later, *The Descent of Man* came out, their number doubled. Only now, in the twilight of his life, had the cascade slowed. Yet he still had a larger postbag, he had been told, than anyone else in Britain apart from the Prime Minister.

The young woman had written to him before.

He knew that only because of the scrupulousness of his secretary in filing his correspondence. He had answered the first letter out of politeness. So many people wrote to him – letters of hate, letters of fantasy, letters describing sad and crippled lives – it was impossible for him to deal with them all. But the young woman had been so evidently serious, however misguided, he had felt bound to send her a brief reply.

Darwin thought that was the end of the matter. Then the second letter arrived, the letter he held in his hand now. Darwin had been about to consign it unread to his secretary's basket, when its opening caught his attention.

From a seventeen-year-old girl in an African mission post to a scientist of over eighty, the most famous scientist in the world, it was a breathtaking declaration of equality. Somehow its very boldness, its sheer confident urgency, made Darwin read on. And then at the foot of the second page he came to what had caused him to think of nothing else since he first glanced through it.

'My friend Xtau . . .'

Xtau was a member of the little people. Xtau's people set their shelters to open towards the east. So, according to the girl from the Kuruman mission post, did the baboons.

Darwin believed her.

The implications of that apparently simple observation

transfixed him. In their way they were as momentous as his own observations of the Galapagos finches. The finches had led him slowly but inexorably to the concept of natural selection. From there he had been led equally inexorably to his theory of the descent of man. But that theory had to bridge a vast abyss in the chain of evolution.

A link was missing.

Man's connection with his past had vanished. It was hidden for ever in the lost and buried middens of prehistory. Or so Darwin had always believed. Now, if this child was right, he had been wrong.

Early man was alive and well and still building his shelters like his cousins and living ancestors, the baboon packs of the great Kalahari desert.

'Charles – !'

Darwin glanced up. A silhouette, haloed by the morning sun, had appeared on the path that led back to the house.

'What on earth are you doing here, dear? Your breakfast has been waiting for a good twenty minutes. We've been looking for you everywhere.'

The voice, fussing and scolding, was his wife's. Behind her another figure came into sight.

'Dr Darwin! You promised me you wouldn't venture into the garden without me. Think what might have happened if you'd tripped.'

Even sterner and more accusing, the second voice belonged to his secretary. The two women converged on him. They pulled him to his feet and propelled him between them back towards the house.

'I was merely enjoying the morning sun, dear ladies,' Darwin protested mildly. 'May a gentleman no longer do that in his own grounds?'

'No gentleman thinks clearly on an empty stomach,' was his secretary's crisp reply. 'Furthermore, what is this you've been taxing yourself with?'

She plucked the letter from his hand.

Over the past few years his secretary, Miss Stanwick,

had taken on a more dominant role in Darwin's life and affairs than even Emma, his wife of almost half a century. Now Emma was quite content to let Miss Stanwick read the letter and reprove her husband more bluntly than she could have done.

'It's from that wretched child in Africa,' she said in outrage. 'She must not be allowed to pester you, the troublesome young minx. I shall write to her myself this very morning –'

'No!'

Darwin cut her off with something close to a bellow.

The sound and the vehemence that accompanied it were so startling that the two women stopped open-mouthed in their tracks.

'You will not write to her, Miss Stanwick,' Darwin went on. 'I will write to her myself. I shall tell her that her observations are so full of potential import that they may well determine the very way humanity views itself over centuries to come. I shall urge her to continue her studies. And I shall send her money to further them.'

'Money?' It was Darwin's wife who spoke. Her voice was almost a whisper. 'You cannot be serious, dear.'

'Emma, Miss Stanwick,' Darwin gazed at each of them in turn, 'I have never been more serious in my life. To prove it I shall show you that even an old lion can still roar –'

He lifted his head and gave a deep-throated bellow. The sound echoed off the walls of the house and rippled away into silence round the garden's yew hedges.

'That, I think, is what the young lady has been waiting to hear. I hope it carries to her in Africa,' Darwin chuckled. 'Now let us go inside. What awaits us this morning, Mrs Welford's scrambled eggs or some more of those excellent kippers from Loch Fyne?'

He tossed his stick away. Then, stumbling slightly but unaided, he made for the door. As he reached it Darwin glanced back.

'Don't tarry, Miss Stanwick,' he called. 'We have matters of high moment to attend to today. I have been a vain and foolish old man. No doubt I shall die one. But for a moment the brilliance of youth, not my youth but a girl's youth, has illuminated me again. I want your writing on at least one of the envelopes we shall dispatch today to be as clear as her own desert sunlight.'

Dumbfounded, the two women followed him into the house.

— 21 —

Mary-Ellen did not believe it.

She read the letter once, a second time, and then a third. Then she put it down on a rock. She weighted it with a stone and walked away. Fifty yards off she stopped.

She closed her eyes and began to count.

In her mind Mary-Ellen knew the letter didn't exist. No one would ever write her a letter like that, certainly not in those extraordinary terms and after all the bitter disappointments of the past months. It was as much a mirage as the sheets of water that sometimes shimmered against the desert's horizon. When she turned round the rock would be bare.

Mary-Ellen forced herself to count to a hundred. Then she opened her eyes. Slowly and fearfully she looked back. On top of the rock four sheets of white paper were fluttering under the stone in the Kalahari wind. The impossible had happened. The letter was still there.

Mary-Ellen burst into tears.

'Dear Miss Ramsay, At the start I owe you a full and sincere apology –'

It had taken Mary-Ellen several minutes to compose herself. Now, in the shade of the mopani thicket beyond the compound fence, Mary-Ellen read the letter for the fourth time.

'I woefully underestimated your commitment, your courage, and your perseverance. Far worse, I misjudged the acuteness of your perceptions. I present myself now as your servant who can only beg forgiveness for an old man's blindness –'

Mary-Ellen shook her head in disbelief.

'So, if I may borrow your phrase, to business. In observing a specific behavioural link between groups of the San people and neighbouring baboon packs you have suggested a line of enquiry as important, in my view, as any I have encountered in my lifetime. It must be pursued. You have my full support and encouragement in doing so. As to any general advice I can give you –'

There followed a list of ideas and suggestions about how she should set to work. Finally Mary-Ellen came to the last paragraph.

'Such studies, as I remember well from my youth, are costly. You will need books and all the required tools of research. It occurs to me you will lack the resources to purchase these. It so happens I am co-founder of an educational trust to aid research in the sciences. It was formed to make grants in just such cases as your own.

'As an earnest of my good faith and in further reparation for my earlier obtuseness, I trust you will allow me to fund your studies. I propose doing this by a quarterly remittance of five sovereigns. You will no doubt advise me of the easiest arrangements for transmitting this to you.

'Your servant, Charles Darwin.'

Five sovereigns a quarter. Mary-Ellen's eyes misted over again. In a full year that was over £20. It was a fortune. More than a fortune, it was freedom.

Although it would take a long while for her to digest the full implications, Mary-Ellen sensed even then that a miracle had happened. She had sent the letter like a note in a bottle tossed at hazard into some vast sea. It had come back to her laden with gold.

She was no longer a prisoner of the mission post, doomed to spend a lifetime in thrall to the dark moods and discipline of her father. Suddenly she had become her own woman. She was free to change her life. She had been given a chance to redeem herself from the sickening events of Oswell's visit.

In time she might even win her father's forgiveness. She

would have to prove herself as a scholar in secret first. But if she did that, if she gained respectability in the academic world, one day she might be able to lay her achievements before him. Her father had a profound respect for learning. For the moment she knew Ramsay hated Darwin and all he represented more virulently than anything else on earth.

The years might change that. Mary-Ellen had an unquenchable belief that in the end truth would triumph over everything – and Darwin held the key to the truth.

It would take time and courage. More courage than she would be able to summon up for a long while, perhaps for ever. But from now on it would always be there as a possibility, influencing everything she thought and did.

Meanwhile there was the work. What was it the great doctor had written? She glanced through the pages again. She found it.

'If an old man may venture advice, I think you may find as I have found, that in the end the work is the most important and most satisfying of the experiences the Almighty has made available to us. All else passes. Work, an arduous task well and diligently carried through to completion, remains.'

Mary-Ellen stood up.

She walked to the rim of the copse and looked north.

The light was just beginning to fade. Namaqua and Cape turtle doves were homing to roost in the darkening air. In the far distance she could see a group of gemsbok against the horizon, the great horns of the antelope curving like scimitars against the sky. Above them the stars were appearing, the wheeling, dazzling constellations that lit up the Kalahari night.

Somewhere out there the little people would be settling down to rest. Like their companions, the members of the baboon packs which shared the desert with them, the San's shelters would be set towards the east. She would go out and study them. She was certain the two species belonged together. She would search for the connections, the links, between them.

And as she did it, who knew what she might find? In the Kalahari, the San said, all was possible because the great spirit of the sun who made the desert had decreed it should be so. She might find relationships between men and the animals that not even Dr Darwin had dreamed of.

The sky darkened. Soon it would be time for dinner. Mary-Ellen turned. She plucked up Darwin's letter, folded it carefully, and tucked it away out of sight under her blouse between her breasts.

As she hurried back to the mission, she heard one of the most familiar of all the sounds of the desert at night – the hunting calls of a pack of hyenas.

— 22 —

Akula, Kala's litter brother, was butting her with his muzzle.

Sleepily Kala reached out her hand and slapped him away. She settled back into the hollow beneath the sandy shelf, lying on her stomach and crossing her hands over her head to shut out the light. Akula backed off for a moment. Then he prodded at her again. His nose was damp. It dug uncomfortably into her ribs.

Kala sat up.

'Nksst!' she snarled at him.

She bared her teeth at the young hyena, opening her jaws and drawing her lips back tight towards the corners of her chin so her whole mouth was exposed. Akula retreated a few yards. He sat down and licked his groin.

Kala rubbed her eyes and stared at the early evening sky.

By now she had been with the Merula Pan hyenas for almost a year. The clan's underground lairs were still the centre of Kala's life, but over the past few months the child's world had begun to change and expand dramatically. She spent a large part of each day above ground in the open with the other cubs. She played with them. She lay dozing with them in the shadows. Above all, just as the rest of Herut's litter was doing, she began to learn about their joint clan family.

The first and most important thing Kala learned was how the hyenas 'talked' to each other.

The gesture she'd made in baring her teeth was the hyenas' main signal of rejection. It was an essential 'word' in the clan's language. After five months the child understood and spoke the language fluently.

Kala couldn't use all of it.

There were some 'words' whose meaning depended on physical equipment she didn't possess. She had no tail to raise in question, to bristle in anxiety, to tuck away in submission. She lacked scent glands to help in the vital daily task of marking the pack's territory. She was without a mane to flare at the approach of prey or danger.

Most frustrating of all, she was handicapped in talking to the clan through the system of calls they used.

The hyenas' sound language was complex and subtle. Kala understood almost everything they 'said' to each other. The calls of warning, of play, of hunger, of loneliness, of sexual arousal, of endearment and comfort, even of loss and grief. For weeks Kala faltered when she tried to use them herself.

Part of the reason was simply physiological. Kala came from a different species. Her own larynx and throat had developed to meet different requirements. But there was something else more troubling and confusing.

Embedded in Kala as deeply as her teeth or her nails was the capability of descriptive speech. Words for her were separate from the signs and signals of a growl, a flared tail, the heavy musky scent of a marking.

Speech was a gift, but it needed nurturing. Once, briefly, she had begun to be imprinted with the skills of using it. That was in her human past, and her human past had gone. It had been obliterated by the trauma of her arrival in the hyenas' lair.

Now she was trapped between man's use of 'words' and the animals'.

The hyenas saw a bank of cumulus clouds pressing down on the setting sun. They felt a change in temperature and pressure. They absorbed the restless flight of the evening birds. Together the signals meant rain. The hyenas told each other so by touch and grunt, endlessly reconfirming the information as they bonded themselves more tightly together to prepare for the challenges of the night's hunting.

Kala saw the same signs and signals.

To her they also heralded rain. But even as Kala registered them, she was aware of something else. She didn't only know rain was coming. She knew how and why she knew – the humped pattern of the clouds, the seeping warmth in the air, the sword-like shapes of the owls' beating wings.

Long after the storm passed, she would be able to describe its approach.

The hyenas would not. The storm came. It emptied its swollen belly in hail and deluge. Then, emaciated, the clouds whirled away. The storm was forgotten and the world began anew until more thunder clouds massed on the desert's horizon. Then the hyenas' perceptions would spark and quiver again, needle-sharp like the hairs on the manes of their backs. Meanwhile they had no awareness of the past because they had no words to record it.

The child, Kala, did.

She had been born with words. She had been dipped into the world of men who used them. Caught between the two systems – the signs and signals of the hyenas, and the fragmentary words she had begun to learn – Kala froze. She had started to use the sounds she heard Herut and the cubs using, like the 'Nksst!' she snarled at Akula. Suddenly she stopped.

The conflict in her mind was too fierce and bewildering.

Growls, whimpers and screams jostled and collided with human speech in a memory designed to store words. Kala would hear the echo of something tapping. She could not decide whether it was Herut cracking a bone against a rock, or something much more remote – the rhythmic rise and fall of a mallet on a chisel from somewhere deep in her past.

Kala was barely three years old.

Like any organism, she had a vibrant unquenchable impulse to live. The fire of being dominated everything.

But Kala was also human, and she had been marked by humans. The struggle between her human beginnings and her new life with the hyena clan proved unsupportable.

When Akula, her litter brother, approached her again playfully on the same afternoon Kala had warned him away with bared teeth and the snarled rejection call of 'Nksst!'. Kala opened her mouth again. Her lips parted and the hostile message of her teeth was still unmistakable. This time no sound came out of her throat – neither human nor hyena.

Kala had become mute.

Kala remained mute for a week.

It was the most hazardous week of her life. Her litter brothers and sisters were almost grown-up. They had overtaken her in weight and strength. The litter's cohesion had almost gone. The other three were separating, acquiring their own identities, preparing to become full hunting members of the clan.

Apart from them, Kala was encircled by over thirty other hyenas. Without the ability to communicate – and body signs without sound to reinforce them were useless – she was no more than a cripple, a diseased burden on the clan. The clan did not tolerate cripples or burdens. They threatened the clan's health and safety. Creatures like Kala were living carrion to be killed and eaten swiftly.

During that week Kala was often close to death. She was saved by two events. Both of them stemmed from her foster mother, the great female hyena Herut.

Herut happened to return to the pan just as Kala's brother, Akula, and her two sisters, Ochla and Kwickwa, registered there was something strange about their litter companion. She was silent. She seemed unable to protect herself. She had gone away from them and changed into something else.

What Kala had changed into, they sensed, was prey.

When Herut appeared, the cubs were jostling and snapping at Kala, and her skin was already flecked with blood. The big female snarled furiously and chased her other three offspring away. She inspected Kala. Then she picked the child up in her jaws. Herut carried her to an underground lair Kala had never seen before.

Herut placed her on the sand in the darkness. Grunting, the female hyena offered Kala her dugs. When the child had sucked, Herut lay down at the lair's entrance.

To Herut, Kala was one of her own. The hyena's nose had told her the child wasn't sick, although her silent posture before the other cubs in her litter had been puzzling. But whether sick or not, the ancient maternal imperative in Herut demanded Kala should be protected.

Herut guarded her for five days.

At the end of the five days Herut's milk gave up. Herut was reluctant to leave the child. If she did, Herut knew, her cubs or the other hyenas would kill her. Instead she tried to prod and tug and goad the silent little bundle back into reacting.

Herut bit Kala's neck. Nothing happened. She reached out with her paw and scraped the child's stomach. Kala flinched and turned away. She made no response. Herut pulled the child by her ankle out from the lair into the open. She shook her vigorously. Still there was nothing.

Finally, in a last despairing effort to arouse her, Herut began to lick Kala.

The hyena's tongue travelled down Kala's face, over her chest, and across her body. As Herut reached the child's groin the hyena encountered something. It wasn't part of the child. It was something else. Something apart and different. Something so old all of its smell had gone. The hyena hesitated.

In guarding the child, Herut hadn't eaten for a week. Now the sense cells on her tongue told her she had found food. Not rich or even nourishing food, but a source of protein nonetheless.

Herut began to gnaw at the leather belt round the child's waist.

Kala had been dreaming.

The child had been dreaming ever since the power of speech, to men or animals, had vanished from her. Nothing mattered any longer. She had simply floated away on a slow dark sea where occasionally she heard the sound of a shipwright's tapping mallet and a girl singing. Now, as the hyena's teeth tore at the belt round her groin, the dreams dissolved.

Kala sat up. She bared her teeth and screamed.

'Nksst!'

The warning, threatening call, the call she had shouted at Akula, rang through the darkness of the lair. Herut's head jerked up. She snarled in response. Then she nuzzled the child for a long time. Finally, satisfied her cub was healthy again and forgetting about the coil of leather she had been chewing, she backed away and loped out into the starlight.

Kala dropped back on to the sand.

She clasped the belt to her stomach. Inside it something was throbbing. It seemed as if she were holding a wild struggling creature. The rhythmic beats settled into the same pattern as the beating of her own heart.

As the child fell asleep, all she knew was that the speech had come back to her. Not the speech of men. That had gone. But she could talk again to her own people.

There was no longer any confusion. Kala was once more a member of the nation of hyenas. This time it would be for ever.

23

Kala panted.

She was travelling on her hands and knees. She covered the ground with an extraordinarily quick scuttling movement, but her chest heaved and the muscles on the underside of her arms ached and throbbed. They were bearing almost a third of the weight of her body. It was a burden nothing in the three million years of Kala's evolution as a human had equipped them to carry for long.

A hundred yards from the pan she sank on her haunches. It was the furthest she had ever been from the lair. Ahead of her the other three cubs loped on.

Kala crawled into the shade of a thorn bush and licked the blood from her scraped knuckles.

A moment later her litter brother, Akula, cantered back. He circled Kala. Then he approached her and nipped her on the thigh. Kala was hot and tired. The heat and exhaustion made her careless. Kala struck him casually on the nose with the flat of her palm. Akula squealed and backed off. He lay down and brushed his paw across his muzzle.

Soon afterwards the hyena stood up.

Kala's blow had been swift, but neither swift nor hard enough. Nor had she snarled at him. Something was wrong with her. In an instant she had changed from his litter sister into something else. Kala was full of meat and Akula was hungry. He approached her again. This time he leapt at Kala's throat. As he sprang Akula was snarling.

Somehow Kala sensed what was coming.

She met the hyena's attack with a blow that was neither weak nor casual. At the same time she gave a deep-throated howl. The full force of her bunched hand crashed down between his ears. Akula reared up in shock and spun round. He twisted and fell on his back. Squirming, he tried to escape.

It was no use.

Kala hurled herself on top of him. Her feet kicked savagely at Akula's ribs and her fingers dug into the tendons of his legs. With her teeth Kala sought his throat, trying to do to him what an instant before Akula had intended to do to her. Screaming, Akula managed to break free. He scampered up the bank and collapsed bleeding under an acacia thorn.

Half an hour later he returned to her.

Akula came crawling down the bank on his belly. His head was lowered submissively. He half-closed his eyes and wagged his tail. Kala greeted him with her tongue. She licked his mouth and rolled him on to his back. Then she took him into her arms and hugged him against her breast.

Thirty minutes before, either one might have killed and eaten the other. Now the entire incident was buried and forgotten. Yet both had learned lessons from it they would never forget. Akula that his strange litter sister was not prey but a fearsome adversary.

Kala that she could never afford to be careless again.

Two years later Kala had grown considerably.

Now she was almost five. On the rich diet of her foster mother Herut's milk she weighed more than most children of her age. Her litter brother and sisters, Akula, Ochla and Kwic-kwa, had grown even faster.

Hardly bigger than newborn puppies when Kala was thrust among them, they were now sturdy juvenile members of the Merula Pan clan. Sleeping among them in her first weeks in the night-black tangle of grass, faeces and carrion, the child was like a whale among blind and helpless minnows. Now they all outweighed her – in the case of Akula, her litter brother, by thirty pounds or half her bodyweight.

The difference in their rates of growth came from the different roles evolution had assigned to them. As meat-eating predators designed to feed off a particular shelf in the planet's larder, the hyena cubs' cells were programmed to mature quickly. To hunt and breed, and then to die.

The cycles of turnover, of life and death, in the world of the spotted hyena were rapid.

As a human child, Kala had been fashioned differently. Stamped out by the blind moulds of the planet's kiln, Kala had been crafted as a more sophisticated version of a baboon or a badger. Baboons and badgers are slow-maturing and omnivorous. They eat everything from plants to insects to birds to animals. Denied protein from meat, hyenas die. They have no alternative food supply to fall back on. When meat is unavailable baboons and badgers turn to plants, to tubers, to grubs, to beehives.

Kala, like every human being, was a baboon or a badger wrapped in a human skin.

The child's problem that evening as she scuttled away from the pan on her hands and knees was that her own natural environment had been exchanged not for one of baboons or even badgers. She had been placed in the infinitely more remote and alien environment of hyenas.

Hyenas travelled on four legs. Kala, the human child, tried to do the same. Moving on four legs, in Kala's case on hands and knees, hadn't been too demanding for her first six months in the pan. Emerging from the lair with the rest of the litter to play and bicker, to romp and doze, she had simply copied the other cubs.

She saw them and Herut moving on four legs. She did the same. The distances involved were only a few yards. To Kala it was barely even a physical challenge – it was natural and undemanding.

The day the cubs cantered away from the pan for the first time, everything changed. Kala tried to follow them. She failed. Her hands-and-knees shuffle was enough for the tumbles round the lair's entrance. Outside on the long hunting corridors of thorn and sand it was inadequate. There Kala was a cripple.

In the Kalahari cripples die.

Kala frowned. For a long time she sat rubbing her knees and licking her painfully lacerated hands as she considered the problem. She was not prepared to be a cripple and she was not about to die. She would have to change and adapt. That, it came to her, meant standing up, balancing herself on her feet, and using her legs to propel herself forward.

She rose from the cone of shadow. Her calf muscles and her quadriceps, the muscles that controlled her thighs, were strong and well exercised, but unused to the different leverage she was putting on them now. She stumbled. Then she found her balance. Swaying and clutching from time to time at tree branches, she set off in Akula's tracks.

Ten minutes afterwards she was running swiftly and confidently.

Kala had re-entered her past, the past of a human child who had been taught how to walk. Ten minutes later that past, the tug of her beginnings and learnings, was lost again. Kala still ran on two feet – but she was running as a predator.

She was running to kill and eat.

Her litter brother and sisters, Akula, Ochla and Kwickwa, had been taken out that day by Herut on their first hunt. Kala caught up with them moments before they brought down their prey.

She was in time to take part in the kill.

Herut had chosen the animal carefully.

The pitiless brain of the big female hyena had been scanning the possibilities for several nights. In time of famine, if Herut and her dependants had been hungry, she wouldn't have had the choice. She would have led the clan to kill whatever the desert offered – regardless of her litter's learning requirements.

But in the Kalahari that year there was no famine. The

rains had been good. The sweet trimedra grasses had flourished. The antelope herds were large. It was a time of feasting, of glut.

The impala ram was one of the bountiful season's few casualties.

He was still comparatively young. He was big and strong, and he had corralled a fine harem of more than thirty does for the second year in succession. He had been challenged, of course, by members of the surrounding bachelor herds. One pretender, in particular, had questioned his authority – his right to sow his semen and his genes – with the budding horns and pumped-out glandular secretions of any ambitious young male impala in rut.

The older impala drove him off with an impressive display of his own larger antlers. The encounter took place at night. Unfortunately, in the battle in the darkness, the dominant ram collided with the branch of a fallen tree and broke his thigh.

To any antelope, to any wild animal, a broken thigh is a death warrant. Herut noticed the impala limping the night after the accident. That night she ignored the ram. Zebra mares were dropping their young. Food for Herut's hyenas, the tremulous-legged newborn zebra calves and their protein-rich placentas, was plentiful. She led the clan to kill and feed on them. She did the same on the second and third nights.

On the fourth night – the night Herut led her litter away from the pan for the first time – she set out to stalk the impala.

By then the ram was weakening. Bold and brave as it was, it could not handle the two competing demands on its system – to feed and at the same time defend its harem. The ram trailed behind the does, dragging its shattered leg. Occasionally it snatched at the grass. More often it had to hurl itself at the ever more frequently intruding bachelor males.

The ram could see their swollen penises. It could smell the scent of their dripping seed. It knew where, with their fearsome youthful urgency, they wanted to plant the seed and it knew that they had to be denied.

Running out from a circle of thorn to head off yet another young male, its broken leg trailing behind, the impala ram never saw Herut.

The female hyena rose like a desert ghost from the grass. She caught the ram by the neck. The impala's impetus carried him over her shoulder. For an instant her teeth tore at the veins in his throat. Then Herut discarded him. The ram, still alive, fell to the earth.

Herut crouched and snarled behind her into the darkness.

The snarl was not a warning but an encouragement. Eleven of the Merula Pan hyenas came forward. Most of them were adults but the eleven also included Herut's litter – Akula, Ochla, Kwic-kwa, and the child, Kala.

The hyenas tore at the ram's body. When the impala was motionless, when the last quivering fibres of its life were stilled, the clan began to feed. They ripped away and discarded its hide to get at the flesh beneath.

Kala elbowed Akula aside. He snarled at her but she bared her teeth again and he gave way. Ochla and Kwic-kwa did the same. She edged forward between them. Her human past had finally been erased. She had taken part in a clan kill. Now she would eat.

Pressed between the hyenas Kala fed hungrily.

— 24 —

A cub came towards Kala.

The cub moved slowly, laboriously dragging a pair of wildebeest horns behind it. Only three months old, the cub was a female. The wildebeest horns weighed more than the little hyena. Its paws scrabbling and sliding on the bank, the cub eventually managed to pull the horns up to Kala.

It deposited them at her feet and wagged its haunches proudly. Then it lay down submissively. It began to lick her face.

Kala had been asleep. The cub's tongue woke her. She registered the hyena's smell. It was instantly familiar, the warm musky smell that in different spore mixtures and concentrations scented all the Merula Pan clan.

Instinctively Kala reached for the cub and licked it too. Kala yawned and sat up. The cub twitched its haunches again and watched her eagerly. Kala reached for the wildebeest horns, and tossed them back down on to the pan below. Delighted, the cub raced after them. As the horns settled in the sand, it gripped them between its teeth.

Then it started on the long wearying task of hauling them up to Kala again.

The cub was a member of Ochla's latest litter. As Ochla was Kala's little sister, the cub was Kala's niece. The cub had to exercise its muscles and rid itself of its milk teeth, so it could start to become a hunter. Kala's duty as its aunt was to help it.

The cub returned the horns to her. Kala picked them up and threw them back. The little animal scampered away, and Kala lay back in the shade of the acacia thorn.

It was eight years since she'd been placed by Go-Ki in Herut's den. Now she was ten. For over two-thirds of her life she had lived with the Merula Pan hyenas. Outwardly she was a normal growing child, although her skin carried some scars that most children of her age lacked. A growing long-legged child with dark matted hair and a smooth coppery skin brushed with little puckers of scar tissue.

Outwardly.

Inwardly, as a person, a human being, a girl poised on the edge of womanhood, there was tumult. Until the age of two Kala had been reared by her own kind. She had been weaned on food cooked over fires. She had learnt the beginnings of speech. She had begun to respond to the patterns of behaviour of humans.

Suddenly all of that had been ripped away from her. The framework of her existence vanished. She was thrust into the world of animals.

Kala had grown up to think as a hyena. She felt as a hyena. She looked out at the landscape through a hyena's eyes. She smelt and tasted it through a hyena's nostrils and tongue – quick and acute and razor-sharp. The desert wind was not a vague drift of air. It was a stack of sharply defined shelves, each one laden with meaning.

A pregnant hartebeest was about to give birth five miles to the west. The air carried the pheromones, the fragile scent spores, from the hartebeest's opening uterus. Its calf was possible prey. Like Akula and Ochla, Kala's nostrils dilated as she filtered the smell and interpreted its message.

A lioness was going into oestrus. The warm wet scent was like a banner on the evening breeze. Male lions would start to gather round the female. They would be restless and irritable. If the clan killed in their vicinity that night, they could expect trouble.

Impala rams were herding up their harems. The musk they gave out from between their thighs was rank on the breeze. Packed close together their females sometimes tripped over each other and broke their slender legs. A broken-legged impala, as Kala had learnt long ago, made for energy-efficient hunting.

It was not only smell.

All of Kala's senses had been honed on the whetstones of a desert hunter's existence. The alarm call of a distant jackal, the far-off spiral of a Cape vulture, the texture of the morning sand after a rare shower of rain, the slant of the light from a rising full moon – everything had meaning and significance. Minute by minute, second by second, the intricate patterns of the Kalahari's life were rearranged like a constantly shaken kaleidescope. To survive Kala had had to understand and react to them all.

For a long time she was protected by Herut.

To the great female hyena, the clan's dominant matriarch, Kala was a difficult, slow-maturing infant. She needed more care and attention, more cherishing, than the rest of the litter. Herut gave it to her. Not out of sentiment. The hyena's brain did not accommodate ideas of affection or compassion.

Instead, out of the blind, urgent self-interest of the forces which created Herut. Wrapped in the pelt of her strangled cub, smeared with the cub's blood and juices, Kala had become Herut's own infant. Kala carried the hyena's genes. For those genes to be carried into the next generation, Kala had to survive.

Herut fed, protected and saved the child. The hyena did exactly what old Go-Ki had intended.

The years in the Merula Pan passed.

As they did, Kala was faced with a new challenge, an increasing threat to her continued survival. It came from the fact that her life and the life of her foster mother were unsynchronized. Herut was a powerful and excellent parent. She could protect the retarded infants of her litter like Kala for a certain period of time.

The time was eight to ten years, the life-expectancy of a healthy spotted hyena. At eight to ten years a human female has not normally even matured to the point where she can breed. Biologically at ten Kala was a normal female child. Only two years older, Herut was a normal female hyena. Yet while Kala was only just edging towards puberty, Herut's effective life was over.

The one-time matriarch of a great clan, Herut had yielded her position to a younger dominant female. She had become a barren scavenger who depended on the other hyenas for kills which provided her – and Kala – with food. Herut was sliding quickly towards death.

Within hours of the big hyena dying, Kala's own life would be at risk.

In the world of the clan, the child was an adult hyena without the essential physical equipment that an adult hyena needed to hunt and survive. Kala lacked the strength of her Merula Pan peers, their speed and claws and devastatingly powerful jaws. Herut had compensated for her. With Herut gone, Kala would be on her own. Alone she was destined to die too. If the clan did not kill her as a defenceless freak, the Kalahari would claim her through thirst or starvation.

That day Herut's death was less than a week away.

Neither the great, now-wasting hyena nor her foster child had any inkling of that when, in the late afternoon, the air over the pan began to thicken and the desert sky darkened.

— 25 —

The Merula Pan hyenas were edgy and restless.

It was midday. The sun was at its height and the white Kalahari sky rippled with long coiling ribbons of haze. The heat was so fierce it had sucked every trace of colour from the desert landscape. The thorn bushes stood pale and drained. The golden and bronze mopani leaves were bleached to greyness. Even the tough little tsama melons were shimmery and translucent.

An ominous lowering stillness pressed down over the pan.

Normally the hyenas would have been asleep in the little pockets of shade under the pan's rim or among the surrounding brush. Not that day. Akula kept getting to his feet. He walked a few steps round the sandy wall and lay down. Then he stood up again and moved on. Ochla, his litter sister, moved her cubs from den to den three times in as many hours. Between each move she stretched herself out, exhausted and panting.

Kwic-kwa, the other female in the original litter, was pregnant. She was only a week from giving birth. More than any of the others she should have been resting in one of the underground caverns. Instead she roamed uncertainly between the other adult females, alternately greeting or snapping at them. Even Herut was disturbed. Old and stiffening, she padded fretfully between the entrances to the tunnels, searching for shadow and abandoning it abruptly as soon as she found it.

Kala lay under a clump of marram grass that curved down over her body like a wave.

Her skin felt raw and prickly. Sweat trickled down her

face and her mouth hung open. The tip of her tongue protruded between her lips like those of the panting hyenas. In Kala's case there was no need for her to stick out her tongue. Unlike the hyenas she had no heavy pelt. Her body had its own and different mechanisms for expelling heat. Yet just as in everything else she did, she copied the behaviour of the clan.

Her head hammered with a dull rhythmic pain and her palms itched. She tried to wriggle into the sand, spraying it over herself with her cupped hands as Akula and Ochla were doing with their paws. It was no use. The heat was merciless and unrelenting.

Kala rolled on to her back and gasped wearily for air.

For the first time the desert seemed to have died.

In the early afternoon the air began to darken.

Kala rose.

The heat was more oppressive than she had ever known. Even standing still, sweat was breaking from her pores and flowing down her skin. She looked over the pan. Every member of the clan was on its feet. Some were clustered together, moaning softly. Others were running backwards and forwards in an aimless frenzy. One, old Mikta, the pack's senior male, lifted his head and howled.

Watching them, Kala felt a chill in the pit of her stomach. Fear flooded over her. The tiny sun-gold hairs on her arms rose and bristled. She had never seen the clan behave like this before. She knew something terrible, something unimaginable, was about to happen.

The light dimmed further.

A few heavy drops of rain spattered down on the sand, raising little puffs of dust. Within moments the drops had turned into a blinding, hammering cataract of water. The downpour was so fierce and sudden it almost swept Kala off her feet. Staggering, she opened her mouth and screamed. As she did the sky above her seemed to tear itself apart.

A vast zigzagging spear of forked lightning slashed down and buried itself in the centre of the pan. Before its brilliance had even begun to fade, a tumultuous detonation of thunder exploded overhead. The roar, the shock, threw Kala forward.

She tumbled down through the thorn bushes on to the floor of the pan. Half-stunned, bleeding and terrified, she struggled back to her feet against the battering press of the cascading rain.

She peered round.

Even in the first minutes of the storm, the baked surface of the pan was beginning to fill with water. Rising every second, the water rippled round Kala's ankles. Lightning flared incessantly. Between the flashes thunder cracked and shook the air. Electric charges rippled through the surrounding scrub, haloing the branches with light. The earth seemed to heave and tremble.

In the pulsing glow Kala could just make out the silhouettes of the hyenas.

The clan had gathered together on a small island mound fifty yards from where she had fallen. They stood in a ring, as terrorized as she was, their heads lowered and their hindquarters pressed together. At their centre was Herut.

Weeping, Kala set out towards her. In that moment of terror Herut was more truly Kala's mother and the clan Kala's family than they had ever been. They were her only safety.

Kala never reached the island.

Midway across the pan Kala saw the hyenas divide. Ochla, her litter sister, jumped into the water and headed for the entrance to the tunnel where Ochla's own cubs had been left. Behind Ochla were two of the pack's spinster females. The three hyenas vanished. They reappeared, each with one of Ochla's cubs in their mouths. Carrying their limp black burdens, the three rejoined the other hyenas on the island.

Then, as if in answer to a silent command, the entire Merula Pan clan turned and sprang down into the water. Trotting, splashing, raising their paws above the swiftly rising level of the surface, they vanished towards the east.

Twenty yards away from them Kala stopped in midstride. Appalled and astounded, it took her only an instant to realize what had happened. The hyenas had gone. Her family had deserted her.

She was abandoned.

Kala was still standing numb with shock as the water surged against her knees, when a familiar shape appeared at the edges of her vision. Although it wavered and blurred with rain, she realized it was Herut. The old hyena waded back to Kala. She nuzzled the child's waist. She pressed her nose into Kala's groin. She reached up and licked her face.

Then Herut set off back in the direction the clan had taken. Every few yards she paused and called encouragingly for Kala to follow her. Kala tried. It was hopeless. Kala couldn't battle the water.

Reeling to a halt, she lifted her head and gazed after Herut. The female hyena was on the far lip of the bank above the pan. A sheet of lightning flared over her. Herut opened her mouth and howled. In terror and despair, Kala howled back. She made a final despairing effort to reach the hyena. She failed. Slipping in the mud Kala fell on her face.

She struggled to her knees. Another flash of lightning crackled down and Kala peered forward again. The bank was empty. Herut had gone.

Kala never saw the old hyena again.

Trembling and sobbing, the child set off on her hands and knees back across the sand. Her eyes were blinded by the sheets of blue-white fire that erupted from the sky every few seconds now. Her head throbbed with the roar of the thunder. Her body ached under the hammering assault of the rain. There was only one thought in her mind.

To escape from the storm.

Kala made her way to one of the tunnel entrances to the den. The den's chambers were already flooded, but there was still some shelter under the rim of the overhanging bank.

Kala wedged herself in beneath the shelf of sand.

With the instinctive reaction of any animal in acute danger, she had sought safety in the only place she knew as home – the clan's lair. The lair betrayed her. Ten minutes later, under the continuing violence of the storm's attack, the bank crumbled. Sand cascaded down over Kala's head and a rush of water swept her back out on to the pan.

Tumbled head over heels in the surge, Kala vanished beneath the surface. She bobbed up, coughing and spluttering. She floated limply on her back, tossing in a sea of muddy, flickering blackness. The rain, the lightning and the thunder explosions were savaging her again.

Kala closed her eyes.

Over the years she had seen many animals do the same when death in the form of the Merula Pan hyenas caught up with them. Hartebeest cows, impala rams, young giraffes, wounded jackals, once even a baby elephant, they had all struggled and fought as she had done. But when the battle for life was lost they had accepted defeat. At the end they lay down and shut their eyes.

Fatalistically, in darkness now, Kala began to drift into sleep.

Like all the prey creatures which had nourished her for eight years, she too was slipping into death. All she knew as the water rose and death inexorably approached was that she had to hold on to something.

Kala's hand slid down over her body. It reached her groin. Under the water, in the storm-racked night and far beyond the understanding of what remained of her conscious mind, her fingers touched something. Not part of her own body. Something different. Something hard and angular. Something that was both bound to her and separate from her.

Kala gripped it. The object seemed to throb. It seemed warm. It seemed to buoy her up and melt the numbing, dying coldness that had crept over her body. Kala clung to it. She let it carry her like a hurricane-driven mopani leaf across the churning ripples of the flooded pan to the bank on the far side.

Her head bumped against the bank as the storm passed. Within minutes the thirsty sand of the Kalahari was sucking the water away.

Kala lay unconscious with the Star of Egypt clasped between her fingers.

— 26 —

'How old are you, lad?'

Ben glanced up. The man was tall and white-haired with plump jowls and a gold watch chain gleaming over a swollen belly. On his head was a black stovepipe top hat.

'Does it matter?' Ben tried to keep the irritation out of his voice.

'I'm the customer, son. What the customer wants always matters.'

'Twenty-five,' Ben said shortly.

'Is that a fact?'

The man paused. It was 1882. He and Ben were standing in Ben's workshop near the village of Buckler's Hard, on the Hampshire coast of Britain a few miles west of the great port of Southampton. The man studied Ben shrewdly as if Ben had been a horse offered for sale.

The young man had an untidy shock of black hair and fierce slate-grey eyes set in a sallow strong-jawed face. Stockily built, he was curiously misshapen. The right side of his body was shrunken and lop-sided from his shoulder to his knee. As if in compensation, the other side bulged with massive muscles.

He was wearing a tattered pair of moleskin breeches and a paint-stained canvas jerkin. A chisel stuck out of one of the jerkin's pockets. He looked confident and determined, but there was a certain strangeness, a wildness, in him too.

'I'd have put you a good couple of years fallower,' the tall man went on. 'Well, if it's the truth you're telling, it makes me a mite happier. *If* it's the truth, mind you.'

'I carve with my hands and my mind,' Ben snapped. 'Not with the date on the Church certificate.'

'And that doesn't hold you back?' The tall man gestured at Ben's withered arm.

'Whenever it does, I use the other one,' Ben replied. 'It serves for both – and then more.'

He raised his left arm and clenched his fist. As broad and heavy as most men's legs, the arm looked like a great menacing blackthorn club.

The man backed away and chuckled.

'Don't lose your rag, lad. I like your spirit. Just remember the customer's always right and we'll make a businessman of you yet. And it's not monkey nuts I'm considering spending either –'

The man paused. He reached into the inside pocket of his jacket and pulled out something wrapped in worn yellow oilskin. He unfolded the package and produced a photograph.

'Take a look at this.'

Ben took the photograph. It showed an elderly woman. She had a granite jaw, white hair wound into a bun, and a mouth set as tight and hard as a vermin trap.

'My mam,' the man added proudly. 'Flower of all women and salt of the earth. Think you can catch her, lad?'

Ben stared at the photograph. 'You want her likeness on top of the mermaid's body?'

'Aye, lad, that's exactly what I want.'

'With the mermaid's bosom naked like you said?'

'Anything wrong with that? You listen to me, lad.' The man bent down over Ben. 'I suckled at my mam's titties. Best damn titties in the world, in my humble opinion. Can you catch them and her, that's all I want to know?'

Ben nodded. 'Yes, I think I can.'

'Excellent. We're half-roads to agreement. Now let's look at the wood.'

The man turned and headed for the door of the loft. Dragging his leg behind him, Ben followed. They climbed down the flight of steps into the muddy yard and stopped beside the cart.

In the back of the cart was a six-foot length of a treetrunk. Ben heaved himself up and examined it. The trunk was dark, straight-grained and heavy. He probed it with his fingernail. He could make no impression on the tightly packed fibres. The wood was as hard as teak, but it wasn't teak, Ben was sure of that. It came from a tree he'd never seen before.

'How do, lad?' the man asked.

'It's a good piece of timber,' Ben said, running his fingers over it. 'It'll carve well. Where does it come from?'

'Came out of Africa, the dark continent, that trunk did. One of my own ships fetched it home to Newcastle. Iroko, the darkies call it. Hard as bloody iron it is, just like my mam.'

Ben clambered down. His fingers were sticky with resin. He wiped them on his breeches and said, 'I can do the job.'

'How much, lad, how much?'

'The guild sets the prices. For a full figurehead, carved, painted and gilded with timber supplied, it comes to five sovereigns.'

'Five sovereigns?' The man roared with laughter. 'I'm from Yorkshire, lad. I'm not asking you to build the whole bloody boat too.'

Ben shrugged. 'That's what it costs. You can ask anyone.'

The man pulled out his purse.

'Four sovereigns and six florins. With the florins down on the table right here and now. Agreed?'

Ben looked at him. He gave a quick hard smile. 'If all my business was done with Yorkshiremen, I'd be carving in the poorhouse.'

The man chuckled. 'You won't regret it, lad. I'm taking a gamble on you, but folk tell me you're the best. With my fleet growing as it is, there could be more –'

He counted out the six florins and handed them over. He stared at Ben. Then his face clouded briefly and his eyes moistened.

'I loved my mam, lad,' he said quietly. 'I loved her and

her titties. Bring them back for me, catch them well. It's a fleet I'm building. I want her riding over the waves at the head of it.'

Ben glanced at the dark whorls and fibres of the trunk. His powerful splayed hands were already beginning to flex instinctively for the chisel and the wooden tapping mallet.

'She will have golden hair and the bosom of Helen,' he said.

'The hair gilded, mind, with leaf of fourteen carats? And madder, isn't that what you call it, on the nipples? Red as a rose with six coats of best ship's varnish against the salt. Right?'

Ben nodded.

'Good lad.'

The man clapped him across the shoulders. He heaved himself up into the cross-seat and shouted at the driver. The driver cracked the reins and the cart lumbered away.

Ben watched them go.

The cart rumbled down the lane and into the forest. Half a mile beyond where it disappeared behind the trees, it would pick up the road that led into Southampton. Within a couple of hours the Yorkshire shipowner would be seated by the hearth of the Golden Fleece calling for his supper.

Ben turned.

He wanted his supper too. Unlike the Yorkshireman he wouldn't be climbing up to his bed afterwards. He had a long night's work in front of him. Stifling a yawn he set out for his lodgings on the western side of Buckler's Hard.

The little settlement of Buckler's Hard was set on the Beaulieu river two miles inland from the sea. Tiny as it was, by 1882 it had been a famous shipbuilding centre for several hundred years. The flagships of the Tudor monarchs had been built there. Drake's own craft, the spearhead of the fleet that had destroyed Spain's Armada, first took to the water in its sheltered creek. A century later Pepys described it as 'the very cradle of our safety and our power'.

The reason was simple.

Apart from the stable horseshoe of land surrounding the village and the fine anchorage on the river below, Buckler's Hard had one asset beyond price. It was the end of a natural funnel that led straight up into the heart of the New Forest. The forest was the source of the finest timber in all Britain.

Almost from the beginning, sea-girt island Britain had depended on its navy – to trade, to defend itself against invaders, to sail out and build its empire. For more than a thousand years the best and stoutest ships had been built of New Forest oak. The finest of them all had come out of the south-coast yards like Buckler's Hard.

The world had been changing for half a century or more, and the vogue now was for ironclads. But still when a fishing fleet owner required an addition to his fleet, he came – if he wanted the best – to the village on the Hampshire coast. There he found not just the best boatbuilders, but the best of all the skills that went with them.

He found craftsmen like young Ben to carve the figurehead.

Ben glanced up at the clock in the bell tower of the church. It was almost six. He calculated quickly.

A short rest. Then he would give himself forty minutes for supper. By a quarter to seven he'd be back at the loft. The trunk weighed, he guessed, close on two hundred-weight. Old Nat, who used the barn opposite for his sailmaking, usually gave him a hand up the steps with heavy pieces of timber, but Nat would be away home long since.

Ben would have to manhandle it on his own. With luck, sweat, and a few levers, he'd have it in place on his bench by seven. Two hours of daylight and then he'd have to use the tallow lamps. He'd work through the darkness with them. By dawn the shape would be roughed out.

He'd go home again for breakfast. He might have a nap then. It would have to be short. He'd need the strong clear light of morning to chisel out the features. Mr Featherstone, as the Yorkshireman had introduced himself, was clearly a perfectionist. He was also a man in a hurry.

That suited Ben. Ben was in a hurry too.

As he limped in through the door, Mrs Patten, the lodging-house keeper, looked at him with concern.

'Your face is grey, Ben. Go and rest for a while until I've readied your meal.'

Ben smiled at her. 'Don't worry, Mrs Patten. I've just got a fine new commission. All I need is one of your best dinners and I'll be ready to take on the world, not to mention Mr Featherstone.'

'Who's he?'

'He comes well recommended from Yorkshire. He wants his dear departed mother portrayed as a mermaid for the figurehead of his new ship. And bare to the waist, too,' he added mischievously.

'Bare to the waist?' Mrs Patten looked at him, shocked. 'I trust you're joking. A man's mother with her bosom exposed? It's a disgrace!'

'So indeed I thought,' Ben answered. 'Then he showed me her photograph. I was most impressed. She was evidently a handsome woman. She reminded me not a little of you.'

'She reminded you of me?' Mrs Patten's voice rose in outrage. 'You are going to carve me naked?'

'Not yet, but Mr Featherstone has given me all manner of ideas.'

As Mrs Patten embarked on a torrent of abuse, Ben limped chuckling from the room.

He climbed to his bedroom. His bed, the iron truckle bed he had slept in for the past seven years, was set against the wall. Its plump mattress, newly filled by Mrs Patten with fresh straw, was ready and inviting. Ben glanced at it yearningly.

Stifling a yawn, he shook his head.

Instead Ben pulled out the pattern-book he kept beneath the bed. He flicked through the pages. Gryphons, dragons, blackamoors, dolphins, Nelson – the great sea-captain recurred in different guises again and again – they were all there, neatly drawn and coloured. Ben didn't want any of them. He wanted mermaids.

He found them towards the end of the book. There were six examples. Ben studied them all carefully. He settled on the last. She had the biggest, boldest breasts. They seemed to represent best what Mr Featherstone had in mind to commemorate his mother.

Ben traced the drawing in the book. He took the suggested measurements, and adjusted them to fit the Yorkshireman's specifications. As he finished he heard Mrs Patten calling.

'Supper, Ben, supper!'

He stood up and yawned again. He was hungry. All he wanted to do was eat and then sleep. He would have his supper, but afterwards he wouldn't rest however sleepy the meal made him. He would go back to the loft and begin to carve.

Something in Ben's life was coming to an end. He had known it for a long time. Now the end was very close. So too was the start of something else. Ben had decided it a long time ago. In fact, sometimes he thought he hadn't decided it at all.

It had been decided for him twenty-five years before when his mother left him outside the Buckler's Hard house, and hurried away into the night. Everything had stemmed from the effects of that brutal winter.

— 27 —

The winter of Ben's birth, the winter of 1857, was bitterly cold.

The Thames froze over. In London, oxen were roasted on the ice that coated the river. For days the prosperous merchants gave skating parties that began at dawn and ended long after dark. Mulled wine was ladled out from great cauldrons over log fires, and the frosty night air was bright with music and lamps and laughter.

In the tenements on the edges of the capital, the poor huddled over the few smouldering lumps of coal they had stolen or scrounged.

It was a fearsome winter for the entire country. For one group in particular, the gypsies, the tinkers, the Romanies – the wandering bands of travelling people were known by many names – it was an unending nightmare. In late January an unmarried sixteen-year-old gypsy girl named Leah decided the nightmare had to stop.

Not for her, but for her child.

Her child was a five-month-old boy. Leah had no idea who his father was. He might have been any one of a dozen men she had lain with for a penny at the country fairs. Driven by the cold, Leah's clan had taken their waggons down through the New Forest, and made camp a mile from Buckler's Hard.

Leah's child was already fever-eyed and wishbone thin. She had nothing to feed him with. There were no gleanings from the wild and none to be had in the villages. Within the next day or two, he would die. One evening Leah placed the child in a basket and carried him in the darkness into the village.

She picked a large house with well-lit windows and a handsome cart outside. She kissed the baby on his hollowed cheek and laid the basket against the coal-shed door. Before she left she found a stick and scored the child's name in the thick frost on the paving stones. 'Ben', she spelt out. Apart from her own name it was the only word she knew how to write.

Then she ran away. Next morning the gypsies struck camp and headed east to try their luck in Southampton.

Leah never saw her son again.

Leah had chosen better for the boy than she could ever have hoped for.

The house belonged to a Quaker chandler named Noakes. Ben was discovered by the family maid. If the maid had come out for the night's coal thirty minutes later, it would have been too late. When she carried him inside, Ben's skin was blue with cold. Frost had furred his face and his heartbeat was slowing.

The family took the foundling in, and Ben remained with them until he was eight. Then, suddenly and disastrously, Noakes' business failed. Noakes was forced to sell up and move. Before he left, Noakes, with a heavy heart, managed to place Ben in the local foundling hospital.

By then, unlike most of his new companions, Ben was a strong, well-nourished and well-educated child.

Three years later at the age of eleven he was picked by one of the best carpenters in Buckler's Hard as an apprentice. If Ben's guardian angel had been watching over him until then, the angel's attention suddenly wandered. A month after Ben started work he was sent out on an errand. Running across the street, he tripped and fell under a waggon. Before the driver could pull up the horses, the iron-clad wheels rolled over Ben and ground the right-hand side of his body against the cobbles.

The injuries Ben suffered would have killed most children of his age. Long afterwards Ben used to think he only survived because his body had somehow been tempered and hardened in the bitter winter of his birth.

Ben survived – but at a terrible price.

When the wounds and the broken bones healed, he was left permanently crippled. From then on he walked with an awkward rolling motion, humping his shoulder to accommodate his writhen arm and dragging his leg behind him like a bird with a broken wing.

'Cackle-hob!'

For the next year Ben was tormented by the taunts of the other foundlings in the home – a cackle-hob was a worthless piece of pottery that had split in the kiln. They jeered at him, they tripped him up, they pinched and scratched and kicked him as he lay helplessly on the ground.

Ben had no defence.

Inwardly he raged. He knew he was strong, far stronger than any of them. Somehow that strength had been seized from him. All that was left was a husk of a body that refused to do what he told it – to rise off the floor, strike back, and scatter his tormenters. He could only watch them through narrowed hate- and tear-filled eyes as their laughter and their blows rained down on him.

The next winter all of that changed.

One Sunday morning Ben slipped out of the foundling hospital. The other orphans would spend their only free day of the week huddled round the hospital's fire. For a few hours at least he could escape them. With plumes of steam rising from his mouth in the chill air, Ben hobbled shivering down towards the mouth of the estuary. Normally in winter there was no one there. Today there was – a grey-bearded and gaunt-flanked old man of about seventy.

As Ben watched, the man stripped off his clothes to reveal a baggy striped swimming suit underneath. Then to Ben's astonishment he plunged into the water and swam away. Ten minutes later he returned. As the man climbed out, he noticed Ben standing on the bank.

The man was a retired doctor. He studied the boy's misshapen frame through shrewd practised eyes.

'Born like that, lad, or was it an accident?' the man asked.

'I fell under a cart, sir,' Ben answered.

'Ever tried swimming?'

Ben shook his head.

'Then you should learn, boy,' the man said sternly. 'Vigorous and regular swimming can heal almost all the ills of the human flesh. In your case it would restore your muscular strength.'

Ben stared at him. Strength. The word echoed and re-echoed through his mind.

'Can you show me how, sir?' Ben asked eagerly.

'Strip to the buff and follow me, lad.'

A moment later, fighting back his panic and gasping from the shock of the icy waves, Ben waded into the sea.

Ben lifted his head above the surface.

He blinked the water from his face. Ten yards away on the river's bank the otter watched him warily. Its eyes were dark and suspicious. The animal twitched its nostrils, searching the warm afternoon air for scents to see if it could learn more about the intruder.

Ben slipped back beneath the river. He swam underwater five yards closer to the bank. Then he surfaced again. This time he barely glimpsed the animal. There was a sinuous flash of copper-brown fur, a stir in the summer-dry reeds, and it had vanished.

Ben chuckled and heaved himself out on to the bank.

Ben was seventeen. Six years had passed since he made the awesome discovery of what swimming could do to his body. At first it hadn't been easy. Floundering, gasping and spluttering, he had learnt the rudiments in the ten minutes of his first and only lesson. Afterwards he had been on his own.

Every day Ben had waded into the icy water of the estuary. Grimly and doggedly, fighting off the salt and the spray, he launched himself into the waves and willed himself to float. When he was floating he flailed out wildly with his arms. Caught up in the tidal whirls, he often came close to drowning. Once he was swept almost a mile out to sea only to be hurled back when the tide turned.

Ben persevered. Then something happened that still seemed to him almost miraculous. He suddenly began to swim as swiftly and effortlessly as the shy and elusive otters that thronged the New Forest rivers. As Ben swam, his former strength did not merely return, but he found himself doubly or even trebly as strong as he'd been before.

Ben used his suddenly found powers sparely. The time of his persecution in the foundling hospital was long past. Instead he became the protector of the orphanage's newcomers. He looked at them and thought of himself, and mercilessly stamped down on anyone who tried to bully them. More than anything, Ben used his strength to guard himself. Not against physical assaults – only a madman would dare attack him now. But against the outside world.

In the water Ben might almost have been an otter. On land it was different. The more Ben swam, the stronger he became. Yet his constantly growing strength only highlighted the wreckage of the bones that lay beneath. His muscles swelled under the press of the waves, but the bent and twisted bones beneath them remained the same. The more powerfully his body filled out, the more grotesque and crippled he looked.

Ben was constantly aware of it.

He ruled the orphanage. But occasionally as he limped up the stairs at night, Ben would hear his nickname whispered by some child in the darkness behind him. It was whispered softly and respectfully, but it was whispered nonetheless.

'Cackle-hob.'

The piece that had cracked in the kiln. The piece that was worthless.

Ben shut his ears to the sound and shuffled up to bed.

That afternoon as he lay on the bank, Ben wasn't thinking of the whispers that followed him up the stairs.

The hot summer day was one of the most momentous in Ben's life. That morning his apprenticeship had come to an end. After seven years learning his craft, Ben had become a qualified carpenter and carver of figureheads. When he returned to work in a week, he would be paid a wage for the first time. Already in anticipation Ben had moved out of the orphanage and taken a room in Mrs Patten's lodging-house.

It was an event that demanded to be celebrated, and Ben knew exactly how he was going to celebrate it. The beginning and end of apprenticeships coincided with the local fair a few miles away at the market town of Otterbury. The fair had many attractions, but far and away the most popular was the travelling theatre which set up its huge tent every year in the market square.

Ben had bought a ticket for that night's performance in Otterbury.

A peal of trumpets rang out and the curtain swept down.

In the centre of the audience Ben gripped the back of the seat in front of him. All round him people were shouting and applauding. Some had risen to their feet as they clapped. The noise was tumultuous. Ben didn't move. He sat transfixed, his knuckles whitening as the cheers cascaded over him like the estuary's surf.

The past two hours had been the most extraordinary Ben had ever spent.

As the theatre lights dimmed, a dazzling new world had been born out of the darkness. Swept by pulsing green and blue beams, women had sung to him. Except they were not women – they were the siren mermaids of the stories he had heard in his childhood from the sailors who clustered the quays of Buckler's Hard.

The mermaids and their songs vanished. In their place were strange slant-eyed jugglers who tossed and caught fountains of golden balls like tumbling stars. The jugglers bowed and melted away. A raucous-voiced old harridan with marble-veined breasts stumped forward. Leering, chuckling, mouthing obscenities, she spewed out a cascade of jokes and stories so raw and filthy Ben could hardly believe what he was hearing.

Buoyed up on waves of laughter, she too disappeared. After her came a pair of dancers. Both were young girls. Their faces were pale and wistful, and their long hair as dark as the river in winter. Fugitive and haunting like ghosts of the forest, they turned and spun in clouds of white muslin to the aching chords of a single fiddle.

Finally the performance ended. When the audience stopped clapping and streamed away, Ben stayed in his seat for a long time. Then, the last person to leave the tent, he stood up.

Still dazed, he walked a short way out into the country. He found a couple of rough hessian sacks, wrapped them round him, and lay down to sleep in a ditch.

Tomorrow Ben was going to see the performance again.

The storm swept in from the Channel and broke over the coast shortly before dawn.

Ben woke to the sound of a howling wind, and the drumming of rain on his body. He lay for a moment, shivering. Then he climbed out of the ditch. He draped the sacks over his shoulders and set off back for Otterbury. As Ben entered the market square, he stopped, appalled.

Only hours earlier the theatre tent had floated in a great golden canopy over the cobbles. Now all that was left of it was the central pole, still pointing defiantly at the sky like a splintered lance. From it hung sodden and bedraggled ribbons of torn canvas. On every side were upended chairs, pieces of frayed rope, broken lanterns, and shattered glass glittering in the puddles.

The theatre, the glittering palace of magic and dreams of the night before, had been destroyed.

Shaking his head in anguish, Ben walked slowly forward. Apart from a couple of early-morning urchins, the square appeared to be deserted. Then, at what had been the entrance to the tent, Ben noticed someone else. It was a woman of about sixty. She was short and almost square, with dark hennaed hair piled high on her head. Dressed in a shawl and baggy black trousers, she was leaning on a stick with an owl's-head handle, surveying the wreckage in front of her.

As Ben approached, the woman turned and inspected him.

'Looking for work, young man?' she snapped. 'And if you are, what are your skills – always supposing you've got any?'

'I'm a carpenter,' Ben answered, startled.

'Carpenter?' She stared at him with interest. Then her eyes narrowed suspiciously. 'You'd better be telling the truth. I've a ferret's nose for liars. But if you are, I'm offering two shillings for a day's hard work starting right now.'

Ben gaped at her. 'You want to employ me?'

'I don't want to hire your pretty face, you silly young bugger,' she replied. 'But if it's a skilled pair of hands, then yes. I've got a theatre in ruins – Mrs Araminta Devon's Travelling Theatre to be exact, and me being the said Mrs Devon – and a show to get on tonight.'

She paused. 'Well, if you want the job, boy, don't just stand there. Get on with it!'

'Yes, Mrs Devon, right away!'

The theatre tent opened its doors again at nine o'clock that evening.

It was two hours later than advertised, but none of the audience minded that. Everyone for miles around had experienced the onslaught of the storm. The crowds outside waited patiently until the lamps glowed above the entrance. Then they eagerly poured in.

Ben squatted on his heels in the darkness of what he learnt were called the wings.

He had been working without a break for sixteen hours. He hadn't even had time to eat. His hair was caked with sweat and dust, and his shoulders were bowed with exhaustion. Yet as soon as the lamps dimmed and an expectant silence fell over the tent, the hairs bristled on the back of his neck.

He watched the performance from a different perspective from the night before. Then he had been sitting among the audience with all the effects, illusions and sounds presented as they were meant to be experienced. Now Ben saw the reality behind them.

He saw the girl dancers stumbling off-stage no longer sirens, but weary, coughing women with grotesquely paint-streaked faces. He saw the dazzling jugglers swearing and arguing among themselves like drunken sailors. He saw the set in front of which they all acted not as a shining creation of gossamer mist and shadow, but a cobbled structure of chipped planks and dirty muslin.

Ben saw it all – and it made no difference.

If anything, the spell of the night before, the magic it had woven round him, was even stronger. He saw the fusion of Mrs Devon's artifice with the flesh-and-blood reality of the Hampshire sailors and farmers in the audience. Through some strange alchemy, Ben knew, they had all been transformed.

It didn't matter how briefly and fleetingly. For an instant at least, there really was an escape from the mire and brutality of common living into a land of dreams that were believable. A land where even a cripple soared and flew. Where he would never be called, even in the quietest and most respectful of whispers, a cackle-hob.

'You – !'

The word cut through the clamour with the rasp of a rusting knife-blade. Ben glanced back. He didn't have to search for the voice's owner. He recognized it instantly. It was Mrs Devon.

'Come here, young man.'

Ben followed her to the side of the set. The performance had just ended and the audience had left.

'Did you do this?'

She was pointing at one of the set's pillars. Made of

wooden beading covered with stretched muslin, the pillar was one of the production's many illusions. It looked solid when it was lit from the front, but when the lights were moved to the back for the finale it glowed transparently.

The muslin had been shredded in the storm. When Ben had examined the damage, he thought of the sacks he had picked up in the farmyard. On his own initiative he cut them up, teased out the hessian strands and used them to patch up the holes.

'Yes,' Ben answered.

Mrs Devon studied him again through her keen, penetrating eyes. She grunted in cautious approval.

'You may only have one fully working foot, young man,' she said, 'but at least you can think on it. Better, it seems, than most people on two. No doubt the Almighty will send me other problems needing equally inventive solutions tomorrow. Consider yourself hired for the week.'

Leaning on her owl's-head stick, Mrs Devon stumped away.

'Two shillings a day for six days.' Mrs Devon counted the coins into Ben's hand. 'A handsome remuneration, but for once not undeserved.'

Ben looked down at his palm.

The little silver discs shone brightly up at him. They were the first money he had ever earned. Their sparkle and gleam, the sweat and effort they represented, the rewards they offered when he traded them for something else, all should have left Ben exhilarated.

They did not. He would keep them only as a talisman and souvenir. He had earned them at a magical feast that meant far more to him than money. The feast was not his own. It belonged to strangers and it was constantly, restlessly movable.

The week was over. The feast of Mrs Araminta Devon's Travelling Theatre was moving on. Ben looked at her in anguish, suddenly desperate not to let her and her players slip from him.

'Maybe you could use a carpenter?' he suggested wildly.

'I can find carpenters wherever I go,' the old woman replied. 'Mercifully, the Almighty doesn't torment me with the need for one more than once every dozen years.'

'If you took me on, I'd work for half pay,' Ben implored.

'Anyone who works for half pay isn't worth paying at all,' Mrs Devon answered crisply.

She paused and looked sharply at Ben.

'You're worth paying in full, young man. Not by me. I don't need you now. But someone will. You're quick, skilful, inventive – what you did with those sacks impressed me. You need to learn more yet, but you've got a future in the theatre.'

Ben shook his head despairingly. All he knew was Mrs Devon's company of players. Once they had departed, his own fragile contact with the theatre had gone too.

'Where?' he demanded.

'London,' she answered. 'Travelling companies like mine, they're not worth a tinker's fart – if you'll pardon my French. London's different. It's got two dozen, three dozen, permanent theatres, all of them needing sets. One day you could design them, make them, paint them –'

Mrs Devon hung her bag over her arm.

For an instant she leant on her stick. She gazed at the bright-eyed owl's head as if she were inspecting an old friend.

'Set up on your own,' she advised. 'Rent an arch in Vauxhall. Once you've got your premises, make a few sketches to show what you can do. Then set out on the rounds of the producers. Offer them your services. It won't be easy. You'll need capital, of course.'

'Capital?' Ben asked. 'How much?'

'Fifty guineas should see you through.'

'Fifty guineas – ?'

Ben broke off, speechless. The sum was so enormous it was almost beyond imagining.

Mrs Devon rubbed the owl's head, polishing its dark eyes. Then she smiled at him.

'Patience, young man, patience,' she said. 'Given time, anyone who can transform hessian into magic will be able to drum up fifty guineas.'

She shook the stick at him. Then she strode away, her baggy trousers flapping in the evening breeze.

Ben set out on the road back home.

As he limped along, his head rang with what Mrs Devon had said. Fifty guineas. It was impossible. Few people in Buckler's Hard left estates worth that much when they died – and that was at the end of their working lives. Even if Ben saved every penny from his meagre earnings as an assistant wood-carver, he would almost be ready for his own coffin before he'd accumulated it.

Like the theatre, the idea was a fantasy. It was something to be dismissed and forgotten. But like the theatre too, it was a fantasy that continued to haunt Ben – a fantasy that wouldn't go away.

For the next five years Ben tried to do exactly what he'd vowed on the road back from Otterbury he would put from his mind. He tried to make the fantasy real.

He applied himself to his work with an intensity that sometimes unnerved his former apprentice-master who was now Ben's employer. The dour old carpenter and figurehead-maker was named Trewithy.

'You want to watch your eyes, lad,' Trewithy would say as he went home at night, leaving Ben still tapping away at some carving by the feeble light of a tallow candle. 'Lose them, and there's nowt but back to charity.'

Ben smiled briefly without answering.

There would be a penny bonus if he finished the carving by morning. His eyes, Ben knew, were as keen as an otter's. When the candle went out, he could continue to work by the light of the moon. As the door closed, Ben angled the chisel carefully and hammered it into the wood.

He had no friends, barely even an acquaintance he

could call his own. Taking every job, every passing piece of work he heard about, there was no time for companionship. For five years Ben carved and laboured and swam – long afterwards he used to think that his contact with the otters who shared the water with him was the only real relationship he ever had.

Ben denied himself everything. Then one night at the end of the five years, Ben counted what he had accumulated.

His savings amounted to exactly four pounds and ninepence.

Five years unremitting effort had produced less than a fifth of what he needed. At that rate he would need a further twenty years to meet his target. By which time he would be in advanced middle age. Ben lay down and closed his eyes in despair.

The next morning he woke to the sound of Mrs Patten's voice calling excitedly for him.

'Ben! Ben! There's a letter come for you in the mails.'

Ben got out of bed and ran downstairs.

He could only think there had been some mistake. He had never had a letter in his life. There was no one he knew anywhere who would write to him. Still blinking from sleep, he took the envelope from Mrs Patten's hands. Ben examined it. His name was written clearly in educated writing on the front.

The envelope had originally been addressed to the orphanage. From there it had been forwarded to Mrs Patten's house. Ben slit it open. As he read the letter inside, his eyes widened in astonishment.

The letter came from a firm of solicitors in Liverpool.

They acted for the executors of the estate of the late Mr Noakes, the chandler who had taken Ben into his household as an infant. Noakes, Ben discovered, had gone to Liverpool and set up in business again. The business had prospered and Noakes' fortunes had been restored. He had never forgotten Ben. Staunch Quaker that he was and haunted to the end of his life by the guilt of having to abandon Ben to the orphanage, Noakes had left Ben a legacy.

The legacy, the solicitors said, was twenty-five guineas. They had pleasure in enclosing a banker's draft for the sum.

As Mrs Patten stood quivering with curiosity beside him, Ben read the letter again. He looked at the banker's draft and saw his name printed out in bold capitals as the payee. Below it, written just as clearly, was the amount.

Ben glanced at his landlady.

'What's your favourite tipple, Mrs P?' he demanded.

'Tipple?' She stared at him, flustered. 'Don't be so disgraceful! I don't tipple. I don't know what on earth you're talking about –'

'Oh, yes, you do.' Ben cut her off. 'A good dark stout of a Saturday night, isn't that it? Well, you're going to get a crate of the best available in Buckler's Hard. You're going to celebrate your lodger's entry into the world of business.'

Ben planted a kiss on the startled woman's cheek. He limped out chuckling into the street.

There was only one way Ben could make the money he needed. There had only ever been one way. That was to set up in business on his own. Ben had known it for years. He had also known the likelihood of ever being able to achieve it was as much a fantasy as the sum itself.

Not now. Now he could do it.

By then, although still only twenty-two, Ben was an outstandingly skilful craftsman – at least the equal and, in many people's view, the superior of his employer.

Ben left his job with Trewithy. He rented the barn opposite old Nat, the sailmaker. He bought himself tools and a stock of timber, and opened his doors for business. It was grindingly hard work, but with his already-established reputation, his skill, and his driving determination to succeed, the business began to prosper.

Over the next three years Ben made almost ten times as much money as he had done in his entire working life before. When Mr Featherstone, the Yorkshire ship-owner, commissioned the figurehead of a mermaid with his mother's breasts, Ben's savings stood at almost fifty pounds.

— 28 —

A week after he started on the mermaid, Ben twisted on his stool and studied her face.

She was almost done. A fraction more carmine on the lips, perhaps, but that was all. Ben dipped his brush in the cup of powdered paint, and carefully gave the mouth another coat. Then he cocked his head and rocked back.

The mermaid was perfect.

His own creation from raw trunk to delicately painted carving she might be, but Ben could think of no other word to describe her. Perfection. She soared upwards from the elegant swirl of her tail. Her naked breasts were tilted proudly, her yellow hair streamed back from a broad, strong brow, her eyes – cobalt-blue and flecked with green –gazed searchingly ahead.

She was the finest, the most beautiful, the most sensual mermaid who had ever left Buckler's Hard.

Ben tapped her affectionately on the buttocks. All that remained was to prepare her for the waves. Six coats of varnish Mr Featherstone had demanded for her. Six coats she would get. Ben set to work again. By evening he had finished.

Leaving the last coat of varnish to dry, Ben climbed down the ladder and limped outside. Dusk was falling. The air was clear and warm with the stored-up heat of the summer's day, and the stars were just appearing in the sky. As he stood there a sense of exhilaration swept over Ben. It was so strong that for a moment it made him giddy.

In forty-eight hours Featherstone would arrive to collect and pay for the mermaid. The money, Ben had suddenly realized, would finally take his savings over the magic figure of fifty pounds. The Otterbury fair was about to start. Eight years almost to the day since Ben had first seen Mrs Araminta Devon's travelling players, he had achieved the goal that for so many of those years had seemed a fantasy.

He was free to leave Buckler's Hard. Free to make his way to London. Free to set up in business there and embark on the life that ever since that moment was the only one Ben had ever wanted. He was about to launch himself into the world of the theatre.

In Buckler's Hard, for all the respect Ben had earned with his skills, he would always be thought of as the penniless foundling from the orphanage. He would always be cackle-hob. Not in London. There he would be a craftsman with his own capital, and his own talents in paint and wood and canvas.

Ben had achieved the impossible. The impossible demanded to be celebrated. In euphoria Ben decided he would do something he had never done before, not even on the day when Noakes' legacy arrived and he had bought Mrs Patten an entire crate of milk stout.

He would find a tavern and have his first drink.

Ben could have had his celebration drink in any one of the five inns that served Buckler's Hard.

He chose not to, although the village lights were glimmering only a few hundred yards away as he walked out of the barn. In Buckler's Hard he was known by everyone. The villagers had learnt to accept his solitude and leave him alone. But his appearance in a tavern would inevitably provoke whispers and comment. Someone might even be bold enough to come up and try to engage him in conversation.

Ben wanted none of that.

Instead he headed for the neighbouring hamlet of Canon St Mary half a mile to the west. Close as it was to Buckler's Hard, St Mary was a different community. People would certainly recognize him – Ben's reputation was spreading along the entire coast – but they would be more wary of approaching him. He would be a stranger, not one of their own, and they would let him have his drink in peace.

Ben found a tavern in Canon St Mary. He went in and ordered what he knew the fishermen drank when they were celebrating – a mug of ale with a nip of rum as a chaser. The ale was cloudy and insipid, but the rum was dark and warm.

Ben abandoned the ale and had another glass of rum. The spirit spread over his body with the same invigorating charge of pleasure that came to him when he dived into the sea. He felt safe and confident. Ben asked for a third glass of rum and then a fourth.

Soon afterwards his knees wavered and he felt a surge of giddiness. Ben gripped the bar counter and blinked. Then he chuckled. He knew what had happened – he had often heard it described before. He was becoming slightly drunk. In his case it didn't matter. He was still sober enough to recognize it. He was in control of himself. He would leave the tavern now.

Ben finished his rum. He thanked the tavern-keeper and walked out.

'Where are you going, mister?'

It was a female voice and it came from somewhere to Ben's right. Ben scanned the darkness.

Clouds had filled the night sky since Ben entered the tavern. The clouds parted. In the moonlight Ben saw a girl was sitting on one of the milestones that marked the road to Southampton. She was about fifteen or sixteen. She was wearing a low-cut blouse and a long, soft dark skirt. Her arms were resting on her knees and her head was propped in her hands.

Dimly Ben thought he had seen her in the tavern earlier in the evening.

'Buckler's Hard,' Ben answered.

'Is that on the Otterbury road?'

'Yes,' he said. He went up to her. 'Are you all right?'

'Course I'm not all right,' the girl replied. 'Had too bloody much to drink, haven't I?'

Ben was right. He had seen her in the tavern. She'd been drinking with another couple of girls. All three of them, he knew, were prostitutes. Every year at the time of the fair they thronged the local villages on their way to Otterbury.

Ben had noticed this one in particular because she was extraordinarily attractive. She had long black hair, a full provocative figure, and wayward eyes that were at once vacant and inviting.

'What happened to your friends?' Ben asked.

'Made arrangements, didn't they?' the girl replied.

She stood up. As she did so she stumbled. Ben reached out his arm to steady her and she fell towards him. Pressed against him her body felt soft and warm.

Her head nuzzled his chest. She felt his muscles and giggled.

'You're strong, aren't you? I like strong fellows. I'm Kate. What's your name?'

'Ben,' he answered.

He tried to disentangle himself, but the girl seemed to be clinging to him like a vine.

'Walk me your way for a while, Ben,' the girl, Kate, said. 'Maybe the air will clear my head –'

As Ben hesitated, she drew back her face and smiled at him.

'Come on, Ben, be a gent. I'm not going to eat you.'

In the moonlight it was the most dazzling, enchanting smile Ben had ever seen. He put his arm round Kate's waist. They set off along the road to Buckler's Hard.

'Had a few drops too, have we?' The girl giggled again.

She had felt the shuffle and drag of Ben's hip as they walked. Ben opened his mouth to explain that the lurching wasn't caused by the rum. It was simply the way he had always moved since the accident. Then he closed his mouth again without speaking.

For some reason it didn't seem to matter. There was a scent coming off her, a heady fragrant scent unlike anything he had ever smelled. It swirled up into his face and invaded his nostrils. It blotted out all the other scents of the night air. Ben glanced down. The girl's head was resting lightly on his shoulder. Below it he could see the swell of her breasts beneath the deep-cut neckline of her blouse.

Ben trembled.

He had never, ever been as close to a woman before. The experience was dizzying. It was stranger, more disturbing and intoxicating than any amount of drink could ever have been. He half tripped. For an instant he had to hold on to the girl for support.

Kate misunderstood what had happened.

'My, oh my, are we having difficulty in holding it, then?'

She laughed at him mischievously.

Ben stopped and recovered his balance. He laughed too. Then he glanced round. They had come to the crossroads outside Buckler's Hard. The track to the left led into the village. The road ahead went on to Otterbury. The track on the right ran up to the group of barns which included Ben's workshop.

'This is as far as I go,' Ben said. 'I'll have to be away to my lodging-house. I've got a customer coming at dawn. Otterbury's straight on. It's a fair walk, but the night's as clean as a tinker's whistle and you won't miss the road.'

Awkwardly Ben held out his hand.

As he spoke he felt an aching sense of regret. As vivid and troubling as the waves of scent that were still swirling up round his face, the loss wasn't in his mind but somewhere much darker and more unknown – somewhere that seemed to be rooted first in the pit of his stomach and then between his legs.

Kate took his hand. She gave an elegant little curtsy. She rose and smiled, the same incandescent smile that had bewitched him before. She stared at him. Suddenly she drew Ben to her.

Startled, Ben tried to step back. She was strong, much stronger than he thought. She caught him round the neck and pulled his face down to hers. Her mouth found his and she pressed her lips against his own. She forced his lips open and slipped her tongue inside.

As she kissed him with a passionate, hungry ferocity, one of her arms left his neck. She searched for his hand. She found it and drew it down over her breast. She pushed and moulded it against her nipple.

'I'm not going on to Otterbury tonight,' she whispered. 'I'm going to lie with you. We're going to be together. A bed and you, that's all I want. And because I love strong men, it won't cost you a penny. I come for free.'

In his stupefaction, Ben had been trying to break away from her again. He stopped. Her mouth searched for his once more. Her nipple was hardening under his fingers. It was a signal she wanted him. Vaguely he was sure of that. But there were other much more urgent and demanding signals coursing over his body and through his blood.

Ben lifted the girl off the ground. For an instant as he held her in his arms, he hesitated. She wanted a bed but his bed was in Mrs Patten's house. He couldn't take her there. By mid-morning everyone in Buckler's Hard would know what had happened. He would have to take her to his workshop.

Ben carried her along the right-hand track. He reached the barn and kicked the doors open. With the girl still in his arms, he clambered up the steps to the loft above. At the top he put her down for a moment. He limped forward and shuffled together a pile of discarded pieces of sailcloth to make a bed.

Ben picked up Kate again and placed her at the centre of the pile. As a bed it was rough and ready, but at least it was warm and comfortable. He smiled down at her. Ben stripped off his clothes. As they came away from his body he was only aware of the quivering spear between his legs and the dreamy smiling shape in front of him.

Kate sleepily shrugged off her own few clothes. Then, lying naked on the canvas, she looked up at him and laughed.

'I like to see my men, Ben,' she said. 'In particular, as you might say, my biggest strongest men. Haven't you got a light here?'

Ben chuckled.

His eyes, his otter's eyes, could see through the deepest darkness. Tonight wasn't dark. A crescent moon was already lifting over the loft's windowsills. But to someone like Kate, he knew the night would be impenetrable.

Ben thought for a moment. There were no candles or lamps in the loft. He had never needed them. But he remembered the little paraffin lamp he used to heat the varnish for the figureheads. That gave a fine delicate glow.

He limped across the floor to light it.

As Ben moved, his footsteps pattered unevenly on the boards. To the girl it meant he was still the worse for wear from drink.

'Taking time to wear off, isn't it?' she called out.

Ben lit the lamp. The light spilled out over the loft and illuminated his body. Naked, Ben turned, smiling, and approached the bed of sailcloth.

The girl screamed. As the scream echoed through the loft, Ben froze. Mingling disgust and fear, the scream was the most appalling sound he had ever heard.

'God Almighty, what are you?' she shouted.

She was staring at him in horror.

Instinctively Ben glanced down. His body was as he'd known it for years now – massively muscled on one side, shrunken and writhen on the other. The girl was seeing it for the first time. She was seeing it too against the little pool of light with the deep shadows from the beams playing over it and exaggerating all its deformities.

To her, Ben realized with a sickening shock, it must have looked grotesque.

'I had an accident,' he stammered. 'It's healed. I'm normal –'

'Normal?' she shouted. 'You're a bloody monster! You think I'm going to sleep with that? You must be mad!'

She leapt to her feet. She swept up her clothes and searched for the steps. Ben limped forward and tried to stop her.

'Don't touch me –'

Ben smelled the drink on her breath as she snarled at him. Her face was pale and taut with anger.

'Why didn't you tell me, you bastard? I go with real men, not with dirty cripples. Get out of my way!'

She drew back her hand. With a speed and ferocity Ben was totally unprepared for, she struck him a stinging blow on the side of the face. Ben was off-balance. He swayed back and fell.

Ben felt something scorch his skin. He had fallen against the paraffin burner. He squirmed away and struggled upright. The girl had found the steps and was starting down them. Ben saw the moonlight flooding across her breasts and down the long enticing white planes of her legs.

He threw himself after her again.

He couldn't let her go. In spite of the trauma of the last few seconds, he was still aching with desire. He wanted to hold her, to enter her, to bury himself in her. Most of all he wanted to explain to her – to make her see that she had misunderstood everything and he was truly as he had said.

She was too fast for him. By the time Ben reached the ground, she had gone. He limped through the barn door and out into the night. Twenty yards ahead he glimpsed a pale silhouette racing away down the track.

'Bastard! Monster!'

The furious drunken abuse floated back through the darkness. Then the shouts died away and the silhouette vanished.

Ben dropped to his knees. He put his hands to his face. With the owls hooting round him, for the first time in years he wept. He didn't know how long he wept for. Shaking and sobbing, it seemed to Ben like an eternity. All he knew was that after a while something was pricking at his nostrils.

Ben coughed. He brushed at his eyes and lifted his head. He tensed. Smoke was drifting out behind him through the barn door. He whirled round and looked up.

The loft was on fire.

— 29 —

Ben realized what had happened as soon as he climbed back into the loft.

When the girl hit him, he had knocked over the paraffin burner. The varnish pot had still been on top of the burner. The boiling varnish had spilled across the boards and set fire to them. Now the entire loft was ablaze.

Choking and coughing, Ben glanced round. The flames were already beginning to lap round the base of the mermaid. For an instant Ben gazed at the carving in shock. The figurehead had taken two weeks of his life. It wasn't only the most valuable commission he had been given. It was the best carving he had ever done.

Ben plunged through the smoke.

His eyes streaming, he somehow managed to heave the mermaid on to his shoulders. He crossed the floor again and stumbled down the ladder. As he reached the ground a section of the floor above caved in and he was showered with blazing fragments of timber.

Some of the firebrands caught in the folds of his cotton jerkin and set the cloth alight.

Haloed with flames like a human torch, Ben staggered outside.

He dropped the mermaid and ripped off his jerkin. Then he rolled over and over on the tall, dew-laden grass. Finally he clambered to his feet and stood trembling in the darkness. Patches of skin on his shoulders and arms were raw and blistering, and an acrid smell of burning hair from his head stung his nostrils. Otherwise he was unhurt.

Ben stared at the workshop.

The entire building was blazing like a furnace. Every few seconds a barrel of paint or varnish exploded and a new pillar of flame leapt high into the air through the gaping rafters or empty window frames. Even as he looked, the heat forced him to step back.

'Fire! Fire!'

Ben swung round.

Over the roar of the conflagration he could just hear a distant voice shouting. The workshop was half a mile from the village and screened from the houses by a copse of beeches, but someone must have seen the glow in the sky. Instinctively Ben began to run towards the voice. He knew water had to be brought, salvage attempted, explanations given.

Ben had taken only a few steps when he stopped. He looked back at the building again.

It was beyond salvation. The timber frame was too dry and the fire too fierce. Within an hour it would be no more than a heap of glowing ash. So would his paints, his tools, his pattern-books, and his stock of wood – all the costly and hard-won materials of his business. Yet even they weren't important.

When Ben leased the barn, he had moved the canvas bag containing his savings from beneath his bed in the lodging-house to a padlocked chest at the back of the loft. As Ben watched, he knew the chest was being incinerated with everything else. All that would be left was a puddle of worthless molten metal.

Eight years of his life and labour were vanishing irrevocably in a pillar of sparks and smoke into the night sky.

Ben's gaze swung back to where he had dropped the figurehead.

Burning planks from the outer wall were beginning to fall away from the building as the flames ate through the frame. One of them bounced across the grass and toppled over the mermaid's breasts. Ben sprang forward. He kicked the plank away and hefted the figurehead on to his shoulders for the second time.

Ben reeled under the weight. He heaved himself upright and stood quite still. Other voices were shouting beyond the trees. In the glare cast by the fire he could see the silhouette of a figure running towards the blaze. Within moments the figure would reach him.

Seconds earlier Ben had thought he would have to offer explanations. The time had gone. Everything had gone. Buckler's Hard was behind him. The little community which had been the context and furniture of his entire life was history now. He had planned to leave it strong and bold and confident with the capital to create a new world for himself in London.

No longer. He had nothing apart from the mermaid. Stumbling under the burden, he turned and limped off into the darkness.

'Mr Featherstone, please,' Ben said.

The innkeeper rubbed his eyes and peered at him suspiciously. In the early-morning light Ben looked like an unkempt and ill-made scarecrow.

'Tell him I'm delivering his figurehead.' Ben jerked his thumb over his shoulder at the bundle on the ground behind him. 'He'll know what it's all about.'

'How do I know he's even up yet?' the innkeeper grumbled. 'At this hour most decent folks are still in bed. So would I be if it hadn't been for your knocking.'

'If he's not awake, I'll wait.'

The man stared at him again.

In spite of Ben's youth and bedraggled appearance, he had spoken with an uncommon authority. Still grumbling, the innkeeper disappeared inside.

Wearily Ben rubbed his face.

Half a mile beyond Buckler's Hard, he'd waved down a night-travelling haycart. Ben had paid the driver sixpence for a ride to the outskirts of Southampton, but he'd still had to carry the carving a further mile at the other end. Now he felt as tired as he'd ever been.

'Well, well, if it isn't the young carver,' a voice said

from beneath the eaves a few minutes later. 'What are you doing here so bright and early?'

Ben glanced round.

It was Mr Featherstone. As the portly shipowner walked out into the yard Ben saw he was fully dressed. Confounding the innkeeper's prophecy, he had obviously been up for an hour or more.

'I've brought the mermaid,' Ben said.

'I thought I was due to pick it up tomorrow,' the Yorkshireman replied.

'I finished a day earlier than I reckoned. As I had to come this way, I decided to bring it with me. I thought we might go halves on the transport.'

'Transport?' Featherstone chuckled. 'Regular little Jew boy, aren't we? Well, no harm in that if you want to get ahead. Let's take a look at her. Not one brass farthing leaves my purse until I'm satisfied.'

Ben stood back.

Featherstone came forward. In silence he peered at the mermaid's face. He scratched the varnish with his fingernail. He ran his fingers gently over the firm full breasts. Then he beamed.

'Congratulations, lad,' he said. 'You've got my mam's titties to the life. I'm well pleased. I'll even add a shilling for the delivery.'

He took out his purse and counted the money into Ben's hand. Ben dropped the coins into his pocket.

'I'm glad you're satisfied,' Ben said.

'Where are you off to, lad?'

Ben was already moving away along the track. He stopped and thought for a moment. Then he looked back.

'London,' Ben replied.

'London? Going to make the figureheads for the Royal Navy's ironclads, are you?'

Featherstone roared with laughter.

Ben shook his head. There was no need to answer the mocking question. He was too exhausted anyway. But somehow he felt he had to, if only to buoy himself up, to steel himself for what lay ahead.

'I'm changing my job,' Ben called back. 'My job and my life. I'm going to work in the theatre.'

Featherstone went on chuckling. 'You're a proper joker, boy. I hope you've got plenty of brass in your pocket – and a damn sight more than I've paid you, too. You'll need it in London.'

Ben managed a quick, grim smile. He lifted his hand and walked on.

Jangling in his pocket were the four sovereigns and one shilling Featherstone had just given him. Apart from the clothes he was wearing, it was all Ben had left in the world. Everything else had vanished.

Everything – except the memory of Mrs Araminta Devon's tent and the world he had seen there in the muslin and trumpets and lights. After the torment and humiliation of the night, Ben knew more certainly than ever it was the only world in which he would ever be at home.

He heard the rumble of wheels behind him. Ben turned. Another cart was approaching, lumbering through the early-morning mist. He raised his hand and the cart stopped.

'London?' Ben said.

'One shilling and you ride with the sheep,' the carter replied.

Ben gave him the shilling then levered himself up over the spokes of the rear wheels. He settled down on the filthy bed of straw among the noisy jostling sheep on their way to slaughter at Leadenhall Market. Ben's head sank on to his chest.

As he began to doze, images of the girl's white legs and her upturned breasts whirled through Ben's mind. Her breasts and legs and the dark space between her thighs – the space he had so longed to enter and fill, but which had been snapped shut in front of him at the sight of his body, like a brutally slamming door closing a secret garden.

Cackle-hob.

She had used almost every other word. If she had known it, she'd have used that one in horror and contempt too. She hadn't, but it underlay everything she had screamed at him. The cripple, the worthless one, the pervert. And she was a whore. She was in business to trade her body to any passing stranger for money, a meal, or a bed.

Ben shuddered.

God knew what ordinary women would make of him. Their revulsion would be so complete and overwhelming, so paralysing, that Ben felt his stomach freeze as he thought about it. All he knew was that he would never approach a woman again. He would never again make himself vulnerable. Never again expose himself to the disgust and humiliation his body provoked.

Bitter, tormented and confused, he slipped into an uneasy sleep as the cart headed for London.

— 30 —

The golden-brown leaf fluttered in the light wind of the Kalahari morning.

The flutter was so slight it was undetectable even to the eyes of the battaleur eagle circling above.

Squatting behind the acacia bush, Khoi! watched the leaf's movements with an intent frozen stillness.

The leaf dipped as the breeze dropped. It trailed limply against the branch of the thorn tree. Then, as another gust came, the leaf lifted and swung westwards away from the rising sun. For a moment, brittle and deeply veined, it seemed to hover – floating from side to side as it was tugged this way and that by the wind funnelling through the scrub.

Suddenly the leaf was still. No longer a fragment of the Kalahari's burnt-out vegetation at the summer's end, it had become a compass point – angled at a clearing out of Khoi!'s sight.

Khoi! drew in his breath.

He checked the woven fibre string of his bow, and the set of the poison-dipped bone-headed arrow nestling between his fingers. He breathed out and steadied himself. Then he moved forward, a shadow slipping from bush to bush.

The 'leaf' he had been watching was his father's hand. The stem on which it had fluttered was the wrist of his father, Deial. Deial was still a mighty hunter and his eyesight was as keen as ever, but his arm had weakened with the years and he preferred to lead his son to the kill now. Khoi! passed him without even acknowledging the old man's presence.

Pressed against the thorn trunk, as gnarled as the wood, the old man might have been part of the tree. Deial watched his son go. With his tiny apricot-coloured body as close to the ground as a crawling jackal, Khoi! was almost as invisible as the old man.

Silently Deial grunted in contentment.

Feeling the bark breathe through his ancient skin, Deial waited.

Khoi! came to the edge of the pan. Until then the pan had only been within his father's sight. Now he could see out over it too. The eland cow they had been following was standing at the pan's centre. As he looked at her, Khoi! briefly closed his eyes in wonderment.

She was a majestic creature.

Almost six feet high at the shoulder and weighing over half a ton, the great antelope had a pale tawny hide marked with slender white stripes. A short brown mane covered her neck and a dewlap hung down from her throat. Below her spiralling horns her eyes were dark and liquid and haunting.

On the barren surface of the pan she was more than majestic. She was godlike – an incarnation of the Kalahari sun and its daughter, *pula*, the desert rain. Above all she was succulent. She would feed the clan with sweetness for a week.

Khoi!'s tongue flicked out across his dry lips.

He and his father had been following her for three days. Three times they had almost approached within arrow range. Each time the eland moved on before Khoi! could fire. Yesterday they thought they had lost her. Late in the afternoon the sky had blackened and the worst storm that even old Deial could ever remember erupted over the desert.

The storm raged for several hours.

When it finally passed, night had fallen. They cast for the eland's tracks in the moonlight, but the battering deluge had obliterated all animal spoor for miles around. Dispirited, they lay down on the sodden earth to sleep. At dawn the old man decided they would make one last circle round where they last saw the antelope before returning to the rest of the clan.

They were in luck. Terrified by the storm's ferocity, the eland had spent the night sheltering in a nearby thicket of mopani. The animal had moved on barely an hour before they found the thicket, leaving its hoofprints cut deep in the still-wet sand as it headed north.

The two hunters caught up with it two hours later.

As Khoi! watched, the eland lowered its head. It licked at the film of mineral salts which the rain must have washed to the surface. Khoi!'s eyes quartered the pan. He saw a scatter of crumbling holes in the bank on the far side. A limp bundle lying in the deep shadow beneath them. A V-shaped gully leading away towards the west.

The holes, he knew, were deserted hyena burrows. The bundle was probably a young jackal drowned in the storm. It was the gully that interested him. It was there that the eland would make her escape.

With infinite caution Khoi! raised his bow. He sighted along the slender arrow and released the cord.

The eland leapt in the air, twisting round as it jumped. The arrow had struck exactly where Khoi! intended, on the animal's haunch close to the artery. Reaching back and butting with its head, the eland broke off the arrow's shaft. Then it snorted angrily.

It was what Khoi! expected. To the antelope the arrow-puncture was no more than an irritating insect bite. The arrow was designed to break quickly and easily. With the shaft removed, the irritation had been dealt with. The eland had been disturbed, but it had not been frightened. It would move on now, but at a pace that would be easy to follow.

In a few hours the poison would start to take effect. The animal would slow even further. It would stumble and finally collapse. By then he and his father would be only yards behind it.

As Khoi! watched, the eland set off unhurriedly towards the gully. Unknown to the animal, the deadly toxin was already pumping into its bloodstream.

Khoi! turned back towards his father. He grinned and gave the low fluting whistle of the Kalahari robin. The old man pushed himself away from the tree where he'd stood for the past hour, and came forward to join his son. He touched Khoi! proudly on his forearm with the flat of his hand. Side by side they set off across the pan.

A moment later the old man stopped.

Deial wrinkled his nose. His son might be younger and faster and stronger, but there were still matters of the desert that he noticed and Khoi! did not. There was one now. The old man glanced to his left. The sun was in his face and the shadow beneath the pan's bank was almost black. Dimly he made out a huddled shape on the sand.

For an instant, like Khoi!, he thought it was a drowned jackal. It was not. The silhouette was wrong, so were the smells. The scent spores drifting over the sand were predominantly hyena. Mixed with them was another smell, a smell that had nothing to do with hyenas.

Deial flared his nostrils and inhaled. He let the air flow through his nose and trickle down his throat. He tensed. The aftertaste of what was coming to him on the air was unmistakable.

It was human.

'Khoi!'

He touched his son's shoulder. The eland, although out of sight now, was only a few hundred yards ahead, and Deial's voice was barely a whisper.

Khoi! glanced round, puzzled. He saw his father set off at right angles from the eland's spoor towards the edge of the pan. Without hesitation, Khoi! followed. A few moments later they were standing in the shadow beneath the bank. At their feet was what both of them had thought was a dead jackal.

It was not a jackal. It was the unconscious body of a female child.

'What is this?' Khoi! asked. 'Where does it come from?'

Bewildered, he turned to his father for explanation. For a long time Deial didn't answer.

The old man studied the child.

She was alive. Deial registered that first in the shallow rise and fall of her breast. Then, as his eyes scanned her limp body, he realized she was not one of their own kind, a member of the San people. She was too long-limbed and pale-skinned. Her matted hair was much longer than the San's ever grew, and her face had a strange angular cast.

There was something else. Clutched in her hand was an object, a chiselled stone. From what he could see of the stone in the shadow, it looked dark and cold. Deial prodded the child with his foot. The bank sloped where she was lying. As Deial's foot touched her, she rolled forward out of the shadow into the sunlight.

Instantly the stone acquired a faint glow. A few moments later the child twitched in the warmth of the sun. Her breathing grew stronger. At the same instant the stone's brightness increased.

Deial glanced wonderingly round the pan.

His gaze took in the ruined hyena burrows in the bank. The fast-drying surface scored only by the eland's spoor. The surrounding waves of grey and umber thorn bush. Beyond the thorn there was nothing except desert.

Deial looked up. It was still early in the morning but the air was already filled with light. For once the Kalahari sky had lost its usual arid whiteness. Instead, in the wake of the cleansing rain, it was a clear, vibrant blue. The sun shone golden and all the desert larks were singing.

'She comes from above,' the old man said.

There was nowhere else the child could have come from. Khoi! knew that too. There wasn't another clan of the San people within a hundred miles of the pan.

'What do we do with her?' Khoi! demanded uncertainly.

'She has been given to us,' his father answered. 'We must take her.'

'And the eland cow I have marked, what of that?'

'The eland will wait for us,' Deial said. 'This child is Kala-Xkung-na-Kjota, the little she-hare that fell from the sky with the rains. She is our gift from the sun. The eland was sent to show us where she slept. Now we must nourish her.'

Deial beckoned to his son. Khoi! stepped forward. As he lifted the child, the stone fell from her hand.

'Wait!' his father instructed.

Round the child's waist was a leather belt with an open pouch and tie-strings hanging loosely from it. The worn bulges on the pouch matched the shape of the stone. Deial picked up the stone. He put it in the pouch and knotted the strings.

'The stone came with her,' he said. 'It belongs to her. Now let us go.'

Khoi! lifted the child again and heaved her up over his back.

The two of them set off towards the south in the direction from which the hunt for the eland had led them. As he walked Khoi! could feel the stone pressing into his shoulder.

— 31 —

Deial and his son, Khoi!, belonged to a clan of the San people, the Stone Age hunter-gatherers of the Kalahari desert.

Tiny and apricot-skinned, the San, as Mary-Ellen wrote to Darwin, believed they were the oldest nation in the world – the first people of all. For hundreds of thousands of years they roamed all of southern Africa in little nomadic groups. Like their fellow nations of the wild, the African animals, they lived off the landscape.

Then at almost the same time the vast territory of their homeland was overwhelmed by twin waves of invaders – the migrant black tribes sweeping down from the north and the white colonists pushing up from the Cape.

Caught between the two waves, hunted like vermin or enslaved by black and white alike, the little people were forced to retreat. By 1875, the year Deial and his son found Kala in the Merula Pan, the San were already being hounded into a last refuge in the Kalahari desert. There, on the great upland plateau too hostile to be coveted by anyone else, they found sanctuary.

Unlike many San clans which were forced to retreat into the Kalahari, Deial's people had always lived there. He and Khoi! belonged to a group called the Lone Tree clan, after a single tall camel-thorn acacia that stood at the centre of their winter hunting-grounds. (Much later, when white anthropologists began to study the San, they were forced to use exclamation marks to render in writing the strange and unfamiliar clicks of the San language.)

Apart from the old man and his son, the clan's

extended family consisted of nine other adults and a dozen children of varying ages. Sometimes they met other groups of wandering San whose territories bordered theirs. For most of the year they lived alone in the immensity of the desert, existing off what the women gathered in the way of nuts, tubers, grubs and fruits, and the occasional animal the male hunters killed.

When the two men found Kala it was the end of the rains. The great storm which had scattered the hyenas was the last of the year. The rains had been good and it was a time of plenty. The clan had ranged far from the Lone Tree to take advantage of the spring harvest. The brief flowering of the desert was almost over. Soon it would be time to return to the Lone Tree for the brutal daytime heat and chill nights of the Kalahari winter.

Deial and Khoi! had left the clan four hours south of the hyena den. Travelling at the steady jog-trot they could keep up all day, the two men returned to the clan's camp soon after midday. The camp was nothing more than a small fire and half a dozen reed and grass shelters.

As Deial and Khoi! approached, the others were standing waiting for them.

The returning hunters had been spotted almost a mile away. As soon as they were seen, everyone knew from their bearing that they had been successful. Closer still it was obvious that Khoi! was carrying what they had killed.

Now as Khoi! put the bundle on the ground beside the fire, the smiles of welcome turned to bewilderment. The bundle wasn't dead, it was breathing. And sticking out from the end of the kaross was not an animal's head, but a child's.

'What have you hunted, my brother?'

The first to speak was a young man named Nuna. Five years younger than Khoi!, he was the hunter's brother. Nuna looked at his brother bemused.

Before Khoi! could answer, an older woman stepped forward. She squatted down by the bundle. She unwrapped the kaross and exposed Kala's body. For several moments she gazed at the child. Then she glanced up.

'What does this mean, Deial?' she said.

The woman, Lys, was Deial's wife. Strong-faced with penetrating eyes and tightly curled grey hair, she was the clan's senior female.

The old man frowned.

He gazed at the sky and stroked his chin. It was a huge matter and difficult to put into words. Yet the words had come to him when his son, Khoi!, had asked the same question. Deial knew he had given the right answer then. The spirits had spoken to him. It was still the right answer now.

'It is the little she-hare that fell from the sky with the rains,' Deial answered. 'I and my son, Khoi! the hunter, found her at the Merula Pan. The eland led us there –'

Proudly Deial told the story.

There were no interruptions or questions. The other members of the clan listened in rapt, unbroken silence. Even when Deial finished, it was a long time before anyone spoke.

The event was more than momentous.

It was unparalleled. In all the long and carefully remembered oral history not just of the Lone Tree clan but of the entire San nation, nothing like this had ever happened before. A human child, a stranger from another race, had been found alive in the middle of the desert.

Deial said she came from the sky. The old man could only be right. They all accepted that. There was nowhere else the child could have come from. And because the eland had led the hunters to the pan and then allowed herself to be mortally wounded by Khoi!'s arrow, the child could only be the sky's gift and blessing to the clan.

It was Deial's wife who finally broke the silence.

'If she is not given water,' Lys said practically, 'the sky will soon take back its gift –'

She touched Kala's face. The child's skin was desiccated and papery, and her breathing was already slowing.

Her illness needed no diagnosis from the people of the desert. It was the most familiar condition of all. The deluge which had almost drowned her was eighteen hours in the past. Since then Kala had spent a night unconscious followed by six hours exposed to the sun, all without drinking.

In the Kalahari, animals and men can survive for up to a month without food. Without water the lifespan of both can be measured in hours. Kala was slipping towards death.

'Fetch the buffalo horns and fill them with mud,' Lys instructed.

She was speaking to her daughter, Poli, the youngest of her three children. The girl hurried away.

The clan had made camp beside another pan. The pan was smaller than the Merula Pan, but deeper. The storm had filled it with water. The girl, Poli, filled a pair of hollow buffalo horns with wet mud from the pan's floor. She and her mother slapped it over Kala's body so that the dampness fed through to the child's skin.

At the same time the clan's two other women put straws into the child's mouth. They blew water sucked up from the sip-wells down into her belly. Then all four women spat saliva on to her face and smeared it over Kala's cheeks with their hands, repeating it again and again as the thin wet film evaporated in the heat.

Deial watched them keenly for a moment. Then he looked up at Khoi! and his brother Nuna.

'The little she-hare will live,' the old man announced confidently. 'But when she wakes, she must eat. The eland is her sister and the sky's gift too, for her and for us. Let us go and find the child's sister. Let us bring her back to camp, so we all may feast.'

With the other two following, Deial set off back for the pan to pick up the wounded eland's spoor again.

It was long after midnight when the three arrived back at the clan's camp.

This time they were not jogging but stumbling slowly and wearily. They were weighed down by the heavy burdens draped across their shoulders. They had found the eland dead a mile beyond the Merula Pan. By then it had already been discovered by two pairs of jackals, a dozen Maribou storks, and a flock of vultures.

More vultures were arriving every minute. Soon lions and hyenas, alerted by the downward spiral of the vultures' flight, would be there too.

The men chased the scavengers away. They butchered the eland's carcass with their razor-sharp stone knives. They set aside the choicest cuts of meat and buried the rest in the sand, piling cairns of stones over the cache to protect it from the inevitable arrival of the predators. Then they heaved the chosen meat across their backs and headed home.

In spite of their exhaustion, Deial and his sons were smiling as they dropped their loads beside the fire. They had saved one being and slain another. The child was rare beyond experience, an eland was the greatest gift the desert had to offer. But each hung equally in the scales of eternity.

Now the clan would eat to celebrate them both.

The feast of Kala and the eland lasted for three days and nights. Twice in that time Khoi! and his brother, Nuna, went back to the cache and returned with more of the animal's meat. By the finish, every adult member of the clan had eaten over forty pounds of flesh, almost half their own bodyweight.

It was a feast no one in the Lone Tree clan would ever forget.

Years later even the youngest child who was there remembered it. There was music and dancing and song. Between every fresh roasting, there were recitations of the clan's history. Finally, with the carcass decomposing and the clan's stomachs so distended they could eat no more, the celebrations came to an end.

'So,' Deial said, leaning back on the sand, barely able to move, 'the sky's gift has been properly welcomed. Tomorrow we travel and the little she-hare travels with us. May she travel with us for ever.'

At dawn the next morning the Lone Tree clan

abandoned its shelters of the past two weeks, and continued its wanderings. By then Kala was fully recovered.

'Take her by the hand,' Deial's wife, Lys, instructed their daughter, Poli, as the clan set out. 'Cut her a digging-stick and teach her where the roots lie.'

Poli stripped a small thorn branch and sharpened its end. She ruffled the child's hair affectionately. Poli pressed the stick into Kala's hand then led her forward, pointing out to the little girl where the edible roots lay beneath the sand's surface.

Lys watched them go. She was a well-made child, Lys thought, but she was strangely silent. In fact Kala hadn't uttered a sound since her arrival.

Puzzled, the woman set off after them.

— 32 —

Kala lay in the shadow beneath the bush with her chin resting on her wrists.

It was early afternoon at the height of the Kalahari winter. In a few hours, when darkness fell, the air would become sharp and chill. By morning the branches which canopied her would be glittering with frost. For the moment the heat was fierce and dry. It was a time for sleeping.

Kala closed her eyes. Beneath her she could hear the soft bird-like chatter of the voices of the Lone Tree clan.

'It is more than twelve moons now since the little she-hare came to us,' Poli, Deial and Lys' daughter, was saying. 'And still she does not speak. She trusts me, I am sure of that. She takes my hand. She gathers with me. She has become skilled with her stick. But her mouth never opens. Why?'

The graceful, golden-skinned girl glanced puzzled at her mother.

Her mother frowned.

'She came from the sky,' Lys said. 'If the sky has taken words from her, then that in its wisdom is what the sky has chosen.'

Lys glanced tentatively at her husband for confirmation.

Old Deial scratched his groin and nodded.

'The sky decides,' he agreed. 'The sky sent her with the eland. Look how she rests –'

He turned and pointed with his throwing spear.

Deial's two sons, the hunter Khoi! and Khoi!'s younger brother, Nuna, were squatting with him alongside his wife and his daughter. The other members of the clan were also there.

All of them followed the movement of the spear's tip.

Kala's head was resting on her wrists. A human's wrists would have been crossed between folded arms to take the weight of her head. Not Kala's. Her wrists were pressed together and angled forward like the paws of a crouching animal.

'It is thus that a lion or a jackal takes its sleep,' Deial went on. 'The sky has fashioned her so. She was made by the stars in their own mould. They even gave her part of themselves. Remember the day the children tried to take her belt for play –'

The others nodded. None of them would ever forget it.

It had happened six months earlier. Kala was lying asleep as she was now. Two of the clan's small children crept up to her and tried to untie the belt round her waist. Kala opened her eyes. In an instant she sprang to her knees and bared her teeth. She snarled at the children with such ferocity that they ran away, sobbing in terror.

'She does not need words,' Deial went on. 'She is at one with the great eland who led us to her. She will always be different.'

The others considered what Deial had said. Then they all nodded again in agreement – all except the young woman, Poli.

Poli stared at the ground.

Kala had spent a year with the clan. Over the year Poli had become closer to the child than anyone. Kala slept nestled against Poli under the young woman's bow-framed shelter of grass. Day after day Poli led Kala out on the women's gathering trips. Painstakingly, Poli had taught her how to probe for grubs, how to uncover the buried tubers, how to find the succulent tsama melons.

Poli had instructed the clan's children before – as the eldest daughter of the clan's dominant male it was her main duty. She had never taught anyone so quick to learn, so skilful and swift at finding sources of food that even Poli had overlooked.

Not once in all that time had Kala attempted to communicate with her. She would hold Poli's hand. She would lie beside her. She would wake and watch her for instructions. But never, by word or expression or gesture, would she indicate anything.

The child's face remained as expressionless as a desert stone. Her voice seemed to have been plucked from her throat. Her eyes were blank.

Yes, like the others Poli believed Kala came from the sky. What Poli could not accept was that the child was fundamentally different from the rest of them in the way her father claimed. Kala was human. She was able to speak, Poli was sure of that. Sometimes Poli even sensed she was listening when the clan talked.

On her journey between the sky and the pan, Poli thought, something fearsome must have happened to her. For some reason the spirits had taken the gift of words away. That day Poli decided to see if she could restore it.

She decided to tell Kala the clan's stories.

'The hunter came and killed the ostrich at his eggs,' Poli said. 'His wife plucked the feathers from the ostrich, and threw them into a bush. As the hunter and his wife ate the ostrich's flesh, a whirlwind came. The wind blew one of the feathers high up in the sky. The feather came to earth far away in a pool of rainwater. There it began to grow –'

The story went on and on with the repetitions and digressions that characterized the telling of all the San's fables. Eventually, with the feather reborn as another ostrich which had learnt to beware of all hunters, it came to an end.

As Poli finished she glanced down.

'What did you think of that?'

Kala was trudging beside her. Slung over the child's back was a little woven basket. One of her hands was gripping Poli's. The other was holding her gathering stick. Until then the stick had been flickering quickly and expertly over the sand like a divining rod. At the change in Poli's voice which accompanied the question, the stick fell limply by Kala's side.

Kala glanced up. Her eyes had been bright and eager as they quartered the earth. Now they were glazed with the numb indifference Poli had come to know so well. Kala had heard the young woman address her, and a barrier had come down over her mind.

She did not understand what Poli was saying. She did not want to understand.

Poli's face wrinkled in exasperation.

It happened a year later.

Kala had been with the Lone Tree clan for two full years. Over the second year Poli had recited the clan's stories to the child every day. She told her the ancient tales of the San nation's beginnings. The fables of the wisdom and mischief of the animals, the San's companions throughout their history. The legends of the clan's own great hunts and feasts and wanderings.

The folklore of the San people was more than a treasury. It was an almost inexhaustible cornucopia, constantly growing and passed down from generation to generation. Poli had an exceptionally retentive memory and a vivid imagination. Still young, she already knew more of the clan's long past than even her father, old Deial.

She had recounted it all to Kala. Nothing made any difference. The child's gaze remained as clouded and impenetrable as when Poli started. Now even Poli was running out of fresh stories to tell her.

Poli controlled her impatience. Still stubbornly convinced she could somewhere find the key to unlock the child's silence, she frowned and racked her brain. Poli was reaching deep into her own past now, ransacking her mind for stories she had been told as a child and had long since mostly forgotten.

There was one, it came back to her, about a honey badger and a hyena. Honey badgers often featured in the tales of the San. They had a common interest with the desert people in the hives of the wild bees. Hyenas seldom came into the stories. They were creatures of the night when, like most foraging hunter-gatherers, the San slept.

'One day,' Poli started wearily again, 'a honey badger was led by a honey guide to the foot of a tall mopani tree. There to his surprise was a hyena. Not far above the hyena's head, the badger could see the bees' nest. "If you will move aside," the badger said, "I will climb the tree and bring down the nest, so we may share it." "No," the hyena replied, "I cannot move from here." And to show he meant just what he said, the hyena howled –'

Poli raised her head and howled.

Like all the San, Poli was a superb mimic of the songs and calls of the Kalahari's birds and animals. She used the sounds to illustrate her stories, although she'd never had occasion to mimic a hyena before. As its call lifted from her mouth, she felt a sudden piercing pain on the back of her hand.

Wincing, Poli leapt aside and glanced down.

Kala was holding her hand. At the sound of the call, the child's fingers had tightened like a claw and her nails had cut deep into Poli's skin. Blood was trickling down over the young woman's fingers. To Poli's astonishment the child was staring up at her with a burning intensity. Her eyes were even brighter than when she scanned the Kalahari sand.

Brilliant and unblinking, they were transfixed.

'Nksst –!'

The sound came out of Kala's mouth in a warning growl.

Poli stared at her. For an instant she was bewildered. Then she understood.

Poli went down on her knees. She lowered her head. She reached out her arms. She pulled Kala to her and began to lick her body. She started at her groin and moved her tongue slowly upwards until it was caressing the child's face. Kala knelt and returned her embrace. She licked Poli too. Soon, tangled round each other, they were lying together on the earth.

As she held the child, her lips wet with Kala's sweat and

her nostrils pricking with the scents of her body, Poli looked at the sky.

The fragments of what had happened had arranged themselves in her mind like a pattern shaken out by a kaleidoscope. In the story, Poli had given the hyena's hunting call, its warning of intent and aggression. Kala recognized it. She had replied with a snarl of defiance – the blood was still dripping from Poli's fingers.

Now the misunderstanding – the collision between the story and reality – was finished. They had made peace. What was not finished was the impulse that made Kala behave as she did.

Her father was right, Poli thought as she held the child to her. The child was different. She would always be different. Deial did not know the sky had given Kala to the nation of the hyenas. Only Poli had discovered that. It was a secret she would keep to herself.

The young woman hugged Kala in her arms. It meant nothing to Poli whether the child was a hyena or a human. She was a small being of the desert and Poli loved her. Poli licked the child's face and slept.

Kala did not sleep.

She lay in Poli's arms with her eyes wide open. Something had happened to Kala. Something extraordinary. Speech had not returned to her, but the recognition of words, their association with people, had. Poli's use of the hyena's call had thrown a bridge across the immense abyss that separated Kala from her beginnings.

Time had no meaning for Kala. But she knew the call came out of Poli's mouth. Once in her past, other human beings had used sounds to represent ideas and objects, to forge a connection between them. It was before her wanderings with the clan. Before her long years with the Merula Pan hyenas. Before anything she could remember.

The words belonged to the darkness. Now the darkness had been pierced by a resonating wave of sound. Sound in the form of words was only light in another form. Light had begun to invade her.

At her groin the child felt the stone begin to quiver and stir.

With the sinuous grace of a night animal, Kala disengaged herself from Poli's arms. Leaving the young woman asleep on the sand, she slipped silently away. Kala climbed on to a mound above where the clan had made its camp. She drew out the diamond from its pouch.

There in the starlight she gazed down into the stone's depths.

— 33 —

In the starlight the diamond seemed to expand until it became a huge mirror.

For a while the surface was blurred with mist. Slowly the mist cleared. Kala began to see shapes emerging behind the greyness. On the level of her unconscious mind, the mind that had been formed by the hyenas, the shapes were so alien and incomprehensible they might have come from the hidden landscape of the moon.

Kala wasn't interpreting them consciously. Poli had broken through to the lost world of her past. There, buried deep in the caverns of Kala's memory, there had once been shapes like these – shapes and words and people like the ones she was seeing and hearing now.

The diamond was the vehicle that carried them to her. Stored up in the glittering stone was everything she had ever been. Everything that had ever happened to her. Everything that made her what she was.

Holding her breath, kneeling so still that even the hunting owls saw her only as part of the rock and thorn bush, Kala stared at the stone. Above her head the moon was rising in the Kalahari night.

In the diamond two thousand years earlier it was dawn.

A great marshy inlet spread out before her, a bay where the many veins and arteries of a vast river emptied sluggishly into the sea. A huge crescent of watery pastures of quick green rice, with buffaloes lowing and fishermen casting their nets at the sea's edge. A sprawling cluster of towers and buildings at the bay's centre, a teeming city just awakening, with its walls dazzling white under the early sun.

Kala leant forward.

A column of horses, waggons and soldiers emerged from the city's southern gates. The column was travelling swiftly. There was a frightening urgency in the way the drivers beat the animals to make the waggons move faster; in the anxiety of the racing soldiers as they drove their spears into the horses' flanks, spattering the sandy track with blood.

The waggons and the soldiers were escaping from something, Kala realized that. They were escaping and heading south.

A man mounted on a bright bay horse was riding beside the leading waggon. He was young and sturdy with powerful sloping shoulders and keen intelligent features. In spite of his youth, his beard was greying and his skin was already deeply trenched with lines. From the way the soldiers kept running up and consulting him, he was clearly in command of the column.

Seated inside the waggon was a woman. She was propped upright on a stool made of ebony, and she was immensely old – older than anyone Kala had ever seen. Her little monkey's face was sunken and wrinkled, and her eyes, as black as the ebony on which she sat, were sharp and malevolent. The old woman was holding something on her lap.

Kala tried to see what it was. The man on the horse leant towards the waggon to speak to the woman, and Kala's view was obscured.

'In an hour we will come to where the roads part,' the man said. 'Which track do we follow, Osiris?'

'South in the path of the sun, always south,' the woman replied. 'Do not concern yourself about where we go, Herontas. I will always tell you. In Egypt's star you have the best navigator you will ever have!'

The old woman, Osiris, gave a cackling laugh. The rider, the man she had addressed as Herontas, wheeled his horse away. As he cantered off, Kala saw what Osiris was holding.

Gleaming in the old woman's claw-like hand was the diamond.

Kala gasped.

The great stone was not only in Kala's own hand as she knelt under the desert stars. At the same instant two thousand years away in time, the jewel was clutched between the sparrow bones of Osiris' fingers in the jolting waggon.

A haze covered the column then. The waggons and the soldiers vanished. Kala recognized the haze. It was the same hot and grainy curtain that often swept the Kalahari when the dew lifted and morning began. The haze parted and the diamond's surface cleared again.

Now it was midday and the column had vanished. In its place Kala saw a fleet of ships leaving the city and heading out to sea. The ships were under sail, but most of the power that drove them forward came from beating banks of oars. On the prow of the ship that led the fleet were two fighters.

Kala peered at them.

One of the figures was a man. His bearing was commanding but he had wine-blotched skin and a dissolute, ravaged face that kept restlessly searching the waves ahead. The other was a woman. Her back was towards Kala, but Kala knew she was a queen. Circling her head was a diadem of gold. Apart from that, all Kala could see was a strong, full figure and a mane of tawny hair.

The ship's bows rose and fell through the sea spray. A simple fishing dhow passed it running inshore towards the city. The woman put her arm lovingly round the man's sholders. Then she turned to watch the dhow's passage.

As she swung round, her face and the golden diadem above it came into Kala's view. There was a jagged gap at the diadem's centre. Something had been ripped from it. Kala knew what it was. It was the stone that lay in Kala's hand now.

The woman was smiling but her expression was wistful and charged with an infinite regret, with an immensity of loss. She brushed the wind-blown strands of hair from her forehead and Kala saw her eyes.

Kala froze.

The woman's eyes were flecked with chips of silver. They were eyes that Kala had never seen before. Not in the fugitive dreams of her own beginnings. Not among the hyenas of the Merula Pan. Not among the myriads of other animals she had watched and hunted. Not even among the nomadic San who had adopted her.

Never – except when she knelt and drank at the desert's pools and streams. Then she had seen them often. They gazed back at her in reflection from the water's surface.

They were Kala's own eyes.

Suddenly a lion gave a rumbling roar of challenge and warning. Kala's head jerked up. The roar came from somewhere close to her in the darkness. Kala tucked the diamond into its pouch. Then she ran back to the tiny shelter and curled up alongside Poli.

That night Kala's dreams were filled with images of a woman with silver-flecked eyes, and of a column of men riding hurriedly south from the white city beside the sea.

'Wait!'

Old Deial lifted his hand in warning. Beside him his sons, Khoi! and Nuna, came to a halt with their bows in their hands. All three watched Kala intently.

Kala was a few yards in front of them. Leaning forward with one foot half-raised from the ground like a hunting animal, she stood utterly still. She scanned the air with her nostrils. Then she pointed to the left and stepped back.

Deial waved the two younger men on.

With Khoi! leading, they crept round an outcrop of rock and peered through a screen of thorn. Beyond the thorn was a small open glade. At its centre a male impala leapt in the air, shook itself, and galloped away through the bush. Khoi! gave a fluting whistle. As his younger brother followed, he set off in pursuit.

Two hours later when Deial caught up with them, they had already begun to cut up the now-dead antelope. Deial inspected the meat and nodded in satisfaction. The animal was healthy and well fleshed. The clan would eat well.

Deial turned. Kala was standing at his side. He reached out his hand and ruffled her hair.

'With you as our honey guide, little hare,' he said, chuckling happily, 'we could feast every week.'

Kala stared at him through blank, expressionless eyes. Then she glanced down at the impala. The tip of her tongue flickered out and ran over her lips.

'Carve a piece for her now,' Deial instructed Khoi!. 'She has earned it more than any of us. Let her enjoy it in her own way.'

Khoi! sliced a length of the tender flesh from one of the impala's shoulders, and handed it to Kala. The girl dropped to her haunches and gnawed hungrily at the raw meat. As she ate, the animal's blood flowed down her chin and over her chest.

The three San watched her affectionately. They might have been rewarding a trained falcon. They didn't mind how much she took from their kills. All they knew was that the child who had fallen from the sky was the best hunter the desert had ever known. She had brought fortune to the clan. To the San fortune meant food.

A year had passed since Poli had given the hyena's call and had felt Kala's fingers crush her hand. Within a month Kala's relationship with the wandering group of San had changed. Even before that, Poli sensed the child was listening to the clan talk. Afterwards Kala seemed to be alert to everything they said and did.

It was Deial who realized the significance of the change.

For three weeks after Poli told Kala the fable of the hyena, the surrounding pastures were empty of game. Every hunting expedition was fruitless. The entire clan was forced to depend on what the women managed to gather. One day as the hunters forlornly debated where to set out into the bush, Kala came up and touched Deial's arm.

Deial looked down at her.

Kala pointed westwards. Deial lifted his head. He stared in the direction of her outstretched arm. He could see nothing except the blank shimmering whiteness of the desert sky. Insistently Kala plucked at him again.

Kala took Deial's wrist and dragged him forward. The other hunters followed. Thirty minutes later they saw the downward spiral of vultures and Maribou storks. The hunters began to run. On the ground below the wheeling birds, they found a buffalo with a broken leg. The San chased the other predators away. They killed the buffalo and plundered its meat.

Acute as their eyes were, none of the hunters had picked up the distant flight pattern of the birds. Kala had.

'From now on the little hare will hunt with us,' Deial announced when they returned to camp.

His wife, Lys, gazed at him in bewilderment and consternation. Among the San no woman had ever hunted. The women's role in the clan's survival was to gather.

'She cannot hunt,' Lys said. 'She is not only a girl, but still a child girl.'

'I, Deial, was a great hunter in my youth,' her husband answered. 'My brother, Xa!, was greater still. Yet she sees further, she tracks faster, she scents more truly, than either of us ever did. Is that not so, Xa!?'

Deial's brother, a wizened, gap-toothed old man and the eldest member of the clan, grunted in agreement.

'What my brother states is so,' Xa! said.

'And you,' Deial turned to his sons, 'do you not say it is true too?'

Among the San no major decision could be made without the agreement of all the clan. For a woman to join the hunters, let alone a girl, was unprecedented. It needed everyone's consent.

The two brothers, Khoi! and Nuna, inclined their heads.

'We did not make her a hunter.' Deial turned back to Lys. 'That was the sky's choice. The sky sent her as a gift to us. We must respect the sky. For surely, Lys, does not the sky require us to eat?'

Lys frowned for a moment in silence.

Her glance wandered to the buffalo haunches lying on the ground ready for the fire. They would make a rich feast. Like the rest of the clan, Lys' stomach was hollow and grumbling. Without Kala the meat would not have been there to fill it.

What Deial had proposed was against all the San's most ancient traditions, but perhaps he was right. The girl did indeed come from the sky. Maybe she had been sent to lead the men in the hunt in this season of famine. Lys hungrily eyed the meat again. She nodded.

Behind her the other female members of the clan nodded too.

'Good,' Deial said. 'It is agreed then. From now on when the land is barren and the game is scattered far, the little she-hare will hunt for us. Today let us build the fire and eat.'

An hour later, columns of sparks were rising into the evening sky, and the air was filled with the hissing, spitting sounds of the buffalo meat roasting on the flames.

In the gathering darkness beyond the fire, Kala lay watching the clan. As always her eyes were remote and unfathomable.

— 34 —

Kala lived with the Lone Tree clan for seven years.

Unlike the Merula Pan hyenas, whose lives until the great storm were tied to a single space of earth in the northern desert, the San were nomadic. The San had their winter and their summer feeding grounds, and the vast areas of territory they travelled between them.

Their wanderings depended on the year's rains. If the rains were good, the desert flowered and the Kalahari's pastures were flooded with rich grasses. The grasses increased the numbers of the wild herds which cropped them. With thriving populations of animals all round, there was no need for the clan to journey far.

When the rains were sparse or, worse, when they failed altogether, it was very different. Then the San were forced to travel for days and miles on end in search of food. The rains tended to come in ten-year cycles. During a bad cycle, a cycle of continuing drought, the clan might wander for months, losing up to half its members from starvation and disease.

Kala was fortunate.

Apart from a few short periods of drought, her stay with the Lone Tree clan coincided with a good rain cycle. The San made their usual winter and summer migrations, but the distances they had to travel were small. In many ways, Kala's life among them as they journeyed was very like the pattern of her life with the hyenas.

Just as with the hyenas, the clan's members acquired their own identities. There were no exact parallels. Kala was older now. She was living among a different species with different patterns of behaviour. But the similarities were so close that, had Kala been able to consider them, she might have found them awesome.

Poli, the apricot-skinned daughter of Deial and Lys, was like Kala's litter sister, Ochla. The female hyena had been the same age as Kala. Poli was older. Yet the young woman performed many of the functions the hyena had done. She slept with Kala. She warmed her and groomed her and tutored her. She was a constant unvarying presence in the child's life.

The two young San hunters, Khoi! and Nuna, resembled members of the litter, too. Khoi! might have been the bold and aggressive Akula, the ambitious young hunter in the Merula Pan pack and Kala's litter brother. Nuna could easily have passed for the hyenas' younger sister, the cunning and often troublesome Kwic-kwa.

Then there were Lys and old Deial.

Somehow the two, the matriarch and patriarch of the clan, blended into the single figure of Kala's foster mother, the great female hyena, Herut. Between them they combined Herut's qualities of wisdom, authority and power.

Over the seven years Kala blended into the clan as closely as she had blended into the hyena pack. When the seasons were hard and the prey animals scarce, she used her extraordinary skills in the bush – the skills that had been honed among the hyenas – to guide the hunters. When the desert blossomed and prey was abundant, she reverted to her role as a gatherer with the women.

Yet however close Kala became to the San, she always remained apart.

The reason was her silence. Poli had broken through to the child. The young woman had established a connection between the human voice and what its sounds conveyed. Kala fastened on to the link. Over the years, watching and listening to the San, she came to understand much of their language.

Kala was helped by the fact that the San used gesture almost as much as words. Gestures were familiar to her. When one of the hunters indicated a spoor mark with a stiffened finger, or knelt with flared nostrils to sniff a pile of faeces left by a passing antelope, she knew exactly what he was doing. The hyenas had done the same.

Words were simply an added layer of communication. They were the San's equivalent of the hyenas' growls and calls. Kala had learnt one system of vocalization. Now she learnt another.

She learnt it – but she could not use it. Words eluded her. Sometimes, alone, she tried to frame with her mouth the sounds she had heard the clan make. The sounds would not come. What emerged from Kala's lips instead were the deep-throated chuckles and snarls of the animals which had patterned her.

Confused and frustrated, Kala would retreat into the one sanctuary which was truly her own – the world of the diamond.

Late at night or early in the morning when the clan was still asleep, Kala would slip away from the camp. She would slide the stone out from its pouch at her waist, and stare down at it. Often it revealed nothing. It glittered back at her with the mindless brilliance of one of the Kalahari stars in the sky above. Then she let the play of its blind facets calm and still her.

Often – but not always.

Occasionally the stone became the mirror she had gazed at on the night Poli gave the hyena's call. Sounds and smells and images crossed its surface as they had done then. Again and again she saw the column of waggons and soldiers travelling south. They were following, it seemed to Kala, the fissure of a great valley – a rift in the earth's surface.

They encountered swollen rivers. They waded through flood plains. They struggled over icy mountain crests and through damp airless jungles. They were attacked by land-hungry tribes of black warriors surging down from the north. They were ravaged by fever – by bilharzia, sleeping sickness, and the terrible yellowing malaria. Their waggons were charged and wrecked by elephant herds, their camps were raided by hungry prides of lion.

Two-thirds of the force which had set out died. The man Kala knew as Herontas became almost skeletally thin, and his hair turned white. The venomous old woman, Osiris, shrank inside her already tiny body until she seemed to be no more than the dried-up kernel inside a wrinkled nut.

And yet still, guided by the diamond, they struggled on.

It was an epic journey they were making. The diamond revealed its progress to Kala in fragments, strung out at intervals of months and sometimes years like the ostrich-shell beads on one of the San women's bracelets. Kala had no idea of the expedition's purpose.

All she knew was that the column was coming closer and closer to her in time and space. Each time she glimpsed Herontas, Osiris, or any of the survivors – the soldiers, carpenters, engineers and jewellers, the women and children who travelled with them – their faces were more vivid and more determined.

They had a goal in front of them. Osiris and the diamond were their guides. But their destination had been determined by the woman with the silver-flecked eyes – the eyes that were Kala's, too.

Tantalizingly, the end of the column's journey eluded Kala as much as the words of the San. She was certain it was near to her. She was certain it belonged to her. She was certain it would explain the confused and troubled dreams about her past that had haunted her since she first looked into the diamond's surface.

Time. That was all that was needed. Time. Time for the diamond to reveal its secrets to her.

Kala wasn't given time. Her life with the Lone Tree clan had started three years into the ten-year cycle of good rains. Seven years later, when Kala was seventeen, the rains failed.

'We must move on,' Deial said one evening by the fire.

The old man was frowning. Round him in the dusk the earth was drying and hardening. At that time of year the rains should have started. The rains were already a month late. Each morning's sky was still hot and clear and blue.

Deial knew the signs and he was worried.

'Where do we move to, Father?' Khoi! asked.

'You must ask Xa!,' Deial replied.

Out of respect for age and experience, the eldest of the clan was always consulted first.

Deial's elder brother, Xa!, coughed and wrinkled his face. Shrivelled, ancient, and a bachelor – his wife had left him long ago when his seed proved infertile – Xa! had been the most famous hunter in the whole northern Kalahari.

His hunting days were long past. Xa! had become lame. He tottered and limped like a broken-legged honey badger searching for the wild bees' hives. Yet his knowledge of the Kalahari and its ways was a legend among all the desert clans.

A decision taken without consulting Xa!, the San said, was a decision taken with the rocks for counsellor.

'I spoke four sunrises ago with the elephants,' Xa! said. 'Hole-in-the-Ear came up and talked to me, near as you are to me now –'

The white-headed old man chuckled. He scratched his stomach with the unburnt end of a branch he had plucked from the smouldering fire.

'You know Hole-in-the-Ear?'

All the clan nodded.

They had seen the great matriarchal elephant whose right ear had been punctured by the horn of a charging rhinoceros. They propped themselves up and listened.

'Old Hole-in-the-Ear, she came up to me on the pan,' Xa! went on. 'She stamped her foot and said, "Listen. I'm taking my family south," she said. "Look at this crust. It won't break even under my feet –" '

Xa! stamped his own foot on the baked earth beside the fire.

' "The water's going. I'm going too. The winter dry will be long and hard this year. Behind me all the other nations will scatter. If you've got any sense, old Xa!," she said, "you'll come with me. There'll only be sad hunting for you here this season. Follow me back towards the Thamalakhani river. Keep your children away from mine – and I'll keep mine away from yours." '

Xa! tossed the stick into the fire and rocked back on his heels. He heaved with laughter.

Khoi! watched him.

He trusted his uncle as much as he did his father. Yet there was something menacing in Xa!'s jovial laugh, the menace of the old and wise who knew what they said was true and did not care whether anyone else believed it because for them, for the old, it would soon be a matter beyond caring.

Khoi! reached out and gripped the hand of his brother, Nuna. Nuna held him tightly. He too was afraid. Poli, their sister, hunched her knees to her chest and shivered.

They had all seen the old man and the elephant at the pan's edge. Only feet had separated the two. The tiny Xa! on his spindly legs and the massive shape of Hole-in-the-Ear, dusty and grey as a cloud running behind a dawn sand storm, towering above him with her tusks probing the earth.

Khoi! had no idea whether, as Xa! claimed, they had 'talked', in the sense of exchanging messages in sound. The concept had no meaning for him. What Khoi! did know was that the two, the frail old man and the giant beast, had communicated. Hole-in-the-Ear had told Xa! the water was drying up. The elephants were leaving the pan. The rest of the plain's game would follow them.

Soon the ripples of the animals' retreat would vanish and the northern desert would be left bare. Hunting would be difficult and arduous. A time of peril lay ahead for them all.

'Xa! has spoken to the elephants and now to us,' Deial said. 'He is my brother and the elephants are our brothers. We will do as he and they say. In the morning we will journey south –'

Deial paused.

What he had said was both a statement and a question

– a question because it needed the others' assent. Deial received the clan's answer in the murmurs of agreement that followed.

'We journey south,' Deial repeated, this time with confidence. 'We will take the sky's gift of the little hare with us. She will guard our steps.'

The Lone Tree clan seldom ranged south in their wanderings. Their normal range was east and west. The southern regions of the desert were increasingly known among the San to be dangerous. White men and their cattle had settled there. The white men had built kraals.

One of the kraals, it was said, was named Kuruman.

— 35 —

Gert Frouw reined in his horse and peered ahead. Behind him the other riders, their arms shielding their eyes, halted too.

A wind had risen at dawn and had blown steadily in their faces all day. With it had come stinging curtains of sand. For a moment, as the sand lifted, Grouw thought he'd been mistaken. The dust whirled away over his head and he glimpsed it again. A clump of trees, a hardwood stockade, the roof of a building. It was the Kuruman mission post.

Frouw lifted his arm and beckoned the others forward.

At close to fifty, Frouw was a big, heavy-boned man with a bull neck and a laconic voice. He came from old Afrikaner stock and he'd grown up on a pioneer farm in the Transvaal. Quarrelling with his father in his youth, Frouw had left the farm and set out to make his own way. Since then he'd been a deckhand on a whaler, a cattle herder, an ivory hunter, and a gold prospector.

Frouw had found his latest employment by chance. Five years earlier when a succession of claims proved worthless, he abandoned prospecting and went to Cape Town to look for work. In a Cape Town bar he met an American showman called Wagnell. Wagnell had come to Africa to acquire some wild animals he could exhibit in the new entertainment park on Coney Island.

Frouw told the American he could get them for him. He did the job and shipped the animals to New York. The animals were a success with the public, but most of them died during the winter. Wagnell wrote asking for another consignment for the following season. Other Coney

Island showmen learnt of Frouw's name and copied Wagnell. Frouw soon found himself with a flourishing business exporting African game to the United States.

The year before, when Wagnell had asked for a group of Bushmen, it made no difference to Frouw. As far as Frouw was concerned, the tiny yellow-skinned kaffirs were animals. In some ways they were simpler to catch. They were cunning but they couldn't run as fast as animals with four legs. And once caught they tended to be easier to handle.

If they proved as vulnerable to northern winters as the other animals he shipped over – the yearly death toll was one of the main attractions of exporting to the New World – they would be a useful addition to his business. Frouw personally took the consignment of Bushmen to New York. He spent several months in the United States. In London on his way home to South Africa he was introduced to another American showman, a man named Farini.

Farini also wanted Bushmen. Frouw had been happy to accept the American's commission. Unfortunately, this time it wasn't proving as easy to get them as before.

Frouw sat scowling on his horse as old Parl van der Reik, the eldest of the three hands he'd hired in Johannesburg, rode up to his side.

'It's straight ahead,' Frouw said. 'About half a mile.'

'It's a bastard,' van der Reik replied sourly as another wave of sand tore at their faces. 'I told you before we left, man. Anyone who goes into the Kalahari this time of year needs his head examined.'

'Then examine yours. It'll tell you you're being paid enough to cross the desert on your hands and knees.'

The trees had disappeared again. Frouw kicked his horse forward towards where he'd last seen them. His head sunk morosely on his chest, van der Reik followed.

It was four months since Frouw had left Britain. When his ship docked at Cape Town, he discovered no one knew of any San available locally. He sent telegraphs as far afield as Durban without success. Then he decided to trek inland to Johannesburg. The story was the same there, too. The little people were vanishing as the farms spread out.

Frouw heard of a group who'd been raiding cattle on a ranch to the west, and set out to track them down. He reached the ranch only to find the farmer had killed three of them with his rifle from horseback the week before. The rest had disappeared.

Frouw didn't blame the farmer – the San were marauding vermin and barely deserved the price of a bullet in their lungs. He sat up with the man over steins of home-brewed beer discussing hunting late into the night. When he rode back to Jo'burg with a thick head next day, he was cursing his luck. Frouw wasn't there to talk about shooting game. He was there to bring it back alive.

Finally he decided on the Kalahari.

'That's where the little monkeys hide now,' an old desert pioneer told him in a bar one evening. 'If you want to catch yourself some, that's where you'll have to go. Your best jumping-off point's the mission post at Kuruman. The minister's named Ramsay. He's a *rouinekk* but he's not a bad bloke. He lets his kaffirs use the little buggers as herders. Last time I was there, they were swarming all over the place for his mealy-meal like bees round a hive.'

Frouw hired van der Reik, the other two white outriders, and half a dozen native servants. Then he set off north.

Now, a week's riding later, they were almost there. The sun was setting and the wind was dropping with the approach of evening. As the venomous screens of sand settled back on to the earth, Frouw saw the compound gates in front of him.

He dropped wearily from his horse and walked through.

'May God welcome you to Kuruman!'

The Revd Ramsay came warily down the steps of the mission house.

It was rare for visitors to come to the mission. On the few occasions they did, the dust raised by their horses was normally spotted several miles away by one of the staff. That day, with the wind blowing and the sand hanging high in the air, the travellers had been at the gates before they were noticed. Ramsay barely had time to hurry outside before they knocked at the door.

'Greetings, *meneer*!' Frouw replied.

As Frouw removed his sweat-stained leather hat and held out his hand, Ramsay saw a burly, heavily bearded figure with narrow eyes, red-veined from the desert dust, and a shrewd, jowled face.

'I travel with three of my men and a handful of kaffirs,' Frouw went on. 'May we have your permission to outspan and make our fire within the kraal?'

'May it be your home – !'

Ramsay's voice warmed slightly. He spread out his arms in a gesture of welcome.

Cold and taciturn as he was, Ramsay enjoyed the occasional company of Europeans. It had been months since he'd talked to one. This one was obviously an Afrikaner, and the Afrikaners were men after his own heart. Their talk made a pleasant change from the banal observations of his wife.

'I will get a boy to show you where you may take water. And then I hope you and your companions will share our table.'

'My men will make their own *braii*,' Frouw said. 'But if there is space for one, I would be glad to sit with you.'

An hour later Frouw was seated beside Ramsay at the mission house dining table. Facing him was Mrs Ramsay.

At the far end of the table, separated from the others by the table's length, sat Mary-Ellen.

Mary-Ellen took no part in the conversation. She listened in silence as her father questioned Frouw about Johannesburg and the news from the south. When Ramsay learnt that Frouw had recently come from England, his questions came even faster. England, home of the mighty Queen-Empress and her even mightier empire, was the lodestone on which all of their destinies depended.

At last Ramsay leant back in his chair.

'You are a much-travelled man, *meneer*,' he said. 'I fear I have wearied you with my importunate requests for information. Forgive me. Now, instead, tell us what brings you to lonely little Kuruman.'

Frouw looked thoughtfully at the table.

The old man in the Johannesburg bar who had directed him to Kuruman was an Afrikaner. He had described Ramsay as a *rouinekk*, a redneck, the derisive term for the British settlers whose necks turned scarlet under the African sun. The old man also called him 'not a bad bloke'.

For an Afrikaner speaking of a Briton, that was high praise.

It meant very simply that Ramsay was a spiritual *broeder* – a brother who shared the values and attitudes of the Afrikaner nation. Above all it meant that he viewed the kaffirs, the blacks, as they did. It was a good start, but Frouw needed something more. Glancing round the house and compound earlier, Frouw had realized what it was.

The stakes supporting the compound wall were rotting. So were the house's door and window frames. The mission was financed by the Church Missionary Society. It was widely known that the Society was short of funds.

The mission in Kuruman needed money.

'*Mevrou*,' Frouw turned to Mrs Ramsay, 'even for an unexpected guest, your table beggars the best in Johannesburg. After such a feast I cannot ask you and your fine daughter to listen to the tedious matters of which your husband asks me.'

Frouw stood up. Mrs Ramsay and Mary-Ellen got to their feet too. They both understood the unspoken request. What would follow was men's business.

Mrs Ramsay shook Frouw's hand.

'It was my pleasure, *meneer*,' she said. 'When you

finish your deliberations with my husband, may you sleep well.'

With Mary-Ellen behind her, she left the room.

'Now, Mary, mark him well,' Mrs Ramsay said in the passage outside. 'They are not often gentlemen, those Afrikaners. But the exception always proves the rule. And if Menheer Frouw's not the exception, then I'm a Dutchman – !'

She laughed happily at her own joke. 'What a pleasure it is to have him with us.'

Mary-Ellen kissed her mother goodnight. Then she walked to her room.

The walls of the mission house were fashioned out of the same iroko that provided the building's frame. Apart from the ravages of the white ants, they were durable enough, but they were also thin. Thin enough to let pass almost any sound in the house.

Mary-Ellen's room shared a common wall with the dining room. As her father and Frouw talked, she lay awake in bed. Even if she had not been interested in what they discussed, it would have been impossible for her not to hear them.

Mary-Ellen listened very carefully.

— 36 —

The following morning Mary-Ellen woke very early.

The sky outside the window was dark and the air was grainy with slowly shifting curtains of mist from the river. She dressed quickly and slipped out of the house. She crossed the compound, and walked down to the river.

As she reached the bank the sun broke over the horizon. Its first keen shafts of light cut through the thorn bush, steel-blue and then a translucent lemon and afterwards a flooding rose. The rose spread out and seemed to stain the river to its depths. A late-hunting jackal called. Birds filled the air with morning song, and an adventurous kingfisher arrowed down into the depths.

Mary-Ellen stood quite still, gazing at the water.

It was four years since the arrival of Darwin's letter. Even now Mary-Ellen sometimes found it hard to believe that what had happened was true. The old man had done exactly as he promised. With the help of her friend, Beth Appleby, Mary-Ellen had opened an account in a Mafeking bank. She sent Dr Darwin the details. By return mail she learnt the account had been credited with the first of the quarterly payments. The payments had continued uninterrupted ever since.

That was not all. Dr Darwin's first letter was followed by a stream of others. The letters offered ideas for lines of study, suggestions for books she should order, summaries of the work of other scientists who had published their findings since Darwin published his, even enquiries about her health and her life in Kuruman.

Mary-Ellen was overwhelmed.

The money was extraordinary enough. She ordered every book and periodical Dr Darwin recommended, and others she saw advertised in journals. The costs seemed barely to dent her account. Every quarter the balance grew larger and larger. Three times she wrote pointing out she was receiving far more than she needed. Twice Darwin ignored her. The third time he touched on the matter briefly.

'You say the trust provides more than you require,' Darwin wrote. 'I beg you to listen to me, young lady. As a child I was taught never to look a gift-horse in the mouth. One year a hard winter will come. The gift-horse's foal will then require hay. The hay merchants will ask for payment.

'Keep the money for the foal, the merchants and the hard winters that I as an old man can say with certainty and sadness will surely come.'

It was the last time the subject was mentioned between them.

As the money continued to accumulate in the Mafeking account, the books and journals kept on arriving at the Appleby ranch. At first Mary-Ellen stored them in Beth's room, riding over escorted by Moffat to consult them when she needed. Soon there were too many. Moffat was the only person apart from Beth Appleby who knew what Mary-Ellen was doing. It was Moffat who provided the solution.

Riding back with him to Kuruman one day, Mary-Ellen was fretting about finding an excuse to make yet another visit to the Applebys the following week, and about where, sooner or later, she could store the ever-growing library.

'There's a rondavel up the river from the mission,' Moffat said. 'It belonged to one of the old chief's headmen before the mission came to Kuruman. It's abandoned now. It's hidden in some mopani trees. No one goes there. If I repaired the walls and made the roof good, you could keep the books there. Then you could read them whenever you wanted –'

Moffat grinned. 'Also I wouldn't always have a sore behind from all this riding.'

Mary-Ellen thought for a moment. She glanced at Moffat. Then she burst into laughter.

The Mashona always marched to war on foot. Like all his tribe, Moffat had an instinctive dislike of horses. He rode with her out of duty and loyalty, but he hated the trips to the ranch. Yet, Mary-Ellen realized, it was a brilliant idea. It would solve not only Moffat's problems, but her own.

'You've just become an entry in my notebooks,' she said. 'A demonstration of the superior power of human reasoning as compared to our cousins, the apes. Fix the rondavel up as soon as you can.'

Mary-Ellen kissed him on the cheek. Moffat beamed with pleasure. Together they rode on through the thorn bush.

Two weeks later the library was secretly installed in a round hut, its roof rethatched with reeds and its mud walls repaired by Moffat, half a mile up the river from the mission compound.

Now the books and journals were available to Mary-Ellen whenever she wanted. The library was vitally important to her. Even more important were Mary-Ellen's own notebooks, the journals in which she painstakingly chronicled her observations of the behaviour of the baboon packs that thronged the river.

The notebooks were the tangible expression of her bond with Darwin, of the sacred compact she'd made with the old scientist.

A female baboon would give birth to an infant. Mary-Ellen would watch the baby's response to its mother as the day unfolded. She noted its feeding times, its first cries of hunger, alarm or contentment, its periods of sleeping and waking. Hour by hour she entered them meticulously in her journal. Then as the baby baboon grew up she followed its progress week after week, month after month.

The work needed infinite patience.

It was demanding and exhausting. If a pack Mary-Ellen was watching set off to forage, she would have to follow them for hours through the midday heat. Sometimes she despaired of its worth. The sweat- and often bloodstained columns of notes she scrawled in her own shorthand amid the Kalahari thorn seemed meagre and infinitely remote from the elegant writings in which real scientists presented their discoveries to the world.

Real scientists had rows of letters after their names. In their papers they referred to their laboratories and research assistants. Mary-Ellen had no letters after her name. She didn't even know what the letters meant. Her laboratory was a mud-walled rondavel. Apart from Moffat her only assistance came from the naked grandchildren of old Mama Chi-mona.

Even in her most desolate moments, Mary-Ellen never once considered giving up. The swarming flies and mosquitoes, the ferocity of the Kalahari sun, the constant presence of the desert's predators, lion, leopard and hyena, all were unimportant. A torch, the torch of scientific enquiry, had been passed to her. It was a gift beyond price. Mary-Ellen knew she would carry it proudly to her grave.

Then, too, there were Dr Darwin's letters. They sustained and encouraged her more than anything else.

Twice a year Mary-Ellen sent Darwin a summary of what she had been doing during the past six months. Darwin replied, always with encouragement and usually with comments. Mary-Ellen had received his response to her last report only a few months before Frouw's arrival.

Darwin's letter was rather different from the ones he had sent over the past three years. It was that, together with the appearance of the bearded South African and what she had overheard of Frouw's conversation with her father, which brought Mary-Ellen down to the Kuruman river.

She had Darwin's letter with her. Mary-Ellen opened it and read it again.

'Your baboon studies now fill an entire drawer of my

new teak and brass-bound filing cabinet,' Darwin wrote. 'The cabinet is a "gift" from the manufacturer. He will request in due course, no doubt, my endorsement for his wares. I will certainly recommend him, for it is a sturdy and serviceable piece. But pity the poor deluded man! The public, little does he seem to know, have no interest in science. They seek to ape what they learn of the habits of popular singers, not of scientists, and I use the word ape advisedly –'

Mary-Ellen turned the page.

'So much for my musings on my benefactor, the generous but misguided craftsman, whose work now harbours yours,' Darwin went on. 'Let me return to where I started. Namely, your baboons, young lady. You have, as I say, done much. Interesting patterns are emerging – patterns of procreation, nurture, learning and group assimilation which bear striking resemblances to our own. Much remains to be tested further, but not for the first time I congratulate you. It has been a truly noble endeavour –'

On occasions Dr Darwin, confronted by sloppy or haphazard work, could be a chill and stern critic. It made the praise he gave all the more valuable and heartening.

'Yet the time has come, I believe, for a change in direction,' the letter continued. 'I suggest you turn your attention away from the baboons for a while and concentrate on their cousins, namely ourselves. More specifically I mean the people who prompted this whole study – the Bushmen, or San, as you tell me you prefer to call them. The moment has arrived for us to consider them.'

Mary-Ellen had been half-expecting the suggestion. She set to work immediately. From the great doctor it was not so much a recommendation as a command from on high.

Very quickly she ran into difficulties. Mary-Ellen spoke the San language. She had known the San people intimately from her earliest childhood. At the mission she was surrounded by them. The problem was that at Kuruman they were living in artificial conditions. Not out in the desert where they belonged, but as a satellite community of the Tswana and the mission itself.

For Mary-Ellen's observations to be of any value she had to study them in the Kalahari.

Although the north and centre remained virtually inaccessible, the nearer regions of the desert had opened up a little since Mary-Ellen's childhood. White cattle ranchers had begun to sink bore-holes for their herds along its eastern edge. But any journey into the Kalahari remained a daunting undertaking. Mary-Ellen knew that her parents would never consider allowing her to set out on one.

Where she really wanted to go was not even east towards the ranches but north to where the San lived. Any suggestion she might do that would be greeted with disbelief and, in her father's case, fury. Yet ever since the arrival of Darwin's last letter, Mary-Ellen had been searching her mind for some way to do it.

For months the idea had seemed impossible. Suddenly, with Frouw's arrival, Mary-Ellen saw an extraordinary opportunity.

In spite of her mother's characteristically empty-headed opinion, Mary-Ellen was sure the South African was a villain. She sensed it as soon as she saw him. When she overheard what Frouw proposed to her father, Mary-Ellen knew beyond any doubt.

Frouw told Ramsay he had been commissioned to acquire a group of San to be shipped to Britain for a Christian 'educational' project. The San would be well paid and looked after, and a handsome donation was being offered to any institution or person who helped secure them. It was an enterprise, Frouw suggested, which might well interest the mission.

Mary-Ellen didn't believe a word Frouw said.

Men like Frouw didn't become involved in educational projects, let alone Christian ones. Their business was guns, hunting, and the ostensibly outlawed but in reality still flourishing African slave trade. Although Mary-Ellen didn't know what it was, there was obviously a much more sinister motive behind what the South African was doing.

Her father was either blind to the truth or simply didn't care. All that mattered to Ramsay, as was clear in his response to the South African, was the money. The mission was desperately short of funds. It was also overrun, in Ramsay's words, with the tiny apricot-skinned heathens. To let Frouw select a group of them in return for a donation to Christ's work made admirable sense in every way.

The two men parted on excellent terms and slept well.

Mary-Ellen had slept very little. Darwin's request – his instruction as she saw it – had been weighing on her for a long time. Now to that worry was added the imprecise but acute anxiety she felt about the San that Frouw had in effect offered to buy from her father like so many head of cattle.

What Mary-Ellen had in mind wouldn't solve everything. If she could achieve it, it would take her further into the desert than she had ever been. It would also keep her at Frouw's side. She had no confidence in her ability to protect the San entirely. But at least she would be there to try to help them if her worst fears were realized.

She had nothing to lose in trying – and she started at a huge advantage. Mary-Ellen knew something about the San that neither her father nor Frouw did.

She turned from the bank and walked resolutely back towards the mission.

— 37 —

'Father, may I speak with you, please? And you too, of course, Mama.'

Mary-Ellen's parents were seated at the breakfast table.

Both of them looked at her, surprised. It was almost unheard of for their daughter to want to address them both. There was an expression on Mary-Ellen's face that Mrs Ramsay had never seen before.

Ramsay glanced at his watch.

'You will have to be brief,' he said. 'Mr Frouw is due here any moment. We have important matters to discuss concerning the mission.'

'This concerns Mr Frouw and the mission –'

Mary-Ellen took a deep breath. She gripped the back of the chair in front of her.

'Father, from my bedroom it's impossible not to hear what's being said in here. I couldn't help listening to what you and Mr Frouw discussed last night.'

Ramsay stared at her. His face began to redden with anger.

'You were eavesdropping?'

'No, Father.'

'You must have been. It is utterly despicable –'

In his outrage Ramsay broke off. He fumbled for words. Before he could go on Mrs Ramsay interrupted.

'Calm yourself, George,' Mrs Ramsay said. 'Of course Mary-Ellen couldn't avoid overhearing you. We've had this out before. In her room it's quite impossible to avoid it. What did you expect the poor child to do – sit outside in the compound until you'd finished?'

Ramsay continued to scowl furiously for several moments. Then his head jerked away.

'Something must be done,' he snapped. 'I insist on it. It's intolerable that children should be able to listen to private adult conversations.'

'Father, I believe I may be able to help,' Mary-Ellen put in quickly before he could start again.

'Help? What do you mean, help?'

'I believe Mr Frouw wishes to take a group of Bushmen to Britain,' Mary-Ellen said.

'Indeed he does,' Ramsay replied. 'He has satisfied me the cause is excellent and they will be well treated. I see it as an admirable opportunity for some of those wretched unregenerate creatures out at the back. Goodness knows, we harbour enough of them.'

'Not at the moment, Father,' Mary-Ellen said quietly. 'It is the time of the Bushmen's winter festival. All of them who dwell here left for the desert a few days ago. It will be weeks before they return. There are none at the mission at all.'

Ramsay gazed at Mary-Ellen again. This time his expression was one of astonishment. Swiftly it gave way to alarm.

Like his wife, Ramsay seldom ventured outside the compound. When he did it was only as far as the Tswana village. He'd given up years ago trying to minister to the tiny nomads in the hovels beyond. It was months since he'd even cast eyes on them.

His daughter, on the other hand, was out there every day. If Mary-Ellen said the Bushmen had gone, it was undoubtedly true – and the news was disastrous.

'There are none left at all?' Ramsay asked.

Mary-Ellen shook her head. 'None. There never are at this time of year.'

'This is grave news.' Ramsay frowned. 'I promised Mr Frouw I would use my good offices to see he got what he wanted. In return –'

Ramsay coughed. The way he had been about to phrase it made the transaction sound embarrassingly mercenary.

'I mean Mr Frouw has kindly offered to assist the mission by way of compensation. Now I foresee his offer being placed in jeopardy.'

There was silence in the room. Ramsay drummed his fingers on the dining table.

The mission's finances were in the worst state Ramsay had known during the twenty-five years he had been at Kuruman. For years the Society had been sending him less and less money. Recently they had written informing him that from now on he would have to make up any deficit in his annual budget by raising money locally among the 'faithful'.

The faithful!

Ramsay had laughed bitterly. The white believers in the area owed their allegiance to the Dutch Reformed Church. Ramsay's own flock consisted of the handful of boneheaded kaffirs he'd managed to whip into more or less regular and always uncomprehending attendance at his services. The most he could expect by way of a donation from them was a handful of mealy-meal – mealy that in any event he'd provided in the first place.

Frouw's arrival had seemed like a literal godsend. Now the little savages had sabotaged even that.

'I know how to find where the Bushmen hold their festival, Father.' Mary-Ellen broke the silence at last.

For an instant Ramsay didn't seem to hear her. Then his head swivelled round.

'You mean you can tell Mr Frouw how to get to them?' he demanded.

'I can help him –' Mary-Ellen began.

'You can? Excellent – !' In his excitement Ramsay cut her off. 'That would indeed be a contribution,' Ramsay said. 'I retract nothing I have said, but for once I may have misjudged you, young woman. How precisely can you help him?'

Ramsay got eagerly to his feet. Mrs Ramsay's gaze was switching anxiously between her husband and her daughter. She knew Mary-Ellen and she had seen the look on her face. Mary-Ellen had not finished.

For some inexplicable reason, Mrs Ramsay dreaded what Mary-Ellen was going to say next.

'Father, it is not as simple as that,' Mary-Ellen said. 'When the Bushmen go to their festivals, they leave spoor for other Bushmen to follow. They have taught me how to read it. Very few people can do that. I certainly doubt whether Mr Frouw or any of his companions can –'

Mary-Ellen paused. 'If they want to find the Bushmen, I would have to go with them.'

'You? Go with them – ?'

Ramsay stared at her. His wife drew in her breath sharply in shock. Mrs Ramsay had known her daughter was about to suggest something terrible. She had never guessed it would be as outrageous as this.

'Go with a group of men into the desert on your own?' Ramsay continued. 'You have taken leave of your senses, child!'

'Father, with the greatest respect to you, I am no longer a child –'

Mary-Ellen's wrists were trembling with nervousness. She gripped the chair. Somehow she managed to keep her voice steady.

'I am twenty-two. Also, I did not consider going alone. Moffat would come with me as he always does. So would one of the old Mamas to sleep with me and look after me. I would be well protected and chaperoned.'

'Moffat!' Ramsay ignored the rest of what Mary-Ellen had said, and seized on the name. 'Surely he knows how to follow them?'

'No, Father. Moffat is a Mashona. He knows no more of the San than I imagine Mr Frouw does.'

Ramsay clenched his hand in frustration. He glowered at his daughter again.

'If you know so much, young woman,' he said, 'how is it that the Bushmen have not told you the site of this festival of theirs, instead of all this mumbo-jumbo about the tracks they leave?'

'I do not know it, Father, because they do not know it –'

Suddenly and almost imperceptibly a note of confidence began to enter Mary-Ellen's voice.

She had always been frightened of her father. Frightened and often, when he shouted at her or beat her, she was filled with a dark, guilty hatred of him. Now for the first time in her life she knew he was floundering. He was uncertain and confused. For once it was not him who was the stronger – it was her.

Ramsay wanted what Frouw had promised him. He wanted it with the frantic greed of lonely, embittered men starved for long in lonely places. Mary-Ellen had it in her power to give it to him.

'The place will be somewhere in the desert to the north of here,' Mary-Ellen went on. 'The Bushmen will not know it until they see it. Until something in the way the sun rises and the wind blows and the animals call tells them they have come to it. Then they will know. And I will know too, because they have shown me how to find it.'

Ramsay gazed at his daughter again.

Although she was white-faced and no longer able to control her trembling, Mary-Ellen looked steadfastly back at him. For what seemed to Mary-Ellen like an eternity they stared at each other. In the background Mrs Ramsay fluttered like a distraught moth.

Finally Ramsay glanced abruptly away. He was trapped and he knew it. Ramsay sensed Mary-Ellen was telling the truth. If she was, it would be pointless even to beat her. She still wouldn't be able to tell him where the Bushmen had gone.

'I sense the operation of deviousness at work here,' he said between clenched teeth. 'But I have concluded that the mission must take precedence because the mission is more important. Kindly guide my good friend, Mr Frouw, to wherever the savages choose to meet. Assist him in any way you can. I depend on you, with deep misgivings, I confess, to preserve the decorum required of a minister's daughter. Do not fail me or the Lord.'

Without speaking, Mary-Ellen lowered her head in acknowledgement.

Ramsay turned to leave the room. As he moved, Toko, the senior houseboy, appeared at the door.

'The bwana who ate at the table last night has come to see you,' Toko said.

'I will talk with him,' Ramsay replied grimly. 'He must ready himself for a journey.'

Ramsay went out.

Mrs Ramsay was sobbing quietly. She wasn't sure what had happened, but she knew that one of the links in the chain which bound her to Mary-Ellen had been broken. She also knew that once one link had snapped, the others would dissolve as if they had all been dipped in acid.

Mary-Ellen put her arms round her mother. She fondled Mrs Ramsay's forehead gently, but she wasn't thinking of her, as Mrs Ramsay bent over the dining table still laden with its complement of breakfast dishes.

Mary-Ellen was thinking of the desert wastes of the Kalahari that stretched away to the north of the little mission compound, and of the little people who inhabited them.

— 38 —

Mary-Ellen rode north with Frouw and his men for nine days.

Each morning they breakfasted at dawn beside the embers of last night's fire. Then, mounted on horses or mules and with two ox-drawn supply waggons following them, the party set off. At mid-morning when the heat was at its highest they stopped and rested. Afterwards as the sun lowered they headed on.

Just before darkness they made camp for the night. After the evening meal they went to bed. Mary-Ellen slept with her childhood nurse, old Mama Otapa, under a canvas awning slanted down from the side of one of the waggons. Moffat lay outside on the sand at the entrance.

In other circumstances the journey would have filled Mary-Ellen with delight. The San's spoor – a twisted stick, a pile of pebbles, a knotted stem of dry grass – was easy to follow. The little people had made no attempt to hide their tracks. On the contrary, for those who knew how to read the messages the route was deliberately and invitingly clear.

They were journeying into the Great Thirst to celebrate. All of a like spirit were welcome to join them in their festival.

With at least half her heart and mind Mary-Ellen considered herself a San. She loved the Kalahari almost as much as they did. She was travelling further into the desert, their desert and her desert, than she had ever been before. Its birds and animals surrounded her. There was old Mama Otapa to cook for her and look after her. Her childhood companion Moffat never left her side.

The occasion should have been joyous, not least because she was doing what Darwin wanted her to do. It was not joyous.

From the start Mary-Ellen was filled with unease.

Frouw and his two white companions rode in a tight little group apart from the others. They ate alone. They spoke little, even among themselves. When they did it was in Afrikaans, a coarse bastard language Mary-Ellen barely understood.

In her brief meeting with the South African at the mission, Frouw was polite and smiling. That, Mary-Ellen realized quickly, had been a mask for the benefit of her father. Now he'd reverted to his usual demeanour – sullen and taciturn. He was violent too. Once when his camp boy was slow in bringing his evening washing water, Frouw kicked him savagely in the thigh. The boy limped away, moaning in pain.

Across the camp site Mary-Ellen watched sickened. She glanced at the other two whites. They were shaking with laughter. By her side Moffat's face was grim.

'Not good men,' Moffat said quietly.

Moffat was right. There was something brutal and menacing about all three.

Mary-Ellen thought that by accompanying them she could somehow control them. Now she began to feel that the idea was nothing more than wish fulfilment, a pathetically inadequate excuse for making the journey at all. She couldn't control these men. She couldn't even influence them.

Mary-Ellen slept little that night.

They were nine days out from Kuruman and almost halfway to Lake Ngami, the great shallow lake that marked the approach to the Okovango delta. Until then Mary-Ellen had scrupulously done what she had told her father. She had led the party north along the course of the spoor the San had left.

When she rose restless and shadow-eyed before the others were awake the following morning, a dark sense of foreboding hung over her. She had been attempting, she believed, to follow Dr Darwin's instructions. Just as much, Mary-Ellen thought, she had been gratifying herself in her desire to see where and how the little people lived in the wild.

Whatever her motive had been, she was suddenly certain the journey would end in disaster.

Mary-Ellen had no idea how far in front of them the San were. She only knew she must tell Frouw she had lost their spoor. It would leave the expedition no choice except to turn back. She waited until the South African was at breakfast. Then she walked over to Frouw's fire.

It happened just as Mary-Ellen got there.

One of the other whites, the gaunt, white-bearded man named van der Reik, had finished eating and had mounted his horse. He was trotting away from the camp to see what the landscape in front of them looked like when he stopped and peered ahead. Then he swung round in his saddle.

'Smoke!' he shouted. 'There's another camp about half a mile ahead. It must be the little buggers we're after.'

Frouw jumped to his feet. 'Are you sure, man?' he shouted back excitedly.

'For Christ's sake, man, who else are we going to find out here?'

Frouw glanced at Mary-Ellen and grinned.

'Good spooring, young lady,' he said. 'It seems you've done just what you promised your dad.'

Frouw mounted his own horse and cantered off to join the other South African.

Mary-Ellen looked after him helplessly. She didn't need to follow Frouw to see if van der Reik was right. The Kalahari was the San people's home and hearth. No one else raised smoke in the immensity of the desert. A day earlier and she could have led the three white men away. She had waited too long. Now it was too late.

Her stomach cold and her mind churning with guilt and worry, Mary-Ellen stared in the direction where the two men had disappeared among the thorn bush.

They returned within minutes. Frouw reined in his

horse beside Mary-Ellen. He leaned down over the saddle.

'It's Bushmen, right enough,' he said. 'Just one fire and maybe eight or ten of them. I guess they're still travelling towards this *braii* of theirs.'

Mary-Ellen thought.

If they'd reached the site of the festival there would have been sixty, eighty, or even a hundred of the San, and several fires. This could only be a small clan on their way to join up with other nomadic groups. For an instant Mary-Ellen felt grateful they hadn't stumbled on the festival itself.

Then she realized it made no difference. If something bad was going to happen to the San, it was the same if it happened to eight of them as to a hundred.

'As soon as everyone's saddled up, we'll go forward and talk to them,' Frouw went on. 'I'll need you along to translate.'

Mary-Ellen racked her brains, desperately trying to think of some way she could warn the clan.

'It might be better if I went ahead and spoke to them alone first,' she suggested.

'Why?'

'They may never have seen Europeans. If we all arrive together, they may get frightened and vanish.'

'From what I've heard of the Bushmen,' Frouw said, 'they'll have known about us since yesterday at least. The birds and animals will have warned them we were coming as clearly as if we'd been beating drums. Last night they must have smelt our fire. They probably came over in the darkness to look at us –'

Frouw paused. 'If they wanted to hide, they'd have done so long before now. You're the expert, young lady. Isn't that so?'

There was nothing Mary-Ellen could say. Numbly, she nodded. Frouw went on staring at her.

At the mission the young woman had seemed nothing more than a useful tool, a docile tracker and translator who would do what her father told her. Since they'd ridden into the desert she had changed. She seemed to have acquired an unpleasant obduracy and independence. Frouw didn't like it – any more than he liked her casual familiarity with the old Mama and the boy who rode at her side.

Frouw had seen it happen before. White children who grew up with kaffirs often became contaminated by them. The whites were useful because, like this one, they acquired black skills. But they could also pick up the worst and most dangerous of the kaffirs' habits of mind.

The Revd Ramsay's daughter appeared to be one of them. The girl, it occurred to him, was not to be trusted.

'No one goes ahead,' Frouw said. 'We all ride together.'

They rode into the San encampment an hour later.

A fire was burning at its centre and an impala doe the clan had killed was roasting over the flames. Not far away was a cluster of the tiny grass and twig shelters which had become so familiar to Mary-Ellen over the years. The two elders of the clan were squatting on their haunches waiting to receive them. The others were scattered about the camp.

As the rest of the expedition stayed behind, Mary-Ellen dismounted.

She'd hoped the clan would be one she knew, perhaps even one who'd colonized the mission. It would have given her at least some authority to affect what she sensed, with a growing sense of despair, might happen.

Mary-Ellen was disappointed. She recognized none of the little people's faces. The clan must have been travelling from the remote north of the Kalahari.

'We saw you coming from afar,' the elder of the two said as Mary-Ellen approached them.

'I too saw you from afar,' she replied gravely.

Mary-Ellen knelt down. Even on her knees her eyes were level with theirs.

She laid out the presents Frouw had handed her to give them. Two packets of cane sugar. A cheap knife of Sheffield steel. A hank of black plug tobacco. The men examined them closely. Their faces creased in delighted smiles and they clapped their hands in appreciation.

Ten minutes later, with plugs of the tobacco burning in crude pipes made from the bases of brass bullet cases, the two elders settled back to listen to what Mary-Ellen had to say.

'I am here at your fire to speak for the white men who stand like giraffes.' She gestured at Frouw and his companions. 'They wish that six of your people travel back with them to their own fire, so that their clans may learn the ways of the San. For this they will exchange much. Sugar in bark containers this high and this wide –' Mary-Ellen indicated with her hands.

At the mission she had often had to translate between the San and the European worlds. Always before, Mary-Ellen enjoyed it. She loved language. It had been a challenge to find terms and images that would bridge the vast gulf between the two races and cultures.

This time it was different. Her voice faltered. The words refused to come. When they did, they lacked conviction. She stumbled on, hesitant and troubled. Finally she finished.

The elders clapped their hands again. They stood up and trotted back to discuss with the other members of the clan what she had said. The discussion lasted almost an hour. In the end only one of the elders returned. He was the one who had spoken first.

A tiny, wizened figure with thoughtful opaque eyes that had blurred with trunk-like circles of age, he squatted before Mary-Ellen. What he had to say lasted barely a moment.

'We hear the words !Nai-njala has brought us –'

Mary-Ellen started. Then she smiled delightedly and clapped her hands in appreciation.

!Nai-njala, 'the talking dove that the sun turned gold', was the childhood name the mission San had given Mary-Ellen. She had never seen this clan before, but they knew who she was and they knew her name. Word of the fair-haired daughter of the mission who spoke the little people's language had spread into even the northern Kalahari.

'I am named as Deial,' the old man went on. 'My brother Xa!, the great hunter, listened with me when you spoke before. We see the white men who stand like giraffes. We respect them and their offer. We have spoken of it with my sons, Khoi! and Nuna, and the other hunters of our clan. Also with my wife, Lys, and the clan's women. But we cannot make an exchange. We are all agreed. It is the turning and we must go towards the hills. That is all.'

Mary-Ellen gazed at him.

The hills were the Tsodilo Hills, the little hummocks of rock where the San drew their blood-red paintings and came together to listen to their spirits. Mary-Ellen had never seen them, but she knew from the mission Bushmen that the hills were the holiest of all the San's shrines.

'The matter is ended?' she asked.

'The matter is ended.'

Deial smiled and clapped his hands once more. Mary-Ellen smiled too.

She stood up and walked back to the others.

A wave of relief swept over her. She suddenly realized the source of her disquiet. She had been wrong in ever thinking the little people should leave the desert. That was what had been tugging fretfully at her ever since they left Kuruman. The San belonged here. It was their home and hearth and the site of their holy places. They should never go away from it.

Frouw was waiting impatiently for her.

'Well?' he demanded.

'They have considered the offer carefully,' Mary-Ellen said. 'They cannot accept. It is time for them to make their journey towards the hills.'

Frouw looked at her in disbelief. 'I've promised them a year's supply of sugar. If it isn't enough, give them more.'

Mary-Ellen shook her head. 'You could offer them anything and they still wouldn't agree. The hills are more important.'

Frouw's disbelief turned to anger. His face darkened and his eyes narrowed.

'Are you saying that whatever they're given, they will not come?'

Mary-Ellen nodded.

Frouw hesitated for barely a moment. He stooped and picked up his rifle. As if sensing what he was about to do, the other two Afrikaners leapt to their feet too, their rifles in their hands. The blacks Frouw had hired were also standing behind their masters.

'Get them,' Frouw said savagely but softly in Afrikaans. 'I want six. Five males and a young female with good titties.'

It was what Farini had commissioned him to provide.

Mary-Ellen had little idea what happened next.

One moment the three whites were on the ground, the next they were on their horses. They galloped out to form a horseshoe round the San encampment. The blacks, wielding knives and knobkerries, raced behind them. Taken by surprise the San froze. Then they broke and ran.

Sick with fear, dazed and uncomprehending, Mary-Ellen watched.

Shots rang out. Puffs of smoke lifted into the air. A knobkerrie rose and slammed brutally down across the neck of a small fleeing silhouette. Blood welled over the apricot-coloured skin of his back, and he toppled to the earth. A San woman carrying a child was tripped by an outstretched leg, and beaten as she fell. Another was gripped by the hair and kicked in the back.

Suddenly, as quickly as it had started, it was over.

Three of the San were dead, shot or clubbed down. The rest retreated helplessly towards the fire at the camp's centre as the men on horseback and the blacks closed in round them. Their shelters, traps, and baskets of patiently gathered berries and tubers had all been trampled into the sand.

As the noise of gunfire and shouting died, and the terrified San clustered together, Mary-Ellen's paralysis dissolved. She opened her mouth to scream out in fury and protest. Before any sound emerged Frouw shouted:

'Heine! Beyond you! Get her!'

Mary-Ellen's head jerked round in the direction of Frouw's outstretched arm.

A slim, naked figure had risen from a thicket of grass and was running towards the scrub that ringed the encampment. The figure was a girl. She was tall, much taller than the San, and her skin was paler than the little people's. Although she ran with extraordinary speed, she did so with a curious loping gait.

Heine, the white horseman on Frouw's left, set off after her. Fast as the girl ran, the galloping horse was faster. The man caught up with her just before she reached the scrub. He lashed her across the shoulders with a rhino-hide whip. As the girl's knees buckled, he leant down and caught her beneath her arms. Then he slung her over the horse's quarters as if she had been a dead antelope, and cantered back.

Frouw leant across and pinched the girl's breasts.

'*Gut*,' Frouw grunted. 'She'll do for the female. I'll pick the others. Then we'll head back.'

He began to wheel his horse. Mary-Ellen sprang forward and caught the reins.

'No!' she shouted. 'You cannot do this.'

Frouw glanced down.

'It is done, young *frau*,' he said. 'They had a good offer. They refused it. That was their stupidity. I came here for six of them and I'm going back with six of them.'

'But they're people!' Mary-Ellen screamed up at him. 'You can't take them as if they were slaves –'

'You listen to me.' Frouw cut her off. 'That is not people. That is animals. They steal stock like leopards do. They are hunted like leopards and vultures are hunted. Look at the way they live –'

He swept out his hand over the encampment. The ruined shelters were like trampled bird's nests.

'They are worse than savages – they are creatures. Your pa knows it, all good Christians know it. That is why I have his permission to take them. That is why he sent you to translate for me. Now, if you make any further trouble, I shall rope you as I am going to rope them. I shall take you back to your father, and believe me, young *frau*, I know how he will deal with you –'

Frouw pushed his face towards hers. His voice was as harsh and ugly as the rock that underlay the Kalahari sand.

'He will beat you as I would beat you if you were my daughter. Maybe he will ask me to do it for him.'

Frouw chuckled and rode off. He shouted an order and his blacks began to move towards the San.

Mary-Ellen's head slumped forward on her chest. Against the three white men with their guns and strength and servants, there was nothing she could do. She was as helpless to resist them as the San were.

She began to weep uncontrollably.

As the tears streamed down her face Mary-Ellen ran towards the waggon and the only comfort available to her, the comfort of Mama Otapa's arms. Mama Otapa gripped her and held her tight. Heaving and trembling, Mary-Ellen pressed herself against the old woman's breast.

When Mary-Ellen eventually lifted her head and looked back, five of the San men had been roped together in a line behind the girl who had been ridden down by the horseman. The other members of the clan had fled into the bush. Frouw shouted and the line stumbled towards the waggon.

The girl had been placed in front because she was the tallest. As one of Frouw's boys lashed the rope round her wrists to the tailboard, the girl lifted her head and stared at Mary-Ellen. Mary-Ellen froze. She stared back almost hypnotized.

The girl's eyes were the strangest she had ever seen. Dark and unblinking and impenetrable, they were not the eyes of a human.

They belonged to an animal.

— 39 —

The expedition returned to Kuruman late in the afternoon eighteen days after it had set out.

The tower of the little chapel came into sight when they were still several miles away. As soon as Frouw spotted it, he spoke to his two white companions. Then he spurred his horse and cantered forward. Sitting on the cross-seat of the waggon beside Mama Otapa, Mary-Ellen watched him disappear with a numbing sense of despair.

Mary-Ellen knew what Frouw was going to do.

He would go to her father. He would give his own version of what had happened when they came upon the San. He would say Mary-Ellen had lied from the start. That she had tried to sabotage the entire expedition. She had deliberately distorted his offer to the savages. She had encouraged the San to flee. Most telling of all, Frouw would say she had put his donation to the mission in jeopardy.

By the time Mary-Ellen reached Kuruman, Ramsay would have accepted Frouw's version as the truth. There had been little hope of challenging it even if they arrived together. Now there was none.

The captured San were trudging in a line behind the waggon. Their hands were manacled and a chain tethered them to the waggon's rear shaft. The tall, pale-skinned girl was still at the front. Her gaze switched restlessly from side to side, scanning the clumps of thorn as if they would somehow provide her with sanctuary.

Suddenly the girl noticed Mary-Ellen watching her. Her head jerked up and she focused on Mary-Ellen's face. Gleaming through the dust cast up by the waggon's wheels, the girl's eyes were fierce and questioning. Once again they were not the eyes of a human but an animal.

Like one of the desert's predators snared in a trap, the girl seemed to be challenging Mary-Ellen. I hunt and I am hunted, the girl's stare conveyed. But hunters kill swiftly and the hunted die swiftly.

Why am I held here between the two worlds of life and death?

Mary-Ellen turned her gaze away. She leant against Mama Otapa with tears of helplessness in her eyes.

Thirty minutes later the waggon came to a halt before the mission gates. Mary-Ellen climbed down. She straightened her sunhat over her face and tried to smooth her skirt, rumpled by the jolting ride. Then she stepped forward into the compound. As she turned the corner of the stockade she saw three figures grouped on the steps of the mission house, waiting for her. They were her father, her mother, and Frouw.

Mary-Ellen felt a chill in the pit of her stomach. She braced herself and walked up to them.

'So, Mary-Ellen,' her father said, 'I understand there have been disturbances, grievous disturbances, on this trek.'

Ramsay's face was mottled with anger and his voice shook. In his hand was the rhino-hide whip he used to punish the compound servants. At his side stood Frouw, his pitted face harsh and sombre. Behind them both Mrs Ramsay was dry-eyed and frozen.

Mary-Ellen opened her mouth to reply. Before she could speak, her father cut her off.

'Let it never be claimed I am not just,' he said. 'Menheer Frouw, I ask you to repeat what you have told us, the parents of this child.'

Frouw cleared his throat and spat on the ground.

'I fear, Reverend, this young lady has greater respect for the heathen than she does for good God-fearing Christians –'

In his flat, nasal accent Frouw told his own story.

Mary-Ellen listened, appalled.

It was even worse than she had believed possible. Without explicitly stating anything, Frouw managed to imply that not only had Mary-Ellen lied to the San, but she had apparently encouraged them to attack the expedition. It was only due to the bravery and quick-wittedness of his men that no one had been lost.

'Is this true?' Ramsay demanded when Frouw had finished.

'No, Father,' Mary-Ellen shouted. 'It is all false!'

'Have you the temerity to suggest Menheer Frouw is lying, young woman?'

Ramsay's voice was quiet and venomous.

'Father, he fired and killed –'

'I did not ask what Mr Frouw did,' Ramsay interrupted her. 'He has been good enough to tell me that himself. I asked you a simple question. Its burden is this. Did you or did you not side with the little savages in defiance of my express instructions and everything you have been brought up to believe?'

'For God's sake, Father, it wasn't like that –'

'Do not add blasphemy to your other sins!'

Ramsay shook the hand that held the whip.

'I give you one last chance,' he shouted. 'Did you or did you not try to sabotage the success of Menheer Frouw's expedition, an expedition undertaken from the worthiest of motives and with your father's full support?'

Mary-Ellen didn't reply. In the miasma of lies and half-truths, there was nothing she could say.

'From your silence I take it you have the grace to acknowledge that Mr Frouw's account is indeed true,' Ramsay went on. 'I am at least glad of that. For you are about to learn a lesson, young woman, a lesson I had wrongly believed was inculcated in you long ago. Grace is not enough. By your works ye shall know them –'

Ramsay took a deep breath.

'Your works are vile, young woman, vile! You have defied and disobeyed your father. You have insulted a Christian guest of the Lord's mission here. You have sided with the animal creatures of the desert against the servants of the Almighty. You have shamed your God, your family and yourself!'

The last vestiges of Ramsay's control broke then.

His voice rose in fury and he lifted the whip. Mrs Ramsay screamed. Frouw stepped quickly back. As the whip came down, Mary-Ellen managed to twist round. Instead of slashing across her face, the rhino-hide thong came down with brutal force on her back.

Mary-Ellen's knees buckled. The pain was agonizing. Her eyes streamed with tears and her entire body convulsed. Somehow she managed to heave herself upright. Blindly, frantically, she fumbled through her mind for somewhere to escape. All she could think of was her bedroom.

Panting and sobbing, Mary-Ellen threw herself up the steps of the mission house.

Maddened with rage and shouting incoherently, Ramsay set off behind her. Mrs Ramsay tried to restrain him. He hurled her arm away. Three times before Mary-Ellen reached her bedroom door, her father succeeded in striking her again. Each blow was delivered with redoubled fury and power as if the whip was being wielded not by Ramsay, but by the avenging angel of God himself.

Finally Mary-Ellen found the sanctuary of her room. She slammed the door shut and rammed home the bolt from the inside. Dizzy and trembling, she leant against the wall. Outside in the passage Ramsay, still bellowing, hammered for several minutes on the panels. Then Mary-Ellen caught the sound of her mother's voice.

There was a long confused exchange as her mother pleaded and her father continued to roar. In the end Mary-Ellen heard footsteps recede and silence fall over the house.

Mary-Ellen stumbled to her bed. She sat down. There was a burning sensation across her shoulder blades, and her back felt cold and damp. She reached her arm behind her and explored her skin. When she examined her fingers, they were wet with blood. She brushed the blood away on the counterpane. Then she stood up.

Mary-Ellen walked to the window.

Like all the windows in the house it was heavily barred on the outside in case the mission was attacked by Tswana raiding parties. As she stood there she heard a sound of hammering from the passage. She glanced round. Her bedroom door was vibrating. It took her only a moment to realize what was happening.

Her father must have summoned Ptulo, the mission carpenter. On her father's orders, Ptulo was nailing her door shut. She was to be imprisoned in her room.

Mary-Ellen slumped down on the window seat.

The Kalahari night had fallen and the air was beginning to chill. The blood welling from the weals on her back was caking and hardening painfully in the cold. Mary-Ellen barely noticed the pain. Frouw's nasal voice, her father's violence, her mother's terrorized immobility, her own hurt and humiliation, they all belonged to the past.

The past was over. It had been extinguished in the spurt of flame from Frouw's rifle. The trudging of the manacled San behind the waggon. Her father's mindless slashing whip. Something irrevocable had gone, something irreparable had been broken.

Mary-Ellen had no idea what lay ahead.

She was not even aware of the Kalahari stars as they began to flare in their immense intricate patterns beyond the bars of her window. They had dazzled and entranced her all her life. From her earliest childhood they had been the stuff of her dreams. They were the magical strands of diamonds that her mother told her were worn by the great ladies of Paris.

Mary-Ellen dozed. For once she did not see the stars that night.

She saw a pair of agate-coloured eyes staring at her, wounded and accusing, from the dust that spiralled over the thorn bush. She saw her notebooks hidden in the abandoned hut, notebooks filled with her painstaking observations of the behaviour and life rhythms of the baboon packs. She saw the white-bearded face of an old man with gold-rimmed glasses staring at her from the frontispiece of a book.

The girl, baboons, Darwin.

They were inextricably linked. In her dreams, Mary-Ellen knew she was answerable to them all. For some strange reason Paris and the diamonds were important in the dreams too. Mary-Ellen had no idea why. What Mary-Ellen did know, even in the darkest and most troubled moments of her sleep, was that all was not lost. In the desert where no water ran she had a life raft.

'Mama Mary, Mama Mary – !'

Mary-Ellen woke. Her head jerked up.

A voice was calling to her softly from beyond the window. She blinked and peered through the bars. In the dim moonlit darkness she saw the face of Moffat.

'*Pula*, Mama Mary,' Moffat went on. 'Are you all right?'

Mary-Ellen wiped the sleep from her eyes.

Her first instinct, as so often in the past, was to instruct him not to call her Mama Mary. Then she remembered. She was inside the mission compound. There they had agreed he could use the form of address her father insisted all the compound Africans should use when they spoke to her.

'*Pula*, Moffat,' she replied. 'Why are you here?'

Moffat frowned.

'In the kraal they say bad matters have happened. That the Reverend has beaten you.' Moffat paused. 'I came immediately in the thought you might have need of me.'

Nothing, Mary-Ellen knew, could be kept from the kraal. If anything happened among the white bwanas in the mission, the native huts in the village knew about it instantly. The smallest incident, the smallest event, the smallest quarrel, whatever it was, it would be the common gossip of Kuruman almost before it had taken place.

'Yes, Moffat,' she said. 'Something very bad has happened. I am trapped here in my room. The door is nailed down from the outside. I wish to walk free. What can you do?'

Moffat smiled. 'There is no problem, Mama Mary. I will go beneath the house and raise the floorboards from below.'

Moffat's face disappeared from beyond the bars.

Mary-Ellen waited.

She heard the muffled tap of a hammer beneath the boards that covered her floor. One board sprang free from the nails that anchored it to the joist, then another. A few minutes later Moffat's face appeared in the gap. He beckoned Mary-Ellen down.

Mary-Ellen slid out through the hole. Hunched on her hands and knees, she crawled to the outer wall of the mission. Then she stood up. In the darkness she placed her hand gratefully on Moffat's face. Moffat beamed in pride.

Mary-Ellen turned and walked towards the mission door.

— 40 —

Mary-Ellen pulled down her dress and tried to straighten her hair. She took a deep breath. Then she opened the door and walked into the room.

Ramsay was seated behind his desk. Mrs Ramsay was standing by the window. They both glanced round. Mary-Ellen's mother reacted first. Pale, dishevelled and dust-streaked, with dark bruises on her face and smears of blood down her cheeks, Mary-Ellen looked like a ghost.

Mrs Ramsay's hand went to her throat. She screamed. Before she could move, her husband was on his feet.

'Who let you out?' he roared.

'I let myself out,' Mary-Ellen replied. 'I am not an animal to be caged.'

'You – !'

The Revd Ramsay broke off incoherently. His face reddened in fury. As he made to move forward from behind the desk, Mrs Ramsay recovered herself. Trembling, she threw herself between him and Mary-Ellen.

'Stand back, Mama,' Mary-Ellen said. 'I wish to speak to him. He will not strike me again.'

There was a strength and authority in Mary-Ellen's voice that had never been there before. All the terror of a few hours earlier had vanished. She was no longer an erring child facing a justly angry parent. She was a grown young woman confronting an equal. She stood gazing implacably over her mother's shoulder at her father's face.

Fearfully Mrs Ramsay stepped aside. For a moment

longer Ramsay stared at Mary-Ellen. His mouth was twitching and a vein pulsed at his temple. Then something in Mary-Ellen's gaze daunted him.

Ramsay's breath hissed out and he retreated behind the desk.

'Have you come to apologize?' he blustered.

'No, I have not,' Mary-Ellen replied. 'I have nothing to apologize for. Any apologies, and there are many due, are owed to me.'

'Mary-Ellen, you must not speak to your father like that,' her mother implored, weeping. Mary-Ellen interrupted her.

'I have not addressed him as Father. I do not recognize him as my father. I shall never think of him so again.'

Both Mr and Mrs Ramsay stood quite still. Their faces were frozen, one in shock and the other in fear.

'I am leaving here,' Mary-Ellen went on. 'I have some arrangements to make, but I shall be gone by mid-morning tomorrow. In due course I shall advise you, Mama, where I am, but I do not intend to return.'

'Leaving? Your wits have deserted you, young woman.' Ramsay's voice began to rise again. 'With whose authority? Where? What do you intend to use for money?'

As the rage began to swell up once more, Mary-Ellen cut him off.

'The authority is mine,' she said. 'My destination is my own affair. The money is my own too – and it is ample.'

'You have *money* of your own?' her mother stammered in bewilderment. 'It's not possible. How could you have money?'

'There is much about me you don't know, Mama, that neither of you know –'

Mary-Ellen turned back to address her father.

'For the past four years I have been working on a scientific enquiry into the relationships between man and the animals – more particularly the primates, the baboons. It is research for which I have been generously, more than generously, funded.'

Ramsay shook his head, stupefied.

Mary-Ellen's mother gasped. Then, more acute at that moment than her husband, she said, 'All those times when you went off with your sketchbooks and notebooks, you were looking at *monkeys*?'

Mary-Ellen nodded.

'Who paid for these so-called studies?' Ramsay demanded.

Mary-Ellen drew in her breath again.

'A very great scientist. Dr Charles Darwin,' she said quietly.

'Darwin? Darwin?' Ramsay blinked. 'You are referring to the evil heretic and blasphemer?'

'I would not call him that, but, yes, some poor and ignorant people still view him so.'

'But –'

Ramsay stopped.

A cloud of madness seemed to have enveloped his world. As shock accumulated on top of shock, his head felt as if it would burst. He opened his mouth to bellow again. Nothing came out. He trembled and slumped down into his chair.

Mrs Ramsay ran over to him. She placed her hand on his forehead and felt the blood pumping violently beneath the suffused skin. She soothed him until his pulse slowed. Then she looked back at Mary-Ellen, torn between concern and confusion.

'What is this, Mary?' she asked pathetically. 'You cannot do it to us, these fairy-tales of money and Dr Darwin and the monkeys. What is the truth?'

'It is the truth, Mama,' Mary-Ellen replied.

Her tone was gentle but beneath lay something adamantine, something that chilled Mrs Ramsay as she listened to Mary-Ellen continue.

Mary-Ellen told them everything, from her reading of Oswell's volumes to Darwin's undertaking to sponsor her. When she finished the two were numb and dazed. Ramsay reached up for his wife's hand. It was the first time he had taken it in years.

The rage had drained out of him. Even the shock was dwindling. Instead he felt despair.

Under his roof, beside his hearth, at the very heart of his family, he had been rearing a serpent. She had become infected with evil and she had brought the poison into the very centre of his being. If Mary-Ellen had declared herself a harlot of the black heathens beyond the stockade and revealed she was smearing the mission with their venereal diseases, the effect would not have been more traumatic or devastating.

'You must leave, young woman,' Ramsay mumbled. 'May God find it within the compass of his infinite mercy to forgive you, for I never will.'

Mary-Ellen looked down at him.

From the first moment she had become aware of his presence as a baby, there had been nothing between them. No love, no interest, not even affection. What she had had of those came first from her mother and then, in far greater measure, from the Tswana and the San in the encampment. From Ramsay all she had known over the years was indifference, disapproval, and the unremitting violence of his beatings.

She had grown up with a perpetual stranger. Yet in spite of everything Mary-Ellen had the imprint of him as her father. Her disavowal of him now was as traumatic to her as it was to him. Half her life and half her past, it seemed, had been a cruel, worthless travesty. She had cast him away. With him she was abandoning a huge part of herself.

Mary-Ellen longed to explain to him how wrong he was and how right she was. Even as the words, the concepts of right and wrong, surfaced in her mind, Mary-Ellen knew it was hopeless. A chasm, a world, a cultural eternity, divided them. She faced him across unbridgeable darkness. Sin and fundamentalism, heathens and blasphemy, monkeys and God's image, were the landmarks on his side.

On hers enquiry, impulsiveness and scepticism, a different notion of the planet, of the planet's man and the planet's animals, of everything of which life consisted.

With the clear-sighted, unforgiving eyes of youth Mary-Ellen saw that his errors were so profound and engrained they would never communicate again.

She looked at him. She hated the man for everything he was and everything he stood for – for all the misery and pain he had caused her and so many others over the years. She wanted nothing more than to be rid of him and his house for ever. She exulted in her power to leave and the triumph she had won over him.

And still tears came to Mary-Ellen's eyes and she wept.

'Come now, child.' Her mother came over and put her arm round her. 'There is no sense or purpose in continuing this any longer. I will take you to your room. The door will not be barred.'

Bewildered and weeping too, Mrs Ramsay was responding instinctively from the most ancient of all maternal impulses – to cut off suffering, to heal, to make good with the best available to her.

Calling for Ptulo the carpenter, she led Mary-Ellen away. Behind them Ramsay sat with his head buried in his hands. As they reached the door Mary-Ellen turned back.

Even in what she had said she had been daughterly. She had been resolute, but aghast even as she was. She had hoped to explain and knew it was impossible. Now, from some deep cavern of childhood, the sleeping beasts of rejection and fear – and the hatred that nourished them – suddenly sprang back into the open.

'You are a cruel, cowardly and bigoted man,' she cried. 'You were never my father, never!'

She broke away from her mother and ran for her room. This time it was Mary-Ellen who locked the door behind her.

In her last few hours at Kuruman she had to be alone.

— 41 —

Mary-Ellen was sitting by the window when she heard the rustle of footsteps in the passage.

She turned. She had no idea what the time was. It was still fully dark but from the movement of the stars outside, dawn could not be far off. She must have been sitting there for most of the night.

She realized she couldn't have turned the lock fully, because the door creaked open. A pool of candlelight appeared, and she saw her mother. Mary-Ellen stood up. The two came together. For a while they clung to each other in silence. Then Mary-Ellen became aware that Mrs Ramsay was shivering.

'You're cold, Mama,' she said. 'Have you not been to bed?'

Mrs Ramsay shook her head. 'I have been in the chapel talking with your father.'

'Where is he now?'

'He is praying.'

Mary-Ellen closed her eyes in anguish.

'You were talking about me, I suppose?' she said.

'Of course, dear. About all of this, about all the terrible things that have happened. We were trying to find out where we went wrong.'

'But you didn't go wrong –'

Mary-Ellen stopped. Mrs Ramsay was still shivering. Mary-Ellen picked up her light, quilted coverlet. She wrapped it round her mother's shoulders and sat her down on the bed.

'Perhaps it's all different.' Mary-Ellen tried again, kneeling beside the bed. 'Perhaps I am right and you are wrong.'

'The name of Darwin is a ruinous scandal all over the civilized world,' Mrs Ramsay replied despairingly. 'He is trying to quench the light and unleash darkness upon us again. That is what your father says.'

Mary-Ellen thought for a moment.

'Mother,' she said, 'whatever you really think, surely you can talk to me in your voice and not in his?'

For several moments Mrs Ramsay didn't speak. Then she gave a small, sad smile.

'I'm sorry,' she said. 'He is my husband and a very learned man.'

'What do *you* really think?'

'That you are my daughter and –'

Mrs Ramsay stopped.

'And he is my father?' Mary-Ellen prompted her. 'And I should honour my father and mother as I have been taught all my life. Isn't that so?'

'I said I was your mother –'

Mrs Ramsay broke off again.

'Mama –'

She knew why her parents had gone to the chapel. Anywhere else in the mission she might have overheard them. The things her father had to say about her were so appalling even she was not allowed to listen to them. But she would not accept them and she would force her mother to understand that – and then confront her on her own terms.

Mary-Ellen was about to chide her, to push her on again.

Suddenly there was something else. Something so strange and awesome she could only sense it, not understand it. Something in her mother's tone, in her strange repetition of the words she'd used, in the agonized turn of her head. Mary-Ellen paused too.

Then she added softly, 'What do you mean?'

Mrs Ramsay gently pushed her away. She stood up and went to the window. Mary-Ellen made to follow her, but her mother waved her back.

'I will speak to you from here –'

Her voice was low and unsteady.

She looked away from Mary-Ellen and out at the fading Kalahari night, out at the stars Mary-Ellen had been watching. When she spoke, she spoke towards the sky as if she could lose herself and what she had to say in its immensity.

'Your father is not your father,' she said. 'Your real father was another man. I never intended you should know. But after tonight I realized I had to tell you. I sat in the chapel and I knew a dam had burst. It was sweeping everything away, you with it. I could not stop the waters but I thought they should carry the truth too.'

Mary-Ellen had only registered her mother's first two statements.

'Your father is not your father. Your real father was another man.' She knelt on the floor by the bed. The words echoed in her head without meaning like the assault of pealing bells.

'Who is my father?' she whispered.

'He was a lovely man –'

Mrs Ramsay's head was turned away. Mary-Ellen could not see her face, but she sensed a smile had come to it. This time the smile was not sad but charged with pleasure. As she went on, warmth crept into her voice.

'The loveliest man I ever saw. He had long fair hair and blue eyes, eyes like gentians, and he danced like no one you could ever imagine dancing. So fast, so light, so strong that if you were the one spinning in his arms all the world vanished and there was only you and him –'

She paused. 'I was the one he chose to dance with. I was the one he loved. You were our child.'

She told Mary-Ellen about the French dancing-master who gave lessons in the little town where she had lived, and how she had fallen in love with him and what her mother had done when she discovered her daughter was pregnant.

'So Father – so he has nothing to do with me?'

Her mother had finished. Mary-Ellen fumbled to find the right words. They eluded her. She had only known one 'father'. Now he was not the person she had always thought him.

'He brought you up –'

'That's not the same.' Mary-Ellen cut her off. 'Anyone can bring anyone else up. It's who you inherit your being from that matters.'

Mary-Ellen hesitated. Darwin was in her mind as she spoke. It was not the right moment to mention him.

'But what happened to him?' Mary-Ellen added. 'Have you no idea where he is now?'

Her mother shook her head. 'A few years after you were born, I wrote to one of my cousins, Louisa. She had been my best friend before – before it all happened. Louisa did her best to find out. She wrote to me every month while she tried, but she got nowhere. After a while I knew it was hopeless. I gave up –'

Mrs Ramsay began to weep. 'Oh, my dear child. I am so sorry. I have failed you so miserably.'

Mary-Ellen had been in a state of shock until then. The tears, the pain in her mother's voice and the guilt in her slumped shoulders, brought her out of it.

Mary-Ellen stood up and hurried to the window.

'Mama, you have not failed me.' She put her arms round Mrs Ramsay and held her tight. 'You were no older than I am now, indeed you were younger. You loved him. I am glad you did what you did, proud of you for being yourself. How could that be failing me?'

Her mother clung to her, sobbing. Mary-Ellen tried to comfort her, but still the tears poured down Mrs Ramsay's cheeks.

'Tell me something –'

A thought had suddenly occurred to Mary-Ellen. Holding her mother by the arms, she pushed her away.

'When your cousin Louisa wrote to you, where did she send her letters? Surely they did not come here?'

'Of course not.' Mrs Ramsay's words came out choked between her sobs. 'She addressed them to your friend Beth's mother. Mrs Appleby was the first friend I made when I came here. She has been a staunch friend ever since. Satimi, the boy we had before Moffat, used to collect them for me.'

Mary-Ellen smiled. The smile welled up into a laugh. She held her mother to her again, the warmth of the laughter flowing through to the trembling and guilt-ridden older woman.

'Mama, how little has changed,' she said.

She told Mrs Ramsay about her letters to Dr Darwin. How she had told Darwin to write back to her care of Beth. How Moffat had brought the letters back to her.

'Nothing's changed,' Mary-Ellen finished. 'Mrs Appleby to Beth, Satimi to Moffat. A generation's gone by and we've simply been doing the same things – solving the same problem in the same way.'

Mrs Ramsay's tears stopped then.

She looked up at her daughter. Mrs Ramsay could not laugh yet. The events of the past twelve hours were still too fresh and momentous to allow that. But she managed to smile.

'You truly do not blame me?' she asked timidly.

'Never, never, never!' Mary-Ellen's answer was as final and emphatic as a roll of drums. 'You are my mother and I am your daughter. The matter ends there.'

'What are you going to do now?'

'Now – ?'

For an instant Mary-Ellen was bemused.

Then over her, rippling the length and breadth of her body from her scalp to her fingertips to her toes, flooded a vast surging tide of well-being – of freedom.

She had fought for and won it on her own. She had battled for the San. She had stood against Frouw and her own father. She had been beaten to the ground and locked away. She had broken out and faced her father again, and this time she had stared him down.

And now she had discovered he wasn't her father at all. He was the Revd Dr Ramsay, a violent and brutal man who had nothing to do with her. If he had truly been her father, some part of her allegiance would have been anchored in him always. He would have shadowed and inhibited her for the rest of her life. But he was not her father. Her fear had vanished. Dr Ramsay had become part of history – a history that was not hers.

Mary-Ellen was free.

'Now I must find the San,' Mary-Ellen said. 'Everything has changed and yet nothing has changed. The San have been herded up like cattle. They must be freed. That is what I shall do.'

She took her mother over to the window. They sat down side by side on the broad hardwood bench that ran below.

Often as a child Mary-Ellen had sat there, curled up in a corner, and ignored the rising or setting sun as she immersed herself in a book she had secretly removed from Ramsay's library. It was on the same bench only a few years ago that she read Darwin's works.

Now she sat holding Mrs Ramsay's hands tightly, their fingers threaded through each other's.

Outside the sun began to rise. A pale band of colour lifted over the horizon. At the edges it was yellow. At the centre it shone a translucent gunmetal grey. The primrose and the metal fused. Animals and windswept bending grass and hunched trees reared against it – imprints on a knife-blade of tempered steel.

'You will not forget your father?' Mrs Ramsay asked tremulously.

As it always did, the desert wind was rising with the approaching morning. Mary-Ellen seemed to be leaning towards it. Flaring her nostrils to catch the air. Opening her lips to trap its still-frosty taste on her tongue. Her eyes were sweeping the ranges of the Kalahari in front of them.

Mrs Ramsay shuddered.

She did not know what had happened to her daughter. She only knew she was in the presence of something much stranger and greater, something above and beyond anything she had ever imagined. Mary-Ellen didn't seem to have heard her. Mrs Ramsay began to repeat the question. Her daughter interrupted her.

'I will not forget him, Mama,' she said. 'Maybe one day I will find him. First I have other things to do. As a dancer, I think he will respect me for that.'

She gripped her mother's fingers and leant forward, staring at the dawn.

Mary-Ellen had forgotten about Ramsay. She had forgotten about the tumult and violence of the past twelve hours. She had forgotten about the blood that was still caked on the back of her dress. She was even unaware of her mother.

Mary-Ellen had tasks to do before she left Kuruman. She had to speak to Moffat. Moffat was not merely her friend, her brother, the most important part of what she had suddenly come to consider as her 'real' life at the mission. He was also the only person she could charge with watching and looking after her mother.

Mrs Ramsay would need care and support in the weeks, the months, the years ahead. Mary-Ellen knew that Moffat, tactfully and silently, would give it to her. There were other matters, too, that Mary-Ellen would have to give her attention to. But as she gazed out of the window she was thinking of none of them.

She was thinking of the pale-skinned girl who had tried to escape from the San encampment. Mary-Ellen saw her eyes as the girl trudged, manacled to the line of little people in the dust behind the waggon. From somewhere those eyes were gazing at Mary-Ellen now.

Ferocious and haunted, they were demanding that Mary-Ellen set her free.

— 42 —

Kala lay in the half-darkness on a shelf of slatted wood.

The space was cramped and hot, and the air was foul-smelling. Kala didn't mind either the heat or the narrowness of the shelf. The dens of the Merula Pan hyenas had been humid and confined. She was used to that.

What Kala hated was the smell.

It was unlike anything she had ever smelled before. Harsh and acrid and gaseous. The dens had often reeked, but the stench there came from life, from meat and bones and faeces. This smell was dead. It stung her nostrils. It tasted sour on her tongue. Its metallic pungency made her head ache.

There was the throbbing too. Somewhere something was pounding with a monotonous, unceasing roar. The sound never stopped by day or night. It filled her ears and made the shelf vibrate tormentingly.

Finally there was the movement beneath her. The earth was constantly heaving and swaying. Sometimes the movement was so mild it was barely noticeable. At other times, like now, it was abrupt and violent. The den rose and fell with sickening swoops. Kala's head kept hitting the shelf above her, and her stomach churned.

Like the hyena cubs who had been her childhood companions, she buried her face in her chest and pressed her wrists against her ears.

Kala tried to sleep.

The 'den' was a steerage-class cabin near the stern of the Cape & Atlantic passenger steamship, *The Veld Star*. The noise came from the ship's engines. The pervasive smell was marine oil. Kala had no concept of the sea. She could only imagine that the rocking, plunging motion below her was caused by the earth being troubled, as it had sometimes seemed to be in the desert before a storm.

The Veld Star was a week out of Cape Town on its regular month-long voyage to London's Tilbury docks.

Its steerage cabins were the most primitive of all the ship's accommodation. They were little different from the livestock pens beside them. Each cabin was built to transport eight passengers, who slept on the two four-tiered racks of bare wood bunks. The passengers were generally illiterate labourers hired to work in the South African gold fields.

On this trip, a northbound sailing, the cabin housed Kala and the five San captured with her. There was old Deial, the clan's surviving elder, his sons Khoi! and Nuna, and two of their cousins, Gwi and Hutse.

Normally, steerage passengers were fed in a squalid mess-room on the deck above. Frouw, who was travelling with the San, had arranged with the steerage purser for Kala and the San to be kept locked in their cabin and fed there.

'They're wild country kaffirs,' Frouw explained. 'If they're allowed out and get lost, Christ knows what they might do, man.'

The ship had transported blacks to Britain before. The purser knew well what they were like. They were worse than the animals. He agreed without question.

For Kala the journey was an unending nightmare.

Most of the time, in a fitful trance between sleeping and waking, she dozed. She was aware of the San's presence only in the passage of shadows on the cabin wall. Occasionally Kala ate with them. More often she chose to go hungry. Her stomach threw back the putrid food almost before she had swallowed it.

As the ship steamed north the weather grew worse. The storms became incessant. A bulkhead split near the bows, and the passageway outside the cabin filled with water. Damp seeped in and the cabin walls furred with green sea-mould. Kala caught a fever. Her body was racked with long bouts of coughing, and she began to spit up blood.

Then one night in the early hours when the ship was battling north across the Bight of Benin, the storms suddenly ended for a time and the sea fell calm. Kala woke in the unaccustomed stillness. She sat up and glanced round the cabin. The San were asleep. She rolled off her bunk and placed her feet warily on the floor. For the first time in weeks she found she could stand without gripping something for support.

The cabin had one small sealed porthole. The glass was coated with dried salt from the waves, but it was still just clear enough to let in a few shafts of light from the night sky. Kala went over and stood beneath it. She pulled out the diamond from her belt and held it up.

The stone caught the faint light of the almost-hidden stars. It filled with radiance. As it did so, it began to throb. Kala had felt the diamond move between her fingers before. Never like this. She gazed into the stone. In the past it had thrown images back at her. Not now. Instead, sounds were coming out of it, sounds so faint that even to Kala's acute ear they were almost inaudible.

Kala lowered her head and listened.

She heard a distant humming. The humming divided into separate strands of noise. The strands became speech – not the speech of hyenas or even the speech of the San, the language that bridged the worlds of the animals and man. It was the speech of an entirely different race.

The sea started to rise again then and the sound faded.

Wonderingly, Kala put away the diamond and stumbled back to her bunk. She lay down as the ship started to heave and toss. In spite of the violence that was soon shaking the cabin, it was a long time before she drifted back into the nauseous semi-consciousness of the rest of the voyage.

For almost fifteen years Kala had lived either among animals or the Kalahari hunter-gatherers. Human speech, the speech of her beginnings, had long been lost to her. She no longer understood it. She didn't even know what it represented. Yet suddenly, extraordinarily, she could hear language again even if the individual sounds and words meant nothing.

The presence of Europeans had returned the possibilities of speech to her – and the diamond had sent her its own message of confirmation.

The barriers that had walled in Kala's past were starting to crumble.

— 43 —

'Fancy your chances, lad?'

Ben looked up at him.

The man was wearing a black frock coat. He was tall and lop-shouldered with a florid face and small red-veined eyes. He kept tugging at a gold watch chain looped across his stomach. As he leered down at Ben, Ben smelt the gin on his breath.

'I reckon as you need training for that,' Ben replied.

'Training is it? Salt in the belly doesn't come natural, then? A bit of guts and gunpowder, we've got to be *trained* for it, have we?'

The man's eyes were melancholy and sadistic. The stench of spirits enveloped him like a cloud. He was drunk and combative. If Ben had been able to escape, he would have done. Ben wasn't frightened, but the man clearly spelt trouble.

Unfortunately the press of the crowd that had carried them both into the square didn't allow him to get away. They were shoulder to shoulder at the front of a densely packed throng. Across the square the crowd was even thicker. For the moment he was trapped.

Ben smiled equably at the man. Then he stared resolutely ahead.

It was two weeks after his disastrous encounter with the prostitute in the Canon St Mary tavern, and the fire which had destroyed his workshop. The cart Ben waved down after delivering the mermaid to the Yorkshire shipowner deposited him at midnight on the outskirts of the capital. Ben walked for two hours until he reached the centre of London.

That first night he slept beneath the trees in Hyde Park. The following day he found himself lodgings in a boarding-house in Chelsea, and set out to look for work. The theatres were easy to find. They were advertised on crude posters throughout the city. Ben toured them one by one, knocking at the stage doors and asking if they had employment for a carpenter.

The answer was the same everywhere. The start of the autumn season was not far ahead. The productions were already in rehearsal. The managements had already engaged everyone they required. They needed no one else.

Dispirited and footsore, Ben returned wearily every night to his lodgings. They were among the cheapest in London, but accommodation in the capital, Ben discovered, was ten times as expensive as in Buckler's Hard. So was food. The four sovereigns he'd earned from Mr Featherstone's figurehead would last him at most for another month.

Ben had walked to Westminster that day because the Aquarium had announced that an 'extraordinary epic event' was to take place to advertise the forthcoming opening of its own autumn revue. The Aquarium was the only theatre in London Ben had so far not visited. He'd decided to see the event – its nature had deliberately been cloaked in mystery – and then, forlornly by now, to make a final attempt at getting a job.

To Ben's right he could see a vast cannon mounted on a wooden platform. To his left and almost enveloped by swarming London urchins was a net suspended on poles. In the open space between, a space that was constantly threatened with invasion by the crowd, a man in a cloak and a blue velvet top hat was pacing up and down as he addressed the watchers.

'It has been achieved in New York!' the man bellowed. 'It has been achieved in Paris, France! Now, God willing, it will be repeated on a grander scale than ever among you all here in the world's greatest city. But before the attempt is made, is there not some bold English youth who will vie for the supreme honour?'

The challenge had been issued twice before. It had prompted the man in the frock coat to start taunting Ben. As the gauntlet was thrown down again, the man suddenly gripped Ben's collar.

'There's a volunteer here!' he bellowed. 'English through and through – and more than a match for a waggonload of your Yankee dandies!'

The crowd cheered. Ben struggled furiously. The man was drunk but he was also immensely strong. His hand was clamped to Ben's collar and Ben couldn't break away.

'Chicken, are you?' The man leant down and hissed at him. 'Yellow-livered and white-feathered? Well, you can swallow that and stand up for England. See these strutting rebels about their business. Here –'

With his other hand the man burrowed in his pocket.

'They've offered five sovereigns. I'm adding another.'

The man slapped the coin down into Ben's palm.

He hurled Ben forward into the open space between the crowds. Ben stumbled. He recovered and caught his balance. He turned, gripping the sovereign and ready to throw it back into the man's face. The audience was shouting and applauding. As he stood there they began to shower the cobbles with coins.

Ben hesitated.

He saw the man's face, bloated and red-veined, in front of him. There was a sneer on his lips. Suddenly the anger that had flooded Ben drained away. He was in the presence of morons – and the morons had thrown him their gold.

Ben slipped the sovereign into his pocket and grinned. As the crowd continued to cheer, he limped over to the platform beside the cannon. The man in the cloak and silk hat stepped forward to greet him.

'Do I take it you are offering yourself to the gun?'

Ben nodded.

'I congratulate you, young sir.' The man held out his hand. 'Let me introduce myself. Farini is the name, the Great Farini as the populace choose to call me. Tell me yours and your occupation.'

'My name is Ben. I'm a carpenter.'

'Excellent.' Farini swung round to the crowd. 'My friends, a young hero has come forward to brave the cannon. Without more ado I give you Ben, a carpenter of this fair city of yours!'

As the applause swelled up, Farini gave Ben his instructions.

Ben listened. He climbed the ladder to the platform and reached for the bar suspended above the gun's mouth. He was about to pull himself up so he could slide down into the barrel, when he paused.

'Where are the five sovereigns?' Ben asked.

'The money?' Farini said. 'That will be presented afterwards, of course. Surely you are not suggesting I am not to be trusted, sir?'

'I was told it was five sovereigns to make the attempt,' Ben replied, 'not to survive it. I'd like the money first.'

For a moment Farini scowled. Then he burst into laughter.

'You drive a hard bargain, young man, but I admire your spirit. Here, does this satisfy you?'

Farini reached into his pocket and held out five silver coins.

Ben took them. He added them to the sovereign in his pocket and sprang for the bar. He heaved himself up and dropped into the darkness of the barrel. He stiffened himself and pressed his arms tightly against his sides. He heard the crackle of a lighted taper somewhere below his feet. Then the charge went off.

Afterwards everything happened so quickly that Ben was barely aware of it. There was a deafening explosion. He felt himself being hurled upwards with a sickening jolt that seemed to crush his knees into his thighs. He glimpsed a flash of sky and sunlight. Then he plummeted down, sprawling into the net.

For several moments Ben lay there dizzy and gasping.

The cheering was louder than ever. Slowly Ben sat up. He examined himself. His shirt had been ripped away and he was bleeding from some cuts on his arms and shoulders. Apart from that he was unhurt. He scrambled across the netting and lowered himself shakily to the ground.

'A triumph, young man, a veritable triumph!'

Farini pushed his way through the throng that had excitedly enveloped Ben. He gripped Ben's hand and shook it delightedly. He raised Ben's arm and held it up in the salute of a prizefighter acknowledging a victory. Still panting, Ben stood beside him as the audience surged round them, applauding and clapping him on the back.

It was ten minutes before the crowd began to drift away. As the courtyard in front of the theatre emptied, Farini glanced at Ben.

'I meant that, boy,' Farini said. 'You did a good job. It takes sand to get into that goddamn gun. No one else wanted to. If you hadn't appeared, I might have been left with a real dud firecracker.'

Ben shrugged.

A few tremors were still running across his body. He'd discovered to his irritation that the explosion had wrenched one of his ankles, but otherwise he'd recovered from the experience.

'For five sovereigns it was worth it,' Ben said. 'If there's more I'd do it again.'

'No use to me, kid,' Farini replied. 'The cannon was strictly for today only, to let people know things are happening here at the Aquarium. It worked. But I'm not doing that again. If you'd overshot and emptied your guts on the sidewalk, it could have kicked back on me. On the other hand –'

Farini paused.

'You said you were a carpenter, right?'

Ben nodded.

'Anything else you can do?'

'I'm a painter. I can turn my hand to most things in wood or paint.'

Farini looked at Ben thoughtfully.

'I reckon I could use you on the set,' he said. 'In fact I'm damn sure I could. If you find a kid with sand, hang on to him, that's what I always say. How about working in the theatre?'

— 44 —

'Mr Farini, Mr Farini! He'll have to stop – he's got the alligators going!'

Farini's head jerked round.

The anguished shout came from the wings. Farini could only just hear it over the uproar. The noise in the theatre was deafening. There were stagehands bellowing, hammers battering, dogs barking, musicians trying to tune their instruments, and somewhere a raucous cacophony of animal calls.

'What the hell do you mean?' Farini shouted.

'The animal impersonator, sir. He's driving the alligators mad. They're trying to eat each other.'

The voice belonged to Farini's assistant, Winters. There were fourteen alligators in all. Like every act in the new extravaganza, they had cost Farini a small fortune.

'All right, Winters,' Farini bellowed back. 'I'll have him shifted outside. You – !'

He seized a passing carpenter.

'You know the guy who does the animal noises?'

'Yes, sir.'

'Tell him to pack it in. Tell him from me he's damaging the livestock. Any 'gator I lose goes against his wages. Find him somewhere out back to do his yodelling. And get him to move his butt – we're about to rehearse the coons again.'

'Yes, Mr Farini.'

The carpenter was a stocky young man with a limp and a withered arm. As he hurried away, Farini turned his attention back to the stage. The frenzy of activity swirled round him, but for an instant he was able to watch the scene without interruption.

Farini was standing midway up the sloping ramp of the stalls. He was also standing on the eve of his greatest triumph. Thanks to Barston and the laconic South African, Gert Frouw, tomorrow night he would present the most spectacular show the capital had ever seen. All of fashionable London would be in the audience. Even, it was rumoured, members of the royal family. And he, Farini, the impresario, would be there to greet them.

Farini gave a slow, thoughtful smile.

It was a cold smile and his lips barely moved, but it was also full of satisfaction. It had been a long journey from the back streets of New York to the world's best-known theatre of varieties. Now the journey was almost over – and he had just the spectacle to bring it to an unforgettable climax.

'I've moved him, Mr Farini –'

Farini glanced round. The carpenter had reappeared.

'I put a stove in one of the box rooms at the side,' the carpenter went on. 'It's warm in there and with the door shut you can't hear him.'

Farini realized the chorus of animal calls had stopped.

'Good thinking, boy.' Farini studied the young man. In spite of his crippled body he had an alert, intelligent face. 'What's your name?'

'Ben, sir.'

Farini nodded. 'I took you on a couple of weeks back after you volunteered for the gun, right?'

'Yes, sir.'

'Well, there's something else you can do.' Farini put his hand in his pocket and pulled out a bunch of keys. 'I'm putting you in charge of the coons. From this moment on they're your responsibility. As a start you can get them up right now.'

Ben took the keys as Farini's darting gaze switched back to the stage.

'I'm having the savages brought up, Winters!' Farini shouted. 'For Christ's sake, this time let's see some fire in their guts!'

Farini strode forward down the aisle. For a moment Ben watched him.

With his tall, gaunt frame, his flowing black hair and heavy moustache, and the opera cloak flaring dramatically from his shoulders, the American was an imposing figure. He was also frightening. His eyes were chill and pale and predatory, and his periodic rages terrified everyone in the company.

Ben sensed one of them was about to erupt now.

He turned and hurried to the back of the stage. Ben climbed down the stairs to the warren of passages beneath and unlocked the doors of the rooms which housed the pygmies. Programmed like automatons to answer the turning of the key, six figures filed out.

Five of them were men and the sixth a girl. The men were tiny, barely larger than children. They had dusky apricot-coloured skin, tight-curled wiry hair, and high, almost Tibetan cheekbones. The girl was paler and much taller, with long umber hair and a dazed, vacant face.

The men were naked apart from loincloths. The girl was dressed in a skirt made from jangling strings of multicoloured glass beads. She had a scarlet leather halter round her breast and a tawdry golden crown on her head. They scrambled up the stairs and trotted out beneath the stage lights.

'Faster, you dumb bastards, faster – !'

As Farini bellowed they all broke into a run.

'That's better! Now let's see the torture dance. Winters, get up there with the fire and act the captive – !'

Winters, a burly, slate-faced young man in a tight-fitting tweed suit, appeared on the stage with a brazier of glowing coals. He lowered the brazier and lay down beside it.

'Right – !'

Farini was shouting at the pygmies again.

'Remember what I taught you? You caught this guy in battle. You're going to slice his nuts off and fry them up like muffins. Then you're going to slit him end to end and fill up the cuts with salt. But first you're going to lick your lips and enjoy what's coming to the bastard. Okay, let's have the pain and the vengeance! And, for Christ's sake, let's hear the shrieks!'

The six had no idea what he was saying, but they had rehearsed the routine again and again. By now it was second nature to them. The men shuffled into a circle while the girl scrambled up on to the ornate papier-mâché throne. As the men wailed and danced round the brazier, she removed the leather halter round her breasts and waved her hands.

Ben stared at the stage.

The Africans were the stars of Farini's production. Billed on the posters pasted up every day on the streets of Westminster as 'the dancing pygmies from the centre of the earth', they had been brought to London from somewhere in the southern half of the dark continent.

Their torture dance was Farini's own creation. They performed it against the backdrop of the set Ben and the other carpenters were building. The set was a wooden citadel with towers and turrets rising out of a ghostly green jungle. According to the posters it represented something called the lost city of the Kalahari.

Ben had glimpsed the dance briefly once or twice before. Watching it now, he felt revulsion. From a distance the leaping silhouettes round the fire, and the eerie calls, calls that belonged more to animals than man, had been frightening and convincing.

Close at hand, the performance was a travesty. The little people's eyes were dull. Their movements were apathetic. Their cries were not a spine-tingling chant of hate, but a weary, leaden chorus lifted into false hysteria by Farini's orchestration. Blank-faced and shivering, they tramped faster and faster round the brazier as Farini's voice goaded and abused them.

'For shit's sake!' Farini's rage spilled out in a torrent of venom. 'You dumb, crawling animals! This isn't ladies' night at the Boston sewing circle. It's Africa red and raw – !'

He hammered his fist so violently on the orchestra pit rail, one of the glass lightshades shattered.

'Get them off, Winters! Make Gert sharpen them up. Tell him to use his whip, and on the girl most of all. She's meant to be their sadistic man-eating queen, and she's sitting there like some goddamn stuffed dummy. I want a torture dance – not a fairies' tea party!'

Winters leapt up from beside the brazier. Wielding one of the carpenters' steel measuring rods, he beat the pygmies away into the wings.

'Lock them up again!' Farini shouted at Ben. He turned and called for the next act.

Sickened, Ben threaded his way between the rows of seats and followed the flailing rod down the steps that led backstage.

— 45 —

Ben put the key into the padlock and opened the door of the room.

In fact it was more like a cell than a room. Tucked away in the basement at the back of the theatre, it was one of three in a row – all of them windowless and almost airless. Once, they had been used for storing paint and props. Now they had been cleared out to provide living accommodation for the pygmies. The five men shared two of the rooms. The girl had one to herself.

Ben lifted his lamp and searched the darkness for her.

She was lying on the straw mattress at the back in the position Ben often found her in – stretched out on her stomach with her head resting on her wrists. It was a strange, dog-like posture which, like so many things about her, Ben found baffling. He put the plate of food on the floor between them.

'Here's today's dinner,' Ben said. 'It's not too bad. I've just had some myself.'

Ben gave an awkward smile.

He knew she didn't understand a word he said. He'd been told by Farini, who in turn had learnt it from the South African, Gert Frouw, that the pygmies referred to her as Kala, and that she was mute. But Ben always spoke to her and always smiled at her. It was the least he could do.

Kala stood up. Dully, she clapped her hands once like the other little people did when he gave them their food. It was, Frouw had told him, a gesture of thanks. Then she began to eat, holding the plate with one hand and cupping the other to scoop the food up into her mouth.

Ben watched her.

It was four weeks since Farini had put him in charge of the 'Tom Thumb darkies' as the other stagehands had named the pygmies. Even before then, their treatment had shocked him. Afterwards, as Ben had to deal with them every day, it filled him with growing disgust and revulsion.

They were treated not merely as animals, but imprisoned animals. Two or three times a day Ben would take them up on stage for rehearsals. As often as not, when Farini's temper snapped at their incomprehension about what they were meant to be doing, his assistant, Winters, was ordered to beat them. Then Ben had to lock them up again.

Apart from Ben's visits with food, they spent the rest of their time in darkness. After Ben's first week's charge of them, he summoned up the courage to confront Farini in his office and protest at their conditions.

Farini listened to Ben for a moment. Then he cut him off.

'Those little coons come out of Africa,' he said. 'Now, I don't know Africa any more than you do. But I have this on authority, damn good authority seeing as how it comes from the minister of God who sent them here. In Africa those heathen little bastards just lie around starving and dying. So do their children and families. They don't know any better. Here, they've got shelter, food and money. My goddamn money! And the money is going straight back to Africa to put food into the bellies of the people back home. Look at this –!'

Farini reached in one of the desk drawers. He pulled out a paper and brandished it in Ben's face.

'Signed by the goddamn minister himself! What the hell's his name?' Farini peered at the foot of the paper. 'Ramsay! The Revd Ramsay of the Kuruman mission. A white man, an educated man, a man who knows what he's talking about. Don't you tell me about the coons' "conditions" –'

Farini stuffed the paper back in the drawer before Ben could look at it.

'You want to stop food filling starving niggers' bellies, fine!' he shouted. 'Just go and do it in some other theatre – if you can find one! Sure as hell, I can find other carpenters!'

Ben was silenced. He stood there for a moment without answering.

Then stubbornly Ben said, 'Mr Farini, couldn't I take them out for a walk once a day – just to let them see the sunlight?'

Farini glowered at Ben across the desk. He rubbed his jaw.

In the month Ben had been there, the crippled carpenter had proved the best worker Farini had ever employed. He was skilful, tireless, and he was astonishingly adept at handling the little savages – he could get them to do things even Winters wielding a rod hadn't achieved.

Angry as he was, Farini didn't want to lose him, least of all now with the opening of the production only a few weeks away.

'Half an hour in the afternoons,' Farini snapped. 'And they've got to be roped to you, too. I paid good money for those coons. I don't want them falling under a carriage or skipping off, though Christ knows where they'd run to. Now get the hell out of here – I've got a show to get on!'

Ben left Farini's office.

Since then Ben had taken the pygmies out every day. He used a length of light cord, tied in loops with fishermen's knots, to bind them to him. For thirty minutes the little procession walked up and down the Thames embankment, or travelled in a circle beneath the trees of Green Park.

The five little men seemed fascinated by their daily exercise. They watched the muddy churning waters of the river. They picked up the falling leaves in the park and shredded them curiously between their fingers. They stared at the sky and exchanged puzzled comments about the birds that thronged it. They picked and chewed the drying grass. They gazed wonderingly at the dogs and horses.

Kala was different.

Ben always looped her so that she was nearest in the line to him. She walked behind him, much taller than the San with her head almost at the height of Ben's own. Kala appeared to notice nothing. The birds and animals, the river, trees and grass, the swirling sights and sounds of London, all of its tumult and clamour, passed her by as if they did not exist.

Kala walked isolated and alone.

She might almost have been lifeless, Ben thought sometimes as he glanced back at her, were it not for her eyes. The girl could have been no more than seventeen, but her eyes were the oldest he had ever seen. Bruised and hardened by time, they bored into his face with the bleakness of the ancient flintstone arrowheads he had found as a child in the copses of the New Forest.

The male pygmies were recognizably African, even if their skins weren't black. The girl was not. At times she looked almost Arab. But far more than any of them, she had the eyes of Africa and Africa's infinitely remote past.

How and where, Ben wondered, had their terrible intensity been forged?

As the weeks went by, Kala remained utterly alien and remote. Somehow, in spite of the immense barriers that separated them, Ben sensed to his bewilderment that a bond was beginning to form between them. He had no idea how or why it started.

Kala was a woman and a savage. She was repellent to him as the first, and incomprehensible as the second. Yet he knew the initiative was his. Ben smiled at her. He talked to her, meaningless as he knew his words were. He tried to protect her, and the others, from the more grotesquely mindless of Winters' beatings.

Scuttling away afterwards, the men always clapped their hands quietly in acknowledgement of Ben's intervention. Kala never did. Except when he brought Kala her food and she gave him the same staccato clap, her gaze remained as blank and glazed as the figureheads he had made. Like them she could have been carved out of dead and dried wood.

Kala was an automaton.

Strangely, bewilderingly, Ben realized she was starting to obsess him. Part of the reason, it occurred to him suddenly one day, came when he saw her running away as Farini once again instructed Winters to lash her for some mistake in the pygmies' dance.

Unlike Ben's, Kala's olive-skinned body was perfect – slim and lithe, supple and balanced. She could run much faster than he would ever be able to. Yet she tried to escape from Winters with the same loping and scuttling strides Ben used when he hurried. In Ben's case the gait was forced on him by his body. With Kala it seemed to be dictated by something else.

Wounded dogs, Ben thought, ran like that. He had been wounded, but wounded in his shattered bones. It had become natural for him to run like an animal with a broken leg. For Kala it was not natural. She was whole – and she still ran as he did. It was something that must have been forced upon her long ago as a child.

She too was a cripple. But whatever had wounded Kala, Ben realized, had damaged not her body but her mind.

'For Christ's sake, man, she can't have disappeared! There's nowhere for her to go – !'

At the stage door Ben paused and listened.

The voice shouting furiously was Farini's. It was only three days before the production opened. For the past week rehearsals had continued day and night. Like everyone else Ben had been working almost round the clock. Half an hour earlier he'd locked the pygmies back in their rooms. Ben had given the keys to Winters, and slipped from the theatre for a short break in the chill winter air outside.

'She's my star, goddamn it! I want the little bitch back, and I want her now!'

Even muffled by the walls and corridors between the

stage door and the theatre itself, the rage in Farini's voice was fearsome. Puzzled and apprehensive, Ben ran forward.

The theatre was a turmoil of racing, searching figures, but as soon as Ben appeared on the stage Farini spotted him.

'Where the hell have you been?' Farini bellowed, enraged. 'God damn you, you're meant to be in charge of her! Shift your butt and find the little coon!'

'Yes, sir!'

Ben didn't need to ask who Farini was referring to. Somehow Kala must have escaped from her room. Ben hesitated for barely an instant. The padlock on the door, he was certain, had been closed. Kala must have found some other way out.

Ben ran to the front of the theatre. He hurried up the stairs to the top landing and pushed open the swing doors that led back into the auditorium. The turmoil was below him now. Ben glanced quickly round.

He stiffened.

A figure was sitting deep in the shadows at the back of the last row of seats. It was too dark to see whether it was a man or a woman. Instinctively Ben felt it was a woman. His hip jolting against the seat backs, Ben ran towards the silhouette. He stopped beside it. A face glanced up at his.

Ben was right. The face belonged to a woman. She was a young woman – but not the African girl.

'What are you doing here?' he demanded.

After six weeks Ben knew everyone involved in the production, from the doormen and cleaners to Farini himself. He had never seen this young woman before.

Dimly he could see she was tall with long fair hair and blue eyes. In spite of the nervousness on her face, her eyes stared back at him levelly and steadily. She was dressed in an ankle-length skirt with a matching jacket. Across her shoulders she was wearing a cloak pinned round her neck with a golden brooch.

'I'm a visitor to London,' she said. 'I was passing the theatre. I saw from the boards outside there were rehearsals. I came in to watch. I thought no one would mind.'

'You shouldn't be here,' Ben snapped at her in frustration. 'We're not open for three days. Then you'll need a ticket.'

The young woman got to her feet.

'I'm sorry if I've disturbed anyone,' she said. 'I'll go now.'

'Just a moment – !'

Ben called out as she turned to leave. The young woman stopped and glanced back at him.

'How long have you been here?'

'About fifteen minutes.' She frowned. 'May I ask why?'

'There's a group of pygmy dancers from Africa in the show,' Ben answered. 'One of them's a girl. She's disappeared from her room. We're looking for her. She could have come up here. I thought you might have seen her.'

The young woman was silent. Then she said, 'What does she look like?'

'She's about seventeen,' Ben replied. 'A leather skirt, dark hair, pale skin – more like an Arab than a black. She can't talk.'

'She can't talk – ?'

The young woman broke off. She stared at Ben. Her gaze was disconcertingly direct, and at the same time troubled. She shook her head.

'No, I'm afraid I can't help you. I've seen no one.'

She swung round again and left.

Ben gazed after her as the doors bumped backwards and forwards. Her accent was one he'd never heard before, and her story sounded more like a speech than a genuine explanation.

Ben tried to puzzle it out. He was interrupted by another furious bellow from below.

'Ben, is the little minx up there?'

Ben ran forward to the edge of the balcony and leaned over.

'No, Mr Farini,' he shouted back. 'There's no one here at all.'

'Then get down and start looking on the next level, for Christ's sake!'

'Yes, sir.'

Ben began to turn. He stopped. His head swung back and he gazed out over the mahogany rail.

He was no longer looking down to the confusion on the auditorium floor. He was staring directly across the top of the theatre below the roof dome. On the far side was a network of catwalks that crisscrossed the darkness high above the stage.

For an instant something had blazed out at him.

A light. A sparkling, multifaceted light that flared incandescently from white to gold and back to white again. Ben's immediate reaction was that it came from a hand-held lantern. A moment later he realized it was far too fierce and brilliant.

Mystified, Ben searched the shadows where the cat-walks hung.

The light had gone now, but its print still dazzled his eyeballs. Briefly he sensed rather than saw another gleam. This time it seemed to come from two tiny agate-coloured pinpricks in the blackness. He blinked and the glow vanished. Ben shook his head, bewildered.

It was impossible. There was nothing up there on the catwalks. Yet for a second he had been staring at what might almost have been a pair of animal's eyes.

— 46 —

'Lower that light! And get some paint on the side of the tower! For Christ's sake, move your butts, everyone! We're about to do the finale again – !'

The stage filled with scurrying figures. The man who had bellowed out the instructions, a tall, bearded figure in a black frock coat, glanced round impatiently.

'Where the hell's Ben?'

The man's gaze swept the theatre. His face was angular and hard, and his cold eyes penetrating.

High above him at the back of the dress circle Mary-Ellen instinctively shrank back in her seat. Then she realized it was much too dark for the man to see her. Cautiously she leant forward again.

'Here, Mr Farini.'

The young man with the withered arm limped forward.

'Unlock the little brutes and bring them up.' The man swung back to the stage. 'Chop, chop, everyone! We're about to try it with the pygmies.'

Mary-Ellen sat very still, staring down.

It was her second visit to the theatre. Yesterday she'd seen nothing. The young carpenter Ben, as she learned he was named, had found her and ordered her out within minutes of Mary-Ellen slipping in. Today she'd been luckier. She'd already spent three hours in the misty seats at the back of the dress circle without being discovered.

From there, hidden in the darkness, Mary-Ellen had watched the final rehearsals of what the posters that covered the walls of London called the 'greatest and most extraordinary production ever mounted at the Aquarium'.

She'd seen almost every act, but she hadn't yet seen the San.

Suddenly, shuffling along in a line, they appeared on stage. Mary-Ellen leant forward. She gripped the brass rail in front of her until her knuckles whitened.

At the back of the line was the girl she knew the San had named Kala.

It was five months since Mary-Ellen had left the mission post at Kuruman.

She had travelled over seven thousand miles. From Kuruman, old Piet Donaar had taken her in one of the waggons accompanying his cattle to the slaughter-yard at Mafeking. In Mafeking, Donaar passed her on to a friend of his, a Dutch-German trader who was trekking south next morning with another column of waggons to the Cape.

Until she reached Cape Town, Mary-Ellen had barely wasted a day. In Cape Town her luck changed. The evening before her arrival, the last boat to Britain for three weeks put out to sea. Mary-Ellen spent the next three weeks in a squalid rooming-house near the docks. Finally in late September she set sail on the passenger steamship the *Ambrosia*.

Four weeks later the *Ambrosia* docked in the Tilbury basin on the Thames just to the east of the City of London. A fellow passenger on the ship had recommended lodgings to Mary-Ellen. Mary-Ellen took a horse-drawn cab from the docks to the address. The lodgings were in a sidestreet in Bloomsbury close to the heart of the city.

'Yes?'

The buxom, stern-faced woman who answered the bell was a widow named Mrs Clopton. Mrs Clopton both owned and ran the house.

'I've just arrived from Cape Town on the *Ambrosia*,' Mary-Ellen said nervously – the woman's gaze was daunting. 'Your establishment was recommended to me by another passenger, a Miss Arthur. She said you might be able to provide me with a room.'

Mrs Clopton vaguely remembered Miss Arthur. If she was right, Miss Arthur had lodged with her several years ago. As far as Mrs Clopton could recollect, she had been polite and respectable.

'I cater to the best types of visitor,' Mrs Clopton said severely. 'The minimum stay is two weeks.'

'Two weeks to begin with would suit me well,' Mary-Ellen replied. 'It may, of course, be longer.'

Mrs Clopton inspected her.

The young woman was dressed in a suitably modest but rather faded travelling coat and skirt. She was tall and striking with long fair hair and bold, over-bold, Mrs Clopton thought, brown eyes. In all she was remarkably handsome, rather too handsome in Mrs Clopton's view. Men would probably consider her beautiful.

Mrs Clopton did not like that at all. On the other hand she had a recommendation and she spoke like a lady, at least a colonial lady. More important, it was early October and most of the rooms were unoccupied.

'I think I can manage to fit you in,' Mrs Clopton said.

Inwardly giving a sigh of relief, Mary-Ellen smiled.

Mrs Clopton took two weeks' rent in advance. Then she showed Mary-Ellen up to her room. It was small and plainly furnished, but quiet and with half a view across the British Museum gardens to the towers and spires beyond. As soon as Mrs Clopton went out, Mary-Ellen sat by the window.

She took a deep breath and closed her eyes. Then in the foggy gathering twilight she gazed out over London.

The journey had been the strangest and in many ways the most momentous event of her life. Until she left Kuruman, all Mary-Ellen had known was the tiny enclosed world of the lonely little mission post. In the five months that followed she had been exposed to jolting treks across the southern African landscape. To villages and towns and crowds. To the great bustling port of Cape Town, with its bewildering population of people and races from every corner of the earth. To the gleaming steamship which had carried her to Britain. To her first sight of the capital – capital of the greatest empire the world had known – and the cold, churning waters of the brown river which had carried the *Ambrosia* into its heart.

Mary-Ellen brushed her hair back from her face.

She shook her head and stared out of the window again. The gas lamps on the street below were haloed with fog. Beneath the lamps the people of London – children, thieves, prostitutes, merchants, businessmen, old ladies, tinkers and vendors – were hurrying home to hide themselves away from the falling chill of the dusk.

Mary-Ellen's eyes were keen and clear and thoughtful.

The journey – and for the daughter of a remote desert mission post, it had been an epic journey – had passed like a dream. She had seen it, she had felt and smelled and tasted it, she had undergone all its rigours and frustrations. But everything had floated over her. Inside herself Mary-Ellen was carried forward by one single driving obsession.

A slender young woman, as fugitive as the desert wind, with a golden sheen to her skin and dark unfathomable eyes. A girl about whom all Mary-Ellen knew was that the San had named her Kala.

A ghost who haunted not only Mary-Ellen's mind, but the landscape of her heart and her studies. The Kalahari.

The very word was an echo of Kala's name.

In the vast untidy tumult of the ant-heap that was Victorian London, a city then of three million people and growing every day in size, searing poverty and soaring wealth, Kala proved surprisingly easy to find.

Confronting the problem on the morning after her arrival in the lodging-house, Mary-Ellen had privately accepted that the search might last weeks or even months.

In fact it took a bare thirty minutes.

Mrs Clopton's 'better type' of London visitor included middle-class foreigners interested in the capital's sights, its monuments, and its more respectable entertainments. Among the last were London's theatres. Every shrewd manager in London took care to see that a broadsheet describing his new production was dropped through the letter-box of a thousand establishments like Mrs Clopton's.

Farini was no exception.

A few discreet enquiries to Mrs Clopton over breakfast – 'the girl was a family servant,' was Mary-Ellen's explanation, 'we think she may have been brought here to perform in the theatre' – and Mary-Ellen was taken to the noticeboard in the hall where the broadsheets were pinned up. In the list of forthcoming attractions at the Westminster Aquarium she read that someone named the Great Farini had great pride in presenting:

'The War Dances of the Black Pygmies from the Centre of the Earth!'

'For the Very First Time the Christian Inhabitants of the Civilized World will be able to witness the Terrifying Rituals in Rhythm and Incantation that these Tiny Savage Monsters perform after Torturing the Captives they have taken in their Murderous Wars!

'The Spectacle is Barbarous and Chilling to the Blood, but also Profoundly Educational and Uplifting to the Moral Spirit in the Epic Contrast it reveals between the God-Fearing and the Human Brutes of Nature! Warmly Recommended by Distinguished Churchmen as a Salutary Caution to Children (who will be permitted for matinee performances, if accompanied by their Farseeing Parents, at half the advertised price).'

'Disgusting what those creatures get up to,' was Mrs Clopton's comment as she read the broadsheet over Mary-Ellen's shoulder. 'I'm surprised your parents let them in the house, dear.'

'We turn them out at dusk and bolt the door,' Mary-Ellen replied.

Mrs Clopton nodded. 'Very prudent. I had a kitchen-maid here once. Black as the ace of spades, she was, if you caught her in a certain light. When a saltcellar went missing after dinner on a Tuesday, I knew exactly where to look –'

She turned away. 'Funnily enough it turned out to be one of the guests. But my instincts were right, if you know what I mean. I got rid of that girl right away just in case –'

Talking to herself, Mrs Clopton bustled off down the passage. Mary-Ellen went on studying the broadsheet.

Mr Farini's new spectacle, she saw, would have a Grand Opening the following week when: 'We would not be surprised if Certain Members of the Most Eminent Family in the Kingdom were present to Enjoy and be Amazed at the Entertainment in company with Their Subjects.' Meanwhile, the production was in the last stages of rehearsal.

Mary-Ellen wrinkled her forehead.

Until a few weeks ago she knew little about London and nothing about its theatres. But on the boat she had questioned her companion, the woman who had given her Mrs Clopton's address, closely about both. The woman proved to be something of an authority on the capital's entertainment.

In the confusion generated by rehearsals, Mary-Ellen was told, it was often possible to enter a theatre without payment and watch a performance before it was offered to the public. The woman had done it herself when she was younger. The secret was to present oneself with confidence at the doors and boldly march in as if one was involved in the production.

Mary-Ellen noted down the address of the Aquarium. She thought for a moment longer. Then she went outside. She hailed a hansom cab, and set off for the river.

A thin, chilling rain was falling. As the cab clattered southwards through the press of the morning traffic, Mary-Ellen leant forward and gazed down into the puddles on the roadway. In the reflection thrown back by the dirty water, she practised hardening her face into an expression of authority. It turned out to be as simple as the woman had said.

When Mary-Ellen alighted outside the Aquarium, a stream of people was running in and out through the doors. All of them, talking, arguing, or shouting at each other, seemed to be concerned only with their own preoccupations. Even the doormen, resplendent in top hats and braided uniforms, seemed to have lost interest in the proceedings.

Mary-Ellen took a deep breath.

Then, her head lowered and her heart pounding, she tacked herself on to a group of cleaning women and hurried up the steps behind them. Inside the foyer the women split up and headed away in different directions, calling out boisterously and bawdily to each other. Mary-Ellen hesitated for barely an instant. She glanced round. She saw a flight of stairs leading upwards. She ran towards them and began to climb.

Mary-Ellen came out on to a dimly lit curved landing. In front of her was a pair of swing doors. She pushed through them and found herself in the darkness of the dress circle. Sweating and panting, her heart beating even more quickly than before, Mary-Ellen lowered herself on to one of the seats.

She glanced down. In front of her and far below was a bright pool of light illuminating the stage. Even before she took in the stage, she registered the commanding presence of a man who could only have been Farini calling directions from the stalls.

That was yesterday. Moments later Ben had found her and she was out on the street again. Today, for the first time since Mary-Ellen had watched her being led away behind Gert Frouw's column at Kuruman, she saw Kala.

'Get them on stage fast!' Farini was shouting. 'This is the big finish. It needs speed. I don't want them limping up like zombies. They've been torturing their goddamn prisoners. Now they're going to kill them! Let's feel it out here!'

Another man, a coarse-faced man in a tweed jacket, ran forward with a steel rod in his hand. As Mary-Ellen gazed down in horror he began to beat the San across the shoulders. The man reached the end of the line and came to Kala. He jabbed her brutally in the ribs.

Kala winced and stumbled. Her mouth opened in a

silent cry of pain. Then Kala broke into the swift loping run she had used when she tried to escape in the desert.

Mary-Ellen gasped.

Before she saw what happened next, the doors clattered behind her and the dress circle was flooded with light. Mary-Ellen's head whirled round. Three men appeared with notebooks in their hands. Checking the seats, they moved towards Mary-Ellen. In a moment they would see her.

Mary-Ellen took a last frantic look at the stage.

Kala was sitting on a throne beside a fire with a golden crown on her head. Her eyes were vacant and terrified. Round her the San were tramping in circles, chanting rhythmically as they moved. No one, Mary-Ellen realized with a sudden piercing perception, could have understood what they were singing – no one apart from herself.

The little people were chanting the fable of the eland that escaped from the lion. It was the San nation's ancient and haunting song of freedom.

Mary-Ellen stood up.

On tiptoe she backed away from the advancing men, and edged silently out on to the landing. As she ran down the stairs her mind was in a turmoil of misery and confusion. What had happened to Kala and the Bushmen was worse, far worse, than anything she had ever imagined. The need to rescue them was urgent and desperate. It wasn't something she could do on her own.

Mary-Ellen had to have help. There was only one person in Britain who could help her, perhaps one person in the entire world.

The old man whose face had stared out at her from the greying frontispiece of his books.

— 47 —

Mary-Ellen tugged on the bell-pull.

From somewhere inside the house she heard a distant ringing. Outside on the doorstep it was bitterly cold. She pulled her cloak round her and waited, shivering.

The whole journey had been chill. She'd sat in an icy carriage on the train from London to Kent. At the station she had hired a cab driven by a taciturn driver. She paid him off and walked in the thin November air up the drive to the door.

The house was bigger and more austere than she'd imagined. Although it was midday, for some reason Mary-Ellen couldn't understand the curtains and blinds were still drawn in all the windows. Coupled with the sombre cawing of the rooks from the winter-bare trees and the leaden grey sky, it made the place look melancholy and forbidding.

Mary-Ellen stamped her feet and rubbed her hands together.

'Yes, miss?'

The door opened a crack. The small, wary face of a maid appeared against the background of a darkened hall.

Mary-Ellen started. 'I'm looking for Dr Darwin,' she said. 'I don't have an appointment, but it's a matter of some urgency. I hope if I give you my name, he will agree to see me.'

The maid frowned. 'How did ye pass the gates?'

'The gates were open. I walked through.'

'They should have been locked.' The maid paused. 'The Doctor died last week, miss. The house is all closed up.'

'Died?'

Mary-Ellen stared at her dumbfounded.

'Aye.' The maid gestured at the drawn blinds. 'Dr Darwin passed on last Friday. He was buried Monday, God bless him. Mrs Darwin is away to stay with her niece. There's nae one here but me.'

Mary-Ellen stood for a moment longer. Then she stammered an apology and turned away. Behind her the door closed and the bolts clattered home.

Still in shock Mary-Ellen walked back down the drive. It was the one possibility that had never occurred to her.

For five years Darwin had stood unseen but all-powerful at the centre of her life. Across the vast distance that separated the Kent mansion from the isolated mission post at Kuruman, the old man had encouraged her, advised her, supported and sustained her. Now at last when she was on the point of meeting him face to face, when she needed him more than she had ever needed him, the inconceivable had happened.

Tears filled Mary-Ellen's eyes and ran down her cheeks. She was still walking along almost blindly when she realized someone was approaching her. She blinked and peered ahead. The figure was a tall, stern-faced woman of about sixty, dressed in mourning black.

The woman stopped in front of her.

'May I ask what you are doing here, young lady?' the woman asked.

Her voice was cold and forbidding. Mary-Ellen wiped her face with her handkerchief. She swallowed nervously.

'I'm extremely sorry,' Mary-Ellen said. 'I came here hoping to see Dr Darwin. I was quite unaware of last week's tragic occurrence until the maid told me a moment ago.'

'But surely you had no appointment in any event?'

Mary-Ellen shook her head. 'I fear not. I simply hoped the Doctor would see me.'

'Young lady, Dr Darwin *never* saw anyone without an appointment. In fact, he rarely saw visitors at all. I know because I was privileged to have charge of his diary –'

The woman paused. When she spoke again her voice was even colder.

'I suggest in future you make the normal prior arrangements to visit anyone. In Dr Darwin's case that is now irrelevant. But by taking a little elementary consideration you could avoid unnecessary travel for yourself, and disturbance for others in a time of sadness.'

Mary-Ellen nodded miserably. 'I can only repeat my apologies. I will of course leave.'

Mary-Ellen hurried on down the drive beneath the wheeling, cawing rooks. The woman watched her go.

The woman was Darwin's redoubtable secretary, Miss Stanwick, the 'dragon', as Darwin called her, who guarded his lair. Gazing at Mary-Ellen's back as she hurried away, Miss Stanwick remembered the girl had been weeping. There was something else. The girl's accent. The girl spoke fluent, educated English, but her accent was alien.

Miss Stanwick knew that accent. She had heard it in the voices of several distinguished men who had visited Darwin over the twenty-five years she had served him. It was the accent of Africa.

'Wait a moment –'

Mary-Ellen turned at the call that rang out behind her. Uncertainly she walked back.

'Are you by any chance Miss Mary-Ellen Ramsay?'

'Yes,' Mary-Ellen replied hesitantly.

'Miss Ramsay from Kuruman, if I recollect the name correctly?'

'Yes.'

Miss Stanwick examined her in silence for several moments. Then her features relaxed, and a brief smile crossed her daunting face.

'Dr Darwin was a law unto himself,' she said. 'His heart and spirit were often, in my view, over-generous. I did not always approve of where they led him. It was my duty to protect him. But he was a great man and he had a considerable affection for you. Indeed, he made provision for you. Please come inside for a moment.'

Miss Stanwick turned. Bewildered, Mary-Ellen followed her back towards the house.

'The will was read two days ago on Wednesday,' Miss Stanwick said. 'It remains to be proved. However, as an executor with considerable knowledge of the Doctor's affairs, I know there is ample in the estate for the legacy to be discharged –'

She handed Mary-Ellen a piece of paper.

'It will save the estate the postage to Africa,' Miss Stanwick added with another quick smile.

Mary-Ellen took the piece of paper. It was banker's draft for one hundred guineas. Mary-Ellen looked up astonished.

They were standing in Darwin's library, surrounded by the glass-framed mahogany cases that contained his books. The blinds were still drawn but the maid had lit the fire and brought in candles.

'Thank you,' Mary-Ellen said inadequately. 'It is extraordinarily generous.'

'The thanks are due not to me but the Doctor,' Miss Stanwick replied. 'He was generous to many, not always advisedly. In your case I am sure the generosity was merited. Now, if you will excuse me, I have many of his affairs to attend to.'

'Yes, of course.'

Mary-Ellen followed Miss Stanwick out of the library and through the cavernous hall. They reached the front door. Miss Stanwick held it open for her.

'Well, I think that concludes the matter,' Miss Stanwick said. 'You have the draft. In due course the bank's acknowledgement of payment will act as a receipt. I trust the funds will further your enjoyment of your visit to Britain. Good day, Miss Ramsay.'

She held out her hand. Mary-Ellen shook it and turned to go.

Then, as Mary-Ellen stepped down on to the drive, Miss Stanwick added, 'I imagine you received the Doctor's last package to you?'

Mary-Ellen glanced back. 'I have never had a package from Dr Darwin,' she said. 'Only letters. The last of those arrived almost a year ago.'

'Not the package with the notebooks and the map?' Miss Stanwick frowned. 'You should have had it for several months. I had the contents copied and sent you the originals. I always kept a record of what the Doctor dispatched in case he needed to refer to it again. I remember having to engage a cartographer for the map –'

Miss Stanwick clicked her teeth in vexation. The unreliability of the mails offended her passionate sense of efficiency.

She shook her head and added, 'Never mind. No doubt it will be waiting for you at Kuruman on your return.'

Miss Stanwick disappeared inside. The door began to close. The latch was about to click shut when Mary-Ellen suddenly called out.

'Excuse me –! '

The door opened again. Miss Stanwick's head re-appeared.

'If you had the map and the notebooks copied,' Mary-Ellen said, 'are the copies still here?'

'Of course. The Doctor's files are in excellent order.'

'I'm not going back to Kuruman,' Mary-Ellen went on, 'but that package could be very important – to what Dr Darwin asked me to do. Would it be possible for me to see what it contains?'

Miss Stanwick studied her again.

Miss Stanwick saw a young woman of almost her own imposing height. The young woman had long fair hair. Her face was still pale and her full lips quivered as she tried to control their trembling.

It was her bold, demanding eyes that held Miss Stanwick's attention. Still sheened with tears, they stared at the older woman steadily, almost implacably.

Since the arrival of Mary-Ellen's letters in Darwin's mailbags, Miss Stanwick had mentally referred to the unknown young woman in remote Kuruman as the

African monkey girl. Miss Stanwick knew nothing about Africa and less about monkeys. What she did know was that she loved the Doctor more than anything in the world. Somehow the monkey girl was more important to Darwin not only than his secretary but than any of his other 'indulgences', as Miss Stanwick called them.

Confronting the girl's gaze, Miss Stanwick knew why. Darwin had had the eyes of a man who would change the world.

The girl's eyes were the same.

'There is little point in simply looking at them,' Miss Stanwick said. 'No one here will have need of them again. You may take them with you.'

An hour later on the train back to London, Mary-Ellen opened the large envelope Miss Stanwick had given her.

She began to read.

— 48 —

'I trust by now you will have received my recent letter,' Darwin had written.

'You will recall I suggested a change in the direction of your studies from the baboon packs to your human companions of the desert, the San hunter-gatherers. Indeed you are no doubt already at work on the endeavour. In this connection, or rather I should perhaps say a closely related connection, a most interesting event has occurred. I doubt I need remind you of a certain Mr Oswell, the gentleman who in a sense introduced you to me –'

Mary-Ellen froze.

She had heard nothing of Oswell since his departure from Kuruman almost four years ago, but his name and his presence would haunt her to the grave. For an instant she closed her eyes as the memory of what had happened by the Kuruman river came flooding back.

As if in a dream she saw herself lying on the grass and Oswell, smiling, hunched over his sketchbook on the bank above her. She saw him leaving the wrapped painting at the mission house door in the grey Kalahari dawn before he rode away. She saw her father's face, reddened and engorged with outrage, as he thrust her head down to look at it. She felt the lash of his belt on her back.

Mary-Ellen shuddered. She felt sick. Somehow she forced herself to read on.

'Recently a gentleman wrote and requested to visit me to discuss certain matters pertaining to Africa. By way of introduction he mentioned Mr Oswell's name. Normally my guardian dragon, the admirable Miss Stanwick, bars all visitors. Happily I remembered Oswell in connection with you. I prevailed on Miss Stanwick to make an appointment for him. He arrived and presented himself as a Mr Hearns. We passed on to his business. Here, I trust I will neither surprise nor distress you. First, he informed me that Oswell had been ambushed and killed by savages shortly after leaving Kuruman –'

For the second time in a few moments Mary-Ellen stiffened. She sat for several moments in shock.

Then she trembled as an overwhelming surge of relief mingled with guilt swept over her body. Oswell had died within days of leaving the mission. For Mary-Ellen, another dark, oppressive shadow lingering from the past had been lifted too. She had lived in dread of one day meeting Oswell again, of being forced to confront once more the nightmare of that afternoon.

Now it would never happen. However long the disgust and the pain remained, they would remain with her alone.

Mary-Ellen turned the page and read further.

'Second, I was informed that Oswell had died owing Hearns – an engaging and colourful individual but not, I venture, a pillar of conventional society – a considerable sum of money. The two were, he told me, fellow officers in our nation's army. Oswell, it seems, was one of nature's wanderers. During his African travels, he acquired ranching rights in the newly settled cattle lands of the western Kalahari. He pledged those rights as collateral for his borrowing from his friend. On belatedly learning of Oswell's death – news from the dark continent is tardy in its arrival – Hearns set out to reclaim the security.

'He had scant success. The documents lodged with him by Oswell were disavowed by the local land registry office – a dignified term for a grass-roofed rondavel on the desert's edge. Hearns sensed, as he said, he was the victim of a fraud. (If I may be permitted a personal and perhaps uncharitable observation, I feel he and Oswell were well matched.) Nonetheless he pressed on. Interested in the possibilities of the virgin grasslands, he entered the even richer pastures of the watery region discovered by Dr Livingstone and known as the Okovango delta.

'Soon a lack of supplies forced him to retire. Before retreating he encountered a group of river-dwelling San. Living with the "little people" were two men of a clearly different race. Handsome and lean, in Hearns' words, Levantine-skinned and featured, and speaking their own tongue, they were midway in height between the San and the average European –'

Increasingly absorbed, Mary-Ellen turned the page.

'The two, who had taken San wives, were wary of him. He observed them on the evening of his arrival and even managed to do some trade with them. They were, to Hearns' astonishment, in possession of cut diamonds. Hearns bargained all his remaining trade goods for a number of the stones. The following morning he rose early in the hope of pursuing the business, but they, their wives and their children had disappeared. Hearns did not see them again.

'Hearns has since ventured twice more into the delta in the hope of encountering them again. He has had no success. Further, on his last trip he was gravely afflicted with fever. He subsequently retired to a sugar plantation in Natal which, he told me, he acquired with the very considerable proceeds that accrued to him from the sale of the diamonds. However, like his friend Oswell, Hearns gratifyingly remains something of a student of my views – or so he claimed. He was sufficiently intrigued by his experience to bring it to my attention. Hearns suggested the two "strangers" among the San might represent an intermediate and hitherto unknown step on the ladder of our evolution. It is a seductive notion, and I confess I found him a plausible and seductive visitor. At which point all of my scientific antennae rise and bristle in protest!

'If I may allow myself the familiarity of a personal

counsel, Miss Ramsay, beware of intellectual seduction above all other. The warning is delivered! And having delivered it, I shall proceed to ignore it. Hearns' theory is pure fanciful speculation. I have little doubt he approached me not so much in a spirit of scientific enquiry, as in the hope that I would lend my influence towards sponsoring an expedition into the delta in search of further diamonds – a search Hearns' health and the current political climate in the region prevent him from undertaking on his own. On the other hand, I do not doubt the accuracy of his observation.

'Somewhere in the lagoons that fringe the north-western Kalahari are two men of Caucasian build and countenance. If there are two, the elementary principles of breeding dynamics tell us there must be more and of both sexes.

'How and why did they get there?

'We do not know – and as scientists we should. Let us then find out. We shall do so only by achieving what Hearns failed to achieve. We must trace these men and their companions, the San. We must discover the men's origins and their forebears. We must dig into their past. We must know –!'

Mary-Ellen came to the foot of the letter's last sheet. Fascinated, she turned the page and read Darwin's concluding words.

'I use the term "we",' Darwin wrote. 'In the context I refer, of course, to you alone. I am not familiar with Africa. Even so I am aware of the hazards and travails such a journey will involve. Yet I am convinced it must be undertaken, for the answers must be found. I am equally convinced that you, young lady, are uniquely qualified and placed to undertake it –'

'I remain your obedient and admiring servant, Charles Darwin.'

Enclosed with the letter was a map on which Hearns had marked the course of his journey into what Dr Livingstone had called the 'watery region' of the northern Kalahari.

Mary-Ellen put the letter down in her lap. She stared through the carriage window. Outside, darkness had fallen. As the train roared through the winter evening, she glimpsed the occasional cluster of lights in one of the little Kentish villages. She barely noticed them. She was hardly even aware of the other passengers in the compartment.

Mary-Ellen was dumbfounded.

'Handsome . . . Levantine-skinned and featured . . . midway in height between the San and the average European . . . Caucasian build and countenance . . .' Dr Darwin had been quoting Hearns' description. Darwin was writing of the men. The women would echo them. They would be slender and pale-skinned too. They would also be taller than the San. And if the men were handsome, the women would be beautiful.

The women would be like Kala. The women would *be* Kala.

Mary-Ellen shook her head slowly, disbelievingly. From beyond the grave, it seemed, Dr Darwin was still directing her life. She had been determined, she had been obsessed with taking the San and Kala home. She knew where the San belonged. That was simple. They belonged in the desert. Kala was different. Mute and wild with her burning, unfathomable eyes, she was an enigma. The diamonds meant nothing to Mary-Ellen. They were irrelevant. What Mary-Ellen knew now was where Kala came from.

Livingstone's 'watery region' was the Okovango delta.

That was where Kala belonged. That was where Mary-Ellen had to take her. There in her own home among her own people – and they could only be her own people – Kala might recover the power to speak. Only there might the barriers of catatonic silence that walled in her secrets be broken down.

First Kala had to be freed. To do that, Mary-Ellen needed assistance. Darwin had done everything else but even he couldn't help Mary-Ellen with that now.

It had to be someone else.

— 49 —

Kala crawled slowly round the floor of her room, exploring the walls with her fingers.

She had done the same many times before. The five San were housed in two other rooms that led off the same subterranean passage beneath the stage. Occasionally as Kala moved she could hear them talking among themselves, or tapping on the wall that separated them to communicate with each other.

Like their rooms, Kala's had no windows. It was always dark and almost airless. The only ventilation came from a barred grille in the locked door. The darkness didn't bother her. There had been no light in the dens of the Merula Pan hyenas.

When she started to hunt with the hyenas, Kala had learned to see in the dark as well as she could by day. The light of a single star was enough for Kala to follow them. On the rare occasions there were no stars, Kala used her hands to feel her way through the bush. Her fingers had become almost as sensitive as her eyes.

She came to the end of the fourth wall and stopped.

There was nothing, not the slightest chink between the bricks that might give her something to work on. Until three days ago it had been different. There had been more than a chink. There had been a gap between the top of the wall and the upper floor joists wide enough for Kala to wriggle through.

She had used it when the diamond started throbbing at her waist. She had climbed out of her room and up on to the narrow platforms above the stage to search for the young woman whose face she had glimpsed in the stone's watery, shifting facets. The woman had escaped her and Kala had fallen asleep on the catwalk.

Kala had eventually been found there. She was taken down and her room was searched. The hole between the wall and the joists was boarded up, and the door was locked again. Now she was trapped.

Kala squatted on her haunches.

If the darkness of the room didn't bother her, its airlessness did. She was used to the vastness of the Kalahari sky and its constantly changing scent-laden breezes. Even in the hyena den as she grew up, she had been able to crawl to the entrance and sniff the air of the pan as her mother, Herut, did restlessly and constantly.

Kala rose and walked to the grille. She put her nose between the iron bars and inhaled.

The stench that came to her was harsh and filthy. Kala coughed and almost vomited. She tried to spit the foul sulphurous odours out of her mouth. Then she sank to her heels in the darkness again.

Kala shivered. She hated the stench of the theatre and she hated its stale metallic air. There was something she hated and feared even more. The cold. She had known cold in the Kalahari. There it was crisp and strong and clean. It showed itself in the brilliance of the winter sky, the crystals on the dawn grass, the plumes of steam that rose from the nostrils of the galloping gemsbok.

When morning came and the sun rose, it was gone.

Here the cold was sour and rancid. It puckered skin and gnawed at bones like a chill cancer. No morning sun came to drive it away. Like the choking London fog, it was ever-present – a grey and icy herald of death.

Kala could do nothing about the stench and the fetid air. There was something she could do about the cold. She reached down between her legs and pulled out the diamond. She held it in her palms, warming not just her hands but her entire body in the radiance that blazed out from it. As she warmed herself, Kala stared into the stone's depths.

As she stared, Kala stiffened.

Once before, in the hold of the ship on the voyage from Africa, the diamond had seemed to resound with noises. The noises became a clamour of voices. The voices meant nothing to Kala because the words they used meant nothing. The stone was ringing again now. Not with words but with sounds she did understand – the call of a singing voice and the tap of a mallet.

There was something more. A face. The face of a young woman. The same face that had led Kala up on to the catwalk. Then it had been blurred and indistinct. Now it was clear. For an instant Kala saw a strong, bold jaw, penetrating brown eyes, and a tumbling wave of golden hair. It was the face, Kala knew, that she had sought for and missed as she lay on the catwalk.

The face that had been covered in blood.

Something stirred in the remote caverns of Kala's mind. There were walls and towers. There was a city like the city she danced before on the stage of the theatre. There were people and carpenters and singers – one, in particular, whose song clung elusively to the corners of her memory. Kala tried to draw them all to her, but suddenly they were gone.

The face and the song, the towers and the tapping mallet had vanished.

Kala put the diamond away. She rubbed her eyes wearily with the backs of her hands. It had been a strange and bewildering evening. For some reason for the first time the whole building was filled with people. It seemed to Kala there were thousands of them. She had felt the heat of their bodies like a physical assault when she was driven up on to the stage.

After she and the San danced, the people roared and shouted in dizzying waves of sound. Even when she had been taken below again, the clamour rang on like distant thunder for minute after minute. The experience had frightened and exhausted her.

Like an animal, Kala coiled herself up on the straw mattress. As she fell asleep she was dimly aware of distant footsteps somewhere above her.

— 50 —

The hansom cab came to a halt with a clatter of hoofs. Farini jumped out and pressed a coin into the driver's hand.

'Keep the change,' he said.

The driver glanced down. His eyes widened. The coin was a gold sovereign.

'Thank you, sir. God bless you!'

Farini waved expansively and the cab clattered away into the fog-laden darkness. Farini turned and looked up at the theatre.

It was after three o'clock in the morning but all the lamps on the façade were still burning. At Farini's instructions they were to stay on all night. Great streamers of grey mist swirled across the front of the Aquarium, dimming their glow, but even from the street he could see the huge lettering of his name on the posters beside the doors.

In a few hours the morning papers would be out with their reviews. He had little doubt what the verdict would be. By midday he'd have selected comments pasted over the boards. Well before then the word of mouth would have people lining up at the box office.

Farini smiled. With a cigar in one hand and two bottles of champagne in the other, he ran up the steps and hammered on the doors. A few moments later a face appeared behind the glass and peered out sleepily.

'Good Lord, it's you, sir –'

There was a hurried rattle. The bolts shot back and Marley, the night doorman, appeared.

'I'm so sorry, Mr Farini. I weren't expecting you back, not at this hour.'

'That's all right, Jack.' Farini stepped inside. 'I just wanted a look round before I went to bed.'

'What a night, sir!' Marley added. 'I've been here twenty years, but I've never seen anything like that. We had the Prince of Wales himself and that Mrs Langtry, too.'

'I know, Jack. I had the honour of welcoming them myself. Here,' he handed Marley one of the bottles of champagne, 'you missed out on the party, so celebrate right here.'

'Thank you, Mr Farini.'

'You can lock up again now. I'll let myself out through the stage door.'

Farini crossed the foyer and entered the auditorium.

The main lights had been extinguished, but the small side lamps were still burning all round the theatre and along the front of the stage. Farini walked midway down the sloping ramp of the stalls. He uncorked the champagne and drank from the bottle's neck. Then he sprawled down on one of the seats.

The evening had been more than a triumph. It had been a sensation. All of London society had been there. The first carriages started arriving two hours before the performance began, and the streets of Westminster were still jammed at midnight. When the Prince of Wales appeared with his mistress, the Jersey lily, Mrs Langtry, on his arm, the cheers of the waiting crowds could be heard as far away as Piccadilly.

Nothing that night could go wrong.

Act had followed act without a single mistimed cue, and each more rapturously received than the last. But it was the finale which provided the greatest triumph. Farini had gambled everything on the African pygmies. They had not let him down.

All evening the lost city had shimmered as a misty backdrop to the stage. Then the theatre lights dimmed and it was bathed in brilliant illumination. No longer a wavering artifice of gauze and paint, it suddenly sprang to life as an ancient pagan fortress, grim and menacing and bloodstained. When the drums started to beat and the tiny naked savages leapt out from the wings, their skin shining golden and their knives flashing, the entire audience rose to its feet.

London had never before seen anything like it.

In an instant the watchers were transported from the grey and icy capital to the unknown pulsing heart of Africa, to the pitiless fire and heat of the dark continent. Spellbound, the audience watched in silence as the Bushmen performed the dances Farini had choreographed for them.

The applause that followed was unlike anything Farini had ever heard. It rang on for minute after minute, so loud that the chandeliers suspended high from the roof vibrated.

'Remarkable, my good sir, quite remarkable!'

The Prince of Wales was the first to congratulate him. A group of courtiers had cleared a way through the throng and there he was in front of Farini, tubby and watery-eyed, his beard nicotine-stained and his nose a drinker's scarlet.

Farini inclined his head. 'Thank you, your Royal Highness. It has been a privilege to have you present.'

'Where did you find those extraordinary little fellows?'

'The deserts of Africa, sir. It was a difficult and hazardous undertaking carried out entirely under my own direction –'

Behind the Prince's shoulder Farini was aware of a handsome young woman with bold humorous eyes. She was gazing at him levelly, a small quizzical smile plucking at her mouth.

'With, of course, a little local help,' Farini added.

'Remarkable,' the Prince muttered. 'Don't you agree, Mrs Langtry?'

'Quite remarkable,' Mrs Langtry replied.

The royal party moved away.

Soon afterwards Farini took a carriage along the river to the Savoy Hotel. He had booked the largest banqueting room, and had orderd champagne and an orchestra.

The celebration party was still going on when Farini slipped away. He had barely slept for five nights and even Farini's energy was beginning to slacken. But before he went to bed he wanted to visit the scene of his triumph again.

Farini got to his feet. He walked forward to the orchestra pit and climbed up to the stage. The set of the lost city towered above him. He tapped one of the pillars that supported the city's battlements, and smiled. Then he strolled across the stage and out through the wings.

A moment later, Farini paused.

Ahead of him was the corridor running to the back of the theatre and the stage door. To his right was a flight of steps leading down to the dressing rooms. To his left was another flight of steps. They led down to the rooms that housed the San.

Farini set off down the left-hand stairs.

An idea had suddenly struck him as he stood, wavering slightly now, in the wings. He'd had everything that night. Success, the adulation of the audience, toasts in champagne, money that would keep pouring into the box office for weeks. Everything – except the one pleasure he always allowed himself. A woman.

After a triumph, to Farini a woman was more than an indulgence. It was a necessity.

There were three keys hanging up at the foot of the stairs. Each unlocked one of the three small and windowless rooms where the savages were kept. Two of the rooms housed the men. Kala had been allocated a room of her own. As soon as he saw her, Farini knew Kala was destined to be the star of the show. He didn't want to risk her being damaged by her companions.

Farini took down the key to Kala's room. Outside her door he paused again.

For some reason he'd never had a coon, although many of his Coney Island colleagues used to trumpet their virtues. They were firm and tight and they'd do anything you wanted. This one didn't look like a real coon. She had mulatto skin and strange wild eyes. But she might be better still – she was the original African product, straight out of the jungle.

Grinning as he felt himself harden, Farini turned the key.

Kala was lying asleep on the floor. At the sound of the key in the lock she woke as quickly as she had done as an infant when the Merula Pan pack returned from the hunt. By the time the door swung open, she was on her feet. Kala's eyes adjusted instantly to the faint light spilling in from the passage.

She saw Farini's face. She tensed.

Kala had no concept of love or hatred. Only of allegiance and submission to those who nourished and looked after her, and fear and aggression toward those who threatened her. But if she had been able to hate, she would have hated this man. She had learned that in the month she had been exposed to him. He was even more dangerous than the bearded white man who'd caught and chained her.

That one had been a hunter. A perverted hunter, but at least a predator Kala could recognize. This one was a brutal and unfathomable threat.

He advanced into the room. He had a weapon, a bottle, in one hand, like the sticks the baboons carried. With his other hand he was unbuckling the belt round his waist. On his face was an expression of greed. Greed not for food but for something else – something terrifying.

Kala backed away into the corner. She half-crouched and bared her teeth in a snarl of warning.

As he approached her, Farini saw only a slim young woman with olive skin and long dark hair. She was naked to the waist and her small bare breasts were tilted up provocatively. Round her thighs she wore a short leather skirt. She was a savage and she was behaving like a savage – squatting and spitting at him.

Farini grinned. It was just what he had expected and it made her even more appetizing. He stepped out of his trousers and bent down to rip her skirt away.

What happened next astounded Farini.

One instant the girl was crouching in the corner. The next she had leapt at him like a leopard. Her clawed hands raked his face and her teeth gouged at his neck. Farini fell back, bellowing in surprise and pain. They tumbled across the floor. Then the girl was on top of him again and her teeth were tearing at his shoulders.

Farini howled.

As he desperately tried to find some way to pull the little monster off him, his hand scrabbled down her back and touched a belt. Farini gripped it and heaved. At the same moment he managed to squirm on to one side. He lifted the elbow of his other arm, and drove it into the side of the girl's face.

Farini weighed almost twice as much as Kala. He was also immensely strong. As his elbow slammed into Kala's jaw, she collapsed unconscious over him. Farini hurled her aside and struggled up. With his other hand he was still gripping her belt. As he rose, the belt broke.

Farini tossed the two pieces of leather away and stood above her. He was panting and shaking, and blood was pouring from a dozen gashes on his face, his arms and his shoulders. Kala was lying slumped face down at his feet. In a frenzy of anger Farini drew back his foot to kick her.

With his foot in midair, he checked.

Farini's eye had been caught by something else. Something that even in the dim half-light of the squalid little room shone with a glittering, incandescent brilliance. The object was resting against the far wall. It must have been concealed in the little savage's belt and had rolled there when the belt broke.

Farini stepped over the girl's body. He walked over and picked the object up. In total disbelief he stared at it as it lay in the palm of his hand.

It was a diamond – the largest diamond Farini had ever seen.

— 51 —

Mary-Ellen stamped her feet.

The skin on her face felt raw and cracked. Her lips were blue, and her fingers seemed to rattle in her gloves like little sticks of ice. It was even colder than when she'd stood on the doorstep of Dr Darwin's house twenty-four hours earlier. Nothing in her past, nothing she'd ever read, had prepared her for the bitter, all-pervading chill of a London winter.

She blinked and glanced round.

Mary-Ellen was standing on the far side of the street from the Aquarium. To her left beyond Parliament Square, the House of Commons and the tower of Big Ben loomed out of the fog like the silhouette of a haunted castle. In front of her a man was pasting posters on the theatre's billboards, announcing the triumphant success of the production which had opened the night before.

To her right, the one glow of warmth in the greyness, was a chestnut-vendor's brazier. Mary-Ellen hurried over and bought a twist of hot chestnuts. She ate them close to the flames that flickered up from the bed of charcoal. Every few moments she glanced through the fog at the theatre's doors.

Mary-Ellen was lucky.

She had been prepared to wait all day if necessary, but she had been there less than ten minutes when she spotted the young carpenter, Ben. He came out and paused on the theatre steps, shivering and rubbing his hands. Then he also spotted the brazier. He made his way limping through the stream of carriages, and stopped beside her.

'Excuse me –'

Ben had bought a twist of chestnuts. He was about to run back to the theatre when Mary-Ellen caught hold of his arm. He glanced round surprised.

'Can I speak to you for a moment?' Mary-Ellen added.

Ben looked at her. There was something familiar about the tall young woman with the fair hair and brown eyes, half-hidden now by the hood of her cape. Ben frowned. Then he remembered.

'Weren't you in the theatre a few nights ago?' he asked.

Mary-Ellen nodded. 'I would like to talk to you. It's very important. There's a tavern over there. I could buy you a hot chocolate or a glass of ale. I only ask that you listen to me.'

Her face was pale and strained. No one, Ben thought, had ever looked at him so tensely and anxiously. Ben glanced down at the wax paper cone he was holding. He shrugged.

A few minutes later they were seated opposite each other in the private saloon of the Star and Garter tavern on the corner of Parliament Square.

Mary-Ellen gazed at Ben across the table. Before, she had only glimpsed the lop-sided silhouette of a sturdy young man in the darkness of the theatre or through the swirling fog outside. His misshapen body was of no consequence to her.

She wanted to see his face.

For the first time she could see it clearly. Mary-Ellen needed only an instant to make up her mind. The carpenter's face was broad and strong-jawed with sallow skin and grey eyes beneath dark rumpled hair. Mary-Ellen had assessed many animals by their eyes. Ben's eyes, like the wary eyes of the baboon pack patriarchs, were fierce and intelligent.

She had acted on instinct. So far her instinct was right.

'I need your help,' Mary-Ellen said bluntly. 'I want to rescue the San.'

'The San?' Ben looked puzzled.

'I'm sorry,' Mary-Ellen shook her head, 'I mean the little people in Mr Farini's show. You probably know them as the pygmies. Their real name is San. They were taken from the Kalahari desert in southern Africa. I've come to London to take them back there –'

As Ben listened, Mary-Ellen told the story of how the San had been captured.

'They should never be here,' Mary-Ellen said. 'It is worse than inhuman, worse than barbaric. It is sadism. They are people and they have been made into dancing toys. They will shrivel and die in the cold. Even before that their spirit and nature will be broken. I want to take them back to where they belong. Most of all I want to save the girl, Kala.'

Mary-Ellen stopped.

There was a mirror above the table. It reflected the square outside. Ben stared at it, watching the swathes of mist coiling round the gas lamps and the light flaring off the brass plates on the carriage horses.

The young woman had told him her name was Mary-Ellen. Ben had assumed she wanted tickets to the production, tickets which were almost unobtainable since the morning newspapers headlined the first night's triumph. Only the urgency in her voice, and the realization that she was the stranger in the dress circle, had made him come with her to the tavern.

Mary-Ellen didn't want tickets. She wanted to steal the stars of Farini's show and take them back with her to Africa.

Ben shook his head, bemused. For a moment he gazed at her disbelievingly.

'I don't think you understand,' Ben said. 'Farini paid a fortune for those Africans. Under law they're almost his property now. Without them the show collapses. If they disappear, he'll call in the police. He'll raise a hue and cry all over London. You'll go to prison.'

'The San aren't anyone's property,' Mary-Ellen answered quietly. 'They're people, not cattle or slaves. I don't mind going to prison, but I won't. There's a boat that sails early tomorrow. If I can get them out tonight, no one will know they've gone until the morning. By the time Farini starts searching we'll all be at sea. Anyway, it's a risk I'm prepared to take.'

'*You're* prepared to take?' Ben gave a quick, harsh laugh. 'What about me?'

'You don't have to take any risk,' Mary-Ellen said. 'All I want is to know how I can get into the theatre, where the little people are kept, and how I can get them out. I don't need anything else –'

She paused. 'Don't you care about what's being done to them?'

Ben looked at her again.

Her face was set in an expression of implacable determination. She was mad, Ben thought, mad and dangerous.

Ben leant forward.

'Listen,' he said. 'I don't like the way the little people are being treated any more than you do. I've done my best to make it better. But at least while they're here they're achieving something. They're being paid. The money's going back to Africa for their families –'

'Who told you that?' Mary-Ellen interrupted.

'Farini,' Ben replied. 'He showed me the contract that brought them here.'

'Who signed the contract?' she demanded.

Ben frowned as he searched his mind for the name Farini had mentioned. Then he remembered.

'A Reverend Ramsay,' he answered.

Mary-Ellen was silent. Then she smiled at him. It was a curiously bitter smile.

'Mr Ramsay is my father,' she said. 'Except he is not my father and the money will not go to the San. It will go to the mission.'

Mary-Ellen told him the rest of the story behind the San's capture.

In astonishment Ben listened again. When she finished he rubbed his face.

It was an extraordinary story, but it didn't make any difference. It was impossible to release the San from the theatre – to smuggle them across London and put them on a ship for Africa. There were endless barriers in the way. The San's locked rooms. The porters at the theatre's front and back. The unpredictability of the ships' departures. The army of police who would inevitably be called in as soon as the little people's disappearance was known.

It had been impossible at the start. It was impossible now. Nothing had changed. She was still mad and still dangerous.

'I'm sorry,' Ben said curtly.

He stood up to leave. As he began to move round the table, Ben paused. He glanced down at her.

Ben didn't know why he hesitated. Perhaps it was the revelation that Mary-Ellen, like him, was a bastard, and that whatever separated them, they had at least that in common. Perhaps it was Kala, the elusive and enigmatic presence who had increasingly come to haunt him. Whatever the reason, he felt a sudden compulsive need to explain.

He bent over the table. Angrily, he caught Mary-Ellen's wrist.

'Look,' Ben said. 'I don't want to save anyone. I'm just a carpenter and a painter. All my life I've wanted to come to London. I wanted to set myself up and work in the theatres here. For eight years I saved up so I could do it. Because I was a fool, I lost everything. But I came anyway and a month ago I got myself a job. It's not what I dreamed of, but it's in the theatre. I'm not going to throw it away and very likely end up in prison too, even if you don't. Understand?'

'So you won't help me?'

'I'll look after Kala and the others as best I can,' Ben said. 'I won't mention this to anyone. But, no, I won't have any part of it.'

He released Mary-Ellen's wrist and began to walk away.

'Wait!'

The call rang out sharply behind him. Startled, Ben checked and glanced back. Mary-Ellen had drawn her cape round her shoulders. Her cheeks were even paler, but if anything her expression was more obdurate than before. She was looking at him with bitter, accusing eyes.

'How much did you lose?' Mary-Ellen asked.

Ben frowned. 'What do you mean?'

'You said you'd saved up the money you needed. The money to set yourself up to work in the theatre. Then you lost it. How much was it?'

'Fifty pounds,' he replied almost without thinking.

Mary-Ellen reached below the table. She produced a leather bag and opened it. She pulled out a thick manilla envelope. She extracted two pieces of engraved and wax-stamped paper. She held one out towards him.

'This is a banker's draft for exactly that amount,' Mary-Ellen said. 'It is yours for you to do with as you wish. All I ask in return is not even your physical help or assistance. Simply your advice and guidance – which I will rid from my mind as soon as you have given them to me – as to how I may free Kala and her companions.'

Slowly Ben came back to the table.

He took the paper from Mary-Ellen's hand. He examined it carefully. He had only seen one banker's draft before in his life, the draft sent to him as the legacy from the chandler, Noakes', will. This looked as real and substantial as the other – and this was for fifty pounds.

Ben hesitated. Then he pulled round a chair and sat down.

He gazed at Mary-Ellen. She had pulled the hood back from her head and her cheeks had warmed in the heat from the tavern's fire. Her face was glowing with a keen, impetuous determination.

'I will take the money,' Ben said. 'It will be difficult, but I think I know of a way to get them out. Once they are freed, I'm finished with the business. You'll be on your own. I want nothing more to do with it.'

Mary-Ellen nodded. 'I accept that. Tell me how I can do it. That's all I need to know. Then you can go.'

'I said *once* they're freed,' Ben replied. 'You can't do it alone. The only chance is if I come with you.'

He leant forward and started to talk.

— 52 —

'Are you sure, Ben?' The voice was doubtful. 'I mean, what if Mr Farini comes back? He did last night.'

'Don't even think about it,' Ben answered.

The confidence in his voice was utterly at odds with the acid surges of fear and uncertainty running across his stomach.

'Last night was the first night,' Ben went on. 'That was different. Tonight he was away to his bed an hour ago. He won't be back. Even if he does, I'll just say your wife was ill and I'm standing in for you.'

It was midnight.

Ben was standing in the lobby at the back of the Aquarium. Downes, the night porter at the stage door, was scratching his head in front of him. Ben had just knocked and entered, and the door was still open. Fog was billowing in from the street and a barge hooted mournfully as it made its way down the river.

'Well, I could certainly do with a night in my own bed for once,' Downes said. 'It's bleeding perishing in here. Maybe, if you really don't mind –'

Ben forced himself to chuckle. In spite of the cold, Ben was sweating. The noise that came out of his throat sounded more like a harsh, hollow rasp. Downes didn't seem to notice.

'The alterations his lordship wants on the set are going to take me the whole night anyway,' Ben replied. 'No point in both of us being here. Take advantage of it. I'll hand over to Charlie in the morning.'

The doorman frowned uncertainly. Then he gave a wink and a sly grin.

'You're a mate, Ben,' Downes said. He handed Ben the key to the door. 'For Christ's sake, see no one gets in.'

'It'll be locked as tight as a drum,' Ben said as he pocketed the key.

Downes put on his coat and disappeared into the night. Ben locked the door behind him. He glanced at the clock above it. Ten minutes, that was what he'd decided to give the doorman in case Downes lost his nerve and returned.

Ben waited.

He was mad, Ben knew that. Even if his plan worked, he'd have ruined the production. At best he was throwing away his job. At worst he could even land up in the hands of the police. The young woman, Mary-Ellen, must somehow have infected him with her own madness. Ben felt a surge of violent anger against her. She had trapped him just as effectively as the prostitute in Buckler's Hard.

Ben cursed her savagely under his breath. He controlled himself.

His fury with Mary-Ellen, he knew, was irrational. She hadn't made him do what he was doing. All that existed between them was a financial arrangement. He'd agreed to it of his own free choice for a fee of fifty pounds, just as he'd once accepted commissions for figureheads. In a single night he'd earn back everything he'd lost in the fire.

Ben shivered. He beat his arms against his body to try to ward off the cold. Then he paused.

In truth it wasn't even the fifty pounds. There was another stronger reason. Kala. The strange and fugitive presence with her dark, bruised eyes. The creature imprisoned like a caged animal in the foul-smelling little cell beneath the stage. Ever since Ben had first seen her, Kala had reminded him of something he couldn't identify.

Now Ben knew what it was.

The Hampshire gypsies used to snare and cage otters, and display them at the summer fair. Kala had the eyes of one of those otters, wrenched from the silence and freedom of the forest and river and exhibited behind bars before a roaring, baying throng of humans. The otters always died within a matter of weeks.

That was how Mary-Ellen had persuaded him, Ben understood suddenly, although she would never be aware of it. She said Kala would shrivel and die. Mary-Ellen was right. Kala belonged to the wild as much as the otters did. She too would never survive captivity. Ben knew that, because with part of his being he felt himself an otter too.

He glanced at the clock again. The ten minutes had passed. Ben unlocked the stage door.

Mary-Ellen must have been waiting on the opposite side of the street. She appeared instantly out of the darkness.

'Where are the cabs?' Ben demanded.

'At the end of the street,' she answered. 'I hired two of them. I had to pay the drivers half the fare in advance to make them wait.'

Ben nodded. 'This way,' he said.

Ben set off in the dim light of the gas lamps along the corridor towards the auditorium. The front-of-house doorman, Marley, would probably be dozing, Ben guessed, in the cubicle by the entrance. Apart from him the theatre was deserted.

As they approached the stage, Ben descended the stairs that led to the floor below. The keys to the three rooms where the San were housed were hanging on a hook at the foot of the stairs. Ben took them down.

Ben opened the first door. Behind him he heard Mary-Ellen gasp and recoil.

The fetid stench that billowed out was like the smell from a sealed pig shed. It was so dark inside that Ben could see nothing except the sheen of slime on the floor, and the reflections of three pairs of eyes. The room was occupied by three of the San. The tiny men were all awake and on their feet. Somehow, Ben realized, they must have known of his and Mary-Ellen's approach before they even came down the stairs.

Ignoring the stench, Mary-Ellen pushed past him.

She started to speak, her voice a whisper. The San replied. Ben had no idea what anyone was saying, except that the conversation sounded like a distant exchange of clicks and birdsong. Then Mary-Ellen brushed by him again. Behind her were the three men.

'The next room,' she said.

The second room held two more. There was the same flash of eyes as Ben opened the door. The same incomprehensible exchange and the same procession out into the passage.

'Now the third,' Mary-Ellen whispered.

Ben turned the key.

This time no eyes reflected the light from the corridor. Inside it was uniformly, impenetrably dark. The room seemed to be empty. At Ben's side, Mary-Ellen hesitated. She stepped forward and vanished. Ben heard a quiet rustling sound. Mary-Ellen, he guessed, was exploring the room with her hands.

There was a pause in the rustling and a soft exclamation. Then Mary-Ellen reappeared. She was not alone. She was supporting Kala under the arms. Kala's eyes were closed and her head was lowered on her breast as if she had been drugged. Two of the San ran forward to help Mary-Ellen. The three began to talk.

Ben glanced anxiously back at the stairs.

It was only minutes since he'd unlocked the stage door. In spite of the confidence he'd shown to Downes, Ben was far from sure Farini wouldn't come back that night. After working for the volatile and unpredictable American for a month, he knew that with Farini anything was possible.

Sweat broke out on his body again and the hairs prickled on the back of his neck.

'Hurry!' he urged.

'Something's happened to her,' he heard Mary-Ellen say in an anguished murmur. 'Kala's sick.'

'You'll have to deal with it later,' Ben snapped. 'We've got to get them out now!'

He forced Mary-Ellen and the two San forward. Carrying Kala between them, the three of them hurried up the stairs, with the others behind. Ben pushed them along the passage to the door. There he made them wait while he slipped out into the street. As far as he could tell in the fog and darkness, it was deserted.

'Where are the cabs?' Ben whispered as he came back.

'Down the street and round the corner,' Mary-Ellen replied.

'I'll come with you until we reach them,' Ben said. 'Then you're on your own. Tell the little people to follow you. I'll carry Kala at the back.'

He reached for Kala. Kala barely stirred when he took her in his arms. As he lifted her, Ben heard the distant clatter of hoofs. His head jerked up. Straining his ears, he listened. It was a cab or a carriage, and it was approaching the theatre.

'Quick!' he called urgently.

He hurried Mary-Ellen and the others out into the street. Ben locked the door behind them. With Mary-Ellen leading and Ben bringing up the rear with Kala, the procession set off.

The journey took only a few minutes.

The fog billowed round them in great clouds of damp, acrid vapour. Sleeping drunks and vagrants littered the pavement. The San, trotting as silently as tiny ghosts, stepped nimbly round the sprawled-out bodies as if they had been thorn bushes. Once or twice over their heads Ben glimpsed Mary-Ellen's yellow hair haloed in the streetlights. Apart from that there was only darkness.

In Ben's arms Kala was as light as a child.

The two cabs were where Mary-Ellen had left them. Through the murk Ben saw plumes of steam rising from the horses' nostrils. Mary-Ellen divided the San into two groups and beckoned them inside. Then she turned to Ben and reached for Kala.

'Thank you,' she said. 'You've done everything you promised. I'm truly grateful. You have the money. I will take her now. By morning we will be gone.'

Ben held Kala for an instant longer.

'What's the matter with her?' he asked frowning.

Mary-Ellen shook her head despairingly. 'The San don't know. They say Farini's man had to beat her up on to the stage. She went through the performance like a zombie. Afterwards the San had to carry her back to the room. Either she's fallen ill or something terrible has happened to her.'

Mary-Ellen stopped.

Her arms were still outstretched to take Kala. Behind him, Ben could hear the sound of the carriage wheels coming closer. He passed the girl over and watched Mary-Ellen climb into the cab. The door slammed shut behind her. The driver cracked his whip and the cab began to rumble away into the fog.

Ben waited a moment longer. Then, as the cab was disappearing into the dank and swirling clouds of greyness that filled the street, Ben launched himself forward and began to run. He reached the front step, caught at the rail, and pulled himself up beside the driver.

'Here!' the driver shouted. 'What the hell are you doing?'

'It's all right,' Ben replied. 'I'm the one who brought you your fares. I'm coming with you.'

The fog streamed over his face. Ben folded his arms round his chest. He narrowed his eyes and lowered his head into his neck as he tried to ward out the bitter chill.

Half an hour later the two cabs drew up before a house where the lights were still burning.

As Ben climbed down, the cab door beside him opened and Mary-Ellen stepped out. She was holding Kala in her arms. Kala was still inert. In the glow of the streetlamp her skin was dull and grey, and there were flecks of foam on the girl's lips. Mary-Ellen glimpsed Ben, and her eyes widened.

'I got her out,' Ben said. 'I had to know if she was all right.'

Mary-Ellen hesitated. Then without speaking she pushed past him and went inside.

Ben followed her. A grim-faced old woman was standing inside the hall. He heard Mary-Ellen address her as Mrs Clopton before heading up the stairs with Kala still in her arms and the San behind her. It was a lodging-house, Ben guessed, and the woman was the landlady. Somehow, Mary-Ellen must have persuaded the woman to allow the San to spend the night there.

'Miss Ramsay says you are to wait for her here,' the woman said to Ben.

She showed him into a room on the ground floor and closed the door behind her as she went out.

Ben paced restlessly up and down. What he'd told Mary-Ellen was true as far as it went. For a month he'd tried to look after Kala. What he'd been able to do was pitifully little, although at least he'd managed to stop the worst of the beatings Farini ordered Winters to give her. Ben had fed her, he'd given her exercise with the San in the open air, he'd talked to her and smiled at her.

It was more than Ben had ever done for anyone else. Yet it still didn't explain his sudden impulse to jump on the cab and ride across London through the night. As he struggled with the question, Ben realized his teeth were chattering and his face and hands were numb with cold. There was a gas fire burning against one of the walls. He stopped the restless striding and hunched himself over the glowing bars.

There, as the warmth slowly seeped back into his body, the answer came to him.

Ben had been abandoned in another fearsome winter in the year of his birth. As Mrs Noakes and the family maid had told him often as a child, he'd almost died. When he'd held the unconscious childlike form of Kala on the icy street, Ben had been holding his own life in his arms.

He had to follow Kala to see whether the African girl lived or died, just as much as if it had been him.

'Ben – !'

He glanced round. It was Mary-Ellen at the door of the room. Her face was drawn and grave.

'May I call you by your name?'

It was a puzzling, incongruous question, but he nodded.

'Will you please come with me.'

Ben stood up and followed her across the hall and up the stairs into a room above.

A single candle was burning inside. In its glow Ben saw Kala lying on a couch covered in cheap scarlet velvet. When Ben carried her, Kala had been drowsy and limp but from time to time she had quivered. Now she looked lifeless. The colour of her skin had paled from grey to white, and there was no movement in her chest.

'She's dying, Ben,' Mary-Ellen said quietly.

'She can't be!' Ben replied. 'I watched her on stage last night. She seemed fine then. What is it? Has she picked up a fever in the cold?'

Mary-Ellen shook her head. 'Her pulse is very slow but it's steady and she isn't sweating. But she's bruised and scratched. The San say they heard noises in her room late last night. Someone must have attacked her. I think it has to do with this –'

She held something up. Ben stepped forward and took it.

It was two pieces of leather.

Ben studied them. They were parts of a belt, he realized, with a pouch at the centre. The belt had been torn apart and the pouch had split open – the stitching was ripped across its length. The inside of the pouch was worn and smooth. For a long time it must have contained something. Now it was crumpled and empty.

'She wouldn't let go of it,' Mary-Ellen went on. 'Not even when she fainted. I had to force her fingers apart to get it away. There was something there, something very important. It's gone.'

Ben held the leather straps between his fingers.

'The San don't know what it was?'

'They say she's always worn the belt, it was almost a part of her. They've no idea what was inside, but she wasn't wearing it tonight.'

'Was she wearing it last night?'

Mary-Ellen nodded. 'Yes, they all remember it. They notice things like that.'

Ben thought for a moment.

Apart from the two doormen, the one person who'd been inside the theatre after the performance the night before was Farini. The front porter, Marley, had been chuckling when Ben came into work that morning about the bottle of champagne Farini had given him. If Kala had been robbed, Ben was almost certain it wasn't by either Marley or Downes.

It left only Farini.

Ben shook his head in confusion. He couldn't think what Kala might conceivably have had that Farini wanted, or why he would have attacked her to get it. Like the rest of the San, Kala had nothing. It made no sense.

Mary-Ellen led Ben back into the hall.

'Ben, I know birds and animals,' she said. 'I know their eyes. I know when they're well, or sick, or dying. Maybe it's all I do know, but I know there's a shadow over Kala's eyes. She's lost something, the one thing that links her to life. If we can't find it, I meant what I said. She'll die –'

Mary-Ellen paused. 'If it's anywhere it must be in the theatre.'

Ben stared at her in silence.

'And you want me to go back to look for it?' Ben said.

She gazed back at him. On Mary-Ellen's face was the same look of implacable resolution Ben had seen in the tavern that morning.

'I would go myself,' she answered. 'Except there are only hours before the ship sails and you know the theatre, while I do not. You have already done all you promised for what I paid you. This is no part of it. But happily, I still have some money left. You are welcome to all of it –'

Mary-Ellen began to reach into her bag.

Ben watched her. Then he struck out at her arm with such violence that the bag went spinning away across the floor. Mary-Ellen stumbled back against the wall.

'Keep your filthy money!' he shouted. 'Just let me be, let me think!'

As Mary-Ellen, white-faced and shaken, pulled herself upright, Ben creased his forehead.

Blood was pouring down his hand. As he'd lashed out

at her, Ben realized, he must have cut his knuckles on the bag's clasp. He raised his hand to his mouth and sucked at the cut. Then he focused his mind.

If Farini had stolen something from Kala, it suddenly occurred to Ben, and hadn't taken it away with him, there was only one place where Farini might have left it – in his office at the rear of the second floor of the theatre.

'What time will you have to leave here to catch the ship?' he asked.

'It sails at ten o'clock in the morning,' Mary-Ellen said. 'We should be away from here by seven.'

Ben calculated quickly. It was close to one o'clock now. He had six hours.

'Wait until then,' he said. 'If I'm not back, go! Don't count on anything. I'm looking for a needle in a haystack without knowing what a needle looks like.'

Mary-Ellen stared steadily back at him.

'Needles stitch up wounds and save lives,' she said. 'If you find it, you'll recognize it.'

Ben gave her in return a look of anger, almost of loathing. Then he turned away. He limped hurriedly outside and into the late-night darkness of the street.

— 53 —

Ben inched his way along the catwalk.

He was crawling on his hands and knees. Like a mountaineer on a high rock face, he kept three points anchored and only moved the fourth. It was a slow and painful way of moving. The catwalk was a narrow span of iron. Its surface had been serrated to provide a foothold. Over the years the serrations had rusted away until they were razor-sharp. They cut painfully into his palms and knees.

Twice Ben heard a soft plop as blood from a cut in his skin fell on to the stage far below. He had tried standing upright, but his weight made the iron sway and the hawsers creak. The only way to move in silence was like the animal the catwalk had been named for.

In spite of the cold, Ben's face was sheeted with sweat. Cautiously he raised a hand and wiped his eyes. He gritted his teeth. Then he edged his way on.

It was almost two o'clock. When he got back to the theatre the stage door was in darkness as he'd left it. Ben let himself in. He walked along the passage and started to climb the stairs towards Farini's office. As he reached the third landing, Ben saw a line of light under the office door. He paused. Then he heard the murmur of voices.

Ben froze.

It could only be Farini. For some reason Farini had come back to the Aquarium. He had at least one other person with him. Farini must have come in through the front. He wouldn't have discovered Downes had gone and there was no doorman at the back. Ben's mind raced. After his month's work on the set, Ben knew that the catwalks were tied into the wall at the level of the ceiling of Farini's office.

Ben had used the catwalks several times. From them, he'd discovered by accident, it was possible to look down into the office through a gap in the joists.

Ben retraced his steps. He crept round to the stage. He climbed the towering ladder that led upwards into the gloom and set out across one of the slender rocking pathways. Now he'd reached the point where it met the wall. He brushed the sweat away again and rested his chin on the cold metal. Then he peered down into a slit of light spilling out between the beams and the brickwork.

Ben was gazing into Farini's sanctum.

There were four men in the room below. Farini himself was sitting behind his desk with Winters, his assistant, standing to one side. The third, a tall burly man of about sixty with cropped grey hair and a jowled face the colour of pitted stone, Ben remembered seeing once or twice before. He was the South African named Gert Frouw who had brought the little people to London.

The fourth man was a stranger. Small and neatly dressed, with gold-rimmed glasses glinting on his nose, he stood immediately in front of Farini.

All four were looking at something wrapped in white tissue paper lying on the desk. The paper had been half-unwrapped. From the angle Ben was peering down, he couldn't see what was inside.

'And you're quite sure, Mr Levy?' Farini was saying.

'I have no doubt at all, sir –' The small man answered in a thin precise voice. 'If you examine the base, you will see what I mean.'

Farini reached into the paper and lifted something out. Ben gasped. What Farini was holding blazed and sparkled between his fingers like a handful of icy white fire.

It could only be a diamond – a huge diamond.

'Look at the way the facets have been cut,' Levy, the small man, went on. 'It was a technique known as trefoil. No one knows who first developed it, perhaps the very early jewellers of the Indus valley. You find it in almost all gemstones from the ancient world right up to the sixteenth century. But to my knowledge it hasn't been used for the past several hundred years –'

Levy polished his glasses.

'It's possible, of course, that in some very remote place the technique is still employed. I have to say, as a jeweller myself and a modest historian of our craft, I doubt it. Improvements on old methods tend to travel swiftly, and trefoil is just too wasteful of carats. I think it much more likely that this is a very old cutting indeed.'

Farini was silent. Then he stood up and stretched out his hand.

'Thank you, Mr Levy,' he said. 'I have your account. It will be settled in the morning. You've been most helpful, not least for making yourself available at this unconscionable hour. I am obliged.'

'Not at all, sir.' Levy stood up too. 'To examine a stone of this quality is a remarkable experience –'

The little man hesitated.

'If I may, I would like to hold it once more.'

Farini passed the diamond to him.

Levy ran the tips of his fingers gently over its surface. Afterwards he gazed down wistfully, almost lovingly, at the patterns of radiance cupped in the palm of his hand. Reluctantly he handed it back.

'It is a noble gem, Mr Farini,' he said quietly. 'It is raw, even barbaric, in its presentation. But it is the finest, truest white stone I have ever seen. Guard it well, if I may recommend, sir, for you possess something not only of incalculable value. It is also one of the marvels from when the world was young.'

Levy put on a broad-brimmed black hat and went out.

Farini sat down again. While Levy was in the room he had been quiet and composed. Now he slammed his clenched fist down on the desk and let out a triumphant roar.

'For Christ's sake!' he shouted. 'Did you hear what he

said? "Incalculable value"! Well, sure as hell he calculated it. It's here in his goddamn report –'

Farini picked up Levy's written appraisal.

' "For a diamond of this remarkable size and quality cut in the ancient trefoil manner," ' Farini read, ' "we would suggest a realizable value in excess of one hundred thousand sovereigns. However, to achieve such a price, professional expertise, a broad knowledge of the market, and kindred advisory skills are, we venture, essential. As London's leading –" '

Farini threw the paper down.

'Balls!' he said. 'The yid's in business. He's pitching. Okay, fine. Maybe we use him. Maybe not. But he says the stone's worth a hundred thousand British sovereigns – and that I do believe.'

'At that price,' Winters observed, 'the buyer may want proof it's really yours.'

'Garbage!' Farini snapped. 'I paid good money for those pygmies. When I bought them, I bought them lock, stock and barrel. That includes everything they had with them. It's in the contract. I had it checked out again today. Who was it who signed it, Gert?'

'The preacher at Kuruman,' the big man with the grizzled hair replied. 'Ramsay, the Reverend Ramsay.'

'Right. And we paid him good money too. He's not going to switch on us. I got the pygmies, I got their baggage, I got the diamond. I also got where the diamond came from –'

He glanced up at Frouw. 'You can find your way back?'

Frouw chuckled.

'I could find Kuruman with my eyes shut, two bottles of whisky on board, and a kaffir on each shoulder.' Frouw paused. 'That's not the problem. The girl doesn't come from Kuruman. I roped her with the Bushmen in the desert. But she's not one of them. She's too tall and pale. She's not from any kaffir stock I ever saw. To tell the truth, Mr Farini, I don't know where the hell she does come from.'

Farini thought for a moment. He lit a cigar and paced the room.

'Levy says the diamond was cut hundreds of years ago,' Farini said. 'We know it came out of the desert with the little coons. Either there are people out there still mining and cutting gems like they did once. Or there's some great stack of stones piled up from way back. Either way, I'll bet a dime to a golden dollar –'

He turned and jabbed out his cigar towards them.

'Where there's one stone, there'll be more. Mine or cache, there's treasure out there. I'm going to find it.'

Winters stared at him. 'What about the show?'

'The show's up and running,' Farini replied. 'You can handle it. You'll have no trouble – least of all when I bounce your salary fifty a month. But you, Gert, you're coming with me –'

He glanced at the big man. 'You're the key to the whole goddamn business. To me that says ten per cent of everything we find. Where do we start?'

Frouw rubbed his massive jaw.

'Kuruman,' he replied. 'I reckon the minister's daughter knows more than she let on. She's as thick as thieves with the little buggers. Another good tanning from her dad, and we could be headed in the right direction.'

'Then get it organized,' Farini instructed him. 'The steamship bookings, everything.'

Gert Frouw left the room.

A few minutes afterwards Ben heard their footsteps on the stage. He glanced down. Far below him he could see the shadowy outlines of two figures heading for the foyer. From the height of the catwalk they looked as tiny as the San.

Ben looked back into Farini's office. Farini was standing in front of Winters.

'Look after the show,' Farini was saying, 'because I'm going to forget about it. I'm going to forget about everything. Something like this happens once in a lifetime, and then only in dreams. Except this isn't a dream. It's real –'

Farini raised his hand. The diamond sparkled and blazed between his fingers.

'I said treasure. It's more than treasure. When I find where this came from, I'll find the biggest goddamn fortune on earth. I want it. Christ help anyone who gets in the way. This is something to kill for!'

The hairs rose on the back of Ben's neck. The look on Farini's face was so savage and hungry that even Winters stood transfixed.

Ben held his breath.

He had never before seen such brutal, naked greed. The diamond, still lying in Farini's palm, seemed to have bewitched him. His eyes were narrowed and the vein in his wrist was pulsing like a ravenous snake beneath his skin. Suddenly Farini laughed. He dropped the diamond into his pocket and let go of Winters' shoulder.

Farini turned towards the door.

'Come on,' he said. 'We could use some sleep too.'

The light went out in the office. Then Ben heard the sound of steps descending the stairs.

High in the darkness on the catwalk Ben hesitated. Once again his mind raced.

The diamond was in Farini's pocket. In a few moments Farini and Winters would cross the stage below him. They would climb down into the stalls and walk up the ramp to the gas-lit foyer, just as Frouw and the little jeweller had done. Once they reached the ramp they were safe. The only place they were vulnerable was on the stage itself.

Ben stood up and twisted round.

Ignoring the creaking of the hawsers, he heaved himself back along the catwalk until he reached the ladder. He scrambled down it until he was fifteen feet above the stage floor. Dangling in front of him was one of the scenery pulley ropes.

Ben reached out and caught the rope. He hauled it up. He made a rapid calculation of the distance, and secured the chock. Then he waited.

He only had to wait a few seconds. He saw two figures,

one taller than the other, appear at the back of the stage below him. The taller one was striding in front. Ben let him approach the centre of the stage. Then Ben launched himself off the ladder.

He swung down out of the darkness like a cannonball. Farini barely even heard the creaking of the rope until it was too late. At the last moment there was a flicker of white as Farini's face began to turn. Then Ben's outstretched legs smashed into Farini's chest. Farini was hurled back, sending Winters sprawling behind him.

Ben let go of the rope and dropped to the stage floor. He landed on all floors. In the dimness in front of him he could make out Winters frantically scrambling to his feet.

'What the hell –' Winters started to shout in terror and bewilderment. Ben sprang at him. He struck Winters twice in the face and saw him slump moaning on to the floor. Ben started to swing round. As he moved something crashed across his neck and shoulders. The blow was so powerful he was almost stunned. Pain flooded his body and his knees buckled.

A second blow followed. This time it caught his withered right arm and hurled him sideways. Ben coiled himself into a ball as he fell. Desperately he rolled over and over until he was brought up by the wings. Somehow he struggled to his knees. His eyes watering, Ben peered back.

The attack had come from Farini. He was standing in the middle of the stage with a steel measuring rod in his hands. His strength and the speed of his recovery were awesome. One moment he'd been lying winded and half-unconscious. The next he was back on his feet, lashing out with the weapon he'd seized from the floor.

Farini's eyes quartered the darkness, searching for his assailant. He spotted Ben. He frowned. Then Farini recognized him.

'Christ, it's the cripple!' he roared.

With the rod raised murderously above his head, he leapt at where Ben was crouching.

Ben came off the boards at the same instant. If he

hadn't moved, if the rod had smashed down on his head, he would have been killed. Ben knew that. But it was much more than self-defence that drove him upwards. Ben was filled with rage. A rage just as powerful and searing as Farini's.

The rod in Farini's hands was the one Winters had so often used on his orders to beat the San. It had drawn blood from the little men's shoulders. It had left dark swollen bruises on Kala's body as it jabbed at her ribs. Worst of all it had shamed and humiliated them because they were powerless against it, because they had no answer to the violence.

The rod shamed and humiliated Ben too. The brutality inflicted on the San was the same in kind as the orphans in the foundling hospital had inflicted on Ben before he learnt how to swim. Ben had no one to protect him. Kala and the San had him – and he had failed them.

Ben and Farini collided. Farini was striking down from above. Ben was surging up from below. Ben had fought many bitter and bloody battles in the orphanage. Providing you were strong, Ben had long since learned, every advantage lay with you if you came from beneath. He was coming from beneath and although Farini was strong, Ben was immeasurably stronger.

Ben's head butted into Farini's stomach.

He heard a hiss and a gasp as the breath was forced out of Farini's body. Ben chopped upwards with his left arm against Farini's wrist. The heavy rod arced away from Farini's hand as easily as if it had been a twig. Blank-eyed and choking, Farini collapsed limply on top of him.

Ben hurled him away. He glanced swiftly round. Winters was spreadeagled on his stomach, dizzily shaking his head. Ben knelt. He had seen Farini place the diamond in the right-hand pocket of his jacket. Ben turned Farini over and grabbed at the pocket. In his haste he ripped the cloth. The diamond tumbled out and rolled away across the stage. For an instant it lay there, a pool of fiery light on the boards.

'What's going on?'

Ben's head jerked up. The shout came from the back of the stalls. Marley, the front-of-house porter, must have heard the noise and come through from the foyer to investigate.

Ben scooped up the diamond. He ran towards the rear of the theatre and threw himself out of the stage door into the street.

He was no longer thinking of Kala or even the young South African woman, who'd somehow goaded him into what he'd done. As he raced away with his swift limping shuffle and the diamond in his jacket, all Ben knew, with a chilling, unalterable certainty, was that he'd compromised himself beyond the point of any return.

In the eyes of the law he'd become a violent robber.

— 54 —

On the street Ben glanced quickly to left and right.

As the fog briefly cleared from the clock face on Big Ben, he saw it was almost 3.00 am. He had never been out in London so late before. The city was eerily silent. He'd taken a cab from Bloomsbury to the theatre. Now there were none. London's wheeled traffic, the carriages, phaetons and horse-drawn omnibuses, had gone. The only life in the misty, dimly lit streets seemed to be vagabonds and prostitutes.

On foot, Ben set off in what he thought was the right direction. He walked up Whitehall, crossed Piccadilly Circus, and headed into Mayfair. In spite of the icy December chill the stench from the gutters was stomach-churning. Wrinkling his nose, Ben limped on until he reached Berkeley Square. There he realized he was lost.

He scanned the darkness and spotted the glow of a brazier. A group of figures was huddled round the coals, their heads hooded against the cold with scarves and cowls. In the dim play of the firelight their faces looked like skulls.

Ben asked directions for Bloomsbury.

'I can take you there, mister –'

A tiny figure detached itself from the group and sidled up to him. Ben glanced down. Beneath a dirty woollen shawl, he saw the face of a ten- or eleven-year-old girl. Her face was pinched and pale, but there was an impish smile on her lips.

'Cost you a penny,' she added.

Ben nodded.

The girl gripped him by the hand. As they walked away

from the brazier, Ben heard chuckles behind him. A hundred yards further on they came to a gas streetlamp. The child let go of Ben's hand and stopped in the wavering circle of light.

'How about this, mister?' she said. 'All yours for sixpence and as long as you want.'

Beneath the shawl the girl was wearing a worn tattered velvet dress. She unbuttoned it in a few quick movements and spread it aside. She stood there naked. She hadn't yet reached puberty, and the skin on her flat hairless body was almost blue with cold.

The child grinned up at Ben provocatively. Ben stared back at her, repelled.

'I just want to get to Bloomsbury,' he said.

'You can have a good time on the way, mister.' The child pirouetted, sending the dress swirling out round her like a cloak. 'Also, seeing as how they've knocked a few bits off you, I'll give you a special price – just fourpence particular to you. For that you get the whole business.'

Ben took a deep breath. 'Bloomsbury,' he said again.

The girl stopped in mid-turn. She gathered the dress round her and gazed at him through eyes that were no longer seductive, but narrow and hard.

'Bloody cripple, aren't we then?' The words were hissed out between her teeth. 'Can't get it up, can you? So instead you cheat and lie and lead a girl on. Well, see where your bloody trickery gets you, Mr Cripple.'

She put her fingers to her mouth and let out an ear-splitting whistle.

Ben was aware they weren't alone. Out of the corner of his eye he had seen two or three silhouettes who seemed to be accompanying them through the fog. When the child's whistle rang out, Ben was ready.

Ben whirled round and dropped to his knees.

There were three of them. The first was almost on him. Ben drove his clenched fist upwards into the man's groin. The man screamed and tumbled away over Ben's shoulders. Then the other two closed on him. Pushing himself off the cobbles Ben took out the second with a head-butt in the man's face. He felt the man's nose break and heard another scream of pain.

The third man stumbled against his companion. Ben gripped him by his hair and jolted his bent elbow into his neck. The man collapsed and lay twitching on the ground. Ben stepped back. He brushed the sweat from his face and glanced round.

The girl had gathered her skirts in her hand and was racing away along the cobbles. Ben set off after her. In spite of his ungainly stride, he was faster than the child.

Ben caught up with her at the end of the alley. He seized her arm and dragged her to a stop.

'Bloomsbury,' he repeated furiously.

Ben laced his fingers through hers. Whimpering, the girl led him forward. When they reached the address Mary-Ellen had given him, Ben unclasped the child's hand. He reached into his pocket and produced a penny.

'Take it,' he instructed her. 'And from now on never forget, us cripples are the most dangerous people on earth.'

The child fled sobbing into the mist.

A faint line of light appeared in the crack beneath the door. The door creaked open and he glimpsed Mary-Ellen's face.

Ben limped inside and slumped down on a chair. Mary-Ellen stiffened as she looked at him.

'You've been hurt,' she said.

Ben frowned. He reached up and touched his cheek. There was a smear of blood on his fingers.

'It's nothing,' he replied. 'I had company on the way back.' Shaking his head dismissively, he pulled out his handkerchief and dabbed at the cut.

'Was I right?' she asked eagerly. 'Had something been stolen from Kala?'

Ben nodded.

'Did you find it?'

Ben put his hand in his pocket and pulled out the diamond. He raised it towards the candle. In the glow of the flame, the diamond flared so brilliantly that his hand seemed to be on fire.

Mary-Ellen gasped.

She stared at it in silence. She shook her head. The jewel was as large as one of the autumn crocus bulbs she used to gather as a child and plant in pots outside the mission.

'Is it real?' she whispered.

'Yes,' Ben said, 'it's real.'

Ben told her what he had heard as he crouched on the catwalk above Farini's office.

As he spoke, Mary-Ellen got to her feet. She walked over to the window. The sky was lightening with the approach of dawn. Mary-Ellen gazed out.

The diamond could only have come with Kala from Africa. There was no conceivable way the girl could have acquired it anywhere else. It was also a vital part of Kala's past. Nothing else could explain her despair at losing it. Yet Kala's despair had nothing to do with the diamond's worth. The girl had no concept of money.

For Kala the diamond's value was totally different.

The San said the belt which held it had always been with her. The diamond had to be Kala's one remaining link with her beginnings. After Darwin's letter, Mary-Ellen was sure where those beginnings lay. She remembered something Darwin had said in an earlier letter, one of the first he had sent her.

'Study man, young woman, but beware of man,' Darwin had written. 'After the experience of a long lifetime I have concluded that man's greed, and the extents to which he will go to nourish that greed, is beyond restraint. Truly it has no bounds. He – by which I mean we – will desist from nothing in pursuit of gold or power. As the philosophers say, power corrodes. But of the two, gold, I venture, is the more deadly toxin.

'Complete your studies in the Kalahari, Miss Ramsay, before man comes. Because once man is there – and he will be there, it is in the biological nature of our species that we will be everywhere – ruin and degradation will follow as the night the day. Be there and have done with it first. You must save what is there while it still remains to be saved.'

The recollected words filled Mary-Ellen with fear. She turned and told Ben the story of her visit to Kent.

'Kuruman's a crossroads,' Mary-Ellen finished. 'All the African peoples of the south pass through it. Kala belongs to a race I've never seen. She's neither San nor Tswana nor Hottentot. If her people live in the delta, that may explain it –'

Mary-Ellen paused.

'Maybe something happened to her when she was very young. Perhaps she was seized by slavers and escaped, and the San adopted her. Maybe she was born dumb. Somehow I don't think so. I think more likely she's suffered terribly, and lost her voice as a result.'

'If she brought the diamond from the desert,' Ben replied, 'then her people are extraordinarily advanced –'

Ben knew nothing about diamonds, but he was a craftsman with a craftsman's instincts and skills. From what he had heard on the catwalk, Ben knew that only a fellow craftsman could have cut the diamond. And not just a fellow craftsman. Wood was relatively simple to carve and shape. It had still taken Ben a seven-year apprenticeship before he could tackle a figurehead on his own.

Diamonds were infinitely more complicated. A single slip and the entire intricate pattern of the hidden facets could be shattered.

'Whoever Kala's people are,' Ben went on, 'they must have been working on a huge number of diamonds for a very long time. Techniques like that take centuries to develop. No wonder Farini's ready to give everything up to find them. If he does, he could make himself the richest man in the world.'

Before Mary-Ellen could speak, a gust of cold air from the landing swept through the room. They both turned. Neither of them had heard the door handle turning, but the door was open.

Kala was standing in the doorway.

Draped across her shoulders was a shawl Mary-Ellen had given her. Apart from that she was naked. She stumbled forward. She looked like a ghost. Her skin was grey and wrinkled, and she was shaking with cold. Her breath came out in slow, spluttering heaves, and her face had the dead, opaque colour of clay.

The only sign of life was in her eyes. Sunken, but fierce and questing, they scanned the two faces. They settled on Ben. She stared at him. Then her glance dropped to the diamond.

Kala ran forward.

She plucked the diamond from Ben's palm with a swift, violent clutch of her fingers. She held it cupped in her own hands. The light from the candle, flaring off the stone's facets, irradiated her face. Kala sank down on her haunches. For a long time she squatted on the floor gazing at the jewel.

As she stared at it the shivering stopped and her breathing slowed. The pallor seemed to fade from her skin, and its texture changed to a vibrant gold. Her eyes softened. They lost their searching ferocity and became almost gentle.

Eventually Kala lifted her head. She gazed at Ben and Mary-Ellen again. For the first time, a smile seemed to pluck at her lips. Then she toppled forward and fainted.

Mary-Ellen ran forward. She gathered Kala up and carried her from the room. A few minutes later Mary-Ellen returned.

'Kala's asleep,' she said. 'She can for rest for another hour. Then we'll have to leave. But her will to live has come back. She's going to survive –'

Mary-Ellen paused. 'You found the needle. I think you saved her life. Thank you.'

The words sounded pathetically inadequate. She had known the young carpenter with his fierce grey eyes and his powerful lop-sided body for less than twenty-four hours. All her instincts had been right. At appalling risk to himself he had rescued Kala and the San, and had recovered the diamond.

Yet Mary-Ellen knew there was nothing else now she could say or do. There was an anger and hostility in him she couldn't fathom. Ben had refused any more money. He would equally, she was certain, reject anything she said.

Ben got to his feet. He stood for a moment without speaking. Then he shrugged.

'Take her back to her home,' he said.

Ben tossed his leather jerkin, bloodstained and dirty now, over his shoulder. He began to walk to the door.

'Where will you go now?' Mary-Ellen asked in desperation.

Ben hesitated.

There was a throbbing pain in his neck and arm where Farini had struck him with the steel rod. The cuts on his face from the fight on the cobbles were still raw and bleeding. He was exhausted, bruised and aching. He had thrown away his job and made himself a wanted criminal.

All he had in return was a banker's draft for fifty pounds. With a murderously vengeful Farini and no doubt half the police in London hunting for him, even the money was largely useless. Ben had wanted to help Kala, but he sensed he'd been ruthlessly manipulated and exploited by the young South African woman. He wasn't the architect of what had happened to him. Mary-Ellen was.

Ben glanced back at her with a look of bitterness that was close to hatred.

'I don't know,' he said savagely. 'I doubt I've many choices. If I have any, maybe one will occur to me on the street.'

Ben headed for the door.

'Wait!' Mary-Ellen called after him.

Ben stopped. He turned again.

'You're a carpenter and shipwright, aren't you?'

Reluctantly, Ben nodded.

'I'm taking Kala and the San back to Africa.' There was an edge almost of frenzy in Mary-Ellen's voice. 'I don't know exactly where Kala comes from, but I'm going to try and find it. I've got to return her there before Farini comes. If I don't he won't destroy only her, he'll destroy everything –'

Mary-Ellen took a deep breath. Her cheeks were pale and the tendons on her wrists were quivering.

'On the way to London I travelled from Cape Town,' she went on. 'It's becoming one of the biggest ports in the world. For people with skills like yours, it has endless work. Why not sail with us on the boat as far as there? No one can touch you in Cape Town.'

Ben remained where he was.

He was even more tired than he thought. Every muscle in his body felt limp and weak. He wanted nothing more to do with either Kala or Mary-Ellen. Puzzled, intrigued, and finally trapped by both of them, by their different demands for help, he had done his best for them.

Now it was over.

He never wanted to see either of them again. All he wanted to do was walk out into the darkness and leave them behind him. Except that in the darkness, in the web they had spun for him, he would find only Farini and the police.

'Will I get a passage?' he asked.

Mary-Ellen nodded. 'At this time of year, the boats are almost empty.'

Ben hesitated an instant longer. Then he limped back from the door and sank down into his chair again.

Ben rubbed his eyes. He knew almost nothing about the dark continent, as he remembered the Yorkshireman, Mr Featherstone, calling it when he told Ben where the iroko wood for the figurehead came from. All Ben knew was that Africa was beyond the reach of British law.

In Africa he would be safe.

— 55 —

'Downes has just returned –!'

Winters came panting into the office at a run. He stopped in front of Farini's desk.

'He's talking to the police now, but it's clear enough,' Winters went on. 'Downes is the back doorman. He says the carpenter, Ben, turned up at midnight. Ben told him you wanted alterations to the set. He said he'd be working through the night. Downes claims his wife was ill. He went off and left the place to Ben.'

'The bastard!'

Farini slammed his fist down on the desktop. For a moment there was silence.

Winters waited.

It was nine in the morning. Winters had often seen Farini angry before. He had never seen him in a fury as chilling as now. Malevolent and brutal, Farini's rage was almost tangible. It seemed to fill the room in pulsing waves like the London fog billowing through the streets outside.

Farini got to his feet. Instinctively Winters stepped back.

'What's that goddamn inspector's name?' Farini snapped.

'Ridell,' Winters answered.

'Get back and find him,' Farini said. 'As soon as he's finished with the doorman, I want to see him.'

Winters hurried out. A few minutes later the door opened again and Inspector Ridell came in.

A short, compact man with the sharp face of a weasel and prematurely white hair, Chief Inspector Ridell was one of the most experienced officers in the Metropolitan Police. The report of a robbery at the Westminster Aquarium had reached him by chance. Ridell happened to be at Vine Grove police station in the early morning when it arrived.

As well as being experienced, Ridell was ambitious. The Prince of Wales, he knew from the newspapers, had been at the theatre's recent triumphant success. So had the Prince's friend, Mrs Langtry. The incident at the Aquarium apparently involved a stolen jewel and some missing African pygmies.

For someone with their eyes on the post of Commissioner of Police itself, it was an investigation to be handled personally.

'Well, sir,' Ridell said crisply as he entered, 'I don't think your doorman can contribute anything more. I believe he's speaking the truth.'

'He'll be speaking the goddamn truth if he says he's fired,' Farini replied.

'No doubt.' Ridell paused. 'Can you tell me anything more about the carpenter?'

'He volunteered for the cannon. After the shot, he said he was looking for work. I took him on.' Farini shrugged. 'It happens.'

'He worked well?'

'He did what I hired him for.'

'So you had no cause for complaint,' Ridell continued.

'I paid him,' Farini said flatly. 'I don't pay people who don't work. I throw them out.'

'And as far as you know he had no previous connection with the Africans or this missing diamond?'

Farini rounded on him.

'This "missing diamond", as you quaintly term it, Inspector, happens to belong to me,' he said furiously. 'It's my goddamn property. I paid through the nose for those little devils and everything they had. That diamond's mine!'

'Yes, sir,' Ridell replied. 'I'm only trying to find a link between the pygmies and the carpenter.'

'Then find the bastard!'

Farini stared at Ridell with a savagery that unsettled even the hardened policeman.

Ridell coughed. 'I already have a hundred men out on the streets, Mr Farini.'

Seething, Farini swung away. Somehow he managed to control himself.

'No, Inspector,' he said, 'I don't think the little swine had anything to do with the coons before they got here.'

'And I gather he didn't have much opportunity to associate with them afterwards?'

'How the hell could he unless he spoke the coons' lingo – and I'm damn sure he didn't. Jesus, those little bastards sound like goddamn animals. A kick in the butt is the only way to get through to them –'

Farini stopped. It suddenly dawned on him that Ridell's questions were directed towards something.

'What are you suggesting, Inspector?' he demanded.

Ridell tugged at the gold watch chain draped across his stomach.

'I'm keeping an open mind, Mr Farini,' he said. 'But this matter may be more complicated than it appears. I think someone else may have been involved. Someone who knew about the diamond, and perhaps hired your employee to steal it and spirit away the pygmies.'

'Someone else –?'

Farini looked at him astonished.

From the moment he'd recovered consciousness on the stage floor, it had never occurred to Farini that the attack was anything other than straightforward robbery. When he learnt Ben had tricked the doorman into leaving the theatre, Farini knew he was right.

'What do you mean?' Farini asked. 'Who the hell else?'

'At the moment I can only guess,' Ridell answered. 'If the diamond was the purpose of the attack, there was no reason to release the pygmies too. So the Africans are also a consideration – a major consideration.'

'Who's interested in a bunch of tiny coons?'

'The no doubt well-intentioned people concerned with

African slavery,' Ridell replied. 'The trade was abolished years ago. Unfortunately the laws of hire and contract still contain untested areas. To many, the matter is still very sensitive.'

'Hire and contract? Sensitive?' Farini shook his head. 'What the hell are you talking about?'

'About slaves, sir,' the inspector said. 'Someone or some group of a radical persuasion may have regarded your Africans as slaves. They could have paid your carpenter to free them. It has been known before.'

'Slaves? For Christ's sake, they weren't slaves. They were jungle coons.'

'I personally agree with you, Mr Farini. Not everyone feels the same.'

'And what about the diamond?'

Ridell frowned. 'I truly don't know, sir. I believe the diamond may be almost incidental to the matter.'

'My diamond is "incidental"?' Farini's face flushed with rage again. 'My coons vanish and my diamond is stolen. And that's the best you can do – ?'

Unable to control himself any longer, Farini reached out and gripped Ridell by the jacket.

'Where the hell are all these "incidental" thefts of my property?'

Ridell struggled to disengage himself. Farini was too strong. His hand clenched like the claw of a leopard, Farini held the inspector up in front of him.

'Kindly control yourself, sir!' Ridell managed to exclaim.

Farini let go of him.

'I appreciate the strength of your feelings, Mr Farini, but I must demand you keep them in check.' Ridell straightened his collar. 'To answer your question. If I am right, the pygmies may be returned to their homeland.'

'To Africa?'

Ridell nodded. 'I cannot think of any other reason for their release.'

'And the diamond?'

'The diamond is a mystery. But if my hypothesis is

correct, the same misguided person or group who hired the robbers may believe the jewel is the Africans' property. I fear the diamond may have the same destination.'

'Then find them!' Farini shouted. 'For Christ's sake, don't just stand here – get out on the goddamn streets and look for them!'

Farini clenched his fists in a renewed frenzy of anger and frustration. This time Ridell stood his ground.

'There is a complication,' Ridell said. 'Ships now leave for the African continent almost every day. It is possible the attack was timed to coincide with a sailing. In which case they may shortly be at sea –'

Farini stared at him, appalled. He understood Ridell's words. For once he didn't respond to them.

'I have dispatched a number of men to the docks to check the passenger lists,' Ridell continued. 'I shall naturally inform you as soon as I learn anything.'

Before Farini could speak again, Ridell left the room. Behind him he left Farini standing in disbelieving silence.

'The ship is a P&O vessel called the *Star of Russia*,' Ridell said. 'She sails every two months out of Tilbury for Cape Town. She left London with the tide at ten this morning. That is seven hours ago. Her passenger list includes the following names –'

Ridell consulted the notes that had reached him an hour before from one of the constables he had sent to the docks.

It was early evening. Ridell was once again in Farini's office. Farini was leaning over his desk listening intently to Ridell as he spoke. He was no longer alone. Beside him were two other men.

One was Farini's assistant, Winters. The other was a big burly man with grizzled hair and the shoulders of an ox, who had been introduced to Ridell as Gert Frouw.

'Ben Noakes is the first.' Ridell referred to the paper in his hand as he continued. 'I take him to be the carpenter. Then there is a Miss Mary-Ellen Ramsay –'

As he spoke the last name, the South African, Frouw, gave a quiet derisive grunt. Ridell glanced up at him. Frouw's face was impassive.

'After that, there are six African names,' Ridell went on. 'I will not attempt to pronounce them, but they are designated as servants. I think it safe to assume they are the pygmies. If I may make another assumption, gentlemen, I believe we have traced the whole group –'

Ridell lifted his head again.

'Ben Noakes carried out the robbery and released the pygmies,' he said. 'Miss Ramsay – whoever she may be – seems to have been the organizer. The bookings were made in her name. Whatever the explanation, they are all now on the high seas.'

'And the diamond?' Farini demanded.

Ridell glanced at him.

Farini's voice was much quieter than before. Quieter – and more deadly. The rage had gone from him. Instead, every time he spoke his words were charged with a venomous and vengeful determination.

'We will keep searching for it, sir,' Ridell answered. 'Every jeweller, every sale room, will be alerted. I would not, I advise you, expect much by way of result. It strains credulity to think they left the jewel behind. My belief is it has gone with them.'

There was little more Ridell could add. A few minutes later the inspector left the room.

As the door closed behind him, Farini looked at Frouw.

'The Ramsay girl,' he said. 'She's the missionary's daughter?'

Frouw nodded. 'Can't be anyone else.'

'And they'll head for this place Kuruman?'

The South African nodded again. 'I guess she's trying to take them back to the desert.'

Farini glanced round at Winters. 'When do they dock?'

Winters had spent the day acquiring the schedules of every steamship that sailed out of London for Africa. He had them in his hand. Winters riffled through them.

'The *Star of Russia* puts in at the Canary Islands,' he said. 'It reaches Cape Town on January the twenty-ninth.'

'And when's the next sailing from here?'

'The Union Castle line has a boat that leaves on Thursday,' Winters replied. 'That's three days later, but it's a faster boat and a direct passage. The ship gets to Cape Town the day before the P&O sailing.'

'I want two bookings on it.'

'Yes, Mr Farini.' Winters paused. 'What about the show?'

'Close the theatre for two days,' Farini answered. 'Put up boards saying the coons are sick with a tropical fever. Then use your goddamn initiative. Hire some kids from one of the drama academies. Rehearse them and paint their skins black. Put them on stage with the lights dimmed. No one's going to know the difference. For Christ's sake, the punters only see what they've been told they're going to see!'

'Yes, sir.'

'And shift your butt – you've got forty-eight hours!'

Winters went out.

'We land a day before the coons.' Farini spoke to Frouw again. 'Can you hire me a bunch of men quickly out there, and I mean hard men?'

Frouw gave him a chill smile. 'I'll find the men. They won't come harder anywhere in Africa.'

'We'll be waiting for the cripple and the rest of them when they dock,' Farini said. 'This bitch from the mission isn't taking anyone to Kuruman. I want that diamond back. Believe me, Gert, I'm ready to kill to get it.'

— 56 —

Mrs Ramsay lay on the bed in the single guest room at the side of the Kuruman mission house.

She had been carried there at her own insistence in her last few minutes of full consciousness twelve hours after she fell ill. The room faced away from the sun and the village. It was cooler and quieter than her own bedroom, and better suited for someone stricken by one of Africa's fevers as they struggled to recover. That was only part of her reason for insisting to be moved.

Mrs Ramsay had had fevers often before in her years at Kuruman. This one was different. She sensed it from the very first moment she began to tremble and sweat. She didn't want to increase the risk of her husband contracting it too, by continuing to share her bedroom with him.

There would be no recovery from this fever.

The smell it left on her skin, Mrs Ramsay knew, was the smell of death.

She had been in the guest room for only forty-eight hours since she scented it. Mr Ramsay and the Tswana women servants of the house looked after her. Ramsay dosed her with quinine. The women cooled her skin with wet cloths, and kept trying to pour liquid down her parched throat.

Nothing made any difference. The fever's grip was too strong for the long-eroded and weakened defences of Mrs Ramsay's body to throw off. The quinine was brushed aside by the tide of infection flooding through her. The water was absorbed and expended by her heated blood faster than she could take it in.

For most of the time she lay shuddering and senseless.

Her skin turned a vivid jaundiced yellow. Her breathing was weak and laboured. The flesh shrank from her face. Her sunken eyes were circled with bruised shadows.

'George –'

Very occasionally, consciousness came back to her. Briefly it returned now on the third evening after the fever began.

'Yes.'

Her husband's voice came to her from across the room.

Unlike the Tswana women who attended her constantly, Ramsay only visited his wife at the six-hourly intervals when he gave her the quinine. His visit that night had taken place as she woke.

'What time is it, dear?' Mrs Ramsay asked.

Her voice was so frail, Ramsay had to strain to hear it.

'I am not sure of the hour,' he replied. 'But darkness has fallen.'

Mrs Ramsay tried to lift her head from the pillow.

It was useless. She was too weak. But momentarily her eyes scanned the room. She saw a pool of light from a single wavering candle, and a hunched, brooding silhouette in the shadows behind. Then she glimpsed the window frame. Beyond she made out the open sky, and the distant Kalahari stars.

They were the same wheeling desert stars she had watched with her daughter on that long-ago night when she told Mary-Ellen about her father. Long-ago? It seemed so for an instant. Then, in a rare moment of lucidity, Mrs Ramsay realized it was not long-ago at all. It was barely five months since Mary-Ellen had held her and smiled her last sad smile, and walked away from Kuruman with the bold decisive confidence Mrs Ramsay had never managed to acquire.

Mrs Ramsay began to weep. There was not enough moisture left in her for tears. All that happened was that her eyes blurred slightly and her chest quivered. Across the room Ramsay didn't even notice.

'Where is she now?' she asked.

'Where is who now?'

'My daughter, Mary. Where has she gone?'

'I have ordered you not to mention her,' Ramsay said brutally. 'Perhaps in your fever you may be forgiven for forgetting my instruction. Let me now remind you. She has twice brought shame and degradation on a house that is dedicated to God. Her name shall never be spoken here again –'

He paused. Then he added, 'It would be advisable for you to compose yourself and rest. The Lord's health will not return to you while your mind is contemplating an abomination in his sight.'

Ramsay got to his feet. He picked up the candle and left the room.

Mrs Ramsay heard the door close. The glow of light vanished. For an instant longer she could see the stars. Then they too vanished and she was left in darkness. Not just in darkness but alone. It would be several minutes before the Tswana women heard the minister's departing footsteps and returned.

It didn't really matter when or even whether they came back. The end was very close now. Mrs Ramsay knew that even more surely than she had recognized the smell of death on her skin.

A sense of desolation overwhelmed her. Her own life had been wasted. A moment's folly had condemned her to almost twenty-five years of misery on the edge of the Kalahari's wastes. Her husband's life had been wasted too. She saw that with a sudden piercing clarity. The Africans, the blacks and Hottentots and the tiny Bushmen, were impervious to salvation.

They all had their own gods and spirits. They shared them with the seasons, the animals, and the ancient landscape. Ramsay had tried to dispossess the spirits. He had failed. The Africans' deities were much older, much stronger and more cunning than the Christian Lord from far across the ocean.

Ramsay had been tormented and violent long before she met him, she realized at last. Africa had turned the torment and the violence into madness.

Worst of all, far worse than what had happened to her or Ramsay, was what had happened to Mary-Ellen. Mrs Ramsay's one daughter had been abused, humiliated, beaten, and cast out from her home. Mary-Ellen's life too was wasted and ruined. Mrs Ramsay blamed herself. She blamed the husband she had never had the strength or conviction to control.

Most of all she blamed Africa.

In a frenzy of guilt and despair, Mrs Ramsay tried to raise herself from the bed again. This time she succeeded. For an instant she propped herself up on emaciated and bleeding elbows. She gazed into the night and saw the stars again.

As she stared at them, she realized she was wrong. Africa was not responsible for Mary-Ellen. It was her birthplace. The dark continent hadn't imprisoned her. It had welcomed and embraced her and made her one of its own. The only chains that bound Mary-Ellen were manacled to her beginnings. And she, Mrs Ramsay, had finally turned the key to open those padlocks.

She had given her daughter the chance to do what Mary-Ellen chose.

Mrs Ramsay stared at the stars for a moment longer. In her clear but fevered mind, the constellations seemed to shape themselves into the outlines of two faces. The dancing-master and Mary Ellen.

The French dancing-master had given his daughter her freedom.

Mrs Ramsay's head dropped back on the sweat-stained pillow. When the mission's woman servants padded into the room, her chest was still.

Moffat squatted on his haunches in the darkness beyond the stockade.

It was midnight and the sickle moon was high. The keening and wailing was still lifting over the mission wall. The laments had been ringing out for five hours. Several times Moffat had heard the furious roar of the Reverend's voice as he tried to still them. To Ramsay the mourning cries of the African women were pagan and obscene.

Ramsay had failed. He could impose his will on Kuruman to some extent over the community's daily life. At the most fundamental moments, at times of birth and death, even his authority was powerless.

'Moffat, Moffat –'

As the call rang out, Moffat's head lifted.

He was squatting just outside the stockade's open gates. From there Moffat could see the front of the mission house. As he watched, the door swung back. Ramsay's silhouette appeared against the oblong of light spilling out from inside.

'Come here! In the name of God, you idle black heathen, where are you?'

Ramsay's anger came out not just in the enraged shouts, but in the set of his heavy body. Every tendon and sinew seemed to be taut and shaking with fury.

Unseen, fifty yards away in the darkness, Moffat gazed at him steadily.

Normally Moffat would have been dressed in the clothes he had always been ordered to wear, the Christian clothes insisted on by the Church Missionary Society who bought and paid for them. A pair of grey Lancashire cotton trousers and a trim white cotton shirt.

Not tonight.

Tonight Moffat was wearing a short leather apron round his hips. Apart from that the lithe and hard-muscled young African was naked. Naked – except for a short, broad-bladed sword lying on the ground beside him.

As Ramsay's bellows continued to rend the night, Moffat rose to his feet and began to walk. Not towards the white man – but away from him into the darkness. Ten minutes later, with Ramsay's maddened cries still echoing distantly in his ears, Moffat broke into a run.

In his mind were the words the old San woman, Mama Chi-mona, had spoken to him that morning.

*

Moffat had gone to her hut at dawn.

'Enter, my child,' Mama Chi-mona said when she saw him.

Moffat ducked under the curved branch that supported the opening.

If the hut had been one of the little people's true desert shelters, he would have had to crawl inside. The old woman had adapted the hut to the fashion of the Tswana, the Hottentots, and the other African races who shared the settlement with her. There was just enough room for Moffat to crouch without his head brushing the roof.

'Why do you come to me?' Mama Chi-mona went on.

The old woman studied him through acute, age-ringed eyes.

Moffat was a Mashona. He had grown up as Mary-Ellen's childhood companion in the mission house itself. At puberty he had been sent back to live in the compound. He was different from the other blacks there, but like them, he had never visited the dwellings of the San at the far end of the settlement.

To all the black tribes of Africa the little people were a race apart. They were wild. Like the animals, they belonged to the desert. Except as cattle herders and menials, they were even more remote from the blacks than the white man.

'Because you are Mama Mary-Ellen's friend,' Moffat answered.

'Not her friend. She is my daughter. *You* are her friend. *I* am her mother.'

The old woman cackled with laughter. In her own way, Moffat knew, she was speaking the truth. He struggled on.

'Her mother – her other mother – lies stricken,' he managed to continue. 'The women of the house say she will die.'

'They speak the truth,' Mama Chi-mona replied bleakly. 'The sun rises now. When it sets, it will reach down from the sky and gather Mama Ram'y to its chest so it may hold her in the dark –'

She paused.

'Your friend Mama Mary-Ellen has been gone for five moons. I say again, why do you come to me now?'

'All her years here she was my sister and I stayed,' Moffat said. 'After she departed, I stayed too because she wished so. Before she left she told me many things. Among them that the Reverend was not her father. She wanted me to remain to watch over her mother. I have done so. But now her mother dies.'

'And so?' Mama Chi-mona demanded.

'I am released,' Moffat answered. 'Released from her – but not from myself. I came here as a child without a name and without a father. I was given a name, but it was not my own. No man should come to manhood unknowing of his name and his father. It is time for me to learn them. You were here the night my mother brought me to the mission.'

Moffat stopped. The old San woman would understand the questions he had put to her without even asking them. If she knew, she would give him the answers.

Mama Chi-mona understood.

The old woman looked beyond him at the halo of light filtering into the hut from the rising sun. Then she spoke.

'It was dark and many years ago,' she said. 'I worked in the mission then. Your mother presented herself at the gates. I was called by Mama Ram'y to give her food that she might suckle you. I brought her here from the house. I made her gruel of maize and milk and insects. You were starved and mewling, but we had to wait until her dugs filled. Oh, how you howled – !'

Mama Chi-mona chuckled.

'While we waited over the fire, she talked,' the old woman went on. 'She was a Mashona, she said. Her husband had been a great chieftain named Sechele in the Mashona lands far to the north. She was his last wife and yours was the last seed he planted. When he seeded you, Sechele was old – as old as the great crocodiles of the Kuruman river here. He died in the same moon of your birth. He left behind him many wives. On his death there were quarrels and dissension –'

Moffat nodded.

'Sechele had counselled a white man, a hunter and trader named Dao,' the old woman continued. 'When Sechele died, his son Mashuana became this white man's adviser in his place. Mashuana was your half-brother. He also became protector to your mother and you. After the rains in the second year of your birth, Dao and your half-brother set out with an impi of the Matabele into the desert. They were going to raid a kraal of other white men in the waters beyond the Thirst –'

Like everyone who lived in the great desert Moffat had heard of the fabled river and lagoons on the remote far side of the Kalahari.

He leant forward, waiting eagerly for her to go on.

'No one knows what happened,' Mama Chi-mona said, 'except that the white man, your brother, and many of the impi were killed. When word came back to your homelands that Mashuana, your protector, was dead, your mother's inheritance from Sechele was seized by his other wives. You and your mother were exiled. Thus she told me, and thus it was you came wandering to be here.'

The old woman stopped. Moffat sat before her in silence.

He believed every word Mama Chi-mona had spoken. Moffat could have asked her to tell him again, and every last syllable would have been the same. It was the truth – but it was not enough.

'You say I am Sechele's son and Mashuana was my brother,' he said. 'How can I know this is truly so?'

African history was not merely related. It had to be proved and accepted before it could be related.

'Come with me –'

Mama Chi-mona climbed to her feet. Crouching, Moffat followed her across the beaten earth floor through an arch into another hut beyond. The roof of the second hut was much higher. He got to his feet.

'It was made so for Mama Mary-Ellen.' The old woman waved at the roof above her head. 'Here she could stand. Here she could undress and clothe herself as a child of the desert should be clothed. Do what she did so many times, black child – take off what you wear!'

It was not a request. It was a command. Moffat stripped and stood naked before her.

Mama Chi-mona peered at his groin.

She reached out a gnarled finger and traced a line at the base of his stomach just above the fringe of the pubic hair.

'Sechele marked his male children,' she said. 'He branded them where I touch you now. His mark was the sign of the ship he once sailed in the northern seas. Below each mark, he scored the child's name. The name he gave you was ratel, the honey badger.'

She rocked back on her heels. Moffat glanced down.

With both hands he drew up the skin she had been feeling. Upside down and almost buried in the hairs of his groin was what always before Moffat thought was a scar from some childhood accident. Now he made out the outline of what might have been a ship. Above it, in Mashona script, he slowly recognized the symbol for a ratel, a honey badger, the most powerful and dangerous animal of the desert.

Moffat looked up again. For a long time he was silent.

He had acquired a father and an ancestry. He had learned his own name. Something was still missing, some part of the puzzle was still unsolved. He frowned. Then it came to him.

'My mother and I were exiled,' Moffat said. 'By custom all exiles are permitted to live close to the borders of their tribal lands. Yet the lands of the Mashona are so far from Kuruman no man knows where they truly lie. Why did my mother bring me here on a journey that killed her?'

Mama Chi-mona grunted.

'So I asked her too,' she replied. 'It seems Mashuana, your brother, led a group of your tribe who marched with the white man and the great Matabele impi. Some of them escaped the destruction that befell the rest. They could not return to their homelands because they were Mashuana's men and he was dead. Instead they fled south. They found the source of the Kuruman and followed it –'

The old woman paused again. 'Do you know of the Kakindi?'

Moffat nodded.

The Kakindi, the 'homeless ones', were a small group of warrior Africans who, it was said, occupied the pastures watered by the Kuruman many miles upriver from the Kuruman mission. Throughout Moffat's childhood they had been a remote and somehow threatening presence on the edge of the mission's world. Even Ramsay, in his first vigorous and optimistic years after his arrival at Kuruman, had never attempted to contact and convert them.

'In truth they are not Kakindi,' Mama Chi-mona continued. 'They are the Mashona who escaped. They are your people. Your mother was searching for them. That is why she came here with you.'

Moffat stared at her transfixed.

If the Kakindi were really Mashona, they were not only his people. He was their chief. His mother had been carrying him to them so Moffat could claim his rights of inheritance and pasture. Much more than that, his rights of leadership.

The discovery was so startling, so awesome, that Moffat stood in silence again. The silence lasted much longer than before. He had found not just a name and a father, but a nation. A fragment of a nation, maybe, but a fragment which was waiting for him to return to them.

Suddenly and violently Moffat kicked the mission clothes aside. Naked, he turned to leave the hut. He was checked by Mama Chi-mona's voice.

'Wait –' she called.

Moffat swung back.

'Go on your long journey,' the old woman said. 'Find your people. Prove if you can that you are their chief. But then you must return to Kuruman.'

'Why?' Moffat demanded.

'You came to my dwelling because of Mama Mary-

Ellen,' Mama Chi-mona replied. 'She has been gone since five moons. She went in search of another child of the desert. But she will come back. That I know because all the children of the desert must come back to their birthplace, to their home. She was born here, and they will both return. When they do, and it will be soon, they will need you –'

The old woman lifted her finger and stabbed it out towards Moffat. Then she raised her head. She gazed beyond him through the first hooped circle of the hut's framework, and then through the second.

The distant sky was filling with light. There were no clouds in the oval of whiteness, only the circling patterns of kites and eagles thronging the uplift of the first warm thermals.

'When she returns, Mama Mary-Ellen and the little hare she brings back will have need of warriors.'

Mama Chi-mona's eyes darkened and her head dropped on to her chest.

Eighteen hours later, with the stars wheeling and tumbling above his head, Moffat ran through the darkness of the Kalahari.

He had kept his word to Mary-Ellen. He stayed at Kuruman until he knew Mrs Ramsay was dead. When he heard the wails from the house, he threw off his mission clothing and dressed himself in the simple leather apron of a Mashona warrior. After a last glance at the mission, he had headed out into the night and the bush.

Before he went to Mama Chi-mona's hut, Moffat thought his responsibilities to Mary-Ellen were discharged when her mother died. He was wrong. Mary-Ellen was returning to the desert and bringing the captured girl with her. How the old woman knew that, Moffat had no idea. It made no difference. All that mattered was that he believed the old woman.

Mary-Ellen was coming back. She was his sister and she had need of warriors. For Mary-Ellen to have them,

Moffat would need to prove himself to the Kakindi, to the so-called homeless ones who were in truth Mashona.

He would need to show them that he was their chief.

— 57 —

Moffat guided the horse down to the river.

At the water's edge the horse pricked its ears and glanced nervously to left and right. There were crocodiles lying on the banks on either side. The horse whinnied in alarm.

'There is no danger.' Moffat patted the animal's neck reassuringly as he spoke to it. 'The water is shallow and the crocodiles are young. You are too large and healthy for them.'

He urged the horse on.

Fretful and tense, it stepped into the water. Three of the crocodiles lumbered down the bank and dropped into the river too. With only their eyes and nostrils showing, they swam forward. The horse screamed in alarm. It galloped through the shallows and raced up the bank on the far side. As it reared, Moffat pulled it to a halt.

'There.' Moffat comforted the animal again. 'Did I not tell you the truth? See, they are retreating.'

He tugged the horse's head round to watch the crocodiles which were already crawling back on to the bank. The animal trembled. Then its flanks became still.

Moffat smiled and kicked the horse forward again.

It was four days since he'd left Kuruman. For the first two days he'd travelled on foot, taking only brief rests in the fiercest heat of the day as he followed the course of the Kuruman river westwards. On the third morning of his journey, Moffat had entered the pastures of a Tswana cattle baron.

Apart from his sword and his leather apron, all Moffat had with him were the savings which represented his payment for almost fifteen years' work at the mission. After hours of haggling, they proved just enough for him to buy one of the Tswana's horses.

Moffat had no need of a horse. He could move through the bush as quickly and surely on foot. But he was coming to the Kakindi as a chieftain, and a Mashona chieftain, he knew, always presented himself to his people mounted.

Now Moffat was very close. Ten minutes after leaving the river, he saw a track running through the grass. Moffat followed it. The track ended at a thick thorn fence, a boma encircling a group of huts.

Moffat reined in the horse. For a moment he hesitated. He breathed in deeply. Then he rode through the boma opening on to the baked earth compound on the other side.

The men were waiting for him.

Moffat knew they would be. The movement of birds and animals in the bush would have signalled his approach. All strangers were potentially dangerous, but he was alone – the animals would have told the villagers that too. That was why only half a dozen of the morans, the warriors, were gathered in the compound. It was, Moffat guessed, about a quarter of the village's males.

Moffat stopped.

The men were gathered in a half-circle facing him. He studied them for a moment, his gaze switching slowly and thoughtfully from one face to the next. Then he swung himself off the horse's back. Moffat tossed the reins aside and unbuckled his belt. He let his leather apron fall to the earth. He turned with his arms above his head, showing that he was carrying no weapons.

Then naked he swung back to them. He crossed his arms over his chest. It was a bold and defiant gesture, signifying that he was unafraid and had nothing to fear.

'I greet you,' he said. 'Who speaks for you?'

One of the men stepped forward. His hair was greying and the deep-cut lines on his scarred face showed him to be older than the others.

'I speak for my people,' he said. 'Why have you come to our kraal and what do you want?'

'I have come first for water and wheat,' Moffat replied. 'I have been a traveller and that is any traveller's due. But I am also a traveller whose journeys are ended. I have come home. I am Sechele's son. I come here to claim my own.'

The man stared at him.

'Sechele had many sons,' the man said after a long silence. 'We recognize only Mashuana.'

'He was my brother. Mashuana is dead.'

'We recognized him. We do not recognize you.'

'That is because Sechele sired me later,' Moffat said. 'From my face you can see I have many years less than Mashuana. But he was my brother and Sechele was my father. See, I bear his mark.'

Moffat tapped the scar on his stomach.

Dubiously, with the others crowding behind him, the man came forward. They clustered round Moffat and peered at his waist. Some of them muttered and spoke quietly among themselves. When the murmurs died away, the older man stepped back.

'Marks may be counterfeited!' He shook his spear angrily. 'How do we know you are truly Sechele's son?'

The other morans began to stamp their feet on the ground. Behind them Moffat could see startled women and children gathering at the entrances to the rondavels.

Moffat took another step forward. The older man instinctively backed away. Moffat paused. There was more to be confronted and dealt with, Moffat knew, much more. But, naked as he was, for the moment the initiative had passed to him.

'You!' He shouted sternly at the youngest warrior he could see. 'Fetch me a cover for my loins so that your chieftain may enter his kraal.'

The young man was barely as old as Moffat. He scurried nervously away and returned with a wrap of buffalo hide. Moffat knotted it round his waist.

'Now,' Moffat addressed the older man again, 'I will give you my name. It is the Ratel. It is such because Sechele named me for the boat he sailed in the foreign seas. For Sechele, the Ratel brought many riches. I come to bring you the same. I must first know your name.'

'It is Batuka,' the man answered.

'Listen to me, Batuka,' Moffat said. 'You have seen Sechele's mark. You have seen my horse. You will expect me to know Sechele's ways. Take me to your kraal's oldest, wisest counsellor. Let him or her examine and test me. Then decide whether it is truly Sechele's son who has come to your kraal.'

The man placed the butt-end of his spear between his feet. Through narrowed eyes he gazed thoughtfully first at Moffat, and then at the horse. Finally he turned and shouted.

'Ipimi!' he called. 'Let Ipimi question the man who offers himself as Sechele's seed.'

Ipimi was a woman.

She was very old. She had glazed and sightless eyes, ringed with circles of nut-brown and night-black ebony, and her teeth had long since dropped away. Her tongue snapped against the roof of her mouth with the clatter of a mopani squirrel. She was as old, or even older, Moffat guessed, than his father Sechele would have been.

In the darkness of her hut, Moffat strained to listen to her.

Sometimes he would lose all track of what she was saying. For minutes on end she seemed to wander and ramble, talking to herself in what might have been a private language. Suddenly Moffat would pick up a question. The questions were direct and particular.

How had Sechele held himself when he walked? Moffat didn't know. He was only a week old when his father died, and he said so. His mother's eyes were very pale, old Ipimi remembered, they had the colour of a buzzard's underwing – wasn't that so? Moffat thought. Yes, he agreed, that was so. And her breasts, they were big and strong and full of milk?

Moffat thought again.

No, that wasn't so. His mother was slim and small and

sharp-breasted. On their wanderings south to the mission at Kuruman, she had hired other women to wet-nurse him. They had been big-breasted, but not his mother. She had had the slender form of an antelope in the wind. He would never forget that.

Moffat said so. Ipimi laughed.

'I always said as much,' she chuckled through the rims of her gums. 'I told Sechele. I told him the girl was dry. She was shaped the wrong way to be seeded. He wouldn't listen. He desired her, he wanted to mount her. What did he give her to wear on her wrist?'

'I do not know that Sechele gave them to her,' Moffat answered. 'But my mother wore seven copper bracelets.'

'Sechele gave them to her right enough,' Ipimi said. 'One of them was mine. He gave it to me when we first lay together, but he took it back when I did not swell –'

She chuckled again. 'He was a hard man, your father. I loved him, but he was a bandit. What of your brothers? Tell me about them.'

The questioning continued through the evening and into the small hours of the night.

Long before it ended, Moffat knew it had become a ritual. He had told the truth. He was Sechele's son and old Ipimi knew it. She had known it from the moment he denied the size of his mother's breasts. Afterwards Moffat had simply been keeping the old woman company as she garrulously talked on.

When Ipimi finally tired, she called for Batuka.

'In truth this is Sechele's son,' she said. 'Only Sechele's seed could know what he knows. I give him back to you.'

Moffat left the hut with the leader of the Mashona. A crescent moon was shining. Batuka looked at him.

'It is told that fountains of seed spilled from Sechele's groin,' Batuka said. 'Like the grain in the pastures, some must have grown taller and stronger than the rest. Sechele sifted the best for himself.'

The man stopped.

Moffat looked at him. Batuka was no longer hostile. He was wary and undecided. So, too, were the warriors gathered in a ring behind him. Before there were only a dozen of them. Now the entire spear-carrying male population of the compound had joined the others. As Moffat's eyes swept over them, he saw there were thirty, even forty men, ranged before him.

Moffat nodded.

They had accepted that he was indeed Sechele's son. It did not mean they accepted he was their chieftain. For that he would have to prove himself in a different way.

'I came to you unarmed,' Moffat said. 'I will need a spear.'

'It is ready for you,' Batuka replied. 'The creatures have been spoored and marked. Everything is ready for you –'

He turned and snapped at one of the young men. The young man ran forward and presented Moffat with a spear.

'The trackers have chosen well.' Batuka smiled. It was a challenging, sneering smile. 'The animals might even test Sechele himself.'

Moffat weighed the spear.

It was well balanced. He struck its base against the earth and felt the vibrations run through his hand. The wood of the shaft was good. So too, when he examined them, were the bindings of the thongs that tied the iron blade to the stem. Moffat threw the spear high in the air. It dropped in a clean arc with the head pulling it down. As it fell he caught it and tossed it on his outspread palms.

Moffat smiled. At least Batuka had been just. The weapon was true.

'Then let us go out,' Moffat said. 'Let us see the strength of Sechele's seed.'

He walked towards the boma entrance. Outside the wall of thorns lay the bush, the wilderness, the ancient testing-grounds of Africa. With the trackers behind him, Moffat stepped out into the darkness.

— 58 —

The first trial was against fear.

The snake was old and cunning.

For four dry summers she had guarded the well against the women who wanted to draw water. There was a time when they could go and pull up the clear, clean liquid which, even when the rains had failed for yet another year, ran sweet and pure from the fossil water table which underlay the desert.

Each year the snake took her toll. This year, the fourth summer of the long drought, she had claimed two young girls not yet with the braided hair of puberty. She struck in the midday sun, coming out of the light without a warning hiss or a rattle of dry scales, to leave the young bodies writhing as the poison worked through their twisted limbs.

The great yellow and black patterned snake did not kill for food. Even her huge maw could not digest the full-grown limbs. She struck carelessly, sometimes not from one moon to the next, defending the territory of which she was mistress, her fanged jaws wide, her head whiplashing like an ox-driver's sjambok.

Lizards and tender little birds were more to her taste. At night she lay motionless in the darkness of the hollow thorn tree which overhung her well.

Moffat waited and watched by the well for one long night and one long day.

The snake, he knew, was fear, and fear was death. To conquer fear, to conquer death, required cunning. Cunning required time. Moffat waited and watched.

He saw the snake quiver as the morning rays touched

her patterned scales as she lay coiled in the root of her thorn tree. He saw how her life blood quickened in the warmth of the midday sun. In the hazy afternoon, when all warm-blooded creatures looked for shade against the desert sun, he watched her hunt the weaver birds, picking them off like ripe plums as they rested among the woven nests which hung from her thorn tree. So many and no more, until her belly was quivering with the tiny half-digested bodies.

Above all, as the night drew in, he saw her plaited muscles heavy and sluggish as the drought-dried river when the sun's warmth no longer quickened her. By the time the sun dropped below the horizon the next night, he knew her weakness.

Moffat killed her with a stab of his spear through her head as the moon rose.

The second test was against hunger.

The bull elephant was solitary now.

Once, in the dim past, he had a mate and walked with the herd, their heavy strong bodies moving together through the plains and woods of the African plateau. No thorn bomas held them back. No danger threatened – unless it might be a buffalo cow protecting her calf as the great beasts walked down to water. Or one of the cats, a cheetah perhaps with a litter of young, or a hungry lioness, stalking one of the elephant calves. Then they all formed a wall, trumpeting and stamping with giant's feet.

When the elephants did that, nothing could harm them. They were invulnerable.

Then it had all changed. The great bull elephant's mate had fallen one sudden terrifying dawn, her flesh torn by a thunder which came from a moving animal, no larger than an antelope, undetected at a distance too great to allow warning of danger. Her screams, and those of the infant calf who suckled her, still rang in his ears ten years later. He had searched for her attacker, even charged the thunder, and felt the pain tearing into his own flesh. And then he, too, had run, blundering in blind anguish, screaming in rage as he crashed through the scrub, heaving trunks and rocks from his path and ripping his own flesh on the jagged branches.

That was in the past. Since then, he had wandered through the dry years, alone and angry.

Now, his great ears cooling him like grey fans in the morning sun, his small eyes quartered the mopani scrub. The danger was outside the range of his limited vision. But he knew it was there. The quick, sharp warning calls of the scrub robin, the scent released from the glands of small animals, even the quickening movement of the wings of insects in the breeze, they all told him of an alien presence.

Tentatively he thrust the sensitive tip of his trunk into the moving air. There it was. The stench he hated.

He moved his great ears from side to side, testing the air for the sounds which would give him range.

Moffat watched the huge creature from the fork of the baobab which marked the limits of the bull's territory. He had been there since dawn. The hollow trunk trapped the dew each night, and he had a well of sweet water to sustain him as the sun climbed the sky.

Moffat had dug the pit between the baobab and the tall acacia which the elephant had spent the previous evening stripping of its tender leaves and branches. The animal had slumbered until dawn, leaning the grey bulk of its body against the strong trunk.

Now, for the past hour or two, he had not moved, squinting as he tested the air with his trunk. The breeze swung round and he caught the scent of the man in the tree.

He laid his great ears flat against the grey leather of his pitted flanks. Blindly he charged.

The bull elephant fell into the leaf-hidden, stake-lined pit. Crashing and thundering, his nostrils filled with the stink of his enemy, his massive bulk dropped on to the stakes. Moffat sprang down from the tree. He weighed the spear again in his hand.

The spear felt sharp and true.

Moffat jumped on to the elephant's back and buried the spear's tip in the artery that ran back from its neck. The huge animal shuddered and collapsed beneath him. Scrambling out of the pit, Moffat looked round for the Mashona. They were advancing warily through the bush, their own spears in their hands.

'Where are your knives?' he shouted. 'Here is enough meat to provision us for a month. Let it be carved and dried!'

The Mashona ran forward. They peered into the pit. Then they jumped down and began butchering the elephant. Only Batuka, the elder who had met Moffat at the kraal's gates, remained on the ground above the trap.

'You have slain the serpent,' he said. 'You have given the morans food. But Sechele had more than cunning. He was more than a great provider for his people. When danger came, he met and defeated it for his tribe himself.'

Moffat glanced at his spear. The shaft was running with the elephant's blood.

'While the spear's throat is moist,' he said, 'let it drink again. Where does the danger lie?'

The leopard in the tree lay along the branch, its eyes half closed.

Suddenly it quivered. The hairs in its spotted coat rose, and its nostrils flared. There were drifts of smells coming towards it on the early morning air. Disturbing and dangerous smells. It crept along the branch and snarled a puzzled, uncertain warning.

The leopard had been crouching in the tree for twelve hours. It had been driven to take refuge there by a group of men. They had found its pug-marks in the sand and had encircled it and herded it towards the tree in the afternoon of the day before. Two of the men had remained there ever since.

Now as the light of dawn began to fill the sky the leopard was hungry and confused. Most of all it was angry.

Over the years, men had registered in the leopard's

brain as quick and cunning fork-legged predators who competed with him for prey. The leopard had learnt to distrust and fear them. They carried metallic smoking branches that were even more deadly than its own talons. Men were to be avoided. When they could not be avoided, they had to be attacked.

To attack anything successfully the leopard needed the fury-producing adrenaline that was flooding its body now.

There was another of the fork-legged creatures below him. A different one from the two who had cautiously kept their distance all night. This one was approaching the tree boldly and provocatively. The man's posture signalled menace. In the animal's mind anger, threat and frustration combined in a single overwhelming wave of aggression.

The leopard snarled again and sprang downwards.

Moffat was half-prepared for it.

When the trackers had silently led him to the copse and fanned out behind, leaving him to go forward alone, Moffat knew what to expect. A tree leopard. He had known leopards all his life. Night hunters, they were among the most wary and elusive animals in Africa. Few people ever saw them. They left no shadow on the grass, it was said, by sun or moon or stars. Yet trapped and cornered they were also among the continent's most dangerous creatures.

This leopard had been cornered. Moffat was ready for that. He was not prepared for the suddenness, the speed and ferocity of its attack.

It came down from the tree in an enraged and murderous arc of muscle, talon and tooth. The animal was responding to his presence in the only way it had been genetically programmed to react – swiftly and lethally. Moffat heard the soft whisper of its claws on the branch as the leopard launched itself. He saw its pelt flare in the starlight. He smelt the carrion vapours on its breath. He glimpsed the needle-like points of its claws and the bared fangs.

Moffat rolled on to his back.

He held the spear above him like a lance. The leopard impaled itself on the spear's arrow-shaped head. The blade entered deep into the animal's body. For a moment the leopard hung there over him, clawing at his body. To Moffat the rocking weight between his hands was almost unendurable. Then the spear's shaft broke. The leopard fell, the soft fur catching briefly on the fierce thorns of the tree. As it tumbled, the animal scrabbled in a last frenzied spasm at Moffat's shoulder.

Moffat felt no pain as the claws ripped into his flesh. The pain came later, long after the weight had rolled away and the patterned fur lay lifeless beneath him.

By then it did not matter. By then he was back in the kraal of the Kakindi who were no longer Kakindi, the homeless ones. Now they had a chief. Now they were Mashona again.

'Where do you lead us – ?'

Moffat propped himself up on his elbow as he heard the question.

The speaker was Batuka, the grey-haired elder of the settlement who had advanced to meet him when Moffat rode through the boma entrance. That was seven days ago. Then Batuka had been suspicious and hostile, like the warriors crowding at his back.

Now everything was different. Batuka was smiling and the tone of his voice was eager. Moffat stretched out his arms. His wounds from the leopard's talons had almost healed, but he could still feel painful twinges where the tissue and skin hadn't yet knitted together.

It would be a day or two more before he was ready to move.

'Do we extend our pastures here,' Batuka went on, 'or do we march south where the river grows broader and, it is said, the grasslands are richer still? In which case, we must be ready to fight for them.'

Moffat looked at him.

The thought of battle – and it was clear Batuka was

eager to trek south – had made the older man's eyes gleam. Moffat smiled back.

'We march south,' he said. 'But we do not march this time to conquer. We march to keep faith with a white woman and a child of the desert.'

— 59 —

'For Christ's sake, Mr Bos'n! Get the monkey up here – the kites have stripped!'

Ben's head jerked up. The captain was bellowing somewhere on deck above him. Ben threw off the rough blanket and scrambled to his feet.

He'd been asleep in the crew's quarters at the *Star of Russia*'s bows. When the ship sailed two weeks earlier, he'd managed to get a passage with the guinea riders – passengers who paid a token pound-and-a-shilling for their berth and rations in return for working throughout the voyage.

Until the night before, the winds had been steady and light. Then the ship rounded the bulge of Africa and headed across the Gulf of Guinea. The Gulf was notorious for the roughest seas in the Atlantic, and the storm had hit them with a vengeance an hour ago. Now the noise in the hold was deafening. The boards creaked and groaned, and the wooden walls thundered as the ship's prow slammed into the rearing breakers.

As Ben lurched unsteadily towards the steps leading upwards, he glanced round for Tom. Tom was the 'monkey', the boy whose job was to climb the mast and set the 'kites', the ship's topsails. If the kites had gone they were in trouble.

Ben couldn't see him. Young Tom was probably already on deck. Ben scrambled up after him.

'Where the hell's that carpenter?' Ben heard the captain bellow above the roaring of the wind.

'Here!' Ben shouted back.

'Get back to the stern, damn you! The wheel cable's

casing has split open on the port side. The cable's already dragging on the splinters. If anything else gets in, it'll ride up tight and we'll be spinning like a whore on a lascar's cock. Clear it and get a covering on it, for Christ's sake!'

'Yes, sir!'

Ben grabbed his tool bag. Clutching the streaming guide rail he slithered towards the stern. Then he set to work with the spray cascading over him, and the ship plunging and heaving sickeningly beneath his feet.

Four hours later, Tom the monkey had cut away the torn topsails and lashed down the sheets. Ben had cleared the broken wood from inside the casing. He freed the cable, and hammered on a shield of planks to protect it. The wind was still howling but the *Star of Russia* was running swiftly and steadily southwards.

When dawn came Ben was suspended in a cradle tossing over the stern as he checked the casing on the starboard side. The cold was bone-chilling, his muscles ached, and there was constant danger. Every few moments he had to jerk his arm back to prevent it being crushed as the cradle smashed against the stern timbers. Yet Ben was happier than he had been for months.

Compared with the filthy chill and damp of London, the icy spray was clean and invigorating. Beneath the vast canopy of the racing clouds, the Aquarium seemed in retrospect grim and claustrophobic. The violent turmoil of the last forty-eight hours before he left was already a fading memory. Farini and the theatre belonged to the past.

Most of all, Ben was working with his hands and his skills again in the element he knew best, where he had always been safest, where no one had ever taunted him. In the world of water.

The waves calmed for an instant. Ben wiped his face and glanced up. Two figures were hunched over the stern rail. He blinked and saw that they were Mary-Ellen and Kala. Mary-Ellen was gazing down from beneath the hood of her cape. Kala was bareheaded and her face was half-hidden by wisps of sea-sodden hair. Her eyes were dark and wide, and her lips were drawn back in an expression of fear.

Ben smiled up at them. He waved confidently. Then the sea rose again and a wave spurted up through the open frame of the cradle's floor. He gripped the rope and went back to work.

By the evening the storm had passed.

Until the storm, Ben had hardly seen Mary-Ellen or Kala during the voyage.

Afterwards, Kala began to search him out. As the ship ran south the weather became warmer, and Ben took to sleeping out on deck. Often Kala would find him when he was resting after work high up near the bows.

However still the air, Ben never heard her approach. It was almost eerie. She moved as stealthily and silently as one of the hunting foxes he'd watched as a child in the New Forest. One moment he would be gazing alone out over the sea. The next a slim shadow would fall across the deck. Ben would glance round, startled, to see her standing or squatting beside him.

Soon Ben realized that for some reason he couldn't fathom, Kala had attached herself to him.

Sometimes as he lay sprawled on the deck, she settled his head in her lap. Kala carefully parted his hair and picked through the strands. Whenever she caught a flea or a louse – Ben picked up plenty of both whenever he went into the ship's holds – she would grunt in satisfaction and nip the insect's carapace between her front teeth. At other times, she would butt him with her head and nip his skin, prodding at him until he responded by rolling over and pushing her away.

Mary-Ellen was never far behind Kala. She would watch the girl, frowning. Occasionally she looked at Ben and gave him a distant smile, but she seldom spoke more than two or three words. All Mary-Ellen was interested in was Kala. Any trace of the brief flash of gratitude and concern she'd shown when she suggested Ben take ship with them to Cape Town had long since gone.

Now that he was of no further use to her, Ben thought in the ship's workshop one day, Mary-Ellen was deliberately distancing herself from him. Sometimes he suspected she even resented Kala's attachment to him.

Ben remembered the night in the theatre. He remembered Farini's murderous attack on him with the steel rod. The risks he'd taken, the job he'd lost, and the peril he'd put himself in. Ben swore out loud so violently that the carpenter hammering on the other side of the workshop stopped and glanced round.

Ben grunted angrily.

At least he had the money, and Kala was on her way home. In Cape Town he would be rid of them all. Ben drove the chisel's head deep into the tenon joint he was cutting, and dismissed Mary-Ellen from his mind.

Four weeks later Ben woke to the rattle of the ship's anchor chains.

He leapt up and gazed over the side. The *Star of Russia* was swinging slowly out in the harbour roads of the wide, calm bay beneath Table Mountain. Through the darkness he could see the lights of Cape Town gleaming across the water. Ben stood for a moment staring at them, and smelling the rank night-time smells of the harbour.

Then he turned and went below. Mary-Ellen's cabin was amidships on the lower deck. Ben knocked on the door and waited. There was a rustle inside and the door opened.

'What is it?' Mary-Ellen said anxiously.

Ben drew in his breath in surprise.

Mary-Ellen was wearing a simple cotton nightgown. Through it he could see the shadowy lines of her body. Her long fair hair was tousled and her face warm with sleep. For a moment she looked quite unlike she'd ever looked before. No longer the forceful and commanding young woman who'd hired him to help her and ignored him ever since. Instead she was soft and vulnerable, like a child woken from nightmares.

For an instant Ben felt a sudden almost overwhelming

urge to smile reassuringly, to reach out and touch her cheek. He stopped himself and the moment passed. Instead he shook his head. When he spoke his voice was rough.

'We've arrived,' he said. 'We've dropped anchor out in the roads half a mile from the shore. In the morning the Port Authorities will come aboard. They'll check the ship's lists and issue a bill of health.'

'Then we'll disembark tomorrow?'

'*You* can disembark when you want,' Ben answered. 'As far as I'm concerned, there'll be a warrant out for my arrest in London. British law applies out here. If the police have discovered I boarded the *Star* and have put the warrant on a navy vessel, it may already be here. Those navy ships sail almost twice as fast as we do. In which case they could be waiting for me. It's happened before. One of the old hands on the boat told me –'

Ben paused. 'I'm going ashore tonight. If you're sensible, you'll come too.'

Mary-Ellen stared at him. Her mind raced.

'But how can we land tonight?'

'There's a lighter lying at the stern,' Ben replied. 'All the officers have turned in. There's only the watch still up. I know them, they won't bother about me. We'll take the lighter and Tom the monkey with us. He'll row it back. No one will be any the wiser.'

Mary-Ellen was silent. Then she said quietly, 'You don't have to become involved again. Why are you doing this?'

Ben hesitated. He shrugged but didn't answer. He wasn't even sure himself.

'Be by the stern gangplank in twenty minutes,' he said abruptly. 'You'll need to tie your skirts up.'

He turned and went out.

An hour later Ben shipped the oars, and the lighter came to rest against one of the waterfront jetties. He helped Mary-Ellen and the others out. Then he swung the bows round and pushed the little boat back into the bay. With Tom sculling at the stern, Ben watched it disappear into the darkness.

He climbed up on to the jetty. Fifteen yards away, Kala and the San were clustered like children round the tall figure of Mary-Ellen. Kala glanced round and saw him. As she stared at him, Ben noticed that her eyes were glittering in the moonlight with a fierce ruby glow.

Mary-Ellen saw Ben too. She came over to him. She had gathered her skirts almost up to her waist for the boat, and looped them round her hips with a wide leather belt. Her legs were long and straight. Unencumbered by the cloth, she moved with a quick firm stride that was more like a young man's than a woman's.

'I spent three weeks here in a boarding-house waiting for a ship to London,' Mary-Ellen said. 'I made friends with the landlady. I think she'll let us in even at this hour. It won't be easy to find anywhere else. I suggest you come with us.'

Ben glanced down. His breeches were sodden. He was tired and he was already beginning to shiver as the warmth from the effort of rowing began to wear off in the chill night air.

He looked up at her again. The vulnerability he'd seen in her an hour earlier had vanished. Once again Mary-Ellen was the confident, determined woman she'd been from the start. On the ship the purser had cashed the banker's draft she'd given him. The water had shrunk the pockets of his breeches, and Ben could feel the coins pressing into his thigh. As the memory of the transaction came back to him, Ben felt a sudden surge of resentment.

Ben shook his head. 'I'll find my own lodging, but I'll see you to yours first. A port at night's no place for a lady. You may think you can buy your way out of almost anything, but not even a purse full of guineas will be any use to you out here in the darkness.'

Ben saw her flush. For a moment she looked so angry Ben thought she might even strike him. Instead she turned on her heel and strode away. She stopped briefly to unbuckle her skirt and shake it to the ground. Then she led the way through the darkened alleyways beyond the quay.

The rooming-house was at the end of a narrow street. Once the landlady had opened the door and recognized Mary-Ellen, she was as helpful as Mary-Ellen had said. As Mary-Ellen led Kala and the San upstairs, she fussed round preparing rooms and lighting fires.

Ben waited in the hall.

He didn't know why he'd stayed. He'd meant to leave as soon as they got to the door. Currents of anger and bitterness were still running through him. In spite of that, Ben regretted what he'd said on the quay. At least Mary-Ellen was fearless, even dauntless. He had taken risks, but so had she, appalling risks from the very start of her journey. And she'd done what she'd set out to do. She'd brought Kala back. All that remained was to return the girl to the desert. With Mary-Ellen's resources and her knowledge of Africa, that wouldn't be difficult now.

For that alone, for the memory he'd always have of the slim mute girl with her haunting eyes, he didn't want to part from Mary-Ellen with anger hanging in the air between them. Ben heard Mary-Ellen's footsteps on the stairs. He turned as she came down into the hall.

'They're all settled,' Mary-Ellen said. 'Soon they'll be asleep.'

'I'm glad,' Ben answered stiffly. 'Tomorrow you should be on your way.'

She nodded. 'I'll find out about the waggon trains north in the morning –'

Mary-Ellen hesitated. Her voice had been awkward and uncertain. Suddenly her cheeks reddened.

'You may not believe this, but I am truly grateful for all you've done,' she added. 'I would like to give you more, but I have a feeling you would not take it.'

'No, I would not,' Ben said. 'Not one penny. But I'm sorry for what I said –'

He broke off. He hadn't meant to apologize. Everything he'd said, he knew stubbornly, had been true. For some reason the words had tumbled out almost of their own accord.

'I must be on my way.' Ben managed to gather himself

together. 'It will soon be dawn. There'll be work in the harbour. Take care of the girl.'

Then he was gone.

As the door closed, Mary-Ellen stared thoughtfully after him. Apart from the fact that he was brave and resourceful, all she knew about the young man was that he was proud, prickly, and filled with a dark brooding hostility towards the world. Only twice had she seen him happy.

Once when he was swinging over the ship's stern in the cradle during the storm. Then, with the wind roaring and the waves cascading round him, for a moment he had been a different creature. As his powerful hands worked deftly at the ropes, he had even laughed. The second time was one day when Kala had fallen asleep with her head on his chest. Stroking her hair, Ben's eyes had closed in contentment.

Mary-Ellen had nothing in common with him. They had been briefly yoked together by chance, by accident. Ben was truculent and abrasive and as wary as a wounded animal. Yet she'd grown used to the distant limping silhouette on the deck. In a sense he'd been the only companion she'd had since she left Kuruman. Even his silent presence on the ship had comforted her.

Now he'd gone she felt a hollow, almost a sense of loss, inside her. Mary-Ellen shook her head irritably. She was used to being alone. She'd always been alone. She was back in Africa and she needed no one to help her now, least of all a crippled stranger. She headed for the stairs.

As she climbed them, Mary-Ellen found that in spite of herself she was thinking of the hard grey eyes that had gazed at her across the table in London as the mist swirled down the mournful street outside.

— 60 —

Kala squatted naked on the deeply recessed sill of her room on the second floor of the old Dutch-built rooming-house.

She had climbed up there as soon as Mary-Ellen closed the door. It was still dark outside, but daybreak was close. The sharp metallic odour of dawn pricked her nostrils. She heard the soft rustle of the breast feathers of birds as they puffed them against the sudden chill that came at the end of the night. She listened to the shrill scream of a tiny pearl-spotted owl returning from its hunting.

Then a movement in the street below caught her eye. Kala glanced down.

The young man who'd just brought them ashore emerged from the door. He yawned and glanced up at the lightening sky. She watched him limp lop-sidedly down the empty street. His shuffle reminded Kala vividly of her litter brother Akula. The hyena, too, had moved awkwardly like that when he returned exhausted from the hunt. Kala had felt a kinship with the young man from the moment she first saw his angular gait in the cold termite mound of the city, and heard the tap of his mallet – a sound that echoed up from somewhere unfathomably deep in her memory. Kala had groomed him on the journey across the waves as she'd once groomed Akula. He wasn't as close to her as the hyena had been. The man didn't hunt with her, he didn't warm her at night or lick her clean in the morning. In every other way he had become her litter brother too.

In the same way the other one, the tall woman with the

pale skin and the hair that shone like the sun, had become Kala's mother. She had to replace not just the old female hyena Herut, but the twin presences who succeeded Herut – the San matriarch, Lys, and her daughter Poli. Lys had been left behind in the desert. Poli had been killed by the men with the smoking sticks.

Kala was left with this strange new substitute for all three.

She nuzzled and licked the white woman when they slept together. Kala watched her, she followed her, she clung to her. Kala offered her food. When they met after even the briefest separation, Kala gave her the sign of submission and respect. She stretched out her arms on the ground, touched her chin against her wrists, and turned her head to one side.

The white woman seemed to accept the gesture, just as Lys and Poli had done. But even as Kala rose, she knew it wasn't the same. It hadn't been the same when the San women acknowledged it too. Only Herut knew what it meant. Only the hyena was her true mother.

Now, perched on the sill, her face stiff with concentration and her nostrils flared, Kala wasn't thinking about either the hyenas of her past or the humans who inhabited her present. She was searching for the desert beyond the town.

The desert was still far, far off, but she had known it was there from the moment she stepped into the little boat and smelled the night air of Africa. Tantalizingly, elusively, it hovered somewhere beyond her reach, hidden by the rising clamour and stench of the wakening harbour.

At last, as the air warmed and the invisible thermals began to spiral upwards, the desert returned to her. Free and wild it came carried on the wind, scented with dew and crushed sage from the trampling of the buffalo herds on their way to water, and all the sharp fragrant smells of the Kalahari morning.

As it reached her Kala pulled the diamond from her belt. She held it cupped in her hand, angling it carefully to catch the sun's first beams. Then she gazed into the stone's glittering surface.

The shadow of a landscape moved across the brilliance. A landscape that suddenly burst into colour with the green and gold of papyrus reeds and the glitter of water between. She could hear cries. She saw a boat. No, many boats. Rafts and makoros, the dugout canoes of the inland waterways. The craft were filled with men with skin like hers, olive in the shadows and golden in the sunlight. The men were soldiers. They were dressed in tattered tunics and they carried short swords in their hands.

The paddlers in the boats were all black. They drove their oars into the water and the boats surged forward. In the first makoro was the man Kala had once seen riding the bright horse at the head of the column. Behind him was the old woman, white-haired and wrinkled and stooped. The old woman was pointing forwards to a distant raft of dark trees, half-suspended between the sky and the water. The man stood up and gazed ahead, his heavy brows lowered against the glare.

Across the glittering water and reedbeds, Kala heard the echo of the man's voice as he urged the paddlers on with swift movements of his hand. Kala narrowed her eyes and peered deeper into the depths.

A mile away Ben shouldered his way through the crowds on the Cape Town waterfront.

A few hours ago at midnight it had been deserted. Now, in the morning sunshine, he was enveloped by the tumult of the harbour's daily business. Tall ebony-skinned negro women pushed past him, their heads and bodies bound in brilliant cotton wraps. Tiny brown-skinned girls balancing huge bundles on their heads trotted by on every side. Linened Europeans, elegantly hatted and caned, threaded their way down the alleys which ringed the port. Turbaned Muslim traders argued the price of spice sacks with frowning Indians. Groups of red-faced Boer farmers handed their *hausfraus* up on to the running boards of heavy-wheeled waggons.

Ben spent the whole day on the waterfront. For a skilled carpenter there was no shortage of work in the busy warehouses and along the crowded quays. By the time the evening came he had received five offers of employment, all of them wanting him to start the following morning.

As dusk fell, Ben leant on the harbour wall considering them.

Below him a sailor was furling the flying squaresail on a graceful little single-masted cutter. On the stern was painted its port of origin, Dublin. Ben thought for a moment. If the cutter came from Dublin, at least he and the sailor would share a common language. Perhaps the sailor knew Cape Town and could give him some advice.

Ben swung himself over the wall. He walked down the steps and greeted the man.

'Straight from London, are ye?' the sailor said. 'Did ye sail out on her?'

He pointed at a tall, graceful clipper riding out in the bay beyond. From the clipper's stern fluttered the blue and white flag of the P&O line.

Ben shook his head. 'I took passage on the *Star of Russia*.'

The sailor nodded.

'I know her too,' he said in a soft Irish lilt. 'She's not a bad boat, but there's nothing to touch the clippers – not even steam. Take that Union Castle ship, she'll have left Tilbury three days behind ye but she docked a day ahead –'

The sailor paused.

'Imagine! Ye could have left your baggage behind, but if someone put it on the clipper, it would still have been here in Cape Town before ye!'

He chuckled. As he coiled his rope, the man went on talking.

Ben stiffened. He stood very still.

He was no longer listening to the sailor. Icy charges of adrenaline were pulsing through his stomach.

He'd allowed for the possibility of a navy vessel

outsailing them. It had never occurred to him that a passenger ship could do the same. If Farini learnt they had sailed on the *Star of Russia*, he could have taken the Union Castle clipper and arrived the day before. In which case he would already be here in the city.

Farini was fuelled by rage now as well as greed. If he'd come, he would have brought the massive South African, Gert Frouw, with him. It made no difference that Ben had managed to slip the others ashore the night before. Cape Town wasn't large and Frouw knew it inside out. It would take him only a matter of hours to trace a group of strangers who'd just arrived from Britain.

Whirling away from the puzzled sailor in mid-conversation, Ben threw himself up the steps again. Running as fast as he could, he set off through the swiftly gathering darkness towards the rooming-house.

Mary-Ellen had been out all day.

She'd hoped to be away from Cape Town by mid-afternoon, but there were no waggon trains leaving for the north until next morning. She bought space on the trek for herself and six 'servants', as Kala and the San would have to travel. Then she spent the rest of the day pricing supplies in the warehouses which lined the waterfront.

As evening approached she returned to the boarding-house. Now, as the sky darkened outside, she placed her single suitcase on the bed and began to unpack its contents.

Carefully hidden at the bottom, beneath a hunting knife Moffat had given her, and the heavy flintlock pistol which like every child of the bush she'd been taught to carry wherever she went, was the precious package she'd received from Miss Stanwick. She opened the package, folded the map into a small square, and tucked it inside her skirt. Then she started to read once more the letter from Dr Darwin which by now she knew almost by heart.

The light was too dusky to make out the delicate copperplate hand. Mary-Ellen took the paper over to the window to catch the last of the sun.

As she reached the window, she noticed a movement on the far side of the street. There was something furtive about it. Instinctively she moved back into the shadow of the casement. She gazed into the dusk. A moment later Mary-Ellen tensed in fear.

In one of the pools of light which spilled out from the windows of the opposite house, she could make out a shadowy group of five or six men. Two of the men were taller than the others. One, gesticulating at the centre, was unmistakably Farini. The other was Gert Frouw.

Mary-Ellen drew back from the window.

For a moment she stood frozen, almost unable to breathe. From the room next door, she head a singsong chant and the sound of laughter. Old Deial was telling the San one of the clan's favourite stories. Kala was asleep in the room above beneath the eaves. Mary-Ellen had glanced in when she got back. Kala was lying curled on the floor with the diamond in her hand. For once the expression on her face was calm and untroubled. Mary-Ellen knew why. Kala had sensed the nearness of the desert. She was close to home.

Kala.

Frantically, Mary-Ellen threw off the paralysing numbness, and tried to think. She had no idea how Farini came to be there. For the moment it didn't matter. All that mattered was that he was outside with Gert Frouw and his men. They might try to enter the boarding-house immediately. Or they might wait a few minutes until complete darkness had fallen and the street emptied. From what she knew of Farini, the first was more likely.

As quickly as she could, Mary-Ellen hitched up her skirts again. She hurriedly tied a few of her belongings in a cloth, and thrust the flintlock pistol into her belt. She filled her pockets with shells and seized the hunting knife. Then she ran out and fetched the San. Gesturing for them to be silent, she led them up to Kala's room.

Kala was awake and crouching in the shadow on the sill. As Mary-Ellen came in, Kala's head whirled round. Her eyes were tiny pinpricks of scarlet light, and her lips were pulled back from her teeth in a snarl of fear. She knew Farini was outside too. Mary-Ellen ran to her side. As she peered down, Kala reached out her arm and pointed.

The men below had been joined by two other men in the blue and gold uniform of the Cape police. Kala wasn't pointing at them. It was something else. Mary-Ellen's gaze swung to the right. The street sloped steeply down towards the harbour. Running up the street, outlined against the harbour lights, was a man. It was too dark to see his face but the powerful silhouette and the limping shuffling stride were unmistakable.

It was Ben.

For a split second Mary-Ellen hesitated in an agony of indecision. If she shouted, the men would know she'd seen them. If she didn't, Ben would run straight into them. Mary-Ellen knew she had no choice.

She opened her mouth and screamed, 'Ben! Ben! Get back, they're here!'

The limping figure came to a halt. He gazed upwards in the direction of the shout. Then he threw himself into the shadows at the side of the street.

At that moment the men below raced across the street and hurled themselves at the front door. The door was locked and bolted. There was a brief silence, followed by the crash of an axe splintering wood. Mary-Ellen ran back to the attic door and slammed home the flimsy bolt. Beckoning to Deial's two sons to help her, she upended the bed and jammed it against the door frame.

Her heart pounding, Mary-Ellen paused.

The front door was heavy but it wouldn't withstand the assault of an axe for long. The men would need a few minutes more to search the house before they reached the attic. The door there wouldn't even need an axe before it gave way.

Suddenly there was a deafening crack, and an explosion shook the house. The men hadn't even waited for the axe to do its work. They'd shot the lock out. The shot was followed by the clatter of the landlady's footsteps on the stairs, and the sound of her screams. Outside, guttural voices shouted back at her.

'Police, *mevrou*! Pull back the bolts and open the door!'

'Why have you come to my house?' the woman screamed back at them. 'Why are you firing? There is no criminals here! Go away!'

She started to bellow abuse at them.

The bolts were still in place, Mary-Ellen realized. It could only be a matter of moments before the men forced the women to open them, or shot them out too. Desperately, Mary-Ellen's gaze swept the little room. Her eyes caught the rafters and the thin shingle boards above. She gripped the sturdy Dutch chair standing by the bed, and swung it violently upwards above her head. The edge of the chair smashed against the ceiling and one of the shingles cracked.

Mary-Ellen set the chair back on its feet. She stepped up on to it, opened the hunting knife, and began to lever the boards away from the rafters. A small dark hole appeared above her, and the cool night air swirled into the room.

'Khoi! Stand on my shoulders! Climb outside and widen the hole!'

The little San hunter scrambled up on to Mary-Ellen's shoulders and wriggled out into the darkness. Mary-Ellen heard the shingles snapping as he tore them away from above. A moment later the hole was twice the size. Khoi!'s face appeared, looking down questioningly through the gap.

'Wait there!' Mary-Ellen said.

She turned to call the San forward. Then Mary-Ellen froze again. The other four little people were standing behind her. Apart from them, the room was empty. Kala had vanished.

Mary-Ellen stood there bewildered. From the stairwell she could hear doors crashing and banging, and the landlady screaming. The men were inside the house and working their way upwards. The only way Kala could have escaped was through the window and on to the gable above. From the roof they might be able to pull her up.

Mary-Ellen seized the nearest of the San and heaved him upwards. Khoi! caught him by the arms and pulled him out. The other three followed. As the last one disappeared, Mary-Ellen launched herself off the chair and reached for Khoi!'s hands.

'Miss Ramsay, open the door! We will not harm you. I want nothing more than the return of my property.'

The shout came from the landing. The voice was Farini's. Mary-Ellen hung for an instant beneath the hole. Then she dropped back on to the chair. She turned to face the door.

Outside she heard the mutter of voices, followed by Farini shouting again.

'I have the police with me, Miss Ramsay. If you do not open the door now, you will be in very serious trouble.'

There was silence.

Mary-Ellen's mind raced. She was panting and she could feel sweat trickling down her face. The San were on the roof. Kala was somewhere out in the darkness. The backstreets of Cape Town were a warren. If she could join them outside and get down to the ground, they might still get away. Even a few more minutes might be enough.

Mary-Ellen pulled the gun from her belt and loaded it from the shells in her pocket.

'Back away from the door!' she called out. 'I'm going to count to five. If everyone out there isn't downstairs by then, I'm going to fire!'

Mary-Ellen's voice was calm, but her hand was shaking as she pulled back the hammer on the gun.

Beyond the door there was another whispered conference. Then without warning there was a crack and a flash of steel, and an axe blade scythed through the door panel. Mary-Ellen steadied the pistol on her arm. Taking careful aim, she fired twice through the centre of the door. As she did so the axe crashed down again. This time it tore the door from its frame.

At the same instant there was a deep-throated howl of pain, and the door caved in, carrying the bed with it. Mary-Ellen reloaded. Then she peered through the smoke from the shells which was swirling through the room in the draught from the roof.

Farini was standing in the doorway with the body of a man twitching at his feet. Behind Farini she could make out the silhouettes of six or eight other men. Farini's face was contorted with rage. As she watched, he stepped over the man on the floor and advanced into the room.

Mary-Ellen backed away across the floor.

It was over now, she knew that. There were too many of them, far too many. There was nothing more she could do. She felt empty and sick, but her fear had gone. Her eyes flickered upwards and then back to Farini. Mary-Ellen's mouth tightened. There *was* something she could do – not to save herself, but perhaps to give the others a chance. She could shoot Farini and shout at the San to run. Even on their own the little people might find Kala and escape.

Mary-Ellen raised the gun again.

She aimed at Farini's body and her finger began to tighten on the trigger. Suddenly Farini whirled away. Something outside the room had caught his attention. From the stairwell Mary-Ellen heard a confused clamour of shouts and curses. She frowned. She released the trigger and gazed over Farini's shoulder.

She saw the length of wood first. It was part of the heavy mahogany banister rail and it was being whirled like a club. Its shadow flickered dizzily off the wall behind as it slashed through the air. Then Ben came into sight, his head first, then his shoulders, then the rest of his twisted body as he mounted the stairs. His face was sheeted in blood and his eyes blazed. In front of him Farini's men were tumbling away.

Mary-Ellen hesitated.

There was nothing she could do to help him. She couldn't fire now. If she missed Farini, she might hit Ben. She thrust the gun back into her belt, leapt back on the chair, and jumped upwards. Khoi! caught her hands and heaved. For a moment her bunched skirts caught in the hole. She twisted and struggled. Then she managed to free them and levered herself on to the roof.

Panting and shaking, Mary-Ellen scanned the darkness.

The house was one of perhaps thirty joined together in pairs. Each pair was separated from the next by a narrow alleyway. Khoi! and the other San had already run down the sloping ridge of the roof and jumped across the gap on to the roof of the neighbouring houses. Mary-Ellen gathered up her skirts in one hand. She ran down the ridge and leapt over to join them.

As she landed she saw with horror that Kala wasn't there.

— 61 —

Kala balanced herself on the narrow gable above the window.

She was thirty feet above the ground, but she was as surefooted as a desert cat, and heights held no fear for her. She lowered her head over the edge, craned her neck, and peered back into the room which had been her den for the past night and day.

Kala's nostrils flared at the scent of blood and smoke, and the hairs on the back of her neck bristled at the scene below.

A few minutes earlier, the tall young woman had picked up the San and pushed them through the hole in the roof to safety. It was the same as Herut had done with her cubs when she moved them from den to den. But the woman had left behind the man who limped, the one who reminded Kala so strongly of her Akula. Kala had seen the man earlier hurrying back through the darkness in the street below, and she'd heard the woman's shout of warning. After that the woman had abandoned him just as in the storm Herut had abandoned her.

As Kala watched, the man burst on to the landing. He was lashing wildly round him with a length of wood. The other men had scattered in surprise, but he was only one and they were many. One of the men who had tumbled into the room struggled back to his feet. In his hands was one of the deadly smoking sticks that had brought death to the San encampment in the desert.

Kala saw him raise it to his shoulder.

The other men were starting to press forward again. They were gathering round the limping man like so many cowardly lions preparing to tear him down by the sheer weight of their numbers. Kala's tongue flickered between her lips. Herut had only deserted her because the hyena was old and tired. Before Herut's strength waned, she had taught Kala to cherish and protect the members of the clan to the death just as they cherished and protected her.

Kala had adopted the limping man as a member of the clan. She had bonded herself to him. Now that he was threatened, it was her duty to defend him. Kala was neither old nor tired – and lions, she knew, were no match for a hyena.

Kala bared her teeth. She gripped the window frame from below and launched herself off the eaves. She swung perilously out into the night, and then forward, like a springing leopard, into the room.

Kala landed on the back of the man with the stick. She seized his hair with one hand and jerked back his head. As he reeled away in panic and opened his mouth to shout, Kala sank her teeth into his exposed throat. The smoking stick seemed to explode in his hands, and a double roar from the detonating shells thundered through the room.

Kala dropped from the man's back to the floor. Blood was dripping from her mouth. She licked her lips impassively and glanced round. The man with the stick was slumped against the wall, clutching the deep wound in his neck and screaming. The air was filled with thick, bitter-smelling smoke. Through the smoke she suddenly saw the advancing silhouette of her two-legged litter brother.

At the same moment, Ben saw Kala. He registered both the girl and the hole in the roof above her head. For an instant, deafened by the discharge of the gun, Farini and the men with him were in disarray. Without hesitating, Ben gripped Kala by the arms and hurled her upwards. He saw her vanish. Then he scrambled up after her into the darkness.

Outside on the roof Ben stared over the houses. Fifty yards to his left, he could see the outlines of Mary-Ellen and the San as they leapt from rooftop to rooftop. Taking Kala by the hand, Ben set off after them.

Fifteen sickening jumps later they came to the last pair of houses. Mary-Ellen was waiting for him by an iron chimney flue. As he stopped, Ben heard a shout. He glanced back. A wavering beam of light lifted over the roofs behind.

'Down!' Mary-Ellen whispered.

Ben landed on the ground in a shower of rusting debris a moment after her. Brushing the flakes from his face, he saw Mary-Ellen tear the shoes from her feet and catch hold of Kala. With the San running ahead, they vanished into the darkness. Ben kicked off his own shoes and followed them.

'Here!' Mary-Ellen called out from somewhere ahead.

They had been running for an hour.

Ben was stumbling behind. Mist was sweeping in from the sea. It had become so thick he could only see a few yards in front of him. He heaved himself forward and glimpsed the glow of a fire in a copse of trees. The shadowy figures of the San were outlined against the flames. Ben dropped to his knees and warmed his hands.

'Where are we?' he asked.

Ben had long since lost track of where they'd been. For a time they seemed to have followed a maze of alleyways leading north. Afterwards, they began to climb. Then, Ben sensed, they had entered open country. The air was cleaner and colder, and the sounds of Cape Town faded behind them.

'We're in the hills above the town,' Mary-Ellen answered. 'Some other San made camp here last night. They've gone now, but Deial and Khoi! scented the smoke of the fire they left. The San only camp where it's safe. It means we should be safe for a while too.'

Mary-Ellen lifted her head and glanced round the copse. As she did so she tensed.

'Kala! Where's Kala?'

Plucking a branch from the flames, Mary-Ellen held

the torch high above the ground. In the wavering light Ben saw a row of footprints in the dew leading away through the trees.

'She's gone!'

Mary-Ellen's voice was distraught. She spoke hurriedly to old Deial and his son, Khoi!. Briefly, her gaze swung back to Ben.

'Stay here with the others,' she said. 'We're going to try to find her.'

Mary-Ellen disappeared before Ben could speak. He stared into the night. The fog was so dense now he could barely see the trunks of the nearest trees.

Kala lay on her stomach below the arch of stone which roofed the cave. She licked the last faint trace of dried blood delicately from the corner of her mouth. Then she gazed into darkness.

Kala had been in the cave since the moon rose two hours earlier.

She'd stayed with the woman and the limping man until they reached the fire. The woman was like Herut. She could look after herself. But the limping man was like Akula when her litter brother returned wounded after a long and dangerous hunt. The man had needed Kala. He needed her first when the men attacked him, and then again while they escaped.

Now he was safe. Kala and the woman between them had brought him to safety. He was tired too, terribly tired. She had smelled the exhaustion on his skin when he sank down by the fire. For the moment there was nothing more she could do for him. He had to rest.

That was why Kala hadn't hesitated when she caught the scent.

She had been squatting behind the San beyond the glow of the flames when it came to her nostrils. She could smell the drying sweat and the smoke and the resin from the burning logs. She could smell the scent of fear too, although it was fainter and more fugitive now. And then suddenly there was something else.

Kala had wrinkled her face. It was elusive and far-off, like the smell of the desert she'd searched for at dawn. This was another smell, even more potent and seductive than the morning scents of the Kalahari. For an instant she lost it. She wrinkled her face and inhaled the air, sifting the mist and the night wind through the membranes of her nose. Kala caught it again. This time it was pungent and unmistakable. She stiffened, and the pulse in her wrist began to throb.

Carried to her from the hill slopes above was the scent of a hyena clan.

It plucked not just at her nostrils, but at her mind – invading her, overwhelming her, drawing her irresistibly towards its source. Silently, while the attention of the others was distracted, she backed away from the fire and slipped through the trees. Beyond the copse Kala began to run with the swift loping stride that could cover the ground faster than any of them, faster even than the little yellow people.

As she climbed into the darkness, Kala could feel the diamond bumping rhythmically in its leather pouch above her groin.

'Deial! Khoi!!'

A few yards in front of Mary-Ellen the two little San came to a halt. They turned and trotted back.

It was half an hour since the three of them had left the others in the shelter of the trees. They'd been climbing steadily all the time. Now they had come out above the mist. It lay below them like a dense blanket, with the distant lights of Cape Town occasionally flickering through the rolling waves of greyness.

As he looked at Mary-Ellen, old Deial shook his head. She was sweating and her chest was heaving. Deial could never understand how the white people, so clever with their tools and weapons, dressed in a manner which tied them in more knots than a spring hare in a trap.

Mary-Ellen looked back at him. She knew what the old man was thinking.

'Do you have your knife, grandfather?'

Deial nodded and plucked his bone-handled blade out of his loincloth.

'Do as I say with it.'

Mary-Ellen began to undress.

On the rocky flanks of the hills, her European dress – the tight boots and ankle-length skirt, the neck-high blouse and complicated undergarments – were as hobbling and constricting as the white canvas jackets that restrained the mad. As the two San watched her through alert, incurious eyes, Mary-Ellen stripped until she was naked.

For an instant she stood quite still. She could feel the wind fresh on her skin, the damp touch of the ocean mist, the almost undetectable warmth of the starlight. Then she picked up her skirt.

'Cut it here and here,' she instructed the old man.

With his razor-sharp knife, Deial cut the cloth into two narrow triangles. Mary-Ellen put them between her thighs and knotted them round her waist.

'And here again,' she said.

The knife flashed in the darkness. She picked up the halter of cloth Deial had slashed out, and tied it over her breasts. She pulled it round until the knot was against her spine.

'Now the boots. Like this and this.'

Deial sliced away the leather of the ankle supports until only two thin sheaths remained to cover Mary-Ellen's feet. She stepped back into them and drew the laces tight. Then she tied on her leather purse.

She stood for a moment. Apart from the halter at her breast, she was as unencumbered as the two little hunters.

Deial studied her and clicked his approval. Now they might make better time. The she-hare that fell from the sky could travel at twice the speed of the tall white woman in her cumbersome clothes, and Kala's tracks had been getting harder to follow as the dew fell.

'You have the spoor?' Mary-Ellen asked.

Both the San nodded in reply.

'Let us follow it,' Mary-Ellen said.
They set off again.

'What is it, Deial?'

Another hour had passed. Mary-Ellen had come to a halt beside the suddenly motionless hunters. The old man scratched his chin with a sharpened stick he had cut from the bush. He paused, frowning, before answering.

'The girl is not running away,' Deial said. 'See how we have moved.'

He made a circling gesture with his hand. His son, Khoi!, grunted in agreement.

Mary-Ellen glanced round. She had noticed it herself. Kala's trail hadn't even followed the natural contours of the landscape. Instead it had jinked, twisted, and doubled back on itself. Sometimes the tracks almost seemed to be leading them back towards the clump of trees.

'What is she doing?' Mary-Ellen said.

Deial frowned again. 'I think the she-hare searches for something.'

The two San trotted on. Finally they stopped again. Mary-Ellen came up to the old man's shoulder.

'She is there.' Deial pointed with his stick.

Mary-Ellen peered forward. For several minutes they had been climbing up a broad rock-floored gully. She could see nothing except the black wall of the gully with the stars gleaming above.

'Where?' she asked.

'The cave,' Deial answered. 'The little she-hare is inside.'

Narrowing her eyes, Mary-Ellen could just make out an oval of even more intense blackness at the foot of the wall. On her own she would have walked past without even noticing it, let alone knowing Kala was there. Yet Deial and Khoi! had brought her unerringly to the cave and said the girl was inside. Mary-Ellen knew Kala would be there.

She walked on. Mary-Ellen saw the cave mouth when she was six feet from it. The entrance reached up from the floor of the gully almost to her own height. Hesitating momentarily, she lowered her head and ducked inside.

What happened in the next few seconds was the most terrifying experience of Mary-Ellen's life.

The smell came first.

Outside in the gully the air was clean and fresh. Inside the cave she was hit by a stench so powerful it was like a physical assault. Rank and acid, a mixture of faeces, musk, and ancient rotting flesh, it jolted her back on her feet. Her nostrils shrivelled and her stomach heaved. Mary-Ellen recoiled. Then she recognized what the smell was.

It was the lair stench of a pack of wild carnivores.

Mary-Ellen swallowed. Grasping the hunting knife at her waist, she walked on.

The interior of the cave was filled with a soft radiance. At the centre of the glow she saw Kala. Kala was lying on her stomach on the earth with her arms stretched out in front of her. She was gazing at her hands.

Cupped inside them was the diamond.

The jewel was shining with a dull fiery glow. Suddenly a ray of moonlight shone into the dim interior. The diamond absorbed the wavering light and hurled it back from a thousand facets until the entire cave blazed. Kala lifted her head. She stared at Mary-Ellen.

Mary-Ellen knew Kala's eyes were a deep almond-brown. They were brown no longer. Blank and unblinking, they were a fierce hungry scarlet. Nor were they the only eyes staring at Mary-Ellen. Behind Kala there were a dozen, fifteen, even twenty pairs of other eyes, all gleaming with the same predatory scarlet.

Eyes – and shadows.

Shadows cast on the cave's walls by the diamond's brilliance. Shadows of heavy, four-legged animals with massive sloping shoulders. Shadows with bared teeth in snarling jaws and bristling hair along their backs. Shadows that merged into a hunting clan that began to close on her.

'Kala – ' Mary-Ellen leapt forward.

Her terror forgotten for an instant, she seized Kala and dragged her to her feet. Behind Kala she could see the eyes growing brighter and the shadows larger as the ravening animals pressed forward. Mary-Ellen knew what they were now. The fetid smell of carrion, the scarlet eyes, the hunched shoulders, the powerful jaws and the bristling hair along the spine.

She had stumbled into a hyena den.

'Run!' Mary-Ellen screamed.

She hurled Kala towards the cave mouth.

Mary-Ellen swung back. In her hand was the hunting knife Moffat had given her. She threw it desperately at the leading animal. She saw the tip cut into its muzzle and blood start to run down its chest. Mary-Ellen turned again.

Mary-Ellen gripped Kala's arm and started to run, frantically tugging the girl after her. The outside air was sweet and fresh.

'Mama Mary!'

Mary-Ellen heard the voice as she cannoned into someone. It was Deial. In her haste to escape, she had tripped over his legs, knocking him backwards. They both fell to the ground.

'Hyenas!' Mary-Ellen panted. 'Why in God's name didn't you warn me?'

Kala had fallen too. All three of them struggled to their feet. They stood together in the darkness, with Mary-Ellen still holding Kala's wrist.

The old man looked at her steadily. 'There were hyenas many rains ago. Now there are no hyenas.'

'Deial, there are hyenas in the cave!' Mary-Ellen shouted. 'Fifteen or twenty of them, a full clan. They have their den there. I saw them. Ask your son, Khoi! Why didn't you tell me?'

Mary-Ellen's chest was heaving violently and her arms were trembling. In the starlight she could see Deial staring at her with a puzzled frown on his face. He turned and consulted Khoi!. The old man looked back at her.

'Not for many many rains. Look –'

He held out his hand to her. On his palm was something that looked like a white pebble.

Mary-Ellen took it and lifted it to her nose. There was no smell. She rolled the pebble between her fingers. It crumbled to powder and she sniffed the fragments again. Still there was nothing.

She knew what the white pebble was. A piece of hyena excrement. The digestive systems of the hyenas were so powerful and efficient they could even process bone. When hyenas finally expelled what little waste they couldn't absorb, it emerged in white pellets like the one Deial had handed her.

The pellets were always as hard as chalk and strangely fragrant. They smelt of wild rosemary. They kept their hardness and scent for a year or more. Only when they were old did they soften and lose their odour.

This pellet must have been very old. It was years since hyenas had used the cave as a lair.

Mary-Ellen gazed at Deial in confusion.

'There are hyenas there,' she insisted. 'I smelt them, I saw them. My nose and my eyes do not lie, Deial!'

'They do not lie,' Deial replied. 'But maybe they have made you dream.'

He spoke to Khoi!. Then he glanced back at her.

'We will go to the cave that you may no longer have fear.'

The hair prickled on Mary-Ellen's neck. Before she could say anything, the two had gone. They approached the gully's wall and vanished into the blackness of the cave's mouth.

They were away only a few moments before Mary-Ellen saw their silhouettes returning. Old Deial trotted up to her.

'There are no hyenas,' he said. 'You dropped the knife you carried in your belt.'

Mary-Ellen looked down. In Khoi!'s hand was the knife. There was no trace of blood on either the blade or the handle.

Mary-Ellen was silent. Her mind was in turmoil. She

had *not* been dreaming. She knew that with absolute certainty. Kala had been lying on the earth with a pack of hyenas behind her. Mary-Ellen had smelt them. She had seen their eyes and the heavy awkward shapes of their bodies. She had known hyenas all her life. They were unmistakable. She knew, too, they were among the most dangerous animals in Africa.

To enter a hyenas's lair was to invade its most private territory and provoke an attack.

When she'd left her room in the boarding-house, she had thrust a candle into her pocket. It was still there in the severed triangle of her skirt. She pulled it out and lit it. Slowly, she walked back up to the cave. Outside she took a deep breath. Then she stepped in.

Fighting against her fear, Mary-Ellen held up the candle and looked round. The cave was empty. There were no hunched shadows. No scarlet eyes. Nothing. She sniffed the air. It was dry and clean. There was no trace of the fetid stench that still seemed to cling to her nostrils.

Almost in despair, Mary-Ellen glanced down. The cave floor was flat and sandy. In the middle of it was the shallow print of a human body, Kala's body. Mary-Ellen could see where her feet and hips and breasts had rested, and then the impression of her knuckles at the end of her outstretched arms.

It was there that Kala had been holding the diamond.

Mary-Ellen went outside. Kala was standing with Khoi!. Dawn was close and light was already beginning to fill the sky from the east, but the gully was still in shadow.

Kala's face was expressionless.

She gazed back at Mary-Ellen as if she was staring at her from another world. Yet there was something different in her eyes. No longer scarlet – the memory of them glowing among the hyenas' eyes seemed to belong to a dream – they were almond-brown again. It was more than that. Kala's eyes were still remote and opaque, but there was something else in them.

Mary-Ellen frowned.

Power. It suddenly came to Mary-Ellen. Kala had been mute, helpless, a lost and haunted creature thrown up from the heart of Africa and snared in the violence which prowled the continent. Kala was still mute. She was still lost and haunted. She was no longer helpless.

Kala had discovered something. In her eyes there were the beginnings not just of the sense of power – but of power itself.

Mary-Ellen turned away sharply.

'Deial,' she said. 'Let us go back to the others.'

Deial grunted in acknowledgement. He lifted his sharpened stick and trotted away with Khoi! down the gully. Mary-Ellen blew out the candle and took Kala's hand. She set off behind the two San.

The sun was rising and the air was warming quickly. In spite of the gathering heat, Mary-Ellen was shivering.

— 62 —

Ben stirred and opened his eyes.

Through the branches of the trees the sky was beginning to pale. Dawn was close. On the other side of the ashes of the fire, the three San who had stayed behind when Mary-Ellen left were awake and talking quietly.

Ben climbed to his feet.

He walked to the edge of the copse and gazed across the hill flanks rising beyond. Spirals of dust and scattered thorn bushes, their leaves flaming scarlet and yellow, rose like islands through the thick haze of morning mist which had drenched his clothes.

Cape Town had been strange enough – but in a way it was still familiar. Hotter, steamier, more exotic and mysterious than any other harbour Ben had known, it nevertheless had ships and quays, warehouses and offices, everything he remembered from Buckler's Hard, Lymington, Southampton, and a dozen other ports where he'd travelled in search of commissions.

This great rock-strewn plateau in front of him was different. It was Africa.

A thick tapestry of wild flowers, vermilion and ochre, emerald and kingfisher blue, lapped his feet. Even the flowers' leaves were strange – fat succulent wedges of thorn-spiked fern fronds, or juicy violet-dusted stems seeded with feathery purple blooms. Beyond the meadow, billowing waves of arrow-twigged heather, their creamy tips spiked with tall orange-tongued lilies, filled the fissures in the rocks.

A flicker of movement caught his eye. Turning his head, Ben was just in time to see Nuna, a knife in his hand, slip like a shadow into an outcrop of stone at the edge of the trees. A moment later he reappeared with a giant lizard gripped in his fist, its saffron throat pumping wildly and its scarlet dinosaur jaws gaping. The length of the creature's shimmering emerald body almost equalled his own height.

Noticing Ben, Nuna grinned and waved, rubbing his stomach and smacking his lips. Ben smiled and waved back. Then he narrowed his eyes and scanned the ridges above the mist.

Like a sleeper waking from the night, Ben knew, it would take time for his eyes to adjust to Africa. The dark continent didn't yield its secrets easily. Its images were at once harsher and more subtle, more difficult to read than the lush meadows and quiet waving woods Ben knew so well. Here nothing was as it seemed. What appeared to be grey rock turned into the twisted silver limbs of thorn trees. Apparent ridges of stone evaporated into coils of vanishing mist.

Gradually Ben's vision cleared.

Another movement at the edge of his sight resolved itself into a sinewy trotting shadow barred with silver flanks. He stared and realized it was a jackal. Following the animal's line of sight, Ben picked up what he thought at first was a copse of shadowy grey and white saplings. The saplings moved across the ground and he saw they were a dozen striped horses.

They looked like the New Forest ponies with slender, more delicate heads, but he knew they were the zebra-like creatures which the South Africans called quagga. Abruptly the herd of quagga disappeared into a cleft in the earth. Keeping a cautious distance behind them, the silver-flanked jackal vanished too.

Ben was still gazing upwards, immobile as a rock, when he became aware of the little group of humans moving down the hillside across the slope where the animals had just disappeared. He strained his eyes and picked them out one by one.

The two San, Deial and his son Khoi!, came first. Tiny

and apricot-skinned, they kept appearing and reappearing through the waves of mist that seemed to sweep like breakers over the hills. Both had spears in their hands that they must have fashioned in the bush. Behind them were Mary-Ellen and the wild girl, Kala. Kala seemed to be hanging in Mary-Ellen's footsteps. With every roll of the mist, with every shifting beam of the rising sun, she vanished like a wraith.

Suddenly Kala ran forward.

She caught Mary-Ellen's hand and tugged her on. Now it was Mary-Ellen who was being led and not by another human – but by an animal, a dog that might have been straining at its leash to pull its mistress home. Ben's mind flashed back to the night before.

Through the smoke on the landing he'd seen the man scramble to his feet and level his rifle. The man's knuckle whitened as his finger tightened on the trigger. Then Kala launched herself through the window and leapt on to his back.

Ben had seen her bury her teeth in the man's neck, and afterwards lift her head with the blood streaming down her chin as the man screamed in agony. Her eyes had been blank and glazed and terrifying. She wasn't Kala then. She was an animal, a predator, but a predator who had adopted him as one of her own.

The little group was closer now. Mary-Ellen's golden hair was tousled, and her skin was powdered with dust. She'd discarded the long heavy skirt she'd always worn before. Instead she was dressed in nothing but a pair of rough cloths loosely tied round her body. With Kala loping beside her, she looked almost like a wild creature herself.

As the group reached the copse, Ben saw that Mary-Ellen's face was harrowed and frowning and her eyes strangely abstracted. She gave him a quick nod of acknowledgement. Without speaking, she strode on through the trees. Puzzled, Ben hurried after her. The rich scent of roasting meat floated through the air, and he suddenly realized he was ravenously hungry.

Nuna had skinned the lizard and was turning it on a spit over the flames. Ben squatted down and they all ate swiftly in silence. When Kala had finished, she slipped away into the shadow of a thorn bush. She lay there motionless on her stomach with her head resting on her arms as she watched them.

'You found her?' Ben asked Mary-Ellen. 'What's the matter? Is something wrong?'

'I don't really understand –'

Hesitant and fumbling for the words, Mary-Ellen tried to tell him.

Even as she spoke, Mary-Ellen could feel the events of the night slipping away like a dream lost within moments of waking. If she hadn't described it then, it would have gone, it might never have happened. Mary-Ellen knew it wasn't a dream. It *had* happened.

In the cave Kala had been surrounded by hyenas. The hyenas had vanished without leaving a sign of their presence behind them, not a trace of their feral scent or even the print of a paw. But they had been there, and when Kala emerged there had been something close to triumph in the girl's eyes. It was almost as if she'd summoned the hyenas to her.

Mary-Ellen stopped. She was shivering. Before Ben could say anything, there was a sharp staccato click from Khoi!.

Ben looked round. Khoi! and his father were standing again. The old man was holding out his spear towards the north. Ben's eyes swung in the same direction. The grass beneath the bush where Kala had been lying still held the print of her body. Kala herself had vanished.

Ben peered through the branches of the trees. A silhouette, etched black against the earth by the rising sun, was moving swiftly up the hillside down which the group had come barely ten minutes before.

'Kala!'

Mary-Ellen was already on her feet. Kala made no attempt to escape. When Mary-Ellen caught up with her, the girl stopped and turned, rubbing her head against

Mary-Ellen's shoulder. Together they returned to the trees.

At the fire Mary-Ellen released Kala. Kala stared at her. Then she turned and ran off again. This time Mary-Ellen caught her before she reached the edge of the trees. Kala swung round and stared at Mary-Ellen. For an instant her eyes shone with the same brilliant scarlet that they had glowed in the cave.

Suddenly the silence was broken by old Deial. He grunted and chuckled.

'The girl has heard the song of the desert robin and the cry of the fish eagle,' he said. 'She must return to her own hunting grounds. That is what she is saying in her runnings. She is a honey guide.'

Beside the old man his son, Khoi!, was laughing too.

Mary-Ellen looked at the two hunters. To them the message in Kala's repeated attempts to escape was as clear as the flight of the little brown bird they called the honey guide. Kala wasn't running away. She was leading them forward. The San were laughing with pleasure at the obviousness of it all.

'What did the old man say?' Ben asked.

Mary-Ellen told him.

Ben frowned. 'What's a honey guide?'

'A bird,' she answered. 'It likes eating the grubs of the wild bees, but their hives are too strong for the honey guide to break open. So when the bird finds a hive, it looks for help. It finds someone – a man or an animal – and flies ahead to lead them there. They take the honey and the bird gets the grubs left behind.'

Ben looked at Kala.

The girl was crouching motionless a few yards away on a low ant-hill, her skin glowing in the slanting sunlight of the early morning. She rocked lightly on her heels as she stared into the distance. Her face was almost animated and her eyes had lost their chilling remoteness – the cold, dead glare that made them look like desert stones under the Kalahari moonlight.

Ben glanced back at Mary-Ellen.

'I've got to take her on,' she said. 'Unless Kala knows she's going home, she'll run off again. Next time I may not be able to find her. If I don't, she'll die. She may be able to survive with the San in the desert. Here she's helpless.'

'What do you intend to do?' Ben asked.

'We can't go back into Cape Town,' Mary-Ellen answered. 'We'll have to go on from here. I should be able to buy horses somewhere close. Then we'll ride to Kuruman.'

'And when you get there, *if* you get there?'

Mary-Ellen was silent.

For months she had pushed Kuruman to the back of her mind. She had deliberately refused even to think about the mission and the nightmare of what had happened there. Now she was forced to face it again.

'I have a friend there,' she said. 'A Mashona called Moffat, I grew up with him. He'll help me find a waggon to carry water into the desert. Then I'll be able to take Kala home –'

Mary-Ellen paused. She looked at Ben, her eyes suddenly troubled.

'What about you?'

'Me –?'

Ben gave a quick harsh laugh.

'Well, I can't go back to Cape Town either, can I? A crippled carpenter with a price on his head won't exactly be difficult to spot. Unless of course I want to get myself arrested on charges of robbery, assault, and maybe even murder now too.'

Ben clenched his fists.

'I came to the rescue of your freak show,' he added brutally. 'Look where it's got me. It's made me into an outlaw everywhere.'

Mary-Ellen's cheeks reddened. Ben went on gazing at her.

The rising sun had haloed the dust-streaked cloud of hair round her face with its wide-set clear brown eyes, flecked with green and gold. Her body, in the simple triangles of cloth she'd covered it with, was slender and muscular, and her skin a soft tawny gold. She was, he suddenly realized, very beautiful – even more beautiful than the girl he'd met on the road from Canon St Mary.

At the thought of that, Ben abruptly wrenched his mind away.

'We are all outlaws,' Mary-Ellen said quietly. 'Kala by some stroke of fate. The San by an accident of birth. You by an act of generosity. Me because of a decision I made –'

She paused. 'Come with us to Kuruman. I don't know what we'll find, but I promise I'll do everything I can to help you make a new start from there.'

Ben shrugged.

'Have I any choice – ?'

He turned to gaze over the sloping hill flanks, their edges turning to violet as the morning mist cleared the valleys. His jaw hardened.

'You'll need to buy another horse,' he said. 'Farini won't be far behind us. As you've probably noticed I travel very slowly on foot.'

Mary-Ellen's cheeks flushed an even deeper scarlet. She stood up. She took Kala by the hand, and called for the San. With Ben trailing behind, they left the copse and set off up into the hills.

— 63 —

'Kaffir, you tell Mr Farini what happened, man,' Frouw said.

The tall South African and Farini were sitting in a room on the first floor of a hotel on the outskirts of Cape Town.

The man standing in front of them was a tall and gaunt half-caste named Mackenzie, although on the Cape Town waterfront he'd never been known as anything but 'Kaffir' because of his skin colour.

Kaffir Mackenzie spat angrily at the floor.

'They got away,' he said. 'You were right, man. They're heading north, but they were too goddamn quick. To get to Kuruman, they've got to go through Elandsvlei. I rode there hell for leather. I get to Elandsvlei maybe by midnight last night. I beat at the inn door. I wake the *menheer* and his wife. Yes, they say, those people stop earlier to eat. Then they pass through. On horses there is one man, the cripple, one woman. On foot some coons –'

Mackenzie scratched his neck.

'I go back outside. There is a good fat moon. I see their spoor heading north. Hoofs of the horses and the coons' little feet. They are travelling fast. I think of following them, but their horses have been rested and mine has not.' He shrugged. 'I can only turn back, man.'

Farini swore. He nodded curtly and Mackenzie left the room.

'Can we catch them before Kuruman?' Farini asked as the half-breed went out.

Frouw shook his head. 'By the time we're ready to leave they'll have two days' start. Kaffir says they're riding fast. They'll keep it up until they reach the mission.'

Farini hammered on the table in frustration. Then he strode out on to the balcony, and leant over the rail, cursing.

Two days ago Farini had had them within his grasp. Not just the diamond and the cripple who'd stolen it from him, but something that might be even more valuable still – something that was literally beyond price. Darwin, without understanding its significance, had mentioned it in his letter.

It was Gert Frouw who'd found the letter when they searched the building after the raid. The South African glanced through it. He frowned and studied the letter again. Then he ran down to the hall, where Farini was still standing amidst the wreckage of the broken doors and the bullet-scarred plasterwork.

'For Christ's sake, look at this, man!' Frouw waved it in Farini's face. 'It was on the floor of the preacher's daughter's room. The bitch must have left it there when she ran. Read what it says.'

Farini seized the letter.

He read it quickly once. Then more slowly again. Then even more slowly for a third time. Afterwards Farini looked up. Almost dazed for an instant, he shook his head.

'So I was right,' Farini said quietly. 'There are more diamonds out there.'

The South African nodded. 'And there's a map, too. Maybe it doesn't show exactly where they are. But it'll show where this *rouinekk* he mentions found the coons who traded a few of them. The rest won't be far away. All we have to do is get there.'

Farini thought for a moment. He remembered the blazing jewel, the size of a pigeon's egg, that had tumbled across the floor of the mute savage's room. He saw the wistful look on the Jew's face when he'd asked to hold it for a moment.

'So where the hell is this map?' Farini shouted.

'I guess the Ramsay girl took it with her,' Frouw answered. 'It was probably the one thing she snatched up when they heard us.'

Farini had trembled with rage then, a vein-throbbing rage which left his mouth dry and his hands shaking. It was then, when he was in a state of unfettered anger, that he liked to take a woman. To hurt her, hear her scream a little, draw a little blood before he pumped and pummelled and took his pleasure. That was what he would like to do to the bitch from the mission. It was what he would do when he caught her.

Now, his eyes narrow bars of fury, Farini gazed down over the compound of the hotel where he'd made his headquarters.

Below him a dozen men were strolling between the rough grey canvas tents they'd pitched on the worn grass. In the chill, fog-laden darkness of London, Frouw had said he could hire the hardest men in South Africa. Farini knew about hard men. He'd grown up with them on the New York docks. He'd dealt with them at Niagara, on Coney Island, at the Aquarium. Immigrant Irish bandits with their native shillelaghs. Sicilian 'soldiers' of the society of omerta. The hammer-wielding gang leaders from the East End banks of the Thames.

Compared with the men Frouw had found, they were children.

The half-caste Kaffir Mackenzie had been charged three times with murder – the last of a child prostitute no more than nine years old. The other twelve were as brutal and violent as Mackenzie. They were exactly what the South African had promised – except they had failed. They had tracked the preacher's daughter and surrounded the boarding-house. But when they attacked, the coon girl and the cripple had managed to escape with the diamond. Now, heading up-country on horses, they were beyond his reach.

Farini gripped the balcony rail until his knuckles whitened. He realized Frouw was standing beside him.

'What the hell do we do now?' Farini snapped.

'Let them ride their butts off,' the South African answered. 'Sure, they'll get to Kuruman. But when they reach the mission, they'll have to outspan.'

Farini frowned.

'Halt and take a rest,' Frouw explained. 'Anyone can ride north from here. But once you've got to Kuruman, you're looking at the desert. The Kalahari's different, man. That's wild country out in front of you, wild and thirsty and dangerous. If they want to head into it, they'll have to provision and ready-up. And, hell, will they have problems.'

'Why?'

'Waggons,' Frouw answered. 'There's no water in the desert. If you trek into the Kalahari, you take water with you. The only way to do that is in waggons. I've been to that goddamn village. There's no waggons at Kuruman.'

Farini still didn't understand.

'Two days' start isn't enough,' the South African went on. 'A week isn't enough. They need a waggon. They'll find one sooner or later. They'll probably try to hire one from one of the cattle ranches round Kuruman. But it's going to take time.'

'And until then they'll be stuck at the village?'

Frouw nodded. 'They can't move without water. We'll find them before they load up with it.'

Farini was silent.

Slowly the fury and frustration drained from him. Farini was used to a world of highways and railroads and the swift sure contact of man-made communications. Africa was alien and bewildering. A world where landscape and climate were all that mattered. Where even something as simple as rainfall could dictate the course of human events.

Kala, the mission girl and the cripple were as much ensnared by Africa as he was. They could run to the desert's edge, but to go any further they needed water – and water meant waggons.

'Then we'll need waggons too,' Farini said. 'Where the Christ are we going to find them?'

Frouw chuckled.

'We already got them,' he said.

The South African pointed forward.

At the end of the compound was a wide barred gate. As Farini looked down, two of the men ran forward and opened it. A cloud of dust filled the entrance. Through the dust a team of oxen appeared. Then a waggon rumbled into sight. Behind the waggon came another and then more. Finally there were ten waggons inside the compound.

They creaked and jolted forward between the tents to an open space beyond. The dust was so thick Farini could barely see them, but he could hear the shouts of the drivers and the cracking of whips. When the dust settled Farini saw the waggons had been drawn up in a circle.

Frouw grunted in satisfaction.

'They've made a laager,' the South African said. 'They know the old ways. Where we're going, we sure as hell need them.'

'Where the hell did you get them?' Farini asked.

'It doesn't matter,' the South African answered. 'I saw the stone. I've seen diamonds before, never one like that. For ten per cent of everything else out there in the desert, you don't need to ask where anything comes from, man. You just get the best. All you got to do is remember the ten per cent.'

He glanced at Farini.

Farini had never seen the South African's eyes before. They always seemed to be hidden in the heavy folds of flesh beneath his grizzled eyebrows. Now, for the first time, in the slanted light Farini did see them. Farini started.

Chill and ruthless, Frouw's eyes were filled with an intensity, a greed Farini had only ever seen once before. It was when Farini looked in a mirror into his own eyes.

Farini clapped the South African on the shoulder.

'We're in your territory,' he laughed. 'Keep on second-guessing what I need, and the ten could go up.'

Farini glanced back at the compound.

The waggons were somehow familiar to him. Farini realized why. With their high, bow-shaped frames and canvas coverings, they might have belonged to a column of American pioneers heading west across the plains towards the Pacific. So might the circle, the laager, in which they'd been drawn up. The Americans used the same formation to defend themselves against the Indians.

There was something different. Farini wrinkled his face as he tried to puzzle out what it was.

These waggons were larger and darker. They carried more canvas on their hooped canopies. Ropes clattered against their sides and rocking lanterns hung from spars angled out over the driver's head. They were more like travelling predators than dwellings on wheels.

In the fading light they suddenly reminded Farini of ships. They were designed not so much to cross land as to range free over the waves in search of plunder. Ships. Farini gripped the rail again.

He was taking a pirate fleet out into the desert.

64

The lioness caught the scent a mile away.

It was no more than a fleeting trace on the air. None of the thirteen other lions with her – four almost-grown cubs and nine young females – had noticed it. But the lioness was not only the eldest member of the group and the cubs' mother. She was the pride's leader. It was her duty to miss nothing.

The lioness lifted her head. She half closed her agate-yellow eyes and sniffed again. For a moment the faint smell had gone. Then it came back. This time it was unmistakable.

Horses.

She gave a deep rumbling growl. Seconds later she broke into a trot. She headed in the direction from where the spoors had been carried to her on the breeze. The other lions followed. The light was fading, and the tawny hide of her scarred and aging body blended almost invisibly into the shoulder-high grass. In her wake the pride tracked the twin black tufts of her ears.

It was how millions of years of evolution had programmed them to hunt behind a dominant female. Ignore everything else, the genetic instructions said. Follow the two dark navigation points in the leader's ears like lodestars. The other lions continued to obey the ancient encoded message, even when they too caught the magical scent.

Horses. Horses signalled cattle, and cattle meant prey. The slowest and most succulent prey in all Africa.

Gathering speed with every stride, the lions ran on.

*

It was almost dusk. Ben swung himself off his horse on the crest of the low ridge.

He rubbed the stiffness out of his legs. Then he stood gazing down at the little bowl in the plain below him. The bowl was already in shadow and a fire was blazing at its centre. Two hours earlier Ben had left the others there to make camp at the end of the day's ride.

Ben glanced up. The first stars had appeared and the air was thickening with night.

They had been travelling for three weeks. The first day, the day they'd left the clump of trees outside Cape Town, had been the hardest Ben had ever known. They had walked almost without break for ten hours. For the five little San and Kala it was nothing. For Mary-Ellen it was an exhausting trek. For Ben with his withered leg and his limp it was a torment.

Somehow he had kept up with them. In the late afternoon, just as he thought he could go on no longer, they came to a small white farming settlement. His feet swollen and bloodied, Ben slumped to the ground in the shade of a tree.

Mary-Ellen rubbed the sweat from her skin. She wrapped herself in Ben's shirt and the remnants of her skirt. Then she went off in search of horses.

An hour later Mary-Ellen returned. She had been lucky. One of the Afrikaner farmers was a horse breeder. He was about to send some for auction at the local market. Offering the farmer well above the auction estimate, Mary-Ellen had managed to persuade him to sell two of them with their tack and harnesses.

Kala circled the horses warily for a while, wrinkling her nostrils. Then she backed away and watched as Mary-Ellen and Ben heaved themselves up into the saddles. With the San trotting on either side and Kala loping ahead, they set off again.

The long twilight dissolved into a moonlit night. Finally they saw the lights of an inn glittering through the darkness ahead. By then Ben had slumped forward over the pommel of his saddle. Mary-Ellen reined in her horse and slid to the ground. She persuaded the dour innkeeper to give them a bowl of beans and sausages in his smoke-streaked parlour.

'Only you and your man inside the house,' the innkeeper said gruffly. 'The kaffirs eat in the stable. You pay in advance and you take their food out to them.'

The meal was good, thick and rich and belly-filling. Ben glanced at Mary-Ellen as they finished. Her face was grey and haggard, and her eyelids were drooping with tiredness.

'Maybe we should rent a room and sleep for a few hours,' she said wearily. 'We'll be away well before daybreak.'

The temptation was almost irresistible. Ben was exhausted too. At that moment there was nothing in the world his crippled body wanted more than to rest. Somehow he managed to force himself to his feet.

'No,' he said grimly. 'Farini can buy horses too. We'll go on until morning.'

Old Deial sniffed the air as he trotted on.

From time to time he thought he could smell the scent of the desert on the night wind's keen metallic coldness. The desert was still far in front of them, infinitely far, but it was coming closer all the time. The old man knew that not just from the elusive scent spoors, but from the set of the stars above his head. They were guiding him home more surely than any compass.

The old man smiled.

For more fattenings and thinnings of the moon than he could remember, Deial had thought he would never see Africa again. Never again with his sons, Khoi! and Nuna, would he dance the dance of the spring hare in the dust of the Great Thirst. Never would he be able to teach his dead brother's sons, Gwi and Hutse, how to shape a bow and string an arrow, how to stalk the tall ostrich and set traps for the blue-helmeted guineafowl, how to hook and pluck the ground squirrels from their burrows.

When the white men took him, Deial believed his life

was ended. No longer would he wait by the termite mounds at twilight to catch the creamy grubs as they shook out their wet wings in the last slanting rays of the sun. No longer would he hear the cry of the fish eagle patrolling the river, or see the leopard's shadow below the fork in the baobob tree.

The white man had fed him, it was true. But the white man's food was such that Deial wouldn't have left it for the jackals to scavenge. The white man had given him shelter against the rain, not knowing that the rain was to be greeted and welcomed. The rain cleansed and nurtured. It was not something to cower from, but to embrace. The white man had also beaten him. That Deial could understand. Madness filled the white man's head. When madness came, the sane and the healthy endured it and waited for the storm to pass.

The storms had blown away. The woman as tall as a giraffe had brought him and his people back.

Deial would have preferred to have slept after they had eaten in the shelter where the innkeeper kept his horses. That was what he would normally have done. But when the woman insisted on riding on, he had agreed. Her limping companion had been at her elbow encouraging her. He was ill-made and awkward and strange, but Deial trusted his level grey eyes and liked the strong hard set of his muscles. He was a man who could break the desert's stones.

Deial paused. He flared his nostrils and tested the wind again. He could smell red earth and thorn and the gland and hide scent of distant antelope. He nodded at his sons and their two cousins. They set off again with Kala running her own wayward course in front of them.

On the long first day's trek, Deial had had to stop often, not for the golden-haired woman who swung easily along in her loose clothing, but for the limping cripple who struggled behind.

Now, horse-borne and well fed, they were making better time.

*

They travelled on until dawn.

When Mary-Ellen reined in her chestnut gelding in the long purple shadow of an acacia tree, Ben hadn't the strength to swing his leg over his horse's back. He simply leant forward, rolled off the animal, and fell to the ground. Then he slept.

At midday they were on their way again.

From then on everything changed. They rode quickly and warily, but without the driving, tormenting fear of their escape from Cape Town. The five San took it in turn to hang back and track them from a mile behind. Each evening they reported there was no sign of pursuit. Either Farini hadn't tried to follow them, or he had lost them in the wilderness of the hills.

They rode on.

The days were hot and clear. The nights were crisp and bright with stars. The countryside was a brimming cornucopia. There was water everywhere, and food, in the form of game and wild fruit, on all sides. They slept on beds of heather and grass, and woke clear-eyed with the dawn's dew on their faces. Ben's skin grew tanned, his muscles hardened, his breathing became slower and stronger. Africa was wrapping its warmth round them like a cloak. Its sun was feeding them.

As Ben led his horse down to their camp that evening, he could see Mary-Ellen silhouetted against the fire. She was bent over the flames with a pan in her hand. The San had taken up their usual position, settled back on their heels in a semicircle round her. Ben searched for Kala. For several moments he couldn't find her. Then his eyes picked her out.

Kala had distanced herself from the others.

As she always did, she had chosen the highest point of ground above the camp site. Tonight it was a rocky mound to the west. Kala was lying on top of the mound with her arms stretched out in front of her. She seemed to be holding something in her hands.

Ben narrowed his eyes and watched her.

The evening sun dipped towards the horizon. Its last

beams tilted down and swept over Kala. Suddenly what Kala was holding seemed to erupt with light. It burned emerald and gold, and then a numbing, dazzling white.

Ben blinked and turned his head away, instinctively shielding his face.

In the soft bowl of shadow, Kala gazed into the bright depths of her life-stone.

Herontas – Kala remembered him from before, although the soldier's hair was white now – gripped the handle of his short flat sword as he stood outside the tent of the wizened old woman, the sibyl Osiris.

'It is I, Herontas,' he called out.

'Enter!' the reply came back.

Kala saw Herontas push aside the heavy hide curtain and step inside.

Gathering the last of the sun's radiance and funnelling it into the stone, Kala watched and listened intently.

She was no longer somewhere high up in the rolling hills of the southern African landscape between Cape Town and the great stone plateau of the Kalahari. She was no longer a passenger, a piece of baggage tugged along by the San, the white woman and the cripple with the hammer.

Kala was herself. She was seeing where she had come from. Two thousand years ago, she knew – and although she could not measure time – it had been thus. Thus, because what she saw, what she heard, was so vivid it could not have been any other way.

Kala watched and listened and learned.

She concentrated on the old woman first. The old woman, Kala sensed, held the key to everything.

The old woman, Osiris, was sitting on a stool.

When the column set out, the old woman had insisted on taking the stool with her. High-backed and wrought from ebony, it was the only possession she demanded. She was sitting on it now, gazing fixedly at the pile of coals glowing in the middle of the floor. For several minutes she ignored Herontas.

In the silence Herontas stared at her.

She had been immensely old when they left Alexandria. Yet in the seven years since then she seemed not to have aged any further. The fearsome toll the great journey had taken on everyone else had not touched her. She was still the same tiny bird-boned figure with sparse white hair, and a face as gnarled and wizened as the root of a thousand-year-old olive tree.

Perhaps she had passed beyond age, Herontas thought.

Perhaps in a sense she had crossed the sacred river and was already dead. He started. Osiris had suddenly swung her head round. Her eyes were as hard and black and unyielding as the wood of her seat. They were also as bright as the coals she had been gazing at a moment before.

'You have chosen who will be sacrificed?' Herontas asked.

'The stone has chosen.' The old woman's eyes gleamed malevolently as she answered. 'It is Damietta.'

Herontas felt a stab of ice in the pit of his stomach.

Damietta was the daughter of the waggon column overseer. When they left Alexandria, Damietta had been thirteen. Over the course of the journey she had grown up into a bold and laughing young woman who had been a constant, buoyant source of support and encouragement to everyone, not least to Herontas himself.

Now, after surviving all the horrors of the seven years and at last having come to safety, she was about to be slaughtered.

Herontas closed his eyes. He shuddered. He hated the ritual sacrifices more than anything, but he knew there was nothing he could do. They were the will of Isis and her vessel, Egypt. Damietta would know the same.

'Make sure the child is present,' Osiris added.

The child was Egypt's daughter. Herontas nodded. Without speaking, Herontas left.

The young woman was sacrificed that evening. As the sun went down she was brought out on to a spit of land in front of the camp. She was stripped naked and held down on the sand. Then, with the entire column watching, she was killed with a single sword cut across her throat.

Osiris was present too. Her ebony stool was carried out from her tent and she sat looking down as the sword fell. It was the only occasion since the start that she had presented herself before the expedition. As the blood poured from Damietta's neck, the old woman jumped down and scuttled over to the young woman's body.

Osiris plucked the diamond from the pouch at her waist. She dipped her hand in the blood and smeared it over the stone. Osiris turned to the gathered watchers. She searched their ranks. The child, Cleopatra's child, was standing terrified at their front, surrounded by her attendants.

'Come here –'

Osiris beckoned to her. Uncertainly the child approached her. The old woman touched the child's face with her still-wet fingers.

'You are Egypt, child,' Osiris said. 'This is now your home. Egypt's stone will come to you. With it will come the power to know what the stone tells. Your mother did not have it, but I have it. It is a gift I alone can pass to you. I give it to you now and you in turn will have the power of bequest.'

The old woman stared at her.

The child stared back. Blood from the print of Osiris' fingers on her forehead was trickling down her face. The blood, mingling with the sweat from the delta's heat, stung her eyes.

As the child cried, Kala wonderingly put the stone away.

Coming down the slope, Ben inhaled deeply.

The evening air was clean and fresh. There would be a meal waiting for him at the fire. Mary-Ellen must have been cooking some bird or animal the San had caught. Tonight they would all sleep well. Tomorrow they would head on. Kuruman, according to Mary-Ellen, was very close.

Ben frowned.

Kuruman. Farini knew about Kuruman.

Ben shivered. The desert air was cold at night. He coiled the reins round his wrist and pressed lightly into his horse's flanks. Normally a steady amiable beast, the animal had been restless for the last half hour as the long slow twilight descended, jinking at shadows and snorting through widespread nostrils.

Ben balanced himself and rose in the saddle to peer round. Perhaps something had alarmed the beast.

At that moment the horse screamed and the roar of the lioness tore at his eardrums.

The pride was desperately hungry.

There was no natural reason for them to be so. The rains had passed over the hills. The vegetation was thick and rich. Game, as Ben had discovered, was abundant everywhere. Under normal conditions, the pride would have had no difficulty in killing and feeding.

The landscape was still natural. The conditions were not. Undetectable to the eye, they had been tampered with by man.

The lions associated the smell of horses with cattle. Cattle were foreign to Africa. They were aliens brought in from the north – and they were wholly unsuited to the dark continent. They were clumsy, inefficient feeders in the bush. They were vulnerable to Africa's diseases. They needed more water than the animals of the wild. Where cattle found water, they trampled the nearby vegetation into powder until they could no longer graze. When they moved on, they left deserts behind them.

Cattle were the most deadly engines of destruction ever visited upon Africa. More lethal than rifles, they destroyed its landscape. Yet cattle were prized by man above everything else. To black and white alike they were wealth. Wealth, according to human lore, corrupts.

The white and black man's cattle had corrupted the lions.

As the herds streamed down towards the slaughterhouses of the Cape, South Africa's lions discovered a new source of prey. Lumbering, dull-witted prey that was much easier to hunt than the elusive antelope. Abandoning their traditional quarry in the bush, the lions turned their attention to the dust-haloed herds on the drovers' roads.

The herds made for rich feeding. Soon the numbers of lions soared. For the new generations of cubs there was no need to learn the age-old hunting skills – with cattle they were unnecessary. Old as she was, the lioness had seldom hunted anything else. It was the same for all the lions along the cattle trails. They had become almost as clumsy as the cattle which fed them. And that evening the situation of the lioness and her companions was perilous.

Like every pride, hers had retained a territory in the bush for the times when, as now, the cattle were absent from the trails. A month earlier her pride's three males, the guardians of the territory, had been killed by hunters. Within days their territory was claimed by neighbouring prides. The lioness, her cubs, and the young females, were evicted.

For the past four weeks they had wandered like gypsies. There were no cattle on the trails. There was game in the bush, but the pride's skills were blunted and they were hunting in occupied territory. Each time they came close to killing, they were chased away by the pride which owned the land.

Dispossessed and constantly harried, in the midst of plenty they were close to starvation.

When the lioness scented the horses, she tested the air for the presence of other lions. The air was clean. She had sniffed it again and again as she followed the drifting spoors. The air remained as clean as before. For once there was no threat, no challenge, on the evening breeze. The air was still clean when the horse and the forked creature on its back came into her sight.

The lioness slowed.

She lowered herself to a crouch. For an instant she was still. Behind her the other thirteen lions dropped to their stomachs. They could see the horse and the man, but their eyes were still concentrated on the two black tufts of her pricked ears. They were the signals, they conveyed her instructions. Now the lioness' tail switched backwards and forwards through the grass with the sinuous movements of a winding snake.

Suddenly the tail stiffened. The black tuft at its end rose up erect and her ears went back against her skull. She leapt from the earth, arcing through the air in one sinuous movement.

Ben was never quite sure what happened next.

At the first sign of danger, he had patted the jinking horse reassuringly, tightened his grip on the reins, and urged the animal on towards the fire. A moment later the horse skittered and screamed again, its nostrils dilated with terror. Over the scream Ben heard a roar. As he jumped to the ground, the reins were torn from his hand.

Stumbling, Ben managed to turn.

Ben had never seen lions before. He saw them now a few yards behind him. Not just two or three but what seemed to be dozens of lions, a tawny surge that reared up and raced forward like a roaring wave in the dusk. One of them was ahead of the others. Its yellow eyes glittered and he smelt the hot feral odour of its breath.

Helplessly he started to raise his hands as if he could fend the wave off. It was useless and too late. His arms were barely level with his waist when the wave broke over him. Ben glimpsed the flash of raking, discoloured fangs. The stench was overwhelming. Something slammed against his shoulder. Ben was spun round and hurled backwards.

For a moment Ben had been lucky. The lioness had targeted the horse as prey. Drawing the other lions behind her as she sprang, she had simply knocked Ben aside.

A moment later everything changed. The horse had bolted in a frenzy of fear. By the time the lioness stretched out her claws to pull it to the ground, the horse had gone. With the pride behind her the lioness bounded after it.

The chase was fruitless. At full gallop the horse increased the distance between the two with every second.

The lioness wheeled round with a chilling roar of anger and frustration. She turned and trotted back towards the pride it was her responsibility to feed. The man was in her path. Food. The lioness dropped to a crouch again.

Ben saw her at the same instant.

It was almost dark now but he could see the flicker of the lioness' tail behind her haunches. Beyond and on either side of her, the other lions were crouching too. Apart from the flare of the early starlight in their eyes they might have been carved out of stone.

Ben froze.

As he stared at them Ben knew he was closer to death than he had ever been. In an instant, he knew, the slashing, foul-smelling wave of teeth and claws and sand-coloured hide would erupt from the earth and obliterate him.

He shifted his weight on to his good leg. The pain in his shoulder throbbed. His gaze held that of the lioness. Ben looked into her eyes, pale and pitiless, agate flecked with obsidian.

Her tail stopped moving and stiffened. Her ears flattened. She tensed her muscles to spring. Behind her the pride shifted and swayed.

'Na-ka, Na-ka!'

The sound came from behind the massed beasts.

Ben's head jerked up at the fury and anguish of the call. He didn't know whether it came from a human or an animal. The lions too were bewildered. The hunting spell, the instant of coiled tension before the charge, had been broken. The lions' heads turned. Like him they scanned the dusk.

It was Kala.

She was running with an odd sideways lope, angled wrists held loose and low. Her teeth were bared and she was snarling. She came to a halt in front of the lioness and howled. The lioness shifted uneasily.

'Na-ka, Na-ka, Na-ka!'

The sound came again. This time it was unmistakably an animal's call. High-pitched and threatening, it trailed away in a series of rapid throaty coughs that to Ben sounded almost like human laughter. Transfixed, Ben watched as the two, the crouching lioness and the snarling human, faced each other.

The lioness retreated a step. Kala gave another screaming call. As the demonic laughter that ended it died away, she hunched herself forward, lips drawn back from her teeth, spitting and growling. The lioness glanced uncertainly back at the pride. The other lions had retreated too.

Suddenly the lioness reared up.

Her talons lashed out at Kala's face. Like a cobra Kala swung her head to one side. The claw missed her face but swept down across her body. Ben saw Kala's skin open and the blood glistened scarlet. Kala howled – not in pain but in anger. She lunged forward, gouging at the lioness' eyes.

The lioness whirled away and fled. The pride streamed after her. As they vanished, Mary-Ellen and the San ran forward carrying burning branches from the fire. The San ran after the lions, hurling the brands into the darkness.

Mary-Ellen glanced quickly at Ben. 'Are you hurt?'

Ben shook his head. 'A glancing blow and a bruise maybe.'

Behind them there was a soft thump. They both turned. Kala had half fallen to the ground. She lay in the dust, her entire upper body sheeted in blood. Mary-Ellen ran to her side and began to lift her.

'I'll do it,' Ben said.

He swung Kala up in his arms and hobbled with her towards the fire. Mary-Ellen hurried after him.

'There are needles and cat-gut in my pouch,' she said urgently. 'Hold the flesh together while I prepare them.'

Mary-Ellen sank down on her heels by the flames and took out a small bundle. Carefully she softened the cat-gut with oil from the cooking pot, and sterilized the needle in the flame.

Ben tore a strip from his shirt. He rinsed it out in water from the kettle, and gently wiped some of the blood from Kala's shoulder.

'She's got four deep cuts almost down to the bone,' Ben said.

Mary-Ellen bent down and set to work. Ben felt first fear, and then a quick surge of sympathy as he watched her. Mary-Ellen might be obsessed by the girl from the desert, but it was an obsession rooted in love. Ben could see it in Mary-Ellen's eyes, in the intense concentration of her face, in the swift gentle movements of her hands.

When Mary-Ellen finished she straightened up.

'She's lost a lot of blood,' she said. 'That's not the real danger. A wound from a carnivore almost always results in an infection. If Kala gets infected, I've nothing to use against it.'

Mary-Ellen's voice was taut with anxiety.

'But why did she do it?' Ben rubbed his bruised shoulder. 'A second later and those lions would have attacked me. Kala came out of nowhere and drove them off. Why?'

For several moments Mary-Ellen didn't answer. She stood frowning in silence.

Then she said slowly, 'Only hyenas challenge lions. It wasn't Kala who drove them away. It was a hyena.'

Ben stared at her. He felt the hairs on the back of his neck prickle.

According to Mary-Ellen he'd been saved by an animal. For a moment his mind went back to the otters in the estuary. They'd accepted and tolerated him as a fellow creature of the waters, but that was different. Ben hadn't crossed into their world, he hadn't become one of them. No one could ever do that. No human could become an animal.

'But Kala's a girl, not an animal,' he protested.

'I think she's both,' Mary-Ellen answered. 'I should have realized it long ago. All the signs were there. Somehow I failed to understand and interpret them –'

Frowning, Mary-Ellen shook her head in irritation. She went on as if she was half speaking to herself.

'The way she treated you and me,' Mary-Ellen said. 'The way she reacted to everyone. They weren't the responses of a human. They were how an animal behaves. The San must have known, but they wouldn't have been puzzled. They wouldn't even think it worth commenting on. They don't see any division between us and the animals. To them all living creatures in their different ways are the same.'

She paused.

Ben glanced back at Kala. He remembered again the man's torn throat in the attic room, and the blood dripping down Kala's chin as she gazed at him impassively through the smoke. He heard the snarl as she faced the lions and saw the snake-like flickering movement of her head as the lioness lashed out at her.

Ben shivered. 'How can she be both?' he demanded in bewilderment.

'Old Deial says they found her in the desert seven rainy seasons ago,' Mary-Ellen replied. 'She must have been about nine then. That leaves the first seven years of her life unexplained. Deial named her the little she-hare that fell from the sky –'

Mary-Ellen's voice was thoughtful. She was puzzling something out, Ben sensed, as much for herself as for him.

'It was Deial's way of explaining what couldn't be explained in any other way. He and the San now believe it's true. Literally of course it can't be true. Kala's human. Somewhere a woman gave birth to her. I think that woman, whoever she was, must have abandoned Kala as a child among a hyena clan, and the animals reared her.'

It was Ben's turn to be silent. He could still feel the girl's weight in his arms, the fragility of her bones, the warm wetness of the blood that had flowed down her body. He could also see the great jewel Kala had clutched as fiercely as if she were holding the very threads that bound her to life.

'Then where did the diamond come from?' Ben asked.

Mary-Ellen lifted her shoulders helplessly.

'I don't know,' she said. 'Maybe from the very

beginnings of her past. From before the San and even before the hyenas. That's Kala's own secret. Possibly even she doesn't know. But whatever the answer is, it lies somewhere out in the desert.'

While they'd been talking, Deial had squatted down beside Kala. Now the old man was watching the girl intently. Carefully he reached out one bony finger to feel the pulse which throbbed at her temple. He stood up shaking his head, and spoke to Mary-Ellen.

'Deial says the poison from the lioness' claws has already entered her,' Mary-Ellen translated, her face white. 'When the moon sets tonight Deial says it will spread through her body. By the time the moon sets tomorrow the fever will have invaded her and she will die.'

Ben looked at Kala again. Blood was still welling from her wounds and there was barely any sign of movement in her chest. Her skin was pallid and her body was furred with sweat. In a sudden mindless eruption of grief and fury Ben rounded on Deial.

'If you know she's dying, for Christ's sake do something!' he shouted.

The old man stared at him, calm and unblinking. Ben managed to control himself. It was no fault of Deial's. Ben cursed himself instead and tapped the little San hunter apologetically on the shoulder. He swung back towards Mary-Ellen.

'We must reach Kuruman and get medicines,' Ben said. 'How far away are we?'

'At least two days, however fast we travel,' she answered. 'It's too far.'

Ben rubbed his eyes wearily. Then he realized Deial was speaking again.

'There's an old woman, a Herero.' Mary-Ellen relayed Deial's words to him a moment later. 'Deial says the woman's a witch with the power to heal. I've never heard of her, but Deial says all the San of the southern desert know about her.'

'How far?' Ben's voice was still sharp and his bruised shoulder was throbbing again.

'Her kraal's somewhere between here and Kuruman. Deial isn't sure where. He says he and his sons can try to find it, but they come from the north and it could take them days.'

Ben saw the misery and helplessness in Mary-Ellen's face. Feeling the same bitter impotence he lifted his head and gazed at the sky.

They were close to the edge of the Kalahari. For the first time the desert stars were above them. Low on the desert's horizon, shimmering in the night haze, hung the glittering banner of the Southern Cross, the dizzying constellation of lodestars which guided all travellers in the southern hemisphere.

Ben tensed in the moonlight.

Kala came from the desert. The stars he was staring at were hers. All it needed was a sextant to take the stars' measure, and a compass to fix their course. They had neither sextant nor compass. They had something infinitely stronger and more accurate. Something that could both read the stars and harness the magnetism of the poles. Something that could guide them of its own accord. They had the jewel.

Ben rose, his exhaustion and fear and the pain in his shoulder forgotten.

'The diamond,' Ben said quietly and confidently. 'Take the diamond from Kala's belt. It feeds on the starlight. If only the witch can save her, the diamond will lead us to her kraal.'

— 65 —

'Here –'

Mary-Ellen stretched out her hand to Ben. The diamond was cradled in her palm.

Beside her, Kala was lying on the ground in the darkness on a stretcher that old Deial and his sons had made from branches and wild vines.

Ben took the jewel.

He held it as delicately as a wild bird's egg. For a second it gleamed and flared in the starlight. Then its incandescence started to dull. It was as if a veil had been drawn over a lighted window. Moments later the brilliance was almost extinguished. Even the diamond's warmth had gone. The lump of stone lay in his hand like a piece of dark frosted ice. A few last glimmers quivered at the jewel's heart. Apart from that it was dead.

Ben's fingers chilled as he held it.

Mary-Ellen had seen the glow fade too. She snatched up the diamond. She caught Kala's hand again and folded the girl's limp fingers round the stone.

Kala stirred.

Her eyelids flickered and her fingers tightened round the diamond. She tried to push herself upright. The effort was too much for her. She sank back. Her skin was running with sweat. Her breath was coming in quick, shallow gasps, and blood was pumping from the festering wounds again.

Ben knelt and leant forward.

His eyes travelled from Kala's shrunken face down across her bloodied and bandaged body to her hand. Between her clenched knuckles the diamond was no longer cold and dead. It was shimmering with light.

The light was pulsing with the strong urgent beam of the south coast lighthouses he'd known as a child. The focus of the radiance was directed at a precise angle towards the northeast. Ben stared into the night. Then he leapt to his feet.

'Over there!' he shouted, pointing at the hills that rose above them.

Mary-Ellen turned and called to the San.

The old man Deial nodded. The little she-hare, he knew, had powerful guardians. He beckoned to his sons. Khoi! and Nuna trotted forward. They picked up Kala's litter and settled it on their shoulders. Gwi and Hutse, the swiftest runners, had caught Ben's horse and brought it back to the camp. Ben limped beside the horse now, holding it by the bridle. In front of him the stretcher swayed in the light of the rising moon. The night passed. As dawn came they reached the crest of a ridge. Deial held up his hand. Behind him Khoi! and Nuna gently lowered Kala's stretcher to the ground and squatted down on their heels. Ben stepped forward to the side of the stretcher.

Mary-Ellen reined in her horse beside Deial. As the old man pointed, she gazed ahead, shading her eyes against the rising sun. Deial spoke to her, the little clicks and chirrups of the San language almost lost in the dawn chorus of birdsong.

Mary-Ellen turned back to translate for Ben.

'There is a Herero village in the valley below. Deial says we must go down slowly and in full view to show we come in peace.'

Ben came forward and looked down over the edge of the ridge.

He saw a tiny circle of mud-walled reed-thatched huts in a clearing beneath them. A woman came out of one of the huts and stood looking up as if she knew they were there. Ben glanced at the litter.

Kala was still grasping the diamond. The diamond should have sparkled and flared and glittered. Instead it lay between Kala's fingers as dull and chill as it had lain in

Ben's hand the night before. The resplendent fire had seeped away from it. Like Kala, the diamond was dying.

The San lifted the litter on their shoulders and the small party wound down the hill towards the woman waiting in the valley below.

'I saw you coming from afar.'

The woman was tall and massively built. Using the San greeting, she inclined her head. Mary-Ellen bowed her head in return.

'Mama, we too saw you from afar,' Mary-Ellen replied in the Herero dialect. 'We present ourselves at your door.'

Mary-Ellen kept her head lowered.

Towering above Mary-Ellen, the woman studied her. She nodded slowly in approval. The young white woman had been on a long trek. She was dirty, tousled and dishevelled. So were her companions. But her face was honest. Her eyes were clear and full of grace. There was serenity and confidence in her expression, and respect in her bearing.

The white woman presented herself as a daughter.

'I embrace you, child,' the Herero woman said.

'I hold you to my soul, Mama,' Mary-Ellen responded.

The two women put their arms round each other.

Ben checked Kala's pulse. It was still beating. He straightened up and looked round.

The Herero was the biggest woman he had ever seen. Standing well over six foot and weighing more than three hundred pounds, her bust and hips strained against a gaudy dress that was draped round her in chequered diamonds of scarlet, turquoise and lemon. The dress reached to her ankles and flapped over her bare feet. On her head was a crimson turban slashed with bars of woven gold.

In the confines of the hot and dusky little hut she looked as if a rainbow had been poured over the quintessence of Africa.

'My wells are your wells,' the Herero said as she finally

released Mary-Ellen. 'My corn is your corn. Yet I think you come to me for more than food and water.'

The woman looked at Mary-Ellen through astute, penetrating eyes. Mary-Ellen nodded.

'One of my companions is sick, Mama, grievously sick,' Mary-Ellen said. 'If she is not treated, she will die. I ask you to heal her.'

'Bring her to me.'

Mary-Ellen turned to Deial. The old man clapped his hands. Khoi! and Nuna came forward with the stretcher. The Herero woman stepped back to allow them to carry their load into the hut.

Mama Ovambo followed behind. The San lowered the stretcher to the earth floor. The woman bent over the stretcher and studied Kala gravely for several moments. Kala's face was grey and filmed with sweat. Her skin was pulled so tightly over her cheekbones that her head looked like a skull. Mama Ovambo glanced up and waved her hand. Ben knew she was dismissing him and the San. He backed out of the hut.

Ben retreated to the shadow of a tree.

He was wearier than he had ever been. As he sat down, his head dropped forward on his chest. A moment later he slept.

'You speak the tongue of the little people?' the woman said.

Mary-Ellen nodded.

'Call for them. They know me as Mama Ovambo. I will tell you what I need, and you will explain to them. I could do the gathering myself if there was time, but there is no time. In the wild they are swifter and more skilful.'

Mary-Ellen clapped her hands again. She waited.

The sun was high outside but the interior of the reed-thatched rondavel was cool and dusky. Kala was lying at the centre of the floor on a rough adze-chipped plank, raised from the earth on tree stumps. Mama Ovambo had removed her bandages and stripped her naked. Kala's skin was waxy and yellow, and her chest barely moved as she breathed.

The wounds from the lioness' claws were crusted and suppurating. Occasionally Kala twitched. Each time trickles of blood seeped out from the lacerations. Mary-Ellen kept trying to wipe the blood away, but the blood caked within moments in the heat.

A shadow fell across the rondavel's entrance. Deial's tiny emaciated silhouette appeared against the light.

'Tell him this,' Mama Ovambo said. 'I want a serpent. A snake from the earth, or best, from the trees. It can be green or brown, but it must be living and holding its venom. Then a good handful of webs from the earth spiders. Five handfuls of mould from the deadness beneath a fallen tree. Lastly, a gourd filled with ants, the big wood-eating termites –'

Mama Ovambo paused.

'Tell him he must run swiftly. For the girl's life, the time we have left is the end of the falling sand in the white man's glass.'

Mary-Ellen turned and translated. Deial's two sons were standing behind him. The old man spoke over his shoulder to them. Deial nodded and the three of them vanished.

They returned an hour later. Khoi! and Nuna were carrying little woven baskets in either hand. Deial himself was holding a snake. The snake was a vivid emerald green. The old man was gripping it behind the head and across its body.

'From the trees,' he said, chuckling.

'Tell him to lay it down,' Mama Ovambo instructed.

Still holding it by the neck and body, Deial placed the snake on the earth. Mama Ovambo produced a machete and sliced off its head. As its body continued to writhe, she forced open the snake's mouth with a twig and squeezed out the poison from its glands into a wooden cup.

Mama Ovambo drank something from a stoppered cane tube. She spat into the cup, and swirled the mixture round. She pulled a small porcupine quill from her head-dress, and snapped off its needle-sharp tip. She dipped the quill into the cup and sucked up a few drops of the poison. Then she plunged the point of the quill into Kala's wrist, and let the venom trickle into her vein.

Mary-Ellen watched her, aghast.

The snake was a young boomslang. Boomslang venom was among the most deadly in the world. The drops that had been injected into Kala were enough to kill an elephant. Mama Ovambo noticed the terrified expression on Mary-Ellen's face. She grinned, showing a line of perfect white teeth.

'Ask the old man. Salt and herbs. Mixed with the poison, they take away its power to kill. What is left of the serpent's juice brings sleep. If the child is to recover, her body must be at rest. Now she will be still.'

Mary-Ellen glanced at Kala.

Until then Kala's body had been arched and shaken with tremors. As she watched, Mary-Ellen saw her limbs relax. Kala's skin was still chalk-white and coated in sweat, but now she seemed to be sleeping.

Mama Ovambo took another length of cane from the floor.

The cane was filled with wild bee honey. She smeared some honey over her palm and put her hand into the woven basket containing the ants. The ants were almost an inch long with heavy, pincer-like jaws. A dozen of them swarmed up on to her hand.

Mama Ovambo lifted her hand from the basket. Using her other hand she picked the ants off one by one and placed them over Kala's wounds. As the ants sensed Kala's blood, they sank their jaws into either side of the girl's torn skin. As soon as the skin was bound together, Mama Ovambo snapped off the ants' bodies. What was left behind was a neat row of stitches.

When all of Kala's skin had been drawn together and pinned in place, Mama Ovambo reached for another of the woven baskets. Spilling from the basket in a soft grey mist came the spiders' webs she had told the San to collect.

The Herero woman drank from the tube.

This time she swallowed. Then she breathed over the webs, filming the strands with moisture. Tiny droplets of water glistened on the cloud-like tangle of fibres. Mama Ovambo scooped up the greyness and smeared it over Kala's wounds.

The webs seemed to evaporate almost before they touched Kala's flesh, but they left a strange pearl-like patina on the broken tissue. Mama Ovambo looked at it approvingly. She grunted and reached for the last basket the San had brought into the hut.

The basket was filled with damp black mould, a mixture of earth, rotting leaves and fungus. It filled the hut with a rich, almost metallic smell. The mould was infested with maggots. Mama Ovambo picked out a handful and sifted through it with sure rapid fingers. She picked out the maggots and ate them. Then she smeared the remaining humus over the wounds on Kala's body.

Finally she stood back. She wiped her hands on her dress and placed them on her massive hips. She stood four-square staring down at the unconscious girl.

'Learn from me, child,' she said to Mary-Ellen. 'The ants' jaws will bind the broken skin together. The nets of the spiders will clean the blood and stop it from flowing. The blood is the girl's vital water. It must remain inside her for her to drink. The mould will fight the poison and break down its power. Remember what you have seen me do.'

Mary-Ellen nodded.

'I have learnt from you, Mama,' Mary-Ellen said. 'I will remember –'

She hesitated. 'Will the young woman live?' she asked.

Mama Ovambo didn't answer.

She continued to gaze at Kala. She frowned. She bent forward and took Kala's hand. Kala was still gripping the diamond. Carefully Mama Ovambo parted Kala's fingers from the stone. Mama Ovambo held the diamond in her own hand and studied it.

Across the table on which Kala was lying, Mary-Ellen

could see that the light had faded from the jewel. When the San carried Kala down to the village, a few flickers of radiance had still flared from it. Now it resembled a lump of cheap dusty glass. Only a tiny faint glow still pulsed somewhere deep at its heart.

Mama Ovambo put the diamond back in Kala's hand. Instinctively Kala closed her fingers tightly over it.

'I have done all I can,' Mama Ovambo said. 'This child is from the wild. I have given her the remedies of the wild. Whether she lives or is taken is not for me to say. She has powerful gods. If you would help her more, go out and speak to them. They will give you their answer in the stone. Pray to the spirits which give it life.'

Mama Ovambo turned away.

Her work was done. She busied herself with the cooking pot that hung over a smouldering fire in the corner of the hut. Mary-Ellen went out, her eyes dazzled by the glare of the sun. Pray, but to whom? she wondered. To Ramsay's vengeful purveyor of hell-fire and brimstone? She knew she could never do that again.

In the shade of the tree across the baked earth of the village street, she saw Ben. She walked over and looked down at him as he slept. A knot of village children were squatting silently in a semicircle around him, watching him with patient curiosity.

Ben's eyelids flickered open as Mary-Ellen's shadow fell across his face.

'Kala's sleeping now,' Mary-Ellen said. 'There's nothing we can do but wait –'

Mary-Ellen paused. Gazing at Ben she thought of Mama Ovambo's words. Impulsively she said, 'Do you know how to pray?'

Ben glanced at her, startled. 'Pray?'

Mary-Ellen nodded. 'I'm not sure I can pray to any god any longer. But Mama Ovambo says it's all we can do. Maybe if we try, the spirits who look after Kala will listen.'

'A daughter of the mission who can't pray –'

There was a tight half-smile on Ben's lips as he spoke.

He regretted the smile and the words as soon as he'd uttered them.

Mary-Ellen's face was drawn tight with weariness. In her eyes he could see both despair and wild hope – a hope that the prayers Mama Ovambo had told her to offer up to the sky would somehow save Kala. Prayers wouldn't help Kala, Ben knew that. The girl was snared by the lethal sickness that had come to her from the lioness' jaws.

Kala was going to die.

Ben knew it and still he hesitated. His mind went back to his childhood, to the years in the Quaker household of Mr Noakes. Ben had gone to the meeting house twice every Sunday then, but it was years now since he'd been.

'Yes,' Ben said. 'I know how to pray. I used to pray to an old man with a white beard. Whether he'll hear me out here is another matter.'

'Try,' Mary-Ellen urged frantically.

It was midday. The heat was torrid. The only living creatures seemed to be the vultures and kites hanging over the lonely little kraal. Out on the great plateau beyond, Ben sensed everything was different. Suddenly in the dreaming furnace of the African morning, with the wilderness gathered in the shadows beyond, the benign old man with his white beard took on a darker face.

Africa lived and died by its own rhythms.

Ben shook his head dizzily.

He opened his eyes and looked up. The day had passed. The last gleams of the sun were fading behind the trees round the kraal, and the air was thick with darkness. Stiff and aching in every muscle, he heaved himself to his feet. In the hut, Mary-Ellen was stretched out on the ground beside Kala's sick-bed.

Mama Ovambo met Ben at the entrance. Her gold and turquoise head-dress blazed out of the dusk. She was holding a burning torch from the fire inside. In its flickering light her face was stern and her dark eyes grave.

'The child is balanced between the two worlds,' she said.

She paused as the torch spat and showered the ground with sparks.

Then she continued, 'The stars have risen and they have custody of the child now. She trembles like a leaf in the wind, like the dust of a shooting star. You must speak to the stars. You must tell the moon to let her go –'

Mama Ovambo thumped the brand angrily against the side of the hut.

'I tell you again, I have done all I can. The girl is in your charge. I have meals to prepare. Leave me to the business of living. Take this if you need to sleep.'

The woman tossed a kaross of genet and jackal hides on to the earth. Then she stormed back into the hut.

Ben walked wearily back to the tree.

He pulled the fur cloak round his body. The night's frost was already beginning to glitter on the ground. Ben leant back and stared up at the great dark arc of the sky, watching the stars turn in their galaxies.

The moon rose. Later he heard the soft rustling of the small creatures of the night. He watched a pair of tiny velvet-winged owls hunting the moths drawn to the light of Mama Ovambo's still-smouldering fire. He saw the vivid green eyes of a bush-baby as it silently climbed above his head.

Ben kept his vigil all night. Then in the deep black silence of the hour before dawn he finally slept.

As the stars began to fade, a dozen shadows with heavy hunched shoulders and pricked ears padded through the silent village. No dog barked and there was no one awake to see them pass. The shadows gathered round the hut. For an instant the doorway was filled with shining scarlet eyes. The eyes bore down on the sleeping girl and fastened on the diamond. Then the shadows slipped silently away again.

A moment later the moon dipped below the horizon and the sky began to lighten. Ben woke and stood up. Stepping quietly he went into the hut and glanced round. Mary-Ellen was still lying beside Kala. The girl was sleeping peacefully now, with the diamond grasped tightly in her hand.

Ben sniffed. Hanging in the air was a smell he'd never smelled before. Pungent and rancid, it reminded him of the stench that clung to the dens of breeding otters when they were weaning their young on prey from the river. This was even stronger and more disturbing. Ben inhaled again and it was gone. He shook his head, puzzled.

Outside the sun lifted over the trees. A shaft of pale dawn light swept the floor. It touched the stone and seemed to be drawn inside it. The diamond began to glow. As Ben watched, Kala opened her eyes. She shook her head dreamily as she came out of sleep. Then she half-raised herself on her elbow.

Unaware of Ben, unaware of anything except what she was looking at, Kala gazed down into the diamond's heart.

A baby.

Kala stared at the tiny child. The baby was a girl. She was crying loudly and insistently, and hammering with tiny pink fists against her nurse's cheek.

'May I hold her?' a young woman asked tentatively. 'Just for a moment – ?'

The young woman was named Flavia. She had put the question to the woman who was holding the baby. The other woman was named Serapis. It was morning and the air was hot. The two women were standing in a courtyard before a large wooden building. The women had olive skins and dark hair. Close to them were other women, and then beyond them many soldiers guarding the gateways that led off the courtyard.

Serapis tossed the infant up and down in her arms. She turned and frowned down at the younger woman.

'She is not a toy to be passed from hand to hand,' Serapis said sternly. 'She may be a child, but she is also your queen.'

'I'm sorry.' Her cheeks flushing, Flavia lowered her head.

Serapis continued to glower at her.

Serapis was tall and imposing with greying hair and penetrating eyes. Her natural authority had been reinforced by her appointment as head of the royal bedchamber. All the other ladies of the court were nervous of her.

Suddenly Serapis relented.

Flavia was young and impetuous, but she was good-hearted. Serapis liked her spirit. In time she would make an excellent addition to the team of privileged women that Serapis ruled with a rod of iron.

'Take her,' Serapis said abruptly. 'Hold her with the greatest care.'

Flavia glanced down rapturously as the child was placed in her arms. She held her tight to her breast, hardly daring to breathe under the weight of the responsibility. The baby scrabbled at Flavia's face with her tiny fingers. Then she opened her eyes.

As she did, in Mama Ovambo's hut Kala sucked in her breath. For an instant she felt dizzy. She swayed, and the dawn light blurred. Her wrist went limp and her fingers loosened their grip round the diamond. The jewel almost dropped to the earth. Somehow she clung on to it.

It wasn't the wounds from the lioness, Kala knew that. It was something else. It was the baby's eyes.

The baby's eyes were the colour of ironwood, a deep, luminous brown but a brown flecked with silver. Silver. Kala had only seen eyes flecked with silver like the child's in two other people. The diamond had shown her the first. It was the long-ago woman Kala had watched in the white-walled palace and then on the ship.

The other person Kala knew infinitely better. Kala saw those eyes every time she looked at her reflection in water. However much time and distance separated them, the woman's and the baby's eyes were her own. Kala knew she was not just looking at her own eyes in the baby – she was looking at herself.

Spellbound, Kala gazed into the diamond's depths again.

'Hold her up,' the older woman, Serapis, was instructing. 'Walk with her to the trees by the guardhouse. Show her what will be hers.'

'She can understand already?' Flavia, the young nurse, whispered doubtingly.

Serapis laughed. 'All babies take in more than people ever give them credit for. This one takes in even more than any I have ever known.'

Flavia turned the child so the baby could see out in front of them.

'Look, little one.' Flavia lifted her hand and pointed as she walked forward. 'Can you see the walls?'

Flavia made gentle clucking noises with her tongue. The child gave no response. She stared fixedly ahead. She seemed not so much to be seeing what lay in front of her, as absorbing it in the very marrow of her being. The child's intensity was almost frightening.

Almost two thousand years had passed since the expedition led by Cleopatra's favourite soldier, Herontas, had set out from Alexandria. What lay before Flavia and the child in the morning sun was the fortress town that the long-ago sibyl, Osiris, had decreed, in her last command before she died, should be named Ophir.

Osiris had chosen the site. Herontas had organized and overseen the building of the city. But it was Mansur, the great queen's architect who had accompanied the column and also survived the journey, who had designed it. Mansur and the Egyptian engineers he brought with him had built well.

Skilled in harnessing the waters of the mighty Nile, the slower and shallower flow of the Okovango posed Mansur fewer difficulties than he thought when he first caught sight of the delta at the end of their seven-year journey. Mansur studied the site for a week. Then he began to draw up his plans.

There was one major difference between building in Egypt and in the Okovango's delta. In Egypt, stone had been available. There was of course stone in the Kalahari. The entire plateau was underpinned by it – the desert sand lay like a deep carpet on its surface. The problem was that the stone beneath was mainly limestone.

Limestone, Mansur knew well, was porous and fragile. Over the years it would crumble away until it was returned to the Kalahari as another layer of sand. Expedition after expedition was sent out to see if the desert harboured harder types of rock. The expeditions ranged deep into the Kalahari but they all returned with the same answer. They could find nothing but limestone.

Eventually Mansur decided there was only one solution.

If Ophir could not be built of stone, he would have to use something else. The alternative was all round them. It was iroko, African hardwood. Heavier and tougher than teak, almost as durable as granite, hardwood trees grew in profusion all over the delta and in the forests to the north.

Mansur already knew he would need timber for the sluice gates to hold back the river's waters. Now he decided to use it for Ophir's houses, temples, and fortifications too. For a city destined to be anchored in the Okovango's waters, wood, Mansur thought, was singularly appropriate.

Mansur drew up his plans and began.

'The fever has passed.'

Ben's head jerked up at the words.

Through the hut door he could see the brilliant sunlight of mid-morning. Moments earlier, it seemed, he had been watching Kala. He must have fallen asleep again. He clambered to his feet. It was Mama Ovambo who had spoken. The huge Herero woman was standing beside him in the early light. Beyond her shoulder Ben could see Kala was sleeping again too. Between her fingers the diamond was glittering as brightly as the sun.

Mama Ovambo put her hands on her hips and laughed. It was a great peal of laughter that started in her belly and rumbled up through her body.

'Wake my daughter, the white girl,' Mama Ovambo

went on. 'Tell her the desert child she brought to me will live. The little one who does not speak must have powerful friends. By the day's end she will have the appetite of a hyena.'

Mama Ovambo went on shaking with laughter.

Ben roused Mary-Ellen. Two hours later they were on their way again. They travelled slowly with the four younger San taking turns to carry Kala in her litter, and old Deial trotting ahead. Kala slept. Her face was thin and drawn and her breathing was still shallow, but her body had thrown off the infection. It would take a week or more for the wounds from the lioness' claws to heal, but within days she would be on her feet again.

Mary-Ellen walked beside her, wiping off the sweat that still occasionally filmed Kala's skin. Her relief at the girl's recovery was so overwhelming that each time she glanced back at him, Ben saw her face was radiant with happiness. Leading his horse, Ben trudged behind. Day by day he felt his leg muscles grow stronger. Even his limp seemed less wearisome. When evening came he still had enough energy to go out with the San scavenging for small animals, birds' eggs and roots.

Then at midday on the fifth day after they left Mama Ovambo's kraal, Deial trotted back and spoke to Mary-Ellen. She listened to him for a few moments and turned to Ben.

'Deial says we're almost there,' Mary-Ellen said. 'Kuruman's two hours ahead. We'll stop here while Khoi! and Nuna go on. They'll cast round the village. If anyone's arrived at the mission recently, they'll see their spoor –'

Mary-Ellen paused. A shadow crossed her face and her eyes seemed to darken.

'We've come all this way safely. There's no point in taking any risks now.'

Ben nodded. He knew exactly what Mary-Ellen was thinking. Kala's wounds had cost them almost a week. If Farini had followed them from the south, it was more than enough time for him to overtake them and get to Kuruman first.

Ben dismounted. Uneasily, he settled down to wait.

— 66 —

'There!'

Gert Frouw pointed between the ears of his horse.

Farini raised himself in his saddle and peered ahead. The waggons and the rest of the expedition were an hour behind them. A mile away over the scrub he could see the tower of a small wooden chapel, and the roof of a house rising above the walls of a stockade.

'The Reverend Mr and Mrs Ramsay and their hellcat of a daughter,' Frouw added.

'How do we handle it?' Farini said.

Frouw pushed back his leather hat. He rubbed his stubbled chin with his hand.

'Five months ago I saw the preacher beat the hell out of the girl,' he replied. 'Maybe they've made peace. It doesn't matter. She's got to stop at Kuruman and find herself a waggon. She has to be here or heading here. Either way we need the preacher's help –'

Frouw gave a harsh chuckle. 'He listens to silver. You're the man with the silver tongue. Best you go alone first. I'll wait here for the waggons.'

Farini rode on.

He turned in through the stockade entrance and dismounted by the steps that led up to the door. The place seemed deserted. Farini glanced round, puzzled. He'd expected the mission to be neat and orderly. Instead it had a dismal and shabby air of neglect, almost as if it had been abandoned. The brittle skeletons of a line of rosebushes fringed the path. The paint was peeling on the window frames. Sections of the stockade were rotting and a plank hung loose from the roof, tapping in the desert breeze with a persistent melancholy rattle.

Farini walked up the steps and tugged at the bell-pull which hung by the door. After a few minutes he heard steps inside. The door was opened by a gaunt-cheeked, bearded man who peered at him suspiciously through narrow bloodshot eyes.

'The Reverend Mr Ramsay?' Farini enquired.

The man nodded.

'It is my pleasure to make your acquaintance, sir.' Farini smiled. 'My name is Farini. I have the advantage of you, I believe. I have heard much of both you and your lady wife. Indeed, I may have contributed in a modest way to your noble work out here in the wilds.'

Ramsay frowned. Then he said curtly, 'Dead. Dead this past month. Sow the wind and ye shall reap the whirlwind. The sins of the fathers, sir. The sins of the fathers unto the tenth generation.'

Farini hesitated. Then he realized Ramsay must be referring to his wife. Mrs Ramsay, it seemed, must have died since Frouw's visit. Farini composed his face solemnly and removed his hat.

'Mrs Ramsay has passed away? I am truly distressed to hear such melancholy news, sir. My deepest condolences –'

He paused and gestured behind him. 'I had so many warm recommendations from my colleague, Mr Gert Frouw, I almost felt I knew her. Mr Frouw visited you on my business previously. I believe he made my appreciation clear.'

Ramsay stared at him.

'Ah, yes.' The minister's tone changed. 'The South African gentleman is in your service?'

'Indeed, sir,' Farini answered. 'He is with me now.'

'Then it is both my duty and my pleasure to welcome you,' Ramsay continued. 'Kindly step inside. I will have your horse fed and watered. For the rest, I shall do what I can. The Society gives me little enough. Also, I fear, you will find the housekeeping in a sorry state since Mrs

Ramsay abandoned her duties. As, considering her history, I should have foreseen would be the case.'

A few minutes later Farini found himself in the mission living room.

Untidy and thick with dust, the room echoed the neglect outside. What must have happened was obvious. Mrs Ramsay had held the household together. After her death, the minister had abandoned any attempt at keeping it functioning in a clean, orderly manner. Now it was starting to disintegrate.

In Africa, as Farini was already beginning to learn, the process could take place in a matter of weeks.

Ramsay beckoned Farini to a chair.

'What brings you to Kuruman, Mr Farini?'

'I have come on a matter of some delicacy,' Farini replied. 'It touches, I am bound to say, on your daughter and the mission.'

Ramsay stared at him and frowned.

'I assume you refer to the grievous incident which took place after I allowed the young woman to accompany your colleague into the desert,' Ramsay replied. 'Are there consequences of which I am unaware?'

'I fear there are, Mr Ramsay. Before I outline them, I feel it prudent to ask you a question. Is your daughter at present at Kuruman?'

As Farini spoke, Ramsay's cheeks reddened with anger.

'You have referred to her earlier as my daughter,' he said. 'I have to tell you, sir, I do not recognize her as such. She is no kin of mine. As far as she was once here, it was as Mrs Ramsay's daughter. She is no longer here. She has not been so for the past five months. She will never be admitted under my roof again. Now please be about your business.'

Farini hesitated. The minister, Farini sensed, had not only let the mission slip out of his control. The man was verging on madness.

Then Farini leant forward. In a deliberately grave and concerned voice, he told Ramsay about the disappearance of the diamond and the San from the Westminster Aquarium. When he finished, Ramsay stood up. He walked to the window and frowned into the darkening air beyond.

For a long time the minister said nothing.

'Your words are bitter to me,' Ramsay replied eventually. 'They confirm a truth I have prayed since the young woman's departure was not so. All the evidence then declared she was a liar. I have knelt and begged every night for the Lord to deny it. You have proved she was not merely a liar but a thief. She has taken your property by violence and deceit, and intends to squander it in the very wilderness which our Lord abominates –'

Ramsay turned. He gazed at Farini. His eyes were vengeful and bitter.

'What do you want of me?' he demanded. 'What can I do to frustrate the evil in the young woman?'

Plucking at his moustache, Farini sat back.

'May I ask whether Miss Ramsay ever received any letters or packages through the mails while she was here?'

Ramsay stiffened. 'Why do you wish to know?'

Farini chose his words with care as he answered.

'I have reason to believe,' Farini said, 'that she may have been in correspondence with an author, a man of so-called science whose heresies all God fearing Christians regard as the work of the devil. His name is Darwin, Dr Charles Darwin.'

Ramsay held himself upright for a moment longer. Then his shoulders sagged and he slumped down in the chair behind his desk.

'So you are privy to that, too?' he said. 'Yes, I neither can nor will deny it. She did receive missives from that infamous blasphemer. My belated discovery of the traffic between the two was the most grievous event in my life.'

'May I ask how it came about?' Farini prompted him softly.

'A young man arrived here,' Ramsay answered. 'Later he proved to be the basest scoundrel and fornicator. Naturally, I did not know it at the time. He bore a much-respected name, Oswell, and I allowed him to make camp in the compound. He professed interest in Mary-Ellen. My foolish wife, God forgive her misguided soul, encouraged the child to visit him in the vainglorious hope she would acquire his "accent" –'

Ramsay spat the word out contemptuously. Then he shuddered.

'Vile incidents took place,' he went on. 'They are the concern of none now but the two of them when they answer, as both will, to the Almighty. But there was a viler matter still. Oswell introduced her to the writings of this creature, Darwin. She wrote to the man. According to her, Darwin provided her with funds to study monkeys –'

Until then, Ramsay had been subdued, almost defeated. When he spoke the word 'monkeys', he jerked upright and his voice shook with outrage.

'Or so the young woman told us before she left,' Ramsay added. 'Whatever the truth, she claimed to be departing with substantial resources. And that, sir, is the substance of the story. May that tainted silver do the young woman much good in hell. It will be the only place where the coin is taken.'

Ramsay broke off.

He was panting, and his face was suffused with scarlet. Veins pulsed on his cheeks and his wrists quivered as he rested his arms on the desktop.

Somehow Ramsay managed to control himself. He heaved himself to his feet. He went to a cupboard in the corner of the room, and pulled out two tumblers, which he polished with a large streaked pocket handkerchief. He took the glasses to the sideboard, and filled them almost to the brim with brandy from a half-empty decanter.

'Enough of my own pain and distress, Mr Farini,' Ramsay said, handing Farini one of the glasses. 'The burden of the evil generated by the girl and her consort is for me to bear and me alone. So is the desolation in which the Society's deprivations have left me. They are no concern of yours. What can I do for you and your excellent colleague, Mr Frouw – ?'

Ramsay emptied half of his tumbler in a single gulp. He gazed at Farini with bleared eyes.

'In which connection, where was I?' Ramsay finished wildly.

Ramsay had already forgotten what he had been talking about. Farini realized he was lost in a haze of alcohol and vengeance. He wasn't just verging on madness. The minister had long since plunged into almost total insanity. Almost – but not quite. Ramsay was still obsessed with his God and the lack of funds which was bringing ruin to the mission.

Avoiding the smears, Farini took a small fastidious sip from the glass. Inwardly as he drank, he smiled.

The long years of futility as Ramsay had tried to battle Africa and its unyielding gods – infinitely older and stronger than any deity he could offer in their place. The girl's banishment in disgrace. The death of Ramsay's wife. The dark presence of impending disaster which hung over Kuruman. And now the emptying decanters of brandy.

All of them had come together to destroy the man. They had combined too at exactly the right moment to assist Farini.

Farini stood up.

'Sore loads have been placed on your shoulders, Minister,' he said. 'I trust I was able to mitigate them in some small way before. Now I would like to do more –'

Farini swept out his arm. The gesture was extravagant but generous and graceful.

'I wish to see your mission here at Kuruman blossom once again like a rose of faith in the wilderness,' he continued. 'Happily, humbly, I can offer the resources which may help it flower. But perhaps first we should consign to history certain unhappy events of the past –'

Farini paused. When he went on, his voice was hard and commanding.

'I spoke of the unfortunate Miss Ramsay,' Farini said.

'I said documents might have arrived here for her after her departure. If they have, I would like to see them and put the issue behind us.'

Ramsay gazed at him in silence.

The minister walked back to the sideboard. Unsteadily, he refilled his glass. He gulped down the drink. Then he went over to his desk. Ramsay opened a drawer and pulled out a package. He handed it to Farini.

As Farini took it, he saw the package had already been opened.

'I have inspected the contents,' Ramsay said. 'There is a letter and a map. They come, it seems, from the blasphemer. I have no wish to see them ever again. You may keep them.'

— 67 —

'*Zhu oka!*'

Khoi! raised his hand. He dropped to one knee as his younger brother Nuna ran up to his side.

The two young San hunters had been scouring the bush round Kuruman since the early afternoon. Now the sun was dipping towards the horizon, and the sky was beginning to darken. From the time of Livingstone onwards the village had been the last outpost of explorers, hunters and traders setting out into the interior. Khoi! and Nuna had been combing the dozen rough tracks that converged on the little settlement from every direction.

The track Khoi! was kneeling on was the last to cross the circle they'd traced round the village. He peered closely at the winding corridor of ridged and packed sand. Then he sucked in his breath between his teeth. This one was different from the others. It was patterned with spoor. The spoor was twenty-four hours old, but to Khoi! its meaning was as clear as if it had been printed there only moments before. A dozen waggons accompanied by outriders had passed that way. Each waggon had been drawn by a team of eight oxen. Many men and many animals, Khoi! thought.

He rocked back on his heels and turned to his brother. Nuna had picked up what looked like a stubby length of stick. Nuna rolled it between his fingers. He sniffed it warily, and held it out for Khoi!'s inspection. Khoi! raised it to his nostrils and sniffed it too. He grunted as he recognized the powerful acrid smell. It came from the charred dry leaves of the tobacco plant.

Although Khoi! didn't know it, the object was a half-smoked Havana cigar. What Khoi! did know was that it had been burned by the tall white devil who had beaten him and Nuna so often in the strange cold building in the great kraal beyond the waves. Khoi! recognized Farini's smell as quickly as he recognized the smell of tobacco itself. He slipped the cigar into the pouch at his waist. Then he stood up. With Nuna trotting beside him, he set off back towards where they had left the others.

Khoi! had found what the golden-haired woman had instructed him to look for. He knew she'd hoped he wouldn't find it. But the spoor was there and a child could have read its message, and he would have to tell her so. The previous day a large well-equipped expedition had rumbled into the village.

As he ran, Khoi! felt in his bones that the wind from Kuruman blew ill.

Mary-Ellen woke before dawn.

She had slept only fitfully in the hours since Khoi! and Nuna came back. She had dreaded their return, dreaded what they might tell her – hoping against hope that it wouldn't be so. As soon as she glimpsed the grave frowning faces of the two little San, Mary-Ellen knew her worst fears had been realized.

Farini had reached Kuruman. He and his waggons and his men were still there.

For an instant she'd looked blindly, despairingly, at Ben. Then before he could speak, she had turned and stridden away into the darkness. Ben hadn't followed her and she'd been glad. To travel into the desert they had to have a waggon. Only Moffat could help her find one. Moffat was her responsibility, not Ben's. In the tiny community of Kuruman Ben would have been even more vulnerable than she was.

She and Ben had argued about it later, but Mary-Ellen had stubbornly refused to yield. In the end Ben had backed down. Now it was time for her to go.

Mary-Ellen stood up. She stretched her limbs in the

darkness to rid them of the stiffness of the night. Then she walked over to the pallet on which Kala lay sleeping. The bandages Mary-Ellen put on her every evening were no longer soaked with blood the next morning, and even in the early grey light the girl's cheeks had regained some of their colour. Lying beside Kala with one arm thrown protectively over her chest, Ben was also asleep.

Mary-Ellen looked at the two of them for a moment. Then she walked away through the bush. To the east, the faintest razor-thin line of light had edged above the horizon. Everywhere else it was dark. On all sides the landscape stretched out beneath the stars in a vast flat expanse of thorn and scrub and sand.

A pearl-spotted owl called. Mary-Ellen saw the white flash of its breast as it hawked for insects. A distant lion roared. Somewhere a group of jackals quarrelled in high-pitched barks over a piece of carrion. The desert air had the crisp, piercing clarity that always grew sharper and cleaner with the approach of morning.

Mary-Ellen stopped. She had known the sights, sounds and scents all her life. They were the same all over the Kalahari. She might have been standing almost anywhere in the immensity of the desert. She was not. She was standing in a very particular place. Here even the dawn breeze had a special feel to it. The owl's cry was achingly familiar. The lion's roar belonged to this one spot alone.

Ahead of her lay Kuruman. By the time the sun rose, she would be able to look down over the roof of the mission house. She had come home. Mary-Ellen shivered at the word. She had been away for months. When she left she'd vowed never to return. She had cut herself off utterly from all the mission represented, including a father who had never been her father. In the turmoil of what happened afterwards, she had wiped Kuruman so completely from her mind it might never have existed.

Or so Mary-Ellen thought.

Now Kuruman's nearness was so vivid she might never have gone. Home, Mary-Ellen remembered reading once, was the place everyone returns to when there is nowhere else left to go. Bitterly she knew she had nowhere else to go – not if Kala was to be returned to the desert. Yet Kuruman was much more than that.

The mission was her birthplace.

It was haunted by the fears and nightmares of her childhood. It brought back the brutality of Ramsay's beatings, the violence and misery of her expedition into the Kalahari with Frouw. But Kuruman also stood for her childhood companion Moffat, her foster mother Mama Chi-mona, the love and tenderness of her hapless real mother, and for so much more – for all that had been best in Mary-Ellen's life.

Her eyes blurred with tears. There was no separating the good and the bad, the happiness and the pain. Inextricably bound together, for Mary-Ellen they would always be lodged in the tiny community beyond the thorn bushes on the edge of the desert.

The warmth of the rising sun dried the salt drops on her cheeks.

She tossed her head, shaking the last of the tears away. Then she walked on. She was going into Kuruman alone. Mary-Ellen had always known it was what she would have to do.

The heavily built white man hauled on the horse's reins.

The animal jerked and plunged. The man swore. He struck it violently on the flank with his whip and pulled harder. The horse came to a stop. The man dismounted and unslung the rifle from his shoulders. He tethered the horse to a tree and walked back.

The white man's name was Piet 'Baobab' Botha.

He'd left the waggon laager they'd set up outside Kuruman just after dawn. According to big Gert Frouw, who'd hired him and the others for the trek on behalf of the American, they would camp at the mission for as long as necessary. They were waiting for the preacher's daughter and the coons who'd managed to slip away from them in Cape Town.

It was their second day there. Botha was a hunter and a

tracker. That morning he'd decided to look for antelope. He was three miles south of the village when he spotted the tracks.

Botha squatted and inspected the ground.

The spoor of the footprints was fresh. The bent grasses told him it had been left there only an hour or two ago. The forward pressure on the toes meant a woman. It wasn't a kaffir woman. The kaffirs went barefoot and this one had been wearing boots. It was a white woman and she was taking care not to be seen – she was avoiding the broad game paths and keeping close to the dense bush.

Botha scratched his jaw. He went back to his horse and untethered it. He swung himself up into the saddle and began to follow the tracks.

They led towards the mission.

Mary-Ellen paused in the shadow of a copse of trees.

She stared down. Shimmering in the early heat, the settlement of Kuruman was spread out below her. Winding away beyond was the bright shining ribbon of the Kuruman river. The voices of the Tswana children playing in the alleys between the rondavels rose to her on the morning wind. She could see the high stockade fence, the little tower of the chapel, and the mission house itself.

As the tears rose in her eyes again, Mary-Ellen blinked and shook them away. She squatted on her heels and clenched her jaw. She needed to think. She would visit Mama Chi-mona first. The old woman would tell her what had been happening in the village and where she could find Moffat. Even before that she would have to slip into Kuruman without being seen.

Keeping close to the edges of the dry pastures, Mary-Ellen headed on until she reached the outskirts of the village. Incurious eyes watched her walk swiftly through the pools of shadow in the winding lane between the Hottentot and San dwellings. The huts had always had an air of neglect, but today they seemed even more forlorn than she remembered.

Ten minutes later she ducked quietly into the familiar doorway.

'Daughter of my heart, you have come home! I saw you last night in my dream, and I knew your spirit was close.'

Mama Chi-mona's voice came from the back of the room. Her voice was husky with pleasure. The tiny dark hut with its pervading smells of chewing tobacco and dried maize husks came back to Mary-Ellen with an aching familiarity.

'How I greet you, my mother!' Mary-Ellen replied when she picked out the old woman through the gloom.

Mary-Ellen folded her arms round her. For a while they held each other, rocking slowly together. Then Mary-Ellen drew back. She had been fondling Mama Chi-mona's head. There was something warm and wet on Mary-Ellen's fingers. Suddenly apprehensive, she tensed and glanced down. On her hand was a dark smear of blood.

Anxiously she studied the old woman's face. There was a long open slash down Mama Chi-mona's cheek. With a flash of anger Mary-Ellen recognized the mark of Mr Ramsay's buffalo-hide whip.

'What has happened, Mama?' she asked.

The old woman gave her a tired smile. 'It is nothing, child. It is not your father's fault. He has been as if bitten by the yellow-patterned snake ever since Mama Ram'y was taken up into the sky.'

Mary-Ellen stared at her. 'My mother has been taken?'

'You did not know? Oh, my daughter, I am sorry. She was gathered by the sun one full moon ago.'

Mary-Ellen was motionless as she gazed at the old woman. Gently Mama Chi-mona stretched out her hand. Sobbing, the young woman flung herself forward into the old woman's arms. She buried her face in Mama Chi-mona's chest as the tears streamed down her face.

Mary-Ellen had no idea how long she wept. When she eventually raised her head, Mama Chi-mona was still stroking her hair. Mary-Ellen drew back and looked at the old woman.

'How did she die?'

'She was taken by the white man's fever,' Mama Chi-mona answered. 'The mission boys made a hole for her in the earth behind the chapel. Your father said spells over it. She lies there. She has the wind to sing to her now and the stars for her companions.'

Mary-Ellen bowed her head.

A wave of desolation swept over her. Her mother, Mary-Ellen had discovered at the end, hadn't chosen either her husband or the desert she had come to hate and fear so much. They had both been forced on her. She had been weak and sad and misguided, a victim of her own romantic dreams and her own ruthless mother.

But she had loved her daughter, Mary-Ellen knew that, and she had done her best to cherish and protect her. If Mary-Ellen had stayed at Kuruman, perhaps the fever wouldn't have struck her down. Or maybe Mary-Ellen would have been able to nurse her back to health. Mary-Ellen hadn't stayed. She had left and her mother, lonely and grieving, had died, and Mary-Ellen felt overwhelmed with guilt and sadness.

'She was my mother and I her true daughter, Mama,' she managed to say between sobs. 'I should not have left her to die alone.'

'Then grieve for her, daughter of her blood and my heart. But do not grieve overlong, for the blame is not yours. Her spirit is free now. Do not howl like a jackal for its return.'

Mary-Ellen choked back her tears and nodded. Somehow she managed to put the grief aside and get possession of herself again.

'But what has happened since? What of this?' she asked.

She touched the skin on the old woman's cheek.

'Since Mama Ram'y went, the minister has snarled and snapped like a lion with a festering thorn in its tongue,' Mama Chi-mona answered. 'He has beaten everyone. Not me at first. But then one day your sister, Mama Beth, came from the Appleby ranch with papers for you. She told me to hide them for you, because she knew Bwana Ram'y would be angry if he found them.'

Mary-Ellen leaned forward. 'Do you have them?'

Mama Chi-mona shook her head. She pointed at the wound on her cheek.

'That is what I have instead. Your father searched the compound. When he found the papers in my dwelling, he beat me and took them.'

Puzzled, Mary-Ellen frowned.

'But what about Moffat?' Mary-Ellen demanded. 'He always looked after my papers. Didn't Mama Beth give them to him?'

To her dismay, the old woman shook her head again.

'Moffat has gone to find his people,' she said. 'He came to me after Mama Ram'y was taken. He said he was released then. I told him of his father. He went into the Thirst to claim his name.'

Mary-Ellen stared at the old woman in despair.

Her mother was dead. Moffat was gone. Ramsay had found the documents Darwin had sent her after she left the mission. Only one thing could make it worse. Mary-Ellen knew the answer even before she spoke.

'I have been spoored by white men, Mama,' she said. 'Have any such men come to the settlement?'

The old woman nodded bleakly.

'Many white men with waggons and horses,' she answered. 'They came two days ago. They have made camp two hours to the east. But they are here in the village all the time. No one talks of anything else.'

Hurriedly Mary-Ellen got to her feet.

'I must go, Mama,' she said. 'There is nothing I can do in Kuruman –'

Mary-Ellen broke off.

A shadow had fallen across the floor, and Mama Chi-mona's eyes had widened in fear. Mary-Ellen whirled round.

A heavy-shouldered white man with a rifle in his hand was standing at the hut's entrance. Mary-Ellen had never seen him before, but she knew in an instant who he was. He was one of Farini's men.

For a big man he moved very fast. He ducked under the arch, crossed the floor, and seized Mary-Ellen's arm. With a strength she was powerless to fight against, he swung her round and twisted her arm up behind her back. The pain made Mary-Ellen gasp.

'So I was right,' the man chuckled. 'The preacher's little daughter has run home. You should have been more careful where you left your spoor, *mehnfrau*. Now you will come and tell your daddy and his friends where you've been.'

Mary-Ellen struggled furiously. It was useless. She felt herself being hauled out of the tiny dusky hut on to the baked earth beyond. Mary-Ellen blinked and her eyes watered in the sunlight. Fiercely she lashed back at the man with her foot. She caught him on the knee. He grunted and cursed. For an instant he paused.

'Mama!' Mary-Ellen called over her shoulder. Her breath was coming in quick gasps. She managed to shout some instructions to the old woman in Sarwa. She glimpsed Mama Chi-mona nod in understanding.

Then the man dragged her away towards the mission.

— 68 —

'So,' Ramsay said. 'You have come back.'

Mary-Ellen looked steadily back at him.

They were standing face to face in the mission living room. As the powerful white man had pushed her through the door, Mary-Ellen's eyes had swept quickly over the room. Apart from Ramsay, there were two other men there. She recognized them both. One was Farini, the other the towering South African, Frouw.

'May I ask why?' Ramsay's voice was little more than a whisper.

For a moment Mary-Ellen didn't answer. She went on staring at him.

It was almost as if she were looking at him for the first time. In a sense, it flashed through Mary-Ellen's mind, she was. The last time she'd seen Ramsay, he had still been her father. Since that appalling night and her mother's confession about the French dancing-master, she hadn't seen him again. Until now.

Ramsay might have been a stranger.

He was older, smaller, and wearier than she remembered. Shabby and dishevelled, his appearance reflected the room. Mrs Ramsay had always kept it meticulously neat and clean. As Mary-Ellen had stumbled in, she'd noticed with a shock that it was filthy and layered with dust. Since her mother had died, both Ramsay and the house had started to fall apart.

Only Ramsay's eyes were exactly as before. They had always been angry and embittered. If anything they were more vengeful and inflamed than ever.

'I wish to be released,' Mary-Ellen said.

The white man was still holding her by the arm. As she spoke, his grip tightened. Across the room Farini made a gesture.

'Let her go, Botha,' Farini said.

The man moved away from Mary-Ellen.

'Yes, I will tell you,' she went on. 'I have come back to return the San, who were cruelly, violently and illegally seized, to their homes in the desert.'

'I have prayed for you, young woman,' Ramsay said. 'Out of charity I have knelt every night to implore Heaven's forgiveness for you –'

Ramsay continued as if he hadn't heard Mary-Ellen. His voice was still strangely, chillingly quiet.

'For you and your mother because, God have pity on her, she was a harlot and a fornicator too. I have even wept for the two of you. My prayers, my tears, have been in vain. The Lord has closed his ears to them. Instead in his righteous anger He has sent you back to torment and persecute me –'

Foam started to fleck Ramsay's mouth. His veins pulsed and his face became contorted.

He was mad, Mary-Ellen realized. She thought she had exorcised him when she confronted and stared him down before. She had not. All she had done was to lose her fear of him. The nightmare, the madness, had remained there locked inside the man, corroding and poisoning him. Now the poison was about to erupt and spill over her more violently than ever.

Mary-Ellen clenched her hands until her nails cut into her skin. She couldn't let the fear return. For Kala, for all of them, she had to hold unflinchingly on to what she had won.

'You shall not do so, young woman!' Ramsay's voice suddenly rose to a hoarse shout. 'This time your correction will be such that even the wrath of the Almighty shall be satisfied!'

Ramsay raised his arm and lurched forward to strike her.

'Minister –!'

Farini's voice cut sharply across the room. He coughed and came forward.

'We have an agreement of some consequence to the mission,' Farini added. 'I feel it would be better implemented in some other fashion.'

Ramsay hesitated. He glanced round.

'What do you mean, sir?' he demanded.

'All I desire on my side is the return of my property,' Farini answered. 'As we both know, Miss Ramsay is the key to that. May I suggest you release her into my charge? With your permission I shall take her back to my camp. There I shall be able to discuss the matter with her –'

Farini paused. 'It would save you further distress, Minister. And I believe that, in private with myself and my companions, Miss Ramsay may prove more than willing to reveal what she knows.'

Ramsay's chest was rising and falling wildly. Bemused, he seemed to think for a moment. Then his arm fell to his side and he turned away.

'Take the little whore,' he said. 'Do with her as you will. Do not hesitate to employ the utmost firmness in acquiring the answers you seek. You will have the Lord's blessing.'

Mary-Ellen felt herself being seized again. With Frouw on one side and Botha on the other she was hurried out of the house and into the compound.

As her feet scuffed and stumbled in the dust, Mary-Ellen felt cold and sick. Conditioned by the years of her childhood beatings, she had deluded herself into thinking Ramsay was the danger that had to be outfaced. He was not. Ramsay was insane and violent, but he was a ghost. The danger was striding in front of her. They turned out through the compound gates. Mary-Ellen was heaved up on to a horse and they set off.

In the mission living room, Ramsay walked unsteadily over to the window. He rested his head against the frame. For some reason sharp pains were running across his chest and he was having difficulty in seeing. He blinked. He managed to glimpse below the once cherished but long since neglected garden of his great predecessor, the Revd Robert Moffat.

Ramsay glanced back into the room. The sideboard was as blurred as everything else. On top of it, although he couldn't see them, were five gold sovereigns and a banker's draft for forty-five more. Fifty sovereigns would support the mission for an entire year. They would also allow him, he thought vaguely, to do something to the garden.

Ramsay set off back across the floor to pour himself another glass of brandy. He never got there. Midway to the decanter he toppled and fell. He was still lying there when the houseboy who had replaced Moffat came into the room the next morning.

'I want the girl and the diamond, Miss Ramsay,' Farini said. 'Where are they?'

Mary-Ellen was silent.

She was standing in Farini's tent. They had ridden there from the mission. As they came out through the trees Mary-Ellen saw Farini had made camp in a meadow upriver from Kuruman. She glimpsed a dozen waggons drawn up in a laager, a number of camp fires, and a large enclosure near the water where the waggon's oxen were penned.

Then Mary-Ellen was pulled down off her horse. Her hands were roped behind her back and she was pushed into the tent. That must have been an hour ago. She'd been alone with him ever since.

'I don't know,' she repeated. 'I left them a week ago on the trek road from the Cape. I rode on alone to Kuruman for supplies. If I wasn't back in three days, they were to return south. I got lost. I didn't get here until this morning. By now they'll be four days on their way back to the Cape.'

'No, young lady,' Farini snapped. 'You were travelling with the cripple, the girl and the little coons. You wouldn't have left them. None of them can talk to each other – for Christ's sake, the girl can't even talk at all! Without you they're lost. So where the hell are they?'

Mary-Ellen didn't answer.

It was the best story she'd been able to think of. Farini hadn't believed it the first time. An hour later he still didn't believe it. But at least she'd gained an hour. If Mama Chi-mona had really understood what Mary-Ellen shouted back at her, and if her grandchildren had done what they were told, then every extra minute might count.

'All right,' Farini went on. 'I'm a businessman. I make deals. I'll make you a last offer –'

Until then he'd been sitting in a jute-backed chair. Farini stood up.

'I want the girl and the coons,' he said. 'I paid good money for them, my money. Without them I've got no show. So I want them back. I want the carpenter too. He attacked me, he robbed me. I'd like to see the bastard swing. But –'

Farini paused. He raised his hand.

'I'll trade them all. The girl, the coons, the cripple, you can have them. Naturally you go free too. Just give me back the diamond and you get the rest.'

Farini moved behind her as he spoke. Mary-Ellen didn't turn her head, but she knew he was standing very close to her. She could hear his breathing and smell the strong, sharp scent of the pomade on his hair.

Mary-Ellen stared in front of her.

Farini didn't understand. No one would understand apart from herself, the San, and now perhaps Ben. The diamond was yoked to Kala's life. It was the main artery of her existence. Through it flowed all of Kala's being, her secret past and maybe her future.

Mary-Ellen had no more idea why than the rest of them. All she knew was that if the stone was taken from Kala, the girl would die. Farini wasn't asking for the diamond. He was asking for Kala's life.

'I don't know what you're talking about,' she said defiantly.

Farini hit her.

He was out of Mary-Ellen's sight and she didn't see

him draw back his hand. One moment she was standing upright. The next she felt a jarring blow on the side of her head. With her hands tied behind her she staggered and tumbled forward.

Her face slammed against the baked earth. For several moments she lay stunned. When she managed to lift her head, there was a warm salty taste in her mouth. Dizzily Mary-Ellen realized her lip was cut and bleeding. There was more blood running down from her nose.

'I want my diamond, you little bitch – !'

Farini was bending down over her. Acid with anger, his voice was like Ramsay's. Except, Mary-Ellen knew, this man's rage was fed by a strength and a greed that not even Ramsay had ever had.

'I'm going to beat the truth out of you if it takes all night, all tomorrow, and the next day as well. You're going to tell me where the hell that stone is!'

Farini stood up.

'Gert!' Mary-Ellen heard him shout.

The tent flap rustled. The shadow of the huge South African fell over the earth beside her.

'Take her out,' Farini said. 'Make the bitch see sense. When she does, bring her back!'

Frouw chuckled.

'I've seen how her daddy instructs her,' Frouw said. 'But I don't need to learn from him. I've been teaching kaffirs for years. Maybe I could even give the minister a lesson or two.'

Frouw hauled Mary-Ellen to her feet. With one arm he swung her over his hip and carried her outside.

It was midday. Mary-Ellen's eyes were dazzled by the light. She felt herself being lifted over a space of earth. Then her head collided with something. She blinked. Her face was in shadow now. She could just make out that she'd been propped against the wheel of one of the waggons. Her arms were untied and roped to the waggon spokes.

'Who's going to do the honours?' The call came from Frouw.

'Seeing as I was the one as catched the cow, I reckon I get the first shout at skinning her – !'

Mary-Ellen recognized the voice. It belonged to the man they called Botha, the man who had captured her. Behind her she heard the sound of laughter and cheering.

'I just need to see what I'm skinning!'

The cheers and the laughter grew louder. Mary-Ellen felt a hand grip her skirt and pull violently. The fabric parted and the skirt fell to her ankles. Then her underclothes were ripped away too.

Mary-Ellen could feel the heat of the sun on her naked buttocks and thighs. The men must have moved closer. The noise of their hungry baying and shouting was almost deafening. She began to twist her head, trying to see them, hoping somehow she could hold them back with her eyes.

Mary-Ellen never saw the men crowding in behind her.

The first blow landed on her then. It came with brutal force from a buffalo-hide whip. She gasped. Her knees buckled and she slumped back against the waggon wheel. A wave of sickening blackness surged over her. The pain was more agonizing than anything she had ever known.

Desperately she tried to remain conscious. She had to. For Kala she had to defy them, she had to remain silent, she had to make them believe her and let her go.

It was the last fragmented thought that crossed Mary-Ellen's mind before she fainted.

— 69 —

For the tenth time that afternoon Ben climbed up the slope that led to the top of the mound.

The sun was already beginning to angle down the sky. Ben peered out to the north, shading his eyes against the glare. It was the most desolate landscape he had ever seen. A flat and seemingly endless plain of barren scrub, blurred at its distant horizons with dust and heat haze. It had no colour, only the bleached-out greyness of the lacerating thorn bushes at the end of a Kalahari winter.

Once again there was nothing in front of him except the occasional flight of a desert bird.

Ben turned and limped back to the clearing where they had camped. Mary-Ellen had said she might not be back until the moon rose. There was still a little while before darkness, but she'd left at dawn and dawn was hours ago. She'd already had ample time to reach Kuruman and return.

Fretful and impatient, Ben paced restlessly round the camp.

He should have gone himself, Ben knew that. He'd argued fiercely with Mary-Ellen, but she'd been adamant. Now as the hours passed with no sign of her, Ben cursed himself more and more angrily for giving way. It didn't matter that he didn't know the village or speak the African languages. All they needed to do was find Mary-Ellen's friend, Moffat. Ben could have done that just as well as her. And if Farini was still at Kuruman, the danger was the same for both of them – except that Ben was infinitely better equipped to take Farini on than she was.

Ben clenched his fists.

At midday he'd seen Deial making ready to take his sons out on a hunting expedition. Frustrated by his own inactivity, Ben went with them. In the Kalahari, food would be scarce, and the old man was preparing for the journey. Ben watched the San set out traps which snared some spring hares, a porcupine, and a flock of guinea-fowl. They skinned and butchered the animals, and left the meat to dry in the sun.

Now the little people were gathering in the strips of protein. They were ready to move. As restless as he was, all they were waiting for was Mary-Ellen's return.

Ben glanced over at Kala who was sleeping in the shadow of a tree. Her wounds still weren't fully healed, but the day before she'd insisted on leaving the litter and walking for several hours. Ben marvelled not just at her own powers of recovery, but at Mama Ovambo's herbs and spiders' webs, at the ant jaws and the leaf mould. Between them they had pulled Kala back from the very edge of death.

There was something else too. The diamond. Ben could see the rays of the setting sun flaring off it as it lay between her fingers. More than anything, it was the jewel which had saved her. It had led them to Mama Ovambo's kraal. Its fire had dulled as the pulse of her life faded. Then the brilliance had welled up again as strength seeped back to her. Now in the dusk the stone was blazing.

The jewel was the girl's lifeline. It was also, it suddenly occurred to Ben, a curse on her existence. Someone, somewhere, must have bound the leather pouch round her waist. They had wanted to guard the child, to give her the stone's protection. Even more, they had wanted to save the diamond itself. They had burdened her with its vast richness – not knowing, perhaps, that it might also be her death.

Ben limped off round the clearing again.

Darkness came over the bush. Old Deial and his sons set about relighting the fire. Deial laid a branch of dry mopani wood on the sand. Khoi! carved out a hole in its middle with his knife. He placed a length of sapling upright in the centre, and then, as Nuna piled moss and grass in a pyramid over the hole, Khoi! began to whirl the sapling between his palms.

The spinning sapling heated the mopani wood until the friction made the wood glow. The moss and grass ignited. Delicately, Nuna piled first twigs and then larger and larger branches on to the growing nest of flames. Finally the fire was blazing.

Ben watched the flames rise. As he lowered himself to the ground beside the glow, he suddenly heard old Deial call out.

'N'da! N'da!'

Ben sprang up again. The noise, fluting away into the darkness, hadn't been so much a shout as an echo of the quick clap of Deial's hands that accompanied it. All the San were standing and gazing forward into the night. Ben gazed after them.

For several moments Ben couldn't see what they were staring at. Then he picked out the silhouette of a figure approaching the camp through the bush. A surge of relief swept over him. It could only be Mary-Ellen. Impulsively he stepped forward and opened his mouth to call out a welcome. As he did so, Ben froze.

On either side of him the faces of the San were puzzled and wary. He peered forward again. The silhouette wasn't Mary-Ellen's. With a sickening sense of disappointment, Ben realized it belonged to a man. Tall and black, his limbs glistening with oil, the man strode on towards the flames. Behind him there were other silhouettes, six, ten, and then as many as twenty of them. Ben reached for the gun Mary-Ellen had handed to him before she left. His face taut with uncertainty, he waited.

As the man reached the edge of the camp, old Deial trotted forward to speak to him. Deial gave the man what Ben recognized was the San greeting. The two stood together talking. Then Deial gestured over his shoulder towards Ben. The man listened and nodded and walked on again.

In the glow of the firelight Ben saw he was in his early twenties. He was tall and lean and muscular, with a spear in one hand and an ox-hide shield in the other. The shield's surface was painted with bars of white. Round his ankles and wrists were bands of leopard fur.

Behind him were twenty other warriors, all armed with the same spears and shields, and three apricot-skinned children. The man studied Ben for a moment. He had a strong, high-cheekboned face, and his eyes were keen and level and searching. Then he slammed down his spear, burying its shaft deep in the sand, and spoke.

'You are the companion who has travelled with Mama Mary-Ellen?' he said.

To Ben's bewilderment the words were in English. An instant later Ben realized the man must be Moffat, the childhood companion Mary-Ellen had set out to find. In his mind Ben had had an image of a European-clothed houseboy, not an armed and half-naked tribal chieftain.

Wary and confused, Ben nodded.

'Then I greet you.'

Moffat held out his hand with his palm open in the European handshake. Ben took the black man's hand and shook it.

'Where is Mary-Ellen?' Ben asked, his voice harsh with anxiety. 'She went into Kuruman to find you.'

Moffat stared at him. For a moment there was silence. Then Moffat said, 'The white men have seized her.'

Ben's stomach went cold and his face tightened. 'But you were at the mission,' Ben said. 'She went there to see you. What happened?'

Moffat shook his head. 'I do not come from the mission. I have been away for a full moon. I went to my lands to summon my warriors –'

He gestured towards the men behind him.

'We were marching towards Kuruman when our path crossed with the children's,' Moffat continued. 'They are the grandchildren of Mama Chi-mona. Chi-mona witnessed Mama Mary-Ellen's capture. The old woman waited until she knew where Mama Mary-Ellen had been taken. Then the children were sent to tell you to leave from here, taking the desert girl, Kala, with you.'

He paused.

'Mama Mary-Ellen said you were not to follow her for you would be taken too. There are many evil men and they have guns. You must go on with Kala on your own. It is the girl's only chance.'

Ben was silent. Farini's saturnine face came to his mind. He remembered the American's rages, his violence and his sadistic cruelty. Ben thought of Mary-Ellen in his hands, and fury of his own suddenly flooded over him.

'No!' Ben shouted. 'I'm not going on without her. We've got to get her away from those bastards. And if I need you to help me do it, that's just what you're going to do.'

Ben leant forward. He caught Moffat by the arm and shook him. Behind Moffat the black warriors stirred and raised their spears. Moffat lifted his arm to calm them.

'I spoke of you, not of myself,' Moffat said. 'Did you not know Mary-Ellen is my sister? Did you truly believe I would leave her among the white creatures who have trekked here from the south?'

Ben was silent. The two men stared at each other.

Moffat saw the young white man's powerful shoulders and his heavy muscular hands. He was strong, Moffat knew, infinitely stronger than his lop-sided body suggested. Moffat also saw his eyes. They were narrow and anguished. Behind the anguish Moffat saw something else, something he recognized.

It was the anger and hostility of an outcast. Moffat knew it well. He knew how it repelled friendship, and could turn the love between men and women into hatred. Mary-Ellen had taught him that anger could be turned away, that it was possible to love and be loved. She had been truly both mother and sister to him, but this man had not learnt the lesson she gave.

He was torn between his anger and his love. The two had come together and both would urge him on, but the anger was the stronger. Moffat knew it and still he resented it. This man had come into Mary-Ellen's life and had been unable to protect her. He had stayed behind while she had walked forward into peril.

Now that Mary-Ellen was trapped, he was protesting he would not leave her. Moffat gazed at him with contempt.

'I will go into Kuruman and bring Mama Mary-Ellen out,' Moffat went on. 'You will wait for us by the river. Then you may take the girl into the desert. No –'

Ben had opened his mouth to protest, but Moffat cut him off. He glanced down at Ben's withered leg and then up at the white man's face again.

'This is a task for warriors,' Moffat went on. 'If Mama Mary-Ellen is to be free, it will need speed and silence and skill. Your lameness will not help her. It will hold us back. Maybe there are other matters for you to manage, but they are not in battle. The scars you bear could cloud your judgement.'

Ben gazed at him.

Often in his life, Ben knew, he had felt anger and resentment towards other people as he trailed his wasted body behind them. Never before had he felt hatred. He felt it now. It coiled and rose in his mind like a poisonous cloud until his entire body was shaking. He looked at the proud, supple young black man, and his brain seemed to boil over.

Somehow Ben managed to control himself.

'Where do I go?' he asked flatly.

'The children say the men have taken Mama Mary-Ellen to their camp,' Moffat replied. 'The camp lies upstream on the river. We will go there. Mama Mary-Ellen was seeking a waggon to carry water. Since her mother died, there has been a waggon at the mission for her father's journeys –'

Moffat turned and called over his shoulder. One of the warriors, a grey-haired man with a scarred face, came forward. Moffat spoke to him and looked back at Ben.

'This man is named Batuka,' Moffat said. 'Before I returned to my people, he was their leader. Now he follows me. He will bring the waggon to where you wait by the river.'

Moffat got to his feet. He plucked the spear from the ground and thrust his arm through the shield lying beside it.

'We have delayed long enough,' the African said. 'We will go to the white men's camp. The San, the little people, will enter the camp before us. No one will see them, but they will scent and find where the white men have imprisoned my sister –'

Moffat raised his spear and shook it. In the moonlight the tip of the weapon blazed and danced like a firefly.

Helpless and weary, Ben watched the small group of warriors being swallowed up into the darkness. Then he turned. Beside him, Kala's eyes were glittering as brightly as the spear's tip.

'All quiet, man?'

Baobab Botha swung his heavy frame over the edge of the huge Cape waggon and jumped down to join his companion in the moonlit compound.

At his side Frenchie Rappaport nodded.

'Quiet as Heini's grave –'

Rappaport pulled out a tin box of cigarettes, hand-rolled in coarse yellow paper. He offered the box to Botha who took one.

'Too many kaffirs,' Rappaport went on. 'They got their cattle pastured all over. Lion and leopard, man, they know when people and herds are around. Unless they're starving, those buggers stay away. Isn't that for true?'

His voice had the hard, clipped accents of the veld. Botha nodded in agreement. He leant forward to light the cigarette with a coal from the fire.

Baobab Botha felt comfortable with Rappaport. They both knew the great upland plateau. The evening they'd met at the start of the trek they'd exchanged views about the desert, its game and its ivory. Since then they'd shared the middle night watch.

That night Rappaport had been patrolling the corral

where the draught oxen were penned, while Botha kept guard over the waggon that temporarily housed the girl. She'd been thrown inside it with her hands and her feet tied after she'd fainted. Botha grinned to himself as he remembered the whipping she'd been given.

'So what about the preacher's kid, then?' Rappaport gestured towards the waggon.

'A couple of hours and I'll give her another little lesson,' Botha answered. 'By morning she'll be eating out of my hand, man –' He laughed coarsely. 'Maybe that won't be all she'll be eating either.'

They both chuckled. They stood for a while talking and smoking. Then Rappaport headed back to check the oxen at the other end of the pasture.

Botha stubbed out his cigarette.

He wrinkled his face thoughtfully. The girl had been butt-naked when Frouw pitched her up inside the waggon. She had a fine white arse on her and good strong flanks too, Botha had noticed that. It might be fun to play around with her a little while she was still sleeping the punishment off.

Botha put his foot on the wheel's spoke to lever himself up on to the waggon's driving platform. He never heard the faint shimmer of movement in the grass as the silhouette rose from the earth behind him. All he felt was a light tap on his shoulder. It was probably Rappaport wanting another match. Unthinkingly, Botha turned his head.

Botha's eyes widened in astonishment. He glimpsed the moonlight flaring off the surface of a scything metal blade. Before he could even react, the blade sliced down across Botha's exposed neck. His head snapped back and blood from the severed artery arced through the air, staining the waggon's canvas hood. Botha crumpled to the ground.

Moffat plunged the short, curved knife deep into the earth and cleaned it in the sand.

Khoi! and Nuna were squatting behind him. They both pointed urgently at the waggon. Moffat raised the spear again. He slashed the blade once, twice, and then a third time across the canvas that covered the waggon's hoops. A section of the heavy tarred fabric fell away. Moffat tugged Botha's body aside and leapt up on to the waggon's jump-board. He peered inside.

Face down on the wooden floor was the hunched figure of Mary-Ellen. She seemed to be unconscious and her hands and feet were tightly bound with cords. Most of her clothes had been ripped from her body and her exposed back and shoulders were striped with thick raised welts where the ox-hide whip had bitten into her flesh.

Moffat's eyes glazed in fury.

Then he knelt and slashed away the bonds. He gathered Mary-Ellen in his arms and sprang back to the earth. Whispering at Khoi! and Nuna to follow him, Moffat set off back for the trees.

'Here –'

Moffat lowered Mary-Ellen to the ground at Ben's feet in the blackness of the copse.

'If you have skills to do so, look to her wounds,' Moffat snapped. 'For until now you have surely failed her.'

Moffat spat the words out between clenched teeth.

'Follow Khoi! and Nuna.' Moffat's voice was as cold as before. 'They will carry Mama Mary-Ellen and lead you to the waggon. We will give you an hour's lead.'

Ben said, 'What is there still to do?'

'It is not finished,' Moffat answered. 'The white men cannot move without the oxen for their waggons. The oxen must be released and scattered. It will take the white men two days to round them up again. By then we will be deep into the Great Thirst. Old Deial will lead you to safety. I will join you before the moon sets.'

Moffat turned and vanished, his warriors melting away in his wake.

As the Africans disappeared, Ben heard the click and rustle of old Deial's whispered instructions. Khoi! and Nuna came forward. They reached down to lift Mary-Ellen.

Fiercely Ben pushed them aside. He bent down and caught Mary-Ellen beneath the chest and legs, and heaved her up into his arms. Then he gestured abruptly onwards. The two little hunters gazed at the angry white man. Then they nodded and set off ahead of him into the darkness.

With the warm, limp body of Mary-Ellen cradled against his own and feeling her pulse flutter in her bruised wrists, Ben hobbled after them.

— 70 —

'That's all the oxen we're going to get back, Mr Farini,' Frouw said. 'Three of the animals were taken for sure by lions. We found the carcasses. Another six have just disappeared. Either the lions got them too, or the kaffirs have rustled them.'

Farini swore.

He and the South African were standing by the corral where the oxen were penned. The men had just driven back inside the last animals they'd managed to round up. Frouw had come over to give Farini the news.

'It means we've lost a full team,' Frouw added. 'We'll have to leave one waggon here.'

'The bastards!'

Farini cursed again.

It was Frouw himself who'd discovered what had happened. He'd woken early and walked over to relieve Botha at the waggon. Farini had heard the South African's shout a moment later. He leapt up and went outside. Frouw was standing over a huddled shape on the ground. His face was grim.

Farini ran over. He glanced down and stepped back, sickened. Botha was lying dead in a huge pool of blood that had stained the sand for several feet on every side. His throat had been cut and his head almost severed from his neck.

Farini glanced up at the waggon. A panel had been slashed out of the canvas hood. The interior was empty. The minister's daughter had gone.

'What happened?' Farini demanded huskily.

Frouw squatted. He inspected the surrounding earth.

Then he rolled Botha on to his back and studied the massive wound that had killed him. Frouw stood up.

'It's not the little coons,' he said. 'The spoor of the feet's too big. It's kaffirs and not Tswana either. They don't kill like that. A spear or a fighting sword did that –'

The South African was interrupted by a shout. The rest of the men had risen and run outside. One of them was standing by the gate of the corral.

'Christ, man!' he bellowed. 'They got Frenchie too, and the beasts have gone!'

Frouw and Farini raced over to where the man was standing. Rappaport was lying dead at the man's feet. He'd been killed in the same way as Botha by a massive lacerating blow to his neck. Farini glanced up. The fence at the far end of the pen had been torn down. The space inside was empty.

'Who the hell did it?' Farini shouted.

The shock he'd felt at seeing Botha's body had gone. What Farini felt instead was a rising surge of anger.

Frouw conferred briefly in Afrikaans with two of the men. Then he nodded.

'They reckon it's Matabele, Mashona, or even Zulu,' the South African answered. 'I think they're right. They surprised Baobab and Frenchie. Then they took down the boma fence and drove the oxen out.'

'Why did they take the bitch with them?' Farini demanded.

Frouw scratched his jaw. He frowned and scowled.

'Maybe it was a raiding impi,' he answered. 'Maybe they searched the waggon and just found her –'

Frouw paused. 'I don't know yet, man. What I do know is that without those goddamn oxen we can't move. We need them back.'

He swung round and began to shout instructions. A few moments afterwards all of the men had mounted. Heads bent low over their horses' flanks to follow the tracks of the oxen, they cantered away through the trees.

The oxen hadn't been stolen. That became clear in the next few hours. The animals had been driven away from the pasture and scattered as widely as possible through the bush. At the same time Frouw started to cast round the camp in search of other tracks.

It was mid-afternoon, deep in the trees, before he found what he was looking for. He examined the tracks for a while. Then he followed the trail until he lost it on a long expanse of limestone. Frouw returned to the camp.

'The cripple,' he said to Farini. 'He was here last night. He headed north carrying something heavy. I'd guess it was the mission girl. Two of the little coons were with him. The spoor of all of them's as clear as daylight.'

'So what the Christ happened?'

'I read it wrong,' the South African answered. 'It was kaffir warriors, but it wasn't a raiding party. I reckon the mission girl must have kaffir friends. Now they're all trekking north.'

North meant away from Kuruman and into the desert. North was where the swamps lay – where the man who had written to Darwin had traded with the olive-skinned men for diamonds.

'What about the coon girl with my diamond?' Farini asked.

Frouw shook his head. 'No sign of her spoor anywhere. But she'll be with them. I'll throw my stake on the table on that.'

Farini stared at him. 'I want them, Gert,' he said softly. 'I want all of them. Not one bastard, not even the smallest coon, is going to get away.'

— 71 —

Kala was tired.

Her limbs ached. Every day she could feel her strength returning, but it was still hard. Although her wounds had healed and her scars no longer tasted salty-sweet when she cleansed them with her tongue, her body would still not do all she asked of it.

All morning she had run alongside the water waggon. Today it was the yellow-haired woman who was guiding the oxen. The woman had been wounded too, but her wounds had been on her hide, not inside herself like the infection that had poisoned Kala. In the desert's clean scouring air the woman had recovered quickly. With Kala it was taking longer.

Kala studied the waggon and wrinkled her nostrils. The animals which the white people rode or led puzzled her. To Kala they smelled of meat, sweet fresh meat. If the woman and the limping man didn't seem to depend on them so much, she would have been tempted to leap for the animals' throats and pull them down. The animals were not just food. Their bodies contained water, and water, Kala sensed, was growing shorter every day.

Kala rubbed her nose and inspected the woman thoughtfully.

Kala had noticed that the woman often sought the company of the tall black-haired man, the leader of the other tall men with the spears who tramped behind. The woman laughed and smiled when the two were together. Sometimes they even shared their meat. They were as close to each other as Kala had once been to her litter family.

Kala had seen too that the limping man was angered at

what they shared. He did not show it openly, maybe he did not even recognize his anger, but Kala could see it in the narrowing of his eyes and the set of his mouth as he watched them. When the limping man rode in the waggon, Kala sometimes climbed up and groomed him. Then she could smell his anger on his skin. At night she could see it in the stiff movements of his limbs as he hunched into his blanket beside the fire.

The others lay close together for warmth. He always slept apart and alone.

Kala scrambled into the waggon and settled herself down between the water barrels. As she lay there she felt the diamond calling to her. Kala twisted on the juddering planks, and plucked the jewel from the pouch. As the waggon rumbled on, she cupped the stone in her hands, and stared into the brilliance of its depths.

She could see the distant shadowy figure of a man standing in a well of shadow at the foot of a shaft sunk deep into the desert sand. The man came closer. She glimpsed his face and she knew he was named Ben-Yacoub. Kala had no idea how she knew his name. It came to her from the stone. Like everything else the diamond told her, she did not question it.

Ben-Yacoub rubbed his arm wearily across his face and glanced upwards.

The entrance to the shaft was thirty feet above him. He had climbed down to the shaft's floor on the palm-fibre ropes that had been woven to lower the diggers from the surface. There wasn't enough room for both him and them, and he had summoned the diggers up before he himself went down.

Now Ben-Yacoub was standing there alone.

'It's useless, *sidi*. It's no different from the others – !'

The call came from his assistant, Neguin. Squinting up at the dazzling desert light, Ben-Yacoub could see Neguin's face silhouetted against the small circle of sky.

'There's nothing but limestone layered with mud down there. We could dig for a month and there would still be nothing.'

Ben-Yacoub grunted. The air inside the shaft was already fetid and stifling. When the sun blazed straight down, the shaft would become a furnace.

Everything Neguin said was true. Logically. Ben-Yacoub hesitated.

Ben-Yacoub was an engineer, one of the best in Herontas' column. He had been sent out as commander of one of the many expeditions dispatched by Herontas to search for stone for the building of Ophir. Guided by river Bushmen from the lagoons, Ben-Yacoub had travelled for three hundred miles southeast of the delta until he reached a lake which, his guides told him, was named Lake Dxau.

The lake emptied into a river leading further south still. Ben-Yacoub followed the river until it exhausted itself in sand. There he made camp and ordered the shaft to be sunk. It had proved to be like all the rest. It started and finished in the same porous and useless limestone.

All his long experience told Ben-Yacoub he should abandon the shaft now. The expedition's supplies were almost exhausted. He should order his men to strike camp and head back to the delta. He would have to report failure. It would be no disgrace. For almost a year every other expedition had returned with the same news.

Logically.

'*Sidi*, please come up. There is no point –'

It was Neguin's voice again.

'Wait!' Ben-Yacoub shouted back. 'Give me five minutes and you may haul me up.'

Ben-Yacoub picked up his iron-headed digging axe. He tapped away the accumulated mud from its blade. Then he paused.

Ben-Yacoub was a logical man. He was also a stubborn man. Somehow, for reasons he couldn't begin to explain, he sensed there was something strange about the way the limestone folded with the mud. In fact, at that depth it wasn't so much mud as clay. Glutinous blue-grey clay. Clay was even more worthless than limestone.

Logic told him he should order the diggers to lift him to

the surface without wasting any more time. Logic, but not his stubbornness. Swinging the digging axe back over his shoulder, he started to hack at a fissure between the stone and the clay.

A shower of limestone chips and clay sprayed over his feet. As the debris settled, Ben-Yacoub noticed a gnarled, almost black pebble half buried in the rubble. He bent and picked it up. For an instant he held it between his fingers. Then he placed his axe on the ground. He put the pebble on the flat surface of the axe-blade and struck it a swift, hard blow with the shaft of his hunting knife.

A tiny sliver flew off the pebble, as if a flake of its skin had been pared away. Beneath its surface, the black pebble glittered with a fiery white light. The light was so vivid and startling that Ben-Yacoub blinked. He rubbed his eyes disbelievingly. Even before his sight returned, Ben-Yacoub knew what he had found.

Lying on the axe-blade was a flawless white diamond.

Ben-Yacoub placed the diamond in the pouch at his waist. He slung his digging axe round his shoulder, and called to Neguin to haul him up to the surface.

'You were right,' Ben-Yacoub said as he clambered on to the desert's floor. 'Limestone and mud, and all of it worthless. Except that even those of us who wallow in mud can sometimes find stars.'

Neguin stared at him. Ben-Yacoub smiled.

'Strike camp, young man,' Ben-Yacoub ordered. 'We will go back to the delta. We will bring Herontas no rock, but we will carry him stones. I think he will be well pleased.'

Ben-Yacoub walked to his tent. Behind him the puzzled Neguin shouted for the soldiers to make ready to leave. He could only think his master had spent too long in the sun.

The place where the river ended and the shaft had been sunk was named Orapa. Ben-Yacoub had stumbled on an outcrop of Orapa's diamond pipe. Rediscovered two thousand years later, it was to prove the richest diamond pipe in the world.

The ancient Alexandrians who made up the bulk of the original expedition were above all traders. Trade was the very life-blood of their cosmopolitan city. And of all trade goods, diamonds were the most valuable – thirty jewellers were among the crafts represented in Herontas' column.

Ophir was built as a self-sufficient sanctuary in the delta. After Ben-Yacoub's discovery of the diamond pipe, a satellite settlement was established at Orapa. The raw gemstones mined there were carried back across the desert to the city. There the stones were cut and polished. For many years the diamonds were stockpiled.

Later, as Phoenician and Arab caravans pressed into Africa from the coast, Ophir began to barter some of its jewels. It did so quietly and discreetly. It used trusted intermediaries from the black tribes to handle the transactions. Ophir always kept its distance. The city's privacy was paramount. The fortress on the delta's waters had to remain inviolate and unknown. With the daunting barriers of the desert on two sides and the jungle on the others, it was not difficult.

The caravans passed, crossing and recrossing the desert. The city prospered. For a thousand years Ophir, unaware of its own wealth, grew richer and richer.

Grey thorn and scrub rippled away until it faded into the haze of the far horizon. Ben knew they would reach the horizon by dusk. At dawn the next morning there would be another identical horizon. He had begun to think that the barren featureless landscape would uncoil in front of them for ever.

Ben shifted in his saddle and glanced back.

Immediately behind him were the Mashona warriors. They marched, as always, in a small tight group with their spears trailing in the dust. Sometimes without apparent reason they would begin to sing. The song was a deep rhythmic chant that echoed overhead for a while and then stopped as abruptly as it started.

The five San were scattered out of sight in the bush. The

little men always travelled their own paths, often not joining the rest of the group until they made camp at night. Then they would appear with snared lizards and small birds, tsama melons and wild cucumbers, to augment the diminishing water supply in the waggon. Everything they had they shared. They seemed to have no notion of personal possessions. All was parcelled out and divided up. Even favourite items of clothing – a brightly coloured ribbon, or a porcupine-quill necklace – would appear first on Gwi and the next day on Nuna.

More and more Ben sought the little people's company in the evening. After they'd eaten, old Deial would tell tales in his own tongue. From the gestures and laughter which accompanied the stories, Ben could guess they were tales of a hunter's prowess or a lover's quest. Sometimes Kala too would watch and seem to listen, leaning her head against Ben's shoulder, her face impassive. If Mary-Ellen joined them, Ben would move away abruptly.

Ben narrowed his eyes against the glare and looked back.

Mary-Ellen and Moffat were walking side by side. The African turned his head towards Mary-Ellen and the two faces, one black and the other sun-bronzed, came together. Moffat said something and they both laughed. Their talk floated forward on the wind.

Savagely Ben kicked his horse's flanks.

The animal broke into a trot, increasing the distance between Ben and the pair behind. Ben gripped the reins until his knuckles whitened. He had come to detest the young black warrior. Trying to explain it to himself, Ben thought it was nothing more than envy. He saw the African's supple grace, he watched the tireless way he could walk for hours on end like the San, he noticed his strength and alertness when the day's trek finished.

Envy was an emotion Ben knew. He despised it, and he'd learned to put it behind him. What he felt about Moffat was something different. Not envy – but jealousy. Mary-Ellen and the black man shared a past. They spoke languages Ben couldn't understand. They used names and referred to incidents that meant nothing to him. Moffat was Mary-Ellen's friend and companion. That was how it was and had always been between the two of them. That was what he could not bear.

They inhabited a world from which he was excluded. Nothing he could do could change that. They shared a past where he would always be a stranger. Ben rocked back in the saddle and gazed bitterly ahead.

The accident happened an hour later. Mary-Ellen had been holding the leading rein of the oxen pulling the waggon. She passed the rein to Moffat and dropped back to see to Kala who had fallen behind. Ben was riding just in front of the waggon. He pulled in his horse and rubbed his face, trying to brush away the dust and sand from his sweat-caked skin. As he did so, Ben glanced backwards.

He and Mary-Ellen saw the burrow at the same instant. It had been tunnelled out of the sand by an aardvark, the strong-jawed ant-eating creature which made its dens in the desert floor. As the waggon's wheels rolled on to the burrow's flimsy roof, they both shouted. Their warning calls came a second too late.

The waggon's front wheel plunged into the hole and the waggon toppled on to its side. Ben threw himself off his horse and hobbled over to the wreckage. Everything inside the waggon had been hurled into the bush. The splintered staves of one of their two remaining water barrels littered the sand.

The water that had been inside was bubbling away and staining the sand. As Ben watched, it began to evaporate in the fierce midday sun. For a moment Ben stared at the fading patch of the precious liquid. Then his head jerked up and his eyes bored into Moffat's.

'Why the Christ weren't you watching?' Ben shouted.

Moffat stared back at him. The African's eyes were hot with anger, but he didn't answer. Ben swore and turned away.

The San had been navigating as they crossed the desert. Once they reached the delta and its lagoons and streams, they would be surrounded by water. Until then the supplies they'd been carrying were critical. In the Kalahari they meant the difference between life and death. Ben glanced round. Apart from himself, Mary-Ellen, Kala and Moffat, there were the twenty Mashona, the five San, and the animals.

They had a week to go. Even with the two barrels, it would have been difficult. In the savage, dehydrating heat of the Kalahari, they could have done with at least twice as much again. With just one barrel the journey was impossible.

From the tight anxious expression on Mary-Ellen's face, Ben knew she'd reached the same conclusion.

'How long will it take to repair the waggon?' Mary-Ellen's voice cut through Ben's thoughts.

Ben glanced down. One of the wheels had come off and the rear axle was splintered. By plundering the upper parts, he could find enough material to mend the damage. It would take at least six hours.

Ben told her. Then he frowned and asked, 'Why?'

'Deial said there are sip-wells somewhere ahead,' Mary-Ellen answered. 'We may just be able to reach them.'

Ben didn't even stop to ask her what sip-wells were – they could only mean water. For once there was something he could do. Ben stripped off his shirt.

Under the full force of the burning sun, Ben set to work.

'Tkama an xhora!' Deial pointed at the ground.

It was two days later and the sun was setting.

Ben, Mary-Ellen and Moffat were standing with the old man and the other San on a low bank. Below them a winding ribbon of bare sand stretched away in either direction through the thorn scrub. To Ben it looked as dusty and barren as the rest of the desert they'd crossed.

'It's the dry riverbed,' Mary-Ellen said. 'If the sip-wells hold water, we'll find it here.'

Her voice was hoarse.

Ben nodded. He didn't speak. Like all of them his mouth was raw and parched. They'd finished the water in the remaining barrel the evening before. The last few mugfuls had been saved for the animals. Since then none of them had had any moisture except a few scrapings of dew during the night and a single bitter desert cucumber Hutse had found. If they didn't drink soon, they were all doomed.

Old Deial climbed down the bank with his sons and nephews behind him. Even the San, far better equipped than the others for the desert, were moving slowly and deliberately to preserve the little moisture left in their bodies. Deial cast around for several long minutes. Then he bent low to sniff the ground. Suddenly the old man straightened up.

He beckoned to Moffat. Moffat stepped forward with the shovel from the waggon, and began to dig. When Ben moved forward to help, the old man waved him back.

'Deial says only one man can dig or the water will not come,' Mary-Ellen told him.

Ben saw sweat break out on the African's shoulders. However much Ben disliked the arrogant young black, he knew that with every drop of precious moisture Moffat's body lost, he was putting himself deeper and deeper into water-debt. If Moffat didn't find water, he would literally have killed himself in the attempt. Ben shuddered in sympathy.

The rest of the group had squatted down in the shade of a copse. Even the late evening sun gave no quarter to their dehydrated bodies. Ben and Mary-Ellen waited tensely. Suddenly Moffat paused. He peered down in the half-light. Then he lifted his head and shouted in delight.

'It's coming!'

They all ran forward and gazed into the hole. From the bottom of the sandy bed a stream of pure clear water was starting to bubble up. Moffat gestured for them to stand back. He wielded the shovel furiously again.

Ten minutes later the water was deep enough not just to drink from, but to bathe in.

*

Kala had drunk deeply from the well.

Then she had splashed the water all over her body, rubbing it into her parched skin and shuddering with pleasure at the softness of the moisture on her skin. Now she lay apart from the others in the darkness with the diamond in her hand. The firelight caught the jewel and the diamond began to blaze.

'Flavia! Flavia!'

Ringing out from the stone, Kala could hear the call as clearly as if it had been addressed to her.

Flavia, Kala knew, was the young woman she had seen before with the infant in her arms. The shout came from the other much older woman, the commanding woman who was named Serapis. Kala saw Flavia hurry back across the courtyard with the child rocking against her breast.

'Give her to me –'

Serapis plucked the child from Flavia's arms almost before the young woman had stopped.

The baby, the last link in the chain of royal inheritance which reached back to the court of Alexandria, crumpled her small fist and rubbed her eyes sleepily. Flavia glanced round nervously. Serapis' face was tense. There'd been an unusual urgency in her voice, and for some reason she was surrounded by a cordon of the royal bodyguards.

'Gallad has called for her,' Serapis went on. 'He has sent word that the day and the sun are right for her to be named and shown the stone.'

Flavia's eyes widened.

Gallad was the old high priest. After Ophir's ruler, Gallad was the most important figure in the city's hierarchy. The high priest, Flavia had been taught, was the spiritual descendant of the legendary founding sibyl, Osiris.

Serapis turned. The bodyguards gathered round her, shouldering Flavia aside. The group began to move away. They were heading for the temple that stood at the base of the dammed river between the two islands on which the rest of Ophir was set.

The young woman hesitated. Then Flavia called out.

'Serapis, may I come with you?'

Without checking her stride, Serapis glanced back. She nodded.

'You may come.'

Flavia ran after them. She caught up with the now swiftly moving procession. Flavia pushed her way through the soldiers until she was at Serapis' shoulder.

'What is she to be named?' Flavia asked excitedly.

'She is to be given the name of her great ancestor,' Serapis replied.

'Cleopatra?'

Flavia stopped in astonishment. The soldiers behind bumped into her. Flavia stumbled and almost fell. Then she was swept forward again.

'And why not?' Serapis demanded. 'She comes of the great queen's line. She carries her blood. Is there any reason the child should not bear her name?'

'No, of course not, no –'

Flavia broke off, flustered and confused.

There was no reason why the infant should not be named Cleopatra. It was just that to Flavia, as to all of Ophir's citizens, the ancient Alexandrian queen had somehow slipped through the winnowing filters of historical reality. She had passed from truth to legend to deity.

To Flavia the child was not being named after a woman. She was being given the name of a god. And once the name had been given, the rest would inexorably follow. The royal child would become a god too.

Flavia's thoughts were interrupted by the child's behaviour. Unsettled by the tramp of feet and the disturbance into which she had been swept up, the child suddenly began to cry.

When the procession reached the temple the old high priest, Gallad, took the child from Serapis and carried her to the wall of the dam behind it. The sluice gates set into the dam had been Mansur's greatest achievement. Like the gates which controlled the water supply to

Cleopatra's lakes in Alexandria, they were hewn out in the rosette shape of a floating lily.

The interlocking petals of Mansur's design had been replaced many times since the white-bearded engineer supervised their making. Termites and rain, sun, storm, wind, and the abrasive action of the Kalahari sand, had destroyed the originals and their successors, time and again across the generations. Always the replacements had been scrupulously fashioned to copy the massive wooden flower that held back the delta's waters.

The dam looked exactly as it did when Mansur created it. So did the intricate carving at the sluice gates' centre. Shaped like a lily's golden heart, a nest of wooden stamens held a pool of white fire. Placed where in Alexandria the stone of Isis had once locked back the Nile from Cleopatra's lakes, the fire was the Star of Egypt.

The high priest shook the child to waken her. He held her up to the curving wooden petals. Behind them, high over both their heads, the water surged and rippled. The child blinked, the incandescence of Egypt's diamond gleaming in the midnight depths of her pupils. Then she closed her eyes again.

Gallad reached out and touched the diamond.

A trickle of water, seeping through from the dam, ran down across the jewel's surface. He placed his moistened finger between the child's lips, and the drops ran on to her tongue. Then the old man named her.

The child felt the wetness on her lips. She nuzzled for the soft milky nipple of her wet nurse. She couldn't find it. She opened her lungs and wailed.

As she did so, the child's cries echoed off the heavy sluice gates.

'Ben!'

Ben stirred. He blinked as he reluctantly came out of the layers of sleep which had engulfed him. It was Mary-Ellen's voice. He heard the urgent whisper again and he felt her hand shaking his shoulder. Ben sat up and glanced round.

The sun had lifted over the horizon, and Moffat and his warriors were already preparing for the day's march. The little San had been down to the riverbed to fill their ostrich-egg water containers from the sip-wells. They were ready to leave too.

'What is it?' Ben asked.

'Look at Kala,' Mary-Ellen answered softly. 'Something's happened to her. Her voice has come back. She must be close to her home.'

She pointed across the smouldering embers of the night's fire. Ben peered forward. He got to his feet and walked round to stand above the girl.

Kala was still asleep, but her body was heaving and twitching as if she were caught up in some turbulent dream. As Ben gazed down at her, Kala suddenly clenched her hands and drew her feet up to her chest. For an instant she lay shuddering in a coiled ball like an unborn foetus. Then her lips parted and she began to wail.

Ben tensed. The sounds he heard were the fretful, disturbed cries of a small baby. Ben leant over the young woman.

On her lips, in the dry cold of the Great Thirst, were crystal drops of water.

— 72 —

'There!' Gert Frouw's voice was a harsh whisper in Farini's ear. 'Take the old one with the tusks in front. If she goes down, hit the calf as well.'

Farini drew in his breath.

The elephants were huge, bigger than he'd believed any animals could ever be. They were also curiously graceful as they threaded delicately down through the thorn trees towards the shining eye of the waterhole. Farini pulled the rifle's butt into his shoulder. He steadied the gun and sited through the metal V at the end of the barrel.

The vast creature he was aiming at disappeared for a moment behind a clump of scrub. Farini waited.

After four weeks in the Kalahari's wilderness of sand and thorn, the landscape had changed abruptly in the last forty-eight hours. The occasional twisted trees of the desert had suddenly become taller. They clustered together in groves, and there was a different feel to the air that swirled through their branches. The constant passage of birds and animals beneath the leaves seemed to be swifter and more crowded with every step they travelled.

They were approaching water. Frouw knew it, and with the instincts of an old hunter, he'd known they would find elephant. The expedition needed meat. The great herds of antelope that swirled round them would have provided it, but elephant was the choicest, sweetest meat of all.

'Aim for the eye.' Farini heard the South African's hoarse whisper again. 'Give her both barrels. Then reload for the calf.'

Farini nodded. As the elephant lowered the tip of her trunk to trickle a stream of water over her calf's upraised head, Farini squeezed the trigger. Once, and then a second time.

The twin report thundered across the clearing. The elephant sank to its knees. It tossed its head wildly, screaming and raising its trunk like a dark tulip. Then it toppled into the water. Farini reloaded and pumped two more shells into the terrified calf. As the calf fell too, the rest of the herd scattered and vanished into the trees. Behind them the river ran bright with blood.

Farini inhaled and spat out his breath to blow away the fumes of cordite that clung to the still air. He turned exultantly towards Frouw. The South African was no longer beside him. He had run forward. For some reason he had stopped midway to the stream and was stooping over the bank.

Frouw studied the earth. He came back and held something out to Farini. It was half of an ostrich eggshell. As worn and yellow as a piece of old ivory, a neat hole had been cut in the shell's base.

Puzzled, Farini glanced up at the South African.

'It's a broken water container,' Frouw said. 'The little yellow people fill them from their sip-wells. Their spoor's all over the ground. So are the prints of the mission girl and the cripple. They've got kaffirs and a waggon with them. They were through here not more than two or three days ago.'

Farini was silent. He turned and stared at the carcass of the elephant as it lay sprawled in the churned-up mud of the river bank. The wounded calf was still alive. It moaned and whimpered as it nudged the great motionless bulk of its mother.

'Get the creature butcherd,' Farini said. 'As soon as the meat's stored in the waggons, we'll ride on. If they're only a couple of days ahead, we're gaining on them.'

Farini swung himself up on to his horse.

For an instant he gazed back at the elephant he'd slaughtered. Its flank glittered with droplets of water that had sprayed over its hide as it collapsed in the river's shallows. Farini didn't see the drops as water. In the glare of the setting sun they seemed to be ropes of diamonds draped over the dead body of Africa.

He galloped away towards the dust plume which marked the distant line of waggons.

It lay in front of her.

Kala had known that as soon as she woke after drinking from the sip-wells. She didn't know exactly what it was or quite where it lay. What she did know was that she was travelling towards it, and the diamond was guiding her. All she could do was follow the silent instructions of the stone.

By day she ran swiftly and surely ahead of the San, with the diamond bouncing and flashing in its pouch at her waist. The arid grey scrub of the Kalahari was no longer the limit of the horizon. Instead there were banks of trees and great rippling meadows of grass. On every side were lagoons and slow-moving streams, separated by low islands and fringed with reeds and tall waving banks of papyrus.

As Kala headed on, old Deial lost track of where they were travelling. On the fifth evening after they'd left the sip-wells he came to a halt. Puzzled and frustrated, he wrinkled his face. Deial knew how to navigate across the Great Thirst. He had brought Mama Mary and her companions to the edge of the waters. Now he was confused.

'It is not our land,' Deial said miserably to Mary-Ellen. 'We cannot read its shape, nor understand its words. Look at the stars. They fall in the waters and confuse us with the way they shine. The trees halt the wind and change its smells –'

Mary-Ellen looked at the old man and then down at the map Darwin had sent her.

She had been consulting it again and again ever since they entered the delta. On the carefully traced paper, the position marked by Hearns had looked precise. On the ground, amid the tortuous sweeps and bends of the myriad streams that threaded the delta's thousands of islands, the map was meaningless.

Deial shook his head. 'This place is not for us to lead you to. This place is for others.'

The old man turned to look for Kala. A moment earlier the wild girl had been squatting close to them, watching them all through her unfathomable eyes. Now she was on her feet and running towards the setting sun, her body bending sinuously from side to side through the beds of reeds.

'Follow her!' Ben shouted.

His hip twisting painfully, Ben plunged after her along the bank. A moment later Moffat pushed past him, then Mary-Ellen, and then the Mashona warriors. They all vanished ahead. Afterwards Ben was left struggling through the dense riverine undergrowth on his own. Grimly he stumbled on.

Leading them westwards through the delta's meandering waterways, Kala ran on through the night. At dawn she dropped briefly to the earth to rest. They caught up with her and rested too. Then at midday Kala woke and headed on. They followed her again, plunging deeper and deeper into the heart of the great delta.

By day the sky above was thronged with vultures and eagles. At night soft-winged owls patrolled the streams. Brilliant-feathered kingfishers hunted the waters. Crimson-breasted bee-eaters searched the air for insects. Crocodiles slipped from the overhanging banks and hung, opaque-eyed and deadly, at the current's centre.

On the fifth day Kala led them out on to the shore of the biggest lagoon they'd come across. This time she didn't skirt its shore and head on again. She came to an abrupt halt on the sand and stood searching the air with her nostrils flared. She was still standing there, wary and hesitant, when Ben forced his way through the reeds and limped down to join the others.

Ben stopped and watched her.

Kala stepped forward tentatively into the lagoon. As

the water began to splash against her ankles, she darted back. She hesitated. Then she tried once more. This time the ripples reached her knees before she retreated. Kala made a third attempt. She waded in almost up to her waist, before she whirled away in terror and threw herself out again.

She paused. For several moments she gazed intently into the depths beyond her. Her lips were drawn back from her teeth in the gesture Mary-Ellen and Ben both recognized as fear. She stood trembling on the sand. Then as if something irresistible were drawing her on, Kala flung herself forward once more.

She plunged her hands beneath the surface and brought them up brimming with water. She threw the water over her shoulder on to the shore, and thrust her hands into the lagoon once more. Frantically, she did the same again and again.

Mary-Ellen watched her. For a moment she was bewildered. Then, with a sudden flash of recognition, she understood. She had seen other animals make the same gesture a thousand times before when she'd been carrying out her observations for Dr Darwin. Kala was doing exactly what the baboons had done. She was excavating. It made no difference that she was trying to dig through water rather than earth. The actions and the impulse behind them were the same. Kala was trying to burrow beneath the lagoon to get at something below.

Mary-Ellen glanced across at Ben. She could see from his face that he too had understood.

'Kala's found what she's looking for,' he said.

Mary-Ellen nodded. 'It's somewhere under the surface.'

Ben scanned the bank. Above their heads, half-hidden in the papyrus, was the waggon. Ever since they'd entered the delta they'd had to heave and manhandle it through the waterways, but it was still with them.

Ben's eyes sized it up. The pioneers who designed the trek waggons had made them not just for travel, but for shelter too. The planks of their floor and sides were caulked with resin. When the winter storms lashed the

Cape uplands, they could be turned upside down and used for protection against the deluge from the skies. What could keep the water out from above, Ben knew, could keep it out from below.

Ben turned back to Mary-Ellen. 'Tell Moffat I'll need some of his men,' he said.

Mary-Ellen went over to the African.

Fifteen minutes later, under Ben's direction, the waggon had been stripped of its hoops, its shafts, its axles and its wheels. The Mashona carried it down to the lagoon and lowered it into the water. It floated there like a cumbersome but buoyant raft.

Moffat himself had picked up one of the boards from the driving platform. With a few swift blows of his sword blade, the African had hacked it into a crude paddle. He jumped into what was now the stern, with Mary-Ellen behind him.

Ben swung the craft round. As he pushed it out into the lagoon, there was a splash in the water beside him. He glanced round. It was Kala. She scrambled on board and ran to the front. She stared down into the depths. In her hand the diamond glittered in the sunlight reflected off the lagoon's surface.

Ben heaved himself up and knelt beside her. The water was as opaque as a sheet of polished black marble. Ben stood up and gestured forward.

'Into the middle!' he shouted.

Moffat's paddle drove into the surface and the raft surged forward. When it reached the centre of the lagoon Ben got to his feet. He stripped off his shirt and boots.

'What are you doing?' Mary-Ellen called out behind him.

'I'm going in,' Ben replied.

'Can you swim?' Mary-Ellen's voice was tense with anxiety.

Ben paused for an instant. He glanced back and gave her one of his rare smiles.

'Like an otter,' he said.

Ben drew in his breath and plunged over the side.

— 73 —

Six feet below the surface Ben flattened out from his dive. He steadied himself against the slow current. Then he opened his eyes and peered round.

From above, the water had looked impenetrably dark. The surface of the lagoon appeared to be covered with a shield of oiled black steel. No light, it seemed, could possibly pass through it. The murky waters beneath might have been countless fathoms deep.

Beneath the surface everything was different. Instead of plunging into darkness, Ben found himself in a glittering world of glass. The water was so clear he could see for yards in every direction. There was pale sand beneath him. Trailing roots of water lilies brushed his face. Feathery fronds of fern and weed wavered at the edge of his vision.

Ben narrowed his eyes and frowned. An instant later the explanation came to him.

Blazing down from above, the fierce Kalahari sunlight had been hurled back in reflection as if it had struck a mirror. Below the surface, where the angle of refraction changed, everything else changed too. There the light was almost as pure and luminous as the desert air overhead. His feet propelling him forward, Ben moved otter-like through the depths, feeling the silky coolness against his sun-parched skin.

Two minutes later he came back to the surface. He shook the water from his eyes and glanced across the lagoon. The raft he'd fashioned from the waggon was fifty yards away. Moffat was standing up and waving frantically. Ben ignored him. He filled his lungs with air and dived again.

'What is it, Moffat?' Mary-Ellen asked.

Moffat had swung the boat round and was paddling furiously towards the circle of ripples where Ben had vanished.

'Your white man does not understand,' Moffat said grimly between the strokes of the paddle. 'Here in the delta there are crocodiles everywhere.'

Mary-Ellen turned and stared into the water.

'He swims strongly,' she said. 'Crocodiles attack the weak or the unwary, and mostly on the bank. Underwater they won't know what to make of him.'

Kala sat motionless in the prow, her gaze fixed on the depths. Every now and then she cupped her hand. She scooped up the water and sniffed it. Then she let the drops trickle back down through her fingers.

'Here – !'

Ben came up to the surface again. He thrust his shoulders above the lagoon's surface and called to Moffat. The raft was only twenty yards away. With quick, strong strokes of the paddle, Moffat sent it scudding forward.

'A reed,' Ben snapped at Moffat from the water. 'A good strong reed, cut between its joints and this length –'

He gestured a span of two feet with his hands.

'Make sure it's hollow and bent in a curve.'

Moffat swung the raft round and paddled it into the shore. He cut and trimmed a length of hollow reed, and bent it to Ben's instructions. Then he headed back to where Ben was treading water at the head of the lagoon. Ben seized the reed and placed one end between his lips. This time Ben didn't dive. Instead he swam away across the lagoon's surface.

As he swam Ben cursed himself for his stupidity.

He'd had no need to dive from the start. The water was so clear all he had needed to do was what he was doing now – provide himself with a source of oxygen and put his head beneath the surface. Yet if he hadn't dived, and dived as deep as he'd done, it was possible he might have missed it.

In the five minutes it had taken Moffat to give him the reed, the current had pushed Ben back from the lagoon's head. He kicked his way upstream. He was searching for what he had only glimpsed before. A few minutes later Ben spotted it again. Lying on the surface, he studied it. Then he lifted his head. The raft was very close to him – Moffat had kept the craft within a few feet of Ben's splashing heels. Ben held up the bent reed.

'Keep it,' he said. 'We may need it again.'

Ben prepared himself to dive. Just before he did, he swung round and glanced along the boat.

'I think we've found it,' Ben said.

He upended his body, and plunged down.

Ten feet below the surface his fingers brushed against the object he'd glimpsed from above. Ben caught hold of it. He levered himself down against his own buoyancy and inspected it carefully.

What he was looking at was a length of black timber. From the lagoon, where it had caught his attention, it might have been an immensely long submerged treetrunk that had somehow become trapped in the weeds close to the bottom. Something about it had puzzled him. It was too straight and symmetrical for a tree. Now Ben saw why.

It was not a tree but a vast beam formed out of the trunks of several trees.

The sections had been so tightly dovetailed together that the joins were almost impossible to trace. Only Ben's long experience as a woodworker enabled him to find them as he pulled himself along the beam's length. Well before then he realized something else. The flat surface of the beam wasn't the product of nature. It had been fashioned with chisel and plane.

The beam wasn't only man-made – it had been wrought with extraordinary skill.

His lungs bursting, Ben kicked up to the surface. Ignoring the raft and pausing only to suck in great gulps of air, he dived again. This time he went even deeper until his feet touched the sand at the floor of the lagoon. There he discovered something else. What he had thought was a shadow beneath the beam wasn't a shadow at all. It was a wall of thick planks running down from the beam and burying itself in the sand. The planks had been jointed as skilfully as the beam itself. There was not even enough space between them to admit his fingernail.

Ben dived for almost an hour.

Finally, his head spinning and his body limp with exhaustion, he struck out for the shore. He saw a little inlet between the papyrus clumps and crawled out of the water. Unable to stand, he collapsed and lay heaving on the earth.

'Ben, are you all right?'

Ben heard the raft crunch ashore and the splash of Mary-Ellen's feet as she jumped over the side. He lifted his head. Ben managed to nod and smile. Still shaking, he propped himself up.

'I'm not sure exactly how it was built,' Ben said, 'but I think I know the outlines –'

He paused and turned to stare at the lagoon. 'Out there under the water is a city.'

Ben began to explain.

'When I started swimming up the lagoon,' Ben said, 'I kept seeing pieces of timber half buried in the sand. I didn't pay any attention to them. I thought they were branches of ironwood which had been swept down by floods. Then towards the lagoon's head I saw a much bigger piece –'

Ben broke off a reed and started to draw in the sand.

'At first I thought it was a huge treetrunk. Then I dived. It wasn't a trunk, it's a great beam. It's lying on top of a massive wooden wall that's almost buried in the sand. There's another beam and another wall at an angle to it.'

He sketched the head of the lagoon and then a V-shape to show the two beams coming to a point at the lagoon's mouth.

'I think they're sluice gates,' Ben continued. 'I guess somewhere there's a mechanism to control them. They've been lowered for years, and the channel silted up round them. But when they were raised, the lagoon would have emptied. Where the water is now was once dry land. I think the pieces of wood are what's left of the houses inside.'

Mary-Ellen gazed at the lagoon. She glanced back at him, frowning.

'Why would anyone want to dam the channel when they could build on the islands?' she asked.

It was only one of the riddles which were already puzzling Ben. He had no idea of the answer. Before he could reply, Kala got to her feet.

She had been squatting behind them in the shadow of a thorn bush. She stared down at Ben for a moment, her eyes intent and unblinking. Then she turned and slipped away into the head-high grass and papyrus. On a sudden impulse Ben stood up and followed her.

The island on which they were standing rose little more than eight feet above the level of the lagoon. Ben climbed the gently sloping bank and walked behind Kala for two or three hundred yards through the bush. Suddenly for no apparent reason Kala stopped. She turned to face him. Standing absolutely still, she gazed at him again.

Ben stared back.

As always, Kala's face was expressionless, yet Ben sensed she was trying to communicate something to him. He spread out his hands, silently pleading with her to make some gesture in return. She remained motionless, her eyes fixed on his. He glanced away and searched the bush. The vegetation was no different from any of the delta's countless islands – waving golden grass, scrub thorn, the feathery, tasselled heads of the papyrus, and occasional trees on the higher ground.

Ben looked back at her. Kala's face was unchanged. It might have been shaped from golden Kalahari stone. Suddenly its blankness, its dead unyielding coldness, infuriated him. In frustration Ben kicked out at the ground between them.

His foot collided with something solid. A tremor of pain ran up his leg. He swore and swung away. Then he hesitated. An instant later Ben turned back. He bent down and parted the grass close to the earth.

What his foot had struck, Ben discovered, was a heavy piece of blackened timber. Like the beams in the lagoon it was African ironwood. Those had been protected from the termites by the water. This piece had been gnawed and ravaged for years, but it was still large and tough enough to have kept its shape.

It too had been hewn with chisel and plane. It had also been charred by fire. The fire, even more than its strength, had preserved it. The flames had sucked the living matter from the wood fibres and left the residue worthless to the insects.

Crawling through the grass, Ben followed the lie of the beam to the right. After a few feet he came to an angle where another piece, equally charred, joined it. The second section was covered by an acacia thorn. Ben circled the thorn and found the end of the second beam on the far side. A third length of timber was sunk in the sand beyond, again at a right angle. Finally there was a fourth, running back to the first.

Ben paused for an instant in thought. Then he pushed further through the bush and continued his search. He was so absorbed that he didn't hear Mary-Ellen until she almost tripped over him.

'What are you looking for?'

Sweating, Ben climbed to his feet. 'I've found it,' he answered.

The entire undergrowth was strewn with pieces of timber. They ranged in size from fragments to beams even larger than the ones he had found at Kala's feet. He had one of the smaller pieces in his hand. Ben held it out to Mary-Ellen.

She examined it uncertainly.

'Look.' He pointed out the chisel notches. 'It's the same as the beams in the lagoon. It's been worked. There are bits like it everywhere.'

Mary-Ellen still didn't understand.

'You asked why people built in the lagoon instead of up here on the dry land,' Ben said. 'The answer is that they did both. This was once part of a house. So are all the other pieces. You can see that from the way the beams are lying.'

'But what happened?'

Ben turned the wood over. On the other side, like the rest of the timber, it was heavily charred.

'There was a fire. Everything burnt down.'

Ben remembered the waves of searing heat that had erupted from the blazing workshop in Buckler's Hard. They had come from just one building. Here there had been hundreds packed together. Ben shivered. The inferno must have been devastating.

'Maybe that explains what happened in the lagoon,' Mary-Ellen suggested. 'Perhaps there were houses on the other side too. If the fire started here, maybe they opened the sluice gates to stop it spreading across –'

She glanced over at the island on the far side of the water. There was no sign of any building in the waving grass and reeds.

'If they did,' she added, 'it doesn't seem to have worked.'

Ben shook his head. 'I'm sure we'll find traces of houses there. I'll wager now they've also been burned to the ground. But it still doesn't make any sense. You don't destroy the centre of a town to save a part on the edge. It also doesn't explain why the lagoon was dammed in the first place. That must have been done for a different reason.'

Ben tossed the piece of wood up and down in his hand.

As he and Mary-Ellen stood there, they became aware that Kala was beside them. Not the slightest noise, not even the faint crack of a broken grass stem, heralded her approach. She appeared as soundlessly as a cat. For several moments her eyes remained fixed on Ben's. Then she glanced down.

Kala stepped forward and plucked the fragment of

wood from Ben's hand. She inspected it, puzzled. It was almost as if she half recognized it. That, Ben knew immediately, was impossible. It was only one of a thousand, ten thousand, scraps of charred timber scattered across the island.

Kala lifted it to her nose. She twisted the wood between her fingers and sniffed enquiringly. Her nostrils flared wide. The dreaming blankness had dropped from her features and her face was suddenly quivering and alert.

Kala had known the city was there. The diamond had told her so.

What it hadn't told her was that something was wrong. She sniffed at the wood once more. She caught the smell again, a scent so faint and ancient it existed only as a ghost now. It was a smell far too elusive for the human nose to register. Only the acute sensitivities of a hunting animal would ever have detected it.

It was the smell that rode before the holocaust. The smell that choked and plundered and killed without discrimination between the elephant and the ant. The smell of fire.

Suddenly Kala opened her mouth and screamed.

'Aieee –'

As the scream died away, Kala turned. One moment there was a slim, golden-skinned figure haloed against the reeds. The next there was nothing. Ben looked round in bewilderment at Mary-Ellen.

'What was it?' he asked.

'She smelled fire,' Mary-Ellen answered. 'To animals, all fires smell of danger, but they all smell differently. The most frightening smells come from the fires that have destroyed things you know. Kala recognized the smell in the wood. The fire that burned it destroyed the houses –'

Mary-Ellen paused.

'Kala was here when the city was burned.'

— 74 —

Darkness was falling when they got back to camp.

Ben slumped down by the fire. He was ravenous, and the exhaustion from the diving was washing over him again. The Mashona warriors had been on a hunting foray, and a young warthog was roasting over the flames. Ben ate the gamy flesh hungrily. Then he glanced round for Mary-Ellen.

She was pacing restlessly round the flames, calling Kala's name out into the darkness. There was no response. The instant Kala had scented the long-ago fire in the charred pieces of timber, she had vanished. Ben stood up and walked down to the shore of the lagoon along the path trampled out by the Mashona's feet.

The trunk of an upended tree had tumbled down the bank and come to rest in the shallows. Ben swung his body up and worked his way along it until he was straddled above the water. A fish owl was hunting the lagoon. Ben heard its raucous call, and then the spatter of spray as the bird struck at the water for its prey. On every side a thousand, maybe a hundred thousand, frogs were grunting.

A cow elephant screamed in irritation as something, perhaps a pair of hunting jackals, wandered into its territory. Somewhere a lion roared, a low, stomach-trembling rumble of warning and hunger. Startled, a herd of reed antelope crashed away splay-footed through the tangle of papyrus. Ben hunched his shoulders. He closed his ears to the clamour of the African night, and tried to concentrate on the puzzle that was tormenting him.

First and foremost, Ben was a carpenter. He was a

craftsman, a worker in wood. There was a logic to everything a craftsman did. The placing of the smallest panel-peg had its reason. The logic didn't change with time and place. It was a constant, as sure in its purpose as the movement of the sun and stars. The sunken sluice beams in the lagoon had been made by craftsmen. So had the wooden walls that supported them. So too had the charred and termite-ridden frames of the lost houses.

The settlement, Ben knew, had been built by carpenters like him. They had built across the two islands and down into the bed of a dammed lagoon. On the face of it, the pattern of the construction was incomprehensible. Stubbornly, Ben knew there must be a reason. They had built in that particular way for a particular purpose.

As he frowned in frustration, he heard a voice below him.

'Ben –'

It was Mary-Ellen. She had followed his footprints down to the shore and seen the silhouette of his body against the stars.

'Kala's returned,' Mary-Ellen called up. 'She must have been running through the bush. She's covered with cuts and there's blood all over her. But at least she's back.'

Ben swung himself off the trunk and dropped to the ground.

In the moonlight he could see that the tension had vanished from Mary-Ellen's face. Her relief was so vivid it made her look as vulnerable as she'd appeared for an instant on her last night aboard the *Star of Russia*.

In spite of himself, Ben reached out and touched her hand.

'I'm glad,' he said.

Then, realizing what he had done, he drew back. In silence Ben waited for her to continue.

'I gave her something to eat,' Mary-Ellen said. 'I thought she would sleep. Not tonight. She walked away. She went down to the lagoon and curled up on the shore. She's lying there staring at the water –'

Through the branches, Ben glanced at the lagoon.

There was no wind and the water was utterly still. Imprinted with the reflection of thousands of stars, it looked more than ever like an impenetrable black shield studded with silver.

'She's haunted, Ben,' Mary-Ellen added quietly. 'Something terrible happened here. I don't know how long ago, but maybe when Kala was a child. Whatever it was, she was here then and it's scarred her. I think that's why she's mute.'

'She may not be able to speak, but she can communicate,' Ben said. 'She led me to the island. That wasn't an accident.'

'The houses are only part of it,' Mary-Ellen replied. 'What's really important is under the water. That's where Kala's ghost lies.'

Ben rubbed his face.

He knew Mary-Ellen was right. Yet the puzzle remained as baffling as ever. Why dam the lagoon and build on its bed when dry land lay all round? Why go to that immense cost and effort when there were other islands stretching away on every side? Why bother to fashion those elaborate sluices and walls and construct the precarious buildings beneath them – a flood could have swept them all away – if there was scope to build in safety for miles in all directions?

A flood.

Ben closed his eyes. A flood. In that one word the answer suddenly came to him. He had assumed the builders had been protecting themselves against the waters. He had been wrong, totally wrong. The builders had been using the waters to protect themselves. They had harnessed the river to defend their city.

If danger came, if they were attacked, all they had to do was open the sluice gates and the settlement's heart would be immersed. The houses on the islands on either side were irrelevant. What mattered was what lay beneath the lagoon. That part of the city was so important to them that they would rather drown it than surrender it.

Ben looked at Mary-Ellen and told her. She stood silent in thought for a long time. Then she nodded.

'It would explain everything,' she said. 'There was a city here and it was attacked. The attackers set fire to the settlements on the islands. Then right at the end, when the defenders knew they couldn't hold out any longer, they let the waters in. If Kala was here as a child, it would explain her too. That's why she knows there's something under the lagoon –'

Mary-Ellen glanced back at the gleaming expanse of water. In the darkness it seemed to stretch out to infinity.

'But it's gone now, everything's gone. We'll never know.'

Ben limped down to the lagoon's edge.

He scanned the surface for the red eyes of the crocodiles. There were none. He stepped forward until the water was lapping round his knees. Then he gazed in the direction of the lagoon's mouth, where he had found the sluice gates.

'If you can lower sluice gates, you can raise them,' he said. 'I've never heard of a mechanism that doesn't work both ways –'

Ben turned. 'Someone drowned this city. It's just possible I can raise it again.'

'Send them out in pairs,' Ben said. 'Tell them to concentrate on the tributary streams. I don't know how far away the gates will be. Maybe half a mile, maybe more, but the barrages are out there somewhere. I want them found.'

Moffat stared back at him.

Dawn hadn't yet broken and the air was grey with darkness. The Mashona warriors were gathered behind their leader, their spears in their hands. Moffat had despised Ben from the moment they'd met. The white man wasn't only a cripple, he was a coward. He'd allowed Mary-Ellen to be captured, humiliated and beaten until the skin on her back was raw.

For that, Moffat would never forgive him. The African

disliked him even more now for the casual arrogance of his orders. Moffat opened his mouth angrily to deny him what he'd demanded. Then he closed his lips without speaking. The white man might trail his withered leg like a bird with a broken wing, he might hide behind women, but he was skilled in his craft. Moffat didn't doubt that.

If there truly was a kraal beneath the waters, and if they were to raise it to the air, they needed a man as practised in the workings of wood as the people who had built the dam. Moffat couldn't do it himself, but Mary-Ellen had told him the carpenter could. He believed Mary-Ellen. For her sake, for the sake of the wild girl she valued so much, he would do what the cripple asked.

'They will do as you say,' Moffat answered.

He turned and relayed Ben's instructions to the Mashona. As the warriors dispersed, Ben turned to gaze at the mist hanging over the water.

It was a guess, of course, but everything about the lagoon and the sluice gates and the charred house frames had been a guess. This time Ben felt more confident. His mind and the minds of the builders worked in the same way. Ben knew why the gates were there. Now he had to find out exactly how they had done it.

It was a matter of engineering. The channel had been dammed and an elaborate wall built across the lagoon. That could not have been done unless the myriad streams of the Okovango river hadn't been diverted somewhere further up its course.

The only way to stop the waters, to win time for the construction of the main sluice gates, was to build a whole series of dams along the tributaries. If Ben was right, once they were found he could cut off the press of the river. He could dig out the sand and silt round the base of the gates, and raise them. When that happened, the lagoon would empty and the heart of the city in its bed would rise again.

It was late in the afternoon when Ben heard the shout. By then he had returned, tired and dispirited, to the camp fire. All day he had himself been searching without success. He knew the barrages were there, they *had* to be there. Somehow they had eluded him. He was hunched dejectedly over the flames when the call came. He lifted his head and listened.

The call rang through the air again.

Ben's fatigue vanished instantly. With the shouts still ringing in his ears, he pushed through the papyrus and reeds and set off along the bank. Half an hour later he had tracked the calls to their source beside a narrow lagoon. There was no sign of Moffat, but a clamour of voices rose from the trees on the shore. Ben glanced up. At least a dozen of the warriors were squatting in the branches. All of them were chattering and gesticulating.

At the sight of Ben they fell silent. Ben heard a footfall behind him. He swung round. It was Moffat. The tall African fired questions at one of the men. Then he turned to Ben.

'Batuka says there are doors in the water everywhere here,' Moffat translated. 'He called out to tell the others. When they came, they all saw many crocodiles where the doors are. So they climbed for safety.'

Ben opened his mouth to swear at them. The men had wasted vital time when they could have been searching further. With an effort of will he controlled his anger.

Moffat saw the impatience draining from the white man's face. The African smiled.

'You are gaining in wisdom, carpenter,' he said. 'The Mashona are a proud people. We hunt the leopard with spears and outrun the cheetah. But we are men of the land. We know nothing of water. You are right to restrain yourself.'

Ben stared at him. 'Your men are brave, Moffat,' he said. 'Ask them to show me where they found the gates.'

At Moffat's instruction, the men climbed down.

Ben hobbled after them to the lagoon's neck. He stared into the water. Just beneath the surface he could see the rippling shape of what was unmistakably a pair of wooden flood gates. One of the Mashona plucked at his elbow. Ben followed him to the neighbouring lagoon, and saw another pair of gates.

Ben shuffled on.

It was the same everywhere. There were submerged gates at the head of every one of the network of lagoons that spread out for over a mile across the delta. Ben waded into the water to inspect a pair of them. He swam down and saw that the wooden mechanisms which raised and lowered them had been perfectly preserved by the Okovango's streams.

Ben arrowed back up to the surface. He shook the spray from his head and searched the bank for Moffat.

'You've found it!' Ben shouted. 'The whole system's here. We can dam the river and raise the city!'

— 75 —

It had been a guess from the start. Until it was tested, it was still a guess.

The eighteen pairs of sluice gates might have been built to irrigate the surrounding pastures, to provide permanent water for satellite settlements, for almost anything. Only if the water drained from the main lagoon would Ben know if the guess was right. The uneasy truce between him and Moffat, between the white carpenter and the black warrior, held throughout the day and the long night which followed.

Under Ben's instruction and at the African's direction, the gates were raised one by one. Most came up quickly and easily. Some had their bases blocked by sand. Whenever that was the case, Ben had to dive down and use his bare hands to scrape away the silt. Often, as he surfaced gasping, Ben would glimpse the Mashona leader studying him through narrowed eyes. Ben sensed he was somehow being tested.

Mary-Ellen and Kala watched. Mary-Ellen, bare-legged and wading through the shallows, gave as much help as she could while Kala squatted on the edge of the water, her face expressionless and the diamond cradled in her fist. Slowly the downward press of the river was checked and diverted. Only the last pair of gates resisted any attempt to be moved.

Ben struggled with them for an hour. Finally in the twilight he returned to the camp. He ate and rested briefly. Then he returned to the stream. Moffat was waiting for him on the bank. Wearily, Ben stripped naked again and plunged back into the water. He arched his body and arrowed downwards. He anchored himself to the base of the gates and scooped at the sand once more.

Neither Ben nor Moffat noticed the old female crocodile.

Almost as tired as Ben was, Moffat leant on his spear waiting with drooping eyelids for the white man to surface. Beneath the water Ben concentrated on the buried wall of wood. Lying in the shadowy darkness of the reeds, the crocodile registered the pulses of movement from Ben's body as he tunnelled away. The pulses were fretful and spasmodic. Like the quivers given out by a drowning animal, they disturbed and excited her.

The crocodile was sixteen feet in length, and hungry. Barely disturbing the lagoon's surface, she dipped into the stream and surged forward. Below her she saw a flickering white shape. To her the shape's convulsive movements meant it was wounded and in distress. She could feel a field of warmth coming off it, and she knew it was living prey.

The crocodile lashed out with her tail to give her purchase against the current and drive her downwards. As she approached the fluttering creature, she rolled sideways and opened her immense jaws.

Moffat's dulled brain had vaguely absorbed the crack of the crocodile's tail on the lagoon's surface. The reverberations echoed in his ears. Suddenly he realized what they meant. He stiffened. He hurled off the numbing tiredness and stared at the stream. He glimpsed the scales that stood erect like a row of deadly teeth on the crocodile's back as they vanished below the water. Without hesitating he plucked his spear from the ground and plunged downwards.

Moffat saw the creature's white belly revolve towards him. He drove the spear forward. The razor-sharp blade cut deep into the pale stomach scales and a film of blood rose to the surface of the water. Twisting and lashing in a frenzy of pain, the crocodile arrowed away. Moffat was pulled after her. His lungs bursting, he kept gouging and stabbing with the spear. He sensed he was being drawn towards the bank. Then he lost consciousness.

Moffat recovered to find himself lying in the water. He coughed and vomited. Then he became aware that a pair of arms was supporting him. The arms were immensely strong. He blinked and saw they belonged to Ben. Ben kicked his way to the bank and pulled the African ashore. He dragged Moffat up into the dry grass above the water line.

For an instant Ben stood gazing down. He'd seen the crocodile a moment before Moffat's spear struck it. If the African hadn't plunged into the water, Ben knew that by now he'd either have been dead or appallingly injured. He owed the black man a debt he could never repay. Curtly, Ben grunted his thanks. Then he returned to the lagoon.

An hour later the gates came free. With Moffat's help Ben winched them up to the surface and stopped the flow of water. The last of the arteries that fed the main lagoon had been cut off. If Ben was right, at some stage during the night the water would begin to drain away.

Wearily, Ben limped back to camp and lay down to wait. Within moments he was asleep.

Ben woke before dawn. Mary-Ellen saw him get to his feet. She rose too and followed him down to the shore.

Ben stood on the bank and gazed across the water. The flow should have stopped several hours ago, but the dark metallic surface was still unchanged. Ben glanced upstream to the point where the river entered the lagoon. The water was still rippling steadily downwards through the reeds and papyrus. For all the difference it had made, none of the eighteen pairs of gates might have been closed against the spill of the distant flood.

Ben turned away, shaking his head in frustration. Suddenly as he moved he heard Mary-Ellen's voice call out behind him.

'Look!'

Ben swung round. She was pointing at the lagoon's mouth, at the place at which he'd been gazing only seconds before.

Ben caught his breath in astonishment. In an instant everything had changed. Before his eyes the waters were vanishing. It was happening so fast Ben could barely believe it. A moment earlier he'd been standing on the bank only inches above the river's surface. Now the level was a full twelve inches below him. As he watched it fell further still.

Ben moved towards the lagoon's mouth. The rustling cascade of water from the river had stopped. In its place there were only a few trickles and the occasional patter of individual drops. Soon even the sound of those died away. The Okovango had been cut off. As Ben stared into the darkness, he shook with delirious laughter.

He had simply miscalculated. He'd underestimated the porousness of the marshes below the gates. For hours after the gates were winched up, the marshes had been releasing their stored-up water into the lagoon. Suddenly they had dried out. There was nothing left to drain away. Now the lagoon itself was emptying.

It was the most awesome sight he had ever seen. Ten minutes earlier they had been on the banks of a huge lake. Now the lake was vanishing. It was as if a plug had been pulled from some gigantic bath. One moment ripples were lapping at their feet. The next Ben was looking down a steep and constantly growing bank of wet mud.

Crocodiles, hundreds of them it seemed, were crawling out of what must have been their sanctuary for years. Ben could see their eyes glowing scarlet in the moonlight as they scrambled up the banks. The ground everywhere rippled with the sheen of their armoured backs. Mary-Ellen shrank back as one of them shouldered its way between the two watching humans, careless of their presence, its massive shoulders cannoning against their legs.

Grunting and indifferent, the crocodiles lumbered on in search of another lagoon.

Stranded fish started to jerk and flap on the exposed ridges along the lagoon's floor. Ben could see fat tilapia and long, silver-flanked tiger fish with their jaws of densely packed teeth hanging open and gasping for air. A pair of hunting owls spotted them and dropped down to feed. A trio of jackals joined them. The jackals' cries alerted other predators.

Before long there were dozens of wraith-like animals flitting along the banks and feeding hungrily off the prey in the dwindling shallows. The jackals drew in a male lion. Behind the lion came the rest of the pride. Roosting marabou storks were woken by the pride's roars and growls. They flapped down on the tree branches to join in the feast.

The last of the water ebbed away and Ben tensed again. Beside him Mary-Ellen drew in her breath in astonishment.

The lagoon was deep – far deeper than Ben had guessed. From where he was standing on the bank, the drop to its floor was well over thirty feet. As the river vanished, buildings emerged. There were towers and battlements, houses and fortifications, walls and gates and the outline of streets. Some of the buildings were blackened by the fire which had consumed the houses on either side of the lagoon. Many had been crushed by the flood unleashed when the great sluice gates were lowered. But enough of them remained. Enough to show that they were staring down over the heart of what must once have been a mighty settlement.

'This wasn't an African kraal,' Mary-Ellen said in a whisper. 'Africans don't build like this. This must have been a city.'

Ben slithered down the bank to the lagoon's floor.

He went over to one of the ruined buildings and crouched down by the foundations. He tugged away a floor joist and peered at its joint with the neighbouring joist. Ben probed at the wood with his knife. He paused and examined it. Then he turned and called for Mary-Ellen.

Mary-Ellen was already on her way down the bank. She dropped to the ground and ran over to him.

'Look at this –'

Ben twisted his knife into the joist and levered out a wedge-shaped plug of wood.

'Do you know what it is?'

Mary-Ellen shook her head.

'It's a joiner's marker,' Ben told her. 'All the old houses in Buckler's Hard have them. Whenever a joist or a beam is replaced, the joiner puts in a plug with a date on it to show when the work was done. This isn't dated, but it's numbered. The number's the Roman numeral X –'

Ben showed her the roughly scored X on the plug.

'It means the joist has been replaced ten times since the house was built.' Ben paused. 'How long does iroko last?'

Mary-Ellen frowned. 'The Tswana say that if the termites don't get it, ironwood lasts ten generations – two hundred years.'

Ben probed further along the joist. He found a second plug and then a third. One was scored IX and the other VIII. From its colouring, each was older than the last.

Ben shook his head, bemused. 'If the system's the same, this house was first raised two thousand years ago.'

He looked at Mary-Ellen in silence. Mary-Ellen stared back at him.

Two thousand years ago, southern Africa was uninhabited apart from the San – and the San made birds'-nest shelters, not sophisticated buildings. Every naturalist and scholar who had come there in the wake of the Dutch colonists knew that. Even the black tribes with whom the whites collided accepted it. Not even the murderous Shaka believed that he and his people were anything other than newcomers to a virgin land.

Suddenly Mary-Ellen raised her head and glanced up.

Kala was running down the bank. She stopped close to them. For an instant her eyes quartered the shadowy network of streets and the jagged stumps of the buildings. She seemed to be examining one building with particular care. It was larger than the others. From the charred square at its centre and the size of the beams scattered round it, it must have been dominated by a tower – a tower taller than any of the others.

Momentarily Kala hesitated. Then her head swivelled round and she began to run, threading her way quickly between the debris.

'Follow her!' Ben whispered to Mary-Ellen.

Kala was heading for the lagoon's mouth. Twice she stopped. She doubled back and retraced her steps. She sniffed at the ground. She searched the sky as if she were expecting to see something there that had inexplicably vanished. Then she ran on.

Finally Kala came to a halt.

Quietly Ben and Mary-Ellen came up behind her. Kala was standing in front of the two great sluice gates at the lagoon's entrance. She explored the wooden beams with her fingers. She scrabbled at the panels, at first tentatively and then with an increasing frenzy, tearing with her nails until her fingertips were streaked with blood.

Mary-Ellen reached forward to pull Kala back, but Ben caught her arm.

'Leave her,' Ben said softly.

Suddenly Kala reached down to her waist. She pulled out the diamond and lifted it up towards the gates. The light reflected from the stone was so brilliant it almost blinded Ben. He blinked and rubbed his eyes.

Kala was frantically trying to push the diamond into the gap between the two vast jambs. Ben stared at her. She was like a child, a baby, attempting to force a toy into a place where it had no reason to go. Except Kala wasn't a child or a baby. Suddenly Ben understood.

He swung round to Mary-Ellen. 'Get Moffat and some of the men!'

Moffat was already on the floor of the lagoon. He ran forward with a dozen of the Mashona.

'Clear the sand from the gates!' Ben shouted as he began to dig at the foundations. 'They must be able to swing free.'

Ten minutes later the sluice gates hung clear. Ben tested them. They had been so well made, they were so finely balanced, that a single tap on either side would move them. Ben pushed them forward. The great iron hinges creaked and the gates swung together.

Moffat climbed up the laddered pole at the gates' centre and lowered the huge latching bar. He dropped back to the ground and glanced up. The gates were locked tight against the river.

Kala was crouching on her haunches. Her eyes had never left the men as they shovelled the sand away. When the gates were back in place, she rose. She came forward and inspected them. Her face thoughtful, she reached out and touched the latching bar. Then she started searching again. Her fingers moved over the wood, not with frenzy now but as if she were seeking something she half remembered from long ago.

Kala found what she was looking for.

She lifted the diamond and pressed it into the panel. The stone clung to the wood in a pool of shimmering blue-white fire. Ben stepped forward. He bent down and stared at the tight vertical line between the two great doors. Overlapping them and sunk deep in the frames was a wooden carving. Split into two so that it married perfectly when the jambs were brought together, the carving represented the petals of a lily. At the centre was a hollow where the tight-packed stamens of the living flower would have been.

Now the space was filled by the diamond.

Ben gazed at it in silence. Slowly, almost disbelievingly, the explanation came to him.

The carved lily was a lock and the diamond its key. The lock was so strong that even if the latching bar were raised, the lily with the diamond in position would still hold the gates together. Only if the stone were removed would the gates spring apart under the press of the water, and the pent-up cataract would burst down to flood the space below.

The diamond, and whoever knew its secret, controlled the fate of the city and its inhabitants.

Ben turned to tell Mary-Ellen. As he opened his mouth, a shout rang out from behind. Both of them whirled round. It was almost dawn. As the lagoon's waters sank, Moffat had posted some of his warriors along what remained of the city's eastern walls. It was from the east, from the desert reaches of the Okovango's delta, that they would be followed if Farini was still behind them. It was from the east that the cry came.

'What is it?' Ben shouted at Mary-Ellen.

The man had called out in the tongue of the Mashona. The cry was urgent, but the words meant nothing to Ben.

Mary-Ellen looked at him, frowning. Her face was anxious and puzzled.

'He says there are ships coming,' she answered.

'Ships?' Ben shook his head in bewilderment.

He glanced back at the diamond. Then they both started to run towards the walls from where the shout was still ringing out.

— 76 —

Ben clambered frantically up the zigzagging staircase that led to the observation platform on the outer wall.

Running faster than Ben could, Mary-Ellen and Moffat were several yards in front of him. By the time Ben reached the top, they were gazing eastwards over the delta. He threw himself against the parapet. Standing panting between them, he stared in the same direction.

The breath hissed out between Ben's teeth in astonishment.

It was still early in the morning, but the sun was already clear of the horizon. Below the platform, reaching far out into the distance, lay the languid spread of the great river as its waters seeped down towards their burial ground in the sands of the Kalahari. Ben had seen the same landscape every day since they'd entered the delta.

Now there was a bizarre difference. In the far distance he could see a fleet of ships under sail.

The ships hovered between the delta's waters and the rising mist. They might have been a mirage, except that there was no mirage in the way their sails caught the morning wind. Ben saw the wooden decks heave and roll. He saw the gunwales tilt and straighten. He saw the pennants streaming out from their bows. Almost, he thought, he could hear the crews calling out as they trimmed the sheets.

At his side Mary-Ellen and Moffat were staring with the same disbelieving intensity at the horizon. It was an illusion, Ben knew. It could only be an illusion. Yet for a few seconds it was so vivid that his stomach contracted with fear.

From somewhere out of the desert a fleet was sailing towards the city.

Then the mist swirled away, and the answer came to all three of them at the same instant. The advancing shapes weren't ships. They were waggons, the great ox-drawn waggons with their towering hoods of hooped canvas used by the South African pioneers. Except that these ones didn't belong to the vortrekkers.

They belonged to Farini. Farini's column was less than three miles from the city.

Ben's head jerked round towards Moffat. 'How long will it take them to get here?' he demanded.

'Four, maybe five hours,' Moffat answered.

Ben calculated.

Farini had about twenty men with him. The Mashona numbers were the same, but all they had were their spears and shields. Farini's men were armed with rifles. However brave the Mashona were, against the white men's guns they were helpless – even a force ten times as large would have been doomed.

There was nothing they could do except abandon the city and try to escape deeper still into the delta. Ben turned and told Mary-Ellen. Moffat stood listening. As the African nodded grimly in agreement, they all heard the patter of feet on the stairs behind.

Kala was running up the steps. She reached the platform and pushed her way between them. She gripped the parapet and stared at the waggons. She froze. Tremors ran through her body. She opened her mouth. For several moments nothing came out. Gripped by a series of convulsions, she quivered as if an immense charge of lightning were pulsing through her.

Then Kala drew back her lips. She bared her teeth and gave a furious, menacing snarl. Afterwards she turned and raced back to the ground.

There was a look of recognition and understanding on Kala's face that had never been there before. Ben and Mary-Ellen ran after her.

*

Kala headed west towards the great sluice gates.

As Ben hurried limping behind her, he saw the city for the first time in the quickly gathering light. The streets were broad and paved with stone. The stone was covered with algae now, and a few fish still flapped and twitched in the slime. Like the sluice gates, the paving had been cut and faced by master craftsmen. They had set and jointed it to last a thousand years or even longer.

The buildings, roofless and wrecked as they were, had the same feeling of permanence. They had not been built as temporary shelters. They were there for ever. Even the explosive eruption of the waters that drowned them had been unable to wash them away.

There were villas with gates and courtyards. The remains of vast formal structures that reminded Ben of the militia barracks outside Winchester and Southampton. Buildings with formal columns, tumbled now across the roadways, that must have been temples, and lines of crumbling arcades that could only have housed shops.

It came to Ben that he was running through what had once been a mighty city, a rich and vital centre of civilization in the immensity of the African desert. Then he saw Kala slow. She was approaching the sluice gates. Before she reached them she stopped. She turned off the roadway beneath the hanging lintel of another building.

Ben paused and glanced round.

From the size of its foundations, the building must have been among the largest in the city. Unlike most of the others it had been virtually scythed to the ground. Ben knew why. It was not only the largest, but the tallest. When the waters came, they had flowed over the smaller buildings. The flood had smashed against this one and crushed it to the sand.

He followed Mary-Ellen into what had once been a courtyard.

Ahead of them, Kala hesitated. She frowned as if she were trying to orientate herself. If Kala had been here as a child, this one place, more than any other, would have been difficult to remember. Everything had gone. All that was left was a jumbled detritus of wood and stone.

Kala seemed to make up her mind. She stepped over a tangle of heaped-up beams. Then she vanished.

With Mary-Ellen still leading, Ben scrambled over the pile of fallen wood. On the other side, a pit opened at his feet. Ben looked down. A shaft led down into the earth. The shaft was roofed and walled with stone. It ran to what Ben guessed was a chamber below the centre of the building where they were standing. A steeply sloping passageway ran from the shaft's mouth to the chamber beneath.

Ben limped down it and stopped.

He found himself at the entrance to a vast underground cavern. The shaft had twisted and turned on the way down. Almost no light reached it from the ground, but the cavern's vaulted roof shone with an ice-white glow. So, too, did the walls and floor. They seemed to be studded with myriads of brilliant stars. It was as if he were standing at midnight in the midst of the Kalahari sky, with the constellations showering down round him.

Ben glanced round.

Kala was kneeling on the ground in front of him. As Ben followed the lines of incandescence flaring out from the cavern, he gasped. The light from above was pouring through thousands of jewels, perhaps not even thousands but hundreds of thousands. They were all diamonds and they were everywhere.

They had been cobbled into the floor. They had been set into the walls. They were piled up in layers and banks. They had been poured into chests until the wood split and the chests overflowed. They were stored in sacks and gourds and cane pipes. Finally they had been tipped out and left to lie where they fell.

'What are they?'

Ben heard Mary-Ellen's bemused voice at his side.

Ben couldn't even turn his head to answer her. He was too spellbound by the sight in front of him. All he could do was speak to her softly over his shoulder.

'They're all diamonds,' Ben said. 'This is where the city stored its treasure. I'd guess it must be the greatest accumulation of wealth that's ever been gathered together.'

Suddenly the iridescence from the sun above died. Within moments, the cavern was in darkness. With Mary-Ellen beside him, Ben backed up the slope that led outside. As they climbed, Kala suddenly burst past them. She ran upwards and vanished.

On the ruined courtyard above, Mary-Ellen looked at Ben, aghast.

'We can't leave the city now,' she said. 'We've got to stop them from finding it.'

Ben frowned at her. His mind was still reeling from the cornucopia of riches beneath their feet.

'Don't you see what it means?' Mary-Ellen went on. 'It means men. Not just Farini, but everyone who'll come behind him. If they discover what's here, they'll tear the delta apart. I went through Johannesburg when I was travelling south. I saw what they've done to the land round Kimberley where they found diamonds too. For miles and miles the land's black and dead. There are no birds, no animals, no trees or grasses, nothing. They've killed it all. They'll do the same here. There'll be nothing left.'

She stretched out her arm.

Ben followed the sweep of her hand round the lagoon bed. The sun had just risen. It was the softest part of the morning. The dense blue-green of the forest on the islands was wreathed with the last of the mist. The landscape beyond shone with the veins and arteries of the delta's waters. The air hummed with dawn birdsong and the echoing calls of late-hunting animals.

Ben saw it all.

Suddenly, vividly, he knew Mary-Ellen was right. Once Farini found the diamonds, the delta would be doomed. It didn't matter how great the treasure was or where it came from. They wouldn't be satisfied until every tree had been felled and every animal killed in their search for more.

The murderous column of waggons, the dark ships as they had appeared on the horizon, had to be stopped.

'Mama Mary!'

The sudden call came from Deial. The old man trotted over. As he started excitedly to speak, Mary-Ellen's face tightened in bewilderment.

'What's he saying?' Ben asked in frustration.

Mary-Ellen looked at him. 'Deial says that Kala's spoken,' she replied slowly. 'She's called out my name.'

They both turned. Kala was kneeling in front of the sluice gates below the diamond. A moment later, Mary-Ellen was kneeling facing her with Ben crouching behind.

For an instant Kala's face was the same vacant, impenetrable mask it had been so often in the past. Then her mouth twisted. Her neck tensed and throbbed and her body heaved, as if some vast tormenting struggle was going on inside her. She managed to force her lips open, but still no sound came out.

Mary-Ellen reached forward and took the girl's hand. Motionless and hardly breathing, Ben waited. With all their strength they both silently willed her to succeed.

Kala strained again and then a third time. Her face flushed dark with effort, and sweat poured from her skin. And then at last it happened. Like a dam breaking, words began to emerge. They were incoherent and almost inaudible at first. Gradually they became stronger and began to form sentences.

Mary-Ellen listened intently. To Ben the words were incomprehensible. All he could tell from the now-familiar clicks and whistles was that Kala was using the language of the San.

She spoke for two or three minutes. Then as abruptly as she'd started, Kala fell silent. The blank, impassive stare returned to her face and she stood up. Mary-Ellen asked her some question, but Kala ignored it. She looked down at Mary-Ellen. Suddenly she raced away.

'What did she say?' Ben demanded.

Mary-Ellen got to her feet.

'She said the city belongs to her,' Mary-Ellen answered. 'She says the ships must not come here, because if they do, then the city will die. She says she can't hunt in the sun to stop them because the light dazzles her eyes. We must keep them out until nightfall. Then we must all leave the city. When night comes she will stay here alone to hunt and kill them –'

Mary-Ellen paused, dazed. 'She also says she is not named the little she-hare that fell from the sky. Kala says her true name is Cleopatra.'

— 77 —

Farini reined in his horse and stared ahead.

'What in the name of Christ is that, Gert?' he said.

At his side the South African unslung the brass hunter's spy-glass from his shoulder, and raised it to his eye.

'It's a kraal, a settlement,' Frouw answered after a moment. 'But it's not like any damn kraal I've ever seen. I can see a kaffir up on the wall, but kaffirs didn't build that. I'd almost reckon it was white man's building –'

He lowered the spy-glass and passed it to Farini. 'Take a look for yourself.'

Farini put the glass to his eye.

It was still early in the morning. The waggons were rumbling forward behind them. Riding ahead, Farini and Frouw had rounded the end of a long belt of trees on one of the delta's endless low islands as the mist cleared in the distance.

Out of the mist rose first one tower, then more, and then a length of fortified wall with a pair of gates at the centre. Behind the wall there were the outlines of buildings. Peering through the glass, Farini could see it was indeed a settlement. It appeared to be almost a city. Built out of wood, it lay in a depression between two islands.

Something had clearly happened to it. Parts of the wall had fallen down. Many of the buildings that Farini could just make out were roofless. Several of the towers were tilted sideways, and all had gaping holes in them. It looked as if the settlement had been sacked and then abandoned.

As Farini lowered the glass in bewilderment, he saw

Frouw wheel his horse and ride away through the reeds and papyrus. He disappeared. A moment later the South African called out. Farini set off in the direction of the shout.

The South African was leaning forward over his horse on the edge of the bank.

'Look at that!'

Farini followed the South African's outstretched arm as Frouw pointed downwards. Eight feet below them was the bed of what only hours before must have been a waterway. There was no water in it now. Only a glistening sheet of sand and mud. The soil hadn't even dried yet after the water had drained from it.

Farini shook his head. It made no sense to him, but it was clear to the South African.

'The river should run straight through where that kraal's standing, and then down through the channel here,' Frouw said. 'It doesn't. The waters have been diverted upstream. Until a few hours ago the kraal out there in front must have been under the surface –'

The South African heaved himself upright in the saddle. He stared at Farini.

'That settlement was buried until last night. Then someone raised it from the waters.'

Farini gazed back at him.

The pieces of the bewildering jigsaw spun across his mind. Slowly at first and then with increasing speed they began to drop into place. As each one did, a pattern started to emerge. The pattern formed a picture. The picture's outlines sharpened – and suddenly Farini saw it all.

He had finally reached the place marked on the map he had taken from the mission. It could only be where the coon girl with the strange pale skin and the diamond came from. Farini had been behind the girl and her companions – the minister's daughter, the cripple, and the blacks travelling with them – ever since they left Kuruman.

They had left first and travelled faster, but there was

only one known trek route across the desert to the delta. Farini, guided by Frouw, had followed it too. On the way the South African and his men had found traces of the others' tracks almost every week as the waggons rolled on.

The girl must have arrived here a day or two ago. She knew about the settlement hidden by the waters. Mute as she was, she had either communicated its existence to the others, or they had all met up with her former companions who knew its secret too – the letter in the Cape Town rooming-house had spoken of pale-skinned men in the swamps.

However it had come about, they had dammed and drained the river, and exposed the city that lay beneath. Now it was only a few miles ahead.

'If it's a city and the river covered it, how the Christ did it come to be here in the first place?' Farini demanded.

Frouw shrugged. 'I don't know, man. All I know is that ever since I was a child, I've heard tales of a lost city beyond the Kalahari. So has everyone else in southern Africa. Ask any hunter, any rancher or trader, anyone else who knows the desert. They'll all tell you the same. I always reckoned they were fairy-tales –'

The South African scraped his jaw.

'Well, maybe not. I saw the coon girl's stone. Now I've seen this. Those stories, they always had diamonds in them.' He paused. 'Maybe they weren't fairy-tales after all.'

Frouw's gaze remained fixed on the half-ruined walls and towers that still hung in the distance as the last shreds of mist lifted in the rising sun. His eyes were dark slits of greed in his heavy-jowled face.

Farini swung round in his saddle. As he stared across the delta at the city, he remembered the words in the rooming-house letter.

'I traded with them for diamonds,' Darwin's correspondent, the man called Hearns, had written. Farini remembered, too, his own response to the report of the little jeweller – so long ago now, it seemed – when the Jew with the pebble glasses had assessed and valued the coon girl's stone at the Aquarium.

Where there is a jewel like that, Farini realized then with a flash of perception born of utter certainty, there would be more – perhaps an infinity more. He had come to that one stone's source. The infinity of stones, if they existed, were here too. Farini knew that with the same absolute certainty.

He lifted the reins from the horse's neck and drew back his spurs to kick the animal forward.

'Then let's go forward and find out!' he shouted.

Before he could drive the spurs into the horse's flanks, Frouw reached forward. The South African seized the bridle and stopped him.

'Wait!' he said. 'Look at the riverbed. It's drying, man, drying. In a few hours it'll be hard enough to support the waggons. When it does, we can ride straight up to the gates. The cripple's got a pistol, that's all. Apart from him there's only the two girls and a few kaffirs –'

Frouw chuckled. It was a deep, coarse sound that rippled up through his body and erupted through his throat.

'We'll take the bastards like ripe pods from a winter acacia!'

— 78 —

Ben hurled himself back up the steps and on to the wall again.

Moffat was gazing through narrowed eyes at the horizon. Ben leant over the parapet beside him. The procession of waggons had come to a halt. In the distance he could see the smoke of fires and the silhouettes of men, dark and sinister against the light.

In quick, urgent sentences, Ben told the African what had happened in the courtyard below. Moffat listened in silence.

'So we are to hold them back until night comes?' Moffat said.

Ben nodded. 'It's all we can do. The city belongs to her and Kala belongs to the night. What happens in the darkness is for her alone.'

Moffat was silent. For a moment the two men stared at each other.

Ben saw once again the arrogance and sinewy grace in the way the young African held himself. Ben thought of his easy familiarity with Mary-Ellen, and Moffat's fury at Ben's failure to protect her from Farini. He remembered Moffat's skill with his spear, and the ease with which he had paced day after day through the desert, an ease that had humiliated Ben as he rode behind. Ben remembered, too, how Moffat had risked his own life to save him from the crocodile.

Across the parapet Moffat gazed equally steadily at Ben.

Moffat saw Ben's crippled body. He remembered Ben's awkwardness, his lack of understanding of the ways of

Africa, his tongue-tied ignorance of its languages and landscapes. Moffat would never forgive him for what had happened to Mary-Ellen, but he also remembered the white man's sureness and suppleness in the water, and his craftsman's skills with the sluice gates.

Each knew what the other was thinking. The hostility on either side, and the grudging, hard-won respect each had come to feel for the other. They also knew that now at the end none of it mattered. All that mattered was the purpose they shared.

'I will fight beside you for what your sister, Mary-Ellen, wishes,' Ben said quietly. 'I will fight as you think best.'

Moffat's face was grim and hard. Gradually, almost imperceptibly, his features relaxed. He stretched out his hand. He gave Ben not a smile, but what Ben knew was the closest to a gesture of acceptance the African would ever give him.

'We will fight together,' Moffat said.

Ben took his hand. For an instant he gripped it firmly.

They would never be friends, Ben knew that. Too much separated them. Their alien cultures, the disturbing presence of Mary-Ellen, so much more stood between them. But at that moment they had become comrades in the approaching battle. The bond was stronger than anything else that could ever have united them.

'What do we do?' Ben asked.

The moment had passed. They were standing shoulder to shoulder looking out over the sweep of the delta.

'The white men will wait until the mud dries,' Moffat answered. 'Underneath, the riverbed is firm. When the surface is hard, it will bear the weight of their waggons. Then they will come forward –'

The African stopped. His face was wrinkled in thought as he studied the landscape below.

'They will still have to ford a stream where the trees close in,' Moffat went on. 'I will send Batuka there with some of the morans. He will delay them for a while.'

Ben nodded.

'There is another place where we can attack them too,' the African continued. 'There we can stay them for longer, but it will need swift and hard work to secure. We will need your skills, and timber from here. If God wills, it will hold them for long enough –'

Moffat paused again. His head swung away from the delta. He stared at Ben again with unblinking eyes.

'Whichever way it turns,' he finished bleakly, 'when night comes, there will be few of us left to greet the stars.'

It was almost midday when the column of waggons moved forward again.

Three horsemen rode out first. They tested the dried-out riverbed and waved the others on. Pulled by their teams of heavy black oxen, the waggons rolled down the bank and began to advance.

Two miles away, Ben, Moffat and a dozen of the Mashona had been toiling for five hours under the blazing morning sun.

Out of sight and half a mile beyond them, Batuka and his warriors were already in position for the first ambush. The place Moffat had chosen for the second was where the riverbed narrowed between towering thickets of papyrus. There they had dug a pit as deep as one of the waggons and twice its length. The base had been set with sharpened stakes. Then using timber from the city, Ben had roofed it over.

The roof, if Ben had judged its strength correctly, would support any horsemen riding ahead. It would only give way when the full weight of the leading waggon and its oxen came on to it. The task was almost finished. The riverbed was already hidden beneath piles of papyrus. Now Moffat and the Mashona cut more papyrus from the banks to hide the pit too.

The last pile was being laid in place when they all heard the distant fierce clamour of Mashona war cries, followed by the repeated crack of rifles.

Ben stiffened.

The column had ridden into the ambush.

'Wait for me here!' Moffat called.

Leaving Ben and the others behind, he vanished towards the noise of battle.

Batuka had placed the Mashona deep in the reeds on either side of the stream which the waggons had to ford. He let the outriders and the first two waggons cross. Then with the third waggon in the middle of the stream, Batuka attacked. The warriors rose up from the reeds like black ghosts in the sunlight. The points of their spears flashed like the wings of the darting kingfishers, and the spears lanced through the air.

Two of them found their targets. The waggon's black driver and one of the white horsemen arched backwards. The warriors drew their killing knives and raced forward.

The men Gert Frouw had recruited were veterans of the African campaigns. They had fought blacks countless times before and they were unafraid of them. They were all expert marksmen too and they were armed with heavy hunting rifles – rifles that could halt a charging elephant at a hundred paces. They swung round in their saddles and began to fire.

Two of the warriors were struck instantly. Lifted by the bullets, they were thrown back screaming as if they had been caught on the tips of their own spears. Then the Mashona were among the column. They slashed and stabbed with their knives. A horse toppled backwards whinnying with fear. Half a dozen of the oxen sank to their knees, bellowing in pain as their tendons were severed.

Above their heads a flock of white egrets flung themselves into the air, whirling and crying as the battle raged. A pair of sitatunga, the splay-footed antelope of the reedbeds, crashed away through the trees.

'Back!' Batuka shouted.

The Mashona who were still on their feet whirled round and retreated. Almost instantly they vanished into the reeds. One of them had fallen wounded. As he tried to crawl away, a white man lifted his rifle again. There was no scream this time. Only the heavy thump of the shell and the ringing echo of the discharge.

Afterwards there was silence.

'Two ox teams have been cut down,' Moffat said to Ben half an hour later when he returned with Batuka and the remaining Mashona. 'Another was stampeded. It has won us two more hours towards darkness. We made graves for two of the white men, but six of my best warriors will lie with them –'

He shook his head bitterly. 'When the waggons get here, more of my people will join their brothers in the earth. Yet after them there will still be others ready to fight. The white man does not have enough of his kind to bleed for ever – and we do. It is the only way they can be defeated. We must have patience. That was what Shaka taught his impis, and he was right –'

Moffat paused. Suddenly he gave a quick, hard smile.

'I learnt my patience from a python,' he said. 'I learnt of the pit from hunting the elephant. Africa is a good teacher. What we must all have now is the courage that can only be learnt from the leopard.'

Ben looked at Moffat in silence. His gaze travelled across the warriors leaning on their spears behind Moffat's shoulder. Each face was a mask of defiance. Every one of them was ready to die facing the rifles. Not for cattle or land or a bride, not for anything that even concerned them. Instead out of loyalty to their leader, and because of Moffat's own loyalty to a young and alien white woman with an obsession about the mute girl from the desert.

If he died with them, Ben thought suddenly, he would die in brave company.

They settled down to wait for the column.

Moffat was right. The ambush at the stream had bought them two more hours. When one of the scouts the African had posted came running back to say the waggons were advancing again, it was mid-afternoon. Moffat's last orders were quick and decisive. Batuka had plucked one fallen rifle and a bandolier of shells from the ground before he retreated.

Moffat gave the gun to Ben.

'Take it,' he said. 'Use it well. You will need it to protect Mama Mary-Ellen if we fail. Now go back to the ridge above us. We will hold them here for as long as we can. Make the rifle talk as we fight. When we have to retire, as we surely must, cover our flanks as we pull back. If the need comes, we will stand again for the last time on the city's walls. By then darkness should be close –'

Moffat paused. He gave his quick fierce smile again.

'The white man has never trusted the night. He fears the demons of the dark. Well he might, for they are African demons which people it. If he is not inside the city by dusk, he will not attack until light comes again.'

Ben nodded. He took the rifle. Bending low, he climbed to the top of the low island ridge that rose up at the back of the riverbed. Then he settled himself in thick grass and waited.

The column was not long in coming. A group of horsemen appeared first. Ben could see them below him following the course of the riverbed. They had been ambushed once and they were moving more warily now. As they reached the covered pit, the leading horse shied. Ben held his breath as the animal snorted and rolled its eyes.

The rider, a lean, sharp-eyed Afrikaner, glanced round. A group of vervet monkeys scampered away through the trees beyond. Otherwise the man could see nothing except the endless beds of reed and papyrus.

'On, you bastard!' The man spurred the horse forward. Ben breathed again. The rider crossed the pit and the other horsemen streamed after him. A moment later the scene below erupted in tumult and carnage.

The oxen pulling the first waggon stepped on to the timber roof. The roof held until the waggon rolled on to it too. Then with a splintering crash the timber gave way. The waggon and the oxen plunged down together with two horsemen who'd been riding alongside.

The air rang with bellows of agony as the animals were impaled on the sharpened stakes. Unable to stop in time, the leading pair of oxen from the second waggon tumbled into the pit too. The waggon lurched and fell on to its side. At the same instant Moffat and the Mashona leapt from the banks. Hurling their spears in front of them, they raced forward.

Above them Ben sighted down the rifle's barrel and began to fire.

Ben had no idea how long it lasted. He saw Farini, his dark face convulsed with anger as his horse reared up. Ben fired at him, but he knew the bullet was wide even as he pulled the trigger. He thought he saw Frouw, and aimed at the South African too. Again the shot missed as the huge man whirled away.

Below Ben there was now only a maelstrom of plunging, screaming animals, torn and flapping lengths of canvas from the waggons' hoods, shouts and puffs of smoke, and the flickering silhouettes of the Mashona warriors. Pumping shells into the breech, Ben went on firing until the rifle's barrel was so hot it burnt his hand.

Twice at least the bullets found their targets. He saw one man, the lean Afrikaner who'd led the column, slump to the ground. Another clutched his shoulder as blood and splinters of bone spattered the reeds. He toppled off his horse and lay moaning on the bundles of papyrus.

Then suddenly, bewilderingly, it was over.

Ben heard Moffat shout and saw him raise his arm. The African raised his spear and pointed up the hill to Ben's stronghold. The Mashona started to pull back, racing low to the ground to make harder targets for the marksmen. Ben remembered Moffat's instructions and slammed more shells into the rifle. As he gripped the barrel, Ben could smell his skin burning. Clenching his jaw against the pain, he fired again.

First one and then another and another of the blood-stained Mashona warriors came over the ridge, pursued by a hail of gunshot. Out of the corner of his eye Ben could see the tall figure of Moffat covering his men's retreat. Bright with blood, Moffat's sword flared like a snake's tongue in the sunlight. Beside him was the grizzled silhouette of Batuka wielding his short-bladed killing knife.

The two Africans turned and ran for the ridge. For a moment the gunfire stopped. Ben raised his head from the gun. He could see the horsemen backing away from the pit. Briefly Farini was retreating. Moffat came closer. His face was streaked with dust and sweat, and his body crusted with runnels of blood. He spotted Ben and raised his arm in salute. Then he angled towards Ben.

As Moffat changed direction, a flash of light glittered behind him.

'Look out!'

The shout came from Mary-Ellen. It was lost in the detonation of a rifle. Moffat lurched forward as if he'd been kicked from behind. For a moment he staggered from side to side. Then he crumpled forward on to his face. As he fell, someone brushed past Ben and ran down the slope towards the African. It was Mary-Ellen.

Ben jerked up his gun again. Through the sight he saw the horseman who'd fired. The man was already aiming again, this time at the racing figure of the young woman. Ben squeezed the trigger. He had no idea if he hit the rider, but when the smoke cleared from the barrel's mouth, both the man and the horse had vanished. Ben leapt up and threw himself down the slope behind Mary-Ellen.

She was kneeling on the ground with Moffat in her arms. As Ben gazed down at the African, his stomach seemed to turn over. Moffat's body was sheeted with blood. The bullet had torn through his lungs and come out through his chest.

'Oh, Christ, no!' Ben's voice was a despairing cry.

Mary-Ellen cradled Moffat's head. Her face was glistening with tears. Moffat gazed up at her. Then he noticed Ben. Moffat lifted his head and tried to speak. Ben crouched and listened.

'She is my sister, white man,' the African whispered. 'I leave her in your care. Remember what you owe me.'

Moffat's breath was coming in quick, short gasps.

With an immense effort of will he heaved himself up and gripped Ben's arm. His features were twisted with pain but his eyes were level and steady.

Ben nodded. 'The debt will be paid,' he said.

The African stared at him for a moment longer. Then he let out a sigh and fell back. Mary-Ellen lowered him gently to the ground. She kissed his forehead and glanced down the slope at the carnage of the ambush. Eight of the Mashona were lying dead in the riverbed. Mary-Ellen looked back at Ben.

'They all died for us,' she said with a fierce misery, 'but this one I loved.'

She turned and ran back towards the city. Ben set off after her. As he hobbled in her wake, he realized his own eyes were blurred with tears.

— 79 —

'Isn't there something else, Ben, anything?'

Anguish and despair filled Mary-Ellen's voice. At her side Ben shook his head.

'Nothing,' he said grimly.

It was almost midnight and the moon was high.

They were standing on the island that rose above the dried-out lagoon to the west of the city. Occasionally through the trees there shone the light of the distant fires of Farini's camp. Moffat had been certain the white men would not come forward again until dawn, but Batuka, who'd taken over command of the Mashona, had posted the remaining warriors to stand guard at the lagoon's approaches.

The city lay spread out beneath Ben and Mary-Ellen. They'd left Kala alone there as darkness fell. Now in the moonlight they could see the walls and towers. The pattern of the roadways. The half-ruined buildings. The dark entrance of the shaft that led down to the treasury, and the great sluice gates with the water rustling against them.

From time to time they saw, too, a flitting shadow moving through the streets. It was Kala.

They had been watching her for more than an hour. Kala seemed to be exploring the city as if it were half-familiar to her, and at the same time as if she were determined to print it so deeply on her mind she would never forget it again. She would run forward, zigzagging as she peered from side to side. Then she would stop. She squatted on her haunches gazing fixedly at something, some building or courtyard. Afterwards she restlessly set off again.

Kala paused now. For an instant she knelt, her slim body sculpted in a shaft of moonlight. She reached out with her hand and explored a piece of stone. She raised her fingers to her face. She sniffed and then delicately licked her fingertips, searching for some smell or taste.

Afterwards she ran on and vanished in the shadows.

'We've brought her home,' Ben went on quietly. 'Even if just for a moment, it's allowed her to speak again. We've done what she asked of us. Now it's for her to decide.'

He glanced at Mary-Ellen. Ben saw she was weeping. He stiffened as he watched the tears pour silently down her face. Ben hesitated. Then something rose up inside him.

It was a tide of warmth that seemed to melt and wash away the icy barriers that had kept them apart, that had always kept Ben apart from everyone except Kala. He had felt closer to the girl from the desert than he had ever done to anyone. Kala was alone, she was mute, she had the swift, loping stride of a cripple. A cripple like him.

Almost, Ben blindly thought once, they belonged together. He was wrong. Kala came from a world that was alien from his own. Alien not just in time and space, but in its very nature. She belonged to herself and the hyenas that had reared her. Now she also belonged to the drowned city of her beginnings and the diamond that had led her back.

Kala had never belonged to him. She never would.

Mary-Ellen was different. She did belong to Ben's world. Watching her tears, the heaving of her chest, the grief that made her tremble, there flashed across Ben's mind what she had done. She had abandoned everything. She had left her home and the father who had never been her father. She had travelled to London. She had brought Kala back to the desert. She had been captured, and beaten until she was unconscious.

Moffat had rescued her and they had been able to travel on. But it was Mary-Ellen, not the African or himself, who had led them. She had taken them across the desert and into the delta. She had brought Kala home. And now, when Kala's city had been raised from the waters, Mary-Ellen had to acknowledge that it was all worthless – that Farini, his men and his rifles were at the city's gates, and there was nothing they could do to stop them.

Harrowed, Ben looked at her. Suddenly he reached out. Awkwardly and roughly he caught her in his arms and held her to him.

Mary-Ellen leant against him. She felt Ben's strength, the misshapen but powerful support of his body. Slowly the tears and the trembling stopped. She gazed across the streams on the far side of the lagoon. A fish eagle screamed, and a far-off jackal howled.

Mary-Ellen's head swam.

She looked at the sky. At the cataracts of stars which she had watched drift in their tumbling constellations since she lay in her cradle under the baobab tree in the courtyard at Kuruman. Images thronged her mind. The faithless dancing-master who had been her father. The brutal beatings Ramsay had given her. The handsome, vainglorious Oswell, and the destructive cynicism of what he'd done.

They were all men. In Mary-Ellen they had created a hatred of men. But they were not *all* men. There was old Deial, too, and his sons Khoi! and Nuna. The three little San were brave and generous and loyal beyond the call of anything she owed them. Then there was Moffat, her blood brother who wore a different skin. Moffat had followed her to the end.

And now there was this other one. This gnarled and strong and difficult man who did not belong to Africa. He had come there only because he had been caught up in the web that Kala wove round herself. Kala and the diamond wove the web – but Mary-Ellen, she knew, had knotted its threads together.

He was here with her in the night. He was holding her in his arms. Mary-Ellen looked up at him. She touched his face. She ran her hand down his body, exploring his chest and his flat stomach and his groin. She felt him harden beneath her fingers. Gently he caressed her own body from her throat to her ankles. His knuckles were hard but as his hands flowed over her, they moved with the softness of birds' wings. They travelled across her breasts, down the length of her stomach, between her legs.

Mary-Ellen felt her clothes slipping from her. Her back arched and her thighs parted. She called out and clung to him, her fingernails cutting into his shoulder blades. Then he entered her.

Suddenly there was a fierce, intemperate ferocity in what he was doing. He drove down on her, piercing her, rocking backwards and forwards until she began to moan. She felt him gather for the final all-consuming plunge into the depths of her being. She tensed herself.

Then she relaxed. Her legs opened and spread. She let herself be swept away in the same explosive surge of darkness and Kalahari starlight that was carrying him away too.

Kala gazed at the diamond.

Set deep and firm under the night sky in the carved petals of the lily, the stone glittered back at her from the centre of the massive wooden gates. Kala had roamed the city since sunset. She had visited every bend and corner in the walls. She had examined the remains of every building. She had loped through every street and courtyard. She had touched and smelled and listened.

Her fingers had felt the flat, hard texture of the wooden beams, chiselled out by the blades and tapping mallets of the carpenters. Her nostrils had caught the scents of the streams that ran beyond, the pollen of the reed flowers and the musky odours of the animals coming down to drink from the waters. She heard the plaintive calls of the fish owls, and the grunting roar of lions as they sleepily raised themselves to hunt on the islands beyond.

Everything had been there before. She remembered it all. The city was hers. Not just the physical space it occupied in the delta, but everything it encompassed. Sometimes, when a particularly vivid memory of her remote past came back, she stopped and urinated. It was her territory and she needed to mark it with the signature of her own scent, just as the hyenas of the Merula Pan had always marked theirs.

Time after time, as she ran and searched and explored, Kala went back to the treasure house. She climbed down the shaft and looked at the diamonds. To Kala, the heaped-up stones were the children of the great jewel that belonged to her alone. Each time she stared at them, they glowed brighter. The radiance from the night sky was being passed from the diamond in the gates through her eyes into the jewels below.

Now it was over.

Kala had taken the city back. She had sniffed and prowled its grounds. She had scented and marked it. Others had travelled there with her. The San, the little people with whom she had once lived, had come back with her to the waters. So had the tall white-skinned woman with the strange golden hair. So, too, had the hump-shouldered man, the man with the tapping mallet, who limped almost as she did.

None of them mattered now, not even the black warriors who had also travelled with them. The city was her territory. It was threatened by something more deadly than anything she had ever confronted – more deadly even than the lions and leopards which once challenged the clan of the Merula Pan hyenas for their prey. Against the white man with his lantern-jawed face and his chill, greedy eyes, Kala had only one defence.

She would hunt and the diamond would summon the creatures to hunt with her.

It was still dark, but dawn was not far off now.

Kala had been kneeling since midnight before the gates. As the sickle moon started to lower in the sky, and the stars began to pale, they came to her.

Akula, her litter brother, was the first. Thick mist was

coiling over the delta. Kala didn't see the hyena until he was at her shoulder. He nuzzled her armpit and sniffed at her groin. Then he lay down before her. He raised his paws in the air and grunted. Afterwards he turned his head aside and stretched out his tongue.

Kala gazed down at him.

For an instant she could not believe it was him. Akula was old. His hide was grey and his limbs creaked as he settled himself. There were lice on his muzzle and his eyes were furred with dark, opaque circles. Kala had known him as a bold, relentless hunter, the bravest and strongest of the litter. He was still heavy and powerful, but he was wasting.

Kala reached out. She put her arms round him and licked his face in greeting. Next came her litter sisters, Ochla and Kwic-kwa. They had aged too, but less than their brother. Kwic-kwa had had cubs not long ago, while Ochla had grown vast. Even bigger and more powerful than her mother Herut, she had become the matriarch and leader of the clan. Kala greeted them both.

She glanced round and there were more, many more. One by one the hyenas loped silently out of the mist and gathered round her, until there were forty pairs of scarlet eyes shining in the darkness. Some of them Kala knew by scent or sight. Others had been born and grown to maturity after she lost the clan in the great storm.

Now she had found them again. She was back among her one true family.

Kala stood up. She thought of the man again, except he was no longer a man – the brutal forked creature who had beaten her and menaced the city. He no longer even had a name. Kala was hungry and the man who had once been Farini was prey.

As she'd done so often before, Kala was going hunting.

She rose to her feet and looked down at the hyenas. They surrounded her in a tawny ring of heavy, sloping shoulders and massive jaws. She gave a deep-throated snarl, the hunting call of the clan. The call was picked up by the hyenas and they snarled back. The roar from forty throats echoed off the walls of the sluice gates.

Kala turned. With the diamond glittering behind her and the hyenas galloping at her side, Kala began to run.

'Gert, quick, take a look at that!'

Farini shook the shoulder of the sleeping South African.

Blinking, Frouw stumbled to his feet. As he rose, Frouw noticed the sky was lightening. It was almost morning. He peered in the direction Farini was pointing.

Half a mile away, mist, rising from the streams on either side, covered the city. It surged and swirled in great coils and banks of greyness over the dry riverbed and what had once been the lagoon. From time to time the mist parted. When it did, Frouw glimpsed the still-dark walls and towers and the ruined buildings beyond.

There was something else. The South African frowned. He narrowed his eyes against the morning chill and gazed ahead.

A glow was rising from the mist at the city's heart. It wasn't the glow of a fire. It was too cold and hard and white. The glow appeared to be coming from beneath the ground. Beyond it a star was flashing. Not a star in the sky, but a star that seemed to have fallen. Shining brilliantly and only just visible above the battlements, it hung somewhere in a space of darkness right at the far end of the city.

'What the Christ is it?' Farini demanded.

Frouw shook his head in bewilderment. The South African had never seen anything like the icy-white fire dancing and glittering before them.

'You don't know?' Farini went on, his voice rising. 'Then I'll tell you. Think, man, think! There's only one thing that gives out a light like that – diamonds!'

Farini swung round. He gripped Frouw's shoulder. Farini shook him furiously, his face blazing with excitement.

'I was right, for God's sake!' he shouted. 'The place must be littered with the goddamn stones. The streets are piled with them. We're not going to wait until morning.

Get the men up! Get the waggons moving! We're going in there now!'

Frouw turned. He ran down the column, bellowing at the men to rise.

Ben was vaguely aware of a noise somewhere a long way off.

He stirred. He could feel the warmth of Mary-Ellen's body beside him on the grass. He put his arms round her and pulled her more tightly against him. Ben closed his eyes again.

A moment later he was on his feet. He strained his ears as he listened. In the distance he could hear shouts and the rumbling of waggons. He froze. Farini's column was moving forward again. He seized Mary-Ellen and pulled her up beside him. Together they ran forward to where they had been standing at midnight looking down over the city. They gazed down on it again.

The air was crisp and chill. Darkness had almost gone, but the day had still not come. Under the fading stars, banners of mist swung through the deserted streets and courtyards, and rippled over the delta beyond. For the animals who hunted by night, it was the killing hour – the last moment to bring down their prey before the sun rose.

Animals were hunting the streets of the city. Ben and Mary-Ellen saw them at the same instant. A great pack of hyenas, a clan bigger than Mary-Ellen had ever seen, were running towards the southern gates. At their head was a slim racing figure. Mary-Ellen gripped Ben's hand. Her eyes blurred and she caught her breath. The figure was Kala.

Mary-Ellen shook her head. She lifted her gaze and looked out again. Beyond the walls two horsemen were galloping towards the city's gates. Behind them the column of waggons was rolling forward too, the oxen treading confidently over the now hard and dry surface of the river's bed.

Mary-Ellen had no need to wonder who the horsemen were. Even at that distance, even through the coiling mist, she recognized the silhouettes of both of them. One belonged to Farini, the other to the giant South African, Frouw.

The two reached the gates. They consulted for a moment. Then they both dismounted and led their horses forward into the city. As they did so, it happened.

Out of the earth in front of them, out of the lingering mist, the hyenas erupted. They came forward as they always hunted and tore down their prey – in a pack, in a wave of driving muscle and lacerating teeth. Grunting and howling, they pulled the two men to the ground. At their centre was Kala. She leapt at Farini. She caught him by the arms. She pressed them to his sides and her teeth sought his neck.

Screaming in pain and fear as he fell, Farini recognized her. She was the girl he had whipped into dancing on the stage of the Aquarium – the girl with the diamond. Only she was a girl no longer. She was a maddened, ravening animal, and her teeth were at his throat.

Somehow Farini tore an arm from her grip. He fumbled for his rifle. His hand grasped it on the ground beside him. He slipped his finger through the trigger guard and levered the gun up until the barrel was pointing at the girl's chest. Then he fired.

The shot echoed over the delta. As it rang out, on the island above the city Ben and Mary-Ellen stiffened in horror. They had seen everything. The two men dismounting at the gates. The tide of snarling hyenas that had risen from the mist and engulfed them. Kala leaping for Farini's throat, and the spasm that convulsed her body when in his last desperate moment he fired.

Now it was over. Except that it was not finished even yet. As Mary-Ellen fell against Ben, sobbing, he tensed once more.

The sun was on the point of breaking the horizon and the waggons were still rumbling forward. Ben's gaze was caught by a flare from the sluice gates. He stared at them. The gates were shimmering and rocking under the press of the water from above. A light that was almost blinding beamed out from them.

The light came from the diamond. Quivering and vibrating, the stone was about to burst free from its mount. The city's key was falling from its lock. Hypnotized, Ben gazed at it. He saw the diamond spring away from the carved frame of lily petals that had held it anchored. He saw the great sluice gates burst open and release the pent-up water on the city. He saw the surging flood of spray and foam and water sweep through the streets, and bury the waggons beneath the rushing cataract.

As Mary-Ellen clung to him, Ben knew he was witnessing the death not only of the men who had wanted to plunder the city, but of the city itself.

Ben held her tightly. His own eyes misted with tears. He blinked them away and looked out again. Swirling among the waters was something that shone with a cold bright radiance. It sank and rose again, tugged backwards and forwards by the roaring current of the river.

It could only be the diamond. As Ben watched, the cataract swept it out of sight on to the flood plain that led to the desert.

— 80 —

In the east the sun was edging over the trees, and daylight was beginning to spill across the delta's landscape.

Morning birds were calling. A pied kingfisher hung above the waters of the lagoon. Its wings fluttered black and white against the dawn sky. It lowered its head and arrowed down into the depths. A moment later it lifted from the surface with a fish in its mouth. Silvery spray shone in the gathering light as the bird flew away.

Old Deial, crouched in the half-light in the tamarisk trees which fringed the lagoon, shivered and pulled the kaross around his thin body. He did not like the watery wilderness. It was not the land of his fathers. His body yearned for the dry wind of the desert. Like a lizard his blood grew cold in the night.

The journey was complete. Deial knew that, as surely as he knew that the little she-hare that fell from the sky belonged to the glittering city of the shining stones. Deial did not know if the city was real or ghostly. He did not know if the fiery-eyed visitors were spirits or creatures of flesh and blood. In his world such distinctions were unimportant. Gods were animals, animals were men. Death and life were all one. There was no difference. What mattered was to hear the song in the small breeze.

The song had told him the time had come.

Batuka too had heard the song. He watched impassively as the San lifted their few belongings and slipped away. The shadows of the little people spread out across the grass and vanished. Batuka and his warriors had laid Moffat and their dead comrades gently to rest in the earth. Now Batuka had returned to take his leave of the white woman and the man who worked with wood.

The African leant on his spear with one leg tucked up across his thigh. His shield was resting against him. The patterned hide of its cover was torn and streaked with blood. There was blood on his skin too, but the blood was dry and the crusted wounds were already healing in the arid and cleansing Kalahari air.

Behind Batuka, the Mashona warriors who had survived the battle were standing in the same supple positions. As the light welled up and glittered over their spears, they looked more and more like statues left behind by some god of war to mark the battle's passing.

Batuka's spear was in his hand. He lifted it and hammered its shaft on the ground. Behind him the Mashona did the same. Then he turned and walked away with the warriors striding behind him.

Mary-Ellen and Ben watched them go. As the Mashona disappeared behind the trees, Mary-Ellen glanced back at Ben.

Ben was staring at her. His face was creased and frowning. In his eyes she could see questions, endless questions. Questions about the past and the future. About the mute, the haunted and tormented Kala, and the diamond that had been her lodestar. About the hyenas which encircled her in a rampaging wave of ferocity. About the city that had been drowned, raised from the waters, and then buried beneath them again.

Mary-Ellen had no answers to the questions, but the questions didn't matter. What mattered were the fish eagles calling now in the dawn, the urgent stamp of the lechwe antelope, the roar of the late-hunting lion. They were Africa. They were the sounds that had always enveloped the cradle where the first man child had been rocked.

Mary-Ellen had work to do there, a lifetime of work that would be dedicated to the old man whom she had only known from his letters and from the grave, thoughtful face on the frontispiece of his books. The work would embrace Kala and the San and the packs and clans of animals which threaded their lives. She would find out what linked them, what bound them together, what made them in the end all one.

She glanced at Ben and smiled. She would need many things if she was to do what she wanted, but more than anything she needed a skilled and brave companion. A craftsman who was fearless, and who loved and understood the wild as much as she did. A man who recognized the wilderness for what it was – a constantly changing theatre of birth, survival and death. A man who had nowhere else to go.

Mary-Ellen took Ben by the hand. She led him down from the island to the edge of the lagoon.

'The girl had many names,' Mary-Ellen said. 'To the San she was the little she-hare that fell from the sky. To the hyenas in the tongue of the wild she was something else. But to herself she was always Cleopatra. This was her kingdom. It always will be.'

As the sun lifted, they both knelt and drank.